THE VIKING C[illegible] LIBRARY

DON [illegible]

White Noise

TEXT AND CRITICISM

EDITED BY
Mark Osteen

PENGUIN BOOKS

PENGUIN BOOKS
Published by the Penguin Group
Penguin Putnam Inc., 375 Hudson Street,
New York, New York 10014, U.S.A.
Penguin Books Ltd, 27 Wrights Lane,
London W8 5TZ, England
Penguin Books Australia Ltd, Ringwood,
Victoria, Australia
Penguin Books Canada Ltd, 10 Alcorn Avenue,
Toronto, Ontario, Canada M4V 3B2
Penguin Books (N.Z.) Ltd, 182–190 Wairau Road,
Auckland 10, New Zealand
Penguin India, 210 Chiranjiv Tower, 43 Nehru Place,
New Delhi 11009, India

Penguin Books Ltd, Registered Offices:
Harmondsworth, Middlesex, England

White Noise first published in the United States of America by
Viking Penguin Inc. 1985
Published in Penguin Books 1986
Viking Critical Library edition published in Penguin Books 1998

9 10 8

A portion of *White Noise* appeared originally in *Vanity Fair*.

Acknowledgments for permission to reprint previously published material
appear on the first page of the respective selection.

LIBRARY OF CONGRESS CATALOGING IN PUBLICATION DATA
DeLillo, Don.
White noise: text and criticism/Don DeLillo; edited by Mark Osteen.
p. cm.—(Viking critical library)
Includes bibliographical references (p.).
ISBN 0 14 02 7498 7 (pbk.)
1. Industrial accidents—Middle West—Fiction. 2. College
teachers—Middle West—Fiction. 3. Stepfamilies—Middle West—
Fiction. 4. DeLillo, Don. White noise. 5. Death—Fiction.
I. Osteen, Mark. II. Title. III. Series.
PS3554.E4425W48 1998
813'.54—dc21 98-28815

Printed in the United States of America
Set in Bodoni
Designed by Kathryn Parise

Contents

Introduction

White Noise has often been dubbed Don DeLillo's "breakout book." This term is usually meant in one of two ways: either that the work has achieved greater commercial success than an author's previous works, or that it has raised the author's art to a higher level. In the case of *White Noise*, the second is arguable, but the first is definitely true, for the novel garnered the best reviews and strongest sales of DeLillo's career to that point. It is not difficult to understand why it became one of the most widely acclaimed fictional works of the 1980s: its mordantly witty anatomy of the postnuclear family; its sly satire of television, advertising, and academia; its letter-perfect portrayal of the sounds and sights of supermarkets, malls, and tabloids all strike chords that reverberate strongly with contemporary Americans.

When *White Noise* was first published in January 1985, reviewers were struck by its timeliness; indeed, appearing only a month after a toxic chemical leak at a Union Carbide plant in Bhopal, India, killed some 2,500 people, DeLillo's novel—with an "airborne toxic event" at its center—seemed almost eerily prescient. Although a few reviewers criticized its plot (or alleged plotlessness), found its witticisms too clever, or accused the author of "trendiness," these voices were drowned out by a chorus of praise. As they did in his earlier novels, reviewers recognized the validity of DeLillo's insights about the oppressive effects of contemporary cultural institutions and applauded the astonishing linguistic gifts *White Noise* displays in its sparkling dialogue and in Jack Gladney's alternately bemused, frightened, and self-critical narrative voice. Many readers found Gladney more approachable than the alienated protagonists of DeLillo's previous works; many adults—especially, I suspect, academics—would echo Gladney's blend of denunciation of and baffled appreciation for popular culture. But the novel's most immediately appealing quality is its humor: it's simply a very funny book. I remember reading aloud to friends Jack and Babette's precoital conversation about "entering," Heinrich's stubborn refusal to accept his senses' evidence of rain, and the uproarious one-upmanship of the American Environments department. Although DeLillo's earlier novels were also humorous, they carried a more sardonic, Swiftian edge that lacerated with a cooler precision. Many readers have found *White Noise*'s humor more palatable because it is leavened by a warmth and compassion less obvious in DeLillo's earlier work.

Much of this warm comedy is derived from DeLillo's slightly skewed depiction of the postmodern family, where the once-solid core of mom, dad, and kids has given way to a loose aggregate of siblings, step-siblings, and ex-spouses rotating in various impermanent groupings. Jack Gladney, professor of Hitler Studies at the College-on-the-Hill in a town called Blacksmith, has four children: Mary Alice (age 19) and Steffie (9), from his first and second marriages to Dana Breedlove; Heinrich (14), from his marriage to Janet Savory (now known as Mother Devi); and Bee (12), from his marriage to Tweedy Browner. Only Heinrich and Steffie live with Jack. His wife Babette's three children are Denise (age 11), Eugene (8), and Wilder (about 2). As Thomas Ferraro points out, since Wilder is not Jack's child, this "family" can have been together no more than two years; moreover, not one child is living with a full sibling (Ferraro 1991, 17). This condition of permanent impermanence affects all of Blacksmith, a place of "tag sales and yard sales" where "failed possessions" testify to failed marriages (*White Noise*, 59). Things change so rapidly that even the family members seem unclear about the details. No wonder Jack sees the family as the "cradle of the world's misinformation" (81).

But though the family's handle on facts is hilariously shaky, their conversations also suggest the unfunny results of living in a high-technology society: there is abundant information around, but nobody seems to know anything. And just as the family members gorge themselves with disposable information and fast food, so are they also inundated by consumer goods, not only when they visit the supermarket and the mall, but also when they are at home watching television, which they seem to do constantly. Indeed, *White Noise* is preoccupied with consumerism and with the values inherent in a consumer society. DeLillo's treatment of these ubiquitous features of contemporary life is surprisingly balanced: although he satirizes the family's addictions, he gives many of the best lines to Jack's colleague Murray Jay Siskind, who enthusiastically celebrates television and shopping as contemporary religious rituals. DeLillo dramatizes the omnipresence of TV and consumerism by punctuating the scenes with disembodied electronic voices and lists of brand names. Simultaneously attesting to the novel's highly textured realism and violating it by reminding us of the author's controlling presence, these mysterious, often acerbic insertions are one reason the novel has been called "postmodern."

Another reason is that *White Noise* flouts the conventions it seems to invoke, imitating a number of different genres, but ultimately fitting none of them. For example, the relatively plotless part 1 presents itself as a hyperintelligent TV sitcom, complete with brainy children, zany friends, and banal conflicts. Even here, however, DeLillo alludes to deeper disturbances: Jack and Babette debate about who will die first; Wilder ululates at length for no apparent reason. Things turn much darker when, in part 2, the family is forced to flee a toxic leak; the book begins to resemble a disaster thriller, except that DeLillo is less interested in providing graphic descriptions of poisoning than in tracing its subtler, long-term effects, especially on Jack, who is exposed to the toxic substance and hence "tentatively scheduled to die" (202). No longer comforted by hunkering in Hitler's penumbra, and bereft of strong ties to religion, community, or family, Jack becomes desperately obsessed with his mortality. The novel seems to veer into a midlife crisis tale. But Jack doesn't take up skydiving or learn to box. Instead, after learning that Babette has been involved in a secret experiment involving Dylar, a drug designed to dispel the fear of death, he schemes to get some at any cost. Jack's less attractive qualities—self-absorption, hypocrisy, rage—emerge, prompting him to devise an implausible plot that itself seems to come from a TV movie. Yet Jack's alternately ludicrous and pathetic confrontation with his nemesis neither solves his problem nor resolves the plot, which does not, after all, "move deathward" (26). With this enigmatic, postmodernist conclusion, the novel moves beyond all the formulae it has employed.

Even those who cherish the novel's comedy cannot ignore its deeply ominous undercurrent, for *White Noise* is most of all a profound study of the American way of death: one of DeLillo's working titles was "The American Book of the Dead." It gains much of its remarkable resonance from its unflinching depiction of the nameless fear pervading postmodern society. Like Murray Siskind, DeLillo is particularly interested in "American magic and dread," and his novel dramatizes how our obsessions with exercise and disease, our millennialist religions, our tabloid stories of resurrection and celebrity worship, and our compulsive consumerism offer charms to counteract the terror of oblivion.

White Noise is thus also a novel about religion—or, perhaps more accurately, about belief. Like DeLillo's later novel, *Mao II* (1991), it asks, "When the old God leaves the world, what happens to all the unexpended faith?" (*Mao II*, 7). DeLillo has long been attracted to books that "open out onto some larger mystery" (LeClair 1982, 26); *White Noise* is such a book, one that alludes constantly to what lies just beyond our hearing, to the mysterious, the untellable, the numinous—to what DeLillo calls the "radiance in dailiness" (see page 330 of this volume). The novel defamiliarizes our familiar world by listening to the sounds and listing the products and places—television, supermarkets, and shopping centers, as well as "The Airport Marriott, the Downtown Travelodge, the Sheraton Inn and Conference Center" (*White Noise*, 15)—that channel the spiritual yearnings of contemporary Americans. In *White Noise* we revisit those temples where Americans seek "[p]eace of mind in a profit-oriented context" (87).

Despite its undeniable originality, *White Noise* also reprises the themes and strategies of DeLillo's earlier works. Like his first three novels, it features a first-person narrator who maintains an uneasy relationship with mass culture. David Bell, the protagonist of DeLillo's first novel, *Americana* (1971), drops out of his job at a television network to make an autobiographical film scrutinizing Americans' worship of televised and advertised images. In one scene (reprinted here on page 335), a character in Bell's film calls television "an electronic form of packaging," a phrase that *White Noise* retransmits in its recurrent litanies of brand names and broadcast voices.

The glut of images and glamour of celebrity displayed in *White Noise*'s tabloids take center stage in *Great Jones Street* (1973) and *Mao II*. Like Gladney, both Bucky Wunderlick, the earlier novel's rock-star protagonist, and *Mao II*'s novelist Bill Gray seek what Wunderlick calls a "moral form to master commerce"—a means of discovering authenticity in a world crowded with images and commodities (*Great Jones Street*, 70). Like Bell, these characters withdraw into cocoons where they script private narratives or pursue semisacred quests, only to find their efforts transformed into just another spectacle or consumer item.

Another theme that *White Noise* shares with DeLillo's earlier novels is the social impact of technology, particularly its most devastating products—atomic weapons and poisonous waste. Gary Harkness, the narrator of *End Zone* (1972), discovers a disturbing fascination with the language and "theology" of nuclear war. *End Zone* foreshadows *White Noise* both in its parody of disaster novels and in its protagonist's ambivalence about technology and its consequences. Similarly, *Ratner's Star* (1976) blends mathematics and Menippean satire to mount a scathing critique of scientific authority, exposing it as an elaborate form of magic that neither consoles nor contains the fear of mortality it conceals. In these earlier novels, as in *White Noise*, science engenders a deep and dangerous alienation from nature. DeLillo has returned to these themes in his most recent novel, *Underworld* (1997), which meditates on the intertwined relationship between waste and weapons.

DeLillo's next three novels, *Players* (1977), *Running Dog* (1978), and *The Names* (1982), offer variations on the terrorist thriller, in which bewildered protagonists seek solace in cathartic violence. *Players* adumbrates *White Noise* not only in its superbly rendered dialogue and its depiction of the sedative effects of television (see the excerpt reprinted on pages 342–43), but also in its sharp portrayal of contemporary marriage. Like Jack Gladney, Lyle and Pammy Wynant, the bored protagonists of *Players*, are at once tranquilized and terrorized by the institutions with which they are inextricably involved. The swift, cinematic *Running Dog* marks DeLillo's first analysis of what Gladney calls the "continuing mass appeal of fascist tyranny" (25). Much of that appeal, according to *Running Dog*, issues from the insinuation of filmed images into every crevice of our lives. If in *White Noise* television is a ubiquitous voice droning at the edges of consciousness, in *Running Dog* the omnipresence of cameras transforms all behavior into acting, disabling characters from discriminating between real things and images. *The Names*, the novel about American expatriates that immediately precedes *White Noise*, explicitly investigated for the first time what had always been DeLillo's implicit subject: the nature and value of language itself. Although the plot outline resembles those of DeLillo's earlier novels, *The Names* leaves us with DeLillo's first hopeful denouement, as narrator James Axton recognizes in his son's exhilaratingly mangled prose a source of redemption that prefigures Jack Gladney's discovery of "splendid transcendence" in the utterances of his children (155).

The works that followed *White Noise* have shown DeLillo continuing to experiment with form and subject. In 1986, *The Day Room*, a play, was first produced. It meditates on the relationship between madness and inspiration and features a straitjacketed actor playing a television set (which, as in *White Noise*, provides absurdly apposite comments). DeLillo's subsequent novels have equalled the critical and commercial triumph of *White Noise*. *Libra* (1988), brilliantly synthesizing a fictional biography of Lee Harvey Oswald with a plausible account of a conspiracy to kill President John Kennedy, earned nearly as many critical plaudits and even more commercial success than *White Noise*. Although distinct in both theme and structure, it shares with *White Noise* a self-reflexive consideration of our need for plots. *Mao II*, like *Libra*, won a major national award and for the first time directly addressed DeLillo's understanding of the writer's place in society.

Underworld, a monumental chronicle of America since 1951, unfolding mostly in reverse, is DeLillo's most universally acclaimed and best-selling work so far. While most of DeLillo's works have been compact, even terse, *Underworld* covers a vast canvas with dozens of characters. One of its protagonists, the haunted "waste analyst" Nick Shay, recalls Gladney in his obsession with the detritus of consumer culture and his attraction to violence and the demonic. Although *Underworld* is at once broader and more personal than DeLillo's earlier novels—drawing for the first time upon his background as an Italian American reared in the Bronx—it expands again on the relationship between "American magic and dread," analyzing the myriad theologies through which Americans seek to reclaim transcendence in a world of fearsome technologies and fulsome messages.

White Noise thus brings together many of DeLillo's obsessions: the deleterious effects of capitalism, the power of electronic images, the tyrannical authority and dangerous byproducts of science, the unholy alliance of consumerism and violence, and the quest for sacredness in a secularized world. Like all of his fiction, it displays his virtuoso command of language and, particularly, his ventriloquistic capacity to mimic the argots of various cultural forms. In it he amplifies the noises around us and permits us to hear again how these sounds shape our own voices and beliefs.

The first critical analysis of *White Noise* appeared only two years after its publication, in Tom LeClair's influential book, *In the Loop: Don DeLillo and the Systems Novel*. LeClair places DeLillo in the canon of other American "systems novelists" (such as Thomas Pynchon), who analyze the effects of institutions on the individual. LeClair's chapter on *White Noise* (reprinted here on pages 387–411) presents the Gladneys' trash compactor as a self-reflexive image of both the novel itself and of postmodern America; he goes on to argue that DeLillo finds in that rubbish a source of transcendence that enables Jack to glean a more satisfactory relationship with nature, his body, and death.

Frank Lentricchia's 1989 essay in *Raritan* (see page 412), together with the two essay collections he subsequently edited, helped attract academic attention to DeLillo's work. Lentricchia discusses the "most photographed barn in America" as one of DeLillo's—and our own—"primal scenes," finding in it a perfect instance of how images have supplanted events in contemporary America.

Both LeClair and Lentricchia discuss DeLillo's language, but they emphasize most his authority as a cultural critic. Their emphasis has been shared by many critics, as *White Noise* has gone on to become one of the most frequently taught and analyzed contemporary novels. With the rise of cultural studies in the academy, many literary critics diverted their attention to the very arenas—TV, advertising, pop culture—depicted in *White Noise*, applying theories such as those propounded by French cultural theorist Jean Baudrillard. In his highly influential book *Simulations*, Baudrillard argues that original ideas and events have now been replaced by simulacra—an infinite regress of reproductions without origins; in turn, the "real" has given way to what he calls the "hyperreal" (Baudrillard 1988, 166). John Frow was the first to elucidate the connection between *White Noise* and Baudrillardian simulacra, arguing that the replacement of originals by simulations has worked both to pervert and preserve American myths of origins and authenticity. One of the main forces behind this shift, Frow argues, is television, which, along with the consumer capitalism it serves, reduces all phenomena to mere information.

Although other critics, most notably Leonard Wilcox, have also interpreted the novel through Baudrillardian paradigms, perhaps the most extreme statement of this viewpoint is that of John Duvall, who argues in the essay reprinted on pages 432–455 that *White Noise* is "an extended gloss . . . on Baudrillard's notion of consumer society." Duvall makes the radical claim that consumer society, which pretends to foster free choice, actually inhibits it and thereby promotes a "protofascist" system that recapitulates the abuses of Nazi Germany. Like Frow, Duvall concentrates on television, which inverts the relationship between mediated and immediate experiences, so that only what is broadcast by the media seems real. Other critics, such as Ferraro, have offered more moderate versions of Duvall's arguments. Still, Duvall's piece is exemplary in its treatment of Murray Siskind as the novel's Mephistophelean spokesman for what, Duvall argues, DeLillo finds most dangerous.

Cornel Bonca opposes critics like Duvall and their inferences about DeLillo's Baudrillardian views (see page 456 of this volume). Drawing evidence from both *White Noise* and *The Names*, Bonca distinguishes between two kinds of "white noise": one issuing from capitalism and commodities, the other deriving from a deeper source in human consciousness. This latter may, he argues, counteract our mortal dread. Bonca isolates three scenes—Wilder's wailing in chapter 16, Steffie's chanting of "Toyota Celica" during the airborne toxic event, and the German nun's words about belief near the end of the novel—to expose the way that DeLillo discovers a "purer speech" beneath and within the novel's babble of voices.

Arthur M. Saltzman also scrutinizes DeLillo's language; unlike Bonca, however, who reads white noise as symbol for the denial or fear of death, Saltzman hears as it as a monotonous, narcotizing sound (see page 480 of this volume). The toxicity of our world resides, for Saltzman, as much in our saturation by formulaic language as in black, billowing clouds; the antidote for this aural poison lies in the incisive originality of DeLillo's metaphorical language. Like Bonca, Saltzman finds the novel groping for something luminous within the quotidian, that "radiance in dailiness" cited earlier.

Saltzman and Bonca suggest a new slant in DeLillo criticism. Both LeClair and Lentricchia noted how DeLillo's work leaves a place for "the poetry of mystery, awe, and commitment" (Lentricchia, *New Essays*, 7), and recent criticism has swerved more decidedly toward reading DeLillo in religious or mystical terms. Paul Maltby sees in DeLillo's faith in the redemptive power of language a reaffirmation of the visionary metaphysics of Romantics such as Wordsworth (see page 498 of this volume). Against postmodernist readings of DeLillo, Maltby describes a humanist seeker of the sublime; thus, although Maltby again focuses on Steffie's chanting of "Toyota Celica," he finds in it not Saltzman's "synthetic and deadly" consumer drug, but a potential for sublimity within banality that nonetheless exposes the emptiness and superficiality of contemporary culture.

Clearly *White Noise* is rich enough to provoke contradictory responses, and it will continue to intrigue us because it eludes full explanation. Its conclusion is particularly noteworthy in this regard. How should we interpret Wilder's tricycle ride across the interstate? Is he divinely protected or just lucky? What does it imply about Jack's faith in the wisdom and innocence of children? What is Jack's—and DeLillo's—attitude toward those "postmodern sunsets" to which the residents of Blacksmith flock? And what is the tone of Jack's final description of the supermarket, with its tabloids offering "Everything that is not food or love" (326)? Is he voicing a dazed acceptance? Issuing a sardonic warning? Declaring a numbed neutrality? The author neither judges, spells out his message, nor provides a tidy conclusion.

This final passage exemplifies how DeLillo operates from the inside of the cultural institutions that he is assessing to instigate a dialogue with postmodern culture that takes place in the very language we speak, albeit one more beautifully rendered and ironically gauged, one that borrows familiar formulae but maintains a measured opposition. Masking its critique in celebration, *White Noise* inhabits the very heart of postmodern culture to weigh its menaces against its marvels, alerting us to its wonder as well as its waste.

—MARK OSTEEN

WORKS CITED

Baudrillard, Jean. *Selected Writings*. Edited by Mark Poster. Stanford, Calif.: Stanford University Press, 1988.

DeLillo, Don. *Americana*. Boston: Houghton Mifflin, 1971. Reprint, New York: Penguin, 1989.

———. *Great Jones Street*. Boston: Houghton Mifflin, 1973.

———. "An Interview with Don DeLillo." By Tom LeClair. *Contemporary Literature* 23 (1982): 19–31.

———. *Mao II*. New York; Viking, 1991.

———. "An Outsider in This Society." Interview by Anthony DeCurtis. In *Introducing Don DeLillo*, edited by Frank Lentricchia. Durham, N.C.: Duke University Press, 1991.

Ferraro, Thomas J. "Whole Families Shopping at Night!" In *New Essays on* White Noise, edited by Frank Lentricchia. Cambridge: Cambridge University Press, 1991.

Lentricchia, Frank. Introduction to *New Essays on* White Noise. Cambridge: Cambridge University Press, 1991.

Wilcox, Leonard. "Baudrillard, DeLillo's *White Noise*, and the End of Heroic Narrative." *Contemporary Literature* 32 (1991): 346–65.

Chronology

1936	Donald Richard DeLillo born on November 20 in the Bronx, New York, to Italian immigrant parents. During childhood moves to Pottsville, Pennsylvania, and then back to the Bronx. Grows up in two-story house near the corner of 182nd Street and Adams Place.
1950–54	Attends Cardinal Hayes High School in the Bronx.
1954–58	Attends Fordham University. Graduates with a degree in communication arts in 1958.
1959	Lives in small apartment in Murray Hill, New York City, and works as a copywriter for Ogilvy & Mather advertising agency.
1960	Publishes first story, "The River Jordan," in *Epoch* magazine.
1962	Publishes "Take the 'A' Train" in *Epoch*.
1964	Quits ad agency job. Earns livelihood by taking freelance assignments.
1965	Publishes "Spaghetti and Meatballs" in *Epoch*.
1966	Begins works on first novel, *Americana*. Publishes "Coming Sun. Mon. Tues." in *Kenyon Review*.
1968	Publishes "Baghdad Towers West" in *Epoch*.
1970	Publishes "The Uniforms" in *Carolina Quarterly*.
1971	Publishes *Americana*. Devotes himself to full-time writing. Begins novel, *End Zone*. Publishes "In the Men's Room of the Sixteenth Century" in *Esquire*.

1972 Publishes *End Zone*. Essay about sports gambling, "Total Loss Weekend," appears in *Sports Illustrated*.

1973 Publishes novel, *Great Jones Street*.

1975 Marries Barbara Bennett, a landscape designer. Moves to Toronto, Canada, where he lives until 1976.

1976 Publishes novel, *Ratner's Star*.

1977 Publishes novel, *Players*.

1978 Publishes novel, *Running Dog*.

1979 Receives a Guggenheim Fellowship, which he uses to travel to Greece, and begins work on novel *The Names*. Publishes story, "Creation," in *Antaeus*. Publishes play, *The Engineer of Moonlight*, in *Cornell Review* (the play has never been performed).

1982 Publishes *The Names*. Settles with wife just outside New York City. Late in the year begins *White Noise*.

1983 Essay on the Kennedy assassination, "American Blood: A Journey through the Labyrinth of Dallas and JFK," appears in *Rolling Stone*. Publishes "Human Moments in World War III" in *Esquire*.

1984 Receives Award in Literature from American Academy of Arts and Letters. Finishes *White Noise*; begins *Libra*.

1985 Publishes *White Noise* in January.

1986 Receives National Book Award for *White Noise*. Second play, *The Day Room*, premieres in April at American Repertory Theater in Cambridge, Massachusetts.

1987 Publishes *The Day Room*, which is performed in December at Manhattan Theater Club in New York.

1988 Publishes novel, *Libra*, which wins *Irish Times*–Aer Lingus International Fiction Prize. *Libra* is nominated for National Book Award and chosen as main selection of Book-of-the-Month Club; reaches *New York Times* best-seller list. Essay on Nazism, "Silhouette City: Hitler, Manson and the Millennium," appears in *Dimensions*, the journal of the Anti-Defamation League of B'nai B'rith. Publishes story, "The

Runner," in *Harper's*. Publishes "The Ivory Acrobat" in *Granta*.

1989 In March, begins novel, *Mao II*, partly in response to Ayatollah Khomeini's *fatwa* condemning novelist Salman Rushdie to death.

1990 Publishes playlet, "The Rapture of the Athlete Assumed into Heaven," in *The Quarterly*.

1991 Publishes *Mao II*.

1992 *Mao II* wins PEN/Faulkner Award for Fiction.

1994 Publishes, with novelist Paul Auster, pamphlet in defense of Salman Rushdie. Actor John Malkovich adapts and directs theatrical production of *Libra* at Steppenwolf in Chicago in May.

1996 Scribner acquires manuscript of *Underworld*.

1997 In May, participates in New York Public Library event, "Stand In for Wei Jingsheng," where he reads "The Artist Naked in a Cage," later published in the *New Yorker*. In September, publishes essay, "The Power of History," discussing the origins of *Underworld*, in the *New York Times Magazine*. In October, *Underworld* published to wide acclaim. Is nominated for National Book Award, reaches *New York Times* best-seller list and is chosen as main selection of Book-of-the-Month Club.

I

The Text

White Noise

To Sue Buck and to Lois Wallace

I

Waves and Radiation

1

The station wagons arrived at noon, a long shining line that coursed through the west campus. In single file they eased around the orange I-beam sculpture and moved toward the dormitories. The roofs of the station wagons were loaded down with carefully secured suitcases full of light and heavy clothing; with boxes of blankets, boots and shoes, stationery and books, sheets, pillows, quilts; with rolled-up rugs and sleeping bags; with bicycles, skis, rucksacks, English and Western saddles, inflated rafts. As cars slowed to a crawl and stopped, students sprang out and raced to the rear doors to begin removing the objects inside; the stereo sets, radios, personal computers; small refrigerators and table ranges; the cartons of phonograph records and cassettes; the hairdryers and styling irons; the tennis rackets, soccer balls, hockey and lacrosse sticks, bows and arrows; the controlled substances, the birth control pills and devices; the junk food still in shopping bags—onion-and-garlic chips, nacho thins, peanut creme patties, Waffelos and Kabooms, fruit chews and toffee popcorn; the Dum-Dum pops, the Mystic mints.

I've witnessed this spectacle every September for twenty-one years. It is a brilliant event, invariably. The students greet each other with comic cries and gestures of sodden collapse. Their summer has been bloated with criminal pleasures, as always. The parents stand sun-dazed near their automobiles, seeing images of themselves in every direction. The conscientious suntans. The well-made faces and wry looks. They feel a sense of renewal, of communal recognition. The women crisp and alert, in diet trim, knowing people's names. Their husbands content to measure out the time, distant but ungrudging, accomplished in parenthood, something about them suggesting massive insurance coverage. This assembly of station wagons, as much as anything they might do in the course of the year, more than formal liturgies or laws, tells the parents they are a collection of the like-minded and the spiritually akin, a people, a nation.

I left my office and walked down the hill and into town. There are houses in town with turrets and two-story porches where people sit in the shade of ancient maples. There are Greek revival and Gothic churches. There is an insane asylum with an elongated portico, ornamented dormers and a steeply pitched roof topped by a pineapple finial. Babette and I and our children by previous marriages live at the end of a quiet street in what was once a wooded area with deep ravines. There is an expressway beyond the backyard now, well below us, and at night as we settle into our brass bed the sparse traffic washes past, a remote and steady murmur around our sleep, as of dead souls babbling at the edge of a dream.

I am chairman of the department of Hitler studies at the College-on-the-Hill. I invented Hitler studies in North America in March of 1968. It was a cold bright day with intermittent winds out of the east. When I suggested to the chancellor that we might build a whole department around Hitler's life and work, he was quick to see the possibilities. It was an immediate and electrifying success. The chancellor went on to serve as adviser to Nixon, Ford and Carter before his death on a ski lift in Austria.

At Fourth and Elm, cars turn left for the supermarket. A policewoman crouched inside a boxlike vehicle patrols the area looking for cars parked illegally, for meter violations, lapsed inspection stickers. On telephone poles all over town there are homemade signs concerning lost dogs and cats, sometimes in the handwriting of a child.

2

Babette is tall and fairly ample; there is a girth and heft to her. Her hair is a fanatical blond mop, a particular tawny hue that used to be called dirty blond. If she were a petite woman, the hair would be too cute, too mischievous and contrived. Size gives her tousled aspect a certain seriousness. Ample women do not plan such things. They lack the guile for conspiracies of the body.

"You should have been there," I said to her.

"Where?"

"It's the day of the station wagons."

"Did I miss it again? You're supposed to remind me."

"They stretched all the way down past the music library and onto the interstate. Blue, green, burgundy, brown. They gleamed in the sun like a desert caravan."

"You know I need reminding, Jack."

Babette, disheveled, has the careless dignity of someone too preoccupied with serious matters to know or care what she looks like. Not that she is a gift-bearer of great things as the world generally reckons them. She gathers and tends the children, teaches a course in an adult education program, belongs to a group of volunteers who read to the blind. Once a week she reads to an elderly man named Treadwell who lives on the edge of town. He is known as Old Man Treadwell, as if he were a landmark, a rock formation or brooding swamp. She reads to him from the *National Enquirer*, the *National Examiner*, the *National Express*, the *Globe*, the *World*, the *Star*. The old fellow demands his weekly dose of cult mysteries. Why deny him? The point is that Babette, whatever she is doing, makes me feel sweetly rewarded, bound up with a full-souled woman, a lover of daylight and dense life, the miscellaneous swarming air of families. I watch her all the time doing things in measured sequence, skillfully, with seeming ease, unlike my former wives, who had a tendency to feel estranged from the objective world—a self-absorbed and high-strung bunch, with ties to the intelligence community.

"It's not the station wagons I wanted to see. What are the people like? Do the women wear plaid skirts, cable-knit sweaters? Are the men in hacking jackets? What's a hacking jacket?"

"They've grown comfortable with their money," I said. "They genuinely believe they're entitled to it. This conviction gives them a kind of rude health. They glow a little."

"I have trouble imagining death at that income level," she said.

"Maybe there is no death as we know it. Just documents changing hands."

"Not that we don't have a station wagon ourselves."

"It's small, it's metallic gray, it has one whole rusted door."

"Where is Wilder?" she said, routinely panic-stricken, calling out to the child, one of hers, sitting motionless on his tricycle in the backyard.

Babette and I do our talking in the kitchen. The kitchen and the bedroom are the major chambers around here, the power haunts, the sources. She and I are alike in this, that we regard the rest of the house as storage space for furniture, toys, all the unused objects of earlier marriages and different sets of children, the gifts of lost in-laws, the hand-me-downs and rummages. Things, boxes. Why do these possessions carry such sorrowful weight? There is a darkness attached to them, a foreboding. They make me wary not of personal failure and defeat but of something more general, something large in scope and content.

She came in with Wilder and seated him on the kitchen counter. Denise and Steffie came downstairs and we talked about the school supplies they would need. Soon it was time for lunch. We entered a period of chaos and noise. We milled about, bickered a little, dropped utensils. Finally we were all satisfied with what we'd been able to snatch from the cupboards and refrigerator or swipe from each other and we began quietly plastering mustard or mayonnaise on our brightly colored food. The mood was one of deadly serious anticipation, a reward hard-won. The table was crowded and Babette and Denise elbowed each other twice, although neither spoke. Wilder was still seated on the counter surrounded by open cartons, crumpled tinfoil, shiny bags of potato chips, bowls of pasty substances covered with plastic wrap, flip-top rings and twist ties, individually wrapped slices of orange cheese. Heinrich came in, studied the scene carefully, my only son, then walked out the back door and disappeared.

"This isn't the lunch I'd planned for myself," Babette said. "I was seriously thinking yogurt and wheat germ."

"Where have we heard that before?" Denise said.

"Probably right here," Steffie said.

"She keeps buying that stuff."

"But she never eats it," Steffie said.

"Because she thinks if she keeps buying it, she'll have to eat it just to get rid of it. It's like she's trying to trick herself."

"It takes up half the kitchen."

"But she throws it away before she eats it because it goes bad," Denise said. "So then she starts the whole thing all over again."

"Wherever you look," Steffie said, "there it is."

"She feels guilty if she doesn't buy it, she feels guilty if she buys it and doesn't eat it, she feels guilty when she sees it in the fridge, she feels guilty when she throws it away."

"It's like she smokes but she doesn't," Steffie said.

Denise was eleven, a hard-nosed kid. She led a more or less daily protest against those of her mother's habits that struck her as wasteful or dangerous. I defended Babette. I told her I was the one who needed to show discipline in matters of diet. I reminded her how much I liked the way she looked. I suggested there was an honesty inherent in bulkiness if it is just the right amount. People trust a certain amount of bulk in others.

But she was not happy with her hips and thighs, walked at a rapid clip, ran up the stadium steps at the neoclassical high school.

She said I made virtues of her flaws because it was my nature to shelter loved ones from the truth. Something lurked inside the truth, she said.

The smoke alarm went off in the hallway upstairs, either to let us know the battery had just died or because the house was on fire. We finished our lunch in silence.

3

Department heads wear academic robes at the College-on-the-Hill. Not grand sweeping full-length affairs but sleeveless tunics puckered at the shoulders. I like the idea. I like clearing my arm from the folds of the garment to look at my watch. The simple act of checking the time is transformed by this flourish. Decorative gestures add romance to a life. Idling students may see time itself as a complex embellishment, a romance of human consciousness, as they witness the chairman walking across campus, crook'd arm emerging from his medieval robe, the digital watch blinking in late summer dusk. The robe is black, of course, and goes with almost anything.

There is no Hitler building as such. We are quartered in Centenary Hall, a dark brick structure we share with the popular culture department, known officially as American environments. A curious group. The teaching staff is composed almost solely of New York émigrés, smart, thuggish, movie-mad, trivia-crazed. They are here to decipher the natural language of the culture, to make a formal method of the shiny pleasures they'd known in their Europe-shadowed childhoods—an Aristotelianism of bubble gum wrappers and detergent jingles. The department head is Alfonse (Fast Food) Stompanato, a broad-chested glowering man whose collection of prewar soda pop bottles is on permanent display in an alcove. All his teachers are male, wear rumpled clothes, need haircuts, cough into their armpits. Together they look like teamster officials assembled to identify the body of a mutilated colleague. The impression is one of pervasive bitterness, suspicion and intrigue.

An exception to some of the above is Murray Jay Siskind, an ex-sportswriter who asked me to have lunch with him in the dining room, where the institutional odor of vaguely defined food aroused in me an obscure and gloomy memory. Murray was new to the Hill, a stoop-shouldered man with little round glasses and an Amish beard. He was a visiting lecturer on living icons and seemed embarrassed by what he'd gleaned so far from his colleagues in popular culture.

"I understand the music, I understand the movies, I even see how comic books can tell us things. But there are full professors in this place who read nothing but cereal boxes."

"It's the only avant-garde we've got."

"Not that I'm complaining. I like it here. I'm totally enamored of this place. A small-town setting. I want to be free of cities and sexual entanglements. Heat. This is what cities mean to me. You get off the train and walk out of the station and you are hit with the full blast. The heat of air, traffic and people. The heat of food and sex. The heat of tall buildings. The heat that floats out of the subways and the tunnels. It's always fifteen degrees hotter in the cities. Heat rises from the sidewalks and falls from the poisoned sky. The buses breathe heat. Heat emanates from crowds of shoppers and office workers. The entire infrastructure is based on heat, desperately uses up heat, breeds more heat. The eventual heat death of the universe that scientists love to talk about is already well underway and you can feel it happening all around you in any large or medium-sized city. Heat and wetness."

"Where are you living, Murray?"

"In a rooming house. I'm totally captivated and intrigued. It's a gorgeous old crumbling house near the insane asylum. Seven or eight boarders, more or less permanent except for me. A woman who harbors a terrible secret. A man with a haunted look. A man who never comes out of his room. A woman who stands by the letter box for hours, waiting for something that never seems to arrive. A man with no past. A woman with a past. There is a smell about the place of unhappy lives in the movies that I really respond to."

"Which one are you?" I said.

"I'm the Jew. What else would I be?"

There was something touching about the fact that Murray was dressed almost totally in corduroy. I had the feeling that since the age of eleven in his crowded plot of concrete he'd associated this sturdy fabric with higher learning in some impossibly distant and tree-shaded place.

"I can't help being happy in a town called Blacksmith," he said. "I'm here to avoid situations. Cities are full of situations, sexually cunning people. There are parts of my body I no longer encourage women to handle freely. I was in a situation with a woman in Detroit. She needed my semen in a divorce suit. The irony is that I love women. I fall apart at the sight of long legs, striding, briskly, as a breeze carries up from the river, on a weekday, in the play of morning light. The second irony is that it's not the bodies of women that I ultimately crave but their minds. The mind of a woman. The delicate chambering and massive unidirectional flow, like a physics experiment. What fun it is to talk to an intelligent woman wearing stockings as she crosses her legs. That little staticky sound of rustling nylon can make me happy on several levels. The third and related irony is that it's the most complex and neurotic and difficult women that I am invariably drawn to. I like simple men and complicated women."

Murray's hair was tight and heavy-looking. He had dense brows, wisps of hair curling up the sides of his neck. The small stiff beard, confined to his chin and unaccompanied by a mustache, seemed an optional component, to be stuck on or removed as circumstances warranted.

"What kind of lectures do you plan giving?"

"That's exactly what I want to talk to you about," he said. "You've established a wonderful thing here with Hitler. You created it, you nurtured it, you made it your own. Nobody on the faculty of any college or university in this part of the country can so much as utter the word Hitler without a nod in your direction, literally or metaphorically. This is the center, the unquestioned source. He is now your Hitler, Gladney's Hitler. It must be deeply satisfying for you. The college is internationally known as a result of Hitler studies. It has an identity, a sense of achievement. You've evolved an entire system around this figure, a structure with countless substructures and interrelated fields of study, a history within history. I marvel at the effort. It was masterful, shrewd and stunningly preemptive. It's what I want to do with Elvis."

Several days later Murray asked me about a tourist attraction known as the most photographed barn in America. We drove twenty-two miles into the country around Farmington. There were meadows and apple orchards. White fences trailed through the rolling fields. Soon the signs started appearing. THE MOST PHOTOGRAPHED BARN IN AMERICA. We counted five signs before we reached the site. There were forty cars and a tour bus in the makeshift lot. We walked along a cowpath to the slightly elevated spot set aside for viewing and photographing. All the people had cameras; some had tripods, telephoto lenses, filter kits. A man in a booth sold postcards and slides—pictures of the barn taken from the elevated spot. We stood near a grove of trees and watched the photographers. Murray maintained a prolonged silence, occasionally scrawling some notes in a little book.

"No one sees the barn," he said finally.

A long silence followed.

"Once you've seen the signs about the barn, it becomes impossible to see the barn."

He fell silent once more. People with cameras left the elevated site, replaced at once by others.

"We're not here to capture an image, we're here to maintain one. Every photograph reinforces the aura. Can you feel it, Jack? An accumulation of nameless energies."

There was an extended silence. The man in the booth sold postcards and slides.

"Being here is a kind of spiritual surrender. We see only what the others see. The thousands who were here in the past, those who will come in the future. We've agreed to be part of a collective perception. This literally colors our vision. A religious experience in a way, like all tourism."

Another silence ensued.

"They are taking pictures of taking pictures," he said.

He did not speak for a while. We listened to the incessant clicking of shutter release buttons, the rustling crank of levers that advanced the film.

"What was the barn like before it was photographed?" he said. "What did it look like, how was it different from other barns, how was it similar to other barns? We can't answer these questions because we've read the signs, seen the people snapping the pictures. We can't get outside the aura. We're part of the aura. We're here, we're now."

He seemed immensely pleased by this.

4

When times are bad, people feel compelled to overeat. Blacksmith is full of obese adults and children, baggy-pantsed, short-legged, waddling. They struggle to emerge from compact cars; they don sweatsuits and run in families across the landscape; they walk down the street with food in their faces; they eat in stores, cars, parking lots, on bus lines and movie lines, under the stately trees.

Only the elderly seem exempt from the fever of eating. If they are sometimes absent from their own words and gestures, they are also slim and healthy-looking, the women carefully groomed, the men purposeful and well dressed, selecting shopping carts from the line outside the supermarket.

I crossed the high school lawn and walked to the rear of the building and toward the small open stadium. Babette was running up the stadium steps. I sat across the field in the first row of stone seats. The sky was full of streaking clouds. When she reached the top of the stadium she stopped and paused, putting her hands to the high parapet and leaning into it to rest diagonally. Then she turned and walked back down, breasts chugging. The wind rippled her oversized suit. She walked with her hands on her hips, fingers spread. Her face was tilted up, catching the cool air, and she didn't see me. When she reached the bottom step she turned to face the seats and did some kind of neck stretching exercise. Then she started running up the steps.

Three times she ascended the steps, walked slowly down. There was no one around. She worked hard, hair floating, legs and shoulders working. Every time she reached the top she leaned into the wall, head down, upper body throbbing. After the last descent I met her at the edge of the playing field and embraced her, putting my hands inside the sweatband of her gray cotton pants. A small plane appeared over the trees. Babette was moist and warm, emitting a creaturely hum.

She runs, she shovels snow, she caulks the tub and sink. She plays word games with Wilder and reads erotic classics aloud in bed at night. What do I do? I twirl the garbage bags and twist-tie them, swim laps in the college pool. When I go walking, joggers come up soundlessly behind me, appearing at my side, making me jump in idiotic fright. Babette talks to dogs and cats. I see colored spots out of the corner of my right eye. She plans ski trips that we never take, her face bright with excitement. I walk up the hill to school, noting the whitewashed stones that line the driveways of newer homes.

Who will die first?

This question comes up from time to time, like where are the car keys. It ends a sentence, prolongs a glance between us. I wonder if the thought itself is part of the nature of physical love, a reverse Darwinism that awards sadness and fear to the survivor. Or is it some inert element in the air we breathe, a rare thing like neon, with a melting point, an atomic weight? I held her in my arms on the cinder track. Kids came running our way, thirty girls in bright shorts, an improbable bobbing mass. The eager breathing, the overlapping rhythms of their footfalls. Sometimes I think our love is inexperienced. The question of dying becomes a wise reminder. It cures us of our innocence of the future. Simple things are doomed, or is that a superstition? We watched the girls come round again. They were strung out now, with faces and particular gaits, almost weightless in their craving, able to land lightly.

The Airport Marriott, the Downtown Travelodge, the Sheraton Inn and Conference Center.

On our way home I said, "Bee wants to visit at Christmas. We can put her in with Steffie."

"Do they know each other?"

"They met at Disney World. It'll be all right."

"When were you in Los Angeles?"

"You mean Anaheim."

"When were you in Anaheim?"

"You mean Orlando. It's almost three years now."

"Where was I?" she said.

My daughter Bee, from my marriage to Tweedy Browner, was just starting seventh grade in a Washington suburb and was having trouble readjusting to life in the States after two years in South Korea. She took taxis to school, made phone calls to friends in Seoul and Tokyo. Abroad she'd wanted to eat ketchup sandwiches with Trix sticks. Now she cooked fierce sizzling meals of scallion bushes and baby shrimp, monopolizing Tweedy's restaurant-quality range.

That night, a Friday, we ordered Chinese food and watched television together, the six of us. Babette had made it a rule. She seemed to think that if kids watched television one night a week with parents or stepparents, the effect would be to de-glamorize the medium in their eyes, make it wholesome domestic sport. Its narcotic undertow and eerie diseased brain-sucking power would be gradually reduced. I felt vaguely slighted by this reasoning. The evening in fact was a subtle form of punishment for us all. Heinrich sat silent over his egg rolls. Steffie became upset every time something shameful or humiliating seemed about to happen to someone on the screen. She had a vast capacity for being embarrassed on other people's behalf. Often she would leave the room until Denise signaled to her that the scene was over. Denise used these occasions to counsel the younger girl on toughness, the need to be mean in the world, thick-skinned.

It was my own formal custom on Fridays, after an evening in front of the TV set, to read deeply in Hitler well into the night.

On one such night I got into bed next to Babette and told her how the chancellor had advised me, back in 1968, to do something about my name and appearance if I wanted to be taken seriously as a Hitler innovator. Jack Gladney would not do, he said, and asked me what other names I might have at my disposal. We finally agreed that I should invent an extra initial and call myself J. A. K. Gladney, a tag I wore like a borrowed suit.

The chancellor warned against what he called my tendency to

make a feeble presentation of self. He strongly suggested I gain weight. He wanted me to "grow out" into Hitler. He himself was tall, paunchy, ruddy, jowly, big-footed and dull. A formidable combination. I had the advantages of substantial height, big hands, big feet, but badly needed bulk, or so he believed—an air of unhealthy excess, of padding and exaggeration, hulking massiveness. If I could become more ugly, he seemed to be suggesting, it would help my career enormously.

So Hitler gave me something to grow into and develop toward, tentative as I have sometimes been in the effort. The glasses with thick black heavy frames and dark lenses were my own idea, an alternative to the bushy beard that my wife of the period didn't want me to grow. Babette said she liked the series J. A. K. and didn't think it was attention-getting in a cheap sense. To her it intimated dignity, significance and prestige.

I am the false character that follows the name around.

5

Let's enjoy these aimless days while we can, I told myself, fearing some kind of deft acceleration.

At breakfast, Babette read all our horoscopes aloud, using her storytelling voice. I tried not to listen when she got to mine, although I think I wanted to listen, I think I sought some clues.

After dinner, on my way upstairs, I heard the TV say: "Let's sit half lotus and think about our spines."

That night, seconds after going to sleep, I seemed to fall through myself, a shallow heart-stopping plunge. Jarred awake, I stared into the dark, realizing I'd experienced the more or less normal muscular contraction known as the myoclonic jerk. Is this what it's like, abrupt, peremptory? Shouldn't death, I thought, be a swan dive, graceful, white-winged and smooth, leaving the surface undisturbed?

Blue jeans tumbled in the dryer.

We ran into Murray Jay Siskind at the supermarket. His basket held generic food and drink, nonbrand items in plain white packages with simple labeling. There was a white can labeled CANNED PEACHES. There was a white package of bacon without a plastic window for viewing a representative slice. A jar of roasted nuts had a white wrapper bearing the words IRREGULAR PEANUTS. Murray kept nodding to Babette as I introduced them.

"This is the new austerity," he said. "Flavorless packaging. It appeals to me. I feel I'm not only saving money but contributing to some kind of spiritual consensus. It's like World War III. Everything is white. They'll take our bright colors away and use them in the war effort."

He was staring into Babette's eyes, picking up items from our cart and smelling them.

"I've bought these peanuts before. They're round, cubical, pock-marked, seamed. Broken peanuts. A lot of dust at the bottom of the jar. But they taste good. Most of all I like the packages themselves. You were right, Jack. This is the last avant-garde. Bold new forms. The power to shock."

A woman fell into a rack of paperback books at the front of the store. A heavyset man emerged from the raised cubicle in the far corner and moved warily toward her, head tilted to get a clearer sightline. A checkout girl said, "Leon, parsley," and he answered as he approached the fallen woman, "Seventy-nine." His breast pocket was crammed with felt-tip pens.

"So then you cook at the rooming house," Babette said.

"My room is zoned for a hot plate. I'm happy there. I read the TV listings, I read the ads in *Ufologist Today*. I want to immerse myself in American magic and dread. My seminar is going well. The students are bright and responsive. They ask questions and I answer them. They jot down notes as I speak. It's quite a surprise in my life."

He picked up our bottle of extra-strength pain reliever and sniffed along the rim of the child-proof cap. He smelled our honeydew melons, our bottles of club soda and ginger ale. Babette went down the frozen food aisle, an area my doctor had advised me to stay out of.

"Your wife's hair is a living wonder," Murray said, looking closely into my face as if to communicate a deepening respect for me based on this new information.

"Yes, it is," I said.

"She has important hair."

"I think I know what you mean."

"I hope you appreciate that woman."

"Absolutely."

"Because a woman like that doesn't just happen."

"I know it."

"She must be good with children. More than that, I'll bet she's great to have around in a family tragedy. She'd be the type to take control, show strength and affirmation."

"Actually she falls apart. She fell apart when her mother died."

"Who wouldn't?"

"She fell apart when Steffie called from camp with a broken bone in her hand. We had to drive all night. I found myself on a lumber company road. Babette weeping."

"Her daughter, far away, among strangers, in pain. Who wouldn't?"

"Not her daughter. My daughter."

"Not even her own daughter."

"No."

"Extraordinary. I have to love it."

The three of us left together, trying to maneuver our shopping carts between the paperback books scattered across the entrance. Murray wheeled one of our carts into the parking lot and then helped us heave and push all our double-bagged merchandise into the back of the station wagon. Cars entered and exited. The policewoman in her zippered minicab scouted the area for red flags on the parking meters. We added Murray's single lightweight bag of white items to our load and headed across Elm in the direction of his rooming house. It seemed to me that Babette and I, in the mass and variety of our purchases, in the sheer plenitude those crowded bags suggested, the weight and size and number, the familiar package designs and vivid lettering, the giant sizes, the family bargain packs with Day-Glo sale stickers, in the sense of replenishment we felt, the sense of well-being, the security and contentment these products brought to some snug home in our souls—it seemed we had achieved a fullness of being that is not known to people who need less, expect less, who plan their lives around lonely walks in the evening.

Murray took Babette's hand on leaving.

"I'd ask you to visit my room but it's too small for two people unless they're prepared to be intimate."

Murray is able to produce a look that is sneaky and frank at the same time. It is a look that gives equal credence to disaster and lecherous success. He says that in the old days of his urban entanglements he believed there was only one way to seduce a woman, with clear and open desire. He took pains to avoid self-depreciation, self-mockery, ambiguity, irony, subtlety, vulnerability, a civilized world-weariness and a tragic sense of history—the very things, he says, that are most natural to him. Of these he has allowed only one element, vulnerability, to insert itself gradually into his program of straightforward lust. He is trying to develop a vulnerability that women will find attractive. He works at it consciously, like a man in a gym with weights and a mirror. But his efforts so far have produced only this half sneaky look, sheepish and wheedling.

He thanked us for the lift. We watched him walk toward the lopsided porch, propped with cinder blocks, where a man in a rocker stared into space.

6

Heinrich's hairline is beginning to recede. I wonder about this. Did his mother consume some kind of gene-piercing substance when she was pregnant? Am I at fault somehow? Have I raised him, unwittingly, in the vicinity of a chemical dump site, in the path of air currents that carry industrial wastes capable of producing scalp degeneration, glorious sunsets? (People say the sunsets around here were not nearly so stunning thirty or forty years ago.) Man's guilt in history and in the tides of his own blood has been complicated by technology, the daily seeping falsehearted death.

The boy is fourteen, often evasive and moody, at other times disturbingly compliant. I have a sense that his ready yielding to our wishes and demands is a private weapon of reproach. Babette is afraid he will end up in a barricaded room, spraying hundreds of rounds of automatic fire across an empty mall before the SWAT teams come for him with their heavy-barreled weapons, their bullhorns and body armor.

"It's going to rain tonight."

"It's raining now," I said.

"The radio said tonight."

I drove him to school on his first day back after a sore throat and fever. A woman in a yellow slicker held up traffic to let some children cross. I pictured her in a soup commercial taking off her oilskin hat as she entered the cheerful kitchen where her husband stood over a pot of smoky lobster bisque, a smallish man with six weeks to live.

"Look at the windshield," I said. "Is that rain or isn't it?"

"I'm only telling you what they said."

"Just because it's on the radio doesn't mean we have to suspend belief in the evidence of our senses."

"Our senses? Our senses are wrong a lot more often than they're right. This has been proved in the laboratory. Don't you know about all those theorems that say nothing is what it seems? There's no past, present or future outside our own mind. The so-called laws of motion are a big hoax. Even sound can trick the mind. Just because you don't hear a sound doesn't mean it's not out there. Dogs can hear it. Other animals. And I'm sure there are sounds even dogs can't hear. But they exist in the air, in waves. Maybe they never stop. High, high, high-pitched. Coming from somewhere."

"Is it raining," I said, "or isn't it?"

"I wouldn't want to have to say."

"What if someone held a gun to your head?"

"Who, you?"

"Someone. A man in a trenchcoat and smoky glasses. He holds a gun to your head and says, 'Is it raining or isn't it? All you have to do is tell the truth and I'll put away my gun and take the next flight out of here.'"

"What truth does he want? Does he want the truth of someone traveling at almost the speed of light in another galaxy? Does he want the truth of someone in orbit around a neutron star? Maybe if these people could see us through a telescope we might look like we were two feet two inches tall and it might be raining yesterday instead of today."

"He's holding the gun to *your* head. He wants your truth."

"What good is my truth? My truth means nothing. What if this guy with the gun comes from a planet in a whole different solar system? What we call rain he calls soap. What we call apples he calls rain. So what am I supposed to tell him?"

"His name is Frank J. Smalley and he comes from St. Louis."

"He wants to know if it's raining *now*, at this very minute?"

"Here and now. That's right."

"Is there such a thing as now? 'Now' comes and goes as soon as you say it. How can I say it's raining now if your so-called 'now' becomes 'then' as soon as I say it?"

"You said there was no past, present, or future."

"Only in our verbs. That's the only place we find it."

"Rain is a noun. Is there rain here, in this precise locality, at whatever time within the next two minutes that you choose to respond to the question?"

"If you want to talk about this precise locality while you're in a vehicle that's obviously moving, then I think that's the trouble with this discussion."

"Just give me an answer, okay, Heinrich?"

"The best I could do is make a guess."

"Either it's raining or it isn't," I said.

"Exactly. That's my whole point. You'd be guessing. Six of one, half dozen of the other."

"But you *see* it's raining."

"You see the sun moving across the sky. But is the sun moving across the sky or is the earth turning?"

"I don't accept the analogy."

"You're so sure that's rain. How do you know it's not sulfuric acid from factories across the river? How do you know it's not fallout from a war in China? You want an answer here and now. Can you prove, here and now, that this stuff is rain? How do I know that what you call rain is really rain? What *is* rain anyway?"

"It's the stuff that falls from the sky and gets you what is called wet."

"I'm not wet. Are you wet?"

"All right," I said. "Very good."

"No, seriously, are you wet?"

"First-rate," I told him. "A victory for uncertainty, randomness and chaos. Science's finest hour."

"Be sarcastic."

"The sophists and the hairsplitters enjoy their finest hour."

"Go ahead, be sarcastic, I don't care."

Heinrich's mother lives in an ashram now. She has taken the name Mother Devi and runs the business end of things. The ashram is located on the outskirts of the former copper-smelting town of Tubb, Montana, now called Dharamsalapur. The usual rumors abound of sexual freedom, sexual slavery, drugs, nudity, mind control, poor hygiene, tax evasion, monkey-worship, torture, prolonged and hideous death.

I watched him walk through the downpour to the school entrance. He moved with deliberate slowness, taking off his camouflage cap ten yards from the doorway. At such moments I find I love him with an animal desperation, a need to take him under my coat and crush him to my chest, keep him there, protect him. He seems to bring a danger to him. It collects in the air, follows him from room to room. Babette bakes his favorite cookies. We watch him at his desk, an unpainted table covered with books and magazines. He works well into the night, plotting chess moves in a game he plays by mail with a convicted killer in the penitentiary.

It was warm and bright the next day and students on the Hill sat on lawns and in dorm windows, playing their tapes, sunbathing. The air was a reverie of wistful summer things, the last languorous day, a chance to go bare-limbed once more, smell the mown clover. I went into the Arts Duplex, our newest building, a winged affair with a facade of anodized aluminum, sea-green, cloud-catching. On the lower level was the movie theater, a sloped and dark-carpeted space with two hundred plush seats. I sat in shallow light at the end of the first row and waited for my seniors to arrive.

They were all Hitler majors, members of the only class I still taught, Advanced Nazism, three hours a week, restricted to qualified seniors, a course of study designed to cultivate historical perspective, theoretical rigor and mature insight into the continuing mass appeal of fascist tyranny, with special emphasis on parades, rallies and uniforms, three credits, written reports.

Every semester I arranged for a screening of background footage. This consisted of propaganda films, scenes shot at party congresses, outtakes from mystical epics featuring parades of gymnasts and mountaineers—a collection I'd edited into an impressionistic eighty-minute documentary. Crowd scenes predominated. Close-up jostled shots of thousands of people outside a stadium after a Goebbels speech, people surging, massing, bursting through the traffic. Halls hung with swastika banners, with mortuary wreaths and death's-head insignia. Ranks of thousands of flagbearers arrayed before columns of frozen light, a hundred and thirty antiaircraft searchlights aimed straight up—a scene that resembled a geometric longing, the formal notation of some powerful mass desire. There was no narrative voice. Only chants, songs, arias, speeches, cries, cheers, accusations, shrieks.

I got to my feet and took up a position at the front of the theater, middle aisle, facing the entranceway.

They came in out of the sun in their poplin walk shorts and limited-edition T-shirts, in their easy-care knits, their polo styling and rugby stripes. I watched them take their seats, noting the subdued and reverent air, the uncertain anticipation. Some had notebooks and pencil lights; some carried lecture material in bright binders. There were whispers, rustling paper, the knocking sound of seats dropping as one by one the students settled in. I leaned against the front of the apron, waiting for the last few to enter, for someone to seal the doors against our voluptuous summer day.

Soon there was a hush. It was time for me to deliver the introductory remarks. I let the silence deepen for a moment, then cleared my arms from the folds of the academic robe in order to gesture freely.

When the showing ended, someone asked about the plot to kill Hitler. The discussion moved to plots in general. I found myself saying to the assembled heads, "All plots tend to move deathward. This is the nature of plots. Political plots, terrorist plots, lovers' plots, narrative plots, plots that are part of children's games. We edge nearer death every time we plot. It is like a contract that all must sign, the plotters as well as those who are the targets of the plot."

Is this true? Why did I say it? What does it mean?

7

Two nights a week Babette goes to the Congregational church at the other end of town and lectures to adults in the basement on correct posture. Basically she is teaching them how to stand, sit and walk. Most of her students are old. It isn't clear to me why they want to improve their posture. We seem to believe it is possible to ward off death by following rules of good grooming. Sometimes I go with my wife to the church basement and watch her stand, turn, assume various heroic poses, gesture gracefully. She makes references to yoga, kendo, trance-walking. She talks of Sufi dervishes, Sherpa mountaineers. The old folks nod and listen. Nothing is foreign, nothing too remote to apply. I am always surprised at their acceptance and trust, the sweetness of their belief. Nothing is too doubtful to be of use to them as they seek to redeem their bodies from a lifetime of bad posture. It is the end of skepticism.

We walked home under a marigold moon. Our house looked old and wan at the end of the street, the porch light shining on a molded plastic tricycle, a stack of three-hour colored-flame sawdust and wax logs. Denise was doing her homework in the kitchen, keeping an eye on Wilder, who had wandered downstairs to sit on the floor and stare through the oven window. Silence in the halls, shadows on the sloping lawn. We closed the door and disrobed. The bed was a mess. Magazines, curtain rods, a child's sooty sock. Babette hummed something from a Broadway show, putting the rods in a corner. We embraced, fell sideways to the bed in a controlled way, then repositioned ourselves, bathing in each other's flesh, trying to kick the sheets off our ankles. Her body had a number of long hollows, places the hand might stop to solve in the dark, tempo-slowing places.

We believed something lived in the basement.

"What do you want to do?" she said.

"Whatever you want to do."

"I want to do whatever's best for you."

"What's best for me is to please you," I said.

"I want to make you happy, Jack."

"I'm happy when I'm pleasing you."

"I just want to do what you want to do."

"I want to do whatever's best for you."

"But you please me by letting me please you," she said.

"As the male partner I think it's my responsibility to please."

"I'm not sure whether that's a sensitive caring statement or a sexist remark."

"Is it wrong for the man to be considerate toward his partner?"

"I'm your partner when we play tennis, which we ought to start doing again, by the way. Otherwise I'm your wife. Do you want me to read to you?"

"First-rate."

"I know you like me to read sexy stuff."

"I thought you liked it too."

"Isn't it basically the person being read to who derives the benefit and the satisfaction? When I read to Old Man Treadwell, it's not because I find those tabloids stimulating."

"Treadwell's blind, I'm not. I thought you liked to read erotic passages."

"If it pleases you, then I like to do it."

"But it has to please you too, Baba. Otherwise how would I feel?"

"It pleases me that you enjoy my reading."

"I get the feeling a burden is being shifted back and forth. The burden of being the one who is pleased."

"I want to read, Jack. Honestly."

"Are you totally and completely sure? Because if you're not, we absolutely won't."

Someone turned on the TV set at the end of the hall, and a woman's voice said: "If it breaks easily into pieces, it is called shale. When wet, it smells like clay."

We listened to the gently plummeting stream of nighttime traffic.

I said, "Pick your century. Do you want to read about Etruscan slave girls, Georgian rakes? I think we have some literature on flagellation brothels. What about the Middle Ages? We have incubi and succubi. Nuns galore."

"Whatever's best for you."

"I want you to choose. It's sexier that way."

"One person chooses, the other reads. Don't we want a balance, a sort of give-and-take? Isn't that what makes it sexy?"

"A tautness, a suspense. First-rate. I will choose."

"I will read," she said. "But I don't want you to choose anything that has men inside women, quote-quote, or men entering women. 'I entered her.' 'He entered me.' We're not lobbies or elevators. 'I wanted him inside me,' as if he could crawl completely in, sign the register, sleep, eat, so forth. Can we agree on that? I don't care what these people do as long as they don't enter or get entered."

"Agreed."

"'I entered her and began to thrust.'"

"I'm in total agreement," I said.

"'Enter me, enter me, yes, yes.'"

"Silly usage, absolutely."

"'Insert yourself, Rex. I want you inside me, entering hard, entering deep, yes, now, oh.'"

I began to feel an erection stirring. How stupid and out of context. Babette laughed at her own lines. The TV said: "Until Florida surgeons attached an artificial flipper."

Babette and I tell each other everything. I have told everything, such as it was at the time, to each of my wives. There is more to tell, of course, as marriages accumulate. But when I say I believe in complete disclosure I don't mean it cheaply, as anecdotal sport or shallow revelation. It is a form of self-renewal and a gesture of custodial trust. Love helps us develop an identity secure enough to allow itself to be placed in another's care and protection. Babette and I have turned our lives for each other's thoughtful regard, turned them in the moonlight in our pale hands, spoken deep into the night about fathers and mothers, childhood, friendships, awakenings, old loves, old fears (except fear of death). No detail must be left out, not even a dog with ticks or a neighbor's boy who ate an insect on a dare. The smell of pantries, the sense of empty afternoons, the feel of things as they rained across our skin, things as facts and passions, the feel of pain, loss, disappointment, breathless delight. In these night recitations we create a space between things as we felt them at the time and as we speak them now. This is the space reserved for irony, sympathy and fond amusement, the means by which we rescue ourselves from the past.

I decided on the twentieth century. I put on my bathrobe and went down the hall to Heinrich's room to find a trashy magazine Babette might read from, the type that features letters from readers detailing their sexual experiences. This struck me as one of the few things the modern imagination has contributed to the history of erotic practices. There is a double fantasy at work in such letters. People write down imagined episodes and then see them published in a national magazine. Which is the greater stimulation?

Wilder was in there watching Heinrich do a physics experiment with steel balls and a salad bowl. Heinrich wore a terry cloth robe, a towel around his neck, another towel on his head. He told me to look downstairs.

In a stack of material I found some family photo albums, one or two of them at least fifty years old. I took them up to the bedroom. We spent hours going through them, sitting up in bed. Children wincing in the sun, women in sun hats, men shading their eyes from the glare as if the past possessed some quality of light we no longer experience, a Sunday dazzle that caused people in their churchgoing clothes to tighten their faces and stand at an angle to the future, somewhat averted it seemed, wearing fixed and fine-drawn smiles, skeptical of something in the nature of the box camera.

Who will die first?

8

My struggle with the German tongue began in mid-October and lasted nearly the full academic year. As the most prominent figure in Hitler studies in North America, I had long tried to conceal the fact that I did not know German. I could not speak or read it, could not understand the spoken word or begin to put the simplest sentence on paper. The least of my Hitler colleagues knew some German; others were either fluent in the language or reasonably conversant. No one could major in Hitler studies at the College-on-the-Hill without a minimum of one year of German. I was living, in short, on the edge of a landscape of vast shame.

The German tongue. Fleshy, warped, spit-spraying, purplish and cruel. One eventually had to confront it. Wasn't Hitler's own struggle to express himself in German the crucial subtext of his massive ranting autobiography, dictated in a fortress prison in the Bavarian hills? Grammar and syntax. The man may have felt himself imprisoned in more ways than one.

I'd made several attempts to learn German, serious probes into origins, structures, roots. I sensed the deathly power of the language. I wanted to speak it well, use it as a charm, a protective device. The more I shrank from learning actual words, rules and pronunciation, the more important it seemed that I go forward. What we are reluctant to touch often seems the very fabric of our salvation. But the basic sounds defeated me, the harsh spurting northernness of the words and syllables, the command delivery. Something happened between the back of my tongue and the roof of my mouth that made a mockery of my attempts to sound German words.

I was determined to try again.

Because I'd achieved high professional standing, because my

lectures were well attended and my articles printed in the major journals, because I wore an academic gown and dark glasses day and night whenever I was on campus, because I carried two hundred and thirty pounds on a six-foot three-inch frame and had big hands and feet, I knew my German lessons would have to be secret.

I contacted a man not affiliated with the college, someone Murray Jay Siskind had told me about. They were fellow boarders in the green-shingled house on Middlebrook. The man was in his fifties, a slight shuffle in his walk. He had thinning hair, a bland face and wore his shirtsleeves rolled up to his forearms, revealing thermal underwear beneath.

His complexion was of a tone I want to call flesh-colored. Howard Dunlop was his name. He said he was a former chiropractor but didn't offer a reason why he was no longer active and didn't say when he'd learned German, or why, and something in his manner kept me from asking.

We sat in his dark crowded room at the boarding house. An ironing board stood unfolded at the window. There were chipped enamel pots, trays of utensils set on a dresser. The furniture was vague, foundling. At the borders of the room were the elemental things. An exposed radiator, an army-blanketed cot. Dunlop sat at the edge of a straight chair, intoning generalities of grammar. When he switched from English to German, it was as though a cord had been twisted in his larynx. An abrupt emotion entered his voice, a scrape and gargle that sounded like the stirring of some beast's ambition. He gaped at me and gestured, he croaked, he verged on strangulation. Sounds came spewing from the base of his tongue, harsh noises damp with passion. He was only demonstrating certain basic pronunciation patterns but the transformation in his face and voice made me think he was making a passage between levels of being.

I sat there taking notes.

The hour went quickly. Dunlop managed a scant shrug when I asked him not to discuss the lessons with anyone. It occurred to me that he was the man Murray had described in his summary of fellow boarders as the one who never comes out of his room.

I stopped at Murray's room and asked him to come home with me for dinner. He put down his copy of *American Transvestite* and slipped into his corduroy jacket. We stopped on the porch long enough for Murray to tell the landlord, who was sitting there, about a dripping faucet in the second-floor bathroom. The landlord was a large florid man of such robust and bursting health that he seemed to be having a heart attack even as we looked on.

"He'll get around to fixing it," Murray said, as we set out on foot in the direction of Elm. "He fixes everything eventually. He's very good with all those little tools and fixtures and devices that people in cities never know the names of. The names of these things are only known in outlying communities, small towns and rural areas. Too bad he's such a bigot."

"How do you know he's a bigot?"

"People who can fix things are usually bigots."

"What do you mean?"

"Think of all the people who've ever come to your house to fix things. They were all bigots, weren't they?"

"I don't know."

"They drove panel trucks, didn't they, with an extension ladder on the roof and some kind of plastic charm dangling from the rearview mirror?"

"I don't know, Murray."

"It's obvious," he said.

He asked me why I'd chosen this year in particular to learn German, after so many years of slipping past the radar. I told him there was a Hitler conference scheduled for next spring at the College-on-the-Hill. Three days of lectures, workshops and panels. Hitler scholars from seventeen states and nine foreign countries. Actual Germans would be in attendance.

At home Denise placed a moist bag of garbage in the kitchen compactor. She started up the machine. The ram stroked downward with a dreadful wrenching sound, full of eerie feeling. Children walked in and out of the kitchen, water dripped in the sink, the washing machine heaved in the entranceway. Murray seemed engrossed in the incidental mesh. Whining metal, exploding bottles, plastic smashed flat. Denise listened carefully, making sure the mangling din contained the correct sonic elements, which meant the machine was operating properly.

Heinrich said to someone on the phone, "Animals commit incest all the time. So how unnatural can it be?"

Babette came in from running, her outfit soaked through. Murray walked across the kitchen to shake her hand. She fell into a chair, scanned the room for Wilder. I watched Denise make a mental comparison between her mother's running clothes and the wet bag she'd dumped in the compactor. I could see it in her eyes, a sardonic connection. It was these secondary levels of life, these extrasensory flashes and floating nuances of being, these pockets of rapport forming unexpectedly, that made me believe we were a magic act, adults and children together, sharing unaccountable things.

"We have to boil our water," Steffie said.

"Why?"

"It said on the radio."

"They're always saying boil your water," Babette said. "It's the new thing, like turn your wheel in the direction of the skid. Here comes Wilder now. I guess we can eat."

The small child moved in a swaying gait, great head wagging, and his mother made faces of delight, happy and outlandish masks, watching him approach.

"Neutrinos go right through the earth," Heinrich said into the telephone.

"Yes yes yes," said Babette.

9

They had to evacuate the grade school on Tuesday. Kids were getting headaches and eye irritations, tasting metal in their mouths. A teacher rolled on the floor and spoke foreign languages. No one knew what was wrong. Investigators said it could be the ventilating system, the paint or varnish, the foam insulation, the electrical insulation, the cafeteria food, the rays emitted by microcomputers, the asbestos fireproofing, the adhesive on shipping containers, the fumes from the chlorinated pool, or perhaps something deeper, finer-grained, more closely woven into the basic state of things.

Denise and Steffie stayed home that week as men in Mylex suits and respirator masks made systematic sweeps of the building with infrared detecting and measuring equipment. Because Mylex is itself a suspect material, the results tended to be ambiguous and a second round of more rigorous detection had to be scheduled.

The two girls and Babette, Wilder and I went to the supermarket. Minutes after we entered, we ran into Murray. This was the fourth or fifth time I'd seen him in the supermarket, which was roughly the number of times I'd seen him on campus. He clutched Babette by the left bicep and sidled around her, appearing to smell her hair.

"A lovely dinner," he said, standing directly behind her. "I like to cook myself, which doubles my appreciation of someone who does it well."

"Come any time," she said, turning in an effort to find him.

We moved together into the ultra-cool interior. Wilder sat in the shopping cart trying to grab items off the shelves as we went by. It occurred to me that he was too old and too big to be sitting in supermarket carts. I also wondered why his vocabulary seemed to be stalled at twenty-five words.

"I'm happy to be here," Murray said.

"In Blacksmith?"

"In Blacksmith, in the supermarket, in the rooming house, on the Hill. I feel I'm learning important things every day. Death, disease, afterlife, outer space. It's all much clearer here. I can think and see."

We moved into the generic food area and Murray paused with his plastic basket to probe among the white cartons and jars. I wasn't sure I understood what he was talking about. What did he mean, much clearer? He could think and see what?

Steffie took my hand and we walked past the fruit bins, an area that extended about forty-five yards along one wall. The bins were arranged diagonally and backed by mirrors that people accidentally punched when reaching for fruit in the upper rows. A voice on the loudspeaker said: "Kleenex Softique, your truck's blocking the entrance." Apples and lemons tumbled in twos and threes to the floor when someone took a fruit from certain places in the stacked array. There were six kinds of apples, there were exotic melons in several pastels. Everything seemed to be in season, sprayed, burnished, bright. People tore filmy bags off racks and tried to figure out which end opened. I realized the place was awash in noise. The toneless systems, the jangle and skid of carts, the loudspeaker and coffee-making machines, the cries of children. And over it all, or under it all, a dull and unlocatable roar, as of some form of swarming life just outside the range of human apprehension.

"Did you tell Denise you were sorry?"

"Maybe later," Steffie said. "Remind me."

"She's a sweet girl and she wants to be your older sister and your friend if you'll let her."

"I don't know about friend. She's a little bossy, don't you think?"

"Aside from telling her you're sorry, be sure to give her back her *Physicians' Desk Reference.*"

"She reads that thing all the time. Don't you think that's weird?"

"At least she reads something."

"Sure, lists of drugs and medicines. And do you want to know why?"

"Why?"

"Because she's trying to find out the side effects of the stuff that Baba uses."

"What does Baba use?"

"Don't ask me. Ask Denise."

"How do you know she uses anything?"

"Ask Denise."

"Why don't I ask Baba?"

"Ask Baba," she said.

Murray came out of an aisle and walked alongside Babette, just ahead of us. He took a twin roll of paper towels out of her cart and smelled it. Denise had found some friends and they went up front to look at the paperback books in spindly racks, the books with shiny metallic print, raised letters, vivid illustrations of cult violence and windswept romance. Denise was wearing a green visor. I heard Babette tell Murray she'd been wearing it fourteen hours a day for three weeks now. She would not go out without it, would not even leave her room. She wore it in school, when there was school, wore it to the toilet, the dentist's chair, the dinner table. Something about the visor seemed to speak to her, to offer wholeness and identity.

"It's her interface with the world," Murray said.

He helped Babette push her loaded cart. I heard him say to her, "Tibetans believe there is a transitional state between death and rebirth. Death is a waiting period, basically. Soon a fresh womb will receive the soul. In the meantime the soul restores to itself some of the divinity lost at birth." He studied her profile as if to detect a reaction. "That's what I think of whenever I come in here. This place recharges us spiritually, it prepares us, it's a gateway or pathway. Look how bright. It's full of psychic data."

My wife smiled at him.

"Everything is concealed in symbolism, hidden by veils of mystery and layers of cultural material. But it is psychic data, absolutely. The large doors slide open, they close unbidden. Energy waves, incident radiation. All the letters and numbers are here, all the colors of the spectrum, all the voices and sounds, all the code words and ceremonial phrases. It is just a question of deciphering, rearranging, peeling off the layers of unspeakability. Not that we would want to, not that any useful purpose would be served. This is not Tibet. Even Tibet is not Tibet anymore."

He studied her profile. She put some yogurt in her cart.

"Tibetans try to see death for what it is. It is the end of attachment to things. This simple truth is hard to fathom. But once we stop denying death, we can proceed calmly to die and then go on to experience uterine rebirth or Judeo-Christian afterlife or out-of-body experience or a trip on a UFO or whatever we wish to call it. We can do so with clear vision, without awe or terror. We don't have to cling to life artificially, or to death for that matter. We simply walk toward the sliding doors. Waves and radiation. Look how well-lighted everything is. The place is sealed off, self-contained. It is timeless. Another reason why I think of Tibet. Dying is an art in Tibet. A priest walks in, sits down, tells the weeping relatives to get out and has the room sealed. Doors, windows sealed. He has serious business to see to. Chants, numerology, horoscopes, recitations. Here we don't die, we shop. But the difference is less marked than you think."

He was almost whispering now and I tried to get up closer without ramming my cart into Babette's. I wanted to hear everything.

"Supermarkets this large and clean and modern are a revelation to me. I spent my life in small steamy delicatessens with slanted display cabinets full of trays that hold soft wet lumpy matter in pale colors. High enough cabinets so you had to stand on tiptoes to give your order. Shouts, accents. In cities no one notices specific dying. Dying is a quality of the air. It's everywhere and nowhere. Men shout as they die, to be noticed, remembered for a second or two. To die in an apartment instead of a house can depress the soul, I would imagine, for several lives to come. In a town there are houses, plants in bay windows. People notice dying better. The dead have faces, automobiles. If you don't know a name, you know a street name, a dog's name. 'He drove an orange Mazda.'

You know a couple of useless things about a person that become major facts of identification and cosmic placement when he dies suddenly, after a short illness, in his own bed, with a comforter and matching pillows, on a rainy Wednesday afternoon, feverish, a little congested in the sinuses and chest, thinking about his dry cleaning."

Babette said, "Where is Wilder?" and turned to stare at me in a way that suggested ten minutes had passed since she'd last seen him. Other looks, less pensive and less guilty, indicated greater time spans, deeper seas of inattention. Like: "*I didn't know whales were mammals.*" The greater the time span, the blanker the look, the more dangerous the situation. It was as if guilt were a luxury she allowed herself only when the danger was minimal.

"How could he get out of the cart without my noticing?"

The three adults each stood at the head of an aisle and peered into the traffic of carts and gliding bodies. Then we did three more aisles, heads set forward, weaving slightly as we changed our sightlines. I kept seeing colored spots off to the right but when I turned there was nothing there. I'd been seeing colored spots for years but never so many, so gaily animated. Murray saw Wilder in another woman's cart. The woman waved at Babette and headed toward us. She lived on our street with a teenage daughter and an Asian baby, Chun Duc. Everyone referred to the baby by name, almost in a tone of proud proprietorship, but no one knew who Chun belonged to or where he or she had come from.

"Kleenex Softique, Kleenex Softique."

Steffie was holding my hand in a way I'd come to realize, over a period of time, was not meant to be gently possessive, as I'd thought at first, but reassuring. I was a little astonished. A firm grip that would help me restore confidence in myself, keep me from becoming resigned to whatever melancholy moods she thought she detected hovering about my person.

Before Murray went to the express line he invited us to dinner, a week from Saturday.

"You don't have to let me know till the last minute."

"We'll be there," Babette said.

"I'm not preparing anything major, so just call beforehand and tell me if something else came up. You don't even have to call. If you don't show up, I'll know that something came up and you couldn't let me know."

"Murray, we'll be there."

"Bring the kids."

"No."

"Great. But if you decide to bring them, no problem. I don't want you to feel I'm holding you to something. Don't feel you've made an ironclad commitment. You'll show up or you won't. I have to eat anyway, so there's no major catastrophe if something comes up and you have to cancel. I just want you to know I'll be there if you decide to drop by, with or without kids. We have till next May or June to do this thing so there's no special mystique about a week from Saturday."

"Are you coming back next semester?" I said.

"They want me to teach a course in the cinema of car crashes."

"Do it."

"I will."

I rubbed against Babette in the checkout line. She backed into me and I reached around her and put my hands on her breasts. She rotated her hips and I nuzzled her hair and murmured, "Dirty blond." People wrote checks, tall boys bagged the merchandise. Not everyone spoke English at the cash terminals, or near the fruit bins and frozen foods, or out among the cars in the lot. More and more I heard languages I could not identify much less understand, although the tall boys were American-born and the checkout women as well, short, fattish in blue tunics, wearing stretch slacks and tiny white espadrilles. I tried to fit my hands into Babette's skirt, over her belly, as the slowly moving line edged toward the last purchase point, the breath mints and nasal inhalers.

It was out in the parking lot that we heard the first of the rumors about a man dying during the inspection of the grade school, one of the masked and Mylex-suited men, heavy-booted and bulky. Collapsed and died, went the story that was going around, in a classroom on the second floor.

10

Tuition at the College-on-the-Hill is fourteen thousand dollars, Sunday brunch included. I sense there is a connection between this powerful number and the way the students arrange themselves physically in the reading areas of the library. They sit on broad cushioned seats in various kinds of ungainly posture, clearly calculated to be the identifying signs of some kinship group or secret organization. They are fetal, splayed, knock-kneed, arched, square-knotted, sometimes almost upside-down. The positions are so studied they amount to a classical mime. There is an element of overrefinement and inbreeding. Sometimes I feel I've wandered into a Far Eastern dream, too remote to be interpreted. But it is only the language of economic class they are speaking, in one of its allowable outward forms, like the convocation of station wagons at the start of the year.

Denise watched her mother pull the little cellophane ribbon on a bonus pack of sixteen individually wrapped units of chewing gum. Her eyes narrowed as she turned back to the address books on the kitchen table before her. The eleven-year-old face was an expert mask of restrained exasperation.

She waited a long moment, then said evenly, "That stuff causes cancer in laboratory animals in case you didn't know."

"You wanted me to chew sugarless gum, Denise. It was your idea."

"There was no warning on the pack then. They put a warning, which I would have a hard time believing you didn't see."

She was transcribing names and phone numbers from an old book to a new one. There were no addresses. Her friends had phone numbers only, a race of people with a seven-bit analog consciousness.

"I'm happy to do it either way," Babette said. "It's totally up to you. Either I chew gum with sugar and artificial coloring or I chew sugarless and colorless gum that's harmful to rats."

Steffie got off the phone. "Don't chew at all," she said. "Did you ever think of that?"

Babette was breaking eggs into a wooden salad bowl. She gave me a look that wondered how the girl could talk on the phone and listen to us at the same time. I wanted to say because she finds us interesting.

Babette said to the girls, "Look, either I chew gum or I smoke. If you want me to start smoking again, take away my chewing gum and my Mentho-Lyptus."

"Why do you have to do one or the other?" Steffie said. "Why not do neither one?"

"Why not do both?" Denise said, the face carefully emptying itself of expression. "That's what you want, isn't it? We all get to do what we want, don't we? Except if we want to go to school tomorrow we can't because they're fumigating the place or whatever."

The phone rang; Steffie grabbed it.

"I'm not a criminal," Babette said. "All I want to do is chew a pathetic little tasteless chunk of gum now and then."

"Well it's not that simple," Denise said.

"It's not a crime either. I chew about two of those little chunks a day."

"Well you can't anymore."

"Well I can, Denise. I want to. Chewing happens to relax me. You're making a fuss over nothing."

Steffie managed to get our attention by the sheer pleading force of the look on her face. Her hand was over the mouthpiece of the phone. She did not speak but only formed the words.

The Stovers want to come over.

"Parents or children?" Babette said.

My daughter shrugged.

"We don't want them," Babette said.

"Keep them out," Denise said.

What do I say?

"Say anything you want."

"Just keep them out of here."

"They're boring."

"Tell them to stay home."

Steffie retreated with the phone, appearing to shield it with her body, her eyes full of fear and excitement.

"A little gum can't possibly hurt," Babette said.

"I guess you're right. Never mind. Just a warning on the pack."

Steffie hung up. "Just hazardous to your health," she said.

"Just rats," Denise said. "I guess you're right. Never mind."

"Maybe she thinks they died in their sleep."

"Just useless rodents, so what's the difference?"

"What's the difference, what's the fuss?" Steffie said.

"Plus I'd like to believe she chews only two pieces a day, the way she forgets things."

"What do I forget?" Babette said.

"It's all right," Denise said. "Never mind."

"What do I forget?"

"Go ahead and chew. Never mind the warning. I don't care."

I scooped Wilder off a chair and gave him a noisy kiss on the ear and he shrank away in delight. Then I put him on the counter and went upstairs to find Heinrich. He was in his room studying the deployment of plastic chessmen.

"Still playing with the fellow in prison? How's it going?"

"Pretty good. I think I got him cornered."

"What do you know about this fellow? I've been meaning to ask."

"Like who did he kill? That's the big thing today. Concern for the victim."

"You've been playing chess with the man for months. What do you know about him except that he's in jail for life, for murder? Is he young, old, black, white? Do you communicate at all except for chess moves?"

"We send notes sometimes."

"Who did he kill?"

"He was under pressure."

"And what happened?"

"It kept building and building."

"So he went out and shot someone. Who did he shoot?"

"Some people in Iron City."

"How many?"

"Five."

"Five people."

"Not counting the state trooper, which was later."

"Six people. Did he care for his weapons obsessively? Did he have an arsenal stashed in his shabby little room off a six-story concrete car park?"

"Some handguns and a bolt-action rifle with a scope."

"A telescopic sight. Did he fire from a highway overpass, a rented room? Did he walk into a bar, a washette, his former place of employment and start firing indiscriminately? People scattering, taking cover under tables. People out on the street thinking they heard firecrackers. 'I was just waiting for the bus when I heard this little popping noise like firecrackers going off.'"

"He went up to a roof."

"A rooftop sniper. Did he write in his diary before he went up to the roof? Did he make tapes of his voice, go to the movies, read books about other mass murderers to refresh his memory?"

"Made tapes."

"Made tapes. What did he do with them?"

"Sent them to people he loved, asking for forgiveness."

"'I can't help myself, folks.' Were the victims total strangers? Was it a grudge killing? Did he get fired from his job? Had he been hearing voices?"

"Total strangers."

"Had he been hearing voices?"

"On TV."

"Talking just to him? Singling him out?"

"Telling him to go down in history. He was twenty-seven, out of work, divorced, with his car up on blocks. Time was running out on him."

"Insistent pressuring voices. How did he deal with the media? Give lots of interviews, write letters to the editor of the local paper, try to make a book deal?"

"There is no media in Iron City. He didn't think of that till it was too late. He says if he had to do it all over again, he wouldn't do it as an ordinary murder, he would do it as an assassination."

"He would select more carefully, kill one famous person, get noticed, make it stick."

"He now knows he won't go down in history."

"Neither will I."

"But you've got Hitler."

"Yes, I have, haven't I?"

"What's Tommy Roy Foster got?"

"All right, he's told you all these things in the letters he sends. What do you say when you respond?"

"I'm losing my hair."

I looked at him. He wore a warmup suit, a towel around his neck, sweatbands on both wrists.

"You know what your mother would say about this chess by mail relationship."

"I know what you would say. You're saying it."

"How is your mother? Hear from her lately?"

"She wants me to go out to the ashram this summer."

"Do you want to go?"

"Who knows what I want to do? Who knows what anyone wants to do? How can you be sure about something like that? Isn't it all a question of brain chemistry, signals going back and forth, electrical energy in the cortex? How do you know whether something is really what you want to do or just some kind of nerve impulse in the brain? Some minor little activity takes place somewhere in this unimportant place in one of the brain hemispheres and suddenly I want to go to Montana or I don't want to go to Montana. How do I know I really want to go and it isn't just some neurons firing or something? Maybe it's just an accidental flash in the medulla and suddenly there I am in Montana and I find out I really didn't want to go there in the first place. I can't control what happens in my brain, so how can I be sure what I want to do ten seconds from now, much less Montana next summer? It's all this activity in the brain and you don't know what's you as a person and what's some neuron that just happens to fire or just happens to misfire. Isn't that why Tommy Roy killed those people?"

In the morning I walked to the bank. I went to the automated teller machine to check my balance. I inserted my card, entered my secret code, tapped out my request. The figure on the screen roughly corresponded to my independent estimate, feebly arrived at after long searches through documents, tormented arithmetic. Waves of relief and gratitude flowed over me. The system had blessed my life. I felt its support and approval. The system hardware, the mainframe sitting in a locked room in some distant city. What a pleasing interaction. I sensed that something of deep personal value, but not money, not that at all, had been authenticated and confirmed. A deranged person was escorted from the bank by two armed guards. The system was invisible, which made it all the more impressive, all the more disquieting to deal with. But we were in accord, at least for now. The networks, the circuits, the streams, the harmonies.

11

I woke in the grip of a death sweat. Defenseless against my own racking fears. A pause at the center of my being. I lacked the will and physical strength to get out of bed and move through the dark house, clutching walls and stair rails. To feel my way, reinhabit my body, re-enter the world. Sweat trickled down my ribs. The digital reading on the clock-radio was 3:51. Always odd numbers at times like this. What does it mean? Is death odd-numbered? Are there life-enhancing numbers, other numbers charged with menace? Babette murmured in her sleep and I moved close, breathing her heat.

Finally I slept, to be awakened by the smell of burning toast. That would be Steffie. She burns toast often, at any hour, intentionally. She loves the smell, she is addicted; it's her treasured scent. It satisfies her in ways wood smoke cannot, or snuffed candles, or the odor of explosive powder drifting down the street from firecrackers set off on the Fourth. She has evolved orders of preference. Burnt rye, burnt white, so on.

I put on my robe and went downstairs. I was always putting on a bathrobe and going somewhere to talk seriously to a child. Babette was with her in the kitchen. It startled me. I thought she was still in bed.

"Want some toast?" Steffie said.

"I'll be fifty-one next week."

"That's not old, is it?"

"I've felt the same for twenty-five years."

"Bad. How old is my mother?"

"She's still young. She was only twenty when we were married the first time."

"Is she younger than Baba?"

"About the same. Just so you don't think I'm one of those men who keeps finding younger women."

I wasn't sure whether my replies were meant for Steffie or Babette. This happens in the kitchen, where the levels of data are numerous and deep, as Murray might say.

"Is she still in the CIA?" Steffie said.

"We're not supposed to talk about that. She's just a contract agent anyway."

"What's that?"

"That's what people do today for a second income."

"What exactly does she do?" Babette said.

"She gets a phone call from Brazil. That activates her."

"Then what?"

"She carries money in a suitcase the length and breadth of Latin America."

"That's all? I could do that."

"Sometimes they send her books to review."

"Have I met her?" Babette said.

"No."

"Do I know her name?"

"Dana Breedlove."

Steffie's lips formed the words as I spoke them.

"You're not planning to eat that, are you?" I said to her.

"I always eat my toast."

The phone rang and I picked it up. A woman's voice delivered a high-performance hello. It said it was computer-generated, part of a marketing survey aimed at determining current levels of consumer desire. It said it would ask a series of questions, pausing after each to give me a chance to reply.

I gave the phone to Steffie. When it became clear that she was occupied with the synthesized voice, I spoke to Babette in low tones.

"She liked to plot."

"Who?"

"Dana. She liked to get me involved in things."

"What kind of things?"

"Factions. Playing certain friends against other friends. Household plots, faculty plots."

"Sounds like ordinary stuff."

"She spoke English to me, Spanish or Portuguese to the telephone."

Steffie twisted around, used her free hand to pull her sweater away from her body, enabling her to read the label.

"Virgin acrylic," she said into the phone.

Babette checked the label on her sweater. A soft rain began to fall.

"How does it feel being nearly fifty-one?" she said.

"No different from fifty."

"Except one is even, one is odd," she pointed out.

That night, in Murray's off-white room, after a spectacular meal of Cornish hen in the shape of a frog, prepared on a two-burner hot plate, we moved from our metal folding chairs to the bunk bed for coffee.

"When I was a sportswriter," Murray said, "I traveled constantly, lived in planes and hotels and stadium smoke, never got to feel at home in my own apartment. Now I have a place."

"You've done wonders," Babette said, her gaze sweeping desperately across the room.

"It's small, it's dark, it's plain," he said in a self-satisfied way. "A container for thought."

I gestured toward the old four-story building on several acres across the street. "Do you get any noise from the insane asylum?"

"You mean beatings and shrieks? It's interesting that people still call it the insane asylum. It must be the striking architecture, the high steep roof, the tall chimneys, the columns, the little flourishes here and there that are either quaint or sinister—I can't make up my mind. It doesn't look like a rest home or psychiatric facility. It looks like an insane asylum."

His trousers were going shiny at the knees.

"I'm sorry you didn't bring the kids. I want to get to know small kids. This is the society of kids. I tell my students they're already too old to figure importantly in the making of society. Minute by minute they're beginning to diverge from each other. 'Even as we sit here,' I tell them, 'you are spinning out from the core, becoming less recognizable as a group, less targetable by advertisers and mass-producers of culture. Kids are a true universal. But you're well beyond that, already beginning to drift, to feel estranged from the products you consume. Who are they designed for? What is your place in the marketing scheme? Once you're out of school, it is only a matter of time before you experience the vast loneliness and dissatisfaction of consumers who have lost their group identity.' Then I tap my pencil on the table to indicate time passing ominously."

Because we were seated on the bed, Murray had to lean well forward, looking past the coffee cup poised in my hand, in order to address Babette.

"How many children do you have, all told?"

She appeared to pause.

"There's Wilder, of course. There's Denise."

Murray sipped his coffee, trying to look at her, sideways, with the cup at his lower lip.

"There's Eugene, who's living with his daddy this year in Western Australia. Eugene is eight. His daddy does research in the outback. His daddy is also Wilder's daddy."

"The boy is growing up without television," I said, "which may make him worth talking to, Murray, as a sort of wild child, a savage plucked from the bush, intelligent and literate but deprived of the deeper codes and messages that mark his species as unique."

"TV is a problem only if you've forgotten how to look and listen," Murray said. "My students and I discuss this all the time. They're beginning to feel they ought to turn against the medium, exactly as an earlier generation turned against their parents and their country. I tell them they have to learn to look as children again. Root out content. Find the codes and messages, to use your phrase, Jack."

"What do they say to that?"

"Television is just another name for junk mail. But I tell them I can't accept that. I tell them I've been sitting in this room for more than two months, watching TV into the early hours, listening carefully, taking notes. A great and humbling experience, let me tell you. Close to mystical."

"What's your conclusion?"

He crossed his legs primly and sat with the cup in his lap, smiling straight ahead.

"Waves and radiation," he said. "I've come to understand that the medium is a primal force in the American home. Sealed-off, timeless, self-contained, self-referring. It's like a myth being born right there in our living room, like something we know in a dream-like and preconscious way. I'm very enthused, Jack."

He looked at me, still smiling in a half sneaky way.

"You have to learn how to look. You have to open yourself to the data. TV offers incredible amounts of psychic data. It opens ancient memories of world birth, it welcomes us into the grid, the network of little buzzing dots that make up the picture pattern. There is light, there is sound. I ask my students, 'What more do you want?' Look at the wealth of data concealed in the grid, in the bright packaging, the jingles, the slice-of-life commercials, the products hurtling out of darkness, the coded messages and endless repetitions, like chants, like mantras. '*Coke is it, Coke is it, Coke is it.*' The medium practically overflows with sacred formulas if we can remember how to respond innocently and get past our irritation, weariness and disgust."

"But your students don't agree."

"Worse than junk mail. Television is the death throes of human consciousness, according to them. They're ashamed of their television past. They want to talk about movies."

He got up and refilled our cups.

"How do you know so much?" Babette said.

"I'm from New York."

"The more you talk, the sneakier you look, as if you're trying to put something over on us."

"The best talk is seductive."

"Have you ever been married?" she said.

"Once, briefly. I was covering the Jets, the Mets and the Nets.

How odd a figure I must seem to you now, a solitary crank who maroons himself with a TV set and dozens of stacks of dust-jacketed comic books. Don't think I wouldn't appreciate a dramatic visit between two and three in the morning," he told her, "from an intelligent woman in spike heels and a slit skirt, with high-impact accessories."

It was drizzling as we walked home, my arm around her waist. The streets were empty. Along Elm all the stores were dark, the two banks were dimly lit, the neon spectacles in the window of the optical shop cast a gimmicky light on the sidewalk.

Dacron, Orlon, Lycra Spandex.

"I know I forget things," she said, "but I didn't know it was so obvious."

"It isn't."

"Did you hear Denise? When was it, last week?"

"Denise is smart and tough. No one else notices."

"I dial a number on the phone and forget who I'm calling. I go to the store and forget what to buy. Someone will tell me something, I'll forget it, they'll tell me again, I'll forget it, they'll tell me again, showing a funny-looking smile."

"We all forget," I said.

"I forget names, faces, phone numbers, addresses, appointments, instructions, directions."

"It's something that's just been happening, more or less to everyone."

"I forget that Steffie doesn't like to be called Stephanie. Sometimes I call her Denise. I forget where I've parked the car and then for a long, long moment I forget what the car looks like."

"Forgetfulness has gotten into the air and water. It's entered the food chain."

"Maybe it's the gum I chew. Is that too farfetched?"

"Maybe it's something else."

"What do you mean?"

"You're taking something besides chewing gum."

"Where did you get that idea?"

"I got it secondhand from Steffie."

"Who did Steffie get it from?"

"Denise."

She paused, conceding the possibility that if Denise is the source of a rumor or theory, it could very well be true.

"What does Denise say I'm taking?"

"I wanted to ask you before I asked her."

"To the best of my knowledge, Jack, I'm not taking anything that could account for my memory lapses. On the other hand I'm not old, I haven't suffered an injury to the head and there's nothing in my family background except tipped uteruses."

"You're saying maybe Denise is right."

"We can't rule it out."

"You're saying maybe you're taking something that has the side effect of impairing memory."

"Either I'm taking something and I don't remember or I'm not taking something and I don't remember. My life is either/or. Either I chew regular gum or I chew sugarless gum. Either I chew gum or I smoke. Either I smoke or I gain weight. Either I gain weight or I run up the stadium steps."

"Sounds like a boring life."

"I hope it lasts forever," she said.

Soon the streets were covered with leaves. Leaves came tumbling and scraping down the pitched roofs. There were periods in every day when a stiff wind blew, baring the trees further, and retired men appeared in the backyards, on the small lawns out front, carrying rakes with curved teeth. Black bags were arrayed at the curbstone in lopsided rows.

A series of frightened children appeared at our door for their Halloween treats.

12

I went to German lessons twice a week, in the late afternoon, darkness crowding in earlier with each succeeding visit. It was Howard Dunlop's working rule that we sit facing each other during the full length of the lesson. He wanted me to study his tongue positions as he demonstrated the pronunciation of consonants, diphthongs, long and short vowels. He in turn would look closely into my mouth as I attempted to reproduce the unhappy sounds.

His was a mild and quiet face, an oval surface with no hint of distinctiveness until he started his vocal routines. Then the warping began. It was an eerie thing to see, shamefully fascinating, as a seizure might be if witnessed in a controlled environment. He tucked his head into his trunk, narrowed his eyes, made grimacing humanoid faces. When it was time for me to repeat the noises I did likewise, if only to please the teacher, twisting my mouth, shutting my eyes completely, conscious of an overarticulation so tortured it must have sounded like a sudden bending of the natural law, a stone or tree struggling to speak. When I opened my eyes he was only inches from my mouth, leaning in to peer. I used to wonder what he saw in there.

There were strained silences before and after each lesson. I tried to make small talk, get him to discuss his years as a chiropractor, his life before German. He would look off into the middle distance, not angry or bored or evasive—just detached, free of the connectedness of events, it seemed. When he did speak, about the other boarders or the landlord, there was something querulous in his voice, a drawn-out note of complaint. It was important for him to believe that he'd spent his life among people who kept missing the point.

"How many students do you have?"

"For German?"

"Yes."

"You're the only one I have for German. I used to have others. German has fallen off. These things go in cycles, like everything else."

"What else do you teach?"

"Greek, Latin, ocean sailing."

"People come here to learn ocean sailing?"

"Not so much anymore."

"It's amazing how many people teach these days," I said. "There is a teacher for every person. Everyone I know is either a teacher or a student. What do you think it means?"

He looked off toward a closet door.

"Do you teach anything else?" I said.

"Meteorology."

"Meteorology. How did that come about?"

"My mother's death had a terrible impact on me. I collapsed totally, lost my faith in God. I was inconsolable, withdrew completely into myself. Then one day by chance I saw a weather report on TV. A dynamic young man with a glowing pointer stood before a multicolored satellite photo, predicting the weather for the next five days. I sat there mesmerized by his self-assurance and skill. It was as though a message was being transmitted from the weather satellite through that young man and then to me in my canvas chair. I turned to meteorology for comfort. I read weather maps, collected books on weather, attended launchings of weather balloons. I realized weather was something I'd been looking for all my life. It brought me a sense of peace and security I'd never experienced. Dew, frost and fog. Snow flurries. The jet stream. I believe there is a grandeur in the jet stream. I began to come out of my shell, talk to people in the street. 'Nice day.' 'Looks like rain.' 'Hot enough for you?' Everyone notices the weather. First thing on rising, you go to the window, look at the weather. You do it, I do it. I made a list of goals I hoped to achieve in meteorology. I took a correspondence course, got a degree to teach the subject in buildings with a legal occupancy of less than one hundred.

I've taught meteorology in church basements, in trailer parks, in people's dens and living rooms. They came to hear me in Millers Creek, Lumberville, Watertown. Factory workers, housewives, merchants, members of the police and the fire. I saw something in their eyes. A hunger, a compelling need."

There were little holes in the cuffs of his thermal undershirt. We were standing in the middle of the room. I waited for him to go on. It was the time of year, the time of day, for a small insistent sadness to pass into the texture of things. Dusk, silence, iron chill. Something lonely in the bone.

When I got home, Bob Pardee was in the kitchen practicing his golf swing. Bob is Denise's father. He said he was driving through town on his way to Glassboro to make a presentation and thought he'd take us all to dinner.

He swung his locked hands in slow motion over his left shoulder, following through smoothly. Denise eyed him from a stool by the window. He wore a half shaggy cardigan with sleeves that draped over the cuffs.

"What kind of presentation?" she said.

"Oh, you know. Charts, arrows. Slap some colors on a wall. It's a basic outreach tool, sweetheart."

"Did you change jobs again?"

"I'm raising funds. Busy as hell, too, better believe."

"What kind of funds?"

"Just whatever's out there, you know? People want to give me food stamps, etchings. Hey, great, I don't mind."

He was bent over a putt. Babette leaned on the refrigerator door with her arms folded, watching him. Upstairs a British voice said: "There are forms of vertigo that do not include spinning."

"Funds for what?" Denise said.

"There's a little thing you might have had occasion to hear of, called the Nuclear Accident Readiness Foundation. Basically a legal defense fund for the industry. Just in case kind of thing."

"Just in case what?"

"Just in case I faint from hunger. Let's sneak up on some ribs, why don't we? You got your leg men, you got your breast men.

Babette, what do you say? I'm about semiprepared to slaughter my own animal."

"How many jobs is this anyway?"

"Don't pester me, Denise."

"Never mind, I don't care, do what you want."

Bob took the three older kids to the Wagon Wheel. I drove Babette to the river-edge house where she would read to Mr. Treadwell, the blind old man who lived there with his sister. Wilder sat between us, playing with the supermarket tabloids that Treadwell favored as reading matter. As a volunteer reader to the blind, Babette had some reservations about the old gent's appetite for the unspeakable and seamy, believing that the handicapped were morally bound to higher types of entertainment. If we couldn't look to them for victories of the human spirit, who could we look to? They had an example to set just as she did as a reader and morale-booster. But she was professional in her duty, reading to him with high earnestness, as to a child, about dead men who leave messages on answering machines.

Wilder and I waited in the car. The plan was that after the reading the three of us would meet the Wagon Wheel group at the Dinky Donut, where they would have dessert and we would have dinner. I'd brought along a copy of *Mein Kampf* for that segment of the evening.

The Treadwell house was an old frame structure with rotting trellises along the porch. Less than five minutes after she'd entered, Babette came out, walked uncertainly to the far end of the porch and peered across the dim yard. Then she walked slowly toward the car.

"Door was open. I went in, nobody. I looked around, nothing, nobody. I went upstairs, no sign of life. There doesn't seem to be anything missing."

"What do you know about his sister?"

"She's older than he is and probably in worse shape if you disregard the fact that he's blind and she isn't."

The two nearest houses were dark, both up for sale, and no one at four other houses in the area knew anything about the Treadwells' movements over the past few days. We drove to the state trooper barracks and talked to a female clerk who sat behind a computer console. She told us there was a disappearance every eleven seconds and taped everything we said.

At the Dinky Donut, outside town, Bob Pardee sat quietly as the family ate and talked. The soft pink golfer's face had begun to droop from his skull. His flesh seemed generally to sag, giving him the hangdog look of someone under strict orders to lose weight. His hair was expensively cut and layered, a certain amount of color combed in, a certain amount of technology brought to bear, but it seemed to need a more dynamic head. I realized Babette was looking at him carefully, trying to grasp the meaning of the four careening years they'd spent as man and wife. The panoramic carnage. He drank, gambled, drove his car down embankments, got fired, quit, retired, traveled in disguise to Coaltown where he paid a woman to speak Swedish to him as they screwed. It was the Swedish that enraged Babette, either that or his need to confess it, and she hit out at him—hit out with the backs of her hands, with her elbows and wrists. Old loves, old fears. Now she watched him with a tender sympathy, a reflectiveness that seemed deep and fond and generous enough to contain all the magical counterspells to his current run of woe, although I knew, of course, as I went back to my book, that it was only a passing affection, one of those kindnesses no one understands.

By noon the next day they were dragging the river.

13

The students tend to stick close to campus. There is nothing for them to do in Blacksmith proper, no natural haunt or attraction. They have their own food, movies, music, theater, sports, conversation and sex. This is a town of dry cleaning shops and opticians. Photos of looming Victorian homes decorate the windows of real estate firms. These pictures have not changed in years. The homes are sold or gone or stand in other towns in other states. This is a town of tag sales and yard sales, the failed possessions arrayed in driveways and tended by kids.

Babette called me at my office in Centenary Hall. She said Heinrich had been down at the river, wearing his camouflage cap and carrying an Instamatic, to watch them drag for the bodies, and while he was there word came that the Treadwells had been found alive but shaken in an abandoned cookie shack at the Mid-Village Mall, a vast shopping center out on the interstate. Apparently they'd been wandering through the mall for two days, lost, confused and frightened, before taking refuge in the littered kiosk. They spent two more days in the kiosk, the weak and faltering sister venturing out to scavenge food scraps from the cartoon-character disposal baskets with swinging doors. It was sheer luck that their stay at the mall coincided with a spell of mild weather. No one knew at this point why they didn't ask for help. It was probably just the vastness and strangeness of the place and their own advanced age that made them feel helpless and adrift in a landscape of remote and menacing figures. The Treadwells didn't get out much. In fact no one yet knew how they'd managed to get to the mall. Possibly their grandniece had dropped them off in her car and then forgotten to pick them up. The grandniece could not be reached, Babette said, for comment.

The day before the happy discovery, the police had called in a psychic to help them determine the Treadwells' whereabouts and fate. It was all over the local paper. The psychic was a woman who lived in a mobile home in a wooded area outside town. She wished to be known only as Adele T. According to the paper, she and the police chief, Hollis Wright, sat in the mobile home while she looked at photos of the Treadwells and smelled articles from their wardrobe. Then she asked the chief to leave her alone for an hour. She did exercises, ate some rice and *dahl*, proceeded to trance in. During this altered state, the report went on, she attempted to put a data trace on whatever distant physical systems she wished to locate, in this case Old Man Treadwell and his sister. When chief Wright re-entered the trailer, Adele T. told him to forget the river and to concentrate on dry land with a moonscape look about it, within a fifteen-mile radius of the Treadwell home. The police went at once to a gypsum processing operation ten miles down river, where they found an airline bag that contained a handgun and two kilos of uncut heroin.

The police had consulted Adele T. on a number of occasions and she had led them to two bludgeoned bodies, a Syrian in a refrigerator and a cache of marked bills totaling six hundred thousand dollars, although in each instance, the report concluded, the police had been looking for something else.

The American mystery deepens.

14

We crowded before the window in Steffie's small room, watching the spectacular sunset. Only Heinrich stayed away, either because he distrusted wholesome communal pleasures or because he believed there was something ominous in the modern sunset.

Later I sat up in bed in my bathrobe studying German. I muttered words to myself and wondered whether I'd be able to restrict my German-speaking at the spring conference to brief opening remarks or whether the other participants would expect the language to be used throughout, in lectures, at meals, in small talk, as a mark of our seriousness, our uniqueness in world scholarship.

The TV said: "And other trends that could dramatically impact your portfolio."

Denise came in and sprawled across the foot of the bed, her head resting on her folded arms, facing away from me. How many codes, countercodes, social histories were contained in this simple posture? A full minute passed.

"What are we going to do about Baba?" she said.

"What do you mean?"

"She can't remember anything."

"Did she ask you whether she's taking medication?"

"No."

"No she's not or no she didn't ask?"

"She didn't ask."

"She was supposed to," I said.

"Well she didn't."

"How do you know she's taking something?"

"I saw the bottle buried in the trash under the kitchen sink. A prescription bottle. It had her name and the name of the medication."

"What is the name of the medication?"

"Dylar. One every three days. Which sounds like it's dangerous or habit-forming or whatever."

"What does your drug reference say about Dylar?"

"It's not in there. I spent hours. There are four indexes."

"It must be recently marketed. Do you want me to double-check the book?"

"I already looked. I *looked*."

"We could always call her doctor. But I don't want to make too much of this. Everybody takes some kind of medication, everybody forgets things occasionally."

"Not like my mother."

"I forget things all the time."

"What do you take?"

"Blood pressure pills, stress pills, allergy pills, eye drops, aspirin. Run of the mill."

"I looked in the medicine chest in your bathroom."

"No Dylar?"

"I thought there might be a new bottle."

"The doctor prescribed thirty pills. That was it. Run of the mill. Everybody takes something."

"I still want to know," she said.

All this time she'd been turned away from me. There were plot potentials in this situation, chances for people to make devious maneuvers, secret plans. But now she shifted position, used an elbow to prop her upper body and watched me speculatively from the foot of the bed.

"Can I ask you something?"

"Sure," I said.

"You won't get mad?"

"You know what's in my medicine chest. What secrets are left?"

"Why did you name Heinrich Heinrich?"

"Fair question."

"You don't have to answer."

"Good question. No reason why you shouldn't ask."

"So why did you?"

"I thought it was a forceful name, a strong name. It has a kind of authority."

"Is he named after anyone?"

"No. He was born shortly after I started the department and I guess I wanted to acknowledge my good fortune. I wanted to do something German. I felt a gesture was called for."

"Heinrich Gerhardt Gladney?"

"I thought it had an authority that might cling to him. I thought it was forceful and impressive and I still do. I wanted to shield him, make him unafraid. People were naming their children Kim, Kelly and Tracy."

There was a long silence. She kept watching me. Her features, crowded somewhat in the center of her face, gave to her moments of concentration a puggish and half-belligerent look.

"Do you think I miscalculated?"

"It's not for me to say."

"There's something about German names, the German language, German *things*. I don't know what it is exactly. It's just there. In the middle of it all is Hitler, of course."

"He was on again last night."

"He's always on. We couldn't have television without him."

"They lost the war," she said. "How great could they be?"

"A valid point. But it's not a question of greatness. It's not a question of good and evil. I don't know what it is. Look at it this way. Some people always wear a favorite color. Some people carry a gun. Some people put on a uniform and feel bigger, stronger, safer. It's in this area that my obsessions dwell."

Steffie came in wearing Denise's green visor. I didn't know what this meant. She climbed up on the bed and all three of us went through my German-English dictionary, looking for words that sound about the same in both languages, like orgy and shoe.

Heinrich came running down the hall, burst into the room.

"Come on, hurry up, plane crash footage." Then he was out the door, the girls were off the bed, all three of them running along the hall to the TV set.

I sat in bed a little stunned. The swiftness and noise of their leaving had put the room in a state of molecular agitation. In the debris of invisible matter, the question seemed to be, What is happening here? By the time I got to the room at the end of the hall, there was only a puff of black smoke at the edge of the screen. But the crash was shown two more times, once in stop-action replay, as an analyst attempted to explain the reason for the plunge. A jet trainer in an air show in New Zealand.

We had two closet doors that opened by themselves.

That night, a Friday, we gathered in front of the set, as was the custom and the rule, with take-out Chinese. There were floods, earthquakes, mud slides, erupting volcanoes. We'd never before been so attentive to our duty, our Friday assembly. Heinrich was not sullen, I was not bored. Steffie, brought close to tears by a sitcom husband arguing with his wife, appeared totally absorbed in these documentary clips of calamity and death. Babette tried to switch to a comedy series about a group of racially mixed kids who build their own communications satellite. She was startled by the force of our objection. We were otherwise silent, watching houses slide into the ocean, whole villages crackle and ignite in a mass of advancing lava. Every disaster made us wish for more, for something bigger, grander, more sweeping.

I walked into my office on Monday to find Murray sitting in the chair adjacent to the desk, like someone waiting for a nurse to arrive with a blood-pressure gauge. He'd been having trouble, he said, establishing an Elvis Presley power base in the department of American environments. The chairman, Alfonse Stompanato, seemed to feel that one of the other instructors, a three-hundred-pound former rock 'n' roll bodyguard named Dimitrios Cotsakis, had established prior right by having flown to Memphis when the King died, interviewed members of the King's entourage and family, been interviewed himself on local television as an Interpreter of the Phenomenon.

A more than middling coup, Murray conceded. I suggested that I might drop by his next lecture, informally, unannounced, simply to lend a note of consequence to the proceedings, to give him the benefit of whatever influence and prestige might reside in my office, my subject, my physical person. He nodded slowly, fingering the ends of his beard.

Later at lunch I spotted only one empty chair, at a table occupied by the New York émigrés. Alfonse sat at the head of the table, a commanding presence even in a campus lunchroom. He was large, sardonic, dark-staring, with scarred brows and a furious beard fringed in gray. It was the very beard I would have grown in 1969 if Janet Savory, my second wife, Heinrich's mother, hadn't argued against it. "Let them see that bland expanse," she said, in her tiny dry voice. "It is more effective than you think."

Alfonse invested everything he did with a sense of all-consuming purpose. He knew four languages, had a photographic memory, did complex mathematics in his head. He'd once told me that the art of getting ahead in New York was based on learning how to express dissatisfaction in an interesting way. The air was full of rage and complaint. People had no tolerance for your particular hardship unless you knew how to entertain them with it. Alfonse himself was occasionally entertaining in a pulverizing way. He had a manner that enabled him to absorb and destroy all opinions in conflict with his. When he talked about popular culture, he exercised the closed logic of a religious zealot, one who kills for his beliefs. His breathing grew heavy, arrhythmic, his brows seemed to lock. The other émigrés appeared to find his challenges and taunts a proper context for their endeavor. They used his office to pitch pennies to the wall.

I said to him, "Why is it, Alfonse, that decent, well-meaning and responsible people find themselves intrigued by catastrophe when they see it on television?"

I told him about the recent evening of lava, mud and raging water that the children and I had found so entertaining.

"We wanted more, more."

"It's natural, it's normal," he said, with a reassuring nod. "It happens to everybody."

"Why?"

"Because we're suffering from brain fade. We need an occasional catastrophe to break up the incessant bombardment of information."

"It's obvious," Lasher said. A slight man with a taut face and slicked-back hair.

"The flow is constant," Alfonse said. "Words, pictures, numbers, facts, graphics, statistics, specks, waves, particles, motes. Only a catastrophe gets our attention. We want them, we need them, we depend on them. As long as they happen somewhere else. This is where California comes in. Mud slides, brush fires, coastal erosion, earthquakes, mass killings, et cetera. We can relax and enjoy these disasters because in our hearts we feel that California deserves whatever it gets. Californians invented the concept of life-style. This alone warrants their doom."

Cotsakis crushed a can of Diet Pepsi and threw it at a garbage pail.

"Japan is pretty good for disaster footage," Alfonse said. "India remains largely untapped. They have tremendous potential with their famines, monsoons, religious strife, train wrecks, boat sinkings, et cetera. But their disasters tend to go unrecorded. Three lines in the newspaper. No film footage, no satellite hookup. This is why California is so important. We not only enjoy seeing them punished for their relaxed life-style and progressive social ideas but we know we're not missing anything. The cameras are right there. They're standing by. Nothing terrible escapes their scrutiny."

"You're saying it's more or less universal, to be fascinated by TV disasters."

"For most people there are only two places in the world. Where they live and their TV set. If a thing happens on television, we have every right to find it fascinating, whatever it is."

"I don't know whether to feel good or bad about learning that my experience is widely shared."

"Feel bad," he said.

"It's obvious," Lasher said. "We all feel bad. But we can enjoy it on that level."

Murray said, "This is what comes from the wrong kind of attentiveness. People get brain fade. This is because they've forgotten how to listen and look as children. They've forgotten how to collect data. In the psychic sense a forest fire on TV is on a lower plane than a ten-second spot for Automatic Dishwasher All. The commercial has deeper waves, deeper emanations. But we have reversed the relative significance of these things. This is why people's eyes, ears, brains and nervous systems have grown weary. It's a simple case of misuse."

Grappa casually tossed half a buttered roll at Lasher, hitting him on the shoulder. Grappa was pale and baby-fattish and the tossed roll was an attempt to get Lasher's attention.

Grappa said to him, "Did you ever brush your teeth with your finger?"

"I brushed my teeth with my finger the first time I stayed overnight at my wife's parents' house, before we were married, when her parents spent a weekend at Asbury Park. They were an Ipana family."

"Forgetting my toothbrush is a fetish with me," Cotsakis said. "I brushed my teeth with my finger at Woodstock, Altamont, Monterey, about a dozen other seminal events."

Grappa looked at Murray.

"I brushed my teeth with my finger after the Ali-Foreman fight in Zaire," Murray said. "That's the southernmost point I've ever brushed my teeth with my finger at."

Lasher looked at Grappa.

"Did you ever crap in a toilet bowl that had no seat?"

Grappa's response was semi-lyrical. "A great and funky men's room in an old Socony Mobil station on the Boston Post Road the first time my father took the car outside the city. The station with the flying red horse. You want the car? I can give you car details down to the last little option."

"These are the things they don't teach," Lasher said. "Bowls with no seats. Pissing in sinks. The culture of public toilets. All those great diners, movie houses, gas stations. The whole ethos of the road. I've pissed in sinks all through the American West. I've slipped across the border to piss in sinks in Manitoba and Alberta. This is what it's all about. The great western skies. The Best Western motels. The diners and drive-ins. The poetry of the road, the plains, the desert. The filthy stinking toilets. I pissed in a sink in Utah when it was twenty-two below. That's the coldest I've ever pissed in a sink in."

Alfonse Stompanato looked hard at Lasher.

"Where were you when James Dean died?" he said in a threatening voice.

"In my wife's parents' house before we were married, listening to 'Make Believe Ballroom' on the old Emerson table model. The Motorola with the glowing dial was already a thing of the past."

"You spent a lot of time in your wife's parents' house, it seems, screwing," Alfonse said.

"We were kids. It was too early in the cultural matrix for actual screwing."

"What were you doing?"

"She's my wife, Alfonse. You want me to tell a crowded table?"

"James Dean is dead and you're groping some twelve-year-old."

Alfonse glared at Dimitrios Cotsakis.

"Where were you when James Dean died?"

"In the back of my uncle's restaurant in Astoria, Queens, vacuuming with the Hoover."

Alfonse looked at Grappa.

"Where the hell were you?" he said, as if the thought had just occurred to him that the actor's death was not complete without some record of Grappa's whereabouts.

"I know exactly where I was, Alfonse. Let me think a minute."

"Where were you, you son of a bitch?"

"I always know these things down to the smallest detail. But I was a dreamy adolescent. I have these gaps in my life."

"You were busy jerking off. Is that what you mean?"

"Ask me Joan Crawford."

"September thirty, nineteen fifty-five. James Dean dies. Where is Nicholas Grappa and what is he doing?"

"Ask me Gable, ask me Monroe."

"The silver Porsche approaches an intersection, going like a streak. No time to brake for the Ford sedan. Glass shatters, metal screams. Jimmy Dean sits in the driver's seat with a broken neck, multiple fractures and lacerations. It is five forty-five in the afternoon, Pacific Coast Time. Where is Nicholas Grappa, the jerk-off king of the Bronx?"

"Ask me Jeff Chandler."

"You're a middle-aged man, Nicky, who trafficks in his own childhood. You have an obligation to produce."

"Ask me John Garfield, ask me Monty Clift."

Cotsakis was a monolith of thick and wadded flesh. He'd been Little Richard's personal bodyguard and had led security details at rock concerts before joining the faculty here.

Elliot Lasher threw a chunk of raw carrot at him, then asked, "Did you ever have a woman peel flaking skin from your back after a few days at the beach?"

"Cocoa Beach, Florida," Cotsakis said. "It was very tremendous. The second or third greatest experience of my life."

"Was she naked?" Lasher said.

"To the waist," Cotsakis said.

"From which direction?" Lasher said.

I watched Grappa throw a cracker at Murray. He skimmed it backhand like a Frisbee.

15

I put on my dark glasses, composed my face and walked into the room. There were twenty-five or thirty young men and women, many in fall colors, seated in armchairs and sofas and on the beige broadloom. Murray walked among them, speaking, his right hand trembling in a stylized way. When he saw me, he smiled sheepishly. I stood against the wall, attempting to loom, my arms folded under the black gown.

Murray was in the midst of a thoughtful monologue.

"Did his mother know that Elvis would die young? She talked about assassins. She talked about the life. The life of a star of this type and magnitude. Isn't the life structured to cut you down early? This is the point, isn't it? There are rules, guidelines. If you don't have the grace and wit to die early, you are forced to vanish, to hide as if in shame and apology. She worried about his sleepwalking. She thought he might go out a window. I have a feeling about mothers. Mothers really do know. The folklore is correct."

"Hitler adored his mother," I said.

A surge of attention, unspoken, identifiable only in a certain convergence of stillness, an inward tensing. Murray kept moving, of course, but a bit more deliberately, picking his way between the chairs, the people seated on the floor. I stood against the wall, arms folded.

"Elvis and Gladys liked to nuzzle and pet," he said. "They slept in the same bed until he began to approach physical maturity. They talked baby talk to each other all the time."

"Hitler was a lazy kid. His report card was full of unsatisfactorys. But Klara loved him, spoiled him, gave him the attention his father failed to give him. She was a quiet woman, modest and religious, and a good cook and housekeeper."

"Gladys walked Elvis to school and back every day. She defended him in little street rumbles, lashed out at any kid who tried to bully him."

"Hitler fantasized. He took piano lessons, made sketches of museums and villas. He sat around the house a lot. Klara tolerated this. He was the first of her children to survive infancy. Three others had died."

"Elvis confided in Gladys. He brought his girlfriends around to meet her."

"Hitler wrote a poem to his mother. His mother and his niece were the women with the greatest hold on his mind."

"When Elvis went into the army, Gladys became ill and depressed. She sensed something, maybe as much about herself as about him. Her psychic apparatus was flashing all the wrong signals. Foreboding and gloom."

"There's not much doubt that Hitler was what we call a mama's boy."

A note-taking young man murmured absently, "*Muttersöhnchen.*" I regarded him warily. Then, on an impulse, I abandoned my stance at the wall and began to pace the room like Murray, occasionally pausing to gesture, to listen, to gaze out a window or up at the ceiling.

"Elvis could hardly bear to let Gladys out of his sight when her condition grew worse. He kept a vigil at the hospital."

"When his mother became severely ill, Hitler put a bed in the kitchen to be closer to her. He cooked and cleaned."

"Elvis fell apart with grief when Gladys died. He fondled and petted her in the casket. He talked baby talk to her until she was in the ground."

"Klara's funeral cost three hundred and seventy kronen. Hitler wept at the grave and fell into a period of depression and self-pity. He felt an intense loneliness. He'd lost not only his beloved mother but also his sense of home and hearth."

"It seems fairly certain that Gladys's death caused a fundamental shift at the center of the King's world view. She'd been his anchor, his sense of security. He began to withdraw from the real world, to enter the state of his own dying."

"For the rest of his life, Hitler could not bear to be anywhere near Christmas decorations because his mother had died near a Christmas tree."

"Elvis made death threats, received death threats. He took mortuary tours and became interested in UFOs. He began to study the *Bardo Thödol*, commonly known as *The Tibetan Book of the Dead*. This is a guide to dying and being reborn."

"Years later, in the grip of self-myth and deep remoteness, Hitler kept a portrait of his mother in his spartan quarters at Obersalzberg. He began to hear a buzzing in his left ear."

Murray and I passed each other near the center of the room, almost colliding. Alfonse Stompanato entered, followed by several students, drawn perhaps by some magnetic wave of excitation, some frenzy in the air. He settled his surly bulk in a chair as Murray and I circled each other and headed off in opposite directions, avoiding an exchange of looks.

"Elvis fulfilled the terms of the contract. Excess, deterioration, self-destructiveness, grotesque behavior, a physical bloating and a series of insults to the brain, self-delivered. His place in legend is secure. He bought off the skeptics by dying early, horribly, unnecessarily. No one could deny him now. His mother probably saw it all, as on a nineteen-inch screen, years before her own death."

Murray, happily deferring to me, went to a corner of the room and sat on the floor, leaving me to pace and gesture alone, secure in my professional aura of power, madness and death.

"Hitler called himself the lonely wanderer out of nothingness. He sucked on lozenges, spoke to people in endless monologues, free-associating, as if the language came from some vastness beyond the world and he was simply the medium of revelation. It's interesting to wonder if he looked back from the *führerbunker*, beneath the burning city, to the early days of his power. Did he think of the small groups of tourists who visited the little settlement where his mother was born and where he'd spent summers with his cousins, riding in ox carts and making kites? They came to honor the site, Klara's birthplace. They entered the farmhouse, poked around tentatively. Adolescent boys climbed on the roof. In time the numbers began to increase. They took pictures, slipped small items into their pockets. Then crowds came, mobs of people overrunning the courtyard and singing patriotic songs, painting swastikas on the walls, on the flanks of farm animals. Crowds came to his mountain villa, so many people he had to stay indoors. They picked up pebbles where he'd walked and took them home as souvenirs. Crowds came to hear him speak, crowds erotically charged, the masses he once called his only bride. He closed his eyes, clenched his fists as he spoke, twisted his sweat-drenched body, remade his voice as a thrilling weapon. 'Sex murders,' someone called these speeches. Crowds came to be hypnotized by the voice, the party anthems, the torchlight parades."

I stared at the carpet and counted silently to seven.

"But wait. How familiar this all seems, how close to ordinary. Crowds come, get worked up, touch and press—people eager to be transported. Isn't this ordinary? We *know* all this. There must have been something different about those crowds. What was it? Let me whisper the terrible word, from the Old English, from the Old German, from the Old Norse. *Death.* Many of those crowds were assembled in the name of death. They were there to attend tributes to the dead. Processions, songs, speeches, dialogues with the dead, recitations of the names of the dead. They were there to see pyres and flaming wheels, thousands of flags dipped in salute, thousands of uniformed mourners. There were ranks and squadrons, elaborate backdrops, blood banners and black dress uniforms. Crowds came to form a shield against their own dying. To become a crowd is to keep out death. To break off from the crowd is to risk death as an individual, to face dying alone. Crowds came for this reason above all others. They were there to be a crowd."

Murray sat across the room. His eyes showed a deep gratitude. I had been generous with the power and madness at my disposal, allowing my subject to be associated with an infinitely lesser figure, a fellow who sat in La-Z-Boy chairs and shot out TVs. It was not a small matter. We all had an aura to maintain, and in sharing mine with a friend I was risking the very things that made me untouchable.

People gathered round, students and staff, and in the mild din of half heard remarks and orbiting voices I realized we were now a crowd. Not that I needed a crowd around me now. Least of all now. Death was strictly a professional matter here. I was comfortable with it, I was on top of it. Murray made his way to my side and escorted me from the room, parting the crowd with his fluttering hand.

16

This was the day Wilder started crying at two in the afternoon. At six he was still crying, sitting on the kitchen floor and looking through the oven window, and we ate dinner quickly, moving around him or stepping over him to reach the stove and refrigerator. Babette watched him as she ate. She had a class to teach in sitting, standing and walking. It would start in an hour and a half. She looked at me in a drained and supplicating way. She'd spoken soothingly to him, hefted and caressed him, checked his teeth, given him a bath, examined him, tickled him, fed him, tried to get him to crawl into his vinyl play tunnel. Her old people would be waiting in the church basement.

It was rhythmic crying, a measured statement of short urgent pulses. At times it seemed he would break off into a whimper, an animal complaint, irregular and exhausted, but the rhythm held, the heightened beat, the washed pink sorrow in his face.

"We'll take him to the doctor," I said. "Then I'll drop you at the church."

"Would the doctor see a crying child? Besides, his doctor doesn't have hours now."

"What about your doctor?"

"I think he does. But a crying child, Jack. What can I say to the man? 'My child is crying.'"

"Is there a condition more basic?"

There'd been no sense of crisis until now. Just exasperation and despair. But once we decided to visit the doctor, we began to hurry, to fret. We looked for Wilder's jacket and shoes, tried to remember what he'd eaten in the last twenty-four hours, anticipated questions the doctor would ask and rehearsed our answers carefully. It seemed vital to agree on the answers even if we weren't sure they were correct. Doctors lose interest in people who contradict each other. This fear has long informed my relationship with doctors, that they would lose interest in me, instruct their receptionists to call other names before mine, take my dying for granted.

I waited in the car while Babette and Wilder went into the medical building at the end of Elm. Doctors' offices depress me even more than hospitals do because of their air of negative expectancy and because of the occasional patient who leaves with good news, shaking the doctor's antiseptic hand and laughing loudly, laughing at everything the doctor says, booming with laughter, with crude power, making a point of ignoring the other patients as he walks past the waiting room still laughing provocatively—he is already clear of them, no longer associated with their weekly gloom, their anxious inferior dying. I would rather visit an emergency ward, some urban well of trembling, where people come in gut-shot, slashed, sleepy-eyed with opium compounds, broken needles in their arms. These things have nothing to do with my own eventual death, nonviolent, small-town, thoughtful.

They came out of the small bright lobby onto the street. It was cold, empty and dark. The boy walked next to his mother, holding her hand, still crying, and they seemed a picture of such amateurish sadness and calamity that I nearly started laughing—laughing not at the sadness but at the picture they made of it, at the disparity between their grief and its appearances. My feelings of tenderness and pity were undermined by the sight of them crossing the sidewalk in their bundled clothing, the child determinedly weeping, his mother drooping as she walked, wild-haired, a wretched and pathetic pair. They were inadequate to the spoken grief, the great single-minded anguish. Does this explain the existence of professional mourners? They keep a wake from lapsing into comic pathos.

"What did the doctor say?"

"Give him an aspirin and put him to bed."

"That's what Denise said."

"I told him that. He said, 'Well, why didn't you do it?'"

"Why didn't we?"

"She's a child, not a doctor—that's why."

"Did you tell him that?"

"I don't know what I told him," she said. "I'm never in control of what I say to doctors, much less what they say to me. There's some kind of disturbance in the air."

"I know exactly what you mean."

"It's like having a conversation during a spacewalk, dangling in those heavy suits."

"Everything drifts and floats."

"I lie to doctors all the time."

"So do I."

"But why?" she said.

As I started the car I realized his crying had changed in pitch and quality. The rhythmic urgency had given way to a sustained, inarticulate and mournful sound. He was keening now. These were expressions of Mideastern lament, of an anguish so accessible that it rushes to overwhelm whatever immediately caused it. There was something permanent and soul-struck in this crying. It was a sound of inbred desolation.

"What do we do?"

"Think of something," she said.

"There's still fifteen minutes before your class is due to start. Let's take him to the hospital, to the emergency entrance. Just to see what they say."

"You can't take a child to an emergency ward because he's crying. If anything is not an emergency, this would be it."

"I'll wait in the car," I said.

"What do I tell them? 'My child is crying.' Do they even have an emergency ward?"

"Don't you remember? We took the Stovers this past summer."

"Why?"

"Their car was being repaired."

"Never mind."

"They inhaled the spray mist from some kind of stain remover."

"Take me to my class," she said.

Posture. When I pulled up in front of the church, some of her students were walking down the steps to the basement entrance. Babette looked at her son—a searching, pleading and desperate look. He was in the sixth hour of his crying. She ran along the sidewalk and into the building.

I thought of taking him to the hospital. But if a doctor who examined the boy thoroughly in his cozy office with paintings on the wall in elaborate gilded frames could find nothing wrong, then what could emergency technicians do, people trained to leap on chests and pound at static hearts?

I picked him up and set him against the steering wheel, facing me, his feet on my thighs. The huge lament continued, wave on wave. It was a sound so large and pure I could almost listen to it, try consciously to apprehend it, as one sets up a mental register in a concert hall or theater. He was not sniveling or blubbering. He was crying out, saying nameless things in a way that touched me with its depth and richness. This was an ancient dirge all the more impressive for its resolute monotony. Ululation. I held him upright with a hand under each arm. As the crying continued, a curious shift developed in my thinking. I found that I did not necessarily wish him to stop. It might not be so terrible, I thought, to have to sit and listen to this a while longer. We looked at each other. Behind that dopey countenance, a complex intelligence operated. I held him with one hand, using the other to count his fingers inside the mittens, aloud, in German. The inconsolable crying went on. I let it wash over me, like rain in sheets. I entered it, in a sense. I let it fall and tumble across my face and chest. I began to think he had disappeared inside this wailing noise and if I could join him in his lost and suspended place we might together perform some reckless wonder of intelligibility. I let it break across my body. It might not be so terrible, I thought, to have to sit here for four more hours, with the motor running and the heater on, listening to this uniform lament. It might be good, it might be strangely soothing. I entered it, fell into it, letting it enfold and cover me. He cried with his eyes open, his eyes closed, his hands in his pockets, his mittens on and off. I sat there nodding sagely.

On an impulse I turned him around, sat him on my lap and started up the car, letting Wilder steer. We'd done this once before, for a distance of twenty yards, at Sunday dusk, in August, our street deep in drowsy shadow. Again he responded, crying as he steered, as we turned corners, as I brought the car to a halt back at the Congregational church. I set him on my left leg, an arm around him, drawing him toward me, and let my mind drift toward near sleep. The sound moved into a fitful distance. Now and then a car went by. I leaned against the door, faintly aware of his breath on my thumb. Some time later Babette was knocking on the window and Wilder was crawling across the seat to lift the latch for her. She got in, adjusted his hat, picked a crumpled tissue off the floor.

We were halfway home when the crying stopped. It stopped suddenly, without a change in tone and intensity. Babette said nothing, I kept my eyes on the road. He sat between us, looking into the radio. I waited for Babette to glance at me behind his back, over his head, to show relief, happiness, hopeful suspense. I didn't know how I felt and wanted a clue. But she looked straight ahead as if fearful that any change in the sensitive texture of sound, movement, expression would cause the crying to break out again.

At the house no one spoke. They all moved quietly from room to room, watching him distantly, with sneaky and respectful looks. When he asked for some milk, Denise ran softly to the kitchen, barefoot, in her pajamas, sensing that by economy of movement and lightness of step she might keep from disturbing the grave and dramatic air he had brought with him into the house. He drank the milk down in a single powerful swallow, still fully dressed, a mitten pinned to his sleeve.

They watched him with something like awe. Nearly seven straight hours of serious crying. It was as though he'd just returned from a period of wandering in some remote and holy place, in sand barrens or snowy ranges—a place where things are said, sights are seen, distances reached which we in our ordinary toil can only regard with the mingled reverence and wonder we hold in reserve for feats of the most sublime and difficult dimensions.

17

Babette said to me in bed one night, "Isn't it great having all these kids around?"

"There'll be one more soon."

"Who?"

"Bee is coming in a couple of days."

"Good. Who else can we get?"

The next day Denise decided to confront her mother directly about the medication she was or was not taking, hoping to trick Babette into a confession, an admission or some minimal kind of flustered response. This was not a tactic the girl and I had discussed but I couldn't help admiring the boldness of her timing. All six of us were jammed into the car on our way to the Mid-Village Mall and Denise simply waited for a natural break in the conversation, directing her question toward the back of Babette's head, in a voice drained of inference.

"What do you know about Dylar?"

"Is that the black girl who's staying with the Stovers?"

"That's Dakar," Steffie said.

"Dakar isn't her name, it's where she's from," Denise said. "It's a country on the ivory coast of Africa."

"The capital is Lagos," Babette said. "I know that because of a surfer movie I saw once where they travel all over the world."

"*The Perfect Wave,*" Heinrich said. "I saw it on TV."

"But what's the girl's name?" Steffie said.

"I don't know," Babette said, "but the movie wasn't called *The Perfect Wave*. The perfect wave is what they were looking for."

"They go to Hawaii," Denise told Steffie, "and wait for these tidal waves to come from Japan. They're called origamis."

"And the movie was called *The Long Hot Summer,*" her mother said.

"*The Long Hot Summer,*" Heinrich said, "happens to be a play by Tennessee Ernie Williams."

"It doesn't matter," Babette said, "because you can't copyright titles anyway."

"If she's an African," Steffie said, "I wonder if she ever rode a camel."

"Try an Audi Turbo."

"Try a Toyota Supra."

"What is it camels store in their humps?" Babette said. "Food or water? I could never get that straight."

"There are one-hump camels and two-hump camels," Heinrich told her. "So it depends which kind you're talking about."

"Are you telling me a two-hump camel stores food in one hump and water in the other?"

"The important thing about camels," he said, "is that camel meat is considered a delicacy."

"I thought that was alligator meat," Denise said.

"Who introduced the camel to America?" Babette said. "They had them out west for a while to carry supplies to coolies who were building the great railroads that met at Ogden, Utah. I remember my history exams."

"Are you sure you're not talking about llamas?" Heinrich said.

"The llama stayed in Peru," Denise said. "Peru has the llama, the vicuña and one other animal. Bolivia has tin. Chile has copper and iron."

"I'll give anyone in this car five dollars," Heinrich said, "if they can name the population of Bolivia."

"Bolivians," my daughter said.

The family is the cradle of the world's misinformation. There must be something in family life that generates factual error. Overcloseness, the noise and heat of being. Perhaps something even deeper, like the need to survive. Murray says we are fragile creatures surrounded by a world of hostile facts. Facts threaten our happiness and security. The deeper we delve into the nature of things, the looser our structure may seem to become. The family process works toward sealing off the world. Small errors grow heads, fictions proliferate. I tell Murray that ignorance and confusion can't possibly be the driving forces behind family solidarity. What an idea, what a subversion. He asks me why the strongest family units exist in the least developed societies. Not to know is a weapon of survival, he says. Magic and superstition become entrenched as the powerful orthodoxy of the clan. The family is strongest where objective reality is most likely to be misinterpreted. What a heartless theory, I say. But Murray insists it's true.

In a huge hardware store at the mall I saw Eric Massingale, a former microchip sales engineer who changed his life by coming out here to join the teaching staff of the computer center at the Hill. He was slim and pale, with a dangerous grin.

"You're not wearing dark glasses, Jack."

"I only wear them on campus."

"I get it."

We went our separate ways into the store's deep interior. A great echoing din, as of the extinction of a species of beast, filled the vast space. People bought twenty-two-foot ladders, six kinds of sandpaper, power saws that could fell trees. The aisles were long and bright, filled with oversized brooms, massive sacks of peat and dung, huge Rubbermaid garbage cans. Rope hung like tropical fruit, beautifully braided strands, thick, brown, strong. What a great thing a coil of rope is to look at and feel. I bought fifty feet of Manila hemp just to have it around, show it to my son, talk about where it comes from, how it's made. People spoke English, Hindi, Vietnamese, related tongues.

I ran into Massingale again at the cash terminals.

"I've never seen you off campus, Jack. You look different without your glasses and gown. Where did you get that sweater? Is that a Turkish army sweater? Mail order, right?"

He looked me over, felt the material of the water-repellent jacket I was carrying draped across my arm. Then he backed up, altering his perspective, nodding a little, his grin beginning to take on a self-satisfied look, reflecting some inner calculation.

"I think I know those shoes," he said.

What did he mean, he knew these shoes?

"You're a different person altogether."

"Different in what way, Eric?"

"You won't take offense?" he said, the grin turning lascivious, rich with secret meaning.

"Of course not. Why would I?"

"Promise you won't take offense."

"I won't take offense."

"You look so harmless, Jack. A big, harmless, aging, indistinct sort of guy."

"Why would I take offense?" I said, paying for my rope and hurrying out the door.

The encounter put me in the mood to shop. I found the others and we walked across two parking lots to the main structure in the Mid-Village Mall, a ten-story building arranged around a center court of waterfalls, promenades and gardens. Babette and the kids followed me into the elevator, into the shops set along the tiers, through the emporiums and department stores, puzzled but excited by my desire to buy. When I could not decide between two shirts they encouraged me to buy both. When I said I was hungry, they fed me pretzels, beer, souvlaki. The two girls scouted ahead, spotting things they thought I might want or need, running back to get me, to clutch my arms, plead with me to follow. They were my guides to endless well-being. People swarmed through the boutiques and gourmet shops. Organ music rose from the great court. We smelled chocolate, popcorn, cologne; we smelled rugs and furs, hanging salamis and deathly vinyl. My family gloried in the event. I was one of them, shopping, at last. They gave me advice, badgered clerks on my behalf. I kept seeing myself unexpectedly in some reflecting surface. We moved from store to store, rejecting not only items in certain departments, not only entire departments but whole stores, mammoth corporations that did not strike our fancy for one reason or another. There was always another store, three floors, eight floors, basement full of cheese graters and paring knives. I shopped with reckless abandon. I shopped for immediate needs and distant contingencies. I shopped for its own sake, looking and touching, inspecting merchandise I had no intention of buying, then buying it. I sent clerks into their fabric books and pattern books to search for elusive designs. I began to grow in value and self-regard. I filled myself out, found new aspects of myself, located a person I'd forgotten existed. Brightness settled around me. We crossed from furniture to men's wear, walking through cosmetics. Our images appeared on mirrored columns, in glassware and chrome, on TV monitors in security rooms. I traded money for goods. The more money I spent, the less important it seemed. I was bigger than these sums. These sums poured off my skin like so much rain. These sums in fact came back to me in the form of existential credit. I felt expansive, inclined to be sweepingly generous, and told the kids to pick out their Christmas gifts here and now. I gestured in what I felt was an expansive manner. I could tell they were impressed. They fanned out across the area, each of them suddenly inclined to be private, shadowy, even secretive. Periodically one of them would return to register the name of an item with Babette, careful not to let the others know what it was. I myself was not to be bothered with tedious details. I was the benefactor, the one who dispenses gifts, bonuses, bribes, *baksheesh*. The children knew it was the nature of such things that I could not be expected to engage in technical discussions about the gifts themselves. We ate another meal. A band played live Muzak. Voices rose ten stories from the gardens and promenades, a roar that echoed and swirled through the vast gallery, mixing with noises from the tiers, with shuffling feet and chiming bells, the hum of escalators, the sound of people eating, the human buzz of some vivid and happy transaction.

We drove home in silence. We went to our respective rooms, wishing to be alone. A little later I watched Steffie in front of the TV set. She moved her lips, attempting to match the words as they were spoken.

18

It is the nature and pleasure of townspeople to distrust the city. All the guiding principles that might flow from a center of ideas and cultural energies are regarded as corrupt, one or another kind of pornography. This is how it is with towns.

But Blacksmith is nowhere near a large city. We don't feel threatened and aggrieved in quite the same way other towns do. We're not smack in the path of history and its contaminations. If our complaints have a focal point, it would have to be the TV set, where the outer torment lurks, causing fears and secret desires. Certainly little or no resentment attaches to the College-on-the-Hill as an emblem of ruinous influence. The school occupies an ever serene edge of the townscape, semidetached, more or less scenic, suspended in political calm. Not a place designed to aggravate suspicions.

In light snow I drove to the airport outside Iron City, a large town sunk in confusion, a center of abandonment and broken glass rather than a place of fully realized urban decay. Bee, my twelve-year-old, was due in on a flight from Washington, with two stops and one change of planes along the way. But it was her mother, Tweedy Browner, who showed up in the arrivals area, a small dusty third-world place in a state of halted renovation. For a moment I thought Bee was dead and Tweedy had come to tell me in person.

"Where is Bee?"

"She's flying in later today. That's why I'm here. To spend some time with her. I have to go to Boston tomorrow. Family business."

"But where is she?"

"With her father."

"I'm her father, Tweedy."

"Malcolm Hunt, stupid. My husband."

"He's your husband, he's not her father."

"Do you still love me, Tuck?" she said.

She called me Tuck, which is what her mother used to call her father. All the male Browners were called Tuck. When the line began to pale, producing a series of aesthetes and incompetents, they gave the name to any man who married into the family, within reason. I was the first of these and kept expecting to hear a note of overrefined irony in their voices when they called me by that name. I thought that when tradition becomes too flexible, irony enters the voice. Nasality, sarcasm, self-caricature and so on. They would punish me by mocking themselves. But they were sweet about it, entirely sincere, even grateful to me for allowing them to carry on.

She wore a Shetland sweater, tweed skirt, knee socks and penny loafers. There was a sense of Protestant disrepair about her, a collapsed aura in which her body struggled to survive. The fair and angular face, the slightly bulging eyes, the signs of strain and complaint that showed about the mouth and around the eyes, the pulsing at the temple, the raised veins in the hands and neck. Cigarette ash clung to the loose weave of her sweater.

"For the third time. Where is she?"

"Indonesia, more or less. Malcolm's working in deep cover, sponsoring a Communist revival. It's part of an elegant scheme designed to topple Castro. Let's get out of here, Tuck, before children come swarming around to beg."

"Is she coming alone?"

"Why wouldn't she be?"

"From the Far East to Iron City can't be that simple."

"Bee can cope when she has to. She wants to be a travel writer as a matter of actual fact. Sits a horse well."

She took a deep drag on her cigarette and exhaled smoke in rapid expert streams from nose and mouth, a routine she used when she wanted to express impatience with her immediate surroundings. There were no bars or restaurants at the airport—just a stand with prepackaged sandwiches, presided over by a man with sect marks on his face. We got Tweedy's luggage, went out to the car and drove through Iron City, past deserted factories, on mainly deserted avenues, a city of hills, occasional cobbled streets, fine old homes here and there, holiday wreaths in the windows.

"Tuck, I'm not happy."

"Why not?"

"I thought you'd love me forever, frankly. I depend on you for that. Malcolm's away so much."

"We get a divorce, you take all my money, you marry a well-to-do, well-connected, well-tailored diplomat who secretly runs agents in and out of sensitive and inaccessible areas."

"Malcolm has always been drawn to jungly places."

We were traveling parallel to railroad tracks. The weeds were full of Styrofoam cups, tossed from train windows or wind-blown north from the depot.

"Janet has been drawn to Montana, to an ashram," I said.

"Janet Savory? Good God, whatever for?"

"Her name is Mother Devi now. She operates the ashram's business activities. Investments, real estate, tax shelters. It's what Janet has always wanted. Peace of mind in a profit-oriented context."

"Marvelous bone structure, Janet."

"She had a talent for stealth."

"You say that with such bitterness. I've never known you to be bitter, Tuck."

"Stupid but not bitter."

"What do you mean by stealth? Was she covert, like Malcolm?"

"She wouldn't tell me how much money she made. I think she used to read my mail. Right after Heinrich was born, she got me involved in a complex investment scheme with a bunch of multilingual people. She said she had information."

"But she was wrong and you lost vast sums."

"We made vast sums. I was entangled, enmeshed. She was always maneuvering. My security was threatened. My sense of a long and uneventful life. She wanted to incorporate us. We got phone calls from Liechtenstein, the Hebrides. Fictional places, plot devices."

"That doesn't sound like the Janet Savory I spent a delightful half hour with. The Janet with the high cheekbones and wry voice."

"You all had high cheekbones. Every one of you. Marvelous bone structure. Thank God for Babette and her long fleshy face."

"Isn't there somewhere we can get a civilized meal?" Tweedy said. "A tableclothy place with icy pats of butter. Malcolm and I once took tea with Colonel Qaddafi. A charming and ruthless man, one of the few terrorists we've met who lives up to his public billing."

The snow had stopped falling. We drove through a warehouse district, more deserted streets, a bleakness and anonymity that registered in the mind as a ghostly longing for something that was far beyond retrieval. There were lonely cafés, another stretch of track, freight cars paused at a siding. Tweedy chain-smoked extra-longs, shooting exasperated streams of smoke in every direction.

"God, Tuck, we were good together."

"Good at what?"

"Fool, you're supposed to look at me in a fond and nostalgic way, smiling ruefully."

"You wore gloves to bed."

"I still do."

"Gloves, eyeshades and socks."

"You know my flaws. You always did. I'm ultrasensitive to many things."

"Sunlight, air, food, water, sex."

"Carcinogenic, every one of them."

"What's the family business in Boston all about?"

"I have to reassure my mother that Malcolm isn't dead. She's taken quite a shine to him, for whatever reason."

"Why does she think he's dead?"

"When Malcolm goes into deep cover, it's as though he never existed. He disappears not only here and now but retroactively. No trace of the man remains. I sometimes wonder if the man I'm married to is in fact Malcolm Hunt or a completely different person who is himself operating under deep cover. It's frankly worrisome. I don't know which half of Malcolm's life is real, which half is intelligence. I'm hoping Bee can shed some light."

Traffic lights swayed on cables in a sudden gust. This was the city's main street, a series of discount stores, check-cashing places, wholesale outlets. A tall old Moorish movie theater, now remarkably a mosque. Blank structures called the Terminal Building, the Packer Building, the Commerce Building. How close this was to a classic photography of regret.

"A gray day in Iron City," I said. "We may as well go back to the airport."

"How is Hitler?"

"Fine, solid, dependable."

"You look good, Tuck."

"I don't feel good."

"You never felt good. You're the old Tuck. You were always the old Tuck. We loved each other, didn't we? We told each other everything, within the limits of one's preoccupation with breeding and tact. Malcolm tells me nothing. Who is he? What does he do?"

She sat with her legs tucked under her, facing me, and flicked ashes into her shoes, which sat on the rubber mat.

"Wasn't it marvelous to grow up tall and straight, among geldings and mares, with a daddy who wore blue blazers and crisp gray flannels?"

"Don't ask me."

"Mother used to stand in the arbor with an armful of cut flowers. Just stand there, being what she was."

At the airport we waited in a mist of plaster dust, among exposed wires, mounds of rubble. Half an hour before Bee was due to arrive, the passengers from another flight began filing through a drafty tunnel into the arrivals area. They were gray and stricken, they were stooped over in weariness and shock, dragging their hand luggage across the floor. Twenty, thirty, forty people came out, without a word or look, keeping their eyes to the ground.

Some limped, some wept. More came through the tunnel, adults with whimpering children, old people trembling, a black minister with his collar askew, one shoe missing. Tweedy helped a woman with two small kids. I approached a young man, a stocky fellow with a mailman's cap and beer belly, wearing a down vest, and he looked at me as if I didn't belong in his space-time dimension but had crossed over illegally, made a rude incursion. I forced him to stop and face me, asked him what had happened up there. As people kept filing past, he exhaled wearily. Then he nodded, his eyes steady on mine, full of a gentle resignation.

The plane had lost power in all three engines, dropped from thirty-four thousand feet to twelve thousand feet. Something like four miles. When the steep glide began, people rose, fell, collided, swam in their seats. Then the serious screaming and moaning began. Almost immediately a voice from the flight deck was heard on the intercom: "We're falling out of the sky! We're going down! We're a silver gleaming death machine!" This outburst struck the passengers as an all but total breakdown of authority, competence and command presence and it brought on a round of fresh and desperate wailing.

Objects were rolling out of the galley, the aisles were full of drinking glasses, utensils, coats and blankets. A stewardess pinned to the bulkhead by the sharp angle of descent was trying to find the relevant passage in a handbook titled "Manual of Disasters." Then there was a second male voice from the flight deck, this one remarkably calm and precise, making the passengers believe there was someone in charge after all, an element of hope: "This is American two-one-three to the cockpit voice recorder. Now we know what it's like. It is worse than we'd ever imagined. They didn't prepare us for this at the death simulator in Denver. Our fear is pure, so totally stripped of distractions and pressures as to be a form of transcendental meditation. In less than three minutes we will touch down, so to speak. They will find our bodies in some smoking field, strewn about in the grisly attitudes of death. I love you, Lance." This time there was a brief pause before the mass wailing recommenced. Lance? What kind of people were in control of this aircraft? The crying took on a bitter and disillusioned tone.

As the man in the down vest told the story, passengers from the tunnel began gathering around us. No one spoke, interrupted, tried to embellish the account.

Aboard the gliding craft, a stewardess crawled down the aisle, over bodies and debris, telling people in each row to remove their shoes, remove sharp objects from their pockets, assume a fetal position. At the other end of the plane, someone was wrestling with a flotation device. Certain elements in the crew had decided to pretend that it was not a crash but a crash landing that was seconds away. After all, the difference between the two is only one word. Didn't this suggest that the two forms of flight termination were more or less interchangeable? How much could one word matter? An encouraging question under the circumstances, if you didn't think about it too long, and there was no time to think right now. The basic difference between a crash and a crash landing seemed to be that you could sensibly prepare for a crash landing, which is exactly what they were trying to do. The news spread through the plane, the term was repeated in row after row. "Crash landing, crash landing." They saw how easy it was, by adding one word, to maintain a grip on the future, to extend it in consciousness if not in actual fact. They patted themselves for ballpoint pens, went fetal in their seats.

By the time the narrator reached this point in his account, many people were crowded around, not only people who'd just emerged from the tunnel but also those who'd been among the first to disembark. They'd come back to listen. They were not yet ready to disperse, to reinhabit their earthbound bodies, but wanted to linger with their terror, keep it separate and intact for just a while longer. More people drifted toward us, milled about, close to the entire planeload. They were content to let the capped and vested man speak on their behalf. No one disputed his account or tried to add individual testimony. It was as though they were being told of an event they hadn't personally been involved in. They were interested in what he said, even curious, but also clearly detached. They trusted him to tell them what they'd said and felt.

It was at this point in the descent, as the term "crash landing" spread through the plane, with a pronounced vocal stress on the second word, that passengers in first class came scrambling and clawing through the curtains, literally climbing their way into the tourist section in order to avoid being the first to strike the ground. There were those in tourist who felt they ought to be made to go back. This sentiment was expressed not so much in words and actions as in terrible and inarticulate sounds, mainly cattle noises, an urgent and force-fed lowing. Suddenly the engines restarted. Just like that. Power, stability, control. The passengers, prepared for impact, were slow to adjust to the new wave of information. New sounds, a different flight path, a sense of being encased in solid tubing and not some polyurethane wrap. The smoking sign went on, an international hand with a cigarette. Stewardesses appeared with scented towelettes for cleaning blood and vomit. People slowly came out of their fetal positions, sat back limply. Four miles of prime-time terror. No one knew what to say. Being alive was a richness of sensation. Dozens of things, hundreds of things. The first officer walked down the aisle, smiling and chatting in an empty pleasant corporate way. His face had the rosy and confident polish that is familiar in handlers of large passenger aircraft. They looked at him and wondered why they'd been afraid.

I'd been pushed away from the narrator by people crowding in to listen, well over a hundred of them, dragging their shoulder bags and garment bags across the dusty floor. Just as I realized I was almost out of hearing range, I saw Bee standing next to me, her small face smooth and white in a mass of kinky hair. She jumped up into my embrace, smelling of jet exhaust.

"Where's the media?" she said.

"There is no media in Iron City."

"They went through all that for nothing?"

We found Tweedy and headed out to the car. There was a traffic jam on the outskirts of the city and we had to sit on a road outside an abandoned foundry. A thousand broken windows, street lights broken, darkness settling in. Bee sat in the middle of the rear seat in the lotus position. She seemed remarkably well rested after a journey that had spanned time zones, land masses, vast oceanic distances, days and nights, on large and small planes, in summer and winter, from Surabaya to Iron City. Now we sat waiting in the dark for a car to get towed or a drawbridge to close. Bee didn't think this familiar irony of modern travel was worth a comment. She just sat there listening to Tweedy explain to me why parents needn't worry about children taking such trips alone. Planes and terminals are the safest of places for the very young and very old. They are looked after, smiled upon, admired for their resourcefulness and pluck. People ask friendly questions, offer them blankets and sweets.

"Every child ought to have the opportunity to travel thousands of miles alone," Tweedy said, "for the sake of her self-esteem and independence of mind, with clothes and toiletries of her own choosing. The sooner we get them in the air, the better. Like swimming or ice skating. You have to start them young. It's one of the things I'm proudest to have accomplished with Bee. I sent her to Boston on Eastern when she was nine. I told Granny Browner not to meet her plane. Getting out of airports is every bit as important as the actual flight. Too many parents ignore this phase of a child's development. Bee is thoroughly bicoastal now. She flew her first jumbo at ten, changed planes at O'Hare, had a near miss in Los Angeles. Two weeks later she took the Concorde to London. Malcolm was waiting with a split of champagne."

Up ahead the taillights danced, the line began to move.

Barring mechanical failures, turbulent weather and terrorist acts, Tweedy said, an aircraft traveling at the speed of sound may be the last refuge of gracious living and civilized manners known to man.

19

Bee made us feel self-conscious at times, a punishment that visitors will unintentionally inflict on their complacent hosts. Her presence seemed to radiate a surgical light. We began to see ourselves as a group that acted without design, avoided making decisions, took turns being stupid and emotionally unstable, left wet towels everywhere, mislaid our youngest member. Whatever we did was suddenly a thing that seemed to need explaining. My wife was especially disconcerted. If Denise was a pint-sized commissar, nagging us to higher conscience, then Bee was a silent witness, calling the very meaning of our lives into question. I watched Babette stare into her cupped hands, aghast.

That chirping sound was just the radiator.

Bee was quietly disdainful of wisecracks, sarcasm and other family business. A year older than Denise, she was taller, thinner, paler, both worldly and ethereal, as though in her heart she was not a travel writer at all, as her mother had said she wished to be, but simply a traveler, the purer form, someone who collects impressions, dense anatomies of feeling, but does not care to record them.

She was self-possessed and thoughtful, had brought us hand-carved gifts from the jungles. She took taxis to school and dance class, spoke a little Chinese, had once wired money to a stranded friend. I admired her in a distant and uneasy way, sensing a nameless threat, as if she were not my child at all but the sophisticated and self-reliant friend of one of my children. Was Murray right? Were we a fragile unit surrounded by hostile facts? Would I promote ignorance, prejudice and superstition to protect my family from the world?

On Christmas Day, Bee sat by the fireplace in our seldom used living room, watching the turquoise flames. She wore a long loose khaki outfit that looked casually expensive. I sat in the armchair with three or four gift boxes in my lap, apparel and tissue paper hanging out. My dog-eared copy of *Mein Kampf* rested on the floor at the side of the chair. Some of the other people were in the kitchen preparing the meal, some had gone upstairs to investigate their gifts in private. The TV said: "This creature has developed a complicated stomach in keeping with its leafy diet."

"I don't like this business with Mother," Bee said in a voice of cultivated distress. "She looks keyed-up all the time. Like she's worried about something but she's not sure what it is. It's Malcolm, of course. He's got his jungle. What does she have? A huge airy kitchen with a stove that belongs in a three-star restaurant in the provinces. She put all her energy into that kitchen, but for what? It's not a kitchen at all. It's her life, her middle age. Baba could enjoy a kitchen like that. It would be a kitchen to her. To Mother it's like a weird symbol of getting through a crisis, except she hasn't gotten through it."

"Your mother is not sure exactly who her husband is."

"That's not the basic problem. The basic problem is that she doesn't know who she is. Malcolm is in the highlands living on tree bark and snake. That's who Malcolm is. He needs heat and humidity. He's got like how many degrees in foreign affairs and economics but all he wants to do is squat under a tree and watch tribal people pack mud all over their bodies. They're fun to watch. What does Mother do for fun?"

Bee was small-featured except for her eyes, which seemed to contain two forms of life, the subject matter and its hidden implications. She talked about Babette's effortless skills in making things work, the house, the kids, the flow of the routine universe, sounding a little like me, but there was a secondary sea-life moving deep in the iris of her eye. What did it mean, what was she really saying, why did she seem to expect me to respond in kind? She wanted to communicate in this secondary way, with optic fluids. She would have her suspicions confirmed, find out about me. But what suspicions did she harbor and what was there to find out? I began to worry. As the odor of burning toast filled the house, I tried to get her to talk about life in the seventh grade.

"Is the kitchen on fire?"

"That's Steffie burning toast. A thing she does from time to time."

"I could have prepared some kind of *kimchi* dish."

"Something from your Korean period."

"It's cabbage pickled with red pepper and a bunch of other things. Fiery hot. But I don't know about ingredients. They're hard enough to find in Washington."

"We're probably having something besides toast," I said.

The mild rebuke made her happy. She liked me best when I was dry, derisive and cutting, a natural talent she believed I'd forfeited through long association with children.

The TV said: "Now we will put the little feelers on the butterfly."

In bed two nights later I heard voices, put on my robe and went down the hall to see what was going on. Denise stood outside the bathroom door.

"Steffie's taking one of her baths."

"It's late," I said.

"She's just sitting in all that dirty water."

"It's my dirt," Steffie said from the other side of the door.

"It's still dirt."

"Well it's my dirt and I don't care."

"It's dirt," Denise said.

"It's my dirt."

"Dirt is dirt."

"Not when it's mine."

Bee appeared at the end of the hall wearing a silver and red kimono. Just stood there, distant and pale. There was a moment in which our locus of pettiness and shame seemed palpably to expand, a cartoon of self-awareness. Denise muttered something violent to Steffie through the crack in the door, then went quietly to her room.

In the morning I drove Bee to the airport. Rides to airports make me quiet and glum. We listened to news updates on the radio, curiously excited reports about firemen removing a burning sofa from a tenement in Watertown, delivered in a background clamor of ticker-tape machines. I realized Bee was watching me carefully, importantly. She sat with her back against the door, her knees up, held tightly together, arms enfolding them. The look was one of solemn compassion. It was a look I did not necessarily trust, believing it had little to do with pity or love or sadness. I recognized it in fact as something else completely. The adolescent female's tenderest form of condescension.

On the way back from the airport, I got off the expressway at the river road and parked the car at the edge of the woods. I walked up a steep path. There was an old picket fence with a sign.

THE OLD BURYING GROUND
Blacksmith Village

The headstones were small, tilted, pockmarked, spotted with fungus or moss, the names and dates barely legible. The ground was hard, with patches of ice. I walked among the stones, taking off my gloves to touch the rough marble. Embedded in the dirt before one of the markers was a narrow vase containing three small American flags, the only sign that someone had preceded me to this place in this century. I was able to make out some of the names, great strong simple names, suggesting a moral rigor. I stood and listened.

I was beyond the traffic noise, the intermittent stir of factories across the river. So at least in this they'd been correct, placing the graveyard here, a silence that had stood its ground. The air had a bite. I breathed deeply, remained in one spot, waiting to feel the peace that is supposed to descend upon the dead, waiting to see the light that hangs above the fields of the landscapist's lament.

I stood there, listening. The wind blew snow from the branches. Snow blew out of the woods in eddies and sweeping gusts. I raised my collar, put my gloves back on. When the air was still again, I walked among the stones, trying to read the names and dates, adjusting the flags to make them swing free. Then I stood and listened.

The power of the dead is that we think they see us all the time. The dead have a presence. Is there a level of energy composed solely of the dead? They are also in the ground, of course, asleep and crumbling. Perhaps we are what they dream.

May the days be aimless. Let the seasons drift. Do not advance the action according to a plan.

20

Mr. Treadwell's sister died. Her first name was Gladys. The doctor said she died of lingering dread, a result of the four days and nights she and her brother had spent in the Mid-Village Mall, lost and confused.

A man in Glassboro died when the rear wheel of his car separated from the axle. An idiosyncrasy of that particular model.

The lieutenant governor of the state died of undisclosed natural causes, after a long illness. We all know what that means.

A Mechanicsville man died outside Tokyo during a siege of the airport by ten thousand helmeted students.

When I read obituaries I always note the age of the deceased. Automatically I relate this figure to my own age. Four years to go, I think. Nine more years. Two years and I'm dead. The power of numbers is never more evident than when we use them to speculate on the time of our dying. Sometimes I bargain with myself. Would I be willing to accept sixty-five, Genghis Khan's age on dying? Suleiman the Magnificent made it to seventy-six. That sounds all right, especially the way I feel now, but how will it sound when I'm seventy-three?

It's hard to imagine these men feeling sad about death. Attila the Hun died young. He was still in his forties. Did he feel sorry for himself, succumb to self-pity and depression? He was the King of the Huns, the Invader of Europe, the Scourge of God. I want to believe he lay in his tent, wrapped in animal skins, as in some internationally financed movie epic, and said brave cruel things to his aides and retainers. No weakening of the spirit. No sense of the irony of human existence, that we are the highest form of life on earth and yet ineffably sad because we know what no other animal knows, that we must die. Attila did not look through the opening in his tent and gesture at some lame dog standing at the edge of the fire waiting to be thrown a scrap of meat. He did not say, "That pathetic flea-ridden beast is better off than the greatest ruler of men. It doesn't know what we know, it doesn't feel what we feel, it can't be sad as we are sad."

I want to believe he was not afraid. He accepted death as an experience that flows naturally from life, a wild ride through the forest, as would befit someone known as the Scourge of God. This is how it ended for him, with his attendants cutting off their hair and disfiguring their own faces in barbarian tribute, as the camera pulls back out of the tent and pans across the night sky of the fifth century A.D., clear and uncontaminated, bright-banded with shimmering worlds.

Babette looked up from her eggs and hash browns and said to me with a quiet intensity, "Life is good, Jack."

"What brings this on?"

"I just think it ought to be said."

"Do you feel better now that you've said it?"

"I have terrible dreams," she murmured.

Who will die first? She says she wants to die first because she would feel unbearably lonely and sad without me, especially if the children were grown and living elsewhere. She is adamant about this. She sincerely wants to precede me. She discusses the subject with such argumentative force that it's obvious she thinks we have a choice in the matter. She also thinks nothing can happen to us as long as there are dependent children in the house. The kids are a guarantee of our relative longevity. We're safe as long as they're around. But once they get big and scatter, she wants to be the first to go. She sounds almost eager. She is afraid I will die unexpectedly, sneakily, slipping away in the night. It isn't that she doesn't cherish life; it's being left alone that frightens her. The emptiness, the sense of cosmic darkness.

MasterCard, Visa, American Express.

I tell her I want to die first. I've gotten so used to her that I would feel miserably incomplete. We are two views of the same person. I would spend the rest of my life turning to speak to her.

No one there, a hole in space and time. She claims my death would leave a bigger hole in her life than her death would leave in mine. This is the level of our discourse. The relative size of holes, abysses and gaps. We have serious arguments on this level. She says if her death is capable of leaving a large hole in my life, my death would leave an abyss in hers, a great yawning gulf. I counter with a profound depth or void. And so it goes into the night. These arguments never seem foolish at the time. Such is the dignifying power of our subject.

She put on a long glossy padded coat—it looked segmented, exoskeletal, designed for the ocean floor—and went out to teach her class in posture. Steffie moved soundlessly through the house carrying small plastic bags she used for lining the wicker baskets scattered about. She did this once or twice a week with the quiet and conscientious air of someone who does not want credit for saving lives. Murray came over to talk to the two girls and Wilder, something he did from time to time as part of his investigation into what he called the society of kids. He talked about the otherworldly babble of the American family. He seemed to think we were a visionary group, open to special forms of consciousness. There were huge amounts of data flowing through the house, waiting to be analyzed.

He went upstairs with the three kids to watch TV. Heinrich walked into the kitchen, sat at the table and gripped a fork tightly in each hand. The refrigerator throbbed massively. I flipped a switch and somewhere beneath the sink a grinding mechanism reduced parings, rinds and animal fats to tiny drainable fragments, with a motorized surge that made me retreat two paces. I took the forks out of my son's hands and put them in the dishwasher.

"Do you drink coffee yet?"

"No," he said.

"Baba likes a cup when she gets back from class."

"Make her tea instead."

"She doesn't like tea."

"She can learn, can't she?"

"The two things have completely different tastes."

"A habit's a habit."

"You have to acquire it first."

"That's what I'm saying. Make her tea."

"Her class is more demanding than it sounds. Coffee relaxes her."

"That's why it's dangerous," he said.

"It's not dangerous."

"Whatever relaxes you is dangerous. If you don't know that, I might as well be talking to the wall."

"Murray would also like coffee," I said, aware of a small note of triumph in my voice.

"Did you see what you just did? You took the coffee can with you to the counter."

"So what?"

"You didn't have to. You could have left it by the stove where you were standing and then gone to the counter to get the spoon."

"You're saying I carried the coffee can unnecessarily."

"You carried it in your right hand all the way to the counter, put it down to open the drawer, which you didn't want to do with your left hand, then got the spoon with your right hand, switched it to your left hand, picked up the coffee can with your right hand and went back to the stove, where you put it down again."

"That's what people do."

"It's wasted motion. People waste tremendous amounts of motion. You ought to watch Baba make a salad sometime."

"People don't deliberate over each tiny motion and gesture. A little waste doesn't hurt."

"But over a lifetime?"

"What do you save if you don't waste?"

"Over a lifetime? You save tremendous amounts of time and energy," he said.

"What will you do with them?"

"Use them to live longer."

The truth is I don't want to die first. Given a choice between loneliness and death, it would take me a fraction of a second to decide. But I don't want to be alone either. Everything I say to

Babette about holes and gaps is true. Her death would leave me scattered, talking to chairs and pillows. Don't let us die, I want to cry out to that fifth century sky ablaze with mystery and spiral light. Let us both live forever, in sickness and health, feeble-minded, doddering, toothless, liver-spotted, dim-sighted, hallucinating. Who decides these things? What is out there? Who are you?

I watched the coffee bubble up through the center tube and perforated basket into the small pale globe. A marvelous and sad invention, so roundabout, ingenious, human. It was like a philosophical argument rendered in terms of the things of the world—water, metal, brown beans. I had never looked at coffee before.

"When plastic furniture burns, you get cyanide poisoning," Heinrich said, tapping the Formica tabletop.

He ate a winter peach. I poured a cup of coffee for Murray and together the boy and I went up the stairs to Denise's room, where the TV set was currently located. The volume was kept way down, the girls engaged in a rapt dialogue with their guest. Murray looked happy to be there. He sat in the middle of the floor taking notes, his toggle coat and touring cap next to him on the rug. The room around him was rich in codes and messages, an archaeology of childhood, things Denise had carried with her since the age of three, from cartoon clocks to werewolf posters. She is the kind of child who feels a protective tenderness toward her own beginnings. It is part of her strategy in a world of displacements to make every effort to restore and preserve, keep things together for their value as remembering objects, a way of fastening herself to a life.

Make no mistake. I take these children seriously. It is not possible to see too much in them, to overindulge your casual gift for the study of character. It is all there, in full force, charged waves of identity and being. There are no amateurs in the world of children.

Heinrich stood in a corner of the room, taking up his critical-observer position. I gave Murray his coffee and was about to leave when I glanced in passing at the TV screen. I paused at the door, looked more closely this time. It was true, it was there. I hissed at the others for silence and they swiveled their heads in my direction, baffled and annoyed. Then they followed my gaze to the sturdy TV at the end of the bed.

The face on the screen was Babette's. Out of our mouths came a silence as wary and deep as an animal growl. Confusion, fear, astonishment spilled from our faces. What did it mean? What was she doing there, in black and white, framed in formal borders? Was she dead, missing, disembodied? Was this her spirit, her secret self, some two-dimensional facsimile released by the power of technology, set free to glide through wavebands, through energy levels, pausing to say good-bye to us from the fluorescent screen?

A strangeness gripped me, a sense of psychic disorientation. It was her all right, the face, the hair, the way she blinks in rapid twos and threes. I'd seen her just an hour ago, eating eggs, but her appearance on the screen made me think of her as some distant figure from the past, some ex-wife and absentee mother, a walker in the mists of the dead. If she was not dead, was I? A two-syllable infantile cry, *ba-ba*, issued from the deeps of my soul.

All this compressed in seconds. It was only as time drew on, normalized itself, returned to us a sense of our surroundings, the room, the house, the reality in which the TV set stood—it was only then that we understood what was going on.

Babette was teaching her class in the church basement and it was being televised by the local cable station. Either she hadn't known there would be a camera on hand or she preferred not to tell us, out of embarrassment, love, superstition, whatever causes a person to wish to withhold her image from those who know her.

With the sound down low we couldn't hear what she was saying. But no one bothered to adjust the volume. It was the picture that mattered, the face in black and white, animated but also flat, distanced, sealed off, timeless. It was but wasn't her. Once again I began to think Murray might be on to something. Waves and radiation. Something leaked through the mesh. She was shining a light on us, she was coming into being, endlessly being formed and reformed as the muscles in her face worked at smiling and speaking, as the electronic dots swarmed.

We were being shot through with Babette. Her image was projected on our bodies, swam in us and through us. Babette of electrons and photons, of whatever forces produced that gray light we took to be her face.

The kids were flushed with excitement but I felt a certain disquiet. I tried to tell myself it was only television—whatever that was, however it worked—and not some journey out of life or death, not some mysterious separation. Murray looked up at me, smiling in his sneaky way.

Only Wilder remained calm. He watched his mother, spoke to her in half-words, sensible-sounding fragments that were mainly fabricated. As the camera pulled back to allow Babette to demonstrate some fine point of standing or walking, Wilder approached the set and touched her body, leaving a handprint on the dusty surface of the screen.

Then Denise crawled up to the set and turned the volume dial. Nothing happened. There was no sound, no voice, nothing. She turned to look at me, a moment of renewed confusion. Heinrich advanced, fiddled with the dial, stuck his hand behind the set to adjust the recessed knobs. When he tried another channel, the sound boomed out, raw and fuzzy. Back at the cable station, he couldn't raise a buzz and as we watched Babette finish the lesson, we were in a mood of odd misgiving. But as soon as the program ended, the two girls got excited again and went downstairs to wait for Babette at the door and surprise her with news of what they'd seen.

The small boy remained at the TV set, within inches of the dark screen, crying softly, uncertainly, in low heaves and swells, as Murray took notes.

The Airborne Toxic Event

21

After a night of dream-lit snows the air turned clear and still. There was a taut blue quality in the January light, a hardness and confidence. The sound of boots on packed snow, the contrails streaked cleanly in the high sky. Weather was very much the point, although I didn't know it at first.

I turned into our street and walked past men bent over shovels in their driveways, breathing vapor. A squirrel moved along a limb in a flowing motion, a passage so continuous it seemed to be its own physical law, different from the ones we've learned to trust. When I was halfway down the street I saw Heinrich crouched on a small ledge outside our attic window. He wore his camouflage jacket and cap, an outfit with complex meaning for him, at fourteen, struggling to grow and to escape notice simultaneously, his secrets known to us all. He looked east through binoculars.

I went around back to the kitchen. In the entranceway the washer and dryer were vibrating nicely. I could tell from Babette's voice that the person she was talking to on the phone was her father. An impatience mixed with guilt and apprehension. I stood behind her, put my cold hands to her cheeks. A little thing I liked to do. She hung up the phone.

"Why is he on the roof?"

"Heinrich? Something about the train yards," she said. "It was on the radio."

"Shouldn't I get him down?"

"Why?"

"He could fall."

"Don't tell him that."

"Why not?"

"He thinks you underestimate him."

"He's on a ledge," I said. "There must be something I should be doing."

"The more you show concern, the closer he'll go to the edge."

"I know that but I still have to get him down."

"Coax him back in," she said. "Be sensitive and caring. Get him to talk about himself. Don't make sudden movements."

When I got to the attic he was already back inside, standing by the open window, still looking through the glasses. Abandoned possessions were everywhere, oppressive and soul-worrying, creating a weather of their own among the exposed beams and posts, the fiberglass insulation pads.

"What happened?"

"The radio said a tank car derailed. But I don't think it derailed from what I could see. I think it got rammed and something punched a hole in it. There's a lot of smoke and I don't like the looks of it."

"What does it look like?"

He handed me the binoculars and stepped aside. Without climbing onto the ledge I couldn't see the switching yard and the car or cars in question. But the smoke was plainly visible, a heavy black mass hanging in the air beyond the river, more or less shapeless.

"Did you see fire engines?"

"They're all over the place," he said. "But it looks to me like they're not getting too close. It must be pretty toxic or pretty explosive stuff, or both."

"It won't come this way."

"How do you know?"

"It just won't. The point is you shouldn't be standing on icy ledges. It worries Baba."

"You think if you tell me it worries her, I'll feel guilty and not do it. But if you tell me it worries you, I'll do it all the time."

"Shut the window," I told him.

We went down to the kitchen. Steffie was looking through the brightly colored mail for coupons, lotteries and contests. This was the last day of the holiday break for the grade school and high school. Classes on the Hill would resume in a week. I sent Heinrich outside to clear snow from the walk. I watched him stand out there, utterly still, his head turned slightly, a honed awareness in his stance. It took me a while to realize he was listening to the sirens beyond the river.

An hour later he was back in the attic, this time with a radio and highway map. I climbed the narrow stairs, borrowed the glasses and looked again. It was still there, a slightly larger accumulation, a towering mass in fact, maybe a little blacker now.

"The radio calls it a feathery plume," he said. "But it's not a plume."

"What is it?"

"Like a shapeless growing thing. A dark black breathing thing of smoke. Why do they call it a plume?"

"Air time is valuable. They can't go into long tortured descriptions. Have they said what kind of chemical it is?"

"It's called Nyodene Derivative or Nyodene D. It was in a movie we saw in school on toxic wastes. These videotaped rats."

"What does it cause?"

"The movie wasn't sure what it does to humans. Mainly it was rats growing urgent lumps."

"That's what the movie said. What does the radio say?"

"At first they said skin irritation and sweaty palms. But now they say nausea, vomiting, shortness of breath."

"This is human nausea we're talking about. Not rats."

"Not rats," he said.

I gave him the binoculars.

"Well it won't come this way."

"How do you know?" he said.

"I just know. It's perfectly calm and still today. And when there's a wind at this time of year, it blows that way, not this way."

"What if it blows this way?"

"It won't."

"Just this one time."

"It won't. Why should it?"

He paused a beat and said in a flat tone, "They just closed part of the interstate."

"They would want to do that, of course."

"Why?"

"They just would. A sensible precaution. A way to facilitate movement of service vehicles and such. Any number of reasons that have nothing to do with wind or wind direction."

Babette's head appeared at the top of the stairway. She said a neighbor had told her the spill from the tank car was thirty-five thousand gallons. People were being told to stay out of the area. A feathery plume hung over the site. She also said the girls were complaining of sweaty palms.

"There's been a correction," Heinrich told her. "Tell them they ought to be throwing up."

A helicopter flew over, headed in the direction of the accident. The voice on the radio said: "Available for a limited time only with optional megabyte hard disk."

Babette's head sank out of sight. I watched Heinrich tape the road map to two posts. Then I went down to the kitchen to pay some bills, aware of colored spots whirling atomically somewhere to the right and behind me.

Steffie said, "Can you see the feathery plume from the attic window?"

"It's not a plume."

"But will we have to leave our homes?"

"Of course not."

"How do you know?"

"I just know."

"Remember how we couldn't go to school?"

"That was inside. This is outside."

We heard police sirens blowing. I watched Steffie's lips form the sequence: *wow wow wow wow.* She smiled in a certain way when she saw me watching, as though gently startled out of some absent-minded pleasure.

Denise walked in, rubbing her hands on her jeans.

"They're using snow-blowers to blow stuff onto the spill," she said.

"What kind of stuff?"

"I don't know but it's supposed to make the spill harmless, which doesn't explain what they're doing about the actual plume."

"They're keeping it from getting bigger," I said. "When do we eat?"

"I don't know but if it gets any bigger it'll get here with or without a wind."

"It won't get here," I said.

"How do you know?"

"Because it won't."

She looked at her palms and went upstairs. The phone rang. Babette walked into the kitchen and picked it up. She looked at me as she listened. I wrote two checks, periodically glancing up to see if she was still looking at me. She seemed to study my face for the hidden meaning of the message she was receiving. I puckered my lips in a way I knew she disliked.

"That was the Stovers," she said. "They spoke directly with the weather center outside Glassboro. They're not calling it a feathery plume anymore."

"What are they calling it?"

"A black billowing cloud."

"That's a little more accurate, which means they're coming to grips with the thing. Good."

"There's more," she said. "It's expected that some sort of air mass may be moving down from Canada."

"There's always an air mass moving down from Canada."

"That's true," she said. "There's certainly nothing new in that. And since Canada is to the north, if the billowing cloud is blown due south, it will miss us by a comfortable margin."

"When do we eat?" I said.

We heard sirens again, a different set this time, a larger sound—not police, fire, ambulance. They were air-raid sirens, I realized, and they seemed to be blowing in Sawyersville, a small community to the northeast.

Steffie washed her hands at the kitchen sink and went upstairs. Babette started taking things out of the refrigerator. I grabbed her by the inside of the thigh as she passed the table. She squirmed deliciously, a package of frozen corn in her hand.

"Maybe we ought to be more concerned about the billowing cloud," she said. "It's because of the kids we keep saying nothing's going to happen. We don't want to scare them."

"Nothing *is* going to happen."

"I know nothing's going to happen, you know nothing's going to happen. But at some level we ought to think about it anyway, just in case."

"These things happen to poor people who live in exposed areas. Society is set up in such a way that it's the poor and the uneducated who suffer the main impact of natural and man-made disasters. People in low-lying areas get the floods, people in shanties get the hurricanes and tornados. I'm a college professor. Did you ever see a college professor rowing a boat down his own street in one of those TV floods? We live in a neat and pleasant town near a college with a quaint name. These things don't happen in places like Blacksmith."

She was sitting on my lap by now. The checks, bills, contest forms and coupons were scattered across the table.

"Why do you want dinner so early?" she said in a sexy whisper.

"I missed lunch."

"Shall I do some chili-fried chicken?"

"First-rate."

"Where is Wilder?" she said, thick-voiced, as I ran my hands over her breasts, trying with my teeth to undo her bra clip through the blouse.

"I don't know. Maybe Murray stole him."

"I ironed your gown," she said.

"Great, great."

"Did you pay the phone bill?"

"Can't find it."

We were both thick-voiced now. Her arms were crossed over my arms in such a way that I could read the serving suggestions on the box of corn niblets in her left hand.

"Let's think about the billowing cloud. Just a little bit, okay? It could be dangerous."

"Everything in tank cars is dangerous. But the effects are mainly long-range and all we have to do is stay out of the way."

"Let's just be sure to keep it in the back of our mind," she said, getting up to smash an ice tray repeatedly on the rim of the sink, dislodging the cubes in groups of two and three.

I puckered my lips at her. Then I climbed to the attic one more time. Wilder was up there with Heinrich, whose fast glance in my direction contained a certain practiced accusation.

"They're not calling it the feathery plume anymore," he said, not meeting my eyes, as if to spare himself the pain of my embarrassment.

"I already knew that."

"They're calling it the black billowing cloud."

"Good."

"Why is that good?"

"It means they're looking the thing more or less squarely in the eye. They're on top of the situation."

With an air of weary decisiveness, I opened the window, took the binoculars and climbed onto the ledge. I was wearing a heavy sweater and felt comfortable enough in the cold air but made certain to keep my weight tipped against the building, with my son's outstretched hand clutching my belt. I sensed his support for my little mission, even his hopeful conviction that I might be able to add the balanced weight of a mature and considered judgment to his pure observations. This is a parent's task, after all.

I put the glasses to my face and peered through the gathering dark. Beneath the cloud of vaporized chemicals, the scene was one of urgency and operatic chaos. Floodlights swept across the switching yard. Army helicopters hovered at various points, shining additional lights down on the scene. Colored lights from police cruisers crisscrossed these wider beams. The tank car sat solidly on tracks, fumes rising from what appeared to be a hole in one end. The coupling device from a second car had apparently pierced the tank car. Fire engines were deployed at a distance, ambulances and police vans at a greater distance. I could hear sirens, voices calling through bullhorns, a layer of radio static causing small warps in the frosty air. Men raced from one vehicle to another, unpacked equipment, carried empty stretchers. Other men in bright yellow Mylex suits and respirator masks moved slowly through the luminous haze, carrying death-measuring instruments. Snow-blowers sprayed a pink substance toward the tank car and the surrounding landscape. This thick mist arched through the air like some grand confection at a concert of patriotic music. The snow-blowers were the type used on airport runways, the police vans were the type to transport riot casualties. Smoke drifted from red beams of light into darkness and then into the breadth of scenic white floods. The men in Mylex suits moved with a lunar caution. Each step was the exercise of some anxiety not provided for by instinct. Fire and explosion were not the inherent dangers here. This death would penetrate, seep into the genes, show itself in bodies not yet born. They moved as if across a swale of moon dust, bulky and wobbling, trapped in the idea of the nature of time.

I crawled back inside with some difficulty.

"What do you think?" he said.

"It's still hanging there. Looks rooted to the spot."

"So you're saying you don't think it'll come this way."

"I can tell by your voice that you know something I don't know."

"Do you think it'll come this way or not?"

"You want me to say it won't come this way in a million years. Then you'll attack with your little fistful of data. Come on, tell me what they said on the radio while I was out there."

"It doesn't cause nausea, vomiting, shortness of breath, like they said before."

"What does it cause?"

"Heart palpitations and a sense of *déjà vu.*"

"*Déjà vu?*"

"It affects the false part of the human memory or whatever. That's not all. They're not calling it the black billowing cloud anymore."

"What are they calling it?"

He looked at me carefully.

"The airborne toxic event."

He spoke these words in a clipped and foreboding manner, syllable by syllable, as if he sensed the threat in state-created terminology. He continued to watch me carefully, searching my face for some reassurance against the possibility of real danger—a reassurance he would immediately reject as phony. A favorite ploy of his.

"These things are not important. The important thing is location. It's there, we're here."

"A large air mass is moving down from Canada," he said evenly.

"I already knew that."

"That doesn't mean it's not important."

"Maybe it is, maybe it isn't. Depends."

"The weather's about to change," he practically cried out to me in a voice charged with the plaintive throb of his special time of life.

"I'm not just a college professor. I'm the head of a department. I don't see myself fleeing an airborne toxic event. That's for people who live in mobile homes out in the scrubby parts of the county, where the fish hatcheries are."

We watched Wilder climb backwards down the attic steps, which were higher than the steps elsewhere in the house. At dinner Denise kept getting up and walking in small stiff rapid strides to the toilet off the hall, a hand clapped to her mouth. We paused in odd moments of chewing or salt-sprinkling to hear her retch incompletely. Heinrich told her she was showing outdated symptoms. She gave him a slit-eyed look. It was a period of looks and glances, teeming interactions, part of the sensory array I ordinarily cherish. Heat, noise, lights, looks, words, gestures, personalities, appliances. A colloquial density that makes family life the one medium of sense knowledge in which an astonishment of heart is routinely contained.

I watched the girls communicate in hooded looks.

"Aren't we eating a little early tonight?" Denise said.

"What do you call early?" her mother said.

Denise looked at Steffie.

"Is it because we want to get it out of the way?" she said.

"Why do we want to get it out of the way?"

"In case something happens," Steffie said.

"What could happen?" Babette said.

The girls looked at each other again, a solemn and lingering exchange that indicated some dark suspicion was being confirmed. Air-raid sirens sounded again, this time so close to us that we were negatively affected, shaken to the point of avoiding each other's eyes as a way of denying that something unusual was going on. The sound came from our own red brick firehouse, sirens that hadn't been tested in a decade or more. They made a noise like some territorial squawk from out of the Mesozoic. A parrot carnivore with a DC-9 wingspan. What a raucousness of brute aggression filled the house, making it seem as though the walls would fly apart. So close to us, so surely upon us. Amazing to think this sonic monster lay hidden nearby for years.

We went on eating, quietly and neatly, reducing the size of our bites, asking politely for things to be passed. We became meticulous and terse, diminished the scope of our movements, buttered our bread in the manner of technicians restoring a fresco. Still the horrific squawk went on. We continued to avoid eye contact, were careful not to clink utensils. I believe there passed among us the sheepish hope that only in this way could we avoid being noticed. It was as though the sirens heralded the presence of some controlling mechanism—a thing we would do well not to provoke with our contentiousness and spilled food.

It wasn't until a second noise became audible in the pulse of the powerful sirens that we thought to effect a pause in our little episode of decorous hysteria. Heinrich ran to the front door and opened it. The night's combined sounds came washing in with a freshness and renewed immediacy. For the first time in minutes we looked at each other, knowing the new sound was an amplified voice but not sure what it was saying. Heinrich returned, walking in an over-deliberate and stylized manner, with elements of stealth. This seemed to mean he was frozen with significance.

"They want us to evacuate," he said, not meeting our eyes.

Babette said, "Did you get the impression they were only making a suggestion or was it a little more mandatory, do you think?"

"It was a fire captain's car with a loudspeaker and it was going pretty fast."

I said, "In other words you didn't have an opportunity to notice the subtle edges of intonation."

"The voice was screaming out."

"Due to the sirens," Babette said helpfully.

"It said something like, 'Evacuate all places of residence. Cloud of deadly chemicals, cloud of deadly chemicals.'"

We sat there over sponge cake and canned peaches.

"I'm sure there's plenty of time," Babette said, "or they would have made a point of telling us to hurry. How fast do air masses move, I wonder."

Steffie read a coupon for Baby Lux, crying softly. This brought Denise to life. She went upstairs to pack some things for all of us. Heinrich raced two steps at a time to the attic for his binoculars, highway map and radio. Babette went to the pantry and began gathering tins and jars with familiar life-enhancing labels.

Steffie helped me clear the table.

Twenty minutes later we were in the car. The voice on the radio said that people in the west end of town were to head for the abandoned Boy Scout camp, where Red Cross volunteers would dispense juice and coffee. People from the east end were to take the parkway to the fourth service area, where they would proceed to a restaurant called the Kung Fu Palace, a multiwing building with pagodas, lily ponds and live deer.

We were among the latecomers in the former group and joined the traffic flow into the main route out of town, a sordid gantlet of used cars, fast food, discount drugs and quad cinemas. As we waited our turn to edge onto the four-lane road we heard the amplified voice above and behind us calling out to darkened homes in a street of sycamores and tall hedges.

"Abandon all domiciles, Now, now. Toxic event, chemical cloud."

The voice grew louder, faded, grew loud again as the vehicle moved in and out of local streets. Toxic event, chemical cloud. When the words became faint, the cadence itself was still discernible, a recurring sequence in the distance. It seems that danger assigns to public voices the responsibility of a rhythm, as if in metrical units there is a coherence we can use to balance whatever senseless and furious event is about to come rushing around our heads.

We made it onto the road as snow began to fall. We had little to say to each other, our minds not yet adjusted to the actuality of things, the absurd fact of evacuation. Mainly we looked at people in other cars, trying to work out from their faces how frightened we should be. Traffic moved at a crawl but we thought the pace would pick up some miles down the road where there is a break in the barrier divide that would enable our westbound flow to utilize all four lanes. The two opposite lanes were empty, which meant police had already halted traffic coming this way. An encouraging sign. What people in an exodus fear most immediately is that those in positions of authority will long since have fled, leaving us in charge of our own chaos.

The snow came more thickly, the traffic moved in fits and starts. There was a life-style sale at a home furnishing mart. Well-lighted men and women stood by the huge window looking out at us and wondering. It made us feel like fools, like tourists doing all the wrong things. Why were they content to shop for furniture while we sat panicky in slowpoke traffic in a snowstorm? They knew something we didn't. In a crisis the true facts are whatever other people say they are. No one's knowledge is less secure than your own.

Air-raid sirens were still sounding in two or more towns. What could those shoppers know that would make them remain behind while a more or less clear path to safety lay before us all? I started pushing buttons on the radio. On a Glassboro station we learned there was new and important information. People already indoors were being asked to stay indoors. We were left to guess the meaning of this. Were the roads impossibly jammed? Was it snowing Nyodene D.?

I kept punching buttons, hoping to find someone with background information. A woman identified as a consumer affairs editor began a discussion of the medical problems that could result from personal contact with the airborne toxic event. Babette and I exchanged a wary glance. She immediately began talking to the girls while I turned the volume down to keep them from learning what they might imagine was in store for them.

"Convulsions, coma, miscarriage," said the well-informed and sprightly voice.

We passed a three-story motel. Every room was lighted, every window filled with people staring out at us. We were a parade of fools, open not only to the effects of chemical fallout but to the scornful judgment of other people. Why weren't they out here, sitting in heavy coats behind windshield wipers in the silent snow? It seemed imperative that we get to the Boy Scout camp, scramble into the main building, seal the doors, huddle on camp beds with our juice and coffee, wait for the all-clear.

Cars began to mount the grassy incline at the edge of the road, creating a third lane of severely tilted traffic. Situated in what had formerly been the righthand lane, we didn't have any choice but to watch these cars pass us at a slightly higher elevation and with a rakish thrust, deviated from the horizontal.

Slowly we approached an overpass, seeing people on foot up there. They carried boxes and suitcases, objects in blankets, a long line of people leaning into the blowing snow. People cradling pets and small children, an old man wearing a blanket over his pajamas, two women shouldering a rolled-up rug. There were people on bicycles, children being pulled on sleds and in wagons. People with supermarket carts, people clad in every kind of bulky outfit, peering out from deep hoods. There was a family wrapped completely in plastic, a single large sheet of transparent polyethylene. They walked beneath their shield in lock step, the man and woman each at one end, three kids between, all of them secondarily wrapped in shimmering rainwear. The whole affair had about it a well-rehearsed and self-satisfied look, as though they'd been waiting for months to strut their stuff. People kept appearing from behind a high rampart and trudging across the overpass, shoulders dusted with snow, hundreds of people moving with a kind of fated determination. A new round of sirens started up. The trudging people did not quicken their pace, did not look down at us or into the night sky for some sign of the wind-driven cloud. They just kept moving across the bridge through patches of snow-raging light. Out in the open, keeping their children near, carrying what they could, they seemed to be part of some ancient destiny, connected in doom and ruin to a whole history of people trekking across wasted landscapes. There was an epic quality about them that made me wonder for the first time at the scope of our predicament.

The radio said: "It's the rainbow hologram that gives this credit card a marketing intrigue."

We moved slowly beneath the overpass, hearing a flurry of automobile horns and the imploring wail of an ambulance stuck in traffic. Fifty yards ahead the traffic narrowed to one lane and we soon saw why. One of the cars had skidded off the incline and barreled into a vehicle in our lane. Horns quacked up and down the line. A helicopter sat just above us, shining a white beam down on the mass of collapsed metal. People sat dazed on the grass, being tended to by a pair of bearded paramedics. Two people were bloody. There was blood on a smashed window. Blood soaked upward through newly fallen snow. Drops of blood speckled a tan handbag. The scene of injured people, medics, smoking steel, all washed in a strong and eerie light, took on the eloquence of a formal composition. We passed silently by, feeling curiously reverent, even uplifted by the sight of the heaped cars and fallen people.

Heinrich kept watching through the rear window, taking up his binoculars as the scene dwindled in the distance. He described for us in detail the number and placement of bodies, the skid marks, the vehicular damage. When the wreck was no longer visible, he talked about everything that had happened since the air-raid siren at dinner. He spoke enthusiastically, with a sense of appreciation for the vivid and unexpected. I thought we'd all occupied the same mental state, subdued, worried, confused. It hadn't occurred to me that one of us might find these events brilliantly stimulating. I looked at him in the rearview mirror. He sat slouched in the camouflage jacket with Velcro closures, steeped happily in disaster. He talked about the snow, the traffic, the trudging people. He speculated on how far we were from the abandoned camp, what sort of primitive accommodations might be available there. I'd never heard him go on about something with such spirited enjoyment. He was practically giddy. He must have known we could all die. Was this some kind of end-of-the-world elation? Did he seek distraction from his own small miseries in some violent and overwhelming event? His voice betrayed a craving for terrible things.

"Is this a mild winter or a harsh winter?" Steffie said.

"Compared to what?" Denise said.

"I don't know."

I thought I saw Babette slip something into her mouth. I took my eye off the road for a moment, watched her carefully. She looked straight ahead. I pretended to return my attention to the road but quickly turned once more, catching her off guard as she seemed to swallow whatever it was she'd put in her mouth.

"What's that?" I said.

"Drive the car, Jack."

"I saw your throat contract. You swallowed something."

"Just a Life Saver. Drive the car please."

"You place a Life Saver in your mouth and you swallow it without an interval of sucking?"

"Swallow what? It's still in my mouth."

She thrust her face toward me, using her tongue to make a small lump in her cheek. A clear-cut amateurish bluff.

"But you swallowed something. I saw."

"That was just saliva that I didn't know what to do with. Drive the car, would you?"

I sensed that Denise was getting interested and decided not to pursue the matter. This was not the time to be questioning her mother about medications, side effects and so on. Wilder was asleep, leaning into Babette's arm. The windshield wipers made sweaty arcs. From the radio we learned that dogs trained to sniff out Nyodene D. were being sent to the area from a chemical detection center in a remote part of New Mexico.

Denise said, "Did they ever think about what happens to the dogs when they get close enough to this stuff to smell it?"

"Nothing happens to the dogs," Babette said.

"How do you know?"

"Because it only affects humans and rats."

"I don't believe you."

"Ask Jack."

"Ask Heinrich," I said.

"It could be true," he said, clearly lying. "They use rats to test for things that humans can catch, so it means we get the same diseases, rats and humans. Besides, they wouldn't use dogs if they thought it could hurt them."

"Why not?"

"A dog is a mammal."

"So's a rat," Denise said.

"A rat is a vermin," Babette said.

"Mostly what a rat is," Heinrich said, "is a rodent."

"It's also a vermin."

"A cockroach is a vermin," Steffie said.

"A cockroach is an insect. You count the legs is how you know."

"It's also a vermin."

"Does a cockroach get cancer? No," Denise said. "That must mean a rat is more like a human than it is like a cockroach, even if they're both vermins, since a rat and a human can get cancer but a cockroach can't."

"In other words," Heinrich said, "she's saying that two things that are mammals have more in common than two things that are only vermins."

"Are you people telling me," Babette said, "that a rat is not only a vermin and a rodent but a mammal too?"

Snow turned to sleet, sleet to rain.

We reached the point where the concrete barrier gives way to a twenty-yard stretch of landscaped median no higher than a curbstone. But instead of a state trooper directing traffic into two extra lanes, we saw a Mylex-suited man waving us away from the opening. Just beyond him was the scrap-metal burial mound of a Winnebago and a snowplow. The huge and tortured wreck emitted a wisp of rusty smoke. Brightly colored plastic utensils were scattered for some distance. There was no sign of victims or fresh blood, leading us to believe that some time had passed since the recreational vehicle mounted the plow, probably in a moment when opportunism seemed an easily defensible failing, given the situation. It must have been the blinding snow that caused the driver to leap the median without noting an object on the other side.

"I saw all this before," Steffie said.

"What do you mean?" I said.

"This happened once before. Just like this. The man in the yellow suit and gas mask. The big wreck sitting in the snow. It was totally and exactly like this. We were all here in the car. Rain made little holes in the snow. Everything."

It was Heinrich who'd told me that exposure to the chemical waste could cause a person to experience a sense of *déjà vu*. Steffie wasn't there when he said it, but she could have heard it on the kitchen radio, where she and Denise had probably learned about sweaty palms and vomiting before developing these symptoms themselves. I didn't think Steffie knew what *déjà vu* meant, but it was possible Babette had told her. *Déjà vu,* however, was no longer a working symptom of Nyodene contamination. It had been preempted by coma, convulsions, and miscarriage. If Steffie had learned about *déjà vu* on the radio but then missed the subsequent upgrading to more deadly conditions, it could mean she was in a position to be tricked by her own apparatus of suggestibility. She and Denise had been lagging all evening. They were late with sweaty palms, late with nausea, late again with *déjà vu*. What did it all mean? Did Steffie truly imagine she'd seen the wreck before or did she only imagine she'd imagined it? Is it possible to have a false perception of an illusion? Is there a true *déjà vu* and a false *déjà vu*? I wondered whether her palms had been truly sweaty or whether she'd simply imagined a sense of wetness. And was she so open to suggestion that she would develop every symptom as it was announced?

I feel sad for people and the queer part we play in our own disasters.

But what if she hadn't heard the radio, didn't know what *déjà vu* was? What if she was developing real symptoms by natural means? Maybe the scientists were right in the first place, with their original announcements, before they revised upward. Which was worse, the real condition or the self-created one, and did it matter? I wondered about these and allied questions. As I drove I found myself giving and taking an oral examination based on the kind of quibbling fine-points that had entertained several centuries' worth of medieval idlers. Could a nine-year-old girl suffer a miscarriage due to the power of suggestion? Would she have to be pregnant first? Could the power of suggestion be strong enough to work backward in this manner, from miscarriage to pregnancy to menstruation to ovulation? Which comes first, menstruation or ovulation? Are we talking about mere symptoms or deeply entrenched conditions? Is a symptom a sign or a thing? What is a thing and how do we know it's not another thing?

I turned off the radio, not to help me think but to keep me from thinking. Vehicles lurched and skidded. Someone threw a gum wrapper out a side window and Babette made an indignant speech about inconsiderate people littering the highways and countryside.

"I'll tell you something else that's happened before," Heinrich said. "We're running out of gas."

The dial quivered on E.

"There's always extra," Babette said.

"How can there be always extra?"

"That's the way the tank is constructed. So you don't run out."

"There can't be *always* extra. If you keep going, you run out."

"You don't keep going forever."

"How do you know when to stop?" he said.

"When you pass a gas station," I told him, and there it was, a deserted and rain-swept plaza with proud pumps standing beneath an array of multicolored banners. I drove in, jumped out of the car, ran around to the pumps with my head tucked under the raised collar of my coat. They were not locked, which meant the attendants had fled suddenly, leaving things intriguingly as they were, like the tools and pottery of some pueblo civilization, bread in the oven, table set for three, a mystery to haunt the generations. I seized the hose on the unleaded pump. The banners smacked in the wind.

A few minutes later, back on the road, we saw a remarkable and startling sight. It appeared in the sky ahead of us and to the left, prompting us to lower ourselves in our seats, bend our heads for a clearer view, exclaim to each other in half finished phrases. It was the black billowing cloud, the airborne toxic event, lighted by the clear beams of seven army helicopters. They were tracking its windborne movement, keeping it in view. In every car, heads shifted, drivers blew their horns to alert others, faces appeared in side windows, expressions set in tones of outlandish wonderment.

The enormous dark mass moved like some death ship in a Norse legend, escorted across the night by armored creatures with spiral wings. We weren't sure how to react. It was a terrible thing to see, so close, so low, packed with chlorides, benzines, phenols, hydrocarbons, or whatever the precise toxic content. But it was also spectacular, part of the grandness of a sweeping event, like the vivid scene in the switching yard or the people trudging across the snowy overpass with children, food, belongings, a tragic army of the dispossessed. Our fear was accompanied by a sense of awe that bordered on the religious. It is surely possible to be awed by the thing that threatens your life, to see it as a cosmic force, so much larger than yourself, more powerful, created by elemental and willful rhythms. This was a death made in the laboratory, defined and measurable, but we thought of it at the time in a simple and primitive way, as some seasonal perversity of the earth like a flood or tornado, something not subject to control. Our helplessness did not seem compatible with the idea of a man-made event.

In the back seat the kids fought for possession of the binoculars.

The whole thing was amazing. They seemed to be spotlighting the cloud for us as if it were part of a sound-and-light show, a bit of mood-setting mist drifting across a high battlement where a king had been slain. But this was not history we were witnessing. It was some secret festering thing, some dreamed emotion that accompanies the dreamer out of sleep. Flares came swooning from the helicopters, creamy bursts of red and white light. Drivers sounded their horns and children crowded all the windows, faces tilted, pink hands pressed against the glass.

The road curved away from the toxic cloud and traffic moved more freely for a while. At an intersection near the Boy Scout camp, two schoolbuses entered the mainstream traffic, both carrying the insane of Blacksmith. We recognized the drivers, spotted familiar faces in the windows, people we customarily saw sitting on lawn chairs behind the asylum's sparse hedges or walking in ever narrowing circles, with ever increasing speed, like spinning masses in a gyration device. We felt an odd affection for them and a sense of relief that they were being looked after in a diligent and professional manner. It seemed to mean the structure was intact.

We passed a sign for the most photographed barn in America.

It took an hour to funnel traffic into the single-lane approach to the camp. Mylex-suited men waved flashlights and set out Day-Glo pylons, directing us toward the parking lot and onto athletic fields and other open areas. People came out of the woods, some wearing headlamps, some carrying shopping bags, children, pets. We bumped along dirt paths, over ruts and mounds. Near the main buildings we saw a group of men and women carrying clipboards and walkie-talkies, non-Mylex-suited officials, experts in the new science of evacuation. Steffie joined Wilder in fitful sleep. The rain let up. People turned off their headlights, sat uncertainly in their cars. The long strange journey was over. We waited for a sense of satisfaction to reach us, some mood in the air of quiet accomplishment, the well-earned fatigue that promises a still and deep-lying sleep. But people sat in their dark cars staring out at each other through closed windows. Heinrich ate a candy bar. We listened to the sound of his teeth getting stuck in the caramel and glucose mass. Finally a family of five got out of a Datsun Maxima. They wore life jackets and carried flares.

Small crowds collected around certain men. Here were the sources of information and rumor. One person worked in a chemical plant, another had overheard a remark, a third was related to a clerk in a state agency. True, false and other kinds of news radiated through the dormitory from these dense clusters.

It was said that we would be allowed to go home first thing in the morning; that the government was engaged in a cover-up; that a helicopter had entered the toxic cloud and never reappeared; that the dogs had arrived from New Mexico, parachuting into a meadow in a daring night drop; that the town of Farmington would be uninhabitable for forty years.

Remarks existed in a state of permanent flotation. No one thing was either more or less plausible than any other thing. As people jolted out of reality, we were released from the need to distinguish.

Some families chose to sleep in their cars, others were forced to do so because there was no room for them in the seven or eight buildings on the grounds. We were in a large barracks, one of three such buildings at the camp, and with the generator now working we were fairly comfortable. The Red Cross had provided cots, portable heaters, sandwiches and coffee. There were kerosene lamps to supplement the existing overhead lights. Many people had radios, extra food to share with others, blankets, beach chairs, extra clothing. The place was crowded, still quite cold, but the sight of nurses and volunteer workers made us feel the children were safe, and the presence of other stranded souls, young women with infants, old and infirm people, gave us a certain staunchness and will, a selfless bent that was pronounced enough to function as a common identity. This large gray area, dank and bare and lost to history just a couple of hours ago, was an oddly agreeable place right now, filled with an eagerness of community and voice.

Seekers of news moved from one cluster of people to another, tending to linger at the larger groups. In this way I moved slowly through the barracks. There were nine evacuation centers, I learned, including this one and the Kung Fu Palace. Iron City had not been emptied out; nor had most of the other towns in the area. It was said that the governor was on his way from the capitol in an executive helicopter. It would probably set down in a bean field outside a deserted town, allowing the governor to emerge, square-jawed and confident, in a bush jacket, within camera range, for ten or fifteen seconds, as a demonstration of his imperishability.

What a surprise it was to ease my way between people at the outer edges of one of the largest clusters and discover that my own son was at the center of things, speaking in his new-found voice, his tone of enthusiasm for runaway calamity. He was talking about the airborne toxic event in a technical way, although his voice all but sang with prophetic disclosure. He pronounced the name itself, Nyodene Derivative, with an unseemly relish, taking morbid delight in the very sound. People listened attentively to this adolescent boy in a field jacket and cap, with binoculars strapped around his neck and an Instamatic fastened to his belt. No doubt his listeners were influenced by his age. He would be truthful and earnest, serving no special interest; he would have an awareness of the environment; his knowledge of chemistry would be fresh and up-to-date.

I heard him say, "The stuff they sprayed on the big spill at the train yard was probably soda ash. But it was a case of too little too late. My guess is they'll get some crop dusters up in the air at daybreak and bombard the toxic cloud with lots more soda ash, which could break it up and scatter it into a million harmless puffs. Soda ash is the common name for sodium carbonate, which is used in the manufacture of glass, ceramics, detergents and soaps. It's also what they use to make bicarbonate of soda, something a lot of you have probably guzzled after a night on the town."

People moved in closer, impressed by the boy's knowledgeability and wit. It was remarkable to hear him speak so easily to a crowd of strangers. Was he finding himself, learning how to determine his worth from the reactions of others? Was it possible that out of the turmoil and surge of this dreadful event he would learn to make his way in the world?

"What you're probably all wondering is what exactly is this Nyodene D. we keep hearing about? A good question. We studied it in school, we saw movies of rats having convulsions and so on. So, okay, it's basically simple. Nyodene D. is a whole bunch of things thrown together that are byproducts of the manufacture of insecticide. The original stuff kills roaches, the byproducts kill everything left over. A little joke our teacher made."

He snapped his fingers, let his left leg swing a bit.

"In powder form it's colorless, odorless and very dangerous, except no one seems to know exactly what it causes in humans or in the offspring of humans. They tested for years and either they don't know for sure or they know and aren't saying. Some things are too awful to publicize."

He arched his brows and began to twitch comically, his tongue lolling in a corner of his mouth. I was astonished to hear people laugh.

"Once it seeps into the soil, it has a life span of forty years. This is longer than a lot of people. After five years you'll notice various kinds of fungi appearing between your regular windows and storm windows as well as in your clothes and food. After ten years your screens will turn rusty and begin to pit and rot. Siding will warp. There will be glass breakage and trauma to pets. After twenty years you'll probably have to seal yourself in the attic and just wait and see. I guess there's a lesson in all this. Get to know your chemicals."

I didn't want him to see me there. It would make him self-conscious, remind him of his former life as a gloomy and fugitive boy. Let him bloom, if that's what he was doing, in the name of mischance, dread and random disaster. So I slipped away, passing a man who wore snow boots wrapped in plastic, and headed for the far end of the barracks, where we'd earlier made camp.

We were next to a black family of Jehovah's Witnesses. A man and woman with a boy about twelve. Father and son were handing out tracts to people nearby and seemed to have no trouble finding willing recipients and listeners.

The woman said to Babette, "Isn't this something?"

"Nothing surprises me anymore," Babette said.

"Isn't that the truth."

"What would surprise me would be if there were no surprises."

"That sounds about right."

"Or if there were little bitty surprises. That would be a surprise. Instead of things like this."

"God Jehovah's got a bigger surprise in store than this," the woman said.

"God Jehovah?"

"That's the one."

Steffie and Wilder were asleep in one of the cots. Denise sat at the other end engrossed in the *Physicians' Desk Reference*. Several air mattresses were stacked against the wall. There was a long line at the emergency telephone, people calling relatives or trying to reach the switchboard at one or another radio call-in show. The radios here were tuned mainly to just such shows. Babette sat in a camp chair, going through a canvas bag full of snack thins and other provisions. I noticed jars and cartons that had been sitting in the refrigerator or cabinet for months.

"I thought this would be a good time to cut down on fatty things," she said.

"Why now especially?"

"This is a time for discipline, mental toughness. We're practically at the edge."

"I think it's interesting that you regard a possible disaster for yourself, your family and thousands of other people as an opportunity to cut down on fatty foods."

"You take discipline where you can find it," she said. "If I don't eat my yogurt now, I may as well stop buying the stuff forever. Except I think I'll skip the wheat germ."

The brand name was foreign-looking. I picked up the jar of

wheat germ and examined the label closely.

"It's German," I told her. "Eat it."

There were people in pajamas and slippers. A man with a rifle slung over his shoulder. Kids crawling into sleeping bags. Babette gestured, wanting me to lean closer.

"Let's keep the radio turned off," she whispered. "So the girls can't hear. They haven't gotten beyond *déjà vu.* I want to keep it that way."

"What if the symptoms are real?"

"How could they be real?"

"Why couldn't they be real?"

"They get them only when they're broadcast," she whispered.

"Did Steffie hear about *déjà vu* on the radio?"

"She must have."

"How do you know? Were you with her when it was broadcast?"

"I'm not sure."

"Think hard."

"I can't remember."

"Do you remember telling her what *déjà vu* means?"

She spooned some yogurt out of the carton, seemed to pause, deep in thought.

"This happened before," she said finally.

"What happened before?"

"Eating yogurt, sitting here, talking about *déjà vu.*"

"I don't want to hear this."

"The yogurt was on my spoon. I saw it in a flash. The whole experience. Natural, whole-milk, low-fat."

The yogurt was still on the spoon. I watched her put the spoon to her mouth, thoughtfully, trying to measure the action against the illusion of a matching original. From my squatting position I motioned her to lean closer.

"Heinrich seems to be coming out of his shell," I whispered.

"Where is he? I haven't seen him."

"See that knot of people? He's right in the middle. He's telling them what he knows about the toxic event."

"What does he know?"

"Quite a lot, it turns out."

"Why didn't he tell us?" she whispered.

"He's probably tired of us. He doesn't think it's worth his while to be funny and charming in front of his family. That's the way sons are. We represent the wrong kind of challenge."

"Funny and charming?"

"I guess he had it in him all the while. It was a question of finding the right time to exercise his gifts."

She moved closer, our heads almost touching.

"Don't you think you ought to go over there?" she said. "Let him see you in the crowd. Show him that his father is present at his big moment."

"He'll only get upset if he sees me in the crowd."

"Why?"

"I'm his father."

"So if you go over there, you'll ruin things by embarrassing him and cramping his style because of the father-son thing. And if you don't go over, he'll never know you saw him in his big moment and he'll think he has to behave in your presence the way he's always behaved, sort of peevishly and defensive, instead of in this new, delightful and expansive manner."

"It's a double bind."

"What if I went over?" she whispered.

"He'll think I sent you."

"Would that be so awful?"

"He thinks I use you to get him to do what I want."

"There may be some truth in that, Jack. But then what are stepparents for if they can't be used in little skirmishes between blood relatives?"

I moved still closer, lowered my voice even more.

"Just a Life Saver," I said.

"What?"

"Just some saliva that you didn't know what to do with."

"It was a Life Saver," she whispered, making an O with her thumb and index finger.

"Give me one."

"It was the last one."

"What flavor—*quick.*"

"Cherry."

I puckered my lips and made little sucking sounds. The black man with the tracts came over and squatted next to me. We engaged in an earnest and prolonged handshake. He studied me openly, giving the impression that he had traveled this rugged distance, uprooting his family, not to escape the chemical event but to find the one person who would understand what he had to say.

"It's happening everywhere, isn't it?"

"More or less," I said.

"And what's the government doing about it?"

"Nothing."

"You said it, I didn't. There's only one word in the language to describe what's being done and you found it exactly. I'm not surprised at all. But when you think about it, what *can* they do? Because what is coming is definitely coming. No government in the world is big enough to stop it. Does a man like yourself know the size of India's standing army?"

"One million."

"I didn't say it, you did. One million soldiers and they can't stop it. Do you know who's got the biggest standing army in the world?"

"It's either China or Russia, although the Vietnamese ought to be mentioned."

"Tell me this," he said. "Can the Vietnamese stop it?"

"No."

"It's here, isn't it? People feel it. We know in our bones. God's kingdom is coming."

He was a rangy man with sparse hair and a gap between his two front teeth. He squatted easily, seemed loose-jointed and comfortable. I realized he was wearing a suit and tie with running shoes.

"Are these great days?" he said.

I studied his face, trying to find a clue to the right answer.

"Do you feel it coming? Is it on the way? Do you *want* it to come?"

He bounced on his toes as he spoke.

"Wars, famines, earthquakes, volcanic eruptions. It's all beginning to jell. In your own words, is there anything that can stop it from coming once it picks up momentum?"

"No."

"You said it, I didn't. Floods, tornados, epidemics of strange new diseases. Is it a sign? Is it the truth? Are you ready?"

"Do people really feel it in their bones?" I said.

"Good news travels fast."

"Do people talk about it? On your door-to-door visits, do you get the impression they want it?"

"It's not do they want it. It's where do I go to sign up. It's get me out of here right now. People ask, 'Is there seasonal change in God's kingdom?' They ask, 'Are there bridge tolls and returnable bottles?' In other words I'm saying they're getting right down to it."

"You feel it's a ground swell."

"A sudden gathering. Exactly put. I took one look and I knew. This is a man who understands."

"Earthquakes are not up, statistically."

He gave me a condescending smile. I felt it was richly deserved, although I wasn't sure why. Maybe it was prissy to be quoting statistics in the face of powerful beliefs, fears, desires.

"How do you plan to spend your resurrection?" he said, as though asking about a long weekend coming up.

"We all get one?"

"You're either among the wicked or among the saved. The wicked get to rot as they walk down the street. They get to feel their own eyes slide out of their sockets. You'll know them by their stickiness and lost parts. People tracking slime of their own making. All the flashiness of Armageddon is in the rotting. The saved know each other by their neatness and reserve. He doesn't have showy ways is how you know a saved person."

He was a serious man, he was matter-of-fact and practical, down to his running shoes. I wondered about his eerie self-assurance, his freedom from doubt. Is this the point of Armageddon? No ambiguity, no more doubt. He was ready to run into the next world. He was forcing the next world to seep into my consciousness, stupendous events that seemed matter-of-fact to him, self-evident, reasonable, imminent, true. I did not feel Armageddon in my bones but I worried about all those people who did, who were ready for it, wishing hard, making phone calls and bank withdrawals. If enough people want it to happen, will it happen? How many people are enough people? Why are we talking to each other from this aboriginal crouch?

He handed me a pamphlet called "Twenty Common Mistakes About the End of the World." I struggled out of the squatting posture, feeling dizziness and back-pain. At the front of the hall a woman was saying something about exposure to toxic agents. Her small voice was almost lost in the shuffling roar of the barracks, the kind of low-level rumble that humans routinely make in large enclosed places. Denise had put down her reference work and was giving me a hard-eyed look. It was the look she usually saved for her father and his latest loss of foothold.

"What's wrong?" I said to her.

"Didn't you hear what the voice said?"

"Exposure."

"That's right," she said sharply.

"What's that got to do with us?"

"Not us," she said. "You."

"Why me?"

"Aren't you the one who got out of the car to fill the gas tank?"

"Where was the airborne event when I did that?"

"Just ahead of us. Don't you remember? You got back in the car and we went a little ways and then there it was in all those lights."

"You're saying when I got out of the car, the cloud may have been close enough to rain all over me."

"It's not your fault," she said impatiently, "but you were practically right in it for about two and a half minutes."

I made my way up front. Two lines were forming. A to M and N to Z. At the end of each line was a folding table with a microcomputer on it. Technicians milled about, men and women with lapel badges and color-coded armbands. I stood behind the life-jacket-wearing family. They looked bright, happy and well-drilled. The thick orange vests did not seem especially out of place even though we were on more or less dry land, well above sea level, many miles from the nearest ominous body of water. Stark upheavals bring out every sort of quaint aberration by the very suddenness of their coming. Dashes of color and idiosyncrasy marked the scene from beginning to end.

The lines were not long. When I reached the A-to-M desk, the man seated there typed out data on his keyboard. My name, age, medical history, so on. He was a gaunt young man who seemed suspicious of conversation that strayed outside certain unspecified guidelines. Over the left sleeve on his khaki jacket he wore a green armband bearing the word SIMUVAC.

I related the circumstances of my presumed exposure.

"How long were you out there?"

"Two and a half minutes," I said. "Is that considered long or short?"

"Anything that puts you in contact with actual emissions means we have a situation."

"Why didn't the drifting cloud disperse in all that wind and rain?"

"This is not your everyday cirrus. This is a high-definition event. It is packed with dense concentrations of byproduct. You could almost toss a hook in there and tow it out to sea, which I'm exaggerating to make a point."

"What about people in the car? I had to open the door to get out and get back in."

"There are known degrees of exposure. I'd say their situation is they're minimal risks. It's the two and a half minutes standing right in it that makes me wince. Actual skin and orifice contact. This is Nyodene D. A whole new generation of toxic waste. What we call state of the art. One part per million million can send a rat into a permanent state."

He regarded me with the grimly superior air of a combat veteran. Obviously he didn't think much of people whose complacent and overprotected lives did not allow for encounters with brain-dead rats. I wanted this man on my side. He had access to data. I was prepared to be servile and fawning if it would keep him from dropping casually shattering remarks about my degree of exposure and chances for survival.

"That's quite an armband you've got there. What does SIMUVAC mean? Sounds important."

"Short for simulated evacuation. A new state program they're still battling over funds for."

"But this evacuation isn't simulated. It's real."

"We know that. But we thought we could use it as a model."

"A form of practice? Are you saying you saw a chance to use the real event in order to rehearse the simulation?"

"We took it right into the streets."

"How is it going?" I said.

"The insertion curve isn't as smooth as we would like. There's a probability excess. Plus which we don't have our victims laid out where we'd want them if this was an actual simulation. In other words we're forced to take our victims as we find them. We didn't get a jump on computer traffic. Suddenly it just spilled out, three-dimensionally, all over the landscape. You have to make allowances for the fact that everything we see tonight is real. There's a lot of polishing we still have to do. But that's what this exercise is all about."

"What about the computers? Is that real data you're running through the system or is it just practice stuff?"

"You watch," he said.

He spent a fair amount of time tapping on the keys and then studying coded responses on the data screen—a considerably longer time, it seemed to me, than he'd devoted to the people who'd preceded me in line. In fact I began to feel that others were watching me. I stood with my arms folded, trying to create a picture of an impassive man, someone in line at a hardware store waiting for the girl at the register to ring up his heavy-duty rope. It seemed the only way to neutralize events, to counteract the passage of computerized dots that registered my life and death. Look at no one, reveal nothing, remain still. The genius of the primitive mind is that it can render human helplessness in noble and beautiful ways.

"You're generating big numbers," he said, peering at the screen.

"I was out there only two and a half minutes. That's how many seconds?"

"It's not just you were out there so many seconds. It's your whole data profile. I tapped into your history. I'm getting bracketed numbers with pulsing stars."

"What does that mean?"

"You'd rather not know."

He made a silencing gesture as if something of particular morbid interest was appearing on the screen. I wondered what he meant when he said he'd tapped into my history. Where was it located exactly? Some state or federal agency, some insurance company or credit firm or medical clearinghouse? What history was he referring to? I'd told him some basic things. Height, weight, childhood diseases. What else did he know? Did he know about my wives, my involvement with Hitler, my dreams and fears?

He had a skinny neck and jug-handle ears to go with his starved skull—the innocent prewar look of a rural murderer.

"Am I going to die?"

"Not as such," he said.

"What do you mean?"

"Not in so many words."

"How many words does it take?"

"It's not a question of words. It's a question of years. We'll know more in fifteen years. In the meantime we definitely have a situation."

"What will we know in fifteen years?"

"If you're still alive at the time, we'll know that much more than we do now. Nyodene D. has a life span of thirty years. You'll have made it halfway through."

"I thought it was forty years."

"Forty years in the soil. Thirty years in the human body."

"So, to outlive this substance, I will have to make it into my eighties. Then I can begin to relax."

"Knowing what we know at this time."

"But the general consensus seems to be that we don't know enough at this time to be sure of anything."

"Let me answer like so. If I was a rat I wouldn't want to be anywhere within a two hundred mile radius of the airborne event."

"What if you were a human?"

He looked at me carefully. I stood with my arms folded, staring over his head toward the front door of the barracks. To look at him would be to declare my vulnerability.

"I wouldn't worry about what I can't see or feel," he said. "I'd go ahead and live my life. Get married, settle down, have kids. There's no reason you can't do these things, knowing what we know."

"But you said we have a situation."

"I didn't say it. The computer did. The whole system says it. It's what we call a massive data-base tally. Gladney, J. A. K. I punch in the name, the substance, the exposure time and then I tap into your computer history. Your genetics, your personals, your medicals, your psychologicals, your police-and-hospitals. It comes back pulsing stars. This doesn't mean anything is going to happen to you as such, at least not today or tomorrow. It just means you are the sum total of your data. No man escapes that."

"And this massive so-called tally is not a simulation despite that armband you're wearing. It is real."

"It is real," he said.

I stood absolutely still. If they thought I was already dead, they might be inclined to leave me alone. I think I felt as I would if a doctor had held an X-ray to the light showing a star-shaped hole at the center of one of my vital organs. Death has entered. It is inside you. You are said to be dying and yet are separate from the dying, can ponder it at your leisure, literally see on the X-ray photograph or computer screen the horrible alien logic of it all. It is when death is rendered graphically, is televised so to speak, that you sense an eerie separation between your condition and yourself. A network of symbols has been introduced, an entire awesome technology wrested from the gods. It makes you feel like a stranger in your own dying.

I wanted my academic gown and dark glasses.

When I got back to the other end of the barracks, the three younger children were asleep, Heinrich was making notations on a road map and Babette was seated some distance away with Old Man Treadwell and a number of other blind people. She was reading to them from a small and brightly colored stack of supermarket tabloids.

I needed a distraction. I found a camp chair and set it near the wall behind Babette. There were four blind people, a nurse and three sighted people arranged in a semicircle facing the reader. Others occasionally paused to listen to an item or two, then moved on. Babette employed her storytelling voice, the same sincere and lilting tone she used when she read fairy tales to Wilder or erotic passages to her husband in their brass bed high above the headlong traffic hum.

She reported a front-page story. "Life After Death Guaranteed with Bonus Coupons." Then turned to the designated page.

"Scientists at Princeton's famed Institute for Advanced Studies have stunned the world by presenting absolute and undeniable proof of life after death. A researcher at the world-renowned Institute has used hypnosis to induce hundreds of people to recall their previous-life experiences as pyramid-builders, exchange students and extraterrestrials."

Babette changed her voice to do dialogue.

"'In the last year alone,' declares reincarnation hypnotist Ling Ti Wan, 'I have helped hundreds to regress to previous lives under hypnosis. One of my most amazing subjects was a woman who was able to recall her life as a hunter-gatherer in the Mesolithic era ten thousand years ago. It was remarkable to hear this tiny senior citizen in polyester slacks describe her life as a hulking male chieftain whose band inhabited a peat bog and hunted wild boar with primitive bow and arrow. She was able to identify features of that era which only a trained archaeologist could know about. She even spoke several phrases in the language of that day, a tongue remarkably similar to modern-day German.'"

Babette's voice resumed its tone of straight narration.

"Dr. Shiv Chatterjee, fitness guru and high-energy physicist, recently stunned a live TV audience by relating the well-documented case of two women, unknown to each other, who came to him for regression in the same week, only to discover that they had been twin sisters in the lost city of Atlantis fifty thousand years ago. Both women describe the city, before its mysterious and catastrophic plunge into the sea, as a clean and well-run municipality where you could walk safely almost any time of day or night. Today they are food stylists for NASA.

"Even more startling is the case of five-year-old Patti Weaver who has made convincing claims to Dr. Chatterjee that in her previous-life experience she was the secret KGB assassin responsible for the unsolved murders of famed personalities Howard Hughes, Marilyn Monroe and Elvis Presley. Known in international espionage circles as 'the Viper' for the deadly and untraceable venom he injected into the balls of the feet of his celebrity victims, the assassin died in a fiery Moscow helicopter crash just hours before little Patti Weaver was born in Popular Mechanics, Iowa. She not only has the same bodily markings as the Viper but seems to have a remarkable knack for picking up Russian words and phrases.

"'I regressed this subject at least a dozen times,' says Dr. Chatterjee. 'I used the toughest professional techniques to get her to contradict herself. But her story is remarkably consistent. It is a tale of the good that can come from evil.' Says little Patti, 'At the moment of my death as the Viper, I saw a glowing circle of light. It seemed to welcome me, to beckon. It was a warm spiritual experience. I just walked right toward it. I was not sad at all.'"

Babette did the voices of Dr. Chatterjee and Patti Weaver. Her Chatterjee was a warm and mellow Indian-accented English, with clipped phrasing. She did Patti as a child-hero in a contemporary movie, the only person on screen who is unawed by mysterious throbbing phenomena.

"In a further startling development it was revealed by little Patti that the three supercelebrities were murdered for the same astonishing reason. Each of them at the time of his or her death was in secret possession of the Holy Shroud of Turin, famed for its sacred curative powers. Entertainers Elvis and Marilyn were drink-and-drug nightmare victims and secretly hoped to restore spiritual and bodily calm to their lives by actually drying themselves with the Holy Shroud after pore-cleansing sessions in the sauna. Multi-faceted billionaire Howard Hughes suffered from stop-action blink syndrome, a bizarre condition which prevented his eyes from re-opening for hours after a simple blink, and he obviously hoped to utilize the amazing power of the Shroud until the Viper intervened with a swift injection of phantom venom. Patti Weaver has further revealed under hypnosis that the KGB has long sought possession of the Shroud of Turin on behalf of the rapidly aging and pain-racked members of the Politburo, the famed executive committee of the Communist Party. Possession of the Shroud is said to be the real motive behind the attempted assassination of Pope John Paul II at the Vatican—an attempt that failed only because the Viper had already died in a horror helicopter crash and been reborn as a freckle-faced girl in Iowa.

"The no-risk bonus coupon below gives you guaranteed access to dozens of documented cases of life after death, everlasting life, previous-life experiences, posthumous life in outer space, transmigration of souls, and personalized resurrection through stream-of-consciousness computer techniques."

I studied the faces in the semicircle. No one seemed amazed by this account. Old Man Treadwell lit a cigarette, impatient with his own trembling hand, forced to shake out the flame before it burned him. There was no interest shown in discussion. The story occupied some recess of passive belief. There it was, familiar and comforting in its own strange way, a set of statements no less real than our daily quota of observable household fact. Even Babette in her tone of voice betrayed no sign of skepticism or condescension. Surely I was in no position to feel superior to these elderly listeners, blind or sighted. Little Patti's walk toward the warm welcoming glow found me in a weakened and receptive state. I wanted to believe at least this part of the tale.

Babette read an ad. The Stanford Linear Accelerator 3-Day Particle-Smashing Diet.

She picked up another tabloid. The cover story concerned the country's leading psychics and their predictions for the coming year. She read the items slowly.

"Squadrons of UFOs will invade Disney World and Cape Canaveral. In a startling twist, the attack will be revealed as a demonstration of the folly of war, leading to a nuclear test-ban treaty between the U.S. and Russia.

"The ghost of Elvis Presley will be seen taking lonely walks at dawn around Graceland, his musical mansion.

"A Japanese consortium will buy Air Force One and turn it into a luxury flying condominium with midair refueling privileges and air-to-surface missile capability.

"Bigfoot will appear dramatically at a campsite in the rugged and scenic Pacific Northwest. The hairy, upright man-beast, who stands eight feet tall and may be evolution's missing link, will gently welcome tourists to gather around him, revealing himself to be an apostle of peace.

"UFOs will raise the lost city of Atlantis from its watery grave in the Caribbean by telekinetic means and the help of powerful cables with properties not known in earthlike materials. The result will be a 'city of peace' where money and passports are totally unknown.

"The spirit of Lyndon B. Johnson will contact CBS executives to arrange an interview on live TV in order to defend itself against charges made in recent books.

"Beatle assassin Mark David Chapman will legally change his name to John Lennon and begin a new career as a rock lyricist from his prison cell on murderer's row.

"Members of an air-crash cult will hijack a jumbo jet and crash it into the White House in an act of blind devotion to their mysterious and reclusive leader, known only as Uncle Bob. The President and First Lady will miraculously survive with minor cuts, according to close friends of the couple.

"Dead multibillionaire Howard Hughes will mysteriously appear in the sky over Las Vegas.

"Wonder drugs mass-produced aboard UFO pharmaceutical labs in the weightless environment of space will lead to cures for anxiety, obesity and mood swings.

"From beyond the grave, dead living legend John Wayne will communicate telepathically with President Reagan to help frame U.S. foreign policy. Mellowed by death, the strapping actor will advocate a hopeful policy of peace and love.

"Sixties superkiller Charles Manson will break out of prison and terrorize the California countryside for weeks before negotiating a surrender on live TV in the offices of International Creative Management.

"Earth's only satellite, the moon, will explode on a humid night in July, playing havoc with tides and raining dirt and debris over much of our planet. But UFO cleanup crews will help avert a worldwide disaster, signalling an era of peace and harmony."

I watched the audience. Folded arms, heads slightly tilted. The predictions did not seem reckless to them. They were content to exchange brief and unrelated remarks, as during a break for a commercial on TV. The tabloid future, with its mechanism of a hopeful twist to apocalyptic events, was perhaps not so very remote from our own immediate experience. Look at us, I thought. Forced out of our homes, sent streaming into the bitter night, pursued by a toxic cloud, crammed together in makeshift quarters, ambiguously death-sentenced. We'd become part of the public stuff of media disaster. The small audience of the old and blind recognized the predictions of the psychics as events so near to happening that they had to be shaped in advance to our needs and wishes. Out of some persistent sense of large-scale ruin, we kept inventing hope.

Babette read an ad for diet sunglasses. The old people listened with interest. I went back to our area. I wanted to be near the children, watch them sleep. Watching children sleep makes me feel devout, part of a spiritual system. It is the closest I can come to God. If there is a secular equivalent of standing in a great spired cathedral with marble pillars and streams of mystical light slanting through two-tier Gothic windows, it would be watching children in their little bedrooms fast asleep. Girls especially.

Most of the lights were out now. The barracks roar had subsided. People were settling in. Heinrich was still awake, sitting on the floor, fully dressed, his back to the wall, reading a Red Cross resuscitation manual. He was not, in any case, a child whose lustrous slumber brought me peace. A restless, teeth-grinding and erratic sleeper, the boy sometimes fell from his bed, to be found in a fetal bundle by early light, shivering on the hardwood floor.

"They seem to have things under control," I said.

"Who?"

"Whoever's in charge out there."

"Who's in charge?"

"Never mind."

"It's like we've been flung back in time," he said. "Here we are in the Stone Age, knowing all these great things after centuries of progress but what can we do to make life easier for the Stone Agers? Can we make a refrigerator? Can we even explain how it works? What is electricity? What is light? We experience these things every day of our lives but what good does it do if we find ourselves hurled back in time and we can't even tell people the basic principles much less actually make something that would improve conditions. Name one thing you could make. Could you make a simple wooden match that you could strike on a rock to make a flame? We think we're so great and modern. Moon landings, artificial hearts. But what if you were hurled into a time warp and came face to face with the ancient Greeks. The Greeks invented trigonometry. They did autopsies and dissections. What could you tell an ancient Greek that he couldn't say, 'Big deal.' Could you tell him about the atom? Atom is a Greek word. The Greeks knew that the major events in the universe can't be seen by the eye of man. It's waves, it's rays, it's particles."

"We're doing all right."

"We're sitting in this huge moldy room. It's like we're flung back."

"We have heat, we have light."

"These are Stone Age things. They had heat and light. They had fire. They rubbed flints together and made sparks. Could you rub flints together? Would you know a flint if you saw one? If a Stoner Ager asked you what a nucleotide is, could you tell him? How do we make carbon paper? What is glass? If you came awake tomorrow in the Middle Ages and there was an epidemic raging, what could you do to stop it, knowing what you know about the progress of medicines and diseases? Here it is practically the twenty-first century and you've read hundreds of books and magazines and seen a hundred TV shows about science and medicine. Could you tell those people one little crucial thing that might save a million and a half lives?"

"'Boil your water,' I'd tell them."

"Sure. What about 'Wash behind your ears.' That's about as good."

"I still think we're doing fairly well. There was no warning. We have food, we have radios."

"What is a radio? What is the principle of a radio? Go ahead, explain. You're sitting in the middle of this circle of people. They use pebble tools. They eat grubs. Explain a radio."

"There's no mystery. Powerful transmitters send signals. They travel through the air, to be picked up by receivers."

"They travel through the air. What, like birds? Why not tell them magic? They travel through the air in magic waves. What is a nucleotide? You don't know, do you? Yet these are the building blocks of life. What good is knowledge if it just floats in the air? It goes from computer to computer. It changes and grows every second of every day. But nobody actually knows anything."

"You know something. You know about Nyodene D. I saw you with those people."

"That was a one-time freak," he told me.

He went back to his reading. I decided to get some air. Outside there were several groups of people standing around fires in fifty-five-gallon drums. A man sold soft drinks and sandwiches from an open-sided vehicle. Parked nearby were school buses, motorcycles, smallish vans called ambulettes. I walked around a while. There were people asleep in cars, others pitching tents. Beams of light swung slowly through the woods, searching out sounds, calm voices calling. I walked past a carload of prostitutes from Iron City. The interior light was on, the faces occupied the windows. They resembled the checkout women at the supermarket, blondish, double-chinned, resigned. A man leaned against the front door on the driver's side, speaking through a small opening in the window, his breath showing white. A radio said: "Hog futures have declined in sympathy, adding bearishness to that market."

I realized the man talking to the prostitutes was Murray Jay Siskind. I walked over there, waited for him to finish his sentence before addressing him. He took off his right glove to shake my hand. The car window went up.

"I thought you were in New York for the term break."

"I came back early to look at car-crash movies. Alfonse arranged a week of screenings to help me prepare for my seminar. I was on the airport bus heading in from Iron City when sirens started blowing. The driver didn't have much choice but to follow the traffic out here."

"Where are you spending the night?"

"The whole bus was assigned to one of the outbuildings. I heard a rumor about painted women and came out to investigate. One of them is dressed in leopard loungewear under her coat. She showed me. Another one says she has a snap-off crotch. What do you think she means by that? I'm a little worried, though, about all these outbreaks of life-style diseases. I carry a reinforced ribbed condom at all times. One size fits all. But I have a feeling it's not much protection against the intelligence and adaptability of the modern virus."

"The women don't seem busy," I said.

"I don't think this is the kind of disaster that leads to sexual abandon. One or two fellows might come skulking out eventually but there won't be an orgiastic horde, not tonight anyway."

"I guess people need time to go through certain stages."

"It's obvious," he said.

I told him I'd spent two and a half minutes exposed to the toxic cloud. Then I summarized the interview I'd had with the SIMUVAC man.

"That little breath of Nyodene has planted a death in my body. It is now official, according to the computer. I've got death inside me. It's just a question of whether or not I can outlive it. It has a life span of its own. Thirty years. Even if it doesn't kill me in a direct way, it will probably outlive me in my own body. I could die in a plane crash and the Nyodene D. would be thriving as my remains were laid to rest."

"This is the nature of modern death," Murray said. "It has a life independent of us. It is growing in prestige and dimension. It has a sweep it never had before. We study it objectively. We can predict its appearance, trace its path in the body. We can take cross-section pictures of it, tape its tremors and waves. We've never been so close to it, so familiar with its habits and attitudes. We know it intimately. But it continues to grow, to acquire breadth and scope, new outlets, new passages and means. The more we learn, the more it grows. Is this some law of physics? Every advance in knowledge and technique is matched by a new kind of death, a new strain. Death adapts, like a viral agent. Is it a law of nature? Or some private superstition of mine? I sense that the dead are closer to us than ever. I sense that we inhabit the same air as the dead. Remember Lao Tse. 'There is no difference between the quick and the dead. They are one channel of vitality.' He said this six hundred years before Christ. It is true once again, perhaps more true than ever."

He placed his hands on my shoulders and looked sadly into my face. He told me in the simplest words how sorry he was about what had happened. He talked to me about the likelihood of a computer error. Computers make mistakes, he said. Carpet static can cause a mistake. Some lint or hair in the circuits. He didn't believe this and neither did I. But he spoke convincingly, his eyes filled with spontaneous emotion, a broad and profound feeling. I felt oddly rewarded. His compassion was equal to the occasion, an impressive pity and grief. The bad news was almost worth it.

"Ever since I was in my twenties, I've had the fear, the dread. Now it's been realized. I feel enmeshed, I feel deeply involved. It's no wonder they call this thing the airborne toxic event. It's an event all right. It marks the end of uneventful things. This is just the beginning. Wait and see."

A talk-show host said: "You are on the air." The fires burned in the oil drums. The sandwich vendor closed down his van.

"Any episodes of *déjà vu* in your group?"

"Wife and daughter," I said.

"There's a theory about *déjà vu.*"

"I don't want to hear it."

"Why do we think these things happened before? Simple. They did happen before, in our minds, as visions of the future. Because these are precognitions, we can't fit the material into our system of consciousness as it is now structured. This is basically supernatural stuff. We're seeing into the future but haven't learned how to process the experience. So it stays hidden until the precognition comes true, until we come face to face with the event. Now we are free to remember it, to experience it as familiar material."

"Why are so many people having these episodes now?"

"Because death is in the air," he said gently. "It is liberating suppressed material. It is getting us closer to things we haven't learned about ourselves. Most of us have probably seen our own death but haven't known how to make the material surface. Maybe when we die, the first thing we'll say is, 'I know this feeling. I was here before.'"

He put his hands back on my shoulders, studied me with renewed and touching sadness. We heard the prostitutes call out to someone.

"I'd like to lose interest in myself," I told Murray. "Is there any chance of that happening?"

"None. Better men have tried."

"I guess you're right."

"It's obvious."

"I wish there was something I could do. I wish I could out-think the problem."

"Work harder on your Hitler," he said.

I looked at him. How much did he know?

The car window opened a crack. One of the women said to Murray, "All right, I'll do it for twenty-five."

"Have you checked with your representative?" he said.

She rolled down the window to peer at him. She had the opaque look of a hair-curlered woman on the evening news whose house had been buried in mud.

"You know who I mean," Murray said. "The fellow who sees to your emotional needs in return for one hundred percent of your earnings. The fellow you depend on to beat you up when you're bad."

"Bobby? He's in Iron City, keeping out of the cloud. He doesn't like to expose himself unless it's absolutely necessary."

The women laughed, six heads bobbing. It was insider's laughter, a little overdone, meant to identify them as people bound together in ways not easily appreciated by the rest of us.

A second window opened half an inch, a bright mouth appeared. "The type pimp Bobby is, he likes to use his mind."

A second round of laughter. We weren't sure whether it was at Bobby's expense, or ours, or theirs. The windows went up.

"It's none of my business," I said, "but what is it she's willing to do with you for twenty-five dollars?"

"The Heimlich maneuver."

I studied the part of his face that lay between the touring cap and beard. He seemed deep in thought, gazing at the car. The windows were fogged, the women's heads capped in cigarette smoke.

"Of course we'd have to find a vertical space," he said absently.

"You don't really expect her to lodge a chunk of food in her windpipe."

He looked at me, half startled. "What? No, no, that won't be necessary. As long as she makes gagging and choking sounds. As long as she sighs deeply when I jolt the pelvis. As long as she collapses helplessly backward into my life-saving embrace."

He took off his glove to shake my hand. Then he went over to the car to work out details with the woman in question. I watched him knock on the rear door. After a moment it opened and he squeezed into the back seat. I walked over to one of the oil drums. Three men and a woman stood around the fire, passing rumors back and forth.

Three of the live deer at the Kung Fu Palace were dead. The governor was dead, his pilot and co-pilot seriously injured after a crash landing in a shopping mall. Two of the men at the switching yard were dead, tiny acid burns visible in their Mylex suits. Packs of German shepherds, the Nyodene-sniffing dogs, had shed their parachutes and were being set loose in the affected communities. There was a rash of UFO sightings in the area. There was widespread looting by men in plastic sheets. Two looters were dead. Six National Guardsmen were dead, killed in a firefight that broke out after a racial incident. There were reports of miscarriages, babies born prematurely. There were sightings of additional billowing clouds.

The people who relayed these pieces of unverified information did so with a certain respectful dread, bouncing on their toes in the cold, arms crossed on their chests. They were fearful that the stories might be true but at the same time impressed by the dramatic character of things. The toxic event had released a spirit of imagination. People spun tales, others listened spellbound. There was a growing respect for the vivid rumor, the most chilling tale. We were no closer to believing or disbelieving a given story than we had been earlier. But there was a greater appreciation now. We began to marvel at our own ability to manufacture awe.

German shepherds. That was the reassuring news I took inside with me. The sturdy body, dense and darkish coat, fierce head, long lapping tongue. I pictured them prowling the empty streets, heavy-gaited, alert. Able to hear sounds we couldn't hear, able to sense changes in the flow of information. I saw them in our house, snouting into closets, tall ears pointed, a smell about them of heat and fur and stored power.

In the barracks almost everyone was sleeping. I made my way along a dim wall. The massed bodies lay in heavy rest, seeming to emit a single nasal sigh. Figures stirred; a wide-eyed Asian child watched me step among a dozen clustered sleeping bags. Colored lights skipped past my right ear. I heard a toilet flush.

Babette was curled on an air mattress, covered in her coat. My son slept sitting in a chair like some boozed commuter, head rolling on his chest. I carried a camp chair over to the cot where the younger children were. Then I sat there, leaning forward, to watch them sleep.

A random tumble of heads and dangled limbs. In those soft warm faces was a quality of trust so absolute and pure that I did not want to think it might be misplaced. There must be something, somewhere, large and grand and redoubtable enough to justify this shining reliance and implicit belief. A feeling of desperate piety swept over me. It was cosmic in nature, full of yearnings and reachings. It spoke of vast distances, awesome but subtle forces. These sleeping children were like figures in an ad for the Rosicrucians, drawing a powerful beam of light from somewhere off the page. Steffie turned slightly, then muttered something in her sleep. It seemed important that I know what it was. In my current state, bearing the death impression of the Nyodene cloud, I was ready to search anywhere for signs and hints, intimations of odd comfort. I pulled my chair up closer. Her face in pouchy sleep might have been a structure designed solely to protect the eyes, those great, large and apprehensive things, prone to color phases and a darting alertness, to a perception of distress in others. I sat there watching her. Moments later she spoke again. Distinct syllables this time, not some dreamy murmur—but a language not quite of this world. I struggled to understand. I was convinced she was saying something, fitting together units of stable meaning. I watched her face, waited. Ten minutes passed. She uttered two clearly audible words, familiar and elusive at the same time, words that seemed to have a ritual meaning, part of a verbal spell or ecstatic chant.

Toyota Celica.

A long moment passed before I realized this was the name of an automobile. The truth only amazed me more. The utterance was beautiful and mysterious, gold-shot with looming wonder. It was like the name of an ancient power in the sky, tablet-carved in cuneiform. It made me feel that something hovered. But how could this be? A simple brand name, an ordinary car. How could these near-nonsense words, murmured in a child's restless sleep, make me sense a meaning, a presence? She was only repeating some TV voice. Toyota Corolla, Toyota Celica, Toyota Cressida. Supranational names, computer-generated, more or less universally pronounceable. Part of every child's brain noise, the substatic regions too deep to probe. Whatever its source, the utterance struck me with the impact of a moment of splendid transcendence.

I depend on my children for that.

I sat a while longer, watching Denise, watching Wilder, feeling selfless and spiritually large. There was an empty air mattress on the floor but I wanted to share Babette's and eased myself next to her body, a dreaming mound. Her hands, feet and face were drawn under the sheltering coat; only a burst of hair remained. I fell at once into marine oblivion, a deep-dwelling crablike consciousness, silent and dreamless.

It seemed only minutes later that I was surrounded by noise and commotion. I opened my eyes to find Denise pounding on my arms and shoulders. When she saw I was awake, she began battering her mother. All around us, people were dressing and packing. The major noise issued from sirens in the ambulettes outside. A voice was instructing us through a bullhorn. In the distance I heard a clanging bell and then a series of automobile horns, the first of what would become a universal bleat, a herd-panic of terrible wailing proportions as vehicles of all sizes and types tried to reach the parkway in the quickest possible time.

I managed to sit up. Both girls were trying to rouse Babette. The room was emptying out. I saw Heinrich staring down at me, an enigmatic grin on his face. The amplified voice said: "Wind change, wind change. Cloud has changed direction. Toxic, toxic, heading here."

Babette turned over on the mattress, sighing contentedly. "Five more minutes," she said. The girls rained blows on her head and arms.

I got to my feet, looked around for a men's room. Wilder was dressed, eating a cookie while he waited. Again the voice spoke, like singsong patter on a department-store loudspeaker, amid the perfumed counters and chiming bells: "Toxic, toxic. Proceed to your vehicle, proceed to your vehicle."

Denise, who was clutching her mother by the wrist, flung the entire arm down on the mattress. "Why does he have to say everything twice? We get it the first time. He just wants to hear himself talk."

They got Babette up on all fours. I hurried off to the toilet. I had my toothpaste but couldn't find the brush. I spread some paste on my index finger and ran the finger across my teeth. When I got back, they were dressed and ready, heading for the exit. A woman with an armband handed out masks at the door, gauzy white surgical masks that covered the nose and mouth. We took six and went outside.

It was still dark. A heavy rain fell. Before us lay a scene of panoramic disorder. Cars trapped in mud, cars stalled, cars crawling along the one-lane escape route, cars taking shortcuts through the woods, cars hemmed in by trees, boulders, other cars. Sirens called and faded, horns blared in desperation and protest. There were running men, tents wind-blown into trees, whole families abandoning their vehicles to head on foot for the parkway. From deep in the woods we heard motorcycles revving, voices raising incoherent cries. It was like the fall of a colonial capital to dedicated rebels. A great surging drama with elements of humiliation and guilt.

We put on our masks and ran through the downpour to our car. Not ten yards away a group of men proceeded calmly to a Land-Rover. They resembled instructors in jungle warfare, men with lean frames and long boxy heads. They drove straight into dense underbrush, not only away from the dirt road but away from all the other cars attempting shortcuts. Their bumper sticker read GUN CONTROL IS MIND CONTROL. In situations like this, you want to stick close to people in right-wing fringe groups. They've practiced staying alive. I followed with some difficulty, our smallish wagon jouncing badly in brush tangles, up inclines, over hidden stones. Inside five minutes the Land-Rover was out of sight.

Rain turned to sleet, sleet to snow.

I saw a line of headlights far to the right and drove fifty yards through a gulley in that direction, the car heeled like a toboggan. We did not seem to be getting closer to the lights. Babette turned on the radio and we were told that the Boy Scout camp evacuees were to head for Iron City, where arrangements were being made to provide food and shelter. We heard horns blowing and thought it was a reaction to the radio announcement but they continued in a rapid and urgent cadence, conveying through the stormy night a sense of animal fear and warning.

Then we heard the rotors. Through the stark trees we saw it, the immense toxic cloud, lighted now by eighteen choppers—immense almost beyond comprehension, beyond legend and rumor, a roiling bloated slug-shaped mass. It seemed to be generating its own inner storms. There were cracklings and sputterings, flashes of light, long looping streaks of chemical flame. The car horns blared and moaned. The helicopters throbbed like giant appliances. We sat in the car, in the snowy woods, saying nothing. The great cloud, beyond its turbulent core, was silver-tipped in the spotlights. It moved horribly and sluglike through the night, the choppers seeming to putter ineffectually around its edges. In its tremendous size, its dark and bulky menace, its escorting aircraft, the cloud resembled a national promotion for death, a multimillion-dollar campaign backed by radio spots, heavy print and billboard, TV saturation. There was a high-tension discharge of vivid light. The horn-blowing increased in volume.

I recalled with a shock that I was technically dead. The interview with the SIMUVAC technician came back to me in terrible detail. I felt sick on several levels.

There was nothing to do but try to get the family to safety. I kept pushing toward the headlights, the sound of blowing horns. Wilder was asleep, planing in uniform spaces. I hit the accelerator, jerked the wheel, arm-wrestled the car through a stand of white pine.

Through his mask Heinrich said, "Did you ever really look at your eye?"

"What do you mean?" Denise said, showing immediate interest, as though we were lazing away a midsummer day on the front porch.

"Your own eye. Do you know which part is which?"

"You mean like the iris, the pupil?"

"Those are the publicized parts. What about the vitreous body? What about the lens? The lens is tricky. How many people even know they have a lens? They think 'lens' must be 'camera.'"

"What about the ear?" Denise said in a muffled voice.

"If the eye is a mystery, totally forget the ear. Just say 'cochlea' to somebody, they look at you like, 'Who's this guy?' There's this whole world right inside our own body."

"Nobody even cares," she said.

"How can people live their whole lives without knowing the names of their own parts of the body?"

"What about the glands?" she said.

"Animal glands you can eat. The Arabs eat glands."

"The French eat glands," Babette said through gauze. "The Arabs eat eyes, speaking of eyes."

"What parts?" Denise said.

"The whole eye. The sheep eye."

"They don't eat the lashes," Heinrich said.

"Do sheep have lashes?" Steffie said.

"Ask your father," Babette said.

The car forded a creek which I didn't know was there until we were in it. I struggled to get us over the opposite bank. Snow fell thickly through the high beams. The muffled dialogue went on. I reflected that our current predicament seemed to be of merely glancing interest to some of us. I wanted them to pay attention to the toxic event. I wanted to be appreciated for my efforts in getting us to the parkway. I thought of telling them about the computer tally, the time-factored death I carried in my chromosomes and blood. Self-pity oozed through my soul. I tried to relax and enjoy it.

"I'll give anybody in this car five dollars," Heinrich said through his protective mask, "if you can tell me whether more people died building the pyramids in Egypt or building the Great Wall of China—and you have to say how many died in each place, within fifty people."

I followed three snowmobiles across an open field. They conveyed a mood of clever fun. The toxic event was still in view, chemical tracers shooting in slow arcs out of its interior. We passed families on foot, saw a line of paired red lights winding through the dark. When we edged out of the woods, people in other cars gave us sleepy looks. It took ninety minutes to reach the parkway, another thirty to get to the cloverleaf, where we spun off toward Iron City. It was here that we met up with the group from the Kung Fu Palace. Tooting horns, waving children. Like wagon trains converging on the Santa Fe Trail. The cloud still hung in the rearview mirror.

Krylon, Rust-Oleum, Red Devil.

We reached Iron City at dawn. There were checkpoints at all the road exits. State troopers and Red Cross workers handed out mimeographed instructions concerning evacuation centers. Half an hour later we found ourselves, with forty other families, in an abandoned karate studio on the top floor of a four-story building on the main street. There were no beds or chairs. Steffie refused to take off her mask.

By nine a.m. we had a supply of air mattresses, some food and coffee. Through the dusty windows we saw a group of turbaned schoolchildren, members of the local Sikh community, standing in the street with a hand-lettered sign: IRON CITY WELCOMES AREA EVACUEES. We were not allowed to leave the building.

On the wall of the studio there were poster-size illustrations of the six striking surfaces of the human hand.

At noon a rumor swept the city. Technicians were being lowered in slings from army helicopters in order to plant microorganisms in the core of the toxic cloud. These organisms were genetic recombinations that had a built-in appetite for the particular toxic agents in Nyodene D. They would literally consume the billowing cloud, eat it up, break it down, decompose it.

This stunning innovation, so similar in nature to something we might come across in the *National Enquirer* or the *Star*, made us feel a little weary, glutted in an insubstantial way, as after a junk food spree. I wandered through the room, as I'd done in the Boy Scout barracks, moving from one conversational knot to another. No one seemed to know how a group of microorganisms could consume enough toxic material to rid the sky of such a dense and enormous cloud. No one knew what would happen to the toxic waste once it was eaten or to the microorganisms once they were finished eating.

Everywhere in the room children were striking mock karate poses. When I got back to our area, Babette sat alone in a scarf and knitted cap.

"I don't like this latest rumor," she said.

"Too far-fetched? You think there's no chance a bunch of organisms can eat their way through the toxic event."

"I think there's every chance in the world. I don't doubt for a minute they have these little organisms packaged in cardboard with plastic see-through bubbles, like ballpoint refills. That's what worries me."

"The very existence of custom-made organisms."

"The very idea, the very existence, the wondrous ingenuity. On the one hand I definitely admire it. Just to think there are people out there who can conjure such things. A cloud-eating microbe or whatever. There is just no end of surprise. All the amazement that's left in the world is microscopic. But I can live with that. What scares me is have they thought it through completely?"

"You feel a vague foreboding," I said.

"I feel they're working on the superstitious part of my nature. Every advance is worse than the one before because it makes me more scared."

"Scared of what?"

"The sky, the earth, I don't know."

"The greater the scientific advance, the more primitive the fear."

"Why is that?" she said.

At three p.m. Steffie was still wearing the protective mask. She walked along the walls, a set of pale green eyes, discerning, alert, secretive. She watched people as if they could not see her watching, as if the mask covered her eyes instead of leaving them exposed. People thought she was playing a game. They winked at her, said hi. I was certain it would take at least another day before she felt safe enough to remove the protective device. She was solemn about warnings, interpreted danger as a state too lacking in detail and precision to be confined to a certain time and place. I knew we would simply have to wait for her to forget the amplified voice, the sirens, the night ride through the woods. In the meantime the mask, setting off her eyes, dramatized her sensitivity to episodes of stress and alarm. It seemed to bring her closer to the real concerns of the world, honed her in its wind.

At seven p.m. a man carrying a tiny TV set began to walk slowly through the room, making a speech as he went. He was middle-aged or older, a clear-eyed and erect man wearing a fur-lined cap with lowered flaps. He held the TV set well up in the air and out away from his body and during the course of his speech he turned completely around several times as he walked in order to display the blank screen to all of us in the room.

"There's nothing on network," he said to us. "Not a word, not a picture. On the Glassboro channel we rate fifty-two words by actual count. No film footage, no live report. Does this kind of thing happen so often that nobody cares anymore? Don't those people know what we've been through? We were scared to death. We still are. We left our homes, we drove through blizzards, we saw the cloud. It was a deadly specter, right there above us. Is it possible nobody gives substantial coverage to such a thing? Half a minute, twenty seconds? Are they telling us it was insignificant, it was piddling? Are they so callous? Are they so bored by spills and contaminations and wastes? Do they think this is just television? 'There's too much television already—why show more?' Don't they know it's real? Shouldn't the streets be crawling with cameramen and soundmen and reporters? Shouldn't we be yelling out the window at them, 'Leave us alone, we've been through enough, get out of here with your vile instruments of intrusion.' Do they have to have two hundred dead, rare disaster footage, before they come flocking to a given site in their helicopters and network limos? What exactly has to happen before they stick microphones in our faces and hound us to the doorsteps of our homes, camping out on our lawns, creating the usual media circus? Haven't we earned the right to despise their idiot questions? Look at us in this place. We are quarantined. We are like lepers in medieval times. They won't let us out of here. They leave food at the foot of the stairs and tiptoe away to safety. This is the most terrifying time of our lives. Everything we love and have worked for is under serious threat. But we look around and see no response from the official organs of the media. The airborne toxic event is a horrifying thing. Our fear is enormous. Even if there hasn't been great loss of life, don't we deserve some attention for our suffering, our human worry, our terror? Isn't fear news?"

Applause. A sustained burst of shouting and hand-clapping. The speaker slowly turned one more time, displaying the little TV to his audience. When he completed his turn, he was face to face with me, no more than ten inches away. A change came over his wind-beaten face, a slight befuddlement, the shock of some minor fact jarred loose.

"I saw this before," he finally said to me.

"Saw what before?"

"You were standing there, I was standing here. Like a leap into the fourth dimension. Your features incredibly sharp and clear. Light hair, washed-out eyes, pinkish nose, nondescript mouth and chin, sweaty-type complexion, average jowls, slumped shoulders, big hands and feet. It all happened before. Steam hissing in the pipes. Tiny little hairs standing out in your pores. That identical look on your face."

"What look?" I said.

"Haunted, ashen, lost."

It was nine days before they told us we could go back home.

Dylarama

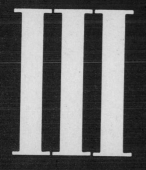

22

The supermarket is full of elderly people who look lost among the dazzling hedgerows. Some people are too small to reach the upper shelves; some people block the aisles with their carts; some are clumsy and slow to react; some are forgetful, some confused; some move about muttering with the wary look of people in institutional corridors.

I pushed my cart along the aisle. Wilder sat inside, on the collapsible shelf, trying to grab items whose shape and radiance excited his system of sensory analysis. There were two new developments in the supermarket, a butcher's corner and a bakery, and the oven aroma of bread and cake combined with the sight of a bloodstained man pounding at strips of living veal was pretty exciting for us all.

"Dristan Ultra, Dristan Ultra."

The other excitement was the snow. Heavy snow predicted, later today or tonight. It brought out the crowds, those who feared the roads would soon be impassable, those too old to walk safely in snow and ice, those who thought the storm would isolate them in their homes for days or weeks. Older people in particular were susceptible to news of impending calamity as it was forecast on TV by grave men standing before digital radar maps or pulsing photographs of the planet. Whipped into a frenzy, they hurried to the supermarket to stock up before the weather mass moved in. Snow watch, said the forecasters. Snow alert. Snowplows. Snow mixed with sleet and freezing rain. It was already snowing in the west. It was already moving to the east. They gripped this news like a pygmy skull. Snow showers. Snow flurries. Snow warnings. Driving snow. Blowing snow. Deep and drifting snow. Accumulations, devastations. The old people shopped in a panic. When

TV didn't fill them with rage, it scared them half to death. They whispered to each other in the checkout lines. Traveler's advisory, zero visibility. When does it hit? How many inches? How many days? They became secretive, shifty, appeared to withhold the latest and worst news from others, appeared to blend a cunning with their haste, tried to hurry out before someone questioned the extent of their purchases. Hoarders in a war. Greedy, guilty.

I saw Murray in the generic food area, carrying a Teflon skillet. I stopped to watch him for a while. He talked to four or five people, occasionally pausing to scrawl some notes in a spiral book. He managed to write with the skillet wedged awkwardly under his arm.

Wilder called out to him, a tree-top screech, and I wheeled the cart over.

"How is that good woman of yours?"

"Fine," I said.

"Does this kid talk yet?"

"Now and then. He likes to pick his spots."

"You know that matter you helped me with? The Elvis Presley power struggle?"

"Sure. I came in and lectured."

"It turns out, tragically, that I would have won anyway."

"What happened?"

"Cotsakis, my rival, is no longer among the living."

"What does that mean?"

"It means he's dead."

"Dead?"

"Lost in the surf off Malibu. During the term break. I found out an hour ago. Came right here."

I was suddenly aware of the dense environmental texture. The automatic doors opened and closed, breathing abruptly. Colors and odors seemed sharper. The sound of gliding feet emerged from a dozen other noises, from the sublittoral drone of maintenance systems, from the rustle of newsprint as shoppers scanned their horoscopes in the tabloids up front, from the whispers of elderly women with talcumed faces, from the steady rattle of cars going over a loose manhole cover just outside the entrance. Gliding feet. I heard them clearly, a sad numb shuffle in every aisle.

"How are the girls?" Murray said.

"Fine."

"Back in school?"

"Yes."

"Now that the scare is over."

"Yes. Steffie no longer wears her protective mask."

"I want to buy some New York cuts," he said, gesturing toward the butcher.

The phrase seemed familiar, but what did it mean?

"Unpackaged meat, fresh bread," he went on. "Exotic fruits, rare cheeses. Products from twenty countries. It's like being at some crossroads of the ancient world, a Persian bazaar or boom town on the Tigris. How are you, Jack?"

What did he mean, how are you?

"Poor Cotsakis, lost in the surf," I said. "That enormous man."

"That's the one."

"I don't know what to say."

"He was big all right."

"Enormously so."

"I don't know what to say either. Except better him than me."

"He must have weighed three hundred pounds."

"Oh, easily."

"What do you think, two ninety, three hundred?"

"Three hundred easily."

"Dead. A big man like that."

"What can we say?"

"I thought I was big."

"He was on another level. You're big on your level."

"Not that I knew him. I didn't know him at all."

"It's better not knowing them when they die. It's better them than us."

"To be so enormous. Then to die."

"To be lost without a trace. To be swept away."

"I can picture him so clearly."

"It's strange in a way, isn't it," he said, "that we can picture the dead."

I took Wilder along the fruit bins. The fruit was gleaming and wet, hard-edged. There was a self-conscious quality about it. It looked carefully observed, like four-color fruit in a guide to photography. We veered right at the plastic jugs of spring water and headed for the checkout. I liked being with Wilder. The world was a series of fleeting gratifications. He took what he could, then immediately forgot it in the rush of a subsequent pleasure. It was this forgetfulness I envied and admired.

The woman at the terminal asked him a number of questions, providing her own replies in a babyish voice.

Some of the houses in town were showing signs of neglect. The park benches needed repair, the broken streets needed resurfacing. Signs of the times. But the supermarket did not change, except for the better. It was well-stocked, musical and bright. This was the key, it seemed to us. Everything was fine, would continue to be fine, would eventually get even better as long as the supermarket did not slip.

Early that evening I drove Babette to her class in posture. We stopped on the parkway overpass and got out to look at the sunset. Ever since the airborne toxic event, the sunsets had become almost unbearably beautiful. Not that there was a measurable connection. If the special character of Nyodene Derivative (added to the everyday drift of effluents, pollutants, contaminants and deliriants) had caused this aesthetic leap from already brilliant sunsets to broad towering ruddled visionary skyscapes, tinged with dread, no one had been able to prove it.

"What else can we believe?" Babette said. "How else can we explain?"

"I don't know."

"We're not at the edge of the ocean or desert. We ought to have timid winter sunsets. But look at the blazing sky. It's so beautiful and dramatic. Sunsets used to last five minutes. Now they last an hour."

"Why is that?"

"Why is that?" she said.

This spot on the overpass offered a broad prospect west. People had been coming here ever since the first of the new sunsets, parking their own cars, standing around in the bitter wind to chat nervously and look. There were four cars here already, others certain to come. The overpass had become a scenic lookout. The police were reluctant to enforce the parking ban. It was one of those situations, like the olympics for the handicapped, that make all the restrictions seem petty.

Later I drove back to the Congregational church to pick her up. Denise and Wilder came along for the ride. Babette in jeans and legwarmers was a fine and stirring sight. Legwarmers lend a note of paramilitary poise, a hint of archaic warriorhood. When she shoveled snow, she wore a furry headband as well. It made me think of the fifth century A.D. Men standing around campfires speaking in subdued tones in their Turkic and Mongol dialects. Clear skies. The fearless exemplary death of Attila the Hun.

"How was class?" Denise said.

"It's going so well they want me to teach another course."

"In what?"

"Jack won't believe this."

"In what?" I said.

"Eating and drinking. It's called Eating and Drinking: Basic Parameters. Which, I admit, is a little more stupid than it absolutely has to be."

"What could you teach?" Denise said.

"That's just it. It's practically inexhaustible. Eat light foods in warm weather. Drink plenty of liquids."

"But everybody knows that."

"Knowledge changes every day. People like to have their beliefs reinforced. Don't lie down after eating a heavy meal. Don't drink liquor on an empty stomach. If you must swim, wait at least an hour after eating. The world is more complicated for adults than it is for children. We didn't grow up with all these shifting facts and attitudes. One day they just started appearing. So people need to be reassured by someone in a position of authority that a certain way to do something is the right way or the wrong way, at least for the time being. I'm the closest they could find, that's all."

A staticky piece of lint clung to the TV screen.

In bed we lay quietly, my head between her breasts, cushioned as if against some remorseless blow. I was determined not to tell her about the computer verdict. I knew she would be devastated to learn that my death would almost surely precede hers. Her body became the agency of my resolve, my silence. Nightly I moved toward her breasts, nuzzling into that designated space like a wounded sub into its repair dock. I drew courage from her breasts, her warm mouth, her browsing hands, from the skimming tips of her fingers on my back. The lighter the touch, the more determined I was to keep her from knowing. Only her own desperation could break my will.

Once I almost asked her to put on legwarmers before we made love. But it seemed a request more deeply rooted in pathos than in aberrant sexuality and I thought it might make her suspect that something was wrong.

23

I asked my German teacher to add half an hour to each lesson. It seemed more urgent than ever that I learn the language. His room was cold. He wore foul weather gear and seemed gradually to be piling furniture against the windows.

We sat facing each other in the gloom. I did wonderfully well with vocabulary and rules of grammar. I could have passed a written test easily, made top grades. But I continued to have trouble pronouncing the words. Dunlop did not seem to mind. He enunciated for me over and over, scintillas of dry spit flying toward my face.

We advanced to three lessons a week. He seemed to shed his distracted manner, to become slightly more engaged. Furniture, newspapers, cardboard boxes, sheets of polyethylene continued to accumulate against the walls and windows—items scavenged from ravines. He stared into my mouth as I did my exercises in pronunciation. Once he reached in with his right hand to adjust my tongue. It was a strange and terrible moment, an act of haunting intimacy. No one had ever handled my tongue before.

German shepherds still patrolled the town, accompanied by men in Mylex suits. We welcomed the dogs, got used to them, fed and petted them, but did not adjust well to the sight of costumed men with padded boots, hoses attached to their masks. We associated these outfits with the source of our trouble and fear.

At dinner Denise said, "Why can't they dress in normal clothes?"

"This is what they wear on duty," Babette said. "It doesn't mean we're in danger. The dogs have sniffed out only a few traces of toxic material on the edge of town."

"That's what we're supposed to believe," Heinrich said. "If they released the true findings, there'd be billions of dollars in law suits. Not to mention demonstrations, panic, violence and social disorder."

He seemed to take pleasure in the prospect. Babette said, "That's a little extreme, isn't it?"

"What's extreme, what I said or what would happen?"

"Both. There's no reason to think the results aren't true as published."

"Do you really believe that?" he said.

"Why shouldn't I believe it?"

"Industry would collapse if the true results of any of these investigations were released."

"What investigations?"

"The ones that are going on all over the country."

"That's the point," she said. "Every day on the news there's another toxic spill. Cancerous solvents from storage tanks, arsenic from smokestacks, radioactive water from power plants. How serious can it be if it happens all the time? Isn't the definition of a serious event based on the fact that it's not an everyday occurrence?"

The two girls looked at Heinrich, anticipating a surgically deft rejoinder.

"Forget these spills," he said. "These spills are nothing."

This wasn't the direction any of us had expected him to take. Babette watched him carefully. He cut a lettuce leaf on his salad plate into two equal pieces.

"I wouldn't say they were nothing," she said cautiously. "They're small everyday seepages. They're controllable. But they're not nothing. We have to watch them."

"The sooner we forget these spills, the sooner we can come to grips with the real issue."

"What's the real issue?" I said.

He spoke with his mouth full of lettuce and cucumber.

"The real issue is the kind of radiation that surrounds us every day. Your radio, your TV, your microwave oven, your power lines just outside the door, your radar speed-trap on the highway. For years they told us these low doses weren't dangerous."

"And now?" Babette said.

We watched him use his spoon to mold the mashed potatoes on his plate into the shape of a volcanic mountain. He poured gravy ever so carefully into the opening at the top. Then he set to work ridding his steak of fat, veins and other imperfections. It occurred to me that eating is the only form of professionalism most people ever attain.

"This is the big new worry," he said. "Forget spills, fallouts, leakages. It's the things right around you in your own house that'll get you sooner or later. It's the electrical and magnetic fields. Who in this room would believe me if I said that the suicide rate hits an all-time record among people who live near high-voltage power lines? What makes these people so sad and depressed? Just the *sight* of ugly wires and utility poles? Or does something happen to their brain cells from being exposed to constant rays?"

He immersed a piece of steak in the gravy that sat in the volcanic depression, then put it in his mouth. But he did not begin chewing until he'd scooped some potatoes from the lower slopes and added it to the meat. A tension seemed to be building around the question of whether he could finish the gravy before the potatoes collapsed.

"Forget headaches and fatigue," he said as he chewed. "What about nerve disorders, strange and violent behavior in the home? There are scientific findings. Where do you think all the deformed babies are coming from? Radio and TV, that's where."

The girls looked at him admiringly. I wanted to argue with him. I wanted to ask him why I should believe these scientific findings but not the results that indicated we were safe from Nyodene contamination. But what could I say, considering my condition? I wanted to tell him that statistical evidence of the kind he was quoting from was by nature inconclusive and misleading. I wanted to say that he would learn to regard all such catastrophic findings with equanimity as he matured, grew out of his confining literalism, developed a spirit of informed and skeptical inquiry, advanced in wisdom and rounded judgment, got old, declined, died.

But I only said, "Terrifying data is now an industry in itself. Different firms compete to see how badly they can scare us."

"I've got news for you," he said. "The brain of a white rat releases calcium ions when it's exposed to radio-frequency waves. Does anyone at this table know what that means?"

Denise looked at her mother.

"Is this what they teach in school today?" Babette said. "What happened to civics, how a bill becomes a law? The square of the hypotenuse is equal to the sum of the squares of the two sides. I still remember my theorems. The battle of Bunker Hill was really fought on Breed's Hill. Here's one. Latvia, Estonia and Lithuania."

"Was it the *Monitor* or the *Merrimac* that got sunk?" I said.

"I don't know but it was Tippecanoe and Tyler too."

"What was that?" Steffie said.

"I want to say he was an Indian running for office. Here's one. Who invented the mechanical reaper and how did it change the face of American agriculture?"

"I'm trying to remember the three kinds of rock," I said. "Igneous, sedimentary and something else."

"What about your logarithms? What about the causes of economic discontent leading up to the Great Crash? Here's one. Who won the Lincoln-Douglas debates? Careful. It's not as obvious as it seems."

"Anthracite and bituminous," I said. "Isosceles and scalene."

The mysterious words came back to me in a rush of confused schoolroom images.

"Here's one. Angles, Saxons and Jutes."

Déjà vu was still a problem in the area. A toll-free hotline had been set up. There were counselors on duty around the clock to talk to people who were troubled by recurring episodes. Perhaps *déjà vu* and other tics of the mind and body were the durable products of the airborne toxic event. But over a period of time it became possible to interpret such things as signs of a deep-reaching isolation we were beginning to feel. There was no large city with a vaster torment we might use to see our own dilemma in some soothing perspective. No large city to blame for our sense of victimization. No city to hate and fear. No panting megacenter to absorb our woe, to distract us from our unremitting sense of time—

time as the agent of our particular ruin, our chromosome breaks, hysterically multiplying tissue.

"Baba," I whispered between her breasts, that night in bed.

Although we are for a small town remarkably free of resentment, the absence of a polestar metropolis leaves us feeling in our private moments a little lonely.

24

It was the following night that I discovered the Dylar. An amber bottle of lightweight plastic. It was taped to the underside of the radiator cover in the bathroom. I found it when the radiator began knocking and I removed the cover to study the valve in an earnest and methodical way, trying to disguise to myself the helplessness I felt.

I went at once to find Denise. She was in bed watching TV. When I told her what I'd found we went quietly into the bathroom and looked at the bottle together. It was easy to see the word *Dylar* through the transparent tape. Neither of us touched a thing, so great was our surprise at finding the medication concealed in this manner. We regarded the little tablets with solemn concern. Then we exchanged a look fraught with implication.

Without a word we replaced the radiator cover, bottle intact, and went back to Denise's room. The voice at the end of the bed said: "Meanwhile here is a quick and attractive lemon garnish suitable for any sea food."

Denise sat on the bed, looking past me, past the TV set, past the posters and souvenirs. Her eyes were narrowed, her face set in a thoughtful scowl.

"We say nothing to Baba."

"All right," I said.

"She'll only say she doesn't remember why she put it there."

"What is Dylar? That's what I want to know. There are only three or four places she could have gone to get the prescription filled, within a reasonable distance. A pharmacist can tell us what the stuff is for. I'll get in the car first thing in the morning."

"I already did that," she said.

"When?"

"Around Christmas. I went to three drugstores and talked to the Indians behind the counters in the back."

"I think they're Pakistanis."

"Whatever."

"What did they tell you about Dylar?"

"Never heard of it."

"Did you ask them to look it up? They must have lists of the most recent medications. Supplements, updates."

"They looked. It's not on any list."

"Unlisted," I said.

"We'll have to call her doctor."

"I'll call him now. I'll call him at home."

"Surprise him," she said, with a certain ruthlessness.

"If I get him at home, he won't be screened by an answering service, a receptionist, a nurse, the young and good-humored doctor who shares his suite of offices and whose role in life is to treat the established doctor's rejects. Once you're shunted from the older doctor to the younger doctor, it means that you and your disease are second-rate."

"Call him at home," she said. "Wake him up. Trick him into telling us what we want to know."

The only phone was in the kitchen. I ambled down the hall, glancing into our bedroom to make sure Babette was still there, ironing blouses and listening to a call-in show on the radio, a form of entertainment she'd recently become addicted to. I went down to the kitchen, found the doctor's name in the phone book and dialed his home number.

The doctor's name was Hookstratten. It sounded sort of German. I'd met him once—a stooped man with a bird-wattled face and deep voice. Denise had said to trick him but the only way to do that was within a context of honesty and truthfulness. If I pretended to be a stranger seeking information about Dylar, he would either hang up or tell me to come into the office.

He answered on the fourth or fifth ring. I told him who I was and said I was concerned about Babette. Concerned enough to call him at home—an admittedly rash act but one I hoped he'd be able to understand. I said I was fairly sure it was the medication he'd prescribed for her that was causing the problem.

"What problem?"

"Memory lapse."

"You would call a doctor at home to talk about memory lapse. If everyone with memory lapse called a doctor at home, what would we have? The ripple effect would be tremendous."

I told him the lapses were frequent.

"Frequent. I know your wife. This is the wife who came to me one night with a crying child. 'My child is crying.' She would come to a medical doctor who is a private corporation and ask him to treat a child for crying. Now I pick up the phone and it's the husband. You would call a doctor in his home after ten o'clock at night. You would say to him, 'Memory lapse.' Why not tell me she has gas? Call me at home for gas?"

"Frequent and prolonged, doctor. It has to be the medication."

"What medication?"

"Dylar."

"Never heard of it."

"A small white tablet. Comes in an amber bottle."

"You would describe a tablet as small and white and expect a doctor to respond, at home, after ten at night. Why not tell me it is round? This is crucial to our case."

"It's an unlisted drug."

"I never saw it. I certainly never prescribed it for your wife. She's a very healthy woman so far as it's within my ability to ascertain such things, being subject as I am to the same human failings as the next fellow."

This sounded like a malpractice disclaimer. Maybe he was reading it from a printed card like a detective informing a suspect of his constitutional rights. I thanked him, hung up, called my own doctor at home. He answered on the seventh ring, said he thought Dylar was an island in the Persian Gulf, one of those oil terminals crucial to the survival of the West. A woman did the weather in the background.

I went upstairs and told Denise not to worry. I would take a tablet from the bottle and have it analyzed by someone in the chemistry department at the college. I waited for her to tell me she'd already done that. But she just nodded grimly and I headed down the hall, stopping in Heinrich's room to say goodnight. He was doing chinning exercises in the closet, using a bar clamped to the doorway.

"Where did you get that?"

"It's Mercator's."

"Who's that?"

"He's this senior I hang around with now. He's almost nineteen and he's still in high school. To give you some idea."

"Some idea of what?"

"How big he is. He bench-presses these awesome amounts."

"Why do you want to chin? What does chinning accomplish?"

"What does anything accomplish? Maybe I just want to build up my body to compensate for other things."

"What other things?"

"My hairline's getting worse, to name just one."

"It's not getting worse. Ask Baba if you don't believe me. She has a sharp eye for things like that."

"My mother told me to see a dermatologist."

"I don't think that's necessary at this stage."

"I already went."

"What did he say?"

"It was a she. My mother told me to go to a woman."

"What did she say?"

"She said I have a dense donor site."

"What does that mean?"

"She can take hair from other parts of my head and surgically implant it where it's needed. Not that it makes any difference. I'd just as soon be bald. I can easily see myself totally bald. There are kids my age with cancer. Their hair falls out from chemotherapy. Why should I be different?"

He was standing in the closet peering out at me. I decided to change the subject.

"If you really think chinning helps, why don't you stand outside the closet and do your exercises facing in? Why stand in that dark musty space?"

"If you think this is strange, you ought to see what Mercator's doing."

"What's he doing?"

"He's training to break the world endurance record for sitting in a cage full of poisonous snakes, for the *Guinness Book of Records*. He goes to Glassboro three times a week where they have this exotic pet shop. The owner lets him feed the mamba and the puff adder. To get him accustomed. Totally forget your North American rattlesnake. The puff adder is the most venomous snake in the world."

"Every time I see newsfilm of someone in his fourth week of sitting in a cage full of snakes, I find myself wishing he'd get bitten."

"So do I," Heinrich said.

"Why is that?"

"He's asking for it."

"That's right. Most of us spend our lives avoiding danger. Who do these people think they are?"

"They ask for it. Let them get it."

I paused a while, savoring the rare moment of agreement.

"What else does your friend do to train?"

"He sits for long periods in one place, getting his bladder accustomed. He's down to two meals a day. He sleeps sitting up, two hours at a time. He wants to train himself to wake up gradually, without sudden movements, which could startle a mamba."

"It seems a strange ambition."

"Mambas are sensitive."

"But if it makes him happy."

"He thinks he's happy but it's just a nerve cell in his brain that's getting too much stimulation or too little stimulation."

I got out of bed in the middle of the night and went to the small room at the end of the hall to watch Steffie and Wilder sleep. I remained at this task, motionless, for nearly an hour, feeling refreshed and expanded in unnameable ways.

I was surprised, entering our bedroom, to find Babette standing at a window looking out into the steely night. She gave no sign that she'd noticed my absence from the bed and did not seem to hear when I climbed back in, burying myself beneath the covers.

25

Our newspaper is delivered by a middle-aged Iranian driving a Nissan Sentra. Something about the car makes me uneasy—the car waiting with its headlights on, at dawn, as the man places the newspaper on the front steps. I tell myself I have reached an age, the age of unreliable menace. The world is full of abandoned meanings. In the commonplace I find unexpected themes and intensities.

I sat at my desk in the office staring down at the white tablet. It was more or less flying-saucer-shaped, a streamlined disk with the tiniest of holes at one end. It was only after moments of intense scrutiny that I'd been able to spot the hole.

The tablet was not chalky like aspirin and not exactly capsule-slick either. It felt strange in the hand, curiously sensitive to the touch but at the same time giving the impression that it was synthetic, insoluble, elaborately engineered.

I walked over to a small domed building known as the Observatory and gave the tablet to Winnie Richards, a young research neurochemist whose work was said to be brilliant. She was a tall gawky furtive woman who blushed when someone said something funny. Some of the New York émigrés liked to visit her cubicle and deliver rapid-fire one-liners, just to see her face turn red.

I watched her sit at the cluttered desk for two or three minutes, slowly rotating the tablet between her thumb and index finger. She licked it and shrugged.

"Certainly doesn't taste like much."

"How long will it take to analyze the contents?"

"There's a dolphin's brain in my in-box but come see me in forty-eight hours."

Winnie was well-known on the Hill for moving from place to

place without being seen. No one knew how she managed this or why she found it necessary. Maybe she was self-conscious about her awkward frame, her craning look and odd lope. Maybe she had a phobia concerning open spaces, although the spaces at the college were mainly snug and quaint. Perhaps the world of people and things had such an impact on her, struck her with the force of some rough and naked body—made her blush in fact—that she found it easier to avoid frequent contact. Maybe she was tired of being called brilliant. In any case I had trouble locating her all the rest of that week. She was not to be seen on the lawns and walks, was absent from her cubicle whenever I looked in.

At home Denise made it a point not to bring up the subject of Dylar. She did not want to put pressure on me and even avoided eye contact, as if an exchange of significant looks was more than our secret knowledge could bear. Babette, for her part, could not seem to produce a look that wasn't significant. In the middle of conversations she turned to gaze at snowfalls, sunsets or parked cars in a sculptured and eternal way. These contemplations began to worry me. She'd always been an outward-looking woman with a bracing sense of particularity, a trust in the tangible and real. This private gazing was a form of estrangement not only from those of us around her but from the very things she watched so endlessly.

We sat at the breakfast table after the older kids were gone.

"Have you seen the Stovers' new dog?"

"No," I said.

"They think it's a space alien. Only they're not joking. I was there yesterday. The animal *is* strange."

"Has something been bothering you?"

"I'm fine," she said.

"I wish you'd tell me. We tell each other everything. We always have."

"Jack, what could be bothering me?"

"You stare out of windows. You're different somehow. You don't quite see things and react to things the way you used to."

"That's what their dog does. He stares out of windows. But not just any window. He goes upstairs to the attic and puts his paws up on the sill to look out the highest window. They think he's waiting for instructions."

"Denise would kill me if she knew I was going to say this."

"What?"

"I found the Dylar."

"What Dylar?"

"It was taped to the radiator cover."

"Why would I tape something to the radiator cover?"

'That's exactly what Denise predicted you would say."

"She's usually right."

"I talked to Hookstratten, your doctor."

"I'm in super shape, really."

"That's what he said."

"Do you know what these cold gray leaden days make me want to do?"

"What?"

"Crawl into bed with a good-looking man. I'll put Wilder in his play tunnel. You go shave and brush your teeth. Meet you in the bedroom in ten minutes."

That afternoon I saw Winnie Richards slip out a side door of the Observatory and go loping down a small lawn toward the new buildings. I hurried out of my office and went after her. She kept close to walls, moving in a long-gaited stride. I felt I had made an important sighting of an endangered animal or some phenomenal subhuman like a yeti or sasquatch. It was cold and still leaden. I found I could not gain on her without breaking into a trot. She hurried around the back of Faculty House and I picked up the pace, fearing I was on the verge of losing her. It felt strange to be running. I hadn't run in many years and didn't recognize my body in this new format, didn't recognize the world beneath my feet, hard-surfaced and abrupt. I turned a corner and picked up speed, aware of floating bulk. Up, down, life, death. My robe flew behind me.

I caught up to her in the empty corridor of a one-story building that smelled of embalming fluids. She stood against the wall in a pale green tunic and tennis sneakers. I was too winded to speak and raised my right arm, requesting a delay. Winnie led me to a table in a small room full of bottled brains. The table was fitted with a sink and covered with note pads and lab instruments. She gave me water in a paper cup. I tried to dissociate the taste of the tap water from the sight of the brains and the general odor of preservatives and disinfectants.

"Have you been hiding from me?" I said. "I've left notes, phone messages."

"Not from you, Jack, or anyone in particular."

"Then why have you been so hard to find?"

"Isn't this what the twentieth century is all about?"

"What?"

"People go into hiding even when no one is looking for them."

"Do you really think that's true?"

"It's obvious," she said.

"What about the tablet?"

"An interesting piece of technology. What's it called?"

"Dylar."

"Never heard of it," she said.

"What can you tell me about it? Try not to be too brilliant. I haven't eaten lunch yet."

I watched her blush.

"It's not a tablet in the old sense," she said. "It's a drug delivery system. It doesn't dissolve right away or release its ingredients right away. The medication in Dylar is encased in a polymer membrane. Water from your gastrointestinal tract seeps through the membrane at a carefully controlled rate."

"What does the water do?"

"It dissolves the medication encased in the membrane. Slowly, gradually, precisely. The medicine then passes out of the polymer tablet through a single small hole. Once again the rate is carefully controlled."

"It took me a while to spot the hole."

"That's because it's laser-drilled. It's not only tiny but stunningly precise in its dimensions."

"Lasers, polymers."

"I'm not an expert in any of this, Jack, but I can tell you it's a wonderful little system."

"What's the point of all this precision?"

"I would think the controlled dosage is meant to eliminate the hit-or-miss effect of pills and capsules. The drug is delivered at specified rates for extended periods. You avoid the classic pattern of overdosage followed by underdosage. You don't get a burst of medication followed by the merest trickle. No upset stomach, queasiness, vomiting, muscle cramps, et cetera. This system is efficient."

"I'm impressed. I'm even dazzled. But what happens to the polymer tablet after the medication is pumped out of it?"

"It self-destructs. It implodes minutely of its own massive gravitation. We've entered the realm of physics. Once the plastic membrane is reduced to microscopic particles, it passes harmlessly out of the body in the time-honored way."

"Fantastic. Now tell me what the medication is designed to do? What is Dylar? What are the chemical components?"

"I don't know," she said.

"Of course you know. You're brilliant. Everyone says so."

"What else can they say? I do neurochemistry. No one knows what that is."

"Other scientists have some idea. They must. And they say you're brilliant."

"We're all brilliant. Isn't that the understanding around here? You call me brilliant, I call you brilliant. It's a form of communal ego."

"No one calls me brilliant. They call me shrewd. They say I latched on to something big. I filled an opening no one knew existed."

"There are openings for brilliance too. It's my turn, that's all. Besides, I'm built funny and walk funny. If they couldn't call me brilliant, they would be forced to say cruel things about me. How awful for everyone."

She clutched some files to her chest.

"Jack, all I can tell you for certain is that the substance contained in Dylar is some kind of psychopharmaceutical. It's probably designed to interact with a distant part of the human cortex. Look around you. Brains everywhere. Sharks, whales, dolphins, great apes. None of them remotely matches the human brain in complexity. The human brain is not my field. I have only a bare working knowledge of the human brain but it's enough to make me proud to be an American. Your brain has a trillion neurons and every neuron has ten thousand little dendrites. The system of intercommunication is awe-inspiring. It's like a galaxy that you can hold in your hand, only more complex, more mysterious."

"Why does this make you proud to be an American?"

"The infant's brain develops in response to stimuli. We still lead the world in stimuli."

I sipped my water.

"I wish I knew more," she said. "But the precise nature of the medication eludes me. I can tell you one thing. It is not on the market."

"But I found it in an ordinary prescription vial."

"I don't care where you found it. I'm pretty sure I'd recognize the ingredients of a known brain-receptor drug. This one is unknown."

She began to shoot quick looks toward the door. Her eyes were bright and fearful. I realized there were noises in the corridor. Voices, shuffling feet. I watched Winnie back toward a rear door. I decided I wanted to see her blush one more time. She put an arm behind her, unlatched the door, turned quickly and went running into the gray afternoon. I tried to think of something funny to say.

26

I sat up in bed with my notes on German grammar. Babette lay on her side staring into the clock-radio, listening to a call-in show. I heard a woman say: "In 1977 I looked in the mirror and saw the person I was becoming. I couldn't or wouldn't get out of bed. Figures moved at the edge of my vision, like with scurrying steps. I was getting phone calls from a Pershing missile base. I needed to talk to others who shared these experiences. I needed a support program, something to enroll in."

I leaned across my wife's body and turned off the radio. She kept on staring. I kissed her lightly on the head.

"Murray says you have important hair."

She smiled in a pale and depleted way. I put down my notes and eased her around slightly so that she looked straight up as I spoke.

"It's time for a major dialogue. You know it, I know it. You'll tell me all about Dylar. If not for my sake, then for your little girl's. She's been worried—worried sick. Besides, you have no more room to maneuver. We've backed you against the wall. Denise and I. I found the concealed bottle, removed a tablet, had it analyzed by an expert. Those little white disks are superbly engineered. Laser technology, advanced plastics. Dylar is almost as ingenious as the microorganisms that ate the billowing cloud. Who would have believed in the existence of a little white pill that works as a pressure pump in the human body to provide medication safely and effectively, and self-destructs as well? I am struck by the beauty of this. We know something else, something crucially damaging to your case. We know Dylar is not available to the general public. This fact alone justifies our demands for an explanation. There's really very little left for you to say. Just tell us the nature of the drug. As you well know, I don't have the temperament to hound people. But Denise is a different kind of person. I've been doing all I can to restrain her. If you don't tell me what I want to know, I'll unleash your little girl. She'll come at you with everything she has. She won't waste time trying to make you feel guilty. Denise believes in a frontal attack. She'll hammer you right into the ground. You know I'm right, Babette."

About five minutes passed. She lay there, staring into the ceiling.

"Just let me tell it in my own way," she said in a small voice.

"Would you like a liqueur?"

"No, thank you."

"Take your time," I said. "We've got all night. If there's anything you want or need, just say so. You have only to ask. I'll be right here for as long as it takes."

Another moment passed.

"I don't know exactly when it started. Maybe a year and a half ago. I thought I was going through a phase, some kind of watermark period in my life."

"Landmark," I said. "Or watershed."

"A kind of settling-in-period, I thought. Middle age. Something like that. The condition would go away and I'd forget all about it. But it didn't go away. I began to think it never would."

"What condition?"

"Never mind that for now."

"You've been depressed lately. I've never seen you like this. This is the whole point of Babette. She's a joyous person. She doesn't succumb to gloom or self-pity."

"Let me tell it, Jack."

"All right."

"You know how I am. I think everything is correctible. Given the right attitude and the proper effort, a person can change a harmful condition by reducing it to its simplest parts. You can make lists, invent categories, devise charts and graphs. This is how I am able to teach my students how to stand, sit and walk, even though I know you think these subjects are too obvious and nebulous and generalized to be reduced to component parts. I'm not a very ingenious person but I know how to break things down, how to separate and classify. We can analyze posture, we can analyze eating, drinking and even breathing. How else do you understand the world, is my way of looking at it."

"I'm right here," I said. "If there's anything you want or need, only say the word."

"When I realized this condition was not about to go away, I set out to understand it better by reducing it to its parts. First I had to find out if it had any parts. I went to libraries and bookstores, read magazines and technical journals, watched cable TV, made lists and diagrams, made multicolored charts, made phone calls to technical writers and scientists, talked to a Sikh holy man in Iron City and even studied the occult, hiding the books in the attic so you and Denise wouldn't find them and wonder what was going on."

"All this without my knowing. The whole point of Babette is that she speaks to me, she reveals and confides."

"This is not a story about your disappointment at my silence. The theme of this story is my pain and my attempts to end it."

"I'll make some hot chocolate. Would you like that?"

"Stay. This is a crucial part. All this energy, this research, study and concealment, but I was getting nowhere. The condition would not yield. It hung over my life, gave me no rest. Then one day I was reading to Mr. Treadwell from the *National Examiner*. An ad caught my eye. Never mind exactly what it said. Volunteers wanted for secret research. This is all you have to know."

"I thought it was my former wives who practiced guile. Sweet deceivers. Tense, breathy, high-cheekboned, bilingual."

"I answered the ad and was interviewed by a small firm doing research in psychobiology. Do you know what that is?"

"No."

"Do you know how complex the human brain is?"

"I have some idea."

"No, you don't. Let's call the company Gray Research, although that's not the true name. Let's call my contact Mr. Gray. Mr. Gray is a composite. I was eventually in touch with three or four or more people at the firm."

"One of those long low pale brick buildings with electrified fencing and low-profile shrubbery."

"I never saw their headquarters. Never mind why. The point is I took test after test. Emotional, psychological, motor response, brain activity. Mr. Gray said there were three finalists and I was one of them."

"Finalists for what?"

"We were to be test subjects in the development of a super experimental and top secret drug, code-name Dylar, that he'd been working on for years. He'd found a Dylar receptor in the human brain and was putting the finishing touches on the tablet itself. But he also told me there were dangers in running tests on a human. I could die. I could live but my brain could die. The left side of my brain could die but the right side could live. This would mean that the left side of my body would live but the right side would die. There were many grim specters. I could walk sideways but not forward. I could not distinguish words from things, so that if someone said 'speeding bullet,' I would fall to the floor and take cover. Mr. Gray wanted me to know the risks. There were releases and other documents for me to sign. The firm had lawyers, priests."

"They let you go ahead, a human test animal."

"No, they didn't. They said it was way too risky—legally, ethically and so forth. They went to work designing computer molecules and computer brains. I refused to accept this. I'd come so far, come so close. I want you to try to understand what happened next. If I'm going to tell you the story at all, I have to include this aspect of it, this grubby little corner of the human heart. You say Babette reveals and confides."

"This is the point of Babette."

"Good. I will reveal and confide. Mr. Gray and I made a private arrangement. Forget the priests, the lawyers, the psychobiologists. We would conduct the experiments on our own. I would be cured of my condition, he would be acclaimed for a wonderful medical breakthrough."

"What's so grubby about this?"

"It involved an indiscretion. This was the only way I could get Mr. Gray to let me use the drug. It was my last resort, my last hope. First I'd offered him my mind. Now I offered my body."

I felt a sensation of warmth creeping up my back and radiating outward across my shoulders. Babette looked straight up. I was propped on an elbow, facing her, studying her features. When I spoke finally it was in a reasonable and inquiring voice—the voice of a man who seeks genuinely to understand some timeless human riddle.

"How do you offer your body to a composite of three or more people? This is a compound person. He is like a police sketch of one person's eyebrows, another person's nose. Let's concentrate on the genitals. How many sets are we talking about?"

"Just one person's, Jack. A key person, the project manager."

"So we are no longer referring to the Mr. Gray who is a composite."

"He is now one person. We went to a grubby little motel room. Never mind where or when. It had the TV up near the ceiling. This is all I remember. Grubby, tacky. I was heartsick. But so, so desperate."

"You call this an indiscretion, as if we haven't had a revolution in frank and bold language. Call it what it was, describe it honestly, give it the credit it deserves. You entered a motel room, excited by its impersonality, the functionalism and bad taste of the furnishings. You walked barefoot on the fire-retardant carpet. Mr. Gray went around opening doors, looking for a full-length mirror. He watched you undress. You lay on the bed, embracing. Then he entered you."

"Don't use that term. You know how I feel about that usage."

"He effected what is called entry. In other words he inserted himself. One minute he was fully dressed, putting the car rental keys on the dresser. The next minute he was inside you."

"No one was inside anyone. That is stupid usage. I did what I had to do. I was remote. I was operating outside myself. It was a capitalist transaction. You cherish the wife who tells you everything. I am doing my best to be that person."

"All right, I'm only trying to understand. How many times did you go to this motel?"

"More or less on a continuing basis for some months. That was the agreement."

I felt heat rising along the back of my neck. I watched her carefully. A sadness showed in her eyes. I lay back and looked at the ceiling. The radio came on. She began to cry softly.

"There's some Jell-O with banana slices," I said. "Steffie made it."

"She's a good girl."

"I can easily get you some."

"No, thank you."

"Why did the radio come on?"

"The auto-timer is broken. I'll take it to the shop tomorrow."

"I'll take it."

"It's all right," she said. "It's no trouble. I can easily take it."

"Did you enjoy having sex with him?"

"I only remember the TV up near the ceiling, aimed down at us."

"Did he have a sense of humor? I know women appreciate men who can joke about sex. I can't, unfortunately, and after this I don't think there's much chance I'll be able to learn."

"It's better if you know him as Mr. Gray. That's all. He's not tall, short, young or old. He doesn't laugh or cry. It's for your own good."

"I have a question. Why didn't Gray Research run tests on animals? Animals must be better than computers in some respects."

"That's just the point. No animal has this condition. This is a human condition. Animals fear many things, Mr. Gray said. But their brains aren't sophisticated enough to accommodate this particular state of mind."

For the first time I began to get an inkling of what she'd been talking about all along. My body went cold. I felt hollow inside. I rose from my supine position, once again propping myself on an elbow to look down at her. She started to cry again.

"You have to tell me, Babette. You've taken me this far, put me through this much. I have to know. What's the condition?"

The longer she wept, the more certain I became that I knew what she was going to say. I felt an impulse to get dressed and leave, take a room somewhere until this whole thing blew over. Babette raised her face to me, sorrowing and pale, her eyes showing a helpless desolation. We faced each other, propped on elbows, like a sculpture of lounging philosophers in a classical academy. The radio turned itself off.

"I'm afraid to die," she said. "I think about it all the time. It won't go away."

"Don't tell me this. This is terrible."

"I can't help it. How can I help it?"

"I don't want to know. Save it for our old age. You're still young, you get plenty of exercise. This is not a reasonable fear."

"It haunts me, Jack. I can't get it off my mind. I know I'm not supposed to experience such a fear so consciously and so steadily. What can I do? It's just there. That's why I was so quick to notice Mr. Gray's ad in the tabloid I was reading aloud. The headline hit home. FEAR OF DEATH, it said. I think about it all the time. You're disappointed. I can tell."

"Disappointed?"

"You thought the condition would be more specific. I wish it was. But a person doesn't search for months and months to corner the solution to some daily little ailment."

I tried to talk her out of it.

"How can you be sure it is death you fear? Death is so vague. No one knows what it is, what it feels like or looks like. Maybe you just have a personal problem that surfaces in the form of a great universal subject."

"What problem?"

"Something you're hiding from yourself. Your weight maybe."

"I've lost weight. What about my height?"

"I know you've lost weight. That's just my point. You practically ooze good health. You reek of it. Hookstratten confirms this, your own doctor. There must be something else, an underlying problem."

"What could be more underlying than death?"

I tried to persuade her it was not as serious as she thought.

"Baba, everyone fears death. Why should you be different? You yourself said earlier it is a human condition. There's no one who has lived past the age of seven who hasn't worried about dying."

"At some level everyone fears death. I fear it right up front. I don't know how or why it happened. But I can't be the only one or why would Gray Research spend millions on a pill?"

"That's what I said. You're not the only one. There are hundreds of thousands of people. Isn't it reassuring to know that? You're like the woman on the radio who got phone calls from a missile base. She wanted to find others whose own psychotic experiences would make her feel less isolated."

"But Mr. Gray said I was extra sensitive to the terror of death. He gave me a battery of tests. That's why he was eager to use me."

"This is what I find odd. You concealed your terror for so long. If you're able to conceal such a thing from a husband and children, maybe it is not so severe."

"This is not the story of a wife's deception. You can't sidestep the true story, Jack. It is too big."

I kept my voice calm. I spoke to her as one of those reclining philosophers might address a younger member of the academy, someone whose work is promising and fitfully brilliant but perhaps too heavily dependent on the scholarship of the senior fellow.

"Baba, I am the one in this family who is obsessed by death. I have always been the one."

"You never said."

"To protect you from worry. To keep you animated, vital and happy. You are the happy one. I am the doomed fool. That's what I can't forgive you for. Telling me you're not the woman I believed you were. I'm hurt, I'm devastated."

"I always thought of you as someone who might *muse* on death. You might take walks and muse. But all those times we talked about who will die first, you never said you were afraid."

"The same goes for you. 'As soon as the kids are grown.' You made it sound like a trip to Spain."

"I do want to die first," she said, "but that doesn't mean I'm not afraid. I'm terribly afraid. I'm afraid all the time."

"I've been afraid for more than half my life."

"What do you want me to say? Your fear is older and wiser than mine?"

"I wake up sweating. I break out in killer sweats."

"I chew gum because my throat constricts."

"I have no body. I'm only a mind or a self, alone in a vast space."

"I seize up," she said.

"I'm too weak to move. I lack all sense of resolve, determination."

"I thought about my mother dying. Then she died."

"I think about everyone dying. Not just myself. I lapse into terrible reveries."

"I felt so guilty. I thought her death was connected to my thinking about it. I feel the same way about my own death. The more I think about it, the sooner it will happen."

"How strange it is. We have these deep terrible lingering fears about ourselves and the people we love. Yet we walk around, talk to people, eat and drink. We manage to function. The feelings are deep and real. Shouldn't they paralyze us? How is it we can survive them, at least for a while? We drive a car, we teach a class. How is it no one sees how deeply afraid we were, last night, this morning? Is it something we all hide from each other, by mutual consent? Or do we share the same secret without knowing it? Wear the same disguise."

"What if death is nothing but sound?"

"Electrical noise."

"You hear it forever. Sound all around. How awful."

"Uniform, white."

"Sometimes it sweeps over me," she said. "Sometimes it insinuates itself into my mind, little by little. I try to talk to it. 'Not now, Death.'"

"I lie in the dark looking at the clock. Always odd numbers. One thirty-seven in the morning. Three fifty-nine in the morning."

"Death is odd-numbered. That's what the Sikh told me. The holy man in Iron City."

"You're my strength, my life-force. How can I persuade you that this is a terrible mistake? I've watched you bathe Wilder, iron my gown. These deep and simple pleasures are lost to me now. Don't you see the enormity of what you've done?"

"Sometimes it hits me like a blow," she said. "I almost physically want to reel."

"Is this why I married Babette? So she would conceal the truth from me, conceal objects from me, join in a sexual conspiracy at my expense? All plots move in one direction," I told her grimly.

We held each other tightly for a long time, our bodies clenched in an embrace that included elements of love, grief, tenderness, sex and struggle. How subtly we shifted emotions, found shadings, using the scantest movement of our arms, our loins, the slightest intake of breath, to reach agreement on our fear, to advance our competition, to assert our root desires against the chaos in our souls.

Leaded, unleaded, super unleaded.

We lay naked after love, wet and gleaming. I pulled the covers up over us. We spoke in drowsy whispers for a while. The radio came on.

"I'm right here," I said. "Whatever you want or need, however difficult, tell me and it's done."

"A drink of water."

"Of course."

"I'll go with you," she said.

"Stay, rest."

"I don't want to be alone."

We put on our robes, went to the bathroom for water. She drank while I pissed. On our way back to the bedroom I put my arm around her and we walked half toppling toward each other, like adolescents on a beach. I waited by the side of the bed as she rearranged the sheets neatly, put the pillows in place. She curled up immediately for sleep but there were still things I wanted to know, things I had to say.

"Precisely what was accomplished by the people at Gray Research?"

"They isolated the fear-of-death part of the brain. Dylar speeds relief to that sector."

"Incredible."

"It's not just a powerful tranquilizer. The drug specifically interacts with neurotransmitters in the brain that are related to the fear of death. Every emotion or sensation has its own neurotransmitters. Mr. Gray found fear of death and then went to worl on finding the chemicals that would induce the brain to make its own inhibitors."

"Amazing and frightening."

"Everything that goes on in your whole life is a result of molecules rushing around somewhere in your brain."

"Heinrich's brain theories. They're all true. We're the sum of our chemical impulses. Don't tell me this. It's unbearable to think about."

"They can trace everything you say, do and feel to the number of molecules in a certain region."

"What happens to good and evil in this system? Passion, envy and hate? Do they become a tangle of neurons? Are you telling me that a whole tradition of human failings is now at an end, that cowardice, sadism, molestation are meaningless terms? Are we being asked to regard these things nostalgically? What about murderous rage? A murderer used to have a certain fearsome size to him. His crime was large. What happens when we reduce it to cells and molecules? My son plays chess with a murderer. He told me all this. I didn't want to listen."

"Can I sleep now?"

"Wait. If Dylar speeds relief, why have you been so sad these past days, staring into space?"

"Simple. The drug's not working."

Her voice broke when she said these words. She raised the comforter over her head. I could only stare at the hilly terrain. A man on talk radio said: "I was getting mixed messages about my sexuality." I stroked her head and body over the quilted bedspread.

"Can you elaborate, Baba? I'm right here. I want to help."

"Mr. Gray gave me sixty tablets in two bottles. This would be more than enough, he said. One tablet every seventy-two hours. The discharge of medication is so gradual and precise that there's no overlapping from one pill to the next. I finished the first bottle sometime in late November, early December."

"Denise found it."

"She did?"

"She's been on your trail ever since."

"Where did I leave it?"

"In the kitchen trash."

"Why did I do that? That was careless."

"What about the second bottle?" I said.

"You found the second bottle."

"I know. I'm asking how many tablets you've taken."

"I've now taken twenty-five from that bottle. That's fifty-five all told. Five left."

"Four left. I had one analyzed."

"Did you tell me that?"

"Yes. And has there been any change at all in your condition.

She allowed the top of her head to emerge.

"At first I thought so. The very beginning was the most hopeful time. Since then no improvement. I've grown more and more discouraged. Let me sleep now, Jack."

"Remember we had dinner at Murray's one night? On the way home we talked about your memory lapses. You said you weren't sure whether or not you were taking medication. You couldn't remember, you said. This was a lie, of course."

"I guess so," she said.

"But you weren't lying about memory lapses in general. Denise and I assumed your forgetfulness was a side effect of whatever drug you were taking."

The whole head emerged.

"Totally wrong," she said. "It wasn't a side effect of the drug. It was a side effect of the condition. Mr. Gray said my loss of memory is a desperate attempt to counteract my fear of death. It's like a war of neurons. I am able to forget many things but I fail when it comes to death. And now Mr. Gray has failed as well."

"Does he know that?"

"I left a message on his answering machine."

"What did he say when he called back?"

"He sent me a tape in the mail, which I took over to the Stovers to play. He said he was literally sorry, whatever that means. He said I was not the right subject after all. He is sure it will work someday, soon, with someone, somewhere. He said he made a mistake with me. It was too random. He was too eager."

It was the middle of the night. We were both exhausted. But we'd come so far, said so much, that I knew we couldn't stop just yet. I took a deep breath. Then I lay back, staring into the ceiling. Babette leaned across my body to turn off the lamp. Then she pressed a button on the radio, killing the voices. A thousand other nights had ended more or less like this. I felt her sink into the bed.

"There's something I promised myself I wouldn't tell you."

"Can it wait until morning?" she said.

"I'm tentatively scheduled to die. It won't happen tomorrow or the next day. But it is in the works."

I went on to tell her about my exposure to Nyodene D., speaking matter-of-factly, tonelessly, in short declarative sentences. I told her about the computer technician, the way he'd tapped into my history to produce a pessimistic massive tally. We are the sum total of our data, I told her, just as we are the sum total of our chemical impulses. I tried to explain how hard I'd struggled to keep the news from her. But after her own revelations, this seemed the wrong kind of secret to be keeping.

"So we are no longer talking about fear and floating terror," I said. "This is the hard and heavy thing, the fact itself."

Slowly she emerged from beneath the covers. She climbed on top of me, sobbing. I felt her fingers clawing at my shoulders and neck. The warm tears fell on my lips. She beat me on the chest, seized my left hand and bit the flesh between the thumb and index finger. Her sobs became a grunting sound, full of terrible desperate effort. She took my head in her hands, gently and yet fiercely, and rocked it to and fro on the pillow, an act I could not connect to anything she'd ever done, anything she seemed to be.

Later, after she'd fallen off my body and into a restless sleep, I kept on staring into the dark. The radio came on. I threw off the covers and went into the bathroom. Denise's scenic paperweights sat on a dusty shelf by the door. I ran water over my hands and wrists. I splashed cold water on my face. The only towel around was a small pink handcloth with a tic-tac-toe design. I dried myself slowly and carefully. Then I tilted the radiator cover away from the wall and stuck my hand underneath. The bottle of Dylar was gone.

27

I had my second medical checkup since the toxic event. No startling numbers on the printout. This death was still too deep to be glimpsed. My doctor, Sundar Chakravarty, asked me about the sudden flurry of checkups. In the past I'd always been afraid to know.

I told him I was still afraid. He smiled broadly, waiting for the punch line. I shook his hand and headed out the door.

On the way home I drove down Elm intending to make a quick stop at the supermarket. The street was full of emergency vehicles. Farther down I saw bodies scattered about. A man with an armband blew a whistle at me and stepped in front of my car. I glimpsed other men in Mylex suits. Stretcher-bearers ran across the street. When the man with the whistle drew closer, I was able to make out the letters on his armband: SIMUVAC.

"Back it out," he said. "Street's closed."

"Are you people sure you're ready for a simulation? You may want to wait for one more massive spill. Get your timing down."

"Move it out, get it out. You're in the exposure swath."

"What's that mean?"

"It means you're dead," he told me.

I backed out of the street and parked the car. Then I walked slowly back down Elm, trying to look as though I belonged. I kept close to storefronts, mingled with technicians and marshals, with uniformed personnel. There were buses, police cars, ambulettes. People with electronic equipment appeared to be trying to detect radiation or toxic fallout. In time I approached the volunteer victims. There were twenty or so, prone, supine, draped over curbstones, sitting in the street with woozy looks.

I was startled to see my daughter among them. She lay in the middle of the street, on her back, one arm flung out, her head tilted the other way. I could hardly bear to look. Is this how she thinks of herself at the age of nine—already a victim, trying to polish her skills? How natural she looked, how deeply imbued with the idea of a sweeping disaster. Is this the future she envisions?

I walked over there and squatted down.

"Steffie? Is that you?"

She opened her eyes.

"You're not supposed to be here unless you're a victim," she said.

"I just want to be sure you're okay."

"I'll get in trouble if they see you."

"It's cold. You'll get sick. Does Baba know you're here?"

"I signed up in school an hour ago."

"They at least should hand out blankets," I said.

She closed her eyes. I spoke to her a while longer but she wouldn't answer. There was no trace of irritation or dismissal in her silence. Just conscientiousness. She had a history of being devout in her victimhood.

I went back to the sidewalk. A man's amplified voice boomed across the street from somewhere inside the supermarket.

"I want to welcome all of you on behalf of Advanced Disaster Management, a private consulting firm that conceives and operates simulated evacuations. We are interfacing with twenty-two state bodies in carrying out this advanced disaster drill. The first, I trust, of many. The more we rehearse disaster, the safer we'll be from the real thing. Life seems to work that way, doesn't it? You take your umbrella to the office seventeen straight days, not a drop of rain. The first day you leave it at home, record-breaking downpour. Never fails, does it? This is the mechanism we hope to employ, among others. O-right, on to business. When the siren sounds three long blasts, thousands of hand-picked evacuees will leave their homes and places of employment, get into their vehicles and head for well-equipped emergency shelters. Traffic directors will race to their computerized stations. Updated instructions will be issued on the SIMUVAC broadcast system. Air-sampling people will deploy along the cloud exposure swath. Dairy samplers will test milk and randomized foodstuffs over the next three days along the ingestion swath. We are not simulating a particular spillage today. This is an all-purpose leak or spill. It could be radioactive steam, chemical cloudlets, a haze of unknown origin. The important thing is movement. Get those people out of the swath. We learned a lot during the night of the billowing cloud. But there is no substitute for a planned simulation. If reality intrudes in the form of a car crash or a victim falling off a stretcher, it is important to remember that we are not here to mend broken bones or put out real fires. We are here to simulate. Interruptions can cost lives in a real emergency. If we learn to work around interruptions now, we'll be able to work around them later when it counts. O-right. When the siren sounds two melancholy wails, street captains will make house-to-house searches for those who may have been inadvertently left behind. Birds, goldfish, elderly people, handicapped people, invalids, shut-ins, whatever. Five minutes, victims. All you rescue personnel, remember this is not a blast simulation. Your victims are overcome but not traumatized. Save your tender loving care for the nuclear fireball in June. We're at four minutes and counting. Victims, go limp. And remember you're not here to scream or thrash about. We like a low-profile victim. This isn't New York or L.A. Soft moans will suffice."

I decided I didn't want to watch. I went back to the car and headed home. The sirens emitted the first three blasts as I pulled up in front of the house. Heinrich was sitting on the front steps, wearing a reflector vest and his camouflage cap. With him was an older boy. He had a powerful compact body of uncertain pigmentation. No one on our street seemed to be evacuating. Heinrich consulted a clipboard.

"What's going on?"

"I'm a street captain," he said.

"Did you know Steffie was a victim?"

"She said she might be."

"Why didn't you tell me?"

"So they pick her up and put her in an ambulance. What's the problem?"

"I don't know what the problem is."

"If she wants to do it, she should do it."

"She seems so well-adjusted to the role."

"It could save her life someday," he said.

"How can pretending to be injured or dead save a person's life?"

"If she does it now, she might not have to do it later. The more you practice something, the less likely it is to actually happen."

"That's what the consultant said."

"It's a gimmick but it works."

"Who's this?"

"This is Orest Mercator. He's going to help me check for left-overs."

"You're the one who wants to sit in a cage full of deadly snakes. Can you tell me why?"

"Because I'm going for the record," Orest said.

"Why would you want to get killed going for a record?"

"What killed? Who said anything about killed?"

"You'll be surrounded by rare and deadly reptiles."

"They're the best at what they do. I want to be the best at what I do."

"What do you do?"

"I sit in a cage for sixty-seven days. That's what it takes to break the record."

"Do you understand that you are risking death for a couple of lines in a paperback book?"

He looked searchingly at Heinrich, obviously holding the boy responsible for this idiotic line of questioning.

"They will bite you," I went on.

"They won't bite me."

"How do you know?"

"Because I know."

"These are real snakes, Orest. One bite, that's it."

"One bite if they bite. But they won't bite."

"They are real. You are real. People get bitten all the time. The venom is deadly."

"People get bitten. But I won't."

I found myself saying, "You will, you will. These snakes don't know you find death inconceivable. They don't know you're young and strong and you think death applies to everyone but you. They will bite and you will die."

I paused, shamed by the passion of my argument. I was surprised to see him look at me with a certain interest, a certain grudging respect. Perhaps the unbecoming force of my outburst brought home to him the gravity of his task, filled him with intimations of an unwieldy fate.

"They want to bite, they bite," he said. "At least I go right away. These snakes are the best, the quickest. A puff adder bites me, I die in seconds."

"What's your hurry? You're nineteen years old. You'll find hundreds of ways to die that are better than snakes."

What kind of name is Orest? I studied his features. He might have been Hispanic, Middle Eastern, Central Asian, a dark-skinned Eastern European, a light-skinned black. Did he have an accent? I wasn't sure. Was he a Samoan, a native North American, a Sephardic Jew? It was getting hard to know what you couldn't say to people.

He said to me, "How many pounds can you bench-press?"

"I don't know. Not very many."

"Did you ever punch somebody in the face?"

"Maybe a glancing blow, once, a long time ago."

"I'm looking to punch somebody in the face. Bare-fisted. Hard as I can. To find out what it feels like."

Heinrich grinned like a stool pigeon in the movies. The siren began to sound—two melancholy blasts. I went inside as the two boys checked the clipboard for house numbers. Babette was in the kitchen giving Wilder some lunch.

"He's wearing a reflector vest," I said.

"It's in case there's haze, he won't get hit by fleeing vehicles."

"I don't think anyone's bothered to flee. How do you feel?"

"Better," she said.

"So do I."

"I think it's being with Wilder that picks me up."

"I know what you mean. I always feel good when I'm with Wilder. Is it because pleasures don't cling to him? He is selfish without being grasping, selfish in a totally unbounded and natural way. There's something wonderful about the way he drops one thing, grabs for another. I get annoyed when the other kids don't fully appreciate special moments or occasions. They let things slide away that should be kept and savored. But when Wilder does it, I see the spirit of genius at work."

"That may be true but there's something else about him that gives me a lift. Something bigger, grander, that I can't quite put my finger on."

"Remind me to ask Murray," I said.

She spooned soup into the child's mouth, creating facial expressions for him to mimic and saying, "Yes yes yes yes yes yes yes."

"One thing I have to ask. Where is the Dylar?"

"Forget it, Jack. Fool's gold or whatever the appropriate term."

"A cruel illusion. I know. But I'd like to keep the tablets in a safe place, if only as physical evidence that Dylar exists. If your left brain should decide to die, I want to be able to sue someone. There are four tablets left. Where are they?"

"Are you telling me they're not behind the radiator cover?"

"That's right."

"I didn't move them, honest."

"Is it possible you threw them away in an angry or depressed moment? I only want them for the sake of historical accuracy. Like White House tapes. They go into the archives."

"You haven't been pretested," she said. "Even one pill can be dangerous to ingest."

"I don't want to ingest."

"Yes, you do."

"We are being coaxed out of the ingestion swath. Where is Mr. Gray? I may want to sue him as a matter of principle."

"We made a pact, he and I."

"Tuesdays and Fridays. The Grayview Motel."

"That's not what I mean. I promised not to reveal his true identity to anyone. Considering what you're after, that promise goes double. It's more for your good than his. I'm not telling, Jack. Let's just resume our lives. Let's tell each other we'll do the best we can. Yes yes yes yes yes."

I drove to the grade school and parked across the street from the main entrance. Twenty minutes later they came surging out, about three hundred kids, babbling, gleeful, casually amuck. They called brilliant insults, informed and spacious obscenities, hit each other with bookbags, knit caps. I sat in the driver's seat scanning the mass of faces, feeling like a dope dealer or pervert.

When I spotted Denise I blew the horn and she came over. This was the first time I'd ever picked her up at school and she gave me a wary and hard-eyed look as she passed in front of the car—a look that indicated she was in no mood for news of a separation or divorce. I took the river road home. She scrutinized my profile.

"It's about Dylar," I said. "The medication has nothing to do with Baba's memory problems. In fact just the opposite. She takes Dylar to improve her memory."

"I don't believe you."

"Why not?"

"Because you wouldn't come and get me at school just to tell me that. Because we already found out you can't get it with a prescription. Because I talked to her doctor and he never heard of it."

"You called him at home?"

"At the office."

"Dylar is a little too special for a G.P."

"Is my mother a drug addict?"

"You're smarter than that," I said.

"No, I'm not."

"We'd like to know what you did with the bottle. There were some tablets left."

"How do you know I took them?"

"I know it, you know it."

"If somebody wants to tell me what Dylar really is, maybe we'll get somewhere."

"There's something you don't know," I said. "Your mother no longer takes the medication. Whatever your reason for holding the bottle, it's just not valid anymore."

We'd looped around to the west and were now driving through the college campus. Automatically I reached into my jacket for the dark glasses and put them on.

"Then I'll throw it away," she said.

Over the next few days I tried an assortment of arguments, some nearly breathtaking in their delicate webby texture. I even enlisted Babette, convincing her that the bottle belonged in adult hands. But the girl's will was supremely resistant. Her life as a legal entity had been shaped by other people's bargaining and haggling and she was determined to follow a code too rigid to allow for the trade-off, the settlement. She would keep the object hidden until we told her its secret.

It was probably just as well. The drug could be dangerous, after all. And I was not a believer in easy solutions, something to swallow that would rid my soul of an ancient fear. But I could not help thinking about that saucer-shaped tablet. Would it ever work, could it work for some but not others? It was the benign counterpart of the Nyodene menace. Tumbling from the back of my tongue down into my stomach. The drug core dissolving, releasing benevolent chemicals into my bloodstream, flooding the fear-of-death part of my brain. The pill itself silently self-destructing in a tiny inward burst, a polymer implosion, discreet and precise and considerate.

Technology with a human face.

28

Wilder sat on a tall stool in front of the stove, watching water boil in a small enamel pot. He seemed fascinated by the process. I wondered if he'd uncovered some splendid connection between things he'd always thought of as separate. The kitchen is routinely rich in such moments, perhaps for me as much as for him.

Steffie walked in saying, "I'm the only person I know who likes Wednesdays." Wilder's absorption seemed to interest her. She went and stood next to him, trying to figure out what attracted him to the agitated water. She leaned over the pot, looking for an egg.

A jingle for a product called Ray-Ban Wayfarer began running through my head.

"How did the evacuation go?"

"A lot of people never showed up. We waited around, moaning."

"They show up for the real ones," I said.

"Then it's too late."

The light was bright and cool, making objects glow. Steffie was dressed for the outdoors, a schoolday morning, but remained at the stove, looking from Wilder to the pot and back, trying to intersect the lines of his curiosity and wonder.

"Baba says you got a letter."

"My mother wants me to visit at Easter."

"Good. Do you want to go? Of course you do. You like your mother. She's in Mexico City now, isn't she?"

"Who'll take me?"

"I'll take you to the airport. Your mother will pick you up at the other end. It's easy. Bee does it all the time. You like Bee."

The enormity of the mission, of flying to a foreign country at nearly supersonic speed, at thirty thousand feet, alone, in a humped container of titanium and steel, caused her to grow momentarily silent. We watched the water boil.

"I signed up to be a victim again. It's just before Easter. So I think I have to stay here."

"Another evacuation? What's the occasion this time?"

"A funny smell."

"You mean some chemical from a plant across the river?"

"I guess so."

"What do you do as the victim of a smell?"

"They have to tell us yet."

"I'm sure they won't mind excusing you just this once. I'll write a note," I said.

My first and fourth marriages were to Dana Breedlove, who is Steffie's mother. The first marriage worked well enough to encourage us to try again as soon as it became mutually convenient. When we did, after the melancholy epochs of Janet Savory and Tweedy Browner, things proceeded to fall apart. But not before Stephanie Rose was conceived, a star-hung night in Barbados. Dana was there to bribe an official.

She told me very little about her intelligence work. I knew she reviewed fiction for the CIA, mainly long serious novels with coded structures. The work left her tired and irritable, rarely able to enjoy food, sex or conversation. She spoke Spanish to someone on the telephone, was a hyperactive mother, shining with an eerie stormlight intensity. The long novels kept arriving in the mail.

It was curious how I kept stumbling into the company of lives in intelligence. Dana worked part-time as a spy. Tweedy came from a distinguished old family that had a long tradition of spying and counterspying and she was now married to a high-level jungle operative. Janet, before retiring to the ashram, was a foreign-currency analyst who did research for a secret group of advanced theorists connected to some controversial think-tank. All she told me is that they never met in the same place twice.

Some of my adoration of Babette must have been sheer relief. She was not a keeper of secrets, at least not until her death fears drove her into a frenzy of clandestine research and erotic deception. I thought of Mr. Gray and his pendulous member. The image was hazy, unfinished. The man was literally gray, giving off a visual buzz.

The water progressed to a rolling boil. Steffie helped the boy down from his perch. I ran into Babette on my way to the front door. We exchanged the simple but deeply sincere question we'd been asking each other two or three times a day since the night of the Dylar revelations. *"How do you feel?"* Asking the question, hearing it asked, made us both feel better. I bounded upstairs to find my glasses.

The National Cancer Quiz was on TV.

In the lunchroom in Centenary Hall, I watched Murray sniff his utensils. There was a special pallor in the faces of the New York émigrés. Lasher and Grappa in particular. They had the wanness of obsession, of powerful appetites confined to small spaces. Murray said that Elliot Lasher had a *film noir* face. His features were sharply defined, his hair perfumed with some oily extract. I had the curious thought that these men were nostalgic for black-and-white, their longings dominated by achromatic values, personal extremes of postwar urban gray.

Alfonse Stompanato sat down, radiating aggression and threat. He seemed to be watching me, one department head measuring the aura of another. There was a Brooklyn Dodger emblem sewed to the front of his gown.

Lasher wadded up a paper napkin and tossed it at someone two tables away. Then he stared at Grappa.

"Who was the greatest influence on your life?" he said in a hostile tone.

"Richard Widmark in *Kiss of Death*. When Richard Widmark pushed that old lady in that wheelchair down that flight of stairs, it was like a personal breakthrough for me. It resolved a number of conflicts. I copied Richard Widmark's sadistic laugh and used it for ten years. It got me through some tough emotional periods. Richard Widmark as Tommy Udo in Henry Hathaway's *Kiss of Death*. Remember that creepy laugh? Hyena-faced. A ghoulish titter. It clarified a number of things in my life. Helped me become a person."

"Did you ever spit in your soda bottle so you wouldn't have to share your drink with the other kids?"

"It was an automatic thing. Some guys even spit in their sandwiches. After we pitched pennies to the wall, we'd buy stuff to eat and drink. There was always a flurry of spitting. Guys spit on their fudge pops, their charlotte russes."

"How old were you when you first realized your father was a jerk?"

"Twelve and a half," Grappa said. "I was sitting in the balcony at the Loew's Fairmont watching Fritz Lang's *Clash by Night* with Barbara Stanwyck as Mae Doyle, Paul Douglas as Jerry d'Amato and the great Robert Ryan as Earl Pfeiffer. Featuring J. Carroll Naish, Keith Andes and the early Marilyn Monroe. Shot in thirty-two days. Black and white."

"Did you ever get an erection from a dental hygienist rubbing against your arm while she cleaned your teeth?"

"More times than I can count."

"When you bite dead skin off your thumb, do you eat it or spit it out?"

"Chew it briefly, then propel it swiftly from the end of the tongue."

"Do you ever close your eyes," Lasher said, "while you're driving on a highway?"

"I closed my eyes on 95 North for eight full seconds. Eight seconds is my personal best. I've closed my eyes for up to six seconds on winding country roads but that's only doing thirty or thirty-five. On multilane highways I usually hover at seventy before I close my eyes. You do this on straightaways. I've closed my eyes for up to five seconds on straightaways driving with other people in the car. You wait till they're drowsy is how you do it."

Grappa had a round moist worried face. There was something in it of a sweet boy betrayed. I watched him light up a cigarette, shake out the match and toss it into Murray's salad.

"How much pleasure did you take as a kid," Lasher said, "in imagining yourself dead?"

"Never mind as a kid," Grappa said. "I still do it all the time. Whenever I'm upset over something, I imagine all my friends, relatives and colleagues gathered at my bier. They are very, very sorry they weren't nicer to me while I lived. Self-pity is something I've worked very hard to maintain. Why abandon it just because you grow up? Self-pity is something that children are very good at, which must mean it is natural and important. Imagining yourself dead is the cheapest, sleaziest, most satisfying form of childish self-pity. How sad and remorseful and guilty all those people are, standing by your great bronze coffin. They can't even look each other in the eye because they know that the death of this decent and compassionate man is the result of a conspiracy they all took part in. The coffin is banked with flowers and lined with a napped fabric in salmon or peach. What wonderful cross-currents of self-pity and self-esteem you are able to wallow in, seeing yourself laid out in a dark suit and tie, looking tanned, fit and rested, as they say of presidents after vacations. But there is something even more childish and satisfying than self-pity, something that explains why I try to see myself dead on a regular basis, a great fellow surrounded by sniveling mourners. It is my way of punishing people for thinking their own lives are more important than mine."

Lasher said to Murray, "We ought to have an official Day of the Dead. Like the Mexicans."

"We do. It's called Super Bowl Week."

I didn't want to listen to this. I had my own dying to dwell upon, independent of fantasies. Not that I thought Grappa's remarks were ill-founded. His sense of conspiracy aroused in me a particular ripple of response. This is what we forgive on our deathbeds, not lovelessness or greed. We forgive them for their ability to put themselves at a distance, to scheme in silence against us, do us, effectively, in.

I watched Alfonse reassert his bearish presence with a shoulder-rolling gesture. I took this as a sign that he was warming up to speak. I wanted to bolt, make off suddenly, run.

"In New York," he said, looking directly at me, "people ask if you have a good internist. This is where true power lies. The inner organs. Liver, kidneys, stomach, intestines, pancreas. Internal medicine is the magic brew. You acquire strength and charisma from a good internist totally aside from the treatment he provides. People ask about tax lawyers, estate planners, dope dealers. But it's the internist who really matters. 'Who's your internist?' someone will say in a challenging tone. The question implies that if your internist's name is unfamiliar, you are certain to die of a mushroom-shaped tumor on your pancreas. You are meant to feel inferior and doomed not just because your inner organs may be trickling blood but because you don't know who to see about it, how to make contacts, how to make your way in the world. Never mind the military-industrial complex. The real power is wielded every day, in these little challenges and intimidations, by people just like us."

I gulped down my dessert and slipped away from the table. Outside I waited for Murray. When he emerged I held his arm just above the elbow and we walked across campus like a pair of European senior citizens, heads bowed in conversation.

"How do you listen to that?" I said. "Death and disease. Do they talk like that all the time?"

"When I covered sports, I used to get together with the other writers on the road. Hotel rooms, planes, taxis, restaurants. There was only one topic of conversation. Sex and death."

"That's two topics."

"You're right, Jack."

"I would hate to believe they are inextricably linked."

"It's just that on the road everything is linked. Everything and nothing, to be precise."

We walked past small mounds of melting snow.

"How is your car crash seminar progressing?"

"We've looked at hundreds of crash sequences. Cars with cars. Cars with trucks. Trucks with buses. Motorcycles with cars. Cars with helicopters. Trucks with trucks. My students think these movies are prophetic. They mark the suicide wish of technology.

The drive to suicide, the hurtling rush to suicide."

"What do you say to them?"

"These are mainly B-movies, TV movies, rural drive-in movies. I tell my students not to look for apocalypse in such places. I see these car crashes as part of a long tradition of American optimism. They are positive events, full of the old 'can-do' spirit. Each car crash is meant to be better than the last. There is a constant upgrading of tools and skills, a meeting of challenges. A director says, 'I need this flatbed truck to do a midair double somersault that produces an orange ball of fire with a thirty-six-foot diameter, which the cinematographer will use to light the scene.' I tell my students if they want to bring technology into it, they have to take this into account, this tendency toward grandiose deeds, toward pursuing a dream."

"A dream? How do your students reply?"

"Just the way you did. 'A dream?' All that blood and glass, that screeching rubber. What about the sheer waste, the sense of a civilization in a state of decay?"

"What about it?" I said.

"I tell them it's not decay they are seeing but innocence. The movie breaks away from complicated human passions to show us something elemental, something fiery and loud and head-on. It's a conservative wish-fulfillment, a yearning for naïveté. We want to be artless again. We want to reverse the flow of experience, of worldliness and its responsibilities. My students say, 'Look at the crushed bodies, the severed limbs. What kind of innocence is this?'"

"What do you say to that?"

"I tell them they can't think of a car crash in a movie as a violent act. It's a celebration. A reaffirmation of traditional values and beliefs. I connect car crashes to holidays like Thanksgiving and the Fourth. We don't mourn the dead or rejoice in miracles. These are days of secular optimism, of self-celebration. We will improve, prosper, perfect ourselves. Watch any car crash in any American movie. It is a high-spirited moment like old-fashioned stunt flying, walking on wings. The people who stage these crashes are able to capture a lightheartedness, a carefree enjoyment that car crashes in foreign movies can never approach."

"Look past the violence."

"Exactly. Look past the violence, Jack. There is a wonderful brimming spirit of innocence and fun."

29

Babette and I moved down the wide aisle, each with a gleaming cart. We passed a family shopping in sign language. I kept seeing colored lights.

"How do you feel?" she said.

"I'm fine. I feel good. How are you?"

"Why don't you have a checkup? Wouldn't you feel better if you found out nothing was there?"

"I've had two checkups. Nothing is there."

"What did Dr. Chakravarty say?"

"What could he say?"

"He speaks English beautifully. I love to hear him speak."

"Not as much as he loves to speak."

"What do you mean he loves to speak? Do you mean he takes every possible opportunity to speak? He's a doctor. He has to speak. In a very real sense you are paying him to speak. Do you mean he flaunts his beautiful English? He rubs your face in it?"

"We need some Glass Plus."

"Don't leave me alone," she said.

"I'm just going to aisle five."

"I don't want to be alone, Jack. I believe you know that."

"We're going to come through this thing all right," I said. "Maybe stronger than ever. We're determined to be well. Babette is not a neurotic person. She is strong, healthy, outgoing, affirmative. She says yes to things. This is the point of Babette."

We stayed together in the aisles and at the checkout. Babette bought three tabloids for her next session with Old Man Treadwell. We read them together as we waited on line. Then we went together to the car, loaded the merchandise, sat very close to each other as I drove home.

"Except for my eyes," I said.

"What do you mean?"

"Chakravarty thinks I ought to see an eye man."

"Is it the colored spots again?"

"Yes."

"Stop wearing those dark glasses."

"I can't teach Hitler without them."

"Why not?"

"I need them, that's all."

"They're stupid, they're useless."

"I've built a career," I said. "I may not understand all the elements involved but this is all the more reason not to tamper."

The *déjà vu* crisis centers closed down. The hotline was quietly discontinued. People seemed on the verge of forgetting. I could hardly blame them even if I felt abandoned to a certain extent, left holding the bag.

I went faithfully to German lessons. I began to work with my teacher on things I might say in welcoming delegates to the Hitler conference, still a number of weeks off. The windows were totally blocked by furniture and debris. Howard Dunlop sat in the middle of the room, his oval face floating in sixty watts of dusty light. I began to suspect I was the only person he ever talked to. I also began to suspect he needed me more than I needed him. A disconcerting and terrible thought.

There was a German-language book on a ruined table near the door. The title was lettered in black in a thick heavy ominous typeface: *Das Aegyptische Todtenbuch.*

"What's that?" I said.

"*The Egyptian Book of the Dead,*" he whispered. "A best-seller in Germany."

Every so often, when Denise wasn't home, I wandered into her room. I picked up things, put them down, looked behind a curtain, glanced into an open drawer, stuck my foot under the bed and felt around. Absentminded browsing.

Babette listened to talk radio.

I started throwing things away. Things in the top and bottom of my closet, things in boxes in the basement and attic. I threw away correspondence, old paperbacks, magazines I'd been saving to read, pencils that needed sharpening. I threw away tennis shoes, sweat socks, gloves with ragged fingers, old belts and neckties. I came upon stacks of student reports, broken rods for the seats of director's chairs. I threw these away. I threw away every aerosol can that didn't have a top.

The gas meter made a particular noise.

That night on TV I saw newsfilm of policemen carrying a body bag out of someone's backyard in Bakersville. The reporter said two bodies had been found, more were believed buried in the same yard. Perhaps many more. Perhaps twenty bodies, thirty bodies—no one knew for sure. He swept an arm across the area. It was a big backyard.

The reporter was a middle-aged man who spoke clearly and strongly and yet with some degree of intimacy, conveying a sense of frequent contact with his audience, of shared interests and mutual trust. Digging would continue through the night, he said, and the station would cut back to the scene as soon as developments warranted. He made it sound like a lover's promise.

Three nights later I wandered into Heinrich's room, where the TV set was temporarily located. He sat on the floor in a hooded sweatshirt, watching live coverage of the same scene. The backyard was floodlit, men with picks and shovels worked amid mounds of dirt. In the foreground stood the reporter, bareheaded, in a sheepskin coat, in a light snow, giving an update. The police said they had solid information, the diggers were methodical and skilled, the work had been going on for over seventy-two hours. But no more bodies had been found.

The sense of failed expectations was total. A sadness and emptiness hung over the scene. A dejection, a sorry gloom. We felt it ourselves, my son and I, quietly watching. It was in the room, seeping into the air from pulsing streams of electrons. The reporter seemed at first merely apologetic. But as he continued to discuss the absense of mass graves, he grew increasingly forlorn, gesturing at the diggers, shaking his head, almost ready to plead with us for sympathy and understanding.

I tried not to feel disappointed.

30

In the dark the mind runs on like a devouring machine, the only thing awake in the universe. I tried to make out the walls, the dresser in the corner. It was the old defenseless feeling. Small, weak, deathbound, alone. Panic, the god of woods and wilderness, half goat. I moved my head to the right, remembering the clock-radio. I watched the numbers change, the progression of digital minutes, odd to even. They glowed green in the dark.

After a while I woke up Babette. Warm air came rising from her body as she shifted toward me. Contented air. A mixture of forgetfulness and sleep. Where am I, who are you, what was I dreaming?

"We have to talk," I said.

She mumbled things, seemed to fend off some hovering presence. When I reached for the lamp, she gave me a backhand punch in the arm. The light went on. She retreated toward the radio, covering her head and moaning.

"You can't get away. There are things we have to talk about. I want access to Mr. Gray. I want the real name of Gray Research."

All she could do was moan, "No."

"I'm reasonable about this. I have a sense of perspective. No huge hopes or expectations. I only want to check it out, give it a try. I don't believe in magical objects. I only say, 'Let me try, let me see.' I've been lying here for hours practically paralyzed. I'm drenched in sweat. Feel my chest, Babette."

"Five more minutes. I need to sleep."

"Feel. Give me your hand. See how wet."

"We all sweat," she said. "What is sweat?"

"There are rivulets here."

"You want to ingest. No good, Jack."

"All I ask is a few minutes alone with Mr. Gray, to find out if I qualify."

"He'll think you want to kill him."

"But that's crazy. I'd be crazy. How can I kill him?"

"He'll know I told you about the motel."

"The motel is over and done. I can't change the motel. Do I kill the only man who can relieve my pain? Feel under my arms if you don't believe me."

"He'll think you're a husband with a grudge."

"The motel is frankly small grief. Do I kill him and feel better? He doesn't have to know who I am. I make up an identity, I invent a context. Help me, please."

"Don't tell me you sweat. What is sweat? I gave the man my word."

In the morning we sat at the kitchen table. The clothes dryer was running in the entranceway. I listened to the tapping sound of buttons and zippers as they struck the surface of the drum.

"I already know what I want to say to him. I'll be descriptive, clinical. No philosophy or theology. I'll appeal to the pragmatist in him. He's bound to be impressed by the fact that I'm actually scheduled to die. This is frankly more than you could claim. My need is intense. I believe he'll respond to this. Besides, he'll want another crack at a live subject. That's the way these people are."

"How do I know you won't kill him?"

"You're my wife. Am I a killer?"

"You're a man, Jack. We all know about men and their insane rage. This is something men are very good at. Insane and violent jealousy. Homicidal rage. When people are good at something, it's only natural that they look for a chance to do this thing. If I were good at it, I would do it. It happens I'm not. So instead of going into homicidal rages, I read to the blind. In other words I know my limits. I am willing to settle for less."

"What did I do to deserve this? This is not like you. Sarcastic, mocking."

"Leave it alone," she said. "Dylar was my mistake. I won't let you make it yours as well."

We listened to the tap and scratch of buttons and zipper tabs. It was time for me to leave for school. The voice upstairs remarked: "A California think-tank says the next world war may be fought over salt."

All afternoon I stood by the window in my office, watching the Observatory. It was growing dark when Winnie Richards appeared at the side door, looked both ways, then began moving in a wolf-trot along the sloping turf. I hurried out of my office and down the stairs. In seconds I was out on a cobbled path, running. Almost at once I experienced a strange elation, the kind of bracing thrill that marks the recovery of a lost pleasure. I saw her turn a corner in a controlled skid before she disappeared behind a maintenance building. I ran as fast as I could, cutting loose, cutting into the wind, running chest out, head high, my arms pumping hard. She reappeared at the edge of the library, an alert and stealthy figure moving beneath the arched windows, nearly lost to the dusk. When she drew near the steps she suddenly accelerated, going full tilt from what was almost a standing start. This was a deft and lovely maneuver that I was able to appreciate even as it put me at a disadvantage. I decided to cut behind the library and pick her up on the long straight approach to the chemistry labs. Briefly I ran alongside the members of the lacrosse team as they charged off a field after practice. We ran step for step, the players waving their sticks in a ritualized manner and chanting something I couldn't understand. When I reached the broad path I was gasping for breath. Winnie was nowhere in sight. I ran through the faculty parking lot, past the starkly modern chapel, around the administration building. The wind was audible now, creaking in the high bare branches. I ran to the east, changed my mind, stood looking around, removed my glasses to peer. I wanted to run, I was willing to run. I would run as far as I could, run through the night, run to forget why I was running. After some moments I saw a figure loping up a hill at the edge of the campus. It had to be her. I started running again, knowing she was too far away, would disappear over the crest of the hill, would not resurface for weeks. I put everything I had into a final climbing burst, charging over concrete, grass, then gravel, lungs burning in my chest, a heaviness in my legs that seemed the very pull of the earth, its most intimate and telling judgment, the law of falling bodies.

How surprised I was, nearing the top of the hill, to see that she had stopped. She wore a Gore-Tex jacket puffed up with insulation and she was looking to the west. I walked slowly toward her. When I cleared a row of private homes I saw what it was that had made her pause. The edge of the earth trembled in a darkish haze. Upon it lay the sun, going down like a ship in a burning sea. Another postmodern sunset, rich in romantic imagery. Why try to describe it? It's enough to say that everything in our field of vision seemed to exist in order to gather the light of this event. Not that this was one of the stronger sunsets. There had been more dynamic colors, a deeper sense of narrative sweep.

"Hi, Jack. I didn't know you came up here."

"I usually go to the highway overpass."

"Isn't this something?"

"It's beautiful all right."

"Makes me think. It really does."

"What do you think about?"

"What *can* you think about in the face of this kind of beauty? I get scared, I know that."

"This isn't one of the scarier ones."

"It scares me. Boy, look at it."

"Did you see last Tuesday? A powerful and stunning sunset. I rate this one average. Maybe they're beginning to wind down."

"I hope not," she said. "I'd miss them."

"Could be the toxic residue in the atmosphere is diminishing."

"There's a school of thought that says it's not residue from the cloud that causes the sunsets. It's residue from the microorganisms that ate the cloud."

We stood there watching a surge of florid light, like a heart pumping in a documentary on color TV.

"Remember the saucer-shaped pill?"

"Of course," she said. "A super piece of engineering."

"I found out what it's designed to do. It's designed to solve an ancient problem. Fear of death. It encourages the brain to produce fear-of-death inhibitors."

"But we still die."

"Everyone dies, yes."

"We just won't be afraid," she said.

"That's right."

"Interesting, I guess."

"Dylar was designed by a secret research group. I believe some of these people are psychobiologists. I wonder if you've heard rumors of a group working secretly on fear of death."

"I'd be the last to hear. No one can ever find me. When they do find me, it's to tell me something important."

"What could be more important?"

"You're talking about gossip, rumors. This is thin stuff, Jack. Who are these people, where is their base?"

"That's why I've been chasing you. I thought you'd know something about them. I don't even know what a psychobiologist is."

"It's a catchall sort of thing. Interdisciplinary. The real work is in the pits."

"Isn't there anything you can tell me?"

Something in my voice made her turn to look at me. Winnie was barely into her thirties but she had a sane and practiced eye for the half-concealed disasters that constitute a life. A narrow face partly hidden by wispy brown ringlets, eyes bright and excited. She had the beaky and hollow-boned look of a great wading creature. Small prim mouth. A smile that was permanently in conflict with some inner stricture against the seductiveness of humor. Murray told me once he had a crush on her, found her physical awkwardness a sign of an intelligence developing almost too rapidly, and I thought I knew what he meant. She was poking and snatching at the world around, overrunning it at times.

"I don't know what your personal involvement is with this substance," she said, "but I think it's a mistake to lose one's sense of death, even one's fear of death. Isn't death the boundary we need? Doesn't it give a precious texture to life, a sense of definition? You have to ask yourself whether anything you do in this life would have beauty and meaning without the knowledge you carry of a final line, a border or limit."

I watch light climb into the rounded summits of high-altitude clouds. Clorets, Velamints, Freedent.

"People think I'm spacey," she said. "I have a spacey theory about human fear, sure enough. Picture yourself, Jack, a confirmed homebody, a sedentary fellow who finds himself walking in a deep wood. You spot something out of the corner of your eye. Before you know anything else, you know that this thing is very large and that it has no place in your ordinary frame of reference. A flaw in the world picture. Either it shouldn't be here or you shouldn't. Now the thing comes into full view. It is a grizzly bear, enormous, shiny brown, swaggering, dripping slime from its bared fangs. Jack, you have never seen a large animal in the wild. The sight of this grizzer is so electrifyingly strange that it gives you a renewed sense of yourself, a fresh awareness of the self—the self in terms of a unique and horrific situation. You see yourself in a new and intense way. You rediscover yourself. You are lit up for your own imminent dismemberment. The beast on hind legs has enabled you to see who you are as if for the first time, outside familiar surroundings, alone, distinct, whole. The name we give to this complicated process is fear."

"Fear is self-awareness raised to a higher level."

"That's right, Jack."

"And death?" I said.

"Self, self, self. If death can be seen as less strange and unreferenced, your sense of self in relation to death will diminish, and so will your fear."

"What do I do to make death less strange? How do I go about it?"

"I don't know."

"Do I risk death by driving fast around curves? Am I supposed to go rock climbing on weekends?"

"I don't know," she said. "I wish I knew."

"Do I scale the sheer facade of a ninety-story building, wearing a clip-on belt? What do I do, Winnie? Do I sit in a cage full of

African snakes like my son's best friend? This is what people do today."

"I think what you do, Jack, is forget the medicine in that tablet. There is no medicine, obviously."

She was right. They were all right. Go on with my life, raise my kids, teach my students. Try not to think of that staticky figure in the Grayview Motel putting his unfinished hands on my wife.

"I'm still sad, Winnie, but you've given my sadness a richness and depth it has never known before."

She turned away, blushing.

I said, "You're more than a fair-weather friend—you're a true enemy."

She turned exceedingly red.

I said, "Brilliant people never think of the lives they smash, being brilliant."

I watched her blush. She used both hands to pull her knit cap down over her ears. We took a last look at the sky and started walking down the hill.

31

DID YOU REMEMBER: 1) to make out your check to Waveform Dynamics? 2) to write your account number on your check? 3) to sign your check? 4) to send payment in full, as we do not accept partial payment? 5) to enclose your original payment document, not a reproduced copy? 6) to enclose your document in such a way that the address appears in the window? 7) to detach the green portion of your document along the dotted line to retain for your records? 8) to supply your correct address and zip code? 9) to inform us at least three weeks before you plan to move? 10) to secure the envelope flap? 11) to place a stamp on the envelope, as the post office will not deliver without postage? 12) to mail the envelope at least three days before the date entered in the blue box?

CABLE HEALTH, CABLE WEATHER, CABLE NEWS, CABLE NATURE.

No one wanted to cook that night. We all got in the car and went out to the commercial strip in the no man's land beyond the town boundary. The never-ending neon. I pulled in at a place that specialized in chicken parts and brownies. We decided to eat in the car. The car was sufficient for our needs. We wanted to eat, not look around at other people. We wanted to fill our stomachs and get it over with. We didn't need light and space. We certainly didn't need to face each other across a table as we ate, building a subtle and complex cross-network of signals and codes. We were content to eat facing in the same direction, looking only inches past our hands. There was a kind of rigor in this. Denise brought the food out to the car and distributed paper napkins. We settled in to eat. We ate fully dressed, in hats and heavy coats, without speaking, ripping into chicken parts with our hands and teeth. There was a mood of intense concentration, minds converging on a single compelling idea. I was surprised to find I was enormously hungry. I chewed and ate, looking only inches past my hands. This is how hunger shrinks the world. This is the edge of the observable universe of food. Steffie tore off the crisp skin of a breast and gave it to Heinrich. She never ate the skin. Babette sucked a bone. Heinrich traded wings with Denise, a large for a small. He thought small wings were tastier. People gave Babette their bones to clean and suck. I fought off an image of Mr. Gray lazing naked on a motel bed, an unresolved picture collapsing at the edges. We sent Denise to get more food, waiting for her in silence. Then we started in again, half stunned by the dimensions of our pleasure.

Steffie said quietly, "How do astronauts float?"

There was a pause like a missing tick in eternity.

Denise stopped eating to say, "They're lighter than air."

We all stopped eating. A worried silence ensued.

"There is no air," Heinrich said finally. "They can't be lighter than something that isn't there. Space is a vacuum except for heavy molecules."

"I thought space was cold," Babette said. "If there's no air, how can it be cold? What makes warm or cold? Air, or so I thought. If there's no air, there should be no cold. Like a nothing kind of day."

"How can there be nothing?" Denise said. "There has to be something."

"There is something," Heinrich said in exasperation. "There's heavy molecules."

"Do-I-need-a-sweater kind of day," Babette said.

There was another pause. We waited to learn if the dialogue was over. Then we set to eating again. We traded unwanted parts in silence, stuck our hands in cartons of rippled fries. Wilder liked the soft white fries and people picked these out and gave them to him. Denise distributed ketchup in little watery pouches.

The interior of the car smelled of grease and licked flesh. We traded parts and gnawed.

Steffie said in a small voice, "How cold is space?"

We all waited once more. Then Heinrich said, "It depends on how high you go. The higher you go, the colder it gets."

"Wait a minute," Babette said. "The higher you go, the closer you get to the sun. So the warmer it gets."

"What makes you think the sun is high?"

"How can the sun be low? You have to look up to see the sun."

"What about at night?" he said.

"It's on the other side of the earth. But people still look up."

"The whole point of Sir Albert Einstein," he said, "is how can the sun be up if you're standing on the sun?"

"The sun is a great molten ball," she said. "It's impossible to stand on the sun."

"He was just saying 'if.' Basically there is no up or down, hot or cold, day or night."

"What is there?"

"Heavy molecules. The whole point of space is to give molecules a chance to cool down after they come shooting off the surface of giant stars."

"If there's no hot or cold, how can molecules cool down?"

"Hot and cold are words. Think of them as words. We have to use words. We can't just grunt."

"It's called the sun's corolla," Denise said to Steffie in a separate discussion. "We saw it the other night on the weather network."

"I thought Corolla was a car," Steffie said.

"Everything's a car," Heinrich said. "The thing you have to understand about giant stars is that they have actual nuclear explosions deep inside the core. Totally forget these Russian IBMs that are supposed to be so awesome. We're talking about a hundred million times bigger explosions."

There was a long pause. No one spoke. We went back to eating for as long as it took to bite off and chew a single mouthful of food.

"It's supposed to be Russian psychics who are causing this crazy weather," Babette said.

"What crazy weather?" I said.

Heinrich said, "We have psychics, they have psychics, supposedly. They want to disrupt our crops by influencing the weather."

"The weather's been normal."

"For this time of year," Denise put in smartly.

This was the week a policeman saw a body thrown from a UFO. It happened while he was on routine patrol on the outskirts of Glassboro. The rain-soaked corpse of an unidentified male was found later that night, fully clothed. An autopsy disclosed that death was due to multiple fractures and heart failure—the result, perhaps, of a ghastly shock. Under hypnosis, the policeman, Jerry Tee Walker, relived in detail the baffling sight of the neon-bright object that resembled an enormous spinning top as it hovered eighty feet above a field. Officer Walker, a Vietnam vet, said the bizarre scene reminded him of helicopter crews throwing Vietcong suspects out the door. Incredibly, as he watched a hatch come open and the body plummet to the ground, Walker sensed an eerie message being psychically transmitted to his brain. Police hypnotists plan to intensify their sessions in an attempt to uncover the message.

There were sightings all over the area. An energizing mental current, a snaky glow, seemed to pass from town to town. It didn't matter whether you believed in these things or not. They were an excitement, a wave, a tremor. Some voice or noise would crack across the sky and we would be lifted out of death. People drove speculatively to the edges of towns, where some would turn back, some decide to venture toward remoter areas which seemed in these past days to exist under a spell, a hallowed expectation. The air grew soft and mild. A neighbor's dog barked through the night.

In the fast food parking lot we ate our brownies. Crumbs stuck to the heels of our hands. We inhaled the crumbs, we licked the fingers. As we got close to finishing, the physical extent of our awareness began to expand. Food's borders yielded to the wider world. We looked past our hands. We looked through the windows, at the cars and lights. We looked at the people leaving the restaurant, men, women and children carrying cartons of food, leaning into the wind. An impatience began to flow from the three bodies in the rear seat. They wanted to be home, not here. They wanted to blink an eye and find themselves in their rooms, with their things, not sitting in a cramped car on this windswept concrete plain. Journeys home were always a test. I started up the car, knowing it was only a matter of seconds before the massed restlessness took on elements of threat. We could feel it coming, Babette and I. A sulky menace brewed back there. They would attack us, using the classic strategy of fighting among themselves. But attack us for what reason? For not getting them home faster? For being older and bigger and somewhat steadier of mood than they were? Would they attack us for our status as protectors—protectors who must sooner or later fail? Or was it simply who we were that they attacked, our voices, features, gestures, ways of walking and laughing, our eye color, hair color, skin tone, our chromosomes and cells?

As if to head them off, as if she could not bear the implications of their threat, Babette said pleasantly, "Why is it these UFOs are mostly seen upstate? The best sightings are upstate. People get abducted and taken aboard. Farmers see burn marks where saucers landed. A woman gives birth to a UFO baby, so she says. Always upstate."

"That's where the mountains are," Denise said. "Spaceships can hide from radar or whatever."

"Why are the mountains upstate?" Steffie said.

"Mountains are always upstate," Denise told her. "This way the snow melts as planned in the spring and flows downhill to the reservoirs near the cities, which are kept in the lower end of the state for exactly this reason."

I thought, momentarily, she might be right. It made a curious kind of sense. Or did it? Or was it totally crazy? There had to be large cities in the northern part of some states. Or were they just north of the border in the southern part of states just to the north? What she said could not be true and yet I had trouble, momentarily, disproving it. I could not name cities or mountains to disprove it. There had to be mountains in the southern part of some states. Or did they tend to be below the state line, in the northern part of states to the south? I tried to name state capitals, governors. How could there be a north below a south? Is this what I found confusing? Was this the crux of Denise's error? Or was she somehow, eerily, right?

The radio said: "Excesses of salt, phosphorus, magnesium."

Later that night Babette and I sat drinking cocoa. On the kitchen table, among the coupons, the foot-long supermarket receipts, the mail-order catalogs, was a postcard from Mary Alice, my oldest. She is the golden issue of my first marriage to Dana Breedlove, the spy, and is therefore Steffie's full sister, although ten years and two marriages fell between. Mary Alice is nineteen now and lives in Hawaii, where she works with whales.

Babette picked up a tabloid someone had left on the table.

"Mouse cries have been measured at forty thousand cycles per second. Surgeons use high-frequency tapes of mouse cries to destroy tumors in the human body. Do you believe that?"

"Yes."

"So do I."

She put down the newspaper. After a while she said to me urgently, "How do you feel, Jack?"

"I'm all right. I feel fine. Honest. What about you?"

"I wish I hadn't told you about my condition."

"Why?"

"Then you wouldn't have told me you're going to die first. Here are the two things I want most in the world. Jack not to die first. And Wilder to stay the way he is forever."

32

Murray and I walked across campus in our European manner, a serenely reflective pace, heads lowered as we conversed. Sometimes one of us gripped the other near the elbow, a gesture of intimacy and physical support. Other times we walked slightly apart, Murray's hands clasped behind his back, Gladney's folded monkishly at the abdomen, a somewhat worried touch.

"Your German is coming around?"

"I still speak it badly. The words give me trouble. Howard and I are working on opening remarks for the conference."

"You call him Howard?"

"Not to his face. I don't call him anything to his face and he doesn't call me anything to my face. It's that kind of relationship. Do you see him at all? You live under the same roof, after all."

"Fleeting glimpses. The other boarders seem to prefer it that way. He barely exists, we feel."

"There's something about him. I'm not sure what it is exactly."

"He's flesh-colored," Murray said.

"True. But that's not what makes me uneasy."

"Soft hands."

"Is that it?"

"Soft hands in a man give me pause. Soft skin in general. Baby skin. I don't think he shaves."

"What else?" I said.

"Flecks of dry spittle at the corners of his mouth."

"You're right," I said excitedly. "Dry spit. I feel it hit me in the face when he leans forward to articulate. What else?"

"And a way of looking over a person's shoulder."

"You see all this in fleeting glimpses. Remarkable. What else?" I demanded.

"And a rigid carriage that seems at odds with his shuffling walk."

"Yes, he walks without moving his arms. What else, what else?"

"And something else, something above and beyond all this, something eerie and terrible."

"Exactly. But what is it? Something I can't quite identify."

"There's a strange air about him, a certain mood, a sense, a presence, an emanation."

"But what?" I said, surprised to find myself deeply and personally concerned, colored dots dancing at the edge of my vision.

We'd walked thirty paces when Murray began to nod. I watched his face as we walked. He nodded crossing the street and kept nodding all the way past the music library. I walked with him step for step, clutching his elbow, watching his face, waiting for him to speak, not interested in the fact that he'd taken me completely out of my way, and he was still nodding as we approached the entrance to Wilmot Grange, a restored nineteenth-century building at the edge of the campus.

"But what?" I said. "But what?"

It wasn't until four days later that he called me at home, at one in the morning, to whisper helpfully in my ear, "He looks like a man who finds dead bodies erotic."

I went to one last lesson. The walls and windows were obscured by accumulated objects, which seemed now to be edging toward the middle of the room. The bland-faced man before me closed his eyes and spoke, reciting useful tourist phrases. "Where am I?" "Can you help me?" "It is night and I am lost." I could hardly bear to sit there. Murray's remark fixed him forever to a plausible identity. What had been elusive about Howard Dunlop was now pinned down. What had been strange and half creepy was now diseased. A grim lasciviousness escaped his body and seemed to circulate through the barricaded room.

In truth I would miss the lessons. I would also miss the dogs, the German shepherds. One day they were simply gone. Needed elsewhere perhaps or sent back to the desert to sharpen their skills. The men in Mylex suits were still around, however, carrying instruments to measure and probe, riding through town in teams of six or eight in chunky peglike vehicles that resembled Lego toys.

I stood by Wilder's bed watching him sleep. The voice next door said: "In the four-hundred-thousand-dollar Nabisco Dinah Shore."

This was the night the insane asylum burned down. Heinrich and I got in the car and went to watch. There were other men at the scene with their adolescent boys. Evidently fathers and sons seek fellowship at such events. Fires help draw them closer, provide a conversational wedge. There is equipment to appraise, the technique of firemen to discuss and criticize. The manliness of firefighting—the virility of fires, one might say—suits the kind of laconic dialogue that fathers and sons can undertake without awkwardness or embarrassment.

"Most of these fires in old buildings start in the electrical wiring," Heinrich said. "Faulty wiring. That's one phrase you can't hang around for long without hearing."

"Most people don't burn to death," I said. "They die of smoke inhalation."

"That's the other phrase," he said.

Flames roared through the dormers. We stood across the street watching part of the roof give way, a tall chimney slowly fold and sink. Pumper trucks kept arriving from other towns, the men descending heavily in their rubber boots and old-fashioned hats. Hoses were manned and trained, a figure rose above the shimmering roof in the grip of a telescopic ladder. We watched the portico begin to go, a far column leaning. A woman in a fiery nightgown walked across the lawn. We gasped, almost in appreciation. She was white-haired and slight, fringed in burning air, and we could see she was mad, so lost to dreams and furies that the fire around her head seemed almost incidental. No one said a word. In all the heat and noise of detonating wood, she brought a silence to her. How powerful and real. How deep a thing was madness. A fire captain hurried toward her, then circled out slightly, disconcerted, as if she were not the person, after all, he had expected to meet here. She went down in a white burst, like a teacup breaking. Four men were around her now, batting at the flames with helmets and caps.

The great work of containing the blaze went on, a labor that seemed as old and lost as cathedral-building, the men driven by a spirit of lofty communal craft. A Dalmatian sat in the cab of a hook-and-ladder truck.

"It's funny how you can look at it and look at it," Heinrich said. "Just like a fire in a fireplace."

"Are you saying the two kinds of fire are equally compelling?"

"I'm just saying you can look and look."

"'Man has always been fascinated by fire.' Is that what you're saying?"

"This is my first burning building. Give me a chance," he said.

The fathers and sons crowded the sidewalk, pointing at one or another part of the half gutted structure. Murray, whose rooming house was just yards away, sidled up to us and shook our hands without a word. Windows blew out. We watched another chimney slip through the roof, a few loose bricks tumbling to the lawn. Murray shook our hands again, then disappeared.

Soon there was a smell of acrid matter. It could have been insulation burning—polystyrene sheathing for pipes and wires—or one or more of a dozen other substances. A sharp and bitter stink filled the air, overpowering the odor of smoke and charred stone. It changed the mood of the people on the sidewalk. Some put hankies to their faces, others left abruptly in disgust. Whatever caused the odor, I sensed that it made people feel betrayed. An ancient, spacious and terrible drama was being compromised by something unnatural, some small and nasty intrusion. Our eyes began to burn. The crowd broke up. It was as though we'd been forced to recognize the existence of a second kind of death. One was real, the other synthetic. The odor drove us away but beneath it and far worse was the sense that death came two ways, sometimes at once, and how death entered your mouth and nose, how death smelled, could somehow make a difference to your soul.

We hurried to our cars, thinking of the homeless, the mad, the dead, but also of ourselves now. This is what the odor of that burning material did. It complicated our sadness, brought us closer to the secret of our own eventual end.

At home I fixed warm milk for us both. I was surprised to see him drink it. He gripped the mug with both hands, talked about the noise of the conflagration, the air-fed wallop of combustion, like a ramjet thrusting. I almost expected him to thank me for the nice fire. We sat there drinking our milk. After a while he went into his closet to chin.

I sat up late thinking of Mr. Gray. Gray-bodied, staticky, unfinished. The picture wobbled and rolled, the edges of his body flared with random distortion. Lately I'd found myself thinking of him often. Sometimes as Mr. Gray the composite. Four or more grayish figures engaged in a pioneering work. Scientists, visionaries. Their wavy bodies passing through each other, mingling, blending, fusing. A little like extraterrestrials. Smarter than the rest of us, selfless, sexless, determined to engineer us out of our fear. But when the bodies fused I was left with a single figure, the project manager, a hazy gray seducer moving in ripples across a motel room. Bedward, plotward. I saw my wife reclining on her side, voluptuously rounded, the eternal waiting nude. I saw her as he did. Dependent, submissive, emotionally captive. I felt his mastery and control. The dominance of his postion. He was taking over my mind, this man I'd never seen, this half image, the barest smidge of brainlight. His bleak hands enfolded a rose-white breast. How vivid and living it was, what a tactile delight, dusted with russet freckles about the tip. I experienced aural torment. Heard them in their purling foreplay, the love babble and buzzing flesh. Heard the sloppings and smackings, the swash of wet mouths, bedsprings sinking in. An interval of mumbled adjustments. Then gloom moved in around the gray-sheeted bed, a circle slowly closing.

Panasonic.

33

What time was it when I opened my eyes, sensing someone or something nearby? Was it an odd-numbered hour? The room was soft and webby. I stretched my legs, blinked, slowly focused on a familiar object. It was Wilder, standing two feet from the bed, gazing into my face. We spent a long moment in mutual contemplation. His great round head, set as it was on a small-limbed and squattish body, gave him the look of a primitive clay figurine, some household idol of obscure and cultic derivation. I had the feeling he wanted to show me something. As I slipped quietly out of bed, he walked in his quilted booties out of the room. I followed him into the hall and toward the window that looks out on our backyard. I was barefoot and robeless and felt a chill pass through the Hong Kong polyester of my pajamas. Wilder stood looking out the window, his chin about an inch above the sill. It seemed I'd spent my life in lopsided pajamas, the shirt buttons inserted in mismatching slits, the fly undone and drooping. Was it dawn already? Were those crows I heard screaming in the trees?

There was someone sitting in the backyard. A white-haired man sitting erect in the old wicker chair, a figure of eerie stillness and composure. At first, dazed and sleepy, I didn't know what to make of the sight. It seemed to need a more careful interpretation than I was able to provide at the moment. I thought one thing, that he'd been *inserted* there for some purpose. Then fear began to enter, palpable and overwhelming, a fist clenching repeatedly in my chest. Who was he, what was happening here? I realized Wilder was no longer next to me. I reached the doorway to his room just in time to see his head sink into the pillow. By the time I got to the bed, he was fast asleep. I didn't know what to do. I felt cold, white. I worked my way back to the window, gripping a doorknob, a handrail, as if to remind myself of the nature and being of real things. He was still out there, gazing into the hedges. I saw him in profile in the uncertain light, motionless and knowing. Was he as old as I'd first thought—or was the white hair purely emblematic, part of his allegorical force? That was it, of course. He would be Death, or Death's errand-runner, a hollow-eyed technician from the plague era, from the era of inquisitions, endless wars, of bedlams and leprosariums. He would be an aphorist of last things, giving me the barest glance—civilized, ironic—as he spoke his deft and stylish line about my journey out. I watched for a long time, waiting for him to move a hand. His stillness was commanding. I felt myself getting whiter by the second. What does it mean to become white? How does it feel to see Death in the flesh, come to gather you in? I was scared to the marrow. I was cold and hot, dry and wet, myself and someone else. The fist clenched in my chest. I went to the staircase and sat on the top step, looking into my hands. So much remained. Every word and thing a beadwork of bright creation. My own plain hand, crosshatched and whorled in a mesh of expressive lines, a life terrain, might itself be the object of a person's study and wonder for years. A cosmology against the void.

I got to my feet and went back to the window. He was still there. I went into the bathroom to hide. I closed the toilet lid and sat there a while, wondering what to do next. I didn't want him in the house.

I paced for a time. I ran cold water over my hands and wrists, splashed it in my face. I felt light and heavy, muddled and alert. I took a scenic paperweight from the shelf by the door. Inside the plastic disk floated a 3-D picture of the Grand Canyon, the colors zooming and receding as I turned the object in the light. Fluctuating planes. I liked this phrase. It seemed the very music of existence. If only one could see death as just another surface one inhabits for a time. Another facet of cosmic reason. A zoom down Bright Angel Trail.

I turned to immediate things. If I wanted to keep him out of the house, the thing to do was go outside. First I would look in on the smaller children. I moved quietly through the rooms on bare white feet. I looked for a blanket to adjust, a toy to remove from a child's warm grasp, feeling I'd wandered into a TV moment. All was still and well. Would they regard a parent's death as just another form of divorce?

I looked in on Heinrich. He occupied the top left corner of the bed, his body tightly wound like the kind of trick device that uncoils abruptly when it's touched. I stood in the doorway nodding.

I looked in on Babette. She was many levels down, a girl again, a figure running in a dream. I kissed her head, smelling the warm musty air that carried up from sleep. I spotted my copy of *Mein Kampf* in a pile of books and journals. The radio came on. I hurried out of the room, fearing that some call-in voice, some stranger's soul-lament, would be the last thing I heard in this world.

I went down to the kitchen. I looked through the window. He was there in the wicker armchair on the wet grass. I opened the inner door and then the storm door. I went outside, the copy of *Mein Kampf* clutched to my stomach. When the storm door banged shut, the man's head jerked and his legs came uncrossed. He got to his feet and turned in my direction. The sense of eerie and invincible stillness washed off, the aura of knowingness, the feeling he conveyed of an ancient and terrible secret. A second figure began to emerge from the numinous ruins of the first, began to assume effective form, develop in the crisp light as a set of movements, lines and features, a contour, a living person whose distinctive physical traits seemed more and more familiar as I watched them come into existence, a little amazed.

It was not Death that stood before me but only Vernon Dickey, my father-in-law.

"Was I asleep?" he said.

"What are you doing out here?"

"Didn't want to wake you folks."

"Did we know you were coming?"

"I didn't know it myself till yesterday afternoon. Drove straight through. Fourteen hours."

"Babette will be happy to see you."

"I just bet."

We went inside. I put the coffee pot on the stove. Vernon sat at the table in his battered denim jacket, playing with the lid of an old Zippo. He had the look of a ladies' man in the crash-dive of his career. His silvery hair had a wan tinge to it, a yellowish discolor, and he combed it back in a ducktail. He wore about four days' stubble. His chronic cough had taken on a jagged edge, an element of irresponsibility. Babette worried less about his condition than about the fact that he took such sardonic pleasure in his own hackings and spasms, as if there were something fatefully attractive in this terrible noise. He still wore a garrison belt with a longhorn buckle.

"So what the hell. Here I am. Big deal."

"What are you doing these days?"

"Shingling here, rustproofing there. I moonlight, except there's nothing I'm moonlighting from. Moonlight is all that's out there."

I noticed his hands. Scarred, busted, notched, permanently seamed with grease and mud. He glanced around the room, trying to spot something that needed replacing or repair. Such flaws were mainly an occasion for discourse. It put Vernon at an advantage to talk about gaskets and washers, about grouting, caulking, spackling. There were times when he seemed to attack me with terms like ratchet drill and whipsaw. He saw my shakiness in such matters as a sign of some deeper incompetence or stupidity. These were the things that built the world. Not to know or care about them was a betrayal of fundamental principles, a betrayal of gender, of species. What could be more useless than a man who couldn't fix a dripping faucet—fundamentally useless, dead to history, to the messages in his genes? I wasn't sure I disagreed.

"I was saying to Babette the other day. 'If there's one thing your father doesn't resemble, it's a widower.'"

"What did she say to that?"

"She thinks you're a danger to yourself. 'He'll fall asleep smoking. He'll die in a burning bed with a missing woman at his side.

An official missing person. Some poor lost unidentified multi-divorced woman.'"

Vernon coughed in appreciation of the insight. A series of pulmonary gasps. I could hear the stringy mucus whipping back and forth in his chest. I poured his coffee and waited.

"Just so you know where I'm at, Jack, there's a woman that wants to marry my ass. She goes to church in a mobile home. Don't tell Babette."

"That's the last thing I'd do."

"She'd get real exercised. Start in with the discount calls."

"She thinks you've gotten too lawless for marriage."

"The thing about marriage today is you don't have to go outside the home to get those little extras. You can get whatever you want in the recesses of the American home. These are the times we live in, for better or worse. Wives will do things. They want to do things. You don't have to drop little looks. It used to be the only thing available in the American home was the basic natural act. Now you get the options too. The action is thick, let me tell you. It's an amazing comment on our times that the more options you get in the home, the more prostitutes you see in the streets. How do you figure it, Jack? You're the professor. What does it mean?"

"I don't know."

"Wives wear edible panties. They know the words, the usages. Meanwhile the prostitutes are standing in the streets in all kinds of weather, day and night. Who are they waiting for? Tourists? Businessmen? Men who've been turned into stalkers of flesh? It's like the lid's blown off. Didn't I read somewhere the Japanese go to Singapore? Whole planeloads of males. A remarkable people."

"Are you seriously thinking of getting married?"

"I'd have to be crazy to marry a woman that worships in a mobile home."

There was an astuteness about Vernon, a deadpan quality of alert and searching intelligence, a shrewdness waiting for a shapely occasion. This made Babette nervous. She'd seen him sidle up to women in public places to ask some delving question in his blank-faced canny way. She refused to go into restaurants with him, fearing his offhand remarks to waitresses, intimate remarks, technically accomplished asides and observations, delivered in the late-night voice of some radio ancient. He'd given her some jittery moments, periods of anger and embarrassment, in a number of leatherette booths.

She came in now, wearing her sweatsuit, ready for an early morning dash up the stadium steps. When she saw her father at the table, her body seemed to lose its motive force. She stood there bent at the knees. Nothing remained but her ability to gape. She appeared to be doing an imitation of a gaping person. She was the picture of gapingness, the bright ideal, no less confused and alarmed than I had been when I saw him sitting in the yard, deathly still. I watched her face fill to the brim with numb wonder.

"Did we know you were coming?" she said. "Why didn't you call? You never call."

"Here I am. Big deal. Toot the horn."

She remained bent at the knees, trying to absorb his raw presence, the wiry body and drawn look. What an epic force he must have seemed to her, taking shape in her kitchen this way, a parent, a father with all the grist of years on him, the whole dense history of associations and connections, come to remind her who she was, to remove her disguise, grab hold of her maundering life for a time, without warning.

"I could have had things ready. You look awful. Where will you sleep?"

"Where did I sleep last time?"

They both looked at me, trying to remember.

As we fixed and ate breakfast, as the kids came down and warily approached Vernon for kisses and hair-mussings, as the hours passed and Babette became accustomed to the sight of the ambling figure in patched jeans, I began to notice the pleasure she took in hovering nearby, doing little things for him, being there to listen. A delight contained in routine gestures and automatic rhythms. At times she had to remind Vernon which foods were his favorites, how he liked them cooked and seasoned, which jokes he told best, which figures from the past were the plain fools, which the comic heroes. Gleanings from another life poured out of her. The cadences of her speech changed, took on a rural tang. The words changed, the references. This was a girl who'd helped her father sand and finish old oak, heave radiators up from the floorboards. His carpenter years, his fling with motorcycles, his biceps tattoo.

"You're getting string-beany, daddy. Finish those potatoes. There's more on the stove."

And Vernon would say to me, "Her mother made the worst french fries you could ever hope to eat. Like french fries in a state park." And then he'd turn to her and say, "Jack knows the problem I have with state parks. They don't move the heart."

We moved Heinrich down to the sofa and gave Vernon his room. It was unnerving to find him in the kitchen at seven in the morning, at six, at whatever grayish hour Babette or I went down to make coffee. He gave the impression he was intent on outfoxing us, working on our guilt, showing us that no matter how little sleep we got, he got less.

"Tell you what, Jack. You get old, you find out you're ready for something but you don't know what it is. You're always getting prepared. You're combing your hair, standing by the window looking out. I feel like there's some little fussy person whisking around me all the time. That's why I jumped in the car and drove headlong all this way."

"To break the spell," I said. "To get away from routine things. Routine things can be deadly, Vern, carried to extremes. I have a friend who says that's why people take vacations. Not to relax or find excitement or see new places. To escape the death that exists in routine things."

"What is he, a Jew?"

"What's that got to do with it?"

"Your roof gutter's sagging," he told me. "You know how to fix that, don't you?"

Vernon liked to hang around outside the house, waiting for garbagemen, telephone repairmen, the mail carrier, the afternoon newsboy. Someone to talk to about techniques and procedures. Sets of special methods. Routes, time spans, equipment. It tightened his grip on things, learning how work was done in areas outside his range.

He liked to tease the kids in his deadpan way. They answered his bantering remarks reluctantly. They were suspicious of all relatives. Relatives were a sensitive issue, part of the murky and complex past, the divided lives, the memories that could be refloated by a word or a name.

He liked to sit in his tortured hatchback, smoking.

Babette would watch from a window, managing to express love, worry, exasperation and despair, hope and gloom, more or less simultaneously. Vernon had only to shift his weight to arouse in her a series of extreme emotions.

He liked to mingle with shopping mall crowds.

"I'm counting on you to tell me, Jack."

"Tell you what?"

"You're the only person I know that's educated enough to give me the answer."

"The answer to what?"

"Were people this dumb before television?"

One night I heard a voice and thought he was moaning in his sleep. I put on my robe, went into the hall, realized the sound came from the TV set in Denise's room. I went in and turned off the set. She was asleep in a drift of blankets, books and clothes. On an impulse I went quietly to the open closet, pulled the light cord and peered inside, looking for the Dylar tablets. I closed the door against my body, which was half in, half out of the closet. I saw a great array of fabrics, shoes, toys, games and other objects. I poked around, catching an occasional trace of some childhood redolence. Clay, sneakers, pencil shavings. The bottle might be in an abandoned shoe, the pocket of some old shirt wadded in a corner. I heard her stir. I went still, held my breath.

"What are you doing?" she said.

"Don't worry, it's only me."

"I know who it is."

I kept on looking through the closet, thinking this would make me appear less guilty.

"I know what you're looking for, too."

"Denise, I've had a recent scare. I thought something awful was about to happen. It turned out I was wrong, thank goodness. But there are lingering effects. I need the Dylar. It may help me solve a problem."

I continued to rummage.

"What's the problem?"

"Isn't it enough for you to know that a problem exists? I wouldn't be here otherwise. Don't you want to be my friend?"

"I am your friend. I just don't want to be tricked."

"There's no question of tricking. I just need to try the medication. There are four tablets left. I'll take them and that'll be the end of it."

The more casual the voice, the better my chances of reaching her.

"You won't take them. You'll give them to my mother."

"Let's be clear about one thing," I said like a high government official. "Your mother is not a drug addict. Dylar is not that kind of medication."

"What is it then? Just tell me what it is."

Something in her voice or in my heart or in the absurdity of the moment allowed me to consider the possibility of answering her question. A breakthrough. Why not simply tell her? She was responsible, able to gauge the implications of serious things. I realized Babette and I had been foolish all along, keeping the truth from her. The girl would embrace the truth, know us better, love us more deeply in our weakness and fear.

I went and sat at the end of the bed. She watched me carefully. I told her the basic story, leaving out the tears, the passions, the terror, the horror, my exposure to Nyodene D., Babette's sexual arrangement with Mr. Gray, our argument over which of us feared death more. I concentrated on the medication itself, told her everything I knew about its life in the gastrointestinal tract and the brain.

The first thing she mentioned was the side effects. Every drug has side effects. A drug that could eliminate fear of death would have awesome side effects, especially if it is still in a trial stage. She was right, of course. Babette had spoken of outright death, brain death, left brain death, partial paralysis, other cruel and bizarre conditions of the body and mind.

I told Denise the power of suggestion could be more important than side effects.

"Remember how you heard on the radio that the billowing cloud caused sweaty palms? Your palms got sweaty, didn't they? The power of suggestion makes some people sick, others well. It may not matter how strong or weak Dylar is. If I think it will help me, it will help me."

"Up to a point."

"We are talking about death," I whispered. "In a very real sense it doesn't matter what is in those tablets. It could be sugar, it could be spice. I am eager to be humored, to be fooled."

"Isn't that a little stupid?"

"This is what happens, Denise, to desperate people."

There was a silence. I waited for her to ask me if this desperation was inevitable, if she would one day experience the same fear, undergo the same ordeal.

Instead she said, "Strong or weak doesn't matter. I threw the bottle away."

"No, you didn't. Where?"

"I put it in the garbage compactor."

"I don't believe you. When was this?"

"About a week ago. I thought Baba might sneak through my room and find it. So I decided to just get it over with. Nobody wanted to tell me what it was, did they? So I threw it in with all the cans and bottles and other junk. Then I compacted it."

"Like a used car."

"Nobody would tell me. That's all they had to do. I was right here all the time."

"It's all right. Don't worry. You did me a favor."

"About eight words was all they needed to say."

"I'm better off without it."

"It wouldn't have been the first time they tricked me."

"You're still my friend," I said.

I kissed her on the head and went to the door. I realized I was extremely hungry. I went downstairs to find something to eat. The kitchen light was on. Vernon was sitting at the table, fully dressed, smoking and coughing. The ash on his cigarette was an inch long, beginning to lean. It was a habit of his, letting the ash dangle. Babette thought he did it to induce feelings of suspense and anxiety in others. It was part of the reckless weather in which he moved.

"Just the man I want to see."

"Vern, it's the middle of the night. Don't you ever sleep?"

"Let's go out to the car," he said.

"Are you serious?"

"What we have here is a situation we ought to conduct in private. This house is full of women. Or am I wrong?"

"We're alone here. What is it you want to talk about?"

"They listen in their sleep," he said.

We went out the back door to keep from waking Heinrich. I followed him along the pathway at the side of the house and down the steps to the driveway. His little car sat in the dark. He got behind the wheel and I slid in next to him, gathering up my bathrobe and feeling trapped in the limited space. The car held a smell like some dangerous vapor in the depths of a body-and-fender shop, a mixture of exhausted metal, flammable rags and scorched rubber. The upholstery was torn. In the glow of a streetlamp I saw wires dangling from the dash and the overhead fixture.

"I want you to have this, Jack."

"Have what?"

"I've had it for years. Now I want you to have it. Who knows if I'll ever see you folks again? What the hell. Who cares. Big deal."

You're giving me the car? I don't want the car. It's a terrible car."

"In your whole life as a man in today's world, have you ever owned a firearm?"

"No," I said.

"I figured. I said to myself here's the last man in America who doesn't own the means to defend himself."

He reached into a hole in the rear seat, coming out with a small dark object. He held it in the palm of his right hand.

"Take it, Jack."

"What is it?"

"Heft it around. Get the feel. It's loaded."

He passed it to me. Stupidly I said again, "What is it?" There was something unreal about the experience of holding a gun. I kept staring at it, wondering what Vernon's motive might be. Was he Death's dark messenger after all? A loaded weapon. How quickly it worked a change in me, numbing my hand even as I sat staring at the thing, not wishing to give it a name. Did Vernon mean to provoke thought, provide my life with a fresh design, a scheme, a shapeliness? I wanted to give it back.

"It's a little bitty thing but it shoots real bullets, which is all a man in your position can rightly ask of a firearm. Don't worry, Jack. It can't be traced."

"Why would anyone want to trace it?"

"I feel like if you give someone a loaded gun, you ought to supply the particulars. This here is a 25-caliber Zumwalt automatic. German-made. It doesn't have the stopping power of a heavy-barreled weapon but you're not going out there to face down a rhino, are you?"

"That's the point. What am I going out there to face down? Why do I need this thing?"

"Don't call it a thing. Respect it, Jack. It's a well-designed weapon. Practical, lightweight, easy to conceal. Get to know your handgun. It's only a question of time as to when you'll want to use it."

"When will I want to use it?"

"Do we live on the same planet? What century is this? Look how easy I got into your backyard. I pry open a window and I'm in the house. I could have been a professional burglar, an escaped con, one of those drifters with a skimpy beard. A wandering killer type that follows the sun. A weekend mass murderer with an office job. Take your choice."

"Maybe you need a gun where you live. Take it back. We don't want it."

"I got myself a combat magnum parked near my bed. I hate to tell you what mischief it can cause with the placement of a man's features."

He gave me a canny look. I resumed staring at the gun. It occurred to me that this was the ultimate device for determining one's competence in the world. I bounced it in the palm of my hand, sniffed the steely muzzle. What does it mean to a person, beyond his sense of competence and well-being and personal worth, to carry a lethal weapon, to handle it well, be ready and willing to use it? A concealed lethal weapon. It was a secret, it was a second life, a second self, a dream, a spell, a plot, a delirium.

German-made.

"Don't tell Babette. She'd get real put out if she knew you were harboring a firearm."

"I don't want it, Vern. Take it back."

"Don't put it just anywhere neither. A kid gets ahold of it, you have an immediate situation. Be smart. Think about where to put it so it'll be right there at the time. Figure out your field of fire beforehand. If you have an intruder situation, where will he enter, how will he approach the valuables? If you have a mental, where is he going to come at you from? Mentals are unpredictable because they don't know themselves what they're doing. They approach from wherever, from a tree limb, a branch. Think about putting jagged glass on your window ledges. Learn dropping to the floor fast."

"We don't want guns in our little town."

"Be smart for once in your life," he told me in the dark car. "It's not what you want that matters."

Early the next day a crew came to fix the street. Vernon was out there at once, watching them jackhammer and haul the asphalt, staying close to them as they leveled the smoking pitch. When the workmen left, his visit seemed to end, collapsed into its own fading momentum. We began to see a blank space where Vernon stood. He regarded us from a prudent distance, as if we were strangers with secret resentments. An indefinable fatigue collected around our efforts to converse.

Out on the sidewalk, Babette held him and wept. For his departure he'd shaved, washed the car, put a blue bandanna around his neck. She could not seem to get enough of crying. She looked into his face and cried. She cried embracing him. She gave him a Styrofoam hamper full of sandwiches, chicken and coffee, and she cried as he set it down amid the gouged-out seat stuffing and slashed upholstery.

"She's a good girl," he told me grimly.

In the driver's seat he ran his fingers through his ducktail, checking himself in the rearview mirror. Then he coughed a while, giving us one more episode of lashing phlegm. Babette wept anew. We leaned toward the window on the passenger's side, watching him hunch around into his driving posture, setting himself casually between the door and the seat, his left arm hanging out the window.

"Don't worry about me," he said. "The little limp means nothing. People my age limp. A limp is a natural thing at a certain age. Forget the cough. It's healthy to cough. You move the stuff around. The stuff can't harm you as long as it doesn't settle in one spot and stay there for years. So the cough's all right. So is the insomnia. The insomnia's all right. What do I gain by sleeping? You reach an age when every minute of sleep is one less minute to do useful things. To cough or limp. Never mind the women. The women are all right. We rent a cassette and have some sex. It pumps blood to the heart. Forget the cigarettes. I like to tell myself I'm getting away with something. Let the Mormons quit smoking. They'll die of something just as bad. The money's no problem. I'm all set incomewise. Zero pensions, zero savings, zero stocks and bonds. So you don't have to worry about that. That's all taken care of. Never mind the teeth. The teeth are all right. The looser they are, the more you can wobble them with your tongue. It gives the tongue something to do. Don't worry about the shakes. Everybody gets the shakes now and then. It's only the left hand anyway. The way to enjoy the shakes is pretend it's somebody else's hand. Never mind the sudden and unexplained weight loss. There's no point eating what you can't see. Don't worry about the eyes. The eyes can't get any worse than they are now. Forget the mind completely. The mind goes before the body. That's the way it's supposed to be. So don't worry about the mind. The mind is all right. Worry about the car. The steering's all awry. The brakes were recalled three times. The hood shoots up on pothole terrain."

Deadpan. Babette thought this last part was funny. The part about the car. I stood there amazed, watching her walk in little circles of hilarity, weak-kneed, shambling, all her fears and defenses adrift in the sly history of his voice.

34

The time of spiders arrived. Spiders in high corners of rooms. Cocoons wrapped in spiderwork. Silvery dancing strands that seemed the pure play of light, light as evanescent news, ideas borne on light. The voice upstairs said: "Now watch this. Joanie is trying to snap Ralph's patella with a *bushido* stun kick. She makes contact, he crumples, she runs."

Denise passed word to Babette that Steffie was routinely examining her chest for lumps. Babette told me.

Murray and I extended the range of our contemplative walks. In town one day he went into small embarrassed raptures over diagonal parking. There was a charm and a native sense to the rows of slanted vehicles. This form of parking was an indispensable part of the American townscape, even when the cars were foreign-made. The arrangement was not only practical but avoided confrontation, the sexual assault motif of front-to-back parking in teeming city streets.

Murray says it is possible to be homesick for a place even when you are there.

The two-story world of an ordinary main street. Modest, sensible, commercial in an unhurried way, a prewar way, with prewar traces of architectural detail surviving in the upper stories, in copper cornices and leaded windows, in the amphora frieze above the dime-store entrance.

It made me think of the Law of Ruins.

I told Murray that Albert Speer wanted to build structures that would decay gloriously, impressively, like Roman ruins. No rusty hulks or gnarled steel slums. He knew that Hitler would be in favor of anything that might astonish posterity. He did a drawing of a Reich structure that was to be built of special materials, allowing it to crumble romantically—a drawing of fallen walls, half columns furled in wisteria. The ruin is built into the creation, I said, which shows a certain nostalgia behind the power principle, or a tendency to organize the longings of future generations.

Murray said, "I don't trust anybody's nostalgia but my own. Nostalgia is a product of dissatisfaction and rage. It's a settling of grievances between the present and the past. The more powerful the nostalgia, the closer you come to violence. War is the form nostalgia takes when men are hard-pressed to say something good about their country."

A humid spell of weather. I opened the refrigerator, peered into the freezer compartment. A strange crackling sound came off the plastic food wrap, the snug covering for half eaten things, the Ziploc sacks of livers and ribs, all gleaming with sleety crystals. A cold dry sizzle. A sound like some element breaking down, resolving itself into Freon vapors. An eerie static, insistent but near subliminal, that made me think of wintering souls, some form of dormant life approaching the threshold of perception.

No one was around. I walked across the kitchen, opened the compactor drawer and looked inside the trash bag. An oozing cube of semi-mangled cans, clothes hangers, animal bones and other refuse. The bottles were broken, the cartons flat. Product colors were undiminished in brightness and intensity. Fats, juices and heavy sludges seeped through layers of pressed vegetable matter. I felt like an archaeologist about to sift through a finding of tool fragments and assorted cave trash. It was about ten days since Denise had compacted the Dylar. That particular round of garbage had almost certainly been taken outside and collected by now. Even if it hadn't, the tablets had surely been demolished by the compactor ram.

These facts were helpful in my efforts to believe that I was merely passing time, casually thumbing through the garbage.

I unfolded the bag cuffs, released the latch and lifted out the bag. The full stench hit me with shocking force. Was this ours? Did it belong to us? Had we created it? I took the bag out to the garage and emptied it. The compressed bulk sat there like an ironic modern sculpture, massive, squat, mocking. I jabbed at it with the butt end of a rake and then spread the material over the concrete floor. I picked through it item by item, mass by shapeless mass, wondering why I felt guilty, a violator of privacy, uncovering intimate and perhaps shameful secrets. It was hard not to be distracted by some of the things they'd chosen to submit to the Juggernaut appliance. But why did I feel like a household spy? Is garbage so private? Does it glow at the core with personal heat, with signs of one's deepest nature, clues to secret yearnings, humiliating flaws? What habits, fetishes, addictions, inclinations? What solitary acts, behavioral ruts? I found crayon drawings of a figure with full breasts and male genitals. There was a long piece of twine that contained a series of knots and loops. It seemed at first a random construction. Looking more closely I thought I detected a complex relationship between the size of the loops, the degree of the knots (single or double) and the intervals between knots with loops and freestanding knots. Some kind of occult geometry or symbolic festoon of obsessions. I found a banana skin with a tampon inside. Was this the dark underside of consumer consciousness? I came across a horrible clotted mass of hair, soap, ear swabs, crushed roaches, flip-top rings, sterile pads smeared with pus and bacon fat, strands of frayed dental floss, fragments of ballpoint refills, toothpicks still displaying bits of impaled food. There was a pair of shredded undershorts with lipstick markings, perhaps a memento of the Grayview Motel.

But no sign anywhere of a shattered amber vial or the remains of those saucer-shaped tablets. It didn't matter. I would face whatever had to be faced without chemical assistance. Babette had said Dylar was fool's gold. She was right, Winnie Richards was right, Denise was right. They were my friends and they were right.

I decided to take another physical. When the results were in, I went to see Dr. Chakravarty in his little office in the medical building. He sat there reading the printout, a man with a puffy face and shadowy eyes, his long hands set flat on the desk, his head wagging slightly.

"Here you are again, Mr. Gladney. We see you so often these

days. How nice it is to find a patient who regards his status seriously."

"What status?"

"His status as a patient. People tend to forget they are patients. Once they leave the doctor's office or the hospital, they simply put it out of their minds. But you are all permanent patients, like it or not. I am the doctor, you the patient. Doctor doesn't cease being doctor at close of day. Neither should patient. People expect doctor to go about things with the utmost seriousness, skill and experience. But what about patient? How professional is he?"

He did not look up from the printout as he said these things in his meticulous singsong.

"I don't think I like your potassium very much at all," he went on. "Look here. A bracketed number with computerized stars."

"What does that mean?"

"There's no point your knowing at this stage."

"How was my potassium last time?"

"Quite average in fact. But perhaps this is a false elevation. We are dealing with whole blood. There is the question of a gel barrier. Do you know what this means?"

"No."

"There isn't time to explain. We have true elevation and false elevations. This is all you have to know."

"Exactly how elevated is my potassium?"

"It has gone through the roof, evidently."

"What might this be a sign of?"

"It could mean nothing, it could mean a very great deal indeed."

"How great?"

"Now we are getting into semantics," he said.

"What I'm trying to get at is could this potassium be an indication of some condition just beginning to manifest itself, some condition caused perhaps by an ingestion, an exposure, an involuntary spillage-intake, some substance in the air or the rain?"

"Have you in fact come into contact with such a substance?"

"No," I said.

"Are you sure?"

"Positive. Why, do the numbers show some sign of possible exposure?"

"If you haven't been exposed, then they couldn't very well show a sign, could they?"

"Then we agree," I said.

"Tell me this, Mr. Gladney, in all honesty. How do you feel?"

"To the best of my knowledge, I feel very well. First-rate. I feel better than I have in years, relatively speaking."

"What do you mean, relatively speaking?"

"Given the fact I'm older now."

He looked at me carefully. He seemed to be trying to stare me down. Then he made a note on my record. I might have been a child facing the school principal over a series of unexcused absences.

I said, "How can we tell whether the elevation is true or false?"

"I will send you to Glassboro for further tests. Would you like that? There is a brand-new facility called Autumn Harvest Farms. They have gleaming new equipment. You won't be disappointed, wait and see. It gleams, absolutely."

"All right. But is potassium the only thing we have to watch?"

"The less you know, the better. Go to Glassboro. Tell them to delve thoroughly. No stone unturned. Tell them to send you back to me with sealed results. I will analyze them down to the smallest detail. I will absolutely pick them apart. They have the know-how at Harvest Farms, the most delicate of instruments, I promise you. The best of third-world technicians, the latest procedures."

His bright smile hung there like a peach on a tree.

"Together, as doctor and patient, we can do things that neither of us could do separately. There is not enough emphasis on prevention. An ounce of prevention, goes the saying. Is this a proverb or a maxim? Surely professor can tell us."

"I'll need time to think about it."

"In any case, prevention is the thing, isn't it? I've just seen the latest issue of *American Mortician*. Quite a shocking picture. The industry is barely adequate to accommodating the vast numbers of dead."

Babette was right. He spoke English beautifully. I went home and started throwing things away. I threw away fishing lures, dead tennis balls, torn luggage. I ransacked the attic for old furniture, discarded lampshades, warped screens, bent curtain rods. I threw away picture frames, shoe trees, umbrella stands, wall brackets, highchairs and cribs, collapsible TV trays, beanbag chairs, broken turntables. I threw away shelf paper, faded stationery, manuscripts of articles I'd written, galley proofs of the same articles, the journals in which the articles were printed. The more things I threw away, the more I found. The house was a sepia maze of old and tired things. There was an immensity of things, an overburdening weight, a connection, a mortality. I stalked the rooms, flinging things into cardboard boxes. Plastic electric fans, burnt-out toasters, *Star Trek* needlepoints. It took well over an hour to get everything down to the sidewalk. No one helped me. I didn't want help or company or human understanding. I just wanted to get the stuff out of the house. I sat on the front steps alone, waiting for a sense of ease and peace to settle in the air around me.

A woman passing on the street said, "A decongestant, an antihistamine, a cough suppressant, a pain reliever."

35

Babette could not get enough of talk radio.

"I hate my face," a woman said. "This is an ongoing problem with me for years. Of all the faces you could have given me, lookswise, this one has got to be the worst. But how can I not look? Even if you took all my mirrors away, I would still find a way to look. How can I not look on the one hand? But I hate it on the other. In other words I still look. Because whose face is it, obviously? What do I do, forget it's there, pretend it's someone else's? What I'm trying to do with this call, Mel, is find other people who have a problem accepting their face. Here are some questions to get us started. What did you look like before you were born? What will you look like in the afterlife, regardless of race or color?"

Babette wore her sweatsuit almost all the time. It was a plain gray outfit, loose and drooping. She cooked in it, drove the kids to school, wore it to the hardware store and the stationer's. I thought about it for a while, decided there was nothing excessively odd in this, nothing to worry about, no reason to believe she was sinking into apathy and despair.

"How do you feel?" I said. "Tell the truth."

"What is the truth? I'm spending more time with Wilder. Wilder helps me get by."

"I depend on you to be the healthy outgoing former Babette. I need this as badly as you do, if not more."

"What is need? We all need. Where is the uniqueness in this?"

"Are you feeling basically the same?"

"You mean am I sick unto death? The fear hasn't gone, Jack."

"We have to stay active."

"Active helps but Wilder helps more."

"Is it my imagination," I said, "or is he talking less than ever?"

"There's enough talk. What is talk? I don't want him to talk. The less he talks, the better."

"Denise worries about you."

"Who?"

"Denise."

"Talk is radio," she said.

Denise would not let her mother go running unless she promised to apply layers of sunscreen gel. The girl would follow her out of the house to dash a final glob of lotion across the back of Babette's neck, then stand on her toes to stroke it evenly in. She tried to cover every exposed spot. The brows, the lids. They had bitter arguments about the need for this. Denise said the sun was a risk to a fair-skinned person. Her mother claimed the whole business was publicity for disease.

"Besides, I'm a runner," she said. "A runner by definition is less likely to be struck by damaging rays than a standing or walking figure."

Denise spun in my direction, arms flung out, her body beseeching me to set the woman straight.

"The worst rays are direct," Babette said. "This means the faster a person is moving, the more likely she is to receive only partial hits, glancing rays, deflections."

Denise let her mouth fall open, bent her body at the knees. In truth I wasn't sure her mother was wrong.

"It is all a corporate tie-in," Babette said in summary. "The sunscreen, the marketing, the fear, the disease. You can't have one without the other."

I took Heinrich and his snake-handling buddy, Orest Mercator, out to the commercial strip for dinner. It was four in the afternoon, the time of day when Orest's training schedule called for his main meal. At his request we went to Vincent's Casa Mario, a blockhouse structure with slit windows that seemed part of some coastal defense system.

I'd found myself thinking of Orest and his snakes and wanted a chance to talk to him further.

We sat in a blood-red booth. Orest gripped the tasseled menu with his chunky hands. His shoulders seemed broader than ever, the serious head partly submerged between them.

"How's the training going?" I said.

"I'm slowing it down a little. I don't want to peak too soon. I know how to take care of my body."

"Heinrich told me you sleep sitting up, to prepare for the cage."

"I perfected that. I'm doing different stuff now."

"Like what?"

"Loading up on carbohydrates."

"That's why we came here," Heinrich said.

"I load up a little more each day."

"It's because of the huge energy he'll be burning up in the cage, being alert, tensing himself when a mamba approaches, whatever."

We ordered pasta and water.

"Tell me, Orest. As you get closer and closer to the time, are you beginning to feel anxious?"

"What anxious? I just want to get in the cage. Sooner the better. This is what Orest Mercator is all about."

"You're not nervous? You don't think about what might happen?"

"He likes to be positive," Heinrich said. "This is the thing today with athletes. You don't dwell on the negative."

"Tell me this, then. What is the negative? What do you think of when you think of the negative?"

"Here's what I think. I'm nothing without the snakes. That's the only negative. The negative is if it doesn't come off, if the humane society doesn't let me in the cage. How can I be the best at what I do if they don't let me do it?"

I liked to watch Orest eat. He inhaled food according to aerodynamic principles. Pressure differences, intake velocities. He went at it silently and purposefully, loading up, centering himself, appearing to grow more self-important with each clump of starch that slid over his tongue.

"You know you can get bitten. We talked about it last time. Do you think about what happens after the fangs close on your wrist? Do you think about dying? This is what I want to know. Does death scare you? Does it haunt your thoughts? Let me put my cards on the table, Orest. Are you afraid to die? Do you experience fear? Does fear make you tremble or sweat? Do you feel a shadow fall across the room when you think of the cage, the snakes, the fangs?"

"What did I read just the other day? There are more people dead today than in the rest of world history put together. What's one extra? I'd just as soon die while I'm trying to put Orest Mercator's name in the record book."

I looked at my son. I said, "Is he trying to tell us there are more people dying in this twenty-four-hour period than in the rest of human history up to now?"

"He's saying the dead are greater today than ever before, combined."

"What dead? Define the dead."

"He's saying people now dead."

"What do you mean, now dead? Everybody who's dead is now dead."

"He's saying people in graves. The known dead. Those you can count."

I was listening intently, trying to grasp what they meant. A second plate of food came for Orest.

"But people sometimes stay in graves for hundreds of years. Is he saying there are more dead people in graves than anywhere else?"

"It depends on what you mean by anywhere else."

"I don't know what I mean. The drowned. The blown-to-bits."

"There are more dead now than ever before. That's all he's saying."

I looked at him a while longer. Then I turned to Orest.

"You are intentionally facing death. You are setting out to do exactly what people spend their lives trying not to do. Die. I want to know why."

"My trainer says, 'Breathe, don't think.' He says, 'Be a snake and you'll know the stillness of a snake.'"

"He has a trainer now," Heinrich said.

"He's a Sunny Moslem," Orest said.

"Iron City has some Sunnies out near the airport."

"The Sunnies are mostly Korean. Except mine's an Arab, I think."

I said, "Don't you mean the Moonies are mostly Korean?"

"He's a Sunny," Orest said.

"But it's the Moonies who are mostly Korean. Except they're not, of course. It's only the leadership."

They thought about this. I watched Orest eat. I watched him pitchfork the spaghetti down his gullet. The serious head sat motionless, an entryway for the food that flew off the mechanical fork. What purpose he conveyed, what sense of a fixed course of action pursued absolutely. If each of us is the center of his or her existence, Orest seemed intent on enlarging the center, making it everything. Is this what athletes do, occupy the self more fully? It's possible we envy them for a prowess that has little to do with sport. In building toward a danger, they escape it in some deeper sense, they dwell in some angelic scan, able to leap free of everyday dying. But was Orest an athlete? He would do nothing but sit—sit for sixty-seven days in a glass cage, waiting to be publicly bitten.

"You will not be able to defend yourself," I said. "Not only that but you will be in a cage with the most slimy, feared and repulsive creatures on earth. Snakes. People have nightmares about snakes. Crawling slithering cold-blooded egg-laying vertebrates. People go to psychiatrists. Snakes have a special slimy place in our collective unconscious. And you are voluntarily getting into an enclosed space with thirty or forty of the most venomous snakes in the world."

"What slimy? They're not slimy."

"The famous sliminess is a myth," Heinrich said. "He's getting into a cage with Gaboon vipers with two-inch fangs. Maybe a dozen mambas. The mamba happens to be the fastest-moving land snake in the world. Isn't sliminess a little besides the point?"

"That's my argument exactly. Fangs. Snakebite. Fifty thousand people a year die of snakebite. It was on television last night."

"Everything was on television last night," Orest said.

I admired the reply. I guess I admired him too. He was creating an imperial self out of some tabloid aspiration. He would train relentlessly, speak of himself in the third person, load up on carbohydrates. His trainer was always there, his friends drawn to the aura of inspired risk. He would grow in life-strength as he neared the time.

"His trainer is teaching him how to breathe in the old way, the Sunny Moslem way. A snake is one thing. A person can be a thousand things."

"Be a snake," Orest said.

"People are getting interested," Heinrich said. "It's like it's starting to build. Like he's really going to do it. Like they believe him now. The total package."

If the self is death, how can it also be stronger than death?

I called for the check. Extraneous flashes of Mr. Gray. A drizzling image in gray shorts and socks. I lifted several bills from my wallet, rubbing hard with my fingers to make sure there weren't others stuck to them. In the motel mirror was my full-length wife, white-bodied, full-bosomed, pink-kneed, stub-toed, wearing only peppermint legwarmers, like a sophomore leading cheers at an orgy.

When we got home, I found her ironing in the bedroom.

"What are you doing?" I said.

"Listening to the radio. Except it just went off."

"If you thought we were finished with Mr. Gray, it's time to bring you up to date."

"Are we talking about Mr. Gray the composite or Mr. Gray the individual? It makes all the difference."

"It certainly does. Denise compacted the pills."

"Does that mean we're all through with the composite?"

"I don't know what it means."

"Does it mean you've turned your male attention to the individual in the motel?"

"I didn't say that."

"You don't have to say it. You're a male. A male follows the path of homicidal rage. It is the biological path. The path of plain dumb blind male biology."

"How smug, ironing handkerchiefs."

"Jack, when you die, I will just fall to the floor and stay there. Eventually, maybe, after a very long time, they will find me crouching in the dark, a woman without speech or gesture. But in the meantime I will not help you find this man or his medication."

"The eternal wisdom of those who iron and sew."

"Ask yourself what it is you want more, to ease your ancient fear or to revenge your childish dopey injured male pride."

I went down the hall to help Steffie finish packing. A sports announcer said: "They're not booing—they're saying, 'Bruce, Bruce.'" Denise and Wilder were in there with her. I gathered from the veiled atmosphere that Denise had been giving confidential advice on visits to distant parents. Steffie's flight would originate in Boston and make two stops between Iron City and Mexico City but she wouldn't have to change planes, so the situation seemed manageable.

"How do I know I'll recognize my mother?"

"You saw her last year," I said. "You liked her."

"What if she refuses to send me back?"

"We have Denise to thank for that idea, don't we? Thank you, Denise. Don't worry. She'll send you back."

"What if she doesn't?" Denise said. "It happens, you know."

"It won't happen this time."

"You'll have to kidnap her back."

"That won't be necessary."

"What if it is?" Steffie said.

"Would you do it?" Denise said.

"It won't happen in a million years."

"It happens all the time," she said. "One parent takes the child, the other parent hires kidnappers to get her back."

"What if she keeps me?" Steffie said. "What will you do?"

"He'll have to send people to Mexico. That's the only thing he can do."

"But will he do it?" she said.

"Your mother knows she can't keep you," I said. "She travels all the time. It's out of the question."

"Don't worry," Denise told her. "No matter what he says now, he'll get you back when the time comes."

Steffie looked at me with deep interest and curiosity. I told her I would travel to Mexico myself and do whatever had to be done to get her back here. She looked at Denise.

"It's better to hire people," the older girl said helpfully. "That way you have someone who's done it before."

Babette came in and picked up Wilder.

"There you are," she said. "We're going to the airport with Steffie. Yes we are. Yes yes."

"Bruce, Bruce."

The next day there was an evacuation for noxious odor. SIMUVAC vehicles were everywhere. Men in Mylex suits patrolled the streets, many of them carrying instruments to measure harm. The consulting firm that conceived the evacuation gathered a small group of computer-screened volunteers in a police van in the supermarket parking lot. There was half an hour of self-induced gagging and vomiting. The episode was recorded on videotape and sent somewhere for analysis.

Three days later an actual noxious odor drifted across the river. A pause, a careful thoughtfulness, seemed to settle on the town. Traffic moved more slowly, drivers were exceedingly polite. There was no sign of official action, no jitneys or ambulettes painted in primary colors. People avoided looking at each other directly. An irritating sting in the nostrils, a taste of copper on the tongue. As time passed, the will to do nothing seemed to deepen, to fix itself firmly. There were those who denied they smelled anything at all. It is always that way with odors. There were those who professed not to see the irony of their inaction. They'd taken part in the

SIMUVAC exercise but were reluctant to flee now. There were those who wondered what caused the odor, those who looked worried, those who said the absence of technical personnel meant there was nothing to worry about. Our eyes began to water.

About three hours after we'd first become aware of it, the vapor suddenly lifted, saving us from our formal deliberations.

36

Now and then I thought of the Zumwalt automatic hidden in the bedroom.

The time of dangling insects arrived. White houses with caterpillars dangling from the eaves. White stones in driveways. You can walk at night down the middle of the street and hear women talking on the telephone. Warmer weather produces voices in the dark. They are talking about their adolescent sons. How big, how fast. The sons are almost frightening. The quantities they eat. The way they loom in doorways. These are the days that are full of wormy bugs. They are in the grass, stuck to the siding, hanging in the air, hanging from the trees and eaves, stuck to the window screens. The women talk long-distance to the grandparents of the growing boys. They share the Trimline phone, beamish old folks in hand-knit sweaters on fixed incomes.

What happens to them when the commercial ends?

I got a call myself one night. The operator said, "There's a Mother Devi that wishes to talk collect to a Jack Gladney. Do you accept?"

"Hello, Janet. What do you want?"

"Just to say hello. To ask how you are. We haven't talked in ages."

"Talked?"

"Swami wants to know if our son is coming to the ashram this summer."

"Our son?"

"Yours, mine and his. Swami regards the children of his followers as his children."

"I sent a daughter to Mexico last week. When she gets back, I'll be ready to talk about the son."

"Swami says Montana will be good for the boy. He will grow out, fill out. These are his touchy years."

"Why are you calling? Seriously."

"Just to greet you, Jack. We greet each other here."

"Is he one of those whimsical swamis with a snow-white beard? Sort of fun to look at?"

"We're serious people here. The cycle of history has but four ages. We happen to be in the last of these. There is little time for whimsy."

Her tiny piping voice bounced down to me from a hollow ball in geosynchronous orbit.

"If Heinrich wants to visit you this summer, it's all right with me. Let him ride horses, fish for trout. But I don't want him getting involved in something personal and intense, like religion. There's already been some kidnap talk around here. People are edgy."

"The last age is the Age of Darkness."

"Fine. Now tell me what you want."

"Nothing. I have everything. Peace of mind, purpose, true fellowship. I only wish to greet you. I greet you, Jack. I miss you. I miss your voice. I only wish to talk a while, pass a moment or two in friendly reminiscence."

I hung up and went for a walk. The women were in their lighted homes, talking on the phone. Did swami have twinkling eyes? Would he be able to answer the boy's questions where I had failed, provide assurances where I had incited bickering and debate? How final is the Age of Darkness? Does it mean supreme destruction, a night that swallows existence so completely that I am cured of my own lonely dying? I listened to the women talk. All sound, all souls.

When I got home I found Babette in her sweatsuit by the bedroom window, staring into the night.

Delegates to the Hitler conference began arriving. About ninety Hitler scholars would spend the three days of the conference attending lectures, appearing on panels, going to movies. They would wander the campus with their names lettered in gothic type on laminated tags pinned to their lapels. They would exchange Hitler gossip, spread the usual sensational rumors about the last days in the *führerbunker*.

It was interesting to see how closely they resembled each other despite the wide diversity of national and regional backgrounds. They were cheerful and eager, given to spitting when they laughed, given to outdated dress, homeliness, punctuality. They seemed to have a taste for sweets.

I welcomed them in the starkly modern chapel. I spoke in German, from notes, for five minutes. I talked mainly about Hitler's mother, brother and dog. His dog's name was Wolf. This word is the same in English and German. Most of the words I used in my address were the same or nearly the same in both languages. I'd spent days with the dictionary, compiling lists of such words. My remarks were necessarily disjointed and odd. I made many references to Wolf, many more to the mother and the brother, a few to shoes and socks, a few to jazz, beer and baseball. Of course there was Hitler himself. I spoke the name often, hoping it would overpower my insecure sentence structure.

The rest of the time I tried to avoid the Germans in the group. Even in my black gown and dark glasses, with my name in Nazi typeface over my heart, I felt feeble in their presence, death-prone, listening to them produce their guttural sounds, their words, their heavy metal. They told Hitler jokes and played pinochle. All I could do was mutter a random monosyllable, rock with empty laughter. I spent a lot of time in my office, hiding.

Whenever I remembered the gun, lurking in a stack of undershirts like a tropical insect, I felt a small intense sensation pass through me. Whether pleasurable or fearful I wasn't sure. I knew it mainly as a childhood moment, the profound stir of secret-keeping.

What a sly device a handgun is. One so small in particular. An intimate and cunning thing, a secret history of the man who owns it. I recalled how I'd felt some days earlier, trying to find the Dylar. Like someone spying on the family garbage. Was I immersing myself, little by little, in a secret life? Did I think it was my last defense against the ruin worked out for me so casually by the force or nonforce, the principle or power or chaos that determines such things? Perhaps I was beginning to understand my ex-wives and their ties to intelligence.

The Hitler scholars assembled, wandered, ate voraciously, laughed through oversized teeth. I sat at my desk in the dark, thinking of secrets. Are secrets a tunnel to a dreamworld where you control events?

In the evening I sped out to the airport to meet my daughter's plane. She was excited and happy, wore Mexican things. She said the people who sent her mother books to review wouldn't leave her alone. Dana was getting big thick novels every day, writing reviews which she microfilmed and sent to a secret archive. She complained of jangled nerves, periods of deep spiritual fatigue. She told Steffie she was thinking of coming in from the cold.

In the morning I sped out to Glassboro to take the further tests my doctor had advised, at Autumn Harvest Farms. The seriousness of such an occasion is directly proportionate to the number of bodily emissions you are asked to cull for analysis. I carried with me several specimen bottles, each containing some melancholy waste or secretion. Alone in the glove compartment rode an ominous plastic locket, which I'd reverently enclosed in three interlocking Baggies, successively twist-tied. Here was a daub of the most solemn waste of all, certain to be looked upon by the technicians on duty with the mingled deference, awe and dread we have come to associate with exotic religions of the world.

But first I had to find the place. It turned out to be a functional pale brick building, one story, with slab floors and bright lighting. Why would such a place be called Autumn Harvest Farms? Was this an attempt to balance the heartlessness of their gleaming precision equipment? Would a quaint name fool us into thinking we live in pre-cancerous times? What kind of condition might we expect to have diagnosed in a facility called Autumn Harvest Farms? Whooping cough, croup? A touch of the grippe? Familiar old farmhouse miseries calling for bed rest, a deep chest massage with soothing Vicks VapoRub. Would someone read to us from *David Copperfield*?

I had misgivings. They took my samples away, sat me down at a computer console. In response to questions on the screen I tapped out the story of my life and death, little by little, each response eliciting further questions in an unforgiving progression of sets and subsets. I lied three times. They gave me a loose-fitting garment and a wristband ID. They sent me down narrow corridors for measuring and weighing, for blood-testing, brain-graphing, the recording of currents traversing my heart. They scanned and probed in room after room, each cubicle appearing slightly smaller than the one before it, more harshly lighted, emptier of human furnishings. Always a new technician. Always faceless fellow patients in the mazelike halls, crossing from room to room, identically gowned. No one said hello. They attached me to a seesaw device, turned me upside down and let me hang for sixty seconds. A printout emerged from a device nearby. They put me on a treadmill and told me to run, run. Instruments were strapped to my thighs, electrodes planted on my chest. They inserted me in an imaging block, some kind of computerized scanner. Someone sat typing at a console, transmitting a message to the machine that would make my body transparent. I heard magnetic winds, saw flashes of northern light. People crossed the hall like wandering souls, holding their urine aloft in pale beakers. I stood in a room the size of a closet. They told me to hold one finger in front of my face, close my left eye. The panel slid shut, a white light flashed. They were trying to help me, to save me.

Eventually, dressed again, I sat across a desk from a nervous young man in a white smock. He studied my file, mumbling something about being new at this. I was surprised to find that this fact did not upset me. I think I was even relieved.

"How long before the results are in?"

"The results are in," he said.

"I thought we were here for a general discussion. The human

part. What the machines can't detect. In two or three days the actual numbers would be ready."

"The numbers are ready."

"I'm not sure I'm ready. All those gleaming devices are a little unsettling. I could easily imagine a perfectly healthy person being made ill just taking these tests."

"Why should anyone be made ill? These are the most accurate test devices anywhere. We have sophisticated computers to analyze the data. This equipment saves lives. Believe me, I've seen it happen. We have equipment that works better than the latest X-ray machine or CAT scanner. We can see more deeply, more accurately."

He seemed to be gaining confidence. He was a mild-eyed fellow with a poor complexion and reminded me of the boys at the supermarket who stand at the end of the checkout counter bagging merchandise.

"Here's how we usually start," he said. "I ask questions based on the printout and then you answer to the best of your ability. When we're all finished, I give you the printout in a sealed envelope and you take it to your doctor for a paid visit."

"Good."

"Good. We usually start by asking how do you feel."

"Based on the printout?"

"Just how do you feel," he said in a mild voice.

"In my own mind, in real terms, I feel relatively sound, pending confirmation."

"We usually go on to tired. Have you recently been feeling tired?"

"What do people usually say?"

"Mild fatigue is a popular answer."

"I could say exactly that and be convinced in my own mind it's a fair and accurate description."

He seemed satisfied with the reply and made a bold notation on the page in front of him.

"What about appetite?" he said.

"I could go either way on that."

"That's more or less how I could go, based on the printout."

"In other words you're saying sometimes I have appetitive reinforcement, sometimes I don't."

"Are you telling me or asking me?"

"It depends on what the numbers say."

"Then we agree."

"Good."

"Good," he said. "Now what about sleep? We usually do sleep before we ask the person if they'd like some decaf or tea. We don't provide sugar."

"Do you get a lot of people who have trouble sleeping?"

"Only in the last stages."

"The last stages of sleep? Do you mean they wake up early in the morning and can't get back to sleep?"

"The last stages of life."

"That's what I thought. Good. The only thing I have is some low threshold animation."

"Good."

"I get a little restless. Who doesn't?"

"Toss and turn?"

"Toss," I said.

"Good."

"Good."

He made some notes. It seemed to be going well. I was heartened to see how well it was going. I turned down his offer of tea, which seemed to please him. We were moving right along.

"Here's where we ask about smoking."

"That's easy. The answer is no. And it's not a matter of having stopped five or ten years ago. I've never smoked. Even when I was a teenager. Never tried it. Never saw the need."

"That's always a plus."

I felt tremendously reassured and grateful.

"We're moving right along, aren't we?"

"Some people like to drag it out," he said. "They get interested in their own condition. It becomes almost like a hobby."

"Who needs nicotine? Not only that, I rarely drink coffee and certainly never with caffeine. Can't understand what people see in all this artificial stimulation. I get high just walking in the woods."

"No caffeine always helps."

Yes, I thought. Reward my virture. Give me life.

"Then there's milk," I said. "People aren't happy with the caffeine and the sugar. They want the milk too. All those fatty acids. Haven't touched milk since I was a kid. Haven't touched heavy cream. Eat bland foods. Rarely touch hard liquor. Never knew what the fuss was all about. Water. That's my beverage. A man can trust a glass of water."

I waited for him to tell me I was adding years to my life.

"Speaking of water," he said, "have you ever been exposed to industrial contaminants?"

"What?"

"Toxic material in the air or water."

"Is this what you usually ask after the cigarettes?"

"It's not a scheduled question."

"You mean do I work with a substance like asbestos? Absolutely not. I'm a teacher. Teaching is my life. I've spent my life on a college campus. Where does asbestos fit into this?"

"Have you ever heard of Nyodene Derivative?"

"Should I have, based on the printout?"

"There are traces in your bloodstream."

"How can that be if I've never heard of it?"

"The magnetic scanner says it's there. I'm looking at bracketed numbers with little stars."

"Are you saying the printout shows the first ambiguous signs of a barely perceptible condition deriving from minimal acceptable spillage exposure?"

Why was I speaking in this stilted fashion?

"The magnetic scanner is pretty clear," he said.

What had happened to our tacit agreement to advance smartly through the program without time-consuming and controversial delving?

"What happens when someone has traces of this material in his or her blood?"

"They get a nebulous mass," he said.

"But I thought no one knew for sure what Nyodene D. did to humans. Rats, yes."

"You just told me you'd never heard of it. How do you know what it does or doesn't do?"

He had me there. I felt I'd been tricked, carried along, taken for a fool.

"Knowledge changes every day," he said. "We have some conflicting data that says exposure to this substance can definitely lead to a mass."

His confidence was soaring.

"Good. Let's get on to the next topic. I'm in something of a hurry."

"This is where I hand over the sealed envelope."

"Is exercise next? The answer is none. Hate it, refuse to do it."

"Good. I am handing over the envelope."

"What is a nebulous mass, just out of idle curiosity?"

"A possible growth in the body."

"And it's called nebulous because you can't get a clear picture of it."

"We get very clear pictures. The imaging block takes the clearest pictures humanly possible. It's called a nebulous mass because it has no definite shape, form or limits."

"What can it do in terms of worst-case scenario contingencies?"

"Cause a person to die."

"Speak English, for God's sake. I despise this modern jargon."

He took insults well. The angrier I got, the better he liked it. He radiated energy and health.

"Now is where I tell you to pay in the outer office."

"What about potassium? I came here in the first place because my potassium was way above normal limits."

"We don't do potassium."

"Good."

"Good. The last thing I'm supposed to tell you is take the

envelope to your doctor. Your doctor knows the symbols."

"So that's it then. Good."

"Good," he said.

I found myself shaking his hand warmly. Minutes later I was out on the street. A boy walked splay-footed across a public lawn, nudging a soccer ball before him. A second kid sat on the grass, taking off his socks by grabbing the heels and yanking. How literary, I thought peevishly. Streets thick with the details of impulsive life as the hero ponders the latest phase in his dying. It was a partially cloudy day with winds diminishing toward sunset.

That night I walked the streets of Blacksmith. The glow of blue-eyed TVs. The voices on the touch-tone phones. Far away the grandparents huddle in a chair, eagerly sharing the receiver as carrier waves modulate into audible signals. It is the voice of their grandson, the growing boy whose face appears in the snapshots set around the phone. Joy rushes to their eyes but it is misted over, infused with a sad and complex knowing. What is the youngster saying to them? His wretched complexion makes him unhappy? He wants to leave school and work full-time at Foodland, bagging groceries? He tells them he *likes* to bag groceries. It is the one thing in life he finds satisfying. Put the gallon jugs in first, square off the six-packs, double-bag the heavy merch. He does it well, he has the knack, he *sees* the items arranged in the bag before he touches a thing. It's like Zen, grampa. I snap out two bags, fit one inside the other. Don't bruise the fruit, watch the eggs, put the ice cream in a freezer bag. A thousand people pass me every day but no one ever sees me. I like it, gramma, it's totally unthreatening, it's how I want to spend my life. And so they listen sadly, loving him all the more, their faces pressed against the sleek Trimline, the white Princess in the bedroom, the plain brown Rotary in granddad's paneled basement hideaway. The old gentleman runs a hand through his thatch of white hair, the woman holds her folded specs against her face. Clouds race across the westering moon, the seasons change in somber montage, going deeper into winter stillness, a landscape of silence and ice.

Your doctor knows the symbols.

37

The long walk started at noon. I didn't know it would turn into a long walk. I thought it would be a miscellaneous meditation, Murray and Jack, half an hour's campus meander. But it became a major afternoon, a serious looping Socratic walk, with practical consequences.

I met Murray after his car crash seminar and we wandered along the fringes of the campus, past the cedar-shingled condominiums set in the trees in their familiar defensive posture—a cluster of dwellings blending so well with the environment that birds kept flying into the plate-glass windows.

"You're smoking a pipe," I said.

Murray smiled sneakily.

"It looks good. I like it. It works."

He lowered his eyes, smiling. The pipe had a long narrow stem and cubical bowl. It was pale brown and resembled a highly disciplined household implement, perhaps an Amish or Shaker antique. I wondered if he'd chosen it to match his somewhat severe chin whiskers. A tradition of stern virtue seemed to hover about his gestures and expressions.

"Why can't we be intelligent about death?" I said.

"It's obvious."

"It is?"

"Ivan Ilyich screamed for three days. That's about as intelligent as we get. Tolstoy himself struggled to understand. He feared it terribly."

"It's almost as though our fear is what brings it on. If we could learn not to be afraid, we could live forever."

"We talk ourselves into it. Is that what you mean?"

"I don't know what I mean. I only know I'm just going through the motions of living. I'm technically dead. My body is growing a nebulous mass. They track these things like satellites. All this as a result of a byproduct of insecticide. There's something artificial about my death. It's shallow, unfulfilling. I don't belong to the earth or sky. They ought to carve an aerosol can on my tombstone."

"Well said."

What did he mean, well said? I wanted him to argue with me, raise my dying to a higher level, make me feel better.

"Do you think it's unfair?" he said.

"Of course I do. Or is that a trite answer?"

He seemed to shrug.

"Look how I've lived. Has my life been a mad dash for pleasure? Have I been hellbent on self-destruction, using illegal drugs, driving fast cars, drinking to excess? A little dry sherry at faculty parties. I eat bland foods."

"No, you don't."

He puffed seriously on his pipe, his cheeks going hollow. We walked in silence for a while.

"Do you think your death is premature?" he said.

"Every death is premature. There's no scientific reason why we can't live a hundred and fifty years. Some people actually do it, according to a headline I saw at the supermarket."

"Do you think it's a sense of incompleteness that causes you the deepest regret? There are things you still hope to accomplish. Work to be done, intellectual challenges to be faced."

"The deepest regret is death. The only thing to face is death. This is all I think about. There's only one issue here. I want to live."

"From the Robert Wise film of the same name, with Susan Hayward as Barbara Graham, a convicted murderess. Aggressive jazz score by Johnny Mandel."

I looked at him.

"So you're saying, Jack, that death would be just as threatening even if you'd accomplished all you'd ever hoped to accomplish in your life and work."

"Are you crazy? Of course. That's an elitist idea. Would you ask a man who bags groceries if he fears death not because it is death but because there are still some interesting groceries he would like to bag?"

"Well said."

"This is death. I don't want it to tarry awhile so I can write a monograph. I want it to go away for seventy or eighty years."

"Your status as a doomed man lends your words a certain prestige and authority. I like that. As the time nears, I think you'll find that people will be eager to hear what you have to say. They will seek you out."

"Are you saying this is a wonderful opportunity for me to win friends?"

"I'm saying you can't let down the living by slipping into self-pity and despair. People will depend on you to be brave. What people look for in a dying friend is a stubborn kind of gravel-voiced nobility, a refusal to give in, with moments of indomitable humor. You're growing in prestige even as we speak. You're creating a hazy light about your own body. I have to like it."

We walked down the middle of a steep and winding street. There was no one around. The houses here were old and looming, set above narrow stone stairways in partial disrepair.

"Do you believe love is stronger than death?"

"Not in a million years."

"Good," he said. "Nothing is stronger than death. Do you believe the only people who fear death are those who are afraid of life?"

"That's crazy. Completely stupid."

"Right. We all fear death to some extent. Those who claim otherwise are lying to themselves. Shallow people."

"People with their nicknames on their license plates."

"Excellent, Jack. Do you believe life without death is somehow incomplete?"

"How could it be incomplete? Death is what makes it incomplete."

"Doesn't our knowledge of death make life more precious?"

"What good is a preciousness based on fear and anxiety? It's an anxious quivering thing."

"True. The most deeply precious things are those we feel secure about. A wife, a child. Does the specter of death make a child more precious?"

"No."

"No. There is no reason to believe life is more precious because it is fleeting. Here is a statement. A person has to be told he is going to die before he can begin to live life to the fullest. True or false?"

"False. Once your death is established, it becomes impossible to live a satisfying life."

"Would you prefer to know the exact date and time of your death?"

"Absolutely not. It's bad enough to fear the unknown. Faced with the unknown, we can pretend it isn't there. Exact dates would drive many to suicide, if only to beat the system."

We crossed an old highway bridge, screened in, littered with sad and faded objects. We followed a footpath along a creek, approached the edge of the high school playing field. Women brought small children here to play in the long-jump pits.

"How do I get around it?" I said.

"You could put your faith in technology. It got you here, it can get you out. This is the whole point of technology. It creates an appetite for immortality on the one hand. It threatens universal extinction on the other. Technology is lust removed from nature."

"It is?"

"It's what we invented to conceal the terrible secret of our decaying bodies. But it's also life, isn't it? It prolongs life, it provides new organs for those that wear out. New devices, new techniques every day. Lasers, masers, ultrasound. Give yourself up to it, Jack. Believe in it. They'll insert you in a gleaming tube, irradiate your body with the basic stuff of the universe. Light, energy, dreams. God's own goodness."

"I don't think I want to see any doctors for a while, Murray, thanks."

"In that case you can always get around death by concentrating on the life beyond."

"How do I do that?"

"It's obvious. Read up on reincarnation, transmigration, hyperspace, the resurrection of the dead and so on. Some gorgeous systems have evolved from these beliefs. Study them."

"Do you believe in any of these things?"

"Millions of people have believed for thousands of years. Throw in with them. Belief in a second birth, a second life, is practically universal. This must mean something."

"But these gorgeous systems are all so different."

"Pick one you like."

"But you make it sound like a convenient fantasy, the worst kind of self-delusion."

Again he seemed to shrug. "Think of the great poetry, the music and dance and ritual that spring forth from our aspiring to a life beyond death. Maybe these things are justification enough for our hopes and dreams, although I wouldn't say that to a dying man."

He poked me with an elbow. We walked toward the commercial part of town. Murray paused, raised one foot behind him, reached back to knock some ashes from his pipe. Then he pocketed the thing expertly, inserting it bowl-first in his corduroy jacket.

"Seriously, you can find a great deal of long-range solace in the idea of an afterlife."

"But don't I have to believe? Don't I have to feel in my heart that there is something, genuinely, beyond this life, out there, looming, in the dark?"

"What do you think the afterlife is, a body of facts just waiting to be uncovered? Do you think the U.S. Air Force is secretly gathering data on the afterlife and keeping it under wraps because we're not mature enough to accept the findings? The findings would cause panic? No. I'll tell you what the afterlife is. It's a sweet and terribly touching idea. You can take it or leave it. In the meantime what you have to do is survive an assassination attempt. That would be an instant tonic. You would feel specially favored, you would grow in charisma."

"You said earlier that death was making me grow in charisma. Besides, who would want to kill me?"

Once more he shrugged. "Survive a train wreck in which a hundred die. Get thrown clear when your single-engine Cessna crashes on a golf course after striking a power line in heavy rain just minutes after takeoff. It doesn't have to be assassination. The point is you're standing at the edge of a smoldering ruin where others lie inert and twisted. This can counteract the effect of any number of nebulous masses, at least for a time."

We window-shopped a while, then went into a shoe store. Murray looked at Weejuns, Wallabees, Hush Puppies. We wandered out into the sun. Children in strollers squinted up at us, appearing to think we were something strange.

"Has your German helped?"

"I can't say it has."

"Has it ever helped?"

"I can't say. I don't know. Who knows these things?"

"What have you been trying to do all these years?"

"Put myself under a spell, I guess."

"Correct. Nothing to be ashamed of, Jack. It's only your fear that makes you act this way."

"*Only* my fear? *Only* my death?"

"We shouldn't be surprised at your lack of success. How powerful did the Germans prove to be? They lost the war, after all."

"That's what Denise said."

"You've discussed this with the children?"

"Superficially."

"Helpless and fearful people are drawn to magical figures, mythic figures, epic men who intimidate and darkly loom."

"You're talking about Hitler, I take it."

"Some people are larger than life. Hitler is larger than death. You thought he would protect you. I understand completely."

"Do you? Because I wish I did."

"It's totally obvious. You wanted to be helped and sheltered. The overwhelming horror would leave no room for your own death. 'Submerge me,' you said. 'Absorb my fear.' On one level you wanted to conceal yourself in Hitler and his works. On another level you wanted to use him to grow in significance and strength.

I sense a confusion of means. Not that I'm criticizing. It was a daring thing you did, a daring thrust. *To use him.* I can admire the attempt even as I see how totally dumb it was, although no dumber than wearing a charm or knocking wood. Six hundred million Hindus stay home from work if the signs are not favorable that morning. So I'm not singling you out."

"The vast and terrible depth."

"Of course," he said.

"The inexhaustibility."

"I understand."

"The whole huge nameless thing."

"Yes, absolutely."

"The massive darkness."

"Certainly, certainly."

"The whole terrible endless hugeness."

"I know exactly what you mean."

He tapped the fender of a diagonally parked car, half smiling.

"Why have you failed, Jack?"

"A confusion of means."

"Correct. There are numerous ways to get around death. You tried to employ two of them at once. You stood out on the one hand and tried to hide on the other. What is the name we give to this attempt?"

"Dumb."

I followed him into the supermarket. Blasts of color, layers of oceanic sound. We walked under a bright banner announcing a raffle to raise money for some incurable disease. The wording seemed to indicate that the winner would get the disease. Murray likened the banner to a Tibetan prayer flag.

"Why have I had this fear so long, so consistently?"

"It's obvious. You don't know how to repress. We're all aware there's no escape from death. How do we deal with this crushing knowledge? We repress, we disguise, we bury, we exclude. Some people do it better than others, that's all."

"How can I improve?"

"You can't. Some people just don't have the unconscious tools to perform the necessary disguising operations."

"How do we know repression exists if the tools are unconscious and the thing we're repressing is so cleverly disguised?"

"Freud said so. Speaking of looming figures."

He picked up a box of Handi-Wrap II, reading the display type, studying the colors. He smelled a packet of dehydrated soup. The data was strong today.

"Do you think I'm somehow healthier because I don't know how to repress? Is it possible that constant fear is the natural state of man and that by living close to my fear I am actually doing something heroic, Murray?"

"Do you feel heroic?"

"No."

"Then you probably aren't."

"But isn't repression unnatural?"

"Fear is unnatural. Lightning and thunder are unnatural. Pain, death, reality, these are all unnatural. We can't bear these things as they are. We know too much. So we resort to repression, compromise and disguise. This is how we survive in the universe. This is the natural language of the species."

I looked at him carefully.

"I exercise. I take care of my body."

"No, you don't," he said.

He helped an old man read the date on a loaf of raisin bread. Children sailed by in silver carts.

"Tegrin, Denorex, Selsun Blue."

Murray wrote something in his little book. I watched him step deftly around a dozen fallen eggs oozing yolky matter from a busted carton.

"Why do I feel so good when I'm with Wilder? It's not like being with the other kids," I said.

"You sense his total ego, his freedom from limits."

"In what way is he free from limits?"

"He doesn't know he's going to die. He doesn't know death at all. You cherish this simpleton blessing of his, this exemption from harm. You want to get close to him, touch him, look at him, breathe him in. How lucky he is. A cloud of unknowing, an omnipotent little person. The child is everything, the adult nothing. Think about it. A person's entire life is the unraveling of this conflict. No wonder we're bewildered, staggered, shattered."

"Aren't you going too far?"

"I'm from New York."

"We create beautiful and lasting things, build vast civilizations."

"Gorgeous evasions," he said. "Great escapes."

The doors parted photoelectronically. We went outside, walking past the dry cleaner, the hair stylist, the optician. Murray relighted his pipe, sucking impressively at the mouthpiece.

"We have talked about ways to get around death," he said. "We have discussed how you've already tried two such ways, each cancelling the other. We have mentioned technology, train wrecks, belief in an afterlife. There are other methods as well and I would like to talk about one such approach."

We crossed the street.

"I believe, Jack, there are two kinds of people in the world. Killers and diers. Most of us are diers. We don't have the disposition, the rage or whatever it takes to be a killer. We let death happen. We lie down and die. But think what it's like to be a killer. Think how exciting it is, in theory, to kill a person in direct confrontation. If he dies, you cannot. To kill him is to gain life-credit. The more people you kill, the more credit you store up. It explains any number of massacres, wars, executions."

"Are you saying that men have tried throughout history to cure themselves of death by killing others?"

"It's obvious."

"And you call this exciting?"

"I'm talking theory. In theory, violence is a form of rebirth. The dier passively succumbs. The killer lives on. What a marvelous equation. As a marauding band amasses dead bodies, it gathers strength. Strength accumulates like a favor from the gods."

"What does this have to do with me?"

"This is theory. We're a couple of academics taking a walk. But imagine the visceral jolt, seeing your opponent bleeding in the dust."

"You think it adds to a person's store of credit, like a bank transaction."

"Nothingness is staring you in the face. Utter and permanent oblivion. You will cease to be. *To be,* Jack. The dier accepts this and dies. The killer, in theory, attempts to defeat his own death by killing others. He buys time, he buys life. Watch others squirm. See the blood trickle in the dust."

I looked at him, amazed. He drew contentedly on his pipe, making hollow sounds.

"It's a way of controlling death. A way of gaining the ultimate upper hand. Be the killer for a change. Let someone else be the dier. Let him replace you, theoretically, in that role. You can't die if he does. He dies, you live. See how marvelously simple."

"You say this is what people have been doing for centuries."

"They're still doing it. They do it on a small intimate scale, they do it in groups and crowds and masses. Kill to live."

"Sounds pretty awful."

He seemed to shrug. "Slaughter is never random. The more people you kill, the more power you gain over your own death. There is a secret precision at work in the most savage and indiscriminate killings. To speak about this is not to do public relations for murder. We're two academics in an intellectual environment. It's our duty to examine currents of thought, investigate the meaning of human behavior. But think how exciting, to come out a winner in a deathly struggle, to watch the bastard bleed."

"Plot a murder, you're saying. But every plot is a murder in effect. To plot is to die, whether we know it or not."

"To plot is to live," he said.

I looked at him. I studied his face, his hands.

"We start our lives in chaos, in babble. As we surge up into the world, we try to devise a shape, a plan. There is dignity in this. Your whole life is a plot, a scheme, a diagram. It is a failed scheme but that's not the point. To plot is to affirm life, to seek shape and control. Even after death, most particularly after death, the search continues. Burial rites are an attempt to complete the scheme, in ritual. Picture a state funeral, Jack. It is all precision, detail, order, design. The nation holds its breath. The efforts of a huge and powerful government are brought to bear on a ceremony that will shed the last trace of chaos. If all goes well, if they bring it off, some natural law of perfection is obeyed. The nation is delivered from anxiety, the deceased's life is redeemed, life itself is strengthened, reaffirmed."

"Are you sure?" I said.

"To plot, to take aim at something, to shape time and space. This is how we advance the art of human consciousness."

We moved in a wide arc back toward campus. Streets in deep and soundless shade, garbage bags set out for collection. We crossed the sunset overpass, pausing briefly to watch the cars shoot by. Sunlight bouncing off the glass and chrome.

"Are you a killer or a dier, Jack?"

"You know the answer to that. I've been a dier all my life."

"What can you do about it?"

"What can any dier do? Isn't it implicit in his makeup that he can't cross over?"

"Let's think about that. Let's examine the nature of the beast, so to speak. The male animal. Isn't there a fund, a pool, a reservoir of potential violence in the male psyche?"

"In theory I suppose there is."

"We're *talking* theory. That's *exactly* what we're talking. Two friends on a tree-shaded street. What else but theory? Isn't there a deep field, a sort of crude oil deposit that one might tap if and when the occasion warrants? A great dark lake of male rage."

"That's what Babette says. Homicidal rage. You sound like her."

"Amazing lady. Is she right or wrong?"

"In theory? She's probably right."

"Isn't there a sludgy region you'd rather not know about? A remnant of some prehistoric period when dinosaurs roamed the earth and men fought with flint tools? When to kill was to live?"

"Babette talks about male biology. Is it biology or geology?"

"Does it matter, Jack? We only want to know whether it is there, buried in the most prudent and unassuming soul."

"I suppose so. It can be. It depends."

"Is it or isn't it there?"

"It's there, Murray. So what?"

"I only want to hear you say it. That's all. I only want to elicit truths you already possess, truths you've always known at some basic level."

"Are you saying a dier can become a killer?"

"I'm only a visiting lecturer. I theorize, I take walks, I admire the trees and houses. I have my students, my rented room, my TV set. I pick out a word here, an image there. I admire the lawns, the porches. What a wonderful thing a porch is. How did I live a life without a porch to sit on, up till now? I speculate, I reflect, I take constant notes. I am here to think, to see. Let me warn you, Jack. I won't let up."

We passed my street and walked up the hill to the campus.

"Who's your doctor?"

"Chakravarty," I said.

"Is he good?"

"How would I know?"

"My shoulder separates. An old sexual injury."

"I'm afraid to see him. I put the printout of my death in the bottom drawer of a dresser."

"I know how you feel. But the tough part is yet to come. You've said good-bye to everyone but yourself. How does a person say good-bye to himself? It's a juicy existential dilemma."

"It certainly is."

We walked past the administration building.

"I hate to be the one who says it, Jack, but there's something that has to be said."

"What?"

"Better you than me."

I nodded gravely. "Why does this have to be said?"

"Because friends have to be brutally honest with each other.

I'd feel terrible if I didn't tell you what I was thinking, especially at a time like this."

"I appreciate it, Murray. I really do."

"Besides, it's part of the universal experience of dying. Whether you think about it consciously or not, you're aware at some level that people are walking around saying to themselves, 'Better him than me.' It's only natural. You can't blame them or wish them ill."

"Everyone but my wife. She wants to die first."

"Don't be so sure," he said.

We shook hands in front of the library. I thanked him for his honesty.

"That's what it all comes down to in the end," he said. "A person spends his life saying good-bye to other people. How does he say good-bye to himself?"

I threw away picture-frame wire, metal book ends, cork coasters, plastic key tags, dusty bottles of Mercurochrome and Vaseline, crusted paintbrushes, caked shoe brushes, clotted correction fluid. I threw away candle stubs, laminated placemats, frayed pot holders. I went after the padded clothes hangers, the magnetic memo clipboards. I was in a vengeful and near savage state. I bore a personal grudge against these things. Somehow they'd put me in this fix. They'd dragged me down, made escape impossible. The two girls followed me around, observing a respectful silence. I threw away my battered khaki canteen, my ridiculous hip boots. I threw away diplomas, certificates, awards and citations. When the girls stopped me, I was working the bathrooms, discarding used bars of soap, damp towels, shampoo bottles with streaked labels and missing caps.

PLEASE NOTE. In several days, your new automated banking card will arrive in the mail. If it is a red card with a silver stripe, your secret code will be the same as it is now. If it is a green card with a gray stripe, you must appear at your branch, with your card, to devise a new secret code. Codes based on birthdays are popular. WARNING. Do not write down your code.

Do not carry your code on your person. REMEMBER. You cannot access your account unless your code is entered properly. Know your code. Reveal your code to no one. Only your code allows you to enter the system.

38

My head was between her breasts, where it seemed to be spending a lot of time lately. She stroked my shoulder.

"Murray says the problem is that we don't repress our fear."

"Repress it?"

"Some people have the gift, some don't."

"The gift? I thought repression was outdated. They've been telling us for years not to repress our fears and desires. Repression causes tension, anxiety, unhappiness, a hundred diseases and conditions. I thought the last thing we were supposed to do was repress something. They've been telling us to talk about our fears, get in touch with our feelings."

"Getting in touch with death is not what they had in mind. Death is so strong that we have to repress, those of us who know how."

"But repression is totally false and mechanical. Everybody knows that. We're not supposed to deny our nature."

"It's natural to deny our nature, according to Murray. It's the whole point of being different from animals."

"But that's crazy."

"It's the only way to survive," I said from her breasts.

She stroked my shoulder, thinking about this. Gray flashes of a staticky man standing near a double bed. His body distorted, rippling, unfinished. I didn't have to imagine his motel companion. Our bodies were one surface, hers and mine, but the delectations of touch were preempted by Mr. Gray. It was his pleasure I experienced, his hold over Babette, his cheap and sleazy power. Down the hall an eager voice said: "If you keep misplacing your ball of string, cage it in a Barney basket, attach some organizer clips to your kitchen corkboard, fasten the basket to the clips. Simple!"

The next day I started carrying the Zumwalt automatic to school. It was in the flap pocket of my jacket when I lectured, it was in the top drawer of my desk when I received visitors in the office. The gun created a second reality for me to inhabit. The air was bright, swirling around my head. Nameless feelings pressed thrillingly on my chest. It was a reality I could control, secretly dominate.

How stupid these people were, coming into my office unarmed.

Late one afternoon I took the gun out of my desk and examined it carefully. Only three bullets remained in the magazine. I wondered how Vernon Dickey had used the missing ammo (or whatever bullets are called by people familiar with firearms). Four Dylar tablets, three Zumwalt bullets. Why was I surprised to find that the bullets were so unmistakably bullet-shaped? I guess I thought new names and shapes had been given to just about everything in the decades since I first became aware of objects and their functions. The weapon was gun-shaped, the little pointed projectiles reassuringly bullet-shaped. They were like childhood things you might come across after forty years, seeing their genius for the first time.

That evening I heard Heinrich in his room, moodily singing "The Streets of Laredo." I stopped in to ask whether Orest had entered the cage yet.

"They said it was not humane. There was no place that would let him do it officially. He had to go underground."

"Where is underground?"

"Watertown. Orest and his trainer. They found a public notary there who said he would certify a document that said that Orest Mercator spent so many days incarcerated with these venomous reptiles blah blah blah."

"Where would they find a large glass cage in Watertown?"

"They wouldn't."

"What would they find?"

"A room in the only hotel. Plus there were only three snakes. And he got bit in four minutes."

"You mean the hotel let them place poisonous snakes in the room?"

"The hotel didn't know. The man who arranged the snakes carried them up in an airline bag. It was a whole massive deception except the man showed up with three snakes instead of the agreed twenty-seven."

"In other words he told them he had access to twenty-seven snakes."

"Venomous. Except they weren't. So Orest got bit for nothing. The jerk."

"Suddenly he's a jerk."

"They had all this antivenom which they couldn't even use. The first four minutes."

"How does he feel?"

"How would you feel if you were a jerk?"

"Glad to be alive," I said.

"Not Orest. He dropped out of sight. He went into complete seclusion. Nobody's seen him since it happened. He doesn't answer the door, he doesn't answer the phone, he doesn't show up at school. The total package."

I decided to wander over to my office and glance at some final exams. Most of the students had already departed, eager to begin the routine hedonism of another bare-limbed summer. The campus was dark and empty. There was a trembling mist. Passing a line of trees, I thought I sensed someone edge in behind me, maybe thirty yards away. When I looked, the path was clear. Was it the gun that was making me jumpy? Does a gun draw violence to it, attract other guns to its surrounding field of force? I walked on quickly toward Centenary Hall. I heard footsteps on gravel, a conspicuous crunch. Someone was out there, on the edge of the parking area, in the trees and the mist. If I had a gun, why was I scared? If I was scared, why didn't I run? I counted off five paces, looked quickly left, saw a figure moving parallel to the path, in and out of deep shadow. I broke into a shambling trot, my gun hand in my pocket, clutching the automatic. When I looked again, he wasn't there. I slowed down warily, crossed a broad lawn, heard running, the meter of bounding feet. He was coming from the right this time, all-out, closing fast. I broke into a weaving run, hoping I'd make an elusive target for someone firing at my back. I'd never run in a weave before. I kept my head down, swerved sharply and unpredictably. It was an interesting way to run. I was surprised at the range of possibilities, the number of combinations I could put together within a framework of left and right swerves. I did a tight left, widened it, cut sharply right, faked left, went left, went wide right. About twenty yards from the end of the open area, I broke off the weave pattern and ran as fast and straight as I could for a red oak. I stuck out my left arm, went skidding around the tree in a headlong cranking countermotion, simultaneously using my right hand to pluck the Zumwalt from my jacket pocket, so that I now faced the person I'd been fleeing, protected by a tree trunk, my gun at the ready.

This was about as deft a thing as I'd ever done. I looked into the heavy mist as my attacker approached in little thudding footfalls. When I saw the familiar odd loping stride, I put the gun back in my pocket. It was Winnie Richards, of course.

"Hi, Jack. At first I didn't know who it was, so I used evasive tactics. When I realized it was you, I said to myself that's just the person I want to see."

"How come?"

"Remember that time you asked me about a secret research group? Working on fear of death? Trying to perfect a medication?"

"Sure—Dylar."

"There was a journal lying around the office yesterday. *American Psychobiologist.* Curious story in there. Such a group definitely existed. Supported by a multinational giant. Operating in the deepest secrecy in an unmarked building just outside Iron City."

"Why deepest secrecy?"

"It's obvious. To prevent espionage by competitive giants. The point is they came very close to achieving their objective."

"What happened?"

"A lot of things. The resident organizational genius, one of the forces behind the whole project, was a fellow named Willie Mink. He turns out to be a controversial fellow. He does some very, very controversial things."

"I'll bet I know the first thing he does. He runs an ad in a gossip tabloid asking for volunteers for a hazardous experiment. FEAR OF DEATH, it says."

"Very good, Jack. A little ad in some rinky-dink newspaper. He interviews the respondents in a motel room, testing them for emotional integration and about a dozen other things in an attempt to work up a death profile for each person. Interviews in a motel. When the scientists and the lawyers find out about this, they go slightly berserk, they reprimand Mink, they put all their resources into computer testing. Berserk official reaction."

"But that's not the end of it."

"How right you are. Despite the fact that Mink is now a carefully observed person, one of the volunteers manages to slip through the screen of watchfulness and begins a program of more or less unsupervised human experimentation, using a drug that is totally unknown, untested and unapproved, with side effects that could beach a whale. An unsupervised well-built human."

"Female," I said.

"Very correct. She periodically reports to Mink in the very motel where he originally did his interviewing, sometimes arriving in a taxi, sometimes on foot from the shabby and depressing bus terminal. What is she wearing, Jack?"

"I don't know."

"A ski mask. She is the woman in the ski mask. When the others find out about Mink's latest caper, there is a period of prolonged controversy, animosity, litigation and disgrace. Pharmaceutical giants have their code of ethics, just like you and me. The project manager is kicked out, the project goes on without him."

"Did the article say what happened to him?"

"The reporter tracked him down. He is living in the same motel where all the controversy took place."

"Where is the motel?"

"In Germantown."

"Where's that?" I said.

"Iron City. It's the old German section. Behind the foundry."

"I didn't know there was a section in Iron City called Germantown."

"The Germans are gone, of course."

I went straight home. Denise was making check marks in a paperback book called *Directory of Toll-Free Numbers.* I found Babette sitting by Wilder's bed, reading him a story.

"I don't mind running clothes as such," I said. "A sweatsuit is a practical thing to wear at times. But I wish you wouldn't wear it when you read bedtime stories to Wilder or braid Steffie's hair. There's something touching about such moments that is jeopardized by running clothes."

"Maybe I'm wearing running clothes for a reason."

"Like what?"

"I'm going running," she said.

"Is that a good idea? At night?"

"What is night? It happens seven times a week. Where is the uniqueness in this?"

"It's dark, it's wet."

"Do we live in a blinding desert glare? What is wet? We live with wet."

"Babette doesn't speak like this."

"Does life have to stop because our half of the earth is dark? Is there something about the night that physically resists a runner? I need to pant and gasp. What is dark? It's just another name for light."

"No one will convince me that the person I know as Babette actually wants to run up the stadium steps at ten o'clock at night."

"It's not what I want, it's what I need. My life is no longer in the realm of want. I do what I have to do. I pant, I gasp. Every runner understands the need for this."

"Why do you have to run up steps? You're not a professional athlete trying to rebuild a shattered knee. Run on plain land. Don't make a major involvement out of it. Everything is a major involvement today."

"It's my life. I tend to be involved."

"It's not your life. It's only exercise."

"A runner needs," she said.

"I also need and tonight I need the car. Don't wait up for me. Who knows when I'll be back."

I waited for her to ask what mysterious mission would require me to get in the car and drive through the rain-streaked night, time of return unknown.

She said, "I can't walk to the stadium, run up the steps five or six times and then walk all the way back home. You can drive me there, wait for me, drive me back. The car is then yours."

"I don't want it. What do you think of that? You want the car, you take it. The streets are slippery. You know what that means, don't you?"

"What does it mean?"

"Fasten your seat belt. There's also a chill in the air. You know what a chill in the air means."

"What does it mean?"

"Wear your ski mask," I told her.

The thermostat began to buzz.

I put on a jacket and went outside. Ever since the airborne toxic event, our neighbors, the Stovers, had been keeping their car in the driveway instead of the garage, keeping it facing the street, keeping the key in the ignition. I walked up the driveway and got in the car. There were trash caddies fixed to the dashboard and seat-backs, dangling plastic bags full of gum wrappers, ticket stubs, lipstick-smeared tissues, crumpled soda cans, crumpled circulars and receipts, ashtray debris, popsicle sticks and french fries, crumpled coupons and paper napkins, pocket combs with missing teeth. Thus familiarized, I started up the engine, turned on the lights and drove off.

I ran a red light when I crossed Middlebrook. Reaching the end of the expressway ramp, I did not yield. All the way to Iron City, I felt a sense of dreaminess, release, unreality. I slowed down at the toll gate but did not bother tossing a quarter into the basket. An alarm went off but no one pursued. What's another quarter to a state that is billions in debt? What's twenty-five cents when we are talking about a nine-thousand-dollar stolen car? This must be how people escape the pull of the earth, the gravitational leaf-flutter that brings us hourly closer to dying. Simply stop obeying. Steal instead of buy, shoot instead of talk. I ran two more lights on the rainy approach roads to Iron City. The outlying buildings were long and low, fish and produce markets, meat terminals with old wooden canopies. I entered the city and turned on the radio, needing company not on the lonely highway but here on the cobbled streets, in the sodium vapor lights, where the emptiness clings. Every city has its districts. I drove past the abandoned car district, the uncollected garbage district, the sniper-fire district, the districts of smoldering sofas and broken glass. Ground glass crunched under the tires. I headed toward the foundry.

Random Access Memory, Acquired Immune Deficiency Syndrome, Mutual Assured Destruction.

I still felt extraordinarily light—lighter than air, colorless, odorless, invisible. But around the lightness and dreaminess, something else was building, an emotion of a different order. A surge, a will, an agitation of the passions. I reached into my pocket, rubbed my knuckles across the grainy stainless steel of the Zumwalt barrel. The man on the radio said: "Void where prohibited."

39

I drove twice around the foundry, looking for signs of some erstwhile German presence. I drove past the row houses. They were set on a steep hill, narrow-fronted frame houses, a climbing line of pitched roofs. I drove past the bus terminal, through the beating rain. It took a while to find the motel, a one-story building set against the concrete pier of an elevated roadway. It was called the Roadway Motel.

Transient pleasures, drastic measures.

The area was deserted, a spray-painted district of warehouses and light industry. The motel had nine or ten rooms, all dark, no cars out front. I drove past three times, studying the scene, and parked half a block away, in the rubble under the roadway. Then I walked back to the motel. Those were the first three elements in my plan.

Here is my plan. Drive past the scene several times, park some distance from the scene, go back on foot, locate Mr. Gray under his real name or an alias, shoot him three times in the viscera for maximum pain, clear the weapon of prints, place the weapon in the victim's staticky hand, find a crayon or lipstick tube and scrawl a cryptic suicide note on the full-length mirror, take the victim's supply of Dylar tablets, slip back to the car, proceed to the expressway entrance, head east toward Blacksmith, get off at the old river road, park Stover's car in Old Man Treadwell's garage, shut the garage door, walk home in the rain and the fog.

Elegant. My airy mood returned. I was advancing in consciousness. I watched myself take each separate step. With each separate step, I became aware of processes, components, things relating to other things. Water fell to earth in drops. I saw things new.

There was an aluminum awning over the office door. On the

door itself were little plastic letters arranged in slots to spell out a message. The message was: NU MISH BOOT ZUP KO.

Gibberish but high-quality gibberish. I made my way along the wall, looking through the windows. My plan was this. Stand at the edges of windows with my back to the wall, swivel my head to look peripherally into rooms. Some windows were bare, some had blinds or dusty shades. I could make out the rough outlines of chairs or beds in the dark rooms. Trucks rumbled overhead. In the next to last unit, there was the scantest flicker of light. I stood at the edge of the window, listening. I swiveled my head, looked into the room out of the corner of my right eye. A figure sat in a low armchair looking up at the flickering light. I sensed I was part of a network of structures and channels. I knew the precise nature of events. I was moving closer to things in their actual state as I approached a violence, a smashing intensity. Water fell in drops, surfaces gleamed.

It occurred to me that I did not have to knock. The door would be open. I gripped the knob, eased the door open, slipped into the room. Stealth. It was easy. Everything would be easy. I stood inside the room, sensing things, noting the room tone, the dense air. Information rushed toward me, rushed slowly, incrementally. The figure was male, of course, and sat sprawled in the short-legged chair. He wore a Hawaiian shirt and Budweiser shorts. Plastic sandals dangled from his feet. The dumpy chair, the rumpled bed, the industrial carpet, the shabby dresser, the sad green walls and ceiling cracks. The TV floating in the air, in a metal brace, pointing down at him.

He spoke first, without taking his eyes from the flickering screen.

"Are you heartsick or soulsick?"

I stood against the door.

"You're Mink," I said.

In time he looked at me, looked at the large friendly figure with the slumped shoulders and forgettable face.

"What kind of name is Willie Mink?" I said.

"It's a first name and a last name. Same as anybody."

Did he speak with an accent? His face was odd, concave,

forehead and chin jutting. He was watching TV without the sound.

"Some of these sure-footed bighorns have been equipped with radio transmitters," he said.

I could feel the pressure and density of things. So much was happening. I sensed molecules active in my brain, moving along neural pathways.

"You're here for some Dylar, of course."

"Of course. What else?"

"What else? Rid the fear."

"Rid the fear. Clear the grid."

"Clear the grid. That's why they come to me."

This was my plan. Enter unannounced, gain his confidence, wait for an unguarded moment, take out the Zumwalt, shoot him three times in the viscera for maximum slowness of agony, put the gun in his hand to suggest a lonely man's suicide, write semi-coherent things on the mirror, leave Stover's car in Treadwell's garage.

"By coming in here, you agree to a certain behavior," Mink said.

"What behavior?"

"Room behavior. The point of rooms is that they're inside. No one should go into a room unless he understands this. People behave one way in rooms, another way in streets, parks and airports. To enter a room is to agree to a certain kind of behavior. It follows that this would be the kind of behavior that takes place in rooms. This is the standard, as opposed to parking lots and beaches. It is the point of rooms. No one should enter a room not knowing the point. There is an unwritten agreement between the person who enters a room and the person whose room had been entered, as opposed to open-air theaters, outdoor pools. The purpose of a room derives from the special nature of a room. A room is inside. This is what people in rooms have to agree on, as differentiated from lawns, meadows, fields, orchards."

I agreed completely. It made perfect sense. What was I here for if not to define, fix in my sights, take aim at? I heard a noise, faint, monotonous, white.

"To begin your project sweater," he said, "first ask yourself what type sleeve will meet your needs."

His nose was flat, his skin the color of a Planter's peanut. What is the geography of a spoon-shaped face? Was he Melanesian, Polynesian, Indonesian, Nepalese, Surinamese, Dutch-Chinese? Was he a composite? How many people came here for Dylar? Where was Surinam? How was my plan progressing?

I studied the palm-studded print of his loose shirt, the Budweiser pattern repeated on the surface of his Bermuda shorts. The shorts were too big. The eyes were half closed. The hair was long and spiky. He was sprawled in the attitude of a stranded air traveler, someone long since defeated by the stale waiting, the airport babble. I began to feel sorry for Babette. This had been her last hope for refuge and serenity, this weary pulse of a man, a common pusher now, spiky-haired, going mad in a dead motel.

Auditory scraps, tatters, whirling specks. A heightened reality. A denseness that was also a transparency. Surfaces gleamed. Water struck the roof in spherical masses, globules, splashing drams. Close to a violence, close to a death.

"The pet under stress may need a prescription diet," he said.

Of course he hadn't always been like this. He'd been a project manager, dynamic, hard-driving. Even now I could see in his face and eyes the faltering remains of an enterprising shrewdness and intelligence. He reached into his pocket, took a handful of white tablets, tossed them in the direction of his mouth. Some entered, some flew past. The saucer-shaped pills. The end of fear.

"Where are you from originally, if I can call you Willie?"

He lapsed into thought, trying to recall. I wanted to put him at ease, get him to talk about himself, about Dylar. Part and parcel of my plan. My plan was this. Swivel my head to look into rooms, put him at his ease, wait for an unguarded moment, blast him in the gut three times for maximum efficiency of pain, take his Dylar, get off at the river road, shut the garage door, walk home in the rain and the fog.

"I wasn't always as you see me now."

"That's exactly what I was thinking."

"I was doing important work. I envied myself. I was literally embarked. Death without fear is an everyday thing. You can live with it. I learned English watching American TV. I had American sex the first time in Port-O-San, Texas. Everything they said was true. I wish I could remember."

"You're saying there is no death as we know it without the element of fear. People would adjust to it, accept its inevitability."

"Dylar failed, reluctantly. But it will definitely come. Maybe now, maybe never. The heat from your hand will actually make the gold-leafing stick to the wax paper."

"There will eventually be an effective medication, you're saying. A remedy for fear."

"Followed by a greater death. More effective, productwise. This is what the scientists don't understand, scrubbing their smocks with Woolite. Not that I have anything personal against death from our vantage point high atop Metropolitan County Stadium."

"Are you saying death adapts? It eludes our attempts to reason with it?"

This was similar to something Murray had once said. Murray had also said, "Imagine the visceral jolt, watching your opponent bleed in the dust. He dies, you live."

Close to a death, close to the slam of metal projectiles on flesh, the visceral jolt. I watched Mink ingest more pills, throwing them at his face, sucking them like sweets, his eyes on the flickering screen. Waves, rays, coherent beams. I saw things new.

"Just between you and I," he said, "I eat this stuff like candy."

"I was just thinking that."

"How much do you want to buy?"

"How much do I need?"

"I see you as a heavyset white man about fifty. Does this describe your anguish? I see you as a person in a gray jacket and light brown pants. Tell me how correct I am. To convert Fahrenheit to Celsius, this is what you do."

There was a silence. Things began to glow. The dumpy chair, the shabby dresser, the rumpled bed. The bed was equipped with casters. I thought, This is the grayish figure of my torment, the man who took my wife. Did she wheel him around the room as he sat on the bed popping pills? Did each lie prone along one side of the bed, reaching an arm down to paddle? Did they make the bed spin with their lovemaking, a froth of pillows and sheets above the small wheels on swivels? Look at him now, glowing in the dark, showing a senile grin.

"I barely forget the times I had in this room," he said, "before I became misplaced. There was a woman in a ski mask, which her name escapes me at the moment. American sex, let me tell you, this is how I learned my English."

The air was rich with extrasensory material. Nearer to death, nearer to second sight. A smashing intensity. I advanced two steps toward the middle of the room. My plan was elegant. Advance gradually, gain his confidence, take out the Zumwalt, fire three bullets at his midsection for maximum visceral agony, clear the weapon of prints, write suicidal cult messages on the mirrors and walls, take his supply of Dylar, slip back to the car, drive to the expressway entrance, head east toward Blacksmith, leave Stover's car in Treadwell's garage, walk home in the rain and the fog.

He gobbled more pills, flung others down the front of his Budweiser shorts. I advanced one step. There were cracked Dylar tablets all over the fire-retardant carpet. Trod upon, stomped. He tossed some tablets at the screen. The set had a walnut veneer with silvery hardware. The picture rolled badly.

"Now I am picking up my metallic gold tube," he said. "Using my palette knife and my odorless turp, I will thicken the paint on my palette."

I recalled Babette's remarks about the side effects of the medication. I said, as a test, "Falling plane."

He looked at me, gripping the arms of the chair, the first signs of panic building in his eyes.

"Plunging aircraft," I said, pronouncing the words crisply, authoritatively.

He kicked off his sandals, folded himself over into the recommended crash position, head well forward, hands clasped behind his knees. He performed the maneuver automatically, with a double-jointed collapsible dexterity, throwing himself into it, like a child or a mime. Interesting. The drug not only caused the user to confuse words with the things they referred to; it made him act in a somewhat stylized way. I watched him slumped there, trembling. This was my plan. Look peripherally into rooms, enter unannounced, reduce him to trembling, gut-shoot him maximally three times, get off at the river road, shut the garage door.

I took another step toward the middle of the room. As the TV picture jumped, wobbled, caught itself in snarls, Mink appeared to grow more vivid. The precise nature of events. Things in their actual state. Eventually he worked himself out of the deep fold, rising nicely, sharply outlined against the busy air. White noise everywhere.

"Containing iron, niacin and riboflavin. I learned my English in airplanes. It's the international language of aviation. Why are you here, white man?"

"To buy."

"You are very white, you know that?"

"It's because I'm dying."

"This stuff fix you up."

"I'll still die."

"But it won't matter, which comes to the same thing. Some of these playful dolphins have been equipped with radio transmitters. Their far-flung wanderings may tell us things."

I continued to advance in consciousness. Things glowed, a secret life rising out of them. Water struck the roof in elongated orbs, splashing drams. I knew for the first time what rain really was. I knew what wet was. I understood the neurochemistry of my brain, the meaning of dreams (the waste material of premonitions). Great stuff everywhere, racing through the room, racing slowly. A richness, a density. I believed everything. I was a Buddhist, a Jain, a Duck River Baptist. My only sadness was Babette, having to kiss a scooped-out face.

"She wore the ski mask so as not to kiss my face, which she said was un-American. I told her a room is inside. Do not enter a room not agreeing to this. This is the point, as opposed to emerging coastlines, continental plates. Or you can eat natural grains, vegetables, eggs, no fish, no fruit. Or fruit, vegetables, animal proteins, no grains, no milk. Or lots of soybean milk for B-12 and lots of vegetables to regulate insulin release but no meat, no fish, no fruit. Or white meat but no red meat. Or B-12 but no eggs. Or eggs but no grains. There are endless workable combinations."

I was ready to kill him now. But I didn't want to compromise the plan. The plan was elaborate. Drive past the scene several times, approach the motel on foot, swivel my head to look peripherally into rooms, locate Mr. Gray under his real name, enter unannounced, gain his confidence, advance gradually, reduce him to trembling, wait for an unguarded moment, take out the .25-caliber Zumwalt automatic, fire three bullets into his viscera for maximum slowness, depth and intensity of pain, wipe the weapon clear of prints, place the weapon in the victim's hand to suggest the trite and predictable suicide of a motel recluse, smear crude words on the walls in the victim's own blood as evidence of his final cult-related frenzy, take his supply of Dylar, slip back to the car, take the expressway to Blacksmith, leave Stover's car in Treadwell's garage, shut the garage door, walk home in the rain and the fog.

I advanced into the area of flickering light, out of the shadows, seeking to loom. I put my hand in my pocket, gripped the firearm. Mink watched the screen. I said to him gently, "Hail of bullets." Keeping my hand in my pocket.

He hit the floor, began crawling toward the bathroom, looking back over his shoulder, childlike, miming, using principles of heightened design but showing real terror, brilliant cringing fear. I followed him into the toilet, passing the full-length mirror where he'd undoubtedly posed with Babette, his shaggy member dangling like a ruminant's.

"Fusillade," I whispered.

He tried to wriggle behind the bowl, both arms over his head, his legs tight together. I loomed in the doorway, conscious of looming, seeing myself from Mink's viewpoint, magnified, threatening. It was time to tell him who I was. This was part of my plan. My plan was this. Tell him who I am, let him know the reason for his slow and agonizing death. I revealed my name, explained my relationship with the woman in the ski mask.

He put his hands over his crotch, tried to fit himself under the toilet tank, behind the bowl. The intensity of the noise in the room was the same at all frequencies. Sound all around. I took out the Zumwalt. Great and nameless emotions thudded on my chest. I knew who I was in the network of meanings. Water fell to earth in drops, causing surfaces to gleam. I saw things new.

Mink took one hand from his crotch, grabbed more tablets from his pocket, hurled them toward his open mouth. His face appeared at the end of the white room, a white buzz, the inner surface of a sphere. He sat up, tearing open his shirt pocket to find more pills. His fear was beautiful. He said to me, "Did you ever wonder why, out of thirty-two teeth, these four cause so much trouble? I'll be back with the answer in a minute."

I fired the gun, the weapon, the pistol, the firearm, the automatic. The sound snowballed in the white room, adding on reflected waves. I watched blood squirt from the victim's midsection. A delicate arc. I marveled at the rich color, sensed the color-causing action of nonnucleated cells. The flow diminished to a trickle, spread across the tile floor. I saw beyond words. I knew what red was, saw it in terms of dominant wavelength, luminance, purity. Mink's pain was beautiful, intense.

I fired a second shot just to fire it, relive the experience, hear the sonic waves layering through the room, feel the jolt travel up my arm. The bullet struck him just inside the right hipbone. A claret stain appeared on his shorts and shirt. I paused to notice him. He sat wedged between the toilet bowl and wall, one sandal missing, eyes totally white. I tried to see myself from Mink's viewpoint. Looming, dominant, gaining life-power, storing up life-credit. But he was too far gone to have a viewpoint.

It was going well. I was pleased to see how well it was going. The trucks rumbled overhead. The shower curtain smelled of mildewed vinyl. A richness, a smashing intensity. I approached the sitting figure, careful not to step in blood, leave revealing prints. I took out my handkerchief, wiped the weapon clean, placed it in Mink's hand, cautiously removing the handkerchief, painstakingly wrapping his bony fingers, one by one, around the stock, delicately working his index finger through the trigger guard. He was foaming, a little, at the mouth. I stepped back to survey the remains of the shattering moment, the scene of squalid violence and lonely death at the shadowy fringes of society. This was my plan. Step back, regard the squalor, make sure things were correctly placed.

Mink's eyes dropped out of his skull. They gleamed, briefly. He raised his hand and pulled the trigger, shooting me in the wrist.

The world collapsed inward, all those vivid textures and connections buried in mounds of ordinary stuff. I was disappointed. Hurt, stunned and disappointed. What had happened to the higher plane of energy in which I'd carried out my scheme? The pain was searing. Blood covered my forearm, wrist and hand. I staggered back, moaning, watching blood drip from the tips of my fingers. I was troubled and confused. Colored dots appeared at the edge of my field of vision. Familiar little dancing specks. The extra dimensions, the super perceptions, were reduced to visual clutter, a whirling miscellany, meaningless.

"And this could represent the leading edge of some warmer air," Mink said.

I looked at him. Alive. His lap a puddle of blood. With the restoration of the normal order of matter and sensation, I felt I was seeing him for the first time as a person. The old human muddles and quirks were set flowing again. Compassion, remorse, mercy. But before I could help Mink, I had to do some basic repair work on myself. Once again I took out my handkerchief, managed with my right hand and my teeth to tie it firmly just above the bullet hole in my left wrist, or between the wound and the heart. Then I sucked at the wound briefly, not knowing quite why, and spat out the resulting blood and pulp. The bullet had made a shallow penetration and deflected away. Using my good hand, I grabbed Mink by his bare foot and dragged him across the blood-dappled tile, the gun still clutched in his fist. There was something redemptive here. Dragging him foot-first across the tile, across the medicated carpet, through the door and into the night. Something large and grand and scenic. Is it better to commit evil and attempt to balance it with an exalted act than to live a resolutely neutral life? I know I felt virtuous, I felt blood-stained and stately, dragging the badly wounded man through the dark and empty street.

The rain had stopped. I was shocked at the amount of blood we were leaving behind. His, mainly. The sidewalk was striped. An interesting cultural deposit. He reached up feebly, dropped more Dylar down his throat. The gun hand dragged.

We reached the car. Mink kicked free, involuntarily, his body flopping and spinning, a little fishlike. He made spent and gasping noises, short of oxygen. I decided to attempt mouth-to-mouth. I leaned over him, used my thumb and index finger to clothes-pin his nose and then tried to work my face down into his. The awkwardness and grim intimacy of the act made it seem all the more dignified under the circumstances. All the larger, more generous. I kept trying to reach his mouth in order to breathe powerful gusts of air into his lungs. My lips were gathered, ready to funnel. His eyes followed me down. Perhaps he thought he was about to be kissed. I savored the irony.

His mouth was awash in regurgitated Dylar foam, half chewed tablets, flyspeck shards of polymer. I felt large and selfless, above resentment. This was the key to selflessness, or so it seemed to me as I knelt over the wounded man, exhaling rhythmically in the littered street beneath the roadway. Get past disgust. Forgive the foul body. Embrace it whole. After some minutes of this, I felt him come around, take regular breaths. I continued to hover just above him, our mouths almost touching.

"Who shot me?" he said.

"You did."

"Who shot you?"

"You did. The gun is in your hand."

"What was the point I was trying to make?"

"You were out of control. You weren't responsible. I forgive you."

"Who are you, literally?"

"A passerby. A friend. It doesn't matter."

"Some millipedes have eyes, some do not."

With much effort, many false starts, I got him into the back of the car, where he stretched out moaning. It was no longer possible to tell whether the blood on my hands and clothes was his or mine. My humanity soared. I started up the car. The pain in my arm was a throb, less fiery now. I drove one-handed through the empty streets, looking for a hospital. Iron City Lying-In. Mother of Mercy. Commiseration and Rapport. I would take whatever they had, even an emergency ward in the worst part of town. This is where we belonged, after all, with the multiple slash wounds, the entry and exit wounds, the blunt instrument wounds, the traumas, overdoses, acute deliriums. The only traffic was a milk van, a bakery van, some heavy trucks. The sky began to lighten. We came to a place with a neon cross over the entrance. It was a three-story building that might have been a Pentecostal church, a day-care center, world headquarters for some movement of regimented youth.

There was a wheelchair ramp, which meant I could drag Mink to the front door without banging his head on the concrete steps. I got him out of the car, clutched his sleek foot and moved up the ramp. He held one hand at his midsection to stanch the flow. The gun hand dragged behind. Dawn. There was a spaciousness to this moment, an epic pity and compassion. Having shot him, having led him to believe he'd shot himself, I felt I did honor to both of us, to all of us, by merging our fortunes, physically leading him to safety. I took long slow strides, pulling his weight. It hadn't occurred to me that a man's attempts to redeem himself might prolong the elation he felt when he committed the crime he now sought to make up for.

I rang the bell. In a matter of seconds, someone appeared at the door. An old woman, a nun, black-habited, black-veiled, leaning on a cane.

"We're shot," I said, lifting my wrist in the air.

"We see a lot of that here," she answered matter-of-factly, in an accented voice, turning to go back inside.

I dragged Mink across the entranceway. The place appeared to be a clinic. There were waiting rooms, screened cubicles, doors marked X-Ray, Eye Test. We followed the old nun to the trauma room. Two orderlies showed up, great squat men with sumo physiques. They lifted Mink onto a table and tore away his clothes in neat short practiced strokes.

"Inflated-adjusted real income," he said.

More nuns arrived, rustling, ancient, speaking German to each other. They carried transfusion equipment, wheeled in trays of glinting implements. The original nun approached Mink to remove the gun from his hand. I watched her toss it in a desk drawer that held about ten other handguns and half a dozen knives. There was a picture on the wall of Jack Kennedy holding hands with Pope John XXIII in heaven. Heaven was a partly cloudy place.

The doctor arrived, an elderly man in a shabby three-piece suit. He spoke German to the nuns and studied Mink's body, which was now partly clad in sheets.

"No one knows why the sea birds come to San Miguel," Willie said.

I was growing fond of him. The original nun took me into a cubicle to work on my wound. I started to give her a version of the shootings but she showed no interest. I told her it was an old gun with feeble bullets.

"Such a violent country."

"Have you been in Germantown long?" I said.

"We are the last of the Germans."

"Who lives here now, mostly?"

"Mostly no one," she said.

More nuns walked by, heavy rosaries swinging from their belts. I found them a merry sight, the kind of homogeneous presence that makes people smile at airports.

I asked my nun her name. Sister Hermann Marie. I told her I knew some German, trying to gain her favor, as I always did with medical personnel of any kind, at least in the early stages, before my fear and distrust overwhelmed any hope I might have had in maneuvering for advantage.

"*Gut, besser, best,*" I said.

A smile appeared on her seamed face. I counted for her, pointed to objects and gave their names. She nodded happily, cleaning out the wound and wrapping the wrist in sterile pads. She said I would not need a splint and told me the doctor would write a prescription for antibiotics. We counted to ten together.

Two more nuns appeared, wizened and creaky. My nun said something to them and soon all four of us were charmingly engaged in a childlike dialogue. We did colors, items of clothing, parts of the body. I felt much more at ease in this German-speaking company than I had with the Hitler scholars. Is there something so innocent in the recitation of names that God is pleased?

Sister Hermann Marie applied finishing touches to the bullet wound. From my chair I had a clear view of the picture of Kennedy and the Pope in heaven. I had a sneaking admiration for the picture. It made me feel good, sentimentally refreshed. The President still vigorous after death. The Pope's homeliness a kind of radiance. Why shouldn't it be true? Why shouldn't they meet somewhere, advanced in time, against a layer of fluffy cumulus, to clasp hands? Why shouldn't we all meet, as in some epic of protean gods and ordinary people, aloft, well-formed, shining?

I said to my nun, "What does the Church say about heaven today? Is it still the old heaven, like that, in the sky?"

She turned to glance at the picture.

"Do you think we are stupid?" she said.

I was surprised by the force of her reply.

"Then what is heaven, according to the Church, if it isn't the abode of God and the angels and the souls of those who are saved?"

"Saved? What is saved? This is a dumb head, who would come in here to talk about angels. Show me an angel. Please. I want to see."

"But you're a nun. Nuns believe these things. When we see a nun, it cheers us up, it's cute and amusing, being reminded that someone still believes in angels, in saints, all the traditional things."

"You would have a head so dumb to believe this?"

"It's not what I believe that counts. It's what you believe."

"This is true," she said. "The nonbelievers need the believers. They are desperate to have someone believe. But show me a saint. Give me one hair from the body of a saint."

She leaned toward me, her stark face framed in the black veil. I began to worry.

"We are here to take care of sick and injured. Only this. You would talk about heaven, you must find another place."

"Other nuns wear dresses," I said reasonably. "Here you still wear the old uniform. The habit, the veil, the clunky shoes. You must believe in tradition. The old heaven and hell, the Latin mass. The Pope is infallible, God created the world in six days. The great old beliefs. Hell is burning lakes, winged demons."

"You would come in bleeding from the street and tell me six days it took to make a universe?"

"On the seventh He rested."

"You would talk of angels? Here?"

"Of course here. Where else?"

I was frustrated and puzzled, close to shouting.

"Why not armies that would fight in the sky at the end of the world?"

"Why not? Why are you a nun anyway? Why do you have that picture on the wall?"

She drew back, her eyes filled with contemptuous pleasure.

"It is for others. Not for us."

"But that's ridiculous. What others?"

"All the others. The others who spend their lives believing that *we* still believe. It is our task in the world to believe things no one else takes seriously. To abandon such beliefs completely, the human race would die. This is why we are here. A tiny minority. To embody old things, old beliefs. The devil, the angels, heaven, hell. If we did not pretend to believe these things, the world would collapse."

"Pretend?"

"Of course pretend. Do you think we are stupid? Get out from here."

"You don't believe in heaven? A nun?"

"If you don't, why should I?"

"If you did, maybe I would."

"If I did, you would not have to."

"All the old muddles and quirks," I said. "Faith, religion, life everlasting. The great old human gullibilities. Are you saying you don't take them seriously? Your dedication is a pretense?"

"Our pretense is a dedication. Someone must appear to believe. Our lives are no less serious than if we professed real faith, real belief. As belief shrinks from the world, people find it more necessary than ever that *someone* believe. Wild-eyed men in caves. Nuns in black. Monks who do not speak. We are left to believe. Fools, children. Those who have abandoned belief must still believe in us. They are sure that they are right not to believe but they know belief must not fade completely. Hell is when no one believes. There must always be believers. Fools, idiots, those who hear voices, those who speak in tongues. We are your lunatics. We surrender our lives to make your nonbelief possible. You are sure that you are right but you don't want everyone to think as you do. There is no truth without fools. We are your fools, your madwomen, rising at dawn to pray, lighting candles, asking statues for good health, long life."

"You've had long life. Maybe it works."

She rattled out a laugh, showing teeth so old they were nearly transparent.

"Soon no more. You will lose your believers."

"You've been praying for nothing all these years?"

"For the world, dumb head."

"And nothing survives? Death is the end?"

"Do you want to know what I believe or what I pretend to believe?"

"I don't want to hear this. This is terrible."

"But true."

"You're a nun. Act like one."

"We take vows. Poverty, chastity, obedience. Serious vows. A serious life. You could not survive without us."

"There must be some of you who aren't pretending, who truly believe. I know there are. Centuries of belief don't just peter out in a few years. There were whole fields of study devoted to these subjects. Angelology. A branch of theology just for angels. A science of angels. Great minds debated these things. There are great minds today. They still debate, they still believe."

"You would come in from the street dragging a body by the foot and talk about angels who live in the sky. Get out from here."

She said something in German. I failed to understand. She spoke again, at some length, pressing her face toward mine, the words growing harsher, wetter, more guttural. Her eyes showed a terrible delight in my incomprehension. She was spraying me with German. A storm of words. She grew more animated as the speech went on. A gleeful vehemence entered her voice. She spoke faster, more expressively. Blood vessels flared in her eyes and face. I began to detect a cadence, a measured beat. She was reciting something, I decided. Litanies, hymns, catechisms. The mysteries of the rosary perhaps. Taunting me with scornful prayer.

The odd thing is I found it beautiful.

When her voice grew weak, I left the cubicle and wandered around until I found the old doctor. "*Herr Doktor*," I called, feeling like someone in a movie. He activated his hearing aid. I got my prescription, asked if Willie Mink would be all right. He wouldn't, at least not for a while. But he wouldn't die either, which gave him the edge on me.

The drive home was uneventful. I left the car in Stover's driveway. The rear seat was covered with blood. There was blood on the steering wheel, more blood on the dashboard and door handles. The scientific study of the cultural behavior and development of man. Anthropology.

I went upstairs and watched the kids a while. All asleep, fumbling through their dreams, eyes rapidly moving beneath closed lids. I got into bed next to Babette, fully dressed except for my shoes, somehow knowing she wouldn't think it strange. But my mind kept racing, I couldn't sleep. After a while I went down to the kitchen to sit with a cup of coffee, feel the pain in my wrist, the heightened pulse.

There was nothing to do but wait for the next sunset, when the sky would ring like bronze.

40

This was the day Wilder got on his plastic tricycle, rode it around the block, turned right onto a dead end street and pedaled noisily to the dead end. He walked the tricycle around the guard rail and then rode along a paved walkway that went winding past some overgrown lots to a set of twenty concrete steps. The plastic wheels rumbled and screeched. Here our reconstruction yields to the awe-struck account of two elderly women watching from the second-story back porch of a tall house in the trees. He walked the tricycle down the steps, guiding it with a duteous and unsentimental hand, letting it bump right along, as if it were an odd-shaped little sibling, not necessarily cherished. He remounted, rode across the street, rode across the sidewalk, proceeded onto the grassy slope that bordered the expressway. Here the women began to call. Hey, hey, they said, a little tentative at first, not ready to accept the implications of the process unfolding before them. The boy pedaled diagonally down the slope, shrewdly reducing the angle of descent, then paused on the bottom to aim his three-wheeler at the point on the opposite side which seemed to represent the shortest distance across. Hey, sonny, no. Waving their arms, looking frantically for some able-bodied pedestrian to appear on the scene. Wilder, meanwhile, ignoring their cries or not hearing them in the serial whoosh of dashing hatchbacks and vans, began to pedal across the highway, mystically charged. The women could only look, empty-mouthed, each with an arm in the air, a plea for the scene to reverse, the boy to pedal backwards on his faded blue and yellow toy like a cartoon figure on morning TV. The drivers could not quite comprehend. In their knotted posture, belted in, they knew this picture did not belong to the hurtling consciousness of the highway, the broad-ribboned modernist stream. In speed there was sense. In signs, in patterns, in split-second lives. What did it mean, this little rotary blur? Some force in the world had gone awry. They veered, braked, sounded their horns down the long afternoon, an animal lament. The child would not even look at them, pedaled straight for the median strip, a narrow patch of pale grass. He was pumped up, chesty, his arms appearing to move as rapidly as his legs, the round head wagging in a jig of lame-brained determination. He had to slow down to get onto the raised median, rearing up to let the front wheel edge over, extremely deliberate in his movements, following some numbered scheme, and the cars went wailing past, horns blowing belatedly, drivers' eyes searching the rearview mirror. He walked the tricycle across the grass. The women watched him regain a firm placement on the seat. Stay, they called. Do not go. No, no. Like foreigners reduced to simple phrases. The cars kept coming, whipping into the straightaway, endless streaking traffic. He set off to cross the last three lanes, dropping off the median like a bouncing ball, front wheel, rear wheels. Then the head-wagging race to the other side. Cars dodged, strayed, climbed the curbstone, astonished heads appearing in the side windows. The furiously pedaling boy could not know how slow he seemed to be moving from the vantage point of the women on the porch. The women were silent by now, outside the event, suddenly tired. How slow he moved, how mistaken he was in thinking he was breezing right along. It made them tired. The horns kept blowing, sound waves mixing in the air, flattening, calling back from vanished cars, scolding. He reached the other side, briefly rode parallel to the traffic, seemed to lose his balance, fall away, going down the embankment in a multicolored tumble. When he reappeared a second later, he was sitting in a water furrow, part of the intermittent creek that accompanies the highway. Stunned, he made the decision to cry. It took him a moment, mud and water everywhere, the tricycle on its side. The women began to call once more, each raising an arm to revoke the action. Boy in the water, they said. Look, help, drown. And he seemed, on his seat in the creek, profoundly howling, to have heard them for the first time, looking up over the earthen mound and into the trees across the expressway. This frightened them all the more. They called and waved, were approaching the early phases of uncontrollable terror when a passing motorist, as such people are called, alertly pulled over, got out of the car, skidded down the embankment and lifted the boy from the murky shallows, holding him aloft for the clamoring elders to see.

We go to the overpass all the time. Babette, Wilder and I. We take a thermos of iced tea, park the car, watch the setting sun. Clouds are no deterrent. Clouds intensify the drama, trap and shape the light. Heavy overcasts have little effect. Light bursts through, tracers and smoky arcs. Overcasts enhance the mood. We find little to say to each other. More cars arrive, parking in a line that extends down to the residential zone. People walk up the incline and onto the overpass, carrying fruit and nuts, cool drinks, mainly the middle-aged, the elderly, some with webbed beach chairs which they set out on the sidewalk, but younger couples also, arm in arm at the rail, looking west. The sky takes on content, feeling, an exalted narrative life. The bands of color reach so high, seem at times to separate into their constituent parts. There are turreted skies, light storms, softly falling streamers. It is hard to know how we should feel about this. Some people are scared by the sunsets, some determined to be elated, but most of us don't know how to feel, are ready to go either way. Rain is no deterrent. Rain brings on graded displays, wonderful running hues. More cars arrive, people come trudging up the incline. The spirit of these warm evenings is hard to describe. There is anticipation in the air but it is not the expectant midsummer hum of a shirtsleeve crowd, a sandlot game, with coherent precedents, a history of secure response. This waiting is introverted, uneven, almost backward and shy, tending toward silence. What else do we feel? Certainly there is awe, it is all awe, it transcends previous categories of awe, but we don't know whether we are watching in wonder or dread, we don't know what we are watching or what it means, we don't know whether it is permanent, a level of experience to which we will gradually adjust, into which our uncertainty will eventually be absorbed, or just some atmospheric weirdness, soon to pass. The collapsible chairs are yanked open, the old people sit. What is there to say? The sunsets linger and so do we. The sky is under a spell, powerful and storied. Now and then a car actually crosses the overpass, moving slowly, deferentially. People keep coming up the incline, some in wheelchairs, twisted by disease, those who attend them bending low to push against the grade. I didn't know how many handicapped and helpless people there were in town until the warm nights brought crowds to the overpass. Cars speed beneath us, coming from the west, from out of the towering light, and we watch them as if for a sign, as if they carry on their painted surfaces some residue of the sunset, a barely detectable luster or film of telltale dust. No one plays a radio or speaks in a voice that is much above a whisper. Something golden falls, a softness delivered to the air. There are people walking dogs, there are kids on bikes, a man with a camera and long lens, waiting for his moment. It is not until some time after dark has fallen, the insects screaming in the heat, that we slowly begin to disperse, shyly, politely, car after car, restored to our separate and defensible selves.

The men in Mylex suits are still in the area, yellow-snouted, gathering their terrible data, aiming their infrared devices at the earth and sky.

Dr. Chakravarty wants to talk to me but I am making it a point to stay away. He is eager to see how my death is progressing. An interesting case perhaps. He wants to insert me once more in the imaging block, where charged particles collide, high winds blow. But I am afraid of the imaging block. Afraid of its magnetic fields, its computerized nuclear pulse. Afraid of what it knows about me.

I am taking no calls.

The supermarket shelves have been rearranged. It happened one day without warning. There is agitation and panic in the aisles, dismay in the faces of older shoppers. They walk in a fragmented trance, stop and go, clusters of well-dressed figures frozen in the aisles, trying to figure out the pattern, discern the underlying logic, trying to remember where they'd seen the Cream of Wheat. They see no reason for it, find no sense in it. The scouring pads are with the hand soap now, the condiments are scattered. The older the man or woman, the more carefully dressed and groomed. Men in Sansabelt slacks and bright knit shirts. Women with a powdered and fussy look, a self-conscious air, prepared for some anxious event. They turn into the wrong aisle, peer along the shelves, sometimes stop abruptly, causing other carts to run into them. Only the generic food is where it was, white packages plainly labeled. The men consult lists, the women do not. There is a sense of wandering now, an aimless and haunted mood, sweet-tempered people taken to the edge. They scrutinize the small print on packages, wary of a second level of betrayal. The men scan for stamped dates, the women for ingredients. Many have trouble making out the words. Smeared print, ghost images. In the altered shelves, the ambient roar, in the plain and heartless fact of their decline, they try to work their way through confusion. But in the end it doesn't matter what they see or think they see. The terminals are equipped with holographic scanners, which decode the binary secret of every item, infallibly. This is the language of waves and radiation, or how the dead speak to the living. And this is where we wait together, regardless of age, our carts stocked with brightly colored goods. A slowly moving line, satisfying, giving us time to glance at the tabloids in the racks. Everything we need that is not food or love is here in the tabloid racks. The tales of the supernatural and the extraterrestrial. The miracle vitamins, the cures for cancer, the remedies for obesity. The cults of the famous and the dead.

II

Contexts

Anthony DeCurtis

This interview appeared in *Rolling Stone*'s November 17, 1988, issue; a longer version, entitled " 'An Outsider in This Society,' An Interview with Don DeLillo," was later collected in *Introducing Don DeLillo*, edited by Frank Lentricchia.

from MATTERS OF FACT AND FICTION

DECURTIS: . . . Some specific American realities have a draw for you.

DELILLO: Certainly there are themes that recur. Perhaps a sense of secret patterns in our lives. A sense of ambiguity. Certainly the violence of contemporary life is a motif. I see contemporary violence as a kind of sardonic response to the promise of consumer fulfillment in America. Again we come back to these men in small rooms who can't get out and who have to organize their desperation and their loneliness, who have to give it a destiny and who often end up doing this through violent means. I see this desperation against the backdrop of brightly colored packages and products and consumer happiness and every promise that American life makes day by day and minute by minute everywhere we go. . . .

DECURTIS: Humor plays an important role in your novels. Do you see it as providing relief from the grimness of some of your subjects?

DELILLO: I don't think the humor is intended to counteract the fear. It's almost part of it. We ourselves may almost instantaneously use humor to offset a particular moment of discomfort or fear, but this reflex is so deeply woven into the original fear that they almost become the same thing. . . .

DECURTIS: There seems to be a fondness in your writing, particularly in *White Noise*, for what might be described as the trappings of suburban middle-class existence, to the point where one of the characters describes the supermarket as a sacred place.

DELILLO: I would call it a sense of the importance of daily life and of ordinary moments. In *White Noise*, in particular, I tried to find a kind of radiance in dailiness. Sometimes this radiance can be almost frightening. Other times it can be almost holy or sacred. Is it really there? Well, yes. You know, I don't believe as Murray Jay Siskind does in *White Noise* that the supermarket is a form of Tibetan lamasery. But there is something there that we tend to miss.

Imagine someone from the third world who has never set foot in a place like that suddenly transported to an A&P in Chagrin Falls, Ohio. Wouldn't he be elated or frightened? Wouldn't he sense that something transcending is about to happen to him in the midst of all this brightness. So I think that's something that has been in the background of my work: a sense of something extraordinary hovering just beyond our touch and just beyond our vision.

DECURTIS: Hitler and the Holocaust have repeatedly been addressed in your books. In *Running Dog*, a pornographic movie allegedly filmed in Hitler's bunker determines a good deal of the novel's plot. In *White Noise*, university professor Jack Gladney attempts to calm his obsessive fear of death through his work in the Department of Hitler Studies.

DELILLO: In his case, Gladney finds a perverse form of protection. The damage caused by Hitler was so enormous that Gladney feels he can disappear inside it and that his own puny dread will be overwhelmed by the vastness, the monstrosity of Hitler himself. He feels that Hitler is not only bigger than life, as we say of many famous figures, but bigger that death. Our sense of fear—we avoid it because we feel it so deeply, so there is an intense conflict at work. I brought this conflict to the surface in the shape of Jack Gladney.

I think it is something we all feel, something we almost never talk about, something that is *almost* there. I tried to relate it in *White Noise* to this other sense of transcendence that lies just beyond our touch. This extraordinary wonder of things is somehow related to the extraordinary dread, to the death fear we try to keep beneath the surface of our perceptions.

Adam Begley

This interview appeared in the *Paris Review* in 1993.

from DON DELILLO: THE ART OF FICTION

INTERVIEWER: There are a number of characters in your work who discover that they are going to die sooner than they thought, though they don't know exactly when. Bucky Wunderlick isn't going to die, but he's been given something awful, and for all he knows the side effects are deadly; Jack Gladney, poisoned by the toxic spill, is another obvious example; and then we come to Bill Gray with his automobile accident. What does this accelerated but vague mortality mean?

DELILLO: Who knows? If writing is a concentrated form of thinking, then the most concentrated writing probably ends in some kind of reflection on dying. This is what we eventually confront if we think long enough and hard enough.

INTERVIEWER: Could it be related to the idea in *Libra* that—

DELILLO: —all plots lead toward death? I guess that's possible. It happens in *Libra*, and it happens in *White Noise*, which doesn't necessarily mean that these are highly plotted novels. *Libra* has many digressions and meditations, and Oswald's life just meanders along for much of the book. It's the original plotter, Win Everett, who wonders if his conspiracy might grow tentacles that will turn an assassination *scare* into an actual murder, and of course this is what happens. The plot extends its own logic to the ultimate point. And *White Noise* develops a trite adultery plot that enmeshes the hero, justifying his fears about the death energies contained in plot. When I think of highly plotted novels I think of detective fiction or mystery fiction, the kind of work that always produces a few dead bodies. But these bodies are basically plot points, not worked-out characters. The book's plot either moves inexorably toward a dead body or flows directly from it, and the more artificial the situation the better. Readers can play off their fears by encountering the death experience in a superficial way. A mystery novel localizes the awesome force of the real death outside the book, winds it tightly in a plot, makes it less fearful by containing it in a kind of game format.

INTERVIEWER: Could you tell me about the passage in *White Noise* in which Jack listens to his daughter Steffie talking in her sleep, and she is repeating the words *Toyota Celica*?

DELILLO: There's something nearly mystical about certain words and phrases that float through our lives. It's computer mysticism. Words that are computer generated to be used on products that might be sold anywhere from Japan to Denmark—words devised to be pronounceable in a hundred languages. And when you detach one of these words from the product it was designed to serve, the word acquires a chantlike quality. Years ago somebody decided—I don't know how this conclusion was reached—that the most beautiful phrase in the English language was *cellar door.* If you concentrate on the sound, if you disassociate the words from the object they denote, and if you say the words over and over, they become a sort of higher Esperanto. This is how *Toyota Celica* began its life. It was pure chant at the beginning. Then they had to find an object to accommodate the words.

INTERVIEWER: It's been said that you have an "ostentatiously gloomy view of American society."

DELILLO: I don't agree, but I can understand how a certain kind of reader would see the gloomy side of things. My work doesn't offer the comforts of other kinds of fiction, work that suggests that our lives and our problems and our perceptions are no different today than they were fifty or sixty years ago. I don't offer comforts except those that lurk in comedy and in structure and in language, and the comedy is probably not all that soothing. But before everything, there's language. Before history and politics, there's language. And it's language, the sheer pleasure of making it and bending it and seeing it form on the page and hearing it whistle in my head—this is the thing that makes my work go. And art can be exhilarating despite the darkness—and there's certainly much darker material than mine—if the reader is sensitive to the music. What I try to do is create complex human beings, ordinary-extraordinary men and women who live in the particular skin of the late twentieth century. I try to record what I see and hear and sense around me—what I feel in the currents, the electric stuff of the culture. I think these are American forces and energies. And they belong to our time.

Caryn James

This piece appeared alongside a review of *White Noise* in the *New York Times Book Review* on January 13, 1985.

" 'I NEVER SET OUT TO WRITE AN APOCALYPTIC NOVEL' "

"I thought of a college that had a department of Hitler studies and that led to death as a subject," Don DeLillo says in describing the origin of *White Noise.* Talking by phone from his home just outside New York City, he is matter-of-fact. "I haven't a clue where that thought came from, but it seemed innately comic, and everything sprang from it. I never felt that I was writing a comic novel before *White Noise.* Maybe the fact that death permeates the book made me retreat into comedy."

Despite the shadow of Hitler and the topical issue of disastrous toxic leaks, Mr. DeLillo says his novel is about prosaic events—the anxieties and mysteries that infuse daily life. "I never set out to write an apocalyptic novel. It's about death on the individual level. Only Hitler is large enough and terrible enough to absorb and neutralize Jack Gladney's obsessive fear of dying—a very common fear, but one that's rarely talked about. Jack uses Hitler as a protective device; he wants to grasp anything he can."

The conjunction of the apocalyptic and the ordinary may be most evident in the character of Murray J. Siskind, who, Mr. DeLillo says, finds the supermarket "very rich in magic and dread; it's a kind of church. Perhaps the supermarket tabloids are the richest material of all, closest to the spirit of the book. They ask profoundly important questions about death, the afterlife, God, worlds and space, yet they exist in an almost Pop Art atmosphere."

Everyday mysteries are embodied in the book's children as well.

"They are a form of magic. The adults are mystified by all the data that flows through their lives, but the children carry the data and absorb it most deeply. They give family life a buzz and hum; it's almost another form of white noise," Mr. DeLillo says. Although he has no children, he denies that their real-life absence influenced his decision to "populate" *White Noise* with them. "There's very little autobiography in my books," he says.

Mr. DeLillo is working on a new novel, but when asked to talk about it, his reply is characteristically understated: "My lips are sealed."

Don DeLillo

In this excerpt from *Americana* (1971), David Bell films a man playing his father, an advertising executive, as he expounds on television advertising.

from *AMERICANA*

A game show was on TV, young married contestants and a suavely gliding master of ceremonies; there were frequent commercials, the usual daytime spasms on behalf of detergents and oral hygiene. This is what I filmed for roughly eight minutes, the TV set, having to break twice for reloading, as Glenn and I, off camera, read from the wrinkled scattered script. Glenn spoke in a monotone throughout.

"We're going to talk about test patterns and shadows. Certain forms of darkness. A small corner of the twentieth century."

"I have all the answers."

"And I have the questions," I said. "We begin, simply enough, with a man watching television. Quite possibly he is being driven mad, slowly, in stages, program by program, interruption by interruption. Still, he watches. What is there in that box? Why is he watching?"

"The TV set is a package and it's full of products. Inside are detergents, automobiles, cameras, breakfast cereal, other television sets. Programs are not interrupted by commercials; exactly the reverse is true. A television set is an electronic form of packaging. It's as simple as that. Without the products there's nothing. Educational television's a joke. Who in America would want to watch TV without commercials?"

"How does a successful television commercial affect the viewer?"

"It makes him want to change the way he lives."

"In what way?" I said.

"It moves him from first person consciousness to third person. In this country there is a universal third person, the man we all want to be. Advertising has discovered this man. It uses him to express the possibilities open to the consumer. To consume in America is not to buy; it is to dream. Advertising is the suggestion that the dream of entering the third person singular might possibly be fulfilled."

"How then does a TV commercial differ from a movie? Movies are full of people we want to be."

"Advertising is never bigger than life. It tries not to edge too far over the fantasy line; in fact it often mocks different fantasy themes associated with the movies. Look, there's no reason why you can't fly Eastern to Acapulco and share two solid weeks of sex and adventure with a vacationing typist from Iowa City. But advertising never claims you can do it with Ava Gardner. Only Richard Burton can accomplish that. You can change your image but you can't change the image of the woman you take to bed. Advertising has merchandised this distinction. We have exploited the limitation of dreams. It's our greatest achievement."

"What makes a good advertising man?"

"He knows how to move the merch off the shelves. It's as simple as that. If the advertising business shut down tomorrow, I'd go over to Macy's and get a job selling men's underwear."

"Let's get back to images. Do the people who create commercials take into account this third person consciousness you've talked about with such persuasiveness and verve?"

"They just make their twenty-second art films. The third person was invented by the consumer, the great armchair dreamer. Advertising discovered the value of the third person but the consumer invented him. The country itself invented him. He came over on the *Mayflower*. I'm waiting for you to ask me about the anti-image."

"What's that?"

"It's the guerrilla warfare being fought behind the lines of the image. It's a picture of devastating spiritual atrocities. The perfect example of the anti-image in advertising is the slice-of-life commercial. A recognizable scene in a suburban home anywhere in the USA. Some dialogue between dad and junior or between Madge and the members of the bridge club. Problem: Madge is suffering from irregularity. Solution: Drink this stuff and the muses will squat. The rationale behind this kind of advertising is that the consumer will identify with Madge. This is a mistake. The consumer never identifies with the anti-image. He identifies only with the image. The Marlboro man. Frank Gifford and Bobby Hull in their Jantzen bathing suits. Slice-of-life commercials usually deal with the more depressing areas of life—odors, sores, old age, ugliness, pain. Fortunately the image is big enough to absorb the anti-image. Not that I object to the anti-image in principle. It has its possibilities; the time may not be far off when we tire of the dream. But the anti-image is being presented much too literally. The old themes. The stereotyped dialogue. It needs a touch of horror, some mad laughter from the graveyard. One of these days some smart copywriter will perceive the true inner mystery of

America and develop an offshoot to the slice-of-life. The slice-of-death."

"Have you spent the major part of your adult life in the advertising business?"

"All but four years."

"Where were they spent?" I said.

"I served a hitch in the army during the war."

"Where?"

"The Pacific."

"Where in the Pacific?"

"The Philippines."

"Where in the Philippines?"

"Bataan: they made two movies about it."

"Do you ever feel uneasy about your place in the constantly unfolding incorporeal scheme of things?"

"Only when I try to pre-empt the truth."

"What does that mean?"

"One of the clients I service is the Nix Olympica Corporation. They make a whole line of products for the human body. Depilatories, salves, foot powder, styptic pencils, mouthwash, cotton swabs for the ears, deodorants for the armpit, deodorants for the male and female crotch, acne cream medication, sinus remedies, denture cleansers, laxatives, corn plasters. We were preparing a campaign for their Dentex Division; that's mouthwash primarily. Okay, so we zero in on one of the essential ingredients, quasi-cinnamaldehyde-plus. QCP. We take the hard-sell route. Dentex with QCP kills mouth poisons and odor-causing impurities thirty-two percent faster. Be specific. Be factual. Make a promise. Okay, so some little creep says to me in a meeting: thirty-two percent faster than what? Obviously, I tell him: thirty-two percent faster than if Dentex didn't have QCP. The fact that all mouthwashes have this cinnamaldehyde stuff is beside the point; we were the only ones talking about it. This is known as pre-empting the truth. The creative people do a storyboard. Open on Formula One racing car, number six, Watkins Glen. Action, noise, crowd, throttling, crack-ups, explosions. Number six comes in first. Beauty queen rushes up to car, leans over to kiss driver, then turns away with grimace. Bad breath. She doesn't want to kiss him. Cut to medical lab, guy with white smock. This is a dramatization—charts, diagrams, supers, QCP thirty-two percent faster. Back to original guy, number six, different race. Checkered flag drops, he wins, wreath around the neck, beauty queen kisses him, dissolve to victory party as they dance, kiss, whisper, dance, kiss. We took the idea to Dentex. They loved it. We took it upstairs to Nix Olympica. They loved it. They were delighted. They gave us the okay to shoot. We get cars and drivers and extras. We go up to Watkins Glen. We use helicopters, we use tracking shots, we use slow-motion, we use stop-action, we zoom, we wide-angle, we set up two small crashes and one monster explosion with a car turning over that nearly kills half the crew. I called a special meeting of the agency's planning board and ran the final print for them. They loved it. When I told them it cost as much, pro-rated, as the movie *Cleopatra*, they were delighted. They would have something to tell their wives that evening. The next day we showed the commercial to Dentex. They loved it. They were delighted. We took it upstairs to Nix Olympica. They turned it down flat. The money didn't bother them; they were impressed with the money; they would have something to tell their wives. But they turned it down flat. They ordered us to re-shoot both sequences in the winner's circle."

"Why?"

"Because of the Oriental. Because of the old man standing at the edge of the group of extras who were crowding around the winner's circle both times, first when the beauty queen refused to kiss number six and then when she did kiss him. Both times he was there, this small shrunken old man, this Oriental. Who was he? Who hired him? How did he get into the crowd? Nobody knew. But he was there all right and Nix Olympica spotted him. All the other extras were young healthy gleaming men and women. It's a commercial for mouthwash; you want health, happiness, freshness, mouth-appeal. And this sick-looking old man is hovering there, this really depressing downbeat Oriental. Look, I love the business. I thrive on it. But I can't help wondering if I've wasted my life simply because of the old man who ruined the mouthwash commercial. On a spring evening some years ago, during the time when my wife was very ill, when she was nearing the very end, I walked up a street in the upper Thirties and turned right onto Park Avenue and there was the Pan Am Building, a mile high and half-a-mile wide, every light blazing, an impossible slab of squared-off rock hulking above me and crowding everything else out of the way, even the sky. It looked like God. I had never seen the Pan Am Building from that particular spot and I wasn't prepared for the colossal surprise of it, the way it crowded out the sky, that overwhelming tier of lights. I swear to you it looked like God the Father. What was the point I was trying to make?"

"I don't know."

"Neither do I. I guess that's what comes of trying to pre-empt the truth."

"What is the role of commercial television in the twentieth century and beyond?"

"In my blackest moods I feel it spells chaos for all of us."

"How do you get over these moods?" I said.

"I take a mild and gentle Palmolive bath, brush my teeth with Crest, swallow two Sominex tablets, and try desperately to fall asleep on my Simmons Beautyrest mattress."

"Thank you."

Don DeLillo

In this excerpt from *End Zone* (1972), protagonist Gary Harkness describes the origins of his fascination with nuclear war.

from *END ZONE*

It started with a book, an immense volume about the possibilities of nuclear war—assigned reading for a course I was taking on the modes of disaster technology. The problem was simple and terrible: I enjoyed the book. I liked reading about the deaths of tens of millions of people. I liked dwelling on the destruction of great cities. Five to twenty million dead. Fifty to a hundred million dead. Ninety percent population loss. Seattle wiped out by mistake. Moscow demolished. Airbursts over every SAC base in Europe. I liked to think of huge buildings toppling, of firestorms, of bridges collapsing, survivors roaming the charred countryside. Carbon 14 and strontium 90. Escalation ladder and subcrisis situation. Titan, Spartan, Poseidon. People burned and unable to breathe. People being evacuated from doomed cities. People diseased and starving. Two hundred thousand bodies decomposing on the roads outside Chicago. I read several chapters twice. Pleasure in the contemplation of millions dying and dead. I became fascinated by words and phrases like thermal hurricane, overkill, circular error probability, post-attack environment, stark deterrence, dose-rate contours, kill-ratio, spasm war. Pleasure in these words. They were extremely effective, I thought, whispering shyly of cycles of destruction so great that the language of past world wars became laughable, the wars themselves somewhat naive. A thrill almost sensual accompanied the reading of this book. What was wrong with me? Had I gone mad? Did others feel as I did? I became seriously depressed. Yet I went to the library and got more books on the subject. Some of these had been published well after the original volume and things were much more up-to-date. Old weapons vanished. Megatonnage soared. New concepts appeared—the rationality of irrationality, hostage cities, orbital attacks. I became more fascinated, more depressed, and finally I left Coral Gables and went back home to my room and to the official team photo of the Detroit Lions. It seemed the only thing to do. My mother brought lunch upstairs. I took the dog for walks.

Major Staley, who plays nuclear-war games with Gary, theorizes about nuclear weapons.

"There's a kind of theology at work here. The bombs are a kind of god. As his power grows, our fear naturally increases. I get as apprehensive as anyone else, maybe more so. We have too many bombs. They have too many bombs. There's a kind of theology of fear that comes out of this. We begin to capitulate to the overwhelming presence. It's so powerful. It dwarfs us so much. We say let the god have his way. He's so much more powerful than we are. Let it happen, whatever he ordains. It used to be that the gods punished men by using the forces of nature against them or by arousing them to take up their weapons and destroy each other. Now god is the force of nature itself, the fusion of tritium and deuterium. Now he's the weapon. So maybe this time we went too far in creating a being of omnipotent power. All this hardware. Fantastic stockpiles of hardware. The big danger is that we'll surrender to a sense of inevitability and start flinging mud all over the planet."

During a meal, Gary's college roommate Anatole Bloomberg discourses on violence.

"I am interested in the violent man and the ascetic. I am on the verge of concluding that an individual's capacity for violence is closely linked with his ascetic tendencies. We are about to rediscover that austerity is our true mode. In our future meditations we may decide to seek the devil's death. In our silence and terror we may steer our technology toward the metaphysical, toward the creation of some unimaginable weapon able to pierce spiritual barriers, to maim or kill whatever dark presence envelopes the world. You will say this seems an unlikely matter to engage the talents of superrational man. But it is precisely this kind of man who has been confronting the unreal, the paradoxical, the ironic, the satanic. After all, the ultimate genius of modern weapons, from the purely theoretical standpoint, is that they destroy the unborn much more effectively than they destroy the living. We can go on from there to frame any number of provocative remarks but we will resist the temptation. We all know that life, happiness, fulfillment come surging out of particular forms of destructiveness. The moral system is enriched by violence put to positive use. But as the capacity for violence grows in the world, the regenerative effects of specific violent episodes become less significant. The capacity overwhelms everything. The mere potential of one form of violence eclipses the actuality of other forms. I am interested in these things. I am also interested in the discontinuation of contractions. Medial letters are as valid as any others. I have already begun to revise my speech patterns accordingly."

We were all laughing, not knowing exactly why. Maybe we thought Bloomberg was crazy. Or maybe we laughed because it was the only reaction we could trust, the only one that could keep us at a safe distance. Anatole, replying to the laughter, tapped his spoon against the plastic tray to his right. I finished my corn flakes and proceeded, as arranged, to the library.

Don DeLillo

In this excerpt from *Players*, Lyle Wynant practices watching television and his wife, Pammy, provides commentary.

from *PLAYERS*

Lyle passed time watching television. Sitting in near darkness about eighteen inches from the screen, he turned the channel selector every half minute or so, sometimes much more frequently. He wasn't looking for something that might sustain his interest. Hardly that. He simply enjoyed jerking the dial into fresh image-burns. He explored content to a point. The tactile-visual delight of switching channels took precedence, however, transforming even random moments of content into pleasing territorial abstractions. Watching television was for Lyle a discipline like mathematics or Zen. Commercials, station breaks, Spanish-language dramas had more to offer as a rule than standard programming. The repetitive aspect of commercials interested him. Seeing identical footage many times was a test for the resourcefulness of the eye, its ability to re-select, to subdivide an instant of time. He rarely used sound. Sound was best served by those UHF stations using faulty equipment or languages other than English.

Occasionally he watched one of the public-access channels. There was an hour or so set aside every week for locally crafted pornography, the work of native artisans. He found on the screen a blunter truth certainly than in all that twinkling flesh in the slick magazines. He sat in his bowl of curved space, his dusty light. There was a child's conspicuous immodesty in all this genital aggression. People off the streets looking for something to suck. Hand-held cameras searching out the odd crotch. Lyle was immobile through this sequence of small gray bodies. What he saw retained his attention completely even as it continued to dull his senses. The hour seemed like four. Weary as he was, blanked out, bored by all these posturing desperadoes, he could easily have watched through the night, held by the mesh effect of television, the electrostatic glow that seemed a privileged state between wave and visual image, a secret of celestial energy. He wondered if he'd become too complex to look at naked bodies, as such, and be stirred.

"Here, look. We're here, folks. The future has collapsed right in on us. And what does it look like?"

"You made me almost jump."

"It looks like this. It looks like waves and waves of static. It's being beamed in ahead of schedule, which accounts for the buzzing effect. It looks like seedy people from Mercer Street."

"Let me sleep, hey."

"See, look, I'm saying. Just as I speak. I mean it's this. We're sitting watching in the intimacy and comfort of our bedroom and they've got their loft and their camera and it gets shown because that's the law. As soon as they see a camera they take off their clothes. It used to be people waved."

Don DeLillo

In this frightening essay, originally published by the Anti-Defamation League of B'nai B'rith, in *Dimensions*, DeLillo develops links between Nazism and contemporary millenarian movements.

SILHOUETTE CITY: HITLER, MANSON AND THE MILLENNIUM

We find messages of death and danger almost everywhere. On the nightly news, in the medical column, on the health channel, in the images of the homeless and the AIDS-afflicted, in the junk mail, in the public service advisories, in the supermarket tabloids and their cult worship of the celebrity dead. It's all mixed together, routinely braided into our lives—murder, torture, superstition, satire, grueling human ordeal. Information shades into rumor and mass fantasy, which convert to topical entertainment. Our levels of perception begin to blend. It isn't always easy to separate disease from its mythology or violence from its trivialization. Not that we're necessarily eager to make distinctions. We depend on an environment that softens and absorbs, that receives the impact of dangerous things without recoil or echo. The message is processed, assimilated and made into something else entirely. Idi Amin became a T-shirt. Racial hostility is a frequent subtext of commercials for beer, soft drinks and running shoes. In these 20-second sociodramas, danger appears in the form of angry-looking blacks, who are then instantly reconstituted as happy Pepsi drinkers. We try to obscure threats and disruptions by tailoring them to a format of consumer appeal.

There is another danger we must think about. It reaches us across the decades, subject to the same occasional blurring. We know it mainly by its original markings, its blazonry of the death's-head and the swastika.

Is there something missing from your life which the imagination of the Nazis can helpfully provide?

Nazi lore and notation represent a rich source of material to be consulted in the service of fantasy and self-fulfillment. For your sub-erotic side, there are bondage hoods and tooled black leather. For your violent or racist side, there is inspiration to be drawn from Aryan publications and white power music. For wholesome family entertainment, you have the Holocaust thriller. This is the category of book, movie and TV drama in which the madness of Hitler and the suffering of the Jews function as story apparatus, easily inserted components that are recognizable at once for their vivid qualities of suspense and melodrama. For your sentimental side, there are many detailed studies of the last days of the Third Reich running their melancholy course as Bruckner's *Romantic Symphony* is performed in an unheated concert hall before music lovers in overcoats. Even the collapse of the Nazi empire had its play list, designed by Albert Speer as if to organize the longings of future generations. For your collecting pleasure, you'll find Third Reich memorabilia everywhere. There are perhaps 50,000 collectors and most are American. The prizes range from Goering's hunting dagger to Hitler's Mercedes, and the excitement, of course, abides in the touch of objects once owned by the authors of unspeakable crimes.

There is some element in the soul that creates in us a need to know the worst about ourselves. If we are a species called Thinking Creature, then let's think to the limit, let's imagine the worst, let's set out to find the purest representative of the species that can imagine the worst. We are obsessed by the Nazis finally because they were masters of extremity. They not only imagined the worst; they did it. They engineered a level of pain and death that takes us to the end of self-knowledge. Beyond this point, what is there to know? We tend to see even their own eventual death as self-inflicted. Only masters could produce such extravagant ruin. There is also something in the Nazi era that addresses us as individuals. Each of us spins on a life-axis of power and submission. The Nazis were so steeped in the uses of power, so determined to force mass capitulation, that we can't help using them as final measures of our personal flaws. They make us uneasy about ourselves, our occasional blind obedience to authority, our willingness to abandon ourselves to a strong personality. We may refer to them unconsciously when we think about our attempts to dominate certain people, to oppress and control, and when we wonder why our lives seem empty without these routine shows of power. Are there particular words one person says to another when the struggle between them grows intense and unequal? "*Fascist!*" "*Nazi!*" Foolish to use these words so randomly. Ridiculous to compare ourselves to men who subjected innocent millions to extremities of horror. But these men have aroused a watchfulness in us. We see their shadow not only at the nightmare edge of collective perception but in the office where we work and the rooms where we live.

And as we monitor ourselves on one level, we may think about the limits of state power and feel a different kind of disquiet. It is clear that our weakened position in the world, after Vietnam and other emblems of decline, has led us into a moral pause, a homesickness for the experience of power unleashed. It was not so long ago that many Americans watched the Soviets march into Afghanistan and pointed out how quickly and brutally they would crush the rebels—no equivocation here. The air of wistfulness was unmistakable (and seems almost touching in the light of subsequent events). It appears to us today that only terror succeeds, only fanatics win unconditional victories, and that every vital design of our democratic mandate must pass through a network of compromise and distortion. This has caused a wavering of the grace of moral vision. In our confusion we may find ourselves seduced by the imagery of force and domination, by the spectacle of an empire that made a systematic attempt to reach the human limit—the limit of fantasy, myth and murderousness.

And do we have a glimpse, today, of something strange working through the margins of the heartland, a new fantasy that takes us beyond the various pornographies we have minted from the Nazi esthetic? The theme of this fantasy is apocalypse and the rewards it offers the conscientious dreamer are an escape from conflict and a direct route to earthly rapture and salvation. There is a formal sense of millennium here. It not only looks ahead to the year 2000 but recollects as well. The operative nostalgia centers our attention on a small group of true believers clustered in the fuehrerbunker as howitzers fill the night with muzzle flash and holy thunder.

2

In his study of millenarian movements *[The Pursuit of the Millennium: Revolutionary Messianism in Medieval and Reformation Europe and Its Bearing on Modern Totalitarian Movements]*, Norman Cohn traces the secularized form of this ancient longing—for destruction to hammer down, for history to end, for harmony and well-being to sweep the world—directly into the totalitarian core of twentieth century fascism and communism.

In their naive form, millenarian movements may appear as isolated rustlings among oppressed or displaced people, the offscourings of society, flea-ridden and illiterate. These are minds open to mirage, to the strong voices of prophets and wonderworkers, messianic figures who tend to lay their most effective claim to legitimacy against a setting of chaos or terror—plague, famine, revolution, the shock of an encroaching culture. Often these men will make *predictions* of calamity, some utopian disaster that carries salvation with it, the cleansing onset of a perfect age. Here the millenarian group will be free of complicating forces, free of enemies, conspiracies, evil. In the face of these prophecies and astonishments, members of such groups may abandon the patterns of generations, walk away from the landowners' fields, leaving crops to rot. Then the desperate ecstasies begin, the frenzies and aberrations—trance states, dancing manias, self-flagellation. People have visions and speak in tongues.

In medieval Europe certain themes began to develop around the millenarian experience. There were legends of dead men returning, leaders of mass movements (such as Baldwin IX and Frederick II) whose followers had every expectation that the Last Days were near. This wishful credit we extend to heroes is clearly still part of our psychology, detectable at the ironic level of pop culture where dead rock stars routinely reappear in ordinary places, poorly photographed. But there is also, tellingly, our continued reluctance to accept the death of significant figures. It could be argued that our reconstruction of the details of President Kennedy's assassination, a quarter century's grim labor, is in some sense an attempt to rewrite time, to put the man himself back together. A strong leader stands, in Ernest Becker's phrase, as our "bulwark against death." And when a master of death such as Hitler dies, what do his followers do with the secret yearning only he could answer—the yearning to be spellbound, unburdened of free will and self-command? They redirect their feelings to Argentina, where the leader is said to live on, breeding expectations of magical return.

Another early millenarian theme concerns the relationship between a spiritually elevated sense of mission and a harrowing earthbound reality. Or how visionary joy and order tend to float above a landscape of panoramic violence. In Crusader days the central apparition was a jeweled city at the end of time, liberated Jerusalem. Multitudes of the poor, prophecy-driven and racked by disease, formed journeys of exalted purpose, advancing toward the Moslem towers. Carrying a shared fantasy of the Last Days, they passed from town to town, barefoot, with crosses sewn on their shirts, massed in hardship, in imitation of Christ, and wherever they went they searched out Jews and killed them. The massacre of Jews was a preparation for some Crusades, an accompaniment to others. Seen as demon-conspirator, the Jew had to convert or die before the millennium could properly come to pass. With him, at times, went the local bishop and abbot, killed for their worldliness. Ascetics, hermit kings, runaway monks all preached the Crusades and won total devotion from the horde. Crop failures brought messianic hopes, prophecies of apocalypse, new Crusades and new atrocities. Bands of flagellants began moving across parts of Europe, their leather scourges fitted with iron spikes. The movement spread, becoming a penitential epic of torn flesh and a prayer for deliverance from the Black Death. In the eschatological drama of the plague, the flagellants led slaughterous assaults on the Jewish populations of many cities. Death answering death. In time the movement degenerated into obscure sects, officially suppressed. Members were pursued and burned at the stake, but others continued to meet in secret, flogging themselves relentlessly, still assembling the vision of a renewed society, harmonious and whole. Among the many ways we can live secretly, perhaps the most satisfying is in the passionate service of a fantasy, our doors double-locked against the impure world, our sense of expectancy rising to a sacred and dangerous pitch. This is the rapture of living in the Last Days.

When these tides reach our own century and become the transforming rage of nations, we may feel the need to consult the source books, the very prose of apocalyptic struggle. In *Mein Kampf*, Hitler wrote of "the world empire of Jewish satrapies" and "the approaching fulfillment of their testamentary prophecy about the great devouring of nations." The Jew will continue to advance "until another force comes forth to oppose him, and in a mighty struggle hurls the heaven-stormer back to Lucifer."

Once the "millennial Jew empire" is destroyed, the state can comfortably begin its Thousand Year Reich.

Norman Cohn writes, "This is the vision that accounts for the otherwise incomprehensible decision to undertake, in the middle of a desperate war and at immense cost in labour and materials and transport, the massacre of some six million Jewish men, women and children."

In newsreel Germany, the flickering gray country on our TV screens, we see social and political moments dressed up like miracle plays. Torchlight parades, tributes to the martyred dead, halls hung with mortuary wreaths, enormous rallies built around dramatic displays of sound and light. The sound is mainly Hitler's voice and he seems at times to be a medium of revelation, a man in a dream state, able to pick up signals from some layer of race memory and transmit them to the crowd in the form of commandment and harangue. Sometimes the older and more shaky the film, the greater the sense of mystical intensity. We know there is something rising above the geometric ranks of thousands of flag bearers standing among columns of sculptured light and it is the same spirit of world-shattering glory and terror, the same race hatreds and millennial enthrallments that informed the crusader rabble moving across Europe with pitchforks and pointed sticks. The medieval vision of the Holy City has become "the force of the national idea"—Hitler's total state. Even the name of this state, the Third Reich, gains in resonance from its similarity to the Third Age, the late twelfth century formulation of a new order of peace and understanding. Based in large part on a "decoding" of the Book of Revelation, the prophetic themes and patterns of Third Age belief became part of European consciousness, periodically reinterpreted but always centered on the conviction that the third age is the last age. In some cases the doctrinal experts specifically taught that the road to the millennium must pass through the city of death, the shadow city where the godless are arrayed for extermination.

3

In a small frame church in Indiana, people wait for the great tornado. God has spoken to the preacher's wife and said it is coming any time now, a towering column of dust and wind that will cause death and vast destruction. The church members don't send their children to school anymore. They've stopped going to their jobs or attending to their illnesses. The church is their home, their refuge and their seclusion. At night they fold up the metal chairs and set them against the walls. Then they spread out the bedding.

In a little town in Arkansas, not long after the communists took Saigon, two dozen people entered a small house and began a vigil. They were keeping watch for the Second Coming of Christ and the end of the world as we know it. They thought it might happen around Christmas and they put on their white ascension robes and waited. Neighbors complained about "bloodcurdling screams." The sheriff showed up to take custody of the children and the judge who tried to end the vigil couldn't help noticing the hate mail that began to fill his mailbox.

These are instances of one kind of American millenarianism. Its heart is stubborn and fundamentalist and its summons is powerful, carrying believers toward the wondrous year that will begin a new century. The more immediate promise is escape, a release from all the old bitterness and misery and bad luck. King Jesus stands in the safe land that waits behind the wall of fire and wind.

There is another kind of millenarian summons, a militant call that tends to place the faithful in barricaded buildings, often in remote mountain country, with a stock of ready weapons. Groups of white supremacists and neo-Nazis have established retreats, compounds, brotherhoods, networks, all linked to homegrown churches that mix apocalyptic reverie with violent anti-Semitism.

This is a membership of the dispossessed and betrayed. These are the outnumbered—"stout Aryan yeomen," as one manifesto puts it, who have been superseded by immigrants and stricken by "the cancer of racial masochism." They are sometimes joined in deep concealment by tax resisters, polygamists, Klansmen and other fugitives from justice, heavily armed.

The barricaded gunman is a lyrical fixture of our time. He is what remains of the wilderness and he feels a pulse in his brain that beats for desolation. Bring it all down. Down with complex systems, centralization, the whole scheming technocracy of welfare and banking. He knows where to put the blame. The enemy is called ZOG, or the Zionist Occupational Government.

Near the Missouri-Arkansas border a group called the Covenant, the Sword and the Arm of the Lord established a 224-acre compound that included computer equipment, a bomb factory and a church. The spiritual leader issued predictions of famine and race war. In the training area there was a rifle range known to the members of the group as Silhouette City. When police raided the area, they found a series of targets—man-shaped shadows on rectangular white backgrounds. Sketched on the chest area of every shadow was a Star of David.

These groups have been responsible for murders, synagogue bombings and many other crimes. But their deepest ambition has so far been restricted to the level of rhetoric—the overthrow of government and the founding of a separate Aryan nation. They know from the start they can't succeed. This accounts for the theme of heroic fatalism that runs through the movement. Even the far-seeing are resigned to a limited destiny, a warriorhood of the day-to-day. The one unsullied vision is the barricaded cabin in the hills, the sense of taking part in Armageddon, even if the final battle is small-scale and local, with FBI agents lofting tear gas over the ponderosa pine. It is our sense of truth that suffers when we deny that heroes are immortal.

There is a possible reference point for this romance of the isolate, the armed solitary with his mixed wish for survival and doom. It is the handed-down tale of Hitler, folk hero of death, hearing the world come to an end above his study in the bunker. One of the men of the extremist group the Brueder Schweigen, or Silent Brotherhood, built a shrine to Hitler in a crawl space in his house near Sandpoint, Idaho. The founder of the Brotherhood, killed by police, was honored in a memorial service held on Hitler's birthday. His widow said he was murdered because he was "brave enough to stand up and fight for God, truth and (his) race."

His brother said, "I'm not so sure he didn't want to die."

The death that rains on history and entices the modern imagination brings with it the lure of personal destruction. The fuehrerbunker is a myth of self-fulfillment. The Norse legends, the hall of slain warriors, the Heavenly Reich, the fate of all white kinsmen who raise the sword against ZOG. These are glories past naming.

The motto of the Brueder Schweigen reads like this: *We are the army of the already dead.*

4

Before the Aryan groups came to prominence, there was a spree of cult violence not widely recognized as millenarian but in fact showing so many signs of the medieval form as to seem a knife-happy parody. But there was no parody; only a system of belief and a set of actions that pursued traditional paths to world-end rapture. The group in question operated against a background of the Vietnam War and the assassinations of the 1960s—a collection of about seventy people, including drop-ins, drifters, bikers and ranch hands, led by a messianic figure who sent shock after shock down the goat gullet of the media and smack into the faces of gripped millions.

The Manson Family, carrying its own built-in sitcom title, lived for much of the time in Death Valley. Charles Manson, a guitar player and ex-convict, came out of nowhere, poor and dirty, like those charismatics of the Middle Ages who claimed to be risen kings, great leaders returned to life by the need of the people. Charlie told the Family he had lived and died before, almost two thousand years ago, drawing his last breath on a wooden cross. He made much of the fact that his last name, with syllables reversed, works out to Son (of) Man. He had no trouble finding believers. One of them said, "Just before we got busted in the desert, there was twelve of us apostles and Charlie."

The Manson cosmology comes out of the Bible, Scientology, Hopi Indian legend, the Beatles and Hitler. Manson spent serious time with the Book of Revelation, finding contemporary references everywhere. He believed that the last war on earth would be a racial conflict known as Helter Skelter. This phrase, from a Beatles' song, was found printed on a refrigerator door in the blood of one of the Family's victims.

The stranger the material, the more it fits the pattern.

The Adamites, a fifteenth-century millenarian sect, practiced free love but only at the direction of their leader, who didn't always give his consent, much like Charlie, in 1969, orchestrating the sex lives of his followers. The Adamites thought of themselves as holy avengers and ran night missions against local villagers, killing avidly. The Manson Family referred to their own night visits as "creepy-crawlies." Nobody knows how many dead they left behind.

The child in play builds a world of hypnotic intensity. Manson wanted to develop "a strong white race" and he set out to do this by eliminating every vestige of a connection between his followers and society. Family members folded themselves into Manson's world to the point where identities vanished. They entered a spell, a privileged state in which all the old conflicts and restraint yielded to the will of the leader.

It's a magical time. Charlie knows your thoughts.

He tells you what to do and you do it, and what to believe and you believe it. What could be better than this?

Manson was not unaware of the precedents.

He told the Family that "Hitler had the best answer to everything."

He said, "Hitler was a tuned-in guy who leveled the karma of the Jews."

As the murder trial progressed, new members were seen among the original Family every time Charlie made an appearance in court. When Charlie carved a swastika on his forehead, members did the same. And when the guilty verdict was announced, female members shaved their heads and warned America, "You'd better watch your children because Judgment Day is coming."

Charlie wasn't afraid of the death penalty. He'd faced death many times in this life and others.

"Death is Charlie's trip," said a member.

In the American air, with every thought permitted, the distance between thought and action becomes ever slighter, and in the malls and city streets and in the shadows of closed factories there's always someone who will shave his head so he can run with the other shaved heads, and together they will enter the culture, welcomed for their vividness and swagger, their adaptability to consumer format.

The San Francisco skinhead poses for the news camera and appears on TV with his tattoos and swastika T-shirt and that pale stubble on his head. He is a working-class boy proud of being white. It happens there are other skinheads from other cities who are also doing the talk shows and soon they've all been absorbed, exhausted, talked away, put in the product box—declassified. They are part of America's Sunday brunch. But somewhere along the way we've *noticed* something. The skinhead has raised an unexpected image, that of the shorn European Jew filmed by Allied liberators at places like Dachau and Nordhausen more than four decades ago. And we are helpless to break them apart. It is one more dread, one more victory of ignorance. The bullyboy has consumed and incorporated our memory of the victim without even realizing it. They are horribly locked in single bare face, the neo-Nazi and the death camp inmate, and this complex image collapses time and meaning and all sense of distinctions. It is one more haunted message in the river of blur and glut, the painted stream that passes daily through our lives.

Newsweek

When *White Noise* was first published in January 1985, many reviewers remarked that it reminded them of the Bhopal disaster, which had occurred on December 3, 1984. These three stories from *Newsweek*'s December 17, 1984, issue provide an account of the events in Bhopal, a description of the toxic chemical that caused the deaths, and a report on the likelihood of similar disasters in the United States.

from IT WAS LIKE BREATHING FIRE . . .

by Mark Whitaker, et al.

It was an unseasonably cold night in central India. In the shantytowns of Bhopal, thousands of poor families were asleep. At a nearby railway station, a scattering of people waited for early-morning trains. Suddenly, at the local Union Carbide plant, a maintenance worker spotted a problem. A storage tank holding methyl isocyanate (MIC), a chemical used in making pesticides, was showing a dangerously high pressure reading. The worker summoned his boss. The supervisor put out an alert. But it was already too late. A noxious white gas had started seeping from the tank and spreading with the northwesterly winds. At the Vijoy Hotel near the railroad, sociologist Swapan Saha, 33, woke up with a terrible pain in his chest. "It was both a burning and a suffocating sensation," he said. "It was like breathing fire."

Wrapping a damp towel around his nose and mouth, Saha went outside to investigate. Scores of victims lay dead on the train-station platform. "I thought at first there must have been a gigantic railway accident," he recalled. Then he noticed a pall of white smoke on the ground, and an acrid smell in the air. People were running helter-skelter, retching, vomiting and defecating uncontrollably. Many collapsed and died. Dogs, cows and buffaloes were also on the ground, shuddering in death throes. Saha made his way to the railway office, only to find the stationmaster slumped over his desk. For a moment, he thought that an atom bomb had hit Bhopal. Staggering back to the hotel, half blind himself by now, he sat down to write a farewell letter to his wife.

Saha lived, but thousands of others did not escape. For days the body count ticked upward—from 300 to 1,000 to more than 2,500—in the worst industrial accident in history. Across Bhopal, hospitals and mortuaries filled to overflowing. Muslims were buried four and five to a grave, and Hindu funeral pyres burned round the clock. As many as 100,000 survivors may be left with permanent disabilities: blindness, sterility, kidney and liver infections, tuberculosis and brain damage. There were fears that a cholera epidemic could strike. Breaking off a campaign swing through southern India, Prime Minister Rajiv Gandhi rushed to Bhopal. Local officials ordered a full-scale judicial inquiry—and demanded that Union Carbide compensate victims of the disaster.

As a precaution, Union Carbide stopped production and distribution of methyl isocyanate at a plant similar to the Bhopal factory in Institute, W.Va. But it deflected questions about what caused the mishap until it could complete an internal investigation. The prospects of staggering lawsuits helped drive down the company's stock and forced officials to deny rumors that Union Carbide might have to declare bankruptcy. When Warren Anderson, the chairman of the firm, flew to Bhopal to talk about relief, local authorities arrested him on charges of criminal negligence. Later they released him. Union Carbide offered emergency relief, but refused to discuss outright compensation.

For million of Americans, the Bhopal catastrophe raised a frightening question: could it happen here? So far the worst industrial accidents have tended to occur in the Third World, where population density is higher and safety measures often fail to keep up with the spread of technology. By contrast, the U. S. chemical industry can boast of a strong safety record. But with more than 60,000 chemicals produced and stored in America, government regulators and watchdog groups can't even tell where potential time bombs are—let alone guarantee that they won't go off. "It's like a giant roulette game," says Anthony Mazzocchi, an expert on worker safety in New York. "This time the marble came to a stop in a little place in India. But the next time it could be the United States."

Most of Bhopal was asleep when disaster struck. After the leak started, as many as 200,000 people ran through the city streets, coughing, screaming and calling out to each other. At about 2 A.M., the pesticide factory's siren went off. Thinking a fire had broken out, hundreds rushed toward the plant—straight into the path of the deadly gas. The train station was littered with the bodies of railroad employees and red-uniformed porters. The junction was paralyzed for 20 hours, making it impossible for survivors to flee by train. Those wealthy enough to own cars gathered their families and tried to escape. But many drivers were blinded by the gas, and there were scores of accidents.

CITY OF CORPSES

The next morning it looked like a neutron bomb had struck. Buildings were undamaged. But humans and animals littered the low ground, turning hilly Bhopal into a city of corpses. Outside the mortuaries, bodies lay in piles. Those of Muslims were piled on top of each other in hurriedly dug graves. At night the city glowed with the flames of funeral pyres, so many that the local cremation grounds ran out of wood. A fresh supply had to be shipped in overnight before as many as 70 pyres could proceed with Hindu rituals.

Three days after the catastrophe, rescue workers still hadn't uncovered all the dead. Teams broke into the tin, clay and wood shacks of the shantytowns, searching for victims trapped by the gas. One group of volunteers came upon an entire family snuffed out in the night. A small 10-year-old boy named Zahir guided *Newsweek*'s Sudip Mazumdar to the gates of the Union Carbide factory. Zahir wiped his swollen red eyes with a filthy rag, then pointed to the faulty gas tank. "That's the one," he said. Zahir had escaped from the shantytown on Sunday night, wandered through the countryside until daybreak, then returned to find his neighborhood deserted and his parents missing. Hundreds of other kids roamed through the streets. Eventually, the government set up a missing-persons bureau to help all the lost survivors.

The city's hospitals came under siege. Hordes of sufferers, many still vomiting, crowded the emergency rooms. The worst off were old people, children and the poorest shantytown inhabitants. Many of them were chronically ill from malnutrition even before suffering the effects of the methyl isocyanate. Many doctors had also been exposed to the gas and were unable to work. Medical students and policemen had to be brought in from neighboring towns to help out. What the victims needed most, said one harried doctor, were massive doses of antibiotics and vitamins. But some of the inexperienced volunteers treated them with anything at hand—glucose, painkillers, even stomach pills. One house painter named Salim arrived at a hospital with ulcerated eyes and burning pains in his stomach. A medical worker gave him a handful of high-potency antacid tablets.

"KEEP CALM"

Rumors spread like brushfire. One day after the disaster, a blanket of early-morning fog caused people to speculate that another gas leak had taken place. Policemen had to take to the streets in cars to stop everyone from panicking. "Keep calm," they called out through their loudspeakers. "There has been no new leak." There was another report that all the milk and vegetables in the food shops had been contaminated. In the end, that also turned out to be false. However, a local official rekindled fear when he told townspeople to wash their vegetables carefully.

The response of Indian officials was mostly slow and self-interested. Local authorities never set up a crisis-management office. There were even rumors that Arjun Singh, the chief minister of Madhya Pradesh, had fled Bhopal during the gas leak. When Singh finally did talk to reporters, he angrily denied the charge. "If this can be proved," he said, "I will resign from public life forthwith." Later, Rajiv Ghandi showed up briefly, touring two hospitals and talking to relief workers. Then he left Bhopal for a campaign tour of the rest of Madhya Pradesh. For most of a day, Singh dropped his other duties to join the prime minister. . . .

"AN UNSTOPPERED KILLER"
by Matt Clark with Mariana Gosnell

Methyl isocyanate is so unstable and so dangerous that even professional toxicologists are reluctant to study it in the lab. "As soon as you open the bottle, it escapes," says Yves Alarie of the University of Pittsburgh Graduate School of Public Health. "We've done very little on this substance because it is so difficult to control."

MIC belongs to a family of toxins for which there is no antidote and no treatment. It is used in the manufacture of insecticides that kill by attacking the nervous system. But the first effect of exposure is watering of the eyes and damage to the cornea. The substance is quickly absorbed into the corneal cells and renders them opaque. When inhaled, MIC immediately constricts the nasal and bronchial passages and the larynx; "You can compare it to a very dramatic asthma attack," he says. In one of the few human experiments ever done with MIC, a

German researcher several years ago took a whiff to see what would happen; the effect was immediate and frightening. The spasms, Alarie suspects, result from the effect of MIC on nerve endings in the respiratory tract and, if the victim has inhaled enough MIC, can cause sudden death.

MIC can also irritate and inflame the lungs, leading to the accumulation of fluid, or pulmonary edema. Breathing is both difficult and painful, and if the victim has inhaled enough MIC, he will literally drown in the secretions. In the immediate aftermath of exposure, victims are probably more susceptible to lung infections. About the only way doctors can deal with anyone who survives significant exposure is to apply air rich in oxygen and administer sedatives and painkillers.

Just what the long-term effects of exposure will be for the Bhopal survivors is uncertain, since MIC hasn't been studied much in humans. Alarie recalls that, in 1967, firefighters battling a blaze in Britain were exposed to a chemical cousin of MIC called toluene di-isocyanate (TDI). As have many victims of the Indian disaster, some firemen experienced vomiting, possibly because of effects on the nervous system. Some suffered clearly neurological symptoms, including impaired coordination and memory loss. "There was recovery, but not complete recovery in all cases," says Alarie. Some of the Indian victims may have suffered kidney and liver damage. According to William E. Brown, a biologist at Pittsburgh's Carnegie-Mellon University, this can occur because MIC destroys proteins in the bloodstream; the kidneys and liver become overworked trying to rid the body of these aberrant wastes.

SURVIVORS

For most of the victims, especially those whose exposure was relatively slight, the physical effects will probably disappear in time, Brown expects. Many should recover their eyesight, since the cornea is capable of some degree of self-repair. For many, the respiratory problems should also clear up in a matter of weeks or months. Some will have developed antibodies to isocyanates and, therefore, could suffer allergic attacks if exposed again to such compounds—with any luck, an unlikely prospect. But the survivors of heavier exposure will suffer permanent respiratory impairment. "It will appear to be something like emphysema," says Brown, "and there's nothing to do about it."

Lethal as it is, at least one good thing can be said about MIC. It probably won't linger in the environment the way dioxin, PCBs and other noxious substances do. Moisture in the air breaks MIC down or "hydrolizes" it, forming carbon dioxide and a largely inert amine. "In a couple of weeks, the detectable level will be negligible," Brown predicts. Already, the survivors of Bhopal are moving back into their homes, and investigators say "the city's water is safe to drink."

from COULD IT HAPPEN IN AMERICA? *by Melinda Beck with Nikki Finke Greenberg; Mary Hager; Joann Harrison; and Anne Underwood*

A similar disaster is unlikely—but the potential for danger is enormous

Residents of Institute, W. Va., were used to something funny in the air that caused hacking coughs and sometimes chipped the paint off cars. Old-timers affectionately called Union Carbide's big Institute plant "Uncle John's," and its foul odor, "the smell of jobs." The news that more than 2,500 people in India had been killed by methyl isocyanate (MIC)—a chemical made at the plant as well—came as a shock. Union Carbide halted MIC production there last week. But at a town meeting Tuesday night, one man demanded that residents be issued gas masks; another said the poison was so deadly that masks wouldn't help. "I dreamed about it all night long," said Sylvia Parker, a retired social worker. "My immediate concern is that what happened in India doesn't happen here."

That same cloud of concern wafted through communities all across the nation in the wake of the Bhopal tragedy. Chemical-industry experts hastened to say that a similar calamity was unlikely here since most U. S. facilities are not so dependent on unskilled labor and have far more sophisticated emergency-warning systems. Last month, when a small amount of MIC spilled in a plant run by FMC Corp. in Middleport, N.Y., 500 school children and staffers were evacuated in 35 minutes with no serious injuries. In fact, the chemical industry has the best safety record of any U. S. industry. But the potential for danger is enormous. "We have nothing to be comforted by just because we're living in an advanced industrial society," said safety expert Anthony Mazzocchi of the Workers' Policy Project. "On the contrary, we are at greater risk because we have more toxic plants here."

TESTS

The dimensions of the potential risk are staggering. An estimated 6,000 U. S. facilities make possibly hazardous chemicals. There are approximately 180,000 shipments by truck or rail every day in the United

States of everything from nail-polish remover to nuclear weapons. More than 60,000 chemical substances are in use—and federal regulators don't even know how many pose health dangers. The 1976 Toxic Substances Control Act—TOSCA—requires that *new* chemicals be reviewed before they go on the market. But only 20 percent of those already in use have been tested even to minimal standards, according to the National Research Council. Federal disposal regulations do not even classify carbamates—the group of pesticides that use MIC during manufacture—as hazardous waste. That means, says Richard Fortuna of the Hazardous Waste Treatment Council, that "they can be discarded like orange peels."

What's more, responsibility for preventing a Bhopal-like disaster falls between the cracks in the federal bureaucracy. The Labor Department's Office of Safety and Health Administration (OSHA) periodically inspects facilities to ensure that accidents don't harm workers. The Environmental Protection Agency coordinates cleanups of some types of accidents. But EPA was only last month given the authority to regulate underground storage tanks such as the one that leaked in Bhopal. It has not begun to count such tanks, let alone determine what is in them. It will be three years before EPA proposes safety regulations—longer if its budget is cut further. In the meantime, "we've got no regulations and no enforcement," says EPA hazardous-waste expert Hugh Kaufman. "The only reason we haven't had a release with the same disastrous effect is that we've been lucky."

Chemical-industry officials insist it is far more than luck—that they police themselves far more thoroughly than federal regulations ever could. The industry is "obsessed with safety, because of the nature of the product," says Geraldine Cox of the Chemical Manufacturers Association. Because accidents do happen, chemical handlers go to great lengths to minimize the danger, and many are reviewing their safeguards in the wake of the Bhopal tragedy. "Never say never," says Pat Goggin of Dow Chemical in Midland, Mich., which staged a mock "release" of chlorine gas two weeks ago to test its leak-detection and community-warning procedures.

Some chemical firms use elaborate computer models to gauge the likely paths of accident releases. One such model, made by SAFER Emergency Systems in California, not only senses that a leak has occurred, but monitors its rate, concentration and toxicity, evaluates weather conditions and displays the anticipated cloud on a computer screen along with the degree of danger for anything in its path. The system can even dial phone numbers and play a recorded warning message—all within five minutes after the leak is detected.

WHISTLES

But emergency precautions vary widely from plant to plant. In Institute, Union Carbide officials had discussed evacuation plans with a nearby college and a local center for the handicapped. But many residents said they had no idea what to do in case of an accident—nor had many seen a letter that plant spokesmen claimed was sent to residents every year since 1975 outlining the plant's emergency programs.

If they had, they might still be confused. According to the letter, two three-second blasts of the plant's whistle means a fire or medical emergency; three three-second blasts means a gas release; two-second blasts every three seconds for two minutes means a major disaster, with two-second blasts every 30 seconds until the danger has passed. (Last year, when a valve broke on a chemical barge moored at the plant and a neighborhood had to be evacuated at 3 A.M., most people were sleeping with the windows closed and never heard the whistle.) Instructions for what to do next are equally confusing: if the wind is blowing favorably, stay put. If the wind is blowing toward you from the plant, evacuate "by going crosswind." "In some cases, you can see the fumes as a white cloud," the letter added. "However, this is not always the case so don't depend on your eyes."

The very fact that anything so lethal was made nearby stunned many Institute residents. People in Woodbine, Ga., were also surprised to learn that MIC is used at a Union Carbide plant there. Institute plant spokesman Dick Henderson said the company did inform residents—via a newspaper story in 1952. "Do you want an update every six months that we're still making it?" he asked. "For years, we used to tour people around the plant, then interest died down."

Communities elsewhere are pressing for more information about the chemicals next door. Manufacturers are resisting on the ground that disclosing specific names and quantities will reveal trade secrets —and the Reagan administration sympathizes. One of its first acts was to withdraw a Carter administration proposal that all toxic chemicals in the workplace be identified. In defiance, 21 states have passed their own right-to-know laws, but OSHA has moved to pre-empt those with a new rule requiring that substances be labeled only generally as "hazardous." A district court in Newark is set to rule this week on New Jersey's effort to keep its law, which also forces firms to file lists of their chemicals with local safety authorities. "I don't want an orange sign that says 'Danger,' " says Rick Engler of the Philadelphia Area Project on Occupational Safety and Health. "I want to know what the real hazards are."

Areas like New Jersey pose particular hazards because of the dense concentration of chemical facilities. And though few U. S. plants abut crowded shantytowns like Bhopal, some are upwind of large population centers. "All of Niagara County is a trouble spot," says Peter Slocum of the New York State Department of Health. "Those who live in Staten Island live in constant peril of New Jersey." Last October, a derivative of the insecticide malathion escaped from an American Cyanamid tank in Linden, N. J., blanketing a 20-mile area with noxious fumes that drove 100 people to hospitals. Last month there were two more minor chemical releases in the direction of New York City from plants located in Linden.

The prospect of evacuating large sections of any major city is the stuff of nightmares—and most are alarmingly unprepared. The area around the Houston Ship Channel has the nation's highest concentration of petro-chemical installations, yet the city has no plan for coping with an accident like the natural-gas explosion that killed 452 in Mexico City last month. Given Houston's chronic traffic congestion and lack of industrial zoning, "evacuation isn't the answer," says city public-health director James Haughton. "It isn't a possibility. It doesn't even seem like a hope. . . . There would be total chaos." A major chemical disaster would also quickly overwhelm available medical facilities. As it is, most physicians aren't trained to deal with toxicological problems. "I don't know of *any* hospital in the Houston area that specializes in chemical injuries," Houghton says. "We don't even know how many burn units there are."

The potential hazards are also mobile. Given the vast amount of hazardous cargo crisscrossing the nation, accidents could happen anywhere—in rural areas far from the nearest hospital or in congested urban areas. Every day, some 4,000 trucks barrel along Houston's freeways from one petro-chemical plant to another. In 1976, a tank truck went off an elevated freeway, exploded and released 19 tons of anhydrous ammonia, killing seven people. In 1947, a French ship loaded with ammonium nitrate exploded at a dock in Texas City, near Galveston, destroying a Monsanto plant and everything else within blocks. A second ship loaded with the same material exploded 16 hours later. In all, 565 people were killed and more than 2,000 injured.

The Texas City disaster prompted vast improvements in transportation-safety measures. Last year there were only eight deaths and 191 injuries in 5,761 reported "incidents" involving shipments of hazardous material—a remarkable record, considering traffic-accident rates overall. The Department of Transportation requires that the contents of every load be identified with a numerical code—MIC's is 2480—visibly posted on the truck or rail car, and every police and fire vehicle supposedly carries the DOT's Emergency Response Guidebook which identifies the substance and accident procedures. But there are few federal rules governing shipment routes, and DOT has overruled some local restrictions—on the ground that they simply exported the hazards to neighboring areas.

BIG FEAR

The transport trucks and rail cars that carried MIC from Institute to Woodbine stopped rolling last week. Company officials said they might close the Georgia plant, which uses MIC to manufacture the pesticide Temik, until the cause of the Bhopal disaster is found. In Institute, though the plant was no longer making MIC, it was using up 600,000 pounds of the substance on hand, turning it into the pesticide Sevin at a rate of 11,000 pounds per hour. Gov. Jay Rockefeller ordered the state Air Pollution Control Commission to monitor the plant 24 hours a day until the MIC was gone. Ten state agencies were investigating plant safety along with OSHA officials. Some plant workers, meanwhile, were ambivalent. Said one: "I make $620 a week and I don't want to talk about it."

Other Institute residents did give voice to their other big fear: that repercussions from the Bhopal tragedy might put Uncle John's out of work, along with the 1,400 people he employs. The 150 products made at the Institute plant, some pointed out, find their way into everything from shampoo to floor wax; Sevin was airlifted into Egypt one year to save the cotton crop. Experts elsewhere said that many of the victims in India would not have been alive at all if not for chemicals that increased food supplies, reduced the incidence of malaria and improved sanitation. Judged against such benefits, the risks of chemical accidents seem more acceptable. But there is clearly room for improvement in reducing them.

III

Reviews

Sol Yurick

Yurick's review of *White Noise* appeared in the *Philadelphia Inquirer* on January 20, 1985.

FLEEING DEATH IN A WORLD OF HYPER-BABBLE

We in America are assailed by a million messages. Television, newspapers, signs, sounded words and those messages whose import we cannot understand—electromagnetic impulses—that pass through our body, radiated from thousands of channels. Words assail us, icons confront us. They sink into our bodies, become part of us, and, perhaps, reemerge in dreams.

Jack Gladney learns this directly. A professor of Hitler Studies at the College-on-the-Hill, a small liberal arts school in Middle America, this narrator of Don DeLillo's beguiling new novel is sitting at the far end of a barracks in a Boy Scout camp—one of the many shelters to which local people have fled in the wake of an "airborne toxic event." He listens to his daughter Steffie mutter some words in her sleep, then utter a few distinct syllables, then speak two "clearly audible" words:

"*Toyota Celica*. . . . She was only repeating some TV voice. Toyota Corolla, Toyota Celica, Toyota Cressida. Supranational names, computer-generated, more or less universally pronounceable. Part of every child's brain noise, the substatic regions too deep to probe. Whatever its source, the utterance struck me with the impact of a moment of splendid transcendence. . . ."

On the last page of the book, contemplating an eerie scene, Gladney muses, "This is the language of waves and radiation, or how the dead speak to the living." And in time, all these waves seem to become as one.

White noise.

White Noise.

White noise is a susurration, a fusion of signals and messages, a leveling of sounds into one all-sound—its individual components become indistinguishable. White noise is essentially anti-dramatic. No highs, no lows, no emphases, no diminuendos, all utterances made equal. People who have trouble sleeping—perhaps they want to shut out the screams of the world and their minds—put on earphones that emit a monotonous, soothing sound. Auditory entropy. The death of distinction and distinguishability.

The plot of *White Noise* takes place in one academic season—one of the grand cycles of life and death in modern society. Gladney, who invented Hitler Studies in North America in March of 1968, has made the field his own, much in the way that others have possessed Holocaust studies. He runs Hitler conferences and teaches Advanced Nazism. But Jack Gladney doesn't speak German—he's gotten away with this for years. It's not that he hasn't tried to learn. German resists him—he finds the sound of the language ominous and mysterious. Unlike his creator, he doesn't have a good ear.

Gladney's fellow academics have succeeded in making major disciplines out of the fascinations of their youth—trivia. "There are full professors in this place who read nothing but cereal boxes," observes a newcomer. They have elevated the common media (television, the gossip and wonder sheets, jazz, rock music, soap operas, commercials, cartoons, movies) into the focus of intense study.

And, after all, these were made the primal images of their youthful unconscious, not the kind of thing Freud talked about. They discuss their interests with the same fervor as experts in Dante, Kant or Marx. This is very American. (And what is common wisdom other than high-class philosophy in other jargons? The flip side of Hegel is Sancho Panza.)

Murray Jay Siskind, an ex-sportswriter turned teacher, wants to create a power base in the college—Elvis Presley studies. "Where were you when James Dean died?" one of the academics asks. The question and answer are a test of personal memory wedded to public events, a mimicking of the greater ritual: "Do you remember where you were on the day President Kennedy was shot?" Hitler becomes as important as Elvis Presley. White noise.

Jack and his wife, Babette, have been married previously a few times. Children from earlier marriages live with them. DeLillo's children don't speak like ordinary children but rather like adults. One is reminded of Ivy Compton-Burnett. In fact, everyone in *White Noise* speaks the same way. The wonder of DeLillo's art is that it is not boring or monotonous but very funny in a mordant way. White noise, black humor.

DeLillo has a superb but peculiar ear, a first-rate sense of rhythm. Some authors have the ability to listen and record the way people talk. This is not merely an auctorial way of being a tape recorder—it's not as easy as it sounds. The writer must choose what's important and eliminate what's not. The mere act of recognition requires art of the highest order. But DeLillo's technique takes us beyond. After hearing, he transforms what he hears into a kind of new, invented dialogue. On close examination you realize that no one talks like this . . . and yet everyone does.

The Gladneys seem to live a timeless life. Babette teaches yoga and reads to the blind. The blind, rather than wishing to listen to uplifting literature, prefer lurid accounts (miracles, monsters, incredible conspiracies and plots) to be found in the National Enquirer and National Star—they have a wish to believe in the incredible in the midst of white noise. Or perhaps, being overwhelmed by too many signals, they need excitement, anything that signals the presence of the anti-rational and mysterious. The remnants of the ancient gods are to be found in the cheap tabloid pages.

The life of the Gladneys seems serene, but there are deeper currents of disturbance. Babette has a fear of death. She's been taking mysterious pills—something called Dylar—that are supposed to suppress this fear by working on the appropriate part of the brain. Babette has learned of Dylar while reading to the blind from the Enquirer. Her family is worried. Is she becoming a junkie? Before they can find out what drug she takes, the accidental spill of something called Nyodene D intervenes. The spill boils up into a black cloud—the "airborne toxic event."

The cloud seems to have a life of its own . . . black, billowing, cohesive, it is wafting around the countryside. Everyone is uprooted and flees. A nightmare scene, perhaps out of Dante . . . an exodus of panic, an emergency no one is ready for . . . a crawling caravan of American refugees in cars bottlenecked on ribbon-threads of highway (how else can we escape?), chaotic, incoherent, dangerous.

Helicopters surround the cloud at night and play spotlights on it. Beneath, in the winter scene, a procession of the fleeing, listening constantly to their radios to see which way the cloud is going. There is a scheme to drop Nyodene D–eating bacteria into the cloud. The bacteria eat the cloud. Science has created the problem, science can solve it. Absurd.

Jack is exposed to the toxicity.

Language conventions that level and conceal the horror spring up and become common usage, ritual. After his exposure, not so much to a noxious, disgusting, dangerous, poisonous cloud, but to this "airborne toxic event," Jack is examined. His life particulars are fed into a computer to evaluate his life chances. The projection is ominous. He asks: "Am I going to die?"

"Not as such."

"What do you mean?"

"Not in so many words."

That's white noise. In a theme reechoed from *The Names*, his previous novel, DeLillo shows us that the death of language can also mean the death of people. "Not in so many words."

(Considering the recent events at Bhopal, India, one might ask, was DeLillo prescient? Or rather, did he fix on the kind of event that is always taking place in one part of the world or another? White noise prevents us from seeing certain horrifying commonplaces of this modern age.)

Later, the emergency is, so to speak, pre-simulated by a company called Advanced Disaster Management: "Air-sampling people will deploy along the cloud-exposure swath . . . We are not simulating a particular spillage today. This is an all-purpose leak or spill." In our time, disaster simulation is transformed into a rite of avoidance.

Now, with the possibility of death in him, a concrete death, one that can take up to 15 years, Jack turns to the question of Babette and her constant drug taking. He finds out that she made the connection through the Enquirer, but was forced to have sex with the dispenser of the drug. There is a hint of government funding behind it . . . perhaps chemical warfare . . . a program run wild, a chemical escaped, just as LSD was a drug that escaped from a government testing program.

Unable to deal with this infidelity, he decides to kill the man responsible. He traces the man and shoots him, but in a comic way. Jack cannot succeed in killing him. In the end, he and Babette are reconciled.

In a sense, *White Noise* doesn't really have a plot: It is about the intrusion of plot into life, a stringing-together of random events into some kind of meaningful schema:

"Someone asked about the plot to kill Hitler. The discussion moved to plots in general . . . 'All plots tend to move deathward. This is the nature of plots. Political plots, terrorist plots, lovers' plots, narrative plots . . . We edge nearer death every time we plot . . . It is like a contract that all must sign, the plotters as well as those who are the targets of the plot.' "

Plot is both commentary on time and time-related. Plot and time are dangerous. All sequenced events, things and people lead to death. And thus, the peculiar sense of timelessness in *White Noise* becomes threaded together by time by being rethreaded, plotted, by the author. Narrative plots and life have an ending.

According to the common wisdom of our time, all things decline into entropy, reaching, as is said about the universe itself, the heat-death, ultimate blackness that is the opposite of, and yet the same as, whiteness. And, perhaps, it is the art of the writer to string events and to overcome this whiteness by plotting, by structuring people, sounds, conversation, events into a sequence . . . an invocation of structures and signs to avoid the unavoidable. DeLillo's book strives to overcome the death in all of us, at the same time leaving us with a sense of horror . . . the meaninglessness of it all, while being very funny.

White Noise is philosophy as dialogue, events, people, a brilliant commentary on American life. But a short review can't begin to show DeLillo's skill, for the philosophizing doesn't get in the way of our enjoyment and the humor doesn't get in the way of the profundity.

Albert Mobilio

Albert Mobilio's review of *White Noise* appeared in the *Village Voice* on April 30, 1985. He is the author of two books of poetry, *Bendable Siege* and *The Geographics*.

DEATH BY INCHES

In Don DeLillo's first novel, *Americana*, published in 1971, a television producer embarked on a cross-country trip, camera in hand, from Madison Avenue to Dealey Plaza. His desire to nail down the gas-driven, motel-housed American soul indicated the scope of DeLillo's ambition and established one of his abiding themes: Americans' fondness for their own reflection. In seven subsequent novels he's watched us watch ourselves, measuring in keenly observant prose the depth and cost of that self-absorption. His richest conceit in developing this vision has been technology's ability to project the reassuring likeness—hence television's status as a character in many books. But broadcast waves just mediate the fascination; the mirror game is a human one. Its motivation is expressed without embarrassment by *Americana*'s narrator: "When I began to wonder who I was, I took the simple step of lathering my face and shaving. It all became so clear, so wonderful. I was blue-eyed David Bell. Obviously my life depended on this fact."

Working a territory thick with social critics, DeLillo spares us the polemics. In the current *New Criterion*, he's accused of passing cynical judgments, but criticism of that sort misinterprets his tone. His tack is inquisitive, almost anthropological, as he serves up a variety of American specialties like college football (*End Zone*), leftists and the CIA (*Running Dog*), rock music (*Great Jones Street*), and Wall Street (*Players*). An intensely visual writer, DeLillo can locate and dissect the telling freeze—porchfront cocktails on a suburban Sunday or downtown Manhattan's rush-hour ballet. He illuminates the idiosyncrasies of our tribal life with an indulgent grace that imparts a sense of communality where none was ever imagined. Yet the darker side of such attachments, the subterranean warfare Americans wage against their own cultural and ideological inventions, inspires his shrewdest insights.

What sets DeLillo apart from moralists like Heller or Bellow is an understanding of the complicitous bond between individual and institution. His novels actually celebrate the confusion over personal responsibility for public madness. To this end he turns the trick of making Wall Street or the CIA objects of wondrous contemplation, splicing a clipped lyricism with technical detail to produce descriptions of labyrinthine toys, exaggerated sums of private fears.

While DeLillo's Americans nurse paranoias large and small, they're most frightened of themselves. Apprentice schizophrenics living in willful isolation, these characters still maintain a practiced cool. Thinking tends to occur in quotation marks, acute self-awareness permitting only laconic assessments of surface activity. Their cramped, often abstract dialogue suggests that words aren't quite up to the job of saying what's felt. Sex is rendered topologically, in terms of tensed arcs and shifting planes: a poetry for wind-up romance. The implacable aloneness and emotional confinement surface repeatedly as amply qualified passion: "He was lean and agile. She found herself scratching his shoulders, working against his body with uncharacteristic intensity. Who is this son of a bitch, she thought." The narcissism is corrosive, potentially terminal; these people worry themselves to death.

DeLillo's new novel, *White Noise*, takes that possibility seriously, exploring the narcissist's inevitable trap: a preoccupation with dying. It's set in a college town where "the supermarket is the key to the neighborhood" and all traces of morbidity have been scrubbed clean. Here J. A. K. (the triad of initials concocted for effect) Gladney, world's foremost Hitler scholar, heads a Nazi studies department at a small liberal arts school. He's also obsessed to distraction by his own mortality. The study of Hitler, who appears "larger than death," provides an orderly myth; it's as close as Gladney can come to religious faith.

But Gladney's dark dreams aren't the only ones circulating around the College-on-the-Hill. DeLillo has great fun with a faculty composed of New York émigrés who've come to the provinces in search of "American magic and dread." They haunt shopping malls, conduct classes in famous movie car crashes and the semiotics of food labeling, and pass the time recalling their whereabouts the day James Dean died. In an atmosphere where others revel in social pathologies, Gladney spreads some shadows of his own. Presiding over classes in black gown and sunglasses, he interprets films of Nazi party rallies: "Crowds came to form a shield against their own dying. To become a crowd is to keep out death. To break off from the crowd is to risk death as an individual, to face dying alone."

For solace, the professor turns to his family, a middle ground between fervent isolation and mass hysteria. A family took center stage in DeLillo's last novel, *The Names*; he examined its emotional strategies and hermetic codes with sympathetic insight absent from his earlier books. In *White Noise* he extends this evocation of the complex, colloquial textures of contemporary family life.

Gladney's a devoted father, deeply in love with his wife Babette, a stolid earth mother who teaches classes in correct posture to the elderly. The children—products of serial marriages—are a knowing and precocious bunch. Oldest son Heinrich (perversely named for Himmler?) plays mail chess with a death row convict and serves as in-house sophist. The daughters cleave to the television, dispense crafted naiveté at the dinner table, and murmur brand names like Toyota Celica in their sleep. For recreation everyone shops.

DeLillo's surgical analysis of their domestic rituals uncovers the irresistible force proximity exerts on personality, a force that fuels Gladney's obsession. When infant son Wilder begins crying inexplicably and continues for hours, Gladney hears "an anguish so accessible that it rushes to overwhelm whatever immediately caused it. There was something permanent and soul-struck in this crying. It was a sound of inbred desolation." What he hears, of course, is his own unvoiced pain. Every embrace he and Babette share is followed by a silent refrain: Who will die first? . . . But ultimately DeLillo sees these human connections as too vital and necessary to be easily dismissed. In counterpoint he's drawn a compassionate picture of a primitive refuge in a modern "world of hostile fact."

The vulnerability of this refuge to technological assault constitutes the novel's rather thin plot. An overturned railroad car creates an "airborne toxic event" that forces evacuation of the town, and Gladney is exposed to Nyodene D, the rogue chemical. For the 52-year-old professor, news that the dose might prove fatal sometime within 35 years shouldn't be too dispiriting; his anxiety nonetheless reaches fever pitch. Waking in cold sweats becomes a nightly event. Jack's distress is compounded when he learns that his obsession is shared by the outwardly stable Babette, who has secretly volunteered to test Dylar—an experimental drug designed to eliminate the fear of death. The drug—a compact metaphor for technology's power to dim consciousness and blur its definitions—becomes Gladney's would-be cure. Heedless of its quirky side effects, like inducing confusion between nouns and objects, he pursues the pills from the family trash bin to the inventor's motel hideout. Gladney attacks his prey with the words "Hail of bullets," and drops him to the floor. Then, after wounding the scientist with real bullets, he rushes him to the hospital, neglecting to collect the Dylar. In the book's closing scene Gladney describes son Wilder pedaling his tricycle through four lanes of highway traffic. The child, oblivious to the danger, arrives safely on the other side, where he slips in a puddle and only then begins to cry.

The coda affirms the workaday usefulness of faith, however naive or contrived, and recalls its primal, complementary link to mortality. In the emergency room Gladney quizzes a nun who denies believing in heaven. She tells him, "Our pretense is a dedication. Someone must appear to believe. Our lives are no less serious than if we professed real faith, real belief. As belief shrinks from the world, people find it more necessary than ever that *someone* believe." This resolution, no doubt equivocal, still offers some possibility of escaping the self's prison. Indeed, it is the author's most optimistic reading of the situation yet.

In light of this, *White Noise* can be taken as a terse summa of DeLillo's work. Again he shows Americans to be a damaged breed, carnivores devouring their own tails. Our peculiar brand of extinction—which, as Gladney points out, deserves an aerosol spray can for a tombstone—embodies our deepest wishes. The technological prowess evidenced by carcinogens, television, and the fantasy drug Dylar serves a consumptive, and therefore fatal love of self. Its death rattle is heard in TV's electronic din, the book's "white noise." DeLillo, it seems, may lean a bit too hard here. While his grasp of television's fluid grammar and mime of broadcast patter are first-rate, perhaps he's come to regard the box as too sinister, too important. Granted, it lulls us with "coded messages and endless repetitions," and attractive footage of downed jets and hostage shoot-outs offers intimate knowlege of death. But . . . if death has been wrung free of mystery and meaning, larger factors must weigh in alongside the evening news as culprits.

This slight imbalance aside, the novel is perceptively targeted—and the writing, as usual, is sharp as cut glass. DeLillo becomes increasingly elliptical with every book, as if he's paring his prose to the style of a scientist's notebook. Paradoxically, the distillation is matched by a more subtle and convincing treatment of his characters' inner lives. This broadened emotional vocabulary charges *White Noise* with a resonance and credibility that makes it difficult to ignore. Critics who have argued his work is too clever and overly intellectual should take notice: DeLillo's dark vision is now hard-earned. It strikes at both head and heart.

Diane Johnson

Johnson's review of *White Noise* appeared in the *New York Review of Books* on March 14, 1985.

CONSPIRATORS

The horrors of 1984 did not emerge quite in the form that Orwell imagined, reminding us that novelists are usually more gifted with hindsight than with prescience. Many novelists confess to feeling that there are certain things they dare not write, for fear they will come true, and can tell you of things they have written which have afterward happened, proving, if not prescience, the power of wishes. Novelists stay away from prediction. Not to make too much of the "airborne toxic event" in Don DeLillo's new novel, *White Noise*, and the Bhopal tragedy it anticipates, but it is the index of DeLillo's sensibility, so alert is he to the content, not to mention the speech rhythms, dangers, dreams, fears, etc., of modern life that you imagine him having to spend a certain amount of time in a quiet, darkened room. He works with less lead time than other satirists, too—we should have teen-age suicide and the new patriotism very soon—and this must be demanding. But here, as in his other novels, his voice is authoritative, his tone characteristically light. In all his work he seems less angry or disappointed than some critics of society, as if he had expected less in the first place, or perhaps his marvelous power with words is compensation for him.

White Noise is a meditation on themes of whiteness—the pallor of death, and white noise, the sound, so emblematic of modern life, that is meant to soothe human beings by screening out the other, more irritating noises of their civilization. The hero and narrator is Jack Gladney, chairman of Hitler Studies at a small eastern university:

> We are quartered in Centenary Hall, a dark brick structure we share with the popular culture department, known officially as American environments. A curious group. The teaching staff is composed almost solely of New York émigrés, smart, thuggish, movie-mad, trivia-crazed. They are here to decipher the natural language of the culture, to make a formal method of the shiny pleasures they'd known in their Europe-shadowed childhoods—an Aristotelianism of bubble gum wrappers and detergent jingles.

Jack is married to Babette, and they have a number of children from their former marriages. Babette, normally a wholesome, cheerful woman, has taken to sneaking a certain pill, and when challenged denies it. Next, a toxic leak obliges them to evacuate their house and exposes Jack to a chemical cloud which may or will kill him in an unknown length of time.

Now he is seized by the fear of death. He learns that mortality is Babette's preoccupation too, and that she has volunteered as an experimental subject to take a pill being developed to relieve this fear. She has been giving herself to the drug company man, in a shabby motel, on a regular basis, to ensure her continuing supply.

Will Jack be able to discover what Babette's taking? Will he be able to get a supply for himself? Is he really going to die of the whiff of Nyodene Derivative? Will he go through with his plan to kill Willie Mink, the drug company man, to revenge Babette and steal the Dylar pills? This is the armature upon which DeLillo hangs a series of observations, descriptions, jokes, and dialogues, approximately Socratic, on sundry great and lesser subjects:

> "Did you ever spit in your soda bottle so you wouldn't have to share your drink with the other kids?"
>
> "How old were you when you first realized your father was a jerk?"
>
> "Exactly how elevated is my potassium?"

As we read fiction, we are always aware of the operative formal principle—it's either "life" (meandering, inconclusive) or "plot," as in this novel, where the fortune or fate of an individual is opposed to a conspiracy, to a plot within the plot, which serves as a metaphor for the world itself, organized against you, clever, wickedly determined on its own usually illegal ends, and in this mirroring the illicit desires of our own hearts. Thus the pirates, spy rings, smugglers, dope pushers,

CIA, criminal organizations, high-up secret governmental department, terrorist cadre, heartless chemical industry we find in some of the most interesting recent fiction, conspirators representing in microcosm the hostile confusion and formless menace of the big world. A novel whose plot contains a plot might be *the* postmodern novel, an adaptation of an earlier model of fiction, from before the era of the fiction of the self, when we had novels of the person in society or the universe, making his or her way, and making judgments on it. It is a distinguished tradition from Gulliver to Greene, but harder than ever to succeed in, now that plots demand an extreme imagination if they are to surpass what is furnished by mere reality.

> "Remember that time you asked me about a secret research group? Working on fear of death? Trying to perfect a medication? . . . Such a group definitely existed. Supported by a multinational giant. Operating in the deepest secrecy in an unmarked building just outside Iron City."
>
> "Why deepest secrecy?"
>
> "It's obvious. To prevent espionage by competitive giants. The point is they came very close to achieving their objective."

All of Don DeLillo's fictions contain these conspiratorial models of the world. In *Players* two Yuppies get mixed up with urban terrorists. In *Running Dog* a porn ring tries to get its hands on a dirty home movie reputed to have been made *in the bunker*. In *Great Jones Street* a drug syndicate pursues a depressed rock star who unwittingly possesses their stash. Chemical substances and commodities, like the conspiracies, and like the dustheaps in Dickens, embody the moral defects of the society that produces them.

In *White Noise* the conspirators try to find a drug that will take away the fear of death from a society that is fixedly preoccupied with producing death, but the motive is profit. Sometimes the desire for power, or to possess the substance for its own sake, moves the plot, but the Dickensian themes of mistaken, lost, or found identity, themes that have dominated novels ever since the nineteenth century, are deliberately effaced—another gloss on the modern situation. Perhaps a vestige of the struggle for place, that other Victorian obsession, can be seen in Jack's efforts to stake out an academic niche for himself as chairman of Hitler Studies.

One finds these plots, these themes, in other contemporary novels—by Robert Stone, or Gore Vidal (in his *Duluth* or *Kalki* mode), or Joan Didion, and however one might long for the affirmative charm of, say, Grace Paley, one can't but admit that these are powerful observers.

> Our newspaper is delivered by a middle-aged Iranian driving a Nissan Sentra. Something about the car makes me uneasy—the car waiting with its headlights on, at dawn, as the man places the newspaper on the front steps. I tell myself I have reached an age, the age of unreliable menace. The world is full of abandoned meanings. In the commonplace I find unexpected themes and intensities.

Of course people are by no means agreed that the world is a suitable subject for fiction. The distinguished *Washington Post* critic Jonathan Yardley objects to DeLillo's topical agenda: "Could there be a more predictable catalogue of trendy political themes: radiation, addiction to violence, television as religion, the trivialization of suffering, the vulgarity of America?" But is topicality only transmogrified into art by the passage of time? Without a willingness to engage the problems of the world around him, we would not have the novels of Dickens, just as, without an acid tone and interest in abstraction, we would not have the novels of Voltaire, or Peacock, or Huxley. Yardley complains, like others, about "fiction as op-ed material. . . . a novel that simply does not work as *fiction*, which is the novelist's first artistic obligation." The difficulty seems to lie in the definition of fiction: "None of the characters acquires any genuine humanity."

Along with the novel of plot and the novel of character, certain old-fashioned theorists of the novel would sometimes speak of the novel of ideas, implying that it was a special taste, and that there is something distinct, if not antithetical, about ideas and the kind of narrative pleasure one derives from less abstract and more simply suspenseful stories: what will happen next? Perhaps the novel of ideas cannot be as exciting, if the ideas demand, like badly brought-up children, to be noticed. Perhaps, even, the reader's awareness of the restless and skeptical intelligence of the author may in some absolute sense operate against such reader responses as sympathy and identification. One is always slightly too aware of the efforts of, say, Bellow, another novelist of ideas, to try to combat their effect by putting in charming human touches, and DeLillo certainly tries to do that here, strewing the text with kids and endearing details of family life.

A first-person protagonist is at least a concession to our old-fashioned wish for heroines and heroes, somebody to stumble through the narrative, thinking the thoughts, experiencing the emotions, more reassuringly human than in satires like Vidal's equally trenchant but chillier *Duluth*, for instance, where all the jokes are the author's. Authors in their omniscience can be intimidating, and perhaps should be advised to conceal their intelligence, the way girls used to be advised to do. Anyhow, we are happy to have Jack Gladney, a diplomatic creation on DeLillo's part, and necessary to a fiction that could otherwise seem too programmatic or too abstract, a regular guy who, because an airborne toxic event and the fear of death are part of his life, convinces us that these unwelcome universals will soon be part of ours.

A more conventional hapless hero, like Jay McInerney's in his recent *Bright Lights, Big City*, may make us laugh by doing a bunch of bad-boy dumb things—too much cocaine before an office deadline—but he does them with minimum self-awareness, and a kind of irritating (male?) confidence in the total indulgence of his readers, among whom the men are expected to identify with him, the women forgive. But Gladney disarms by his penetration, even if he is a five-times married academic who goes around wearing his robe and dark glasses and has to pretend to know German. ("I talked mainly about Hitler's mother, brother and dog. His dog's name was Wolf. This word is the same in English and German. . . . I'd spent days with the dictionary, compiling lists of such words.")

All the characters are infected by Jack's high interrogative style. The novel is entirely composed of questions, sometimes one you'd like to know the answers to: "Were people this dumb before television?" "Does a man like yourself know the size of India's standing army?" "What if someone held a gun to your head?" "What if the symptoms are real?"

What accounts for the charm of these serious novels on dread subjects? Perhaps Jack's eloquence is such that we are a little less harrowed by his author's exacting and despairing view of civilization. And he is very funny. Besides, there is the special pleasure afforded by the extraordinary language, the coherence of the imagery, saturated with chemicals and whiteness and themes of poisons and shopping, the nice balance of humor and poignance, solemn nonsense and real questions:

> "What do I do to make death less strange? How do I go about it?"
>
> "I don't know."
>
> "Do I risk death by driving fast around curves? Am I supposed to go rock climbing on weekends?"
>
> "I don't know," she said. "I wish I knew."

Pico Iyer

Iyer's review of *White Noise* appeared in *Partisan Review* 53 in 1986.

A CONNOISSEUR OF FEAR

Writing of death, Don DeLillo takes one's breath away. A private man issuing a strangely private kind of fiction, he is the closest thing we have to an Atomic Age Melville. That rarest of birds, a novelist on fire with ideas—and an outlaw epistemologist to boot—he uses his fictional excursions as occasions to think aloud in shadowed sentences, speak in modern tongues, plumb mysteries, fathom depths. In book after cryptic book, DeLillo circles obsessively around the same grand and implacable themes—language, ritual, breakup, death. How to make sense of randomness or piece together identity? How, in a centrifugal world of relativity, to steady oneself with absolutes? How, in the end, to get across the untellable?

The DeLillo universe is an ordinary world transfigured by extraordinary concerns, a quotidian place seen in the terrifying white light of eternity. Thus *White Noise* is furnished with all the suburban props of the all-American novel: an amiably rumpled middle-aged professor, his plump earth-motherly wife, bright children from scattered marriages, a nuclear family in a pleasant postnuclear home. Their story is unlikely, however, to be mistaken for a fifties sitcom. The academic, Jack Gladney, teaches Advanced Nazism at the College-on-the-Hill; the matriarch leads adult education classes in posture; Gladney's three exwives all have ties with the intelligence community; and the fourteen-year-old eldest child of the household, Heinrich Gerhardt, has both a receding hairline and a philosophical bent—on his first appearance in the novel, he solemnly proclaims, "There's no past, present or future outside our own mind. The so-called laws of motion are a big hoax. Even sound can trick the mind."

Nothing in DeLillo's world is casual, nothing free of occult significance. Dark forces swirl around the bright, plastic artifacts of Anytown, U.S.A., and the country seems nothing but a gleaming library of portents. Bills, bank statements, the brand names of cars are recited as if they were mantras; tabloids are read as fragments from an American Book of the Dead; the television is consulted as a mystic oracle in the dark. The very title of the book, we learn, refers to death: the static of our lives is thus the sound track of our dying.

Yet of all the subversions of the everyday, the nightmare turns on the American Dream, the most unnerving comes when the Gladneys pile into the family station wagon and head off on what resembles a picnic. It is in fact a nuclear evacuation. The huge cloud of escaped poison gas that drifts through the novel's central episode as symbol, prophecy, white whale and man-made black death all in one seems at first to be the stuff of routine sci-fi apocalypse (though, in a harrowing, but not unexpected irony, this book came out at the same time as the Bhopal disaster). Yet the effect of the rogue chemical is almost entirely internal. In the wake of the fugitive cloud, Gladney brings up pulsing stars on a computer. What does that mean? The poison has entered his system; he has come to incarnate death.

It is said that DeLillo is funny, but his is the funniness of peculiarity, not mirth. It is, more precisely, the terrible irony of the lone metaphysician, rising to a keening intensity as he registers the black holes in the world about him. In *White Noise*, as in all his novels, DeLillo absorbs the jargon of myriad disciplines and reprocesses them in a terminal deadpan. His is a hard-edged, unsmiling kind of satire. It is not user friendly. And where Thomas Berger, for example, trains the same kind of heightened sensibility on low-down Americana, setting loose an antic concatenation of events that unravels the world and triggers a resistless cycle of repercussions (this is what happens when Archie Bunker makes a pass at Clytemnestra), DeLillo has no time for anarchic pratfalls, Aristophanic gambits, non sequiturs. His humor is pitch black. The National Cancer Quiz is on television. The local college offers courses on "The Cinema of Car Crashes." On family outings, Gladney reads *Mein Kampf* in the neighborhood Dunkin' Donuts.

Just as DeLillo's characters are often not people so much as energies or eccentricities with voices, just as his suburbia is a crowded set of signs fit for a moonlighting Roland Barthes, so his speech is not normal discourse as much as a kind of rhetoric pitched high, a collection of phantom sentences, a chorus of texts without contexts. And his (charnel) house style has the cool metallic sleekness of a hearse: it is all polished angles, black lines, sunless planes. No wasted motion. No extraneous matter. No scraps of the regular world. Words in DeLilloese are stripped dry, sheared clean, given a deadly precision:

> "Am I going to die?"
> "Not as such," he said.
> "What do you mean?"
> "Not in so many words."

It is this stark tonelessness that accounts for the terrible beauty of much of his writing. DeLillo does not put spin on his words; he leaves them hanging—weightless, somber things full of density and gravity. Disconnected, theirs is the kind of bare, brooding blankess that suggests not numbness so much as mystery, a world not empty of meaning, but too full of it, electrically supercharged. The most conspicuous tic in a DeLillo novel, indeed, is to end chapters with a paragraph consisting of nothing but a single sentence:

> "Panasonic."
>
> "I am the false character that follows the name around."
>
> "Who will die first?"

Grist for a paranoid or a nihilist, the words simply stand there in space, mute, momentous, eerie as the pillars of Stonehenge.

DeLillo's other characteristic device is to put together words and rhythms into patterns, sequences, escalating cadences that build a mood and gather momentum and pick up in time a hypnotic and heart-stopping intensity. They turn into riffs, disquisitions, revved-up harangues. They move with the even, pounding purposefulness of footfalls down an alleyway.

This dazzle of Promethean language is largely consecrated to a single driving theme: the rising struggle between tribalism and technology. DeLillo's novels worry and worry at humanity's fight with science; DeLillo's characters are caught between the spirits of their ancestors and the gods of their computer world. The courses in "Eating and Drinking" he satirizes are no idle joke; in Gladney's world, primal instincts are threatened by a conception of progress that would transform men from animals into machines. "The greater the scientific advance, the more primitive the fear," Gladney tells his wife. Science and fear, those are the antagonists in *White Noise*; we need our fear to defeat a science that tries to conquer fear. And the most potent instrument in this contest, the original—and aboriginal—martial art, is language. DeLillo is fascinated with the ways in which language creates and re-creates the world. Names nail down slippery identities; chants mass together crowds into forces stronger even than technology; language is a way, perhaps the only way, of making connections, an ordered system that can withstand the entropic pressure of the world at large. (Like Pynchon, DeLillo everywhere seeks out networks, circuits, codes, connections; and, like Pynchon, he knows that the man who finds connections everywhere is a paranoid.) Words, in the end, make up the fabric of our beings (and so the assurance that Gladney is not dying "in so many words" knells with particular plangency).

Above all, language, for DeLillo, is like fear: it is all we have of certainty, and of humanity. In this novelist's (largely verbal) universe, words are treated as archaeological fragments that can help us recover something of a more primitive and so more human past. Words are runes, atavistic relics, talismans with something of the sacred about them. Language is ritual; language is liturgy. It is no coincidence that the scenes from DeLillo's fiction that hum in the memory are virtuoso set pieces fashioned out of nothing but syllables: the conquest in *The Names* in which the protagonist makes love to an unwilling woman just by mouthing words to her in a crowded Athens restaurant; the episode in *White Noise* in which two professors deliver, simultaneously and in the same room, lectures on Elvis and Hitler, their words and ideas chiming and separating as in some verbal stereo system. At his most reverberant DeLillo at once explores and embodies the power, the fear of sound: recitation, repetition, incantation, words as rough magic, a way of making spells.

At times, perhaps inevitably, DeLillo's rhythms overpower him, acquire a life of their own, race so fast that they overthrow the meaning they are meant to carry. The minute Gladney is given a gun, he thinks of it as "a secret, . . . a second life, a second self, a dream, a spell, a plot, a delirium." Also concealed in the runaway rhetoric is the deeper liability of seeing eternity in a grain of sand: DeLillo and his characters are so eager to read the world, to invest it with significance, that they come on occasion to seem overanxious. Hardly has Gladney begun to rummage through the trash than he is off again: "Is garbage so private? Does it glow at the core with personal heat, with signs of one's deepest nature, clues to secret yearnings, humiliating flaws? What habits, fetishes, addictions, inclinations? What solitary acts, behavioral ruts?" His atmospherics stronger than his aphorisms, DeLillo occasionally builds up menace without meaning, is about profundity rather than full of it, becomes—in a word—portentous. The price he pays for his hubristic ambition is an intermittent bout of pretension; manuals for Zen and the art of emotional maintenance, his books mass-produce fortune cookies along with their koans.

Perhaps the oddest and most enduring mystery of DeLillo's remarkable novels is that, though preoccupied with plotting, they are themselves ill-plotted; portraits of a mind as searching, driven and ceaselessly vagrant as the voice in a Beckett novel, they have trouble with resolutions. Such, perhaps, are the treacheries of a Melvillean course. For DeLillo is determined to take on inquiries that cannot be concluded, to make challenges that cannot be met (just as Gladney resolves to wrestle with the riddle of the Holocaust while his colleagues content themselves with deconstructing detergent jingles, soda bottles, and bubble gum). Writing of the unspeakable, DeLillo is fascinated with the unanswerable. "Is a symptom a sign or a thing? What is a thing and how do we know it's not another thing?" "What is electricity? What is light?" "What is dark?" "How does a person say good-bye to himself?" The questions keep coming and coming, pushing the reader back to metaphysical basics, mocking the answering machine, refuting artificial intelligence, mimicking the manner of a child who goes instantly to the heart of the matter, and with it the heart of darkness.

Next to DeLillo's large and terrifying talent, most modern fiction seems trifling indeed. A connoisseur of fear, he writes novels that leave a chill in one's bones. At the same time, however, it is always difficult to tell what he is about, beyond fear, emptiness, the dark. He knows his data cold; he addresses the great themes with uncommon courage (and so, at moments, heroic presumption and folly); his skills are astonishing. But where is he going, what can he do, with them? Imprisoned, it sometimes seems, within the four walls of his obsessions, he keeps on, in a sense, writing the same book, simply carrying his medicine bag of tricks and theme into a different genre, a new language, with every novel: college football or rock-'n'-roll, science fiction or international business or the academy. Thirteen years ago, his second novel *End Zone* sounded many of the same notes of foreboding that toll through *White Noise*: film clips of hurricanes and tornadoes; some all-American boys with names like "Hauptfuhrer," others burdened by an obscure need to master German; the consoling, earth-bound magnetism of the fat; classes in "the untellable."

For all that, however, *White Noise* remains a far greater book than *End Zone*, in large part because it is something more than cold and curious reason; it offsets its existential shivers with a domestic strength that is touching and true. In the midst of all the Pandoran currents and forces that pulse through the dark is a family that is vulnerable, warm bodies that turn to each other for shelter. Gladney wards off the power of the unknown by holding onto his adored wife at night; his unquiet mind is grounded, and uplifted, when he gazes upon the simple calm of his offspring—"Watching children sleep makes me feel devout, part of a spiritual system. It is the closest I can come to God." The professor's fears for his children as they move through a world of dangers are reminiscent, perhaps, of John Irving's Undertoad. But where Irving was coy and ingratiating, DeLillo is serious and moving. It is a shock to learn after reading his book that DeLillo has no children. All his terrors, his affections, are imagined.

DeLillo can keep one up at night.

IV

Critical Essays

Tom LeClair

Tom LeClair teaches at the University of Cincinnati. He is the author of *In the Loop* and *The Art of Excess* (criticism), *Passing Off* (a novel), and many reviews in *The Nation*, *Atlantic Monthly*, *New York Times Book Review*, *Washington Post*, and other periodicals.

CLOSING THE LOOP: *WHITE NOISE*

"The American mystery deepens," says the native but disoriented narrator of *White Noise* (1985).[1] If DeLillo's three years of living and traveling outside the United States contributed to the scope and intricacy of *The Names*, its "complex systems, endless connections," this period of absence also resensitized him to the glut and blurt of this country, the waste and noise condensed in *White Noise*, which he began after his return in 1982.[2] Throughout his career DeLillo has alternated ways of exploring and creating that mystery he has said fiction should express, expanding his materials and methods to an undecidable spiral of intellectual complication or contracting his subjects and means to drill a test shaft into what he calls, in *Ratner's Star*, "the fear level . . . the starkest tract of awareness."[3] *The Names*, with its wide range and subtlety, is the summation of DeLillo's first seven novels because it unites many of his essential themes and corresponds formally to the multiple collaborative systems we live among. *White Noise*, with its compression and ironic explicitness, is the ghostly double, the photographic negative, of *The Names*. *White Noise* might be termed DeLillo's subtractive or retractive achievement, a deepening of the American and human mystery by means of a narrow and relentless focus on a seemingly ultimate subject—death. *White Noise* is about "closing the loop"—personal and mass dying, the "circle slowly closing" (241) of fear producing its object, and the closed-in structures man erects for safety. Furthermore this novel is itself a tightly looped fiction and is a closing of a large loop in DeLillo's career: he returns not only to America, but also to some of the circumstances and methods of *Americana* and *End Zone*. Because of these returns and the explicitness of *White Noise*, DeLillo's systems orientation is . . . evident . . . and the coherence of his fiction clear. . . .

The title of *White Noise* appears, quite appropriately, in *The Names*. The passage describes air travel, one of that novel's symbols of American-made alienation: "We take no sense impressions with us, no voices, none of the windy blast of aircraft on the tarmac, or the white noise of flight, or the hours waiting" (*The Names*, 7). Like *The Names*, *White Noise* is narrated by a middle-aged father who seeks refuge from the largeness of things—the complexities of information and communication that surround him—in his marriage and children. He finds in family life "the one medium of sense knowledge in which an astonishment of heart is routinely contained" (117), and then, when family is lost to him as a source of safety, succumbs to a visceral obsession with violence; this obsession propels the second halves of the two novels' plots. The fear of death, which infects Owen Brademas and the cult in *The Names*, moves to the center of *White Noise*, driving its narrator/protagonist, a composite of Brademas's anxieties and the cult's responses, into the double binds DeLillo knotted in *The Names*.

The subjects and techniques of *White Noise* are closer to a synthesis of *Americana* and *End Zone*, however, than to the multinational boundary crossings and Venn diagrams of *The Names*. *White Noise* has *Americana*'s small-town setting, its buzzing details of domestic life, an atmosphere polluted by electronic media, and DeLillo's early vision of America as a consumer nation symbolized by the supermarket, where David Bell finds the "white beyond white" of his father's advertising.[4] From *End Zone* DeLillo takes the collegiate setting, intellectual follies, and concern with large-scale ecological disaster. In recombining these earlier materials DeLillo restores a hard-edged explicitness to several methods that had been smoothed to subtlety in his more recent work. *White Noise* has in its action the literal circularity of *Americana*, and it has in its protagonist a character with the repetition compulsion of David Bell. These distinct and pervasive loopings are narrated in the ironic mode of *End Zone*, and *White Noise* also has that novel's sharp declination between "good company" and "madness."

While writing *White Noise*, DeLillo mocked what he called the "around-the-house-and-in-the-yard" school of American fiction, a realism about "marriages and separations and trips to Tanglewood" that gives its readers' reflected lives "a certain luster, a certain significance."[5]

In "Waves and Radiation," the first of the three parts of *White Noise*, DeLillo represents with acute specificity the quotidian life of the Gladney family—Jack and Babette and their four children from various earlier marriages. Though tinged with some satire and foreboding, Part I establishes "around-the-house" expectations, the "good company" of *White Noise*. As in *End Zone*, which has a parallel structure of two balancing sets of chapters surrounding a center of irrational activity, "good company" abruptly shifts in Part II, "The Airborne Toxic Event." *White Noise* becomes a disaster novel. While the Gladneys' safety is suddenly destroyed by the chemical spill that forces them to evacuate their home and town, the reader's expectations of the marital changes and vacations recorded in "around-the-house" realism are deconfirmed. In "The Airborne Toxic Event," DeLillo describes the chemical cloud, the process of evacuation, and several non-Gladney evacuees, but he also quickly subverts the conventions of disaster fiction. The cast of thousands and the long-running suspense of this subgenre are radically contracted in *White Noise*. In DeLillo's disaster, no one dies. The timing of the disaster within the novel is also skewed: preceded by twenty chapters, the 54 pages of Part II are followed by nineteen chapters as DeLillo quickly shifts from the event to his characters' response. Gladney, his family, and the town of Blacksmith look just as they did before this new kind of technological disaster, because its effects are invisible to the naked eye. Their response is to information—quantified measures of exposure, possible long-range consequences—rather than to entities, the scattered corpses or destroyed buildings of conventional disaster fiction. The disaster of *White Noise* is, ultimately, the new knowledge that seeps into the future from the imploded toxic event.

In Part III, "Dylarama," the reader understands that DeLillo is not only successively reversing two subgenres but is also, in the whole of *White Noise*, inverting yet another subgenre—the college novel—to illustrate for whom new knowledge is a threat. The book opens with Professor Jack Gladney, head of the Hitler Studies Department at College-on-the-Hill, describing the return of students in the autumn. It closes with summer recess an academic year later. Several of Gladney's colleagues have roles, and there is one classroom scene; but the political intrigues and intellectual adventures one expects from the college novel occur primarily within the confines of Gladney's home. His very contemporary family is wired to more sources of information than was a college student of Gladney's generation. While the university in *White Noise* is presented as trivialized by the nostalgic study of popular and youth culture, Gladney's children are making his family a center of learning. The irony of this inverted situation is that the professor and his teacher-wife attempt to resist knowledge and regress into nostalgia while their children, despite their fears, move forward and outward into the Age of Information, into awareness of large, complexly related systems. For the parents, this attitude toward knowledge is madness—as, for some readers, is DeLillo's inversion of the college novel, his making the Gladney children fearful prodigies. However, both the rapid shifts and reversals exist within a general verisimilitude, the grounding for DeLillo's mockery and exaggeration.

Although generically and rhetorically doubled, *White Noise*, when compared with *The Names* or even with *Americana*, is structurally and stylistically simple; it lacks their spatial forms, temporal dislocations, framed analogies, overlapping subtexts, and multiple voices. The physical action of *White Noise* is constricted and repetitive: Jack Gladney evades literal death by leaving Blacksmith and traveling to nearby Iron City in the novel's first half, and in the second half he returns to Iron City in quest of a drug that would let him evade his fear of death. Much of the intellectual action—Gladney's dialogues and meditations—is equally looping and reductive, marked by circular logic and sophistical argument. Like David Bell of *Americana*, who does not recognize that the auto test track at the end of the novel is a symbolic repetition of his job at the beginning, Gladney ends in Blacksmith where he began—with the reader unsure of how much the professor has learned from his spatial loops and compulsive repetitions. Other characters offer little assistance to the reader who attempts to gauge Gladney's development. Although *White Noise* displays some of the doubling also seen in *The Names* and *Americana*, the characters in Gladney's family, his acquaintances, and his friends exist primarily as sources of information or stimuli for Gladney, not as persons with plots and complex lives of their own.

DeLillo packs the text with disparate cultural signs and symptoms, but the simple chronological continuity with which Gladney orders his narrative has the effect of reducing it to a collection with apparently minimal connections, more an aggregate than a system. Although Gladney tells his tale primarily in the past tense, he seems to be recording both the trivia and trauma as they happen, not—like David Bell and James Axton—forming the materials from a later perspective. Gladney seldom recalls the past before the novel's events begin, and he plans the future only when forced to. "May the days be aimless. Let the seasons drift. Do not advance the action according to a plan" (98)—these are his desires before the disaster. Gladney allows gaps between episodes, sometime suddenly shifts from description to dialogue or meditation, and composes in short chapters. Gary Harkness of *End Zone* used the same methods to create discontinuity within a basic chronological order. The only technique to intrude upon the novel's illusion of natural or unsophisticated recall is DeLillo's insertion of lists. Always composed of three items, usually the names of products, the lists do not always seem to be in Gladney's consciousness; rather, they are part of the circumambient noise in which he exists, a reminder of the author's presence, his knowledge of a larger context of communications. The lists are also a small analogue of the reductive organization of the text as a whole.

Gladney's sentences are like these lists: short, noun dominated, sometimes fragmentary, with few of the convolutions or Jamesian subordinations that show up in *The Names*. Often lexically and syntactically repetitious, Gladney's strings of declarations effect a primer style, an expression not of ignorance (for Gladney knows the language of the humanities) but of something like shock, a seeming inability to sort into contexts and hierarchies the information he receives and the thinking he does. Gladney's account of his life resembles the narration of a near-disaster that he hears at the Iron City airport, where a man "wearily" and "full of a gentle resignation" (90) describes the terror of preparing for a crash landing. When not neutrally—almost distractedly—recording, Gladney's voice does rise to complaint and, more frequently, to series of rhetorical questions for which he has few answers. A character who has to be forced to think and who resists the process, the self-limiting narrator of *White Noise* resembles Gary Harkness, who is as frozen by guilt as Gladney is by fear. But where the blank-faced narration of *End Zone* occasionally hinted that Harkness was playing a game, was intentionally unreliable, the survivor style of Gladney suggests a shrunken reliability. The reader perceives evasion, rather than power.

This structural and stylistic reductiveness creates a sense of "implosion," a word used several times in *White Noise*. The Gladneys' trash compactor is DeLillo's metaphor in the novel for the novel, for the characters' self-reducing double binds and the narrator's compression of the familiar and wasted. Searching for a wonder drug to relieve his fear of death, Gladney pokes through rubbish compacted into a "compressed bulk [that] sat there like an ironic modern sculpture, massive, squat, mocking":

> I jabbed at it with the butt end of a rake and then spread the material over the concrete floor. I picked through it item by item, mass by shapeless mass, wondering why I felt guilty, a violator of privacy, uncovering intimate and perhaps shameful secrets. It was hard not to be distracted by some of the things they'd chosen to submit to the Juggernaut appliance. But why did I feel like a household spy? Is garbage so private? Does it

> glow at the core with a personal heat, with signs of one's deepest nature, clues to secret yearnings, humiliating flaws? What habits, fetishes, addictions, inclinations? What solitary acts, behavioral ruts? I found crayon drawings of a figure with full breasts and male genitals. There was a long piece of twine that contained a series of knots and loops. It seemed at first a random construction. Looking more closely I thought I detected a complex relationship between the size of the loops, the degree of the knots (single or double) and the intervals between knots with loops and freestanding knots. Some kind of occult geometry or symbolic festoon of obsessions. I found a banana skin with a tampon inside. Was this the dark underside of consumer consciousness? I came across a horrible clotted mass of hair, soap, ear swabs, crushed roaches, flip-top rings, sterile pads smeared with pus and bacon fat, strands of frayed dental floss, fragments of ballpoint refills, toothpicks still displaying bits of impaled food. (258–59)

In its list-like style, discontinuities, and repetition, its jammed subgenres and intellectual foolishness, *White Noise* is—as one meaning of its title suggests—an "ironic modern sculpture," a novelistic heap of waste, the precise opposite of the living system and, as I said earlier, the formal negative of its systems-imitating precursor, *The Names.* This reversal is indicated by the design of the title page of *White Noise* and the first page of each part, where a roman numeral is printed in white on a black background. DeLillo uses this explicit negative to direct attention to the qualities of healthy living systems, which are symbolized in the book by that miniaturized organ, the brain: "Your brain," a colleague tells Gladney, "has a trillion neurons and every neuron has ten thousand little dendrites. The system of inter-communication is awe-inspiring. It's like a galaxy that you can hold in your hand, only more complex, more mysterious" (189).

As a systems novelist, DeLillo recycles American waste into art to warn against entropy, both thermodynamic and informational. *White Noise* has an apocalyptic toxic cloud striking from Pynchon's rocket-pocked heavens, a slow accumulation of garbage heaping up from Gaddis's commercial multimedia, and the self-destructive aberrations of victimization and power that Coover extends from individuals to states. The systems novelists' best works—*Gravity's Rainbow, JR, The Public Burning*—are, like *Ratner's Star,* the DeLillo novel most similar to them, massive disaster novels, industrial-strength "runaway" books. Though about a "runaway calamity" (139), *White Noise* is the compact, accessible model of their warnings, one more example of DeLillo's desire to be in the loop of general readers. Early in the novel DeLillo describes the trash compactor's "dreadful wrenching sound, full of eerie feeling" (33), qualities of *White Noise* that make it his most emotionally demonstrative book, an expression of his passionate concern with human survival, his rage at and pity for what humankind does to itself—reasons why, I believe, DeLillo was finally recognized with the National Book Award for this novel. . . .

In the "ironic modern sculpture" of *White Noise*, the central paradox is "the irony of human existence, that we are the highest form of life on earth and yet ineffably sad because we know what no other animal knows, that we must die" (99). This is the disastrous knowledge in the novel, arising from disaster and leading to it. Saturated with awareness of mortality and denials of that awareness, *White Noise* can be read as a dialogue with Ernest Becker's *The Denial of Death*, which is one of the few "influences" DeLillo will confirm.[6] Becker's book is an identifiable source for a long "looping Socratic walk" (282) and talk that Gladney has with the philosopher/magus of the book, Murray Jay Siskind. In *White Noise* and elsewhere, DeLillo seems to accept Becker's Existential and Rankian positions that the fear of death is the mainspring of human motivation and that man needs to belong to a system of ideas in which mystery exists. But DeLillo differs with Becker's conclusions that repression of the death fear is necessary to live and that "the problem of heroics is the central one of human life," for repression and heroic attempts to overcome death place Gladney in life-threatening situations.[7] Like Pynchon's rocket builders, Gaddis's empire builders, and Coover's high-wire performers, the Gladneys are victims of a self-inflicted double bind: fearing death and desiring transcendence, they engage in evasive artifices and mastering devices that turn back upon them, bringing them closer to the death they fear, even inspiring a longing for disaster, "supreme destruction, a night that swallows existence so completely," as Jack fantasizes, "that I am cured of my own lonely dying" (273).

To demonstrate the self-destructive loops of the Gladneys' sad foolishness, DeLillo employs a continuous ironic reversal, trapping and retrapping his characters in their contradictions. After giving Babette and Jack quite ordinary behavior that they hope will award them a sense of power over their death or protect them from awareness of it, DeLillo has their actions produce dangerous side effects and then the opposite of their intentions. As the Gladneys become increasingly obsessive, DeLillo also includes figures or situations that parody the Gladneys' actions and motives. Finally—and this is the achievement of *White Noise* that particularly needs to be illustrated—DeLillo presses beyond the ironic, extracting from his initially satiric materials a sense of wonderment or mystery, finding in the seeming rubbish of popular culture a kind of knowledge that would provide a more livable set of systemic expectations about life and death. The fundamental questions to which the novel moves forward and backward are: What is natural now? Has the nature of nature changed? If so, has our relation to nature changed? One result of these questions is Murray Jay Siskind's claim, like Ernest Becker's, that "It's natural to deny our nature" (296). If DeLillo begins with some of Becker's assumptions about the effects of mortal fear, the developing theme of nature in *White Noise* undermines the epistemological foundations of Becker's positions and offers the systems approach to mortality that Gregory Bateson presents in his summary book, *Mind and Nature*.[8] Impacted in situation and form, *White Noise* does come to have an intellectual expansiveness accompanying its emotionally enlarging ironies.

Suffering for years from the fear of death, Babette and Jack have settled on essentially three strategies for managing this fear: "mastering" death by expanding the physical self as an entity; evading awareness of their mortality by extending the physical self into protective communications systems; and sheltering the illusion-producing consciousness from awareness of its defensive mechanisms. While these strategies overlap, the novel's conceptual structure based upon them is circular. The simpler strategies manifest themselves at the beginning, then give way to more sophisticated methods, and then reassert themselves at the end when sophistication fails. Jack, at fifty-one, and Babette, in her mid-forties, believe size is power. He takes comfort from his imposing figure and reminds her that he enjoys the protection of her mass: "there was an honesty inherent in bulkiness" (7). If the Gladneys are physically large, their town of Blacksmith is small and safe, far from the violence of big cities. The village center is the supermarket, which provides the setting for numerous scenes in the novel and stands as a symbol of a physical magnitude that can help master death. For Jack, the purchase of goods confers safety: "in the mass and variety of our purchases, in the sheer plenitude those crowded bags suggested, the weight and size and number, the familiar package designs and vivid lettering, the giant sizes, the family bargain packs with Day-Glo sale stickers, in the sense of replenishment we felt, the sense of well-being, the security and contentment these products brought to some snug home in our souls—it seemed we had achieved a fullness of being that is not known to people who need less, expect less" (20). While the supermarket, like so much else in the novel, has an ironic underedge —the poisons in its products—and ultimately has a deeper meaning, initially it gives the Gladneys both a sense of physical expansiveness and what DeLillo elsewhere calls a "mass anesthesia," a means "by which the culture softens the texture of real danger."[9] From the consumption of supermarket perishables, the Gladney family ascends to the acquiring of durable goods at a giant shopping mall. When Jack is told that he appears to be "a big, harmless, aging, indistinct sort of guy" (83), he indulges himself and his family in a shopping spree. Using the quantitative terms that measure life force in the novel, Jack thinks of himself as huge: "I began to grow in value and self-regard. I filled myself out, found new aspects of myself, located a person I'd forgotten existed. Brightness settled around me" (84).

The ironic result of possessions occurs later: Jack's fear of dying is intensified, rather than relieved, by the objects he has collected over the years. When his things seem like weight he must shed, he rampages through his house, throwing objects away, trying to "say goodbye to himself" (294). Material growth requires money, but in *White Noise* money is no longer physical; to possess the simple force of things, Jack must have contact with a complex communication system. When he checks his bank balance by moving through a complicated set of electronic instructions, Jack says, "The system had blessed my life" (46). But since "the system was invisible," created by "the mainframe sitting in a locked room in some distant city" (46), Jack's material power depends on his vulnerable relation to something with few imaginable physical properties. Like the supermarket and the mall, the data bank both gives and takes away security; later, the computer readout of Jack's health history persuades him that his exposure to toxins has planted death within.

At the same time that the Gladneys' physical strategies gradually bring about ironic results, DeLillo includes figures or situations parodying physical mastery. The novel opens with a minutely detailed description of students returning to college. Their station wagons are stuffed with consumer products; their parents, confident in their power, look as though they have "massive insurance coverage" (3). At novel's end, though, panic strikes supermarket shoppers when the shelf locations of their insuring products are changed. The shopping mall is also a literally dangerous place: an aged brother and sister named Treadwell, disoriented by its "vastness and strangeness" (59), spend two days wandering there, and the old woman eventually dies from the shock. Even for the young, the power of the body can fail embarrassingly: Orest Mercator, filled with the best foods and carefully trained, aims to set a world record for days spent sitting with poisonous snakes, testing himself against death. He is bitten within the first two hours, doesn't die, and goes uncovered by the media.

While attempting to master death by ingesting the world, the

Gladneys also try to protect the physical self from consciousness of its lonely finitude by projecting themselves outward into what they trust are protective and safe relationships: forming a marital alliance against mortality, making a family, participating in mass culture as well as mass transactions, creating a public identity. Like their consumerism, this social strategy leads to ironic traps and eventual absurdities. After four marriages each, Babette and Jack believe they have found partners with whom they can feel safe. For Jack, Babette is the opposite of his other wives, who all had ties to the intelligence community and enjoyed plotting. For Babette, Jack is solid, a stay against confusion. To show their concern for each other's happiness, DeLillo has them compete in giving pleasure: they argue over who should choose which pornography to read. They also compete in sadness, arguing about who wants to die first; each says to be without the partner would involve constant suffering. However, love, what Becker calls "the romantic project" (*Denial of Death*, 167), is, for Jack, no match against death. He admits to himself that although Babette may want to die first, he certainly doesn't. They also say they tell each other everything, even their worst anxieties, but both in fact conceal their fear of death. Their mutual secret sets in motion possibly fatal consequences for both of them. Attempting to shelter and be sheltered from awareness in their alliance, the Gladneys bring closer to actuality what they most fear.

A similar ironic reversal characterizes their parenthood. Babette thinks of the children, gathered together from multiple marriages, as a protective charm: "nothing can happen to us as long as there are dependent children in the house. The kids are a guarantee of our relative longevity" (100). Therefore the Gladneys want to keep their children young, especially the last child, Wilder, who speaks very little, thus giving a secret pleasure to his parents. Although Jack argues with Murray Jay Siskind's theory that "the family process works toward sealing off the world," calling it a "heartless theory" (82), he and Babette attempt precisely this enforced ignorance. Ironically, the children are more willing to face threats to existence than are their parents. Steffie volunteers to be a victim in a simulated disaster. Denise pores over medical books to become familiar with toxins. Heinrich, at fourteen, knows science that shows how small are man's chances for survival. When the children's knowledge and questions penetrate their parents' closed environment, the kids become a threat—an inescapable threat, because Babette and Jack have sealed them into the nuclear structure.

The Gladney children are also the primary channel by which another danger—the electronic media, especially television—enters the parents' safe domesticity. In *Americana* television programming was a simplistic threat, a reductive conditioning agent that DeLillo associated with advertising. In *White Noise* television has more complex effects: conditioning and comforting, distorting and informing, even becoming, as I will discuss later, a source of mystery. As in Gaddis's *JR*, radio and television broadcasts frequently interrupt the conversations or narrative of *White Noise*, sometimes infiltrating the characters' consciousness without their awareness. At one level, the media offer Babette and Jack a soothing background noise, evidence beneath their conscious threshold that they are connected to a mass of other listeners. However, when Jack scrutinizes television, he concludes that it causes "fears and secret desires" (85)—despite the fact that most of the fragments to which Jack attends are bits of information, rather than seductive image-creations of the kind described in *Americana*. To reduce the "brain-sucking power" (16) of television, the Gladneys force their children to watch it with them every Friday evening. Irony occurs when disasters are shown, for television's power is increased, rather than reduced: "There were floods, earthquakes, mud slides, erupting volcanoes," says Jack; "We'd never before been so attentive to our duty, our Friday assembly. . . . Every disaster made us wish for more, for something bigger, grander, more sweeping" (64).

The effect of televised death is, like consumerism, anesthetizing. A seeming confrontation with reality is actually a means of evading one's own mortality, giving the viewer a false sense of power. Jack's fear of and desire for television's power lead him to think of the man who cuckolds him, "Mr. Gray," as a "staticky" (241) creature out of television, an unreal being who can be killed with a television character's impunity. This idea turns out to be half true. When Jack finally meets "Mr. Gray," he has little selfhood or memory; his consciousness and speech are filled with the fractured babble of the television he constantly watches. The contradictory effects of this most pervasive communications system are polarized by two parodic background characters—Heinrich's chess-by-mail partner, a convict who has killed five people after hearing voices speaking to him through television, and Jack's German teacher, who has recovered from deep depression by taking an interest in television meteorology. Ultimately both the positive effects and ironic countereffects of television are, like the polarities of the supermarket, recontextualized when DeLillo shifts attention from the content of television to the medium itself.

Unable to maintain family ignorance as a defense, Jack and Babette attempt to master death through professional study and charity, both of which draw a larger, protective crowd around them than their children can supply. Jack's position as founder and chairman of Hitler Studies confers authority and power. Attempting to grow into the role, he changes his name, adds weight, wears dark glasses, enjoys flourishing his black robe. He likes all things German, carries *Mein Kampf* as if it were an amulet, names his son Heinrich, and takes pleasure in owning a German weapon. He also takes secret German lessons. Sensing the "deathly power of the language," he says, "I wanted to speak it well, use it as a charm, a protective device" (31). In his well-attended lectures on the crowd psychology of the Nazis, he does for himself and his students what the Nazis achieved: "Crowds came to form a shield against their own dying. To become a crowd is to keep out death. To break off from the crowd is to risk death as an individual, to face dying alone" (73). As an expert in mass murder, Gladney possesses an intellectual power over death. Ironically, his expertise does not help him accept his own mortality and may well encourage him to attempt, late in the novel, to literally master death by killing "Mr. Gray." Babette's public role as reader to the blind and posture and diet instructor of the elderly gives her a power over others, like Jack's. The age of the students in her "crowd" keeps death in her consciousness, however, and their appetite for tabloid stories starts her on her quest for the ultimate evasion, the fear-relieving and brain-destroying drug Dylar. The crowds that first give Jack and Babette comfort, then prove dangerous, are finally one more source of uncertainty and mystery. DeLillo gathers into Blacksmith and the novel numerous background characters from various races and nations, with different languages and religions, mostly non-Western and exotic-seeming people whose presence questions the white American noise patterns and values within which the Gladneys would conceal themselves. In *White Noise*, the complex multinational world of *The Names* comes to small-town America.

In Part II, "The Airborne Toxic Event," the Gladneys' evasions have more directly harmful and more painfully ironic consequences. Divided into three untitled sections describing the evacuation from Blacksmith, the shelter outside town, and finally further evacuation to Iron City, this Part not only repeats elements of Part I but also repeats itself, drawing tighter and tighter the loop of irony. Déjà vu, one of the symptoms of toxic exposure, is a principle of composition in Part II. The toxic cloud is first spotted by Heinrich. Though its danger is progressively confirmed by observation, the media, and police warnings, Jack and Babette attempt to deny its threat. Their attempt to protect their children from anxiety is revealed as a way of concealing fear from themselves—a doubly guilty action: delay brings increased physical danger to the children and it causes Jack to be exposed to the toxic cloud. The cloud itself cannot be denied, and when it appears overhead it is described, ironically, in terms that recall supermarket plenitude and media distraction: "Packed with chlorides, benzenes, phenols, hydrocarbons" (127), the cloud "resembled a national promotion for death, a multimillion-dollar campaign backed by radio spots, heavy print and billboard, TV saturation" (158). An amorphous, drifting, mysteriously killing mass, the "ATE" is the contemporary complement of Pynchon's pointed, swift, and explosive rockets. Like the rockets, the toxins were engineered to kill and thus give man control over the Earth; instead, they threaten their inventors and nature. DeLillo tips his hat to Pynchon with a radio advertisement that the Gladneys hear during the evacuation: "It's the rainbow hologram that gives this credit card a marketing intrigue" (122).

After demonstrating the ironic effects of unpreparedness in section 1, DeLillo increases the irony in section 2 by having Jack observe people who not only are prepared for disaster but seem to welcome it. Taken out of his safe place and moved to the shelter, the professor becomes the student; he is instructed in the facts of disaster and ways of living with or through it. Persuaded that "death has entered" (141), Jack finds himself filled with dread, needing some comfort, unable to believe in religion, tabloid faith, or the practical delusions Siskind suggests. At the end of section 2 he listens to Steffie's sleep-talk, "words that seemed to have a ritual meaning, part of a verbal spell or ecstatic chant" (155). Even after he realizes the words are "Toyota Celica," a product of consumer conditioning, he calls them a "moment of splendid transcendence"; her mantra allows him to feel "spiritually large" and to pass into a "silent and dreamless" (155) sleep. Jack's delusion and total relief from consciousness would seem to be an appropriate ending for the disaster section, but in section 3 DeLillo has the Gladneys ironically repeat the process of evacuation, this time with a trip to Iron City. Their flight is once again made unduly dangerous because of the Gladneys' denial and delay. When they reach Iron City, what they think will be an overnight stay turns into a nine-day siege among crowds that give none of the comfort Jack has lectured about. The final ironic indignity of Part II is that the disaster receives no television coverage.

In the first few chapters of Part III, "Dylarama," Babette and Jack, having returned to Blacksmith, attempt to drift along with old defenses. But new threats arise—Heinrich informs his family that radiation from electronic devices is more dangerous than airborne toxins—and Jack increasingly believes that his exposure is causing a large nebulous mass (corresponding to the cloud) to grow within. The possibilities for denying death begin to narrow, as does the range of the plot. Babette's importance in the novel, limited from the beginning by Jack's needs and his narration, diminishes as his thanatophobia becomes a symbolic mass, occupying more and more of himself and his story. Now he desperately seeks literal and extreme methods of evasion and mastery, with increasingly ironic and deadly consequences. He finds that Babette had secretly participated in experiments with Dylar, a drug meant to relieve the fear of death. Although Dylar has not worked for her, he plots to obtain a supply from her source, hoping that it will provide an automatic relief from mortal awareness. If Dylar is the ultimate evasion, predicted in *Americana* by a character who says, "Drugs are scheduled to supplant the media" (*Americana*, 347), Jack's means are the ultimate mastery: killing. Already jealous of "Mr. Gray," the chemist to whom Babette has traded sexual favors for Dylar, Jack is also drawn to the expansion of self that Siskind says will occur during a murder. As Jack's actions become more desperate, they also become simpler, imploded. The novel circles back to its beginnings—to Jack's initial faith in ingesting products and growing in physical size; to entities and force replacing, as they do in *Great Jones Street*, participation in communication systems.

Before following out the consequences of Jack's violent quest for Dylar, I want to discuss the role of Murray Jay Siskind. This character appears in *Amazons*, a novel that was published in 1980 under the pseudonym Cleo Birdwell, the name of its protagonist/narrator.[10] *Amazons* is an entertainment about the first woman to play in the National Hockey League; DeLillo says he wrote the book with a collaborator. In it Murray Jay Siskind is a New York sportswriter who carries around a 900-page manuscript chronicling the Mafia takeover of the snowmobile industry. While Siskind is a comic figure in *Amazons*, in *White Noise* he has a much larger and more complex role. As a guest lecturer, he teaches courses on Elvis Presley and car-crash movies. His function is semiotic, "deciphering, rearranging, pulling off the layers of unspeakability" (38) in popular culture and, eventually, in Jack's life. Siskind's methods are to "root out content" and attend to the deep structures, "the codes and messages" (50), of all media. The title of Part I, "Waves and Radiation," is his phrase. Expressing his conclusions with confidence—"It's obvious" is his favorite phrase—Siskind is particularly convincing to Jack on "the nature of modern death": "It has a life independent of us. It is growing in prestige and dimension. It has a sweep it never had before" (150). Although he is important for DeLillo's purposes throughout the novel, Siskind most influences Jack in "Dylarama." There Siskind probes into his friend's repression of death, forcing Jack to recognize how his consciousness has protected itself from itself, the last and most sophisticated strategy of defense. Siskind's influence culminates during his last appearance in the novel when, as he and Jack take a "looping Socratic walk" (282) around Blacksmith, he points out Jack's failures at both evasion and mastery. He then suggests murder as a form of mastery.

Because of Jack's emotional state, Siskind is persuasive; but both Jack and the reader should remember Siskind's limitations, his errors, oddities, and games. He has been blatantly wrong in several of his analyses, including a conclusion about Babette, and unfair in the judgment of his landlord. He says he only speculates, but he also says that for him the best talk is persuasive. He admits a sexual attraction to Babette and admits as well that he covers up the qualities "that are most natural to him" (21) in order to be seductive. Although Siskind does offer Jack, as well as the reader, penetrating interpretations of the world, especially the meaning of its communications systems, Siskind's advice promotes a profoundly immoral act. Like the Gladneys, he compresses—implodes—the context of his thinking, ignoring the murder victim and Jack's role as husband and father, which would be endangered by his crime. A peripatetic Socrates, Siskind turns into Mephistopheles, a sneaky-looking, beard-wearing magus who infiltrates Gladney's consciousness, not by promising an advance in knowledge, as Faust's tempter did, but by claiming, "We know too much" (289). He suggests regression—"We want to reverse the flow of experience" (218)—tempting with ignorance and nostalgia. Siskind is also, in Michel Serres's systemic terms, the "parasite," the guest who exchanges talk for food and (simultaneously, in French) the agent of noise in a cybernetic system.[11]

The plot that Jack formulates in response to Siskind's temptation and disturbing "noise" has secrecy as a major appeal. Now that Jack cannot keep his impending death secret from his consciousness and his fear secret from his wife, he desires something private, a knowledge wholly his own. Such a secret would provide power, what Jack thinks is his "last defense against the ruin" (275) and what Ernest Becker calls "man's illusion par excellence, the denial of the bodily reality of his destiny" (*Denial of Death*, 237–38). By killing his rival Jack will participate in the "secret precision" (291) of murder and will be able to consume a product created by "secret research" (192). Just after Siskind recommends murder to Jack, he quotes a letter from his bank about his "secret code": "Only your code allows you to enter the system" (295). But for DeLillo, here and in his other novels, secrets collapse a system in on itself, destroying necessary reciprocity and collaboration, denying man's place in multiple systems. The irony—perhaps the saving irony—of Jack's secret plotting is that he is no better a plotter than he has been a protector, no better a master than an evader. His murder plan seems based on the improbabilities of television crime, full of holes despite his constant, step-by-step rehearsal. He drives to Iron City in a stolen car, running red lights along the way. He plans to shoot "Mr. Gray" in the stomach and then put the gun in Gray's hand, implying a rather unusual suicide. While confronting and then shooting Gray, whose name is Willie Mink, Jack is mentally intoxicated. He understands "waves, rays, coherent beams" (308) and feels the air is "rich with extrasensory material" (309). Jack's intellectual expansion, his Murray-sight produced by adrenalin, ends when Mink shoots him. Using the metaphor of implosion, Jack says, "The world collapsed inward, all those vivid textures and connections buried in mounds of ordinary stuff. . . . The old human muddles and quirks were set flowing again" (313). Literally reminded of mortality, Jack forgets the Dylar and secrecy; he takes Mink to a hospital, saving his victim's life and, perhaps, his own tenuous humanity. The crazed Gray-Mink—who resembles Clare Quilty during the murder scene at the end of *Lolita*—is an exotic, colored double for Jack to recognize and accept. Like Jack, he has tried to master death by studying it, and to evade consciousness of death by ingesting products and media. Both Mink and Jack also come close to destroying themselves because of their obsessions.

If the novel appears at this point to drive toward a conventional hopeful ending, DeLillo springs several compacted reversals and ironies in its last few pages. Feeling spiritually "large and selfless" (314) after saving Mink's life, Jack discusses heaven with a German nun in the hospital. She undercuts any sentimental religious hope he may now have by saying that even she and her fellow nuns don't believe; they only pretend to for the sake of all those secularists, like Jack, who need belief not to disappear from the world. Immediately after denying Jack his nostalgia for literal transcendence, his vision of heaven as "fluffy cumulus" (317), DeLillo has Jack report in the last chapter what can be only termed a minor miracle, an event out of what Jack has earlier called "the tabloid future, with its mechanism of a hopeful twist to apocalyptic events" (146): Wilder rides his plastic tricycle across six lanes of busy traffic, beating death at odds it would take a computer to calculate. Perhaps Jack's achievement—a possible new relationship to death—is implied by his drawing no conclusions from Wilder's feat. He simply reports it as a fact of uncertain cause and effect, finding in it no evasion or mastery. This uncertain acceptance of the uncertain also marks the episode that follows Wilder's ride. Jack describes his and other Blacksmith residents' hushed viewing of brilliant sunsets, perhaps caused by toxins in the air: "Certainly there is awe, it is all awe, it transcends previous categories of awe, but we don't know what we are watching or what it means, we don't know whether it is permanent, a level of experience to which we will gradually adjust, into which our uncertainty will eventually be absorbed, or just some atmospheric weirdness, soon to pass" (324–25). As the "fluffy cumulus" would make a good religious finale, these naturally or unnaturally "turreted skies" would provide a conventional humanistic ending for *White Noise*. But DeLillo chooses to conclude with a scene in the supermarket, where Jack and elderly shoppers disoriented by the new locations of products "try to work their way through confusion" (326). What the shoppers "see or think they see . . . doesn't matter," Jack says, because the checkout "terminals are equipped with holographic scanners, which decode the binary secret of every item, infallibly. This is the language of waves and radiation, or how the dead speak to the living" (326). In the adjacent tabloid racks, he concludes, is "everything we need that is not food or love . . . the cures for cancer, the remedies for obesity. The cults of the famous and the dead" (326). In this last paragraph DeLillo passes to the reader the uncertainty that Jack has found dangerous throughout the novel. Here Jack may be speaking literally, which would suggest continuing delusion; or ironically, which might imply a reductive reversal of his earlier delusions; or figuratively, which could be a final achievement, the register of doubleness and uncertainty, resistance to the "binary" simplification he mentions. At the end of *White Noise* the American mystery does deepen, as white space follows Jack's final enigmatic words.

The ambiguities of DeLillo's final chapter send the reader back into the novel to consider the crucial question implicit in the book's packed ironies and explicit in many of DeLillo's references to the concept of nature: What is "the nature and being of real things" (243)? The theme of the natural in *White Noise* is both pervasive and piecemeal, stroked into the texture of the book in such a way as to defy categorization, a jumble of perceptions, queries, assertions, and speculations like the mixture in the trash compactor that provides "signs of one's deepest nature" (259). The nature of inorganic matter or processes is discussed by numerous characters, ranging from Siskind, who comments on the "heat death of the universe" (10), to Heinrich, who possesses specialized knowledge of submolecular matter, to others who meditate on such common subjects as rain and sunsets. The Gladney family gets information about plants and animals from "CABLE NATURE" (231). Characters are particularly interested in laboratory animals and "sharks, whales, dolphins, [and] great apes" (189), animals that blur the distinction with humans. If, asks Heinrich, "animals commit incest . . . how unnatural can it be?" (34). The nature of various human groups is a subject for frequent analysis. A colleague of Jack's says, "Self-pity is something that children are very good at, which must mean it is natural and important" (216). Of his fellow Blacksmith residents, Jack states, "It is the nature and pleasure of townspeople to distrust the city" (85). Babette believes that men have a capacity for "insane and violent jealousy. Homicidal rage" and, further, "When people are good at something, it's only natural that they look for a chance to do this thing" (225). Man's physical nature is most thoroughly treated in Heinrich and Jack's several colloquies on the brain. As for "undisclosed natural causes," Jack says, "We all know what that means" (99). Characters define the nature of love, sex, and shopping; they discuss human products from "the nature of the box camera" (30) to the "natural language of the culture" (9). "Technology," says Siskind, "is lust removed from nature" (285). Finally, the nature of individuals is described and judged: Jack says that "it was my nature to shelter loved ones from the truth" (8), that Steffie looks "natural" in her role as victim, and that Wilder is "selfish in a totally unbounded and natural way" (209).

Because of these multiple categories of the natural, the general response of Jack Gladney (and, I believe, of the reader) is uncertainty about some single natural order. "The deeper we delve into the nature of things," Gladney concludes, "the looser our structure may seem to become" (82). This "looseness," what the systems theorist would call "openness" or "equifinality," is an intellectual disaster for Babette and Jack. This dangerous uncertainty is caused not only by *what* they have come to learn, but also *how*. In the inversion of the college novel, they are instructed by their children and receive often fragmented information from the communication loops that penetrate their ignorance. The knowledge that Heinrich and others impose on Jack and Babette is often specialized, taken out of its scientific context and expressed in its own nomenclature. This new information frequently requires the Gladneys to deny the obvious, accept the improbable, and believe in the invisible. The "waves and radiation" are beyond the capability of "natural" perception: knowledge of them cannot be had without the aid of technological extensions of the nervous system. Because of the Gladneys' schooling and expectations, this new world they inhabit seems remarkably strange. Babette believes, "The world is more complicated for adults than it is for children. We didn't grow up with all these shifting facts and attitudes" (171). She and Jack remember the three kinds of rock but are unprepared for the systems-ranging science that Heinrich seems to find natural. Jack's career is based on a nineteenth-century notion of history, the anachronism of charisma and mass movements, the irrational in terms of personal or social—rather than molecular—forces. What he calls the gradual "seepage" of poison and death into the present is alien to him because he has "evolved an entire system" (12) around the charismatic figure of Hitler. Babette's expectations are even more simplistic: she tells Jack, "I think everything is correctible. Given the right attitude and proper effort, a person can change a harmful condition by reducing it to its simplest parts" (191).

Accompanying the obvious irony here is the negative effect of her analytic method. The splitting of reality into smaller and smaller parts has produced both the "finger-grained" (35) physical danger that Jack remarks and the atomized information that resists a structure, a whole.

The emotional consequences of the Gladneys' uncertainty are nostalgia; guilt: "Man's guilt in history and in the tides of his own blood has been complicated by technology, the daily seeping falsehearted death" (22); and fear: "Every advance is worse than the one before because it makes me more scared" (161), says Babette. Like their responses to death, the Gladneys' responses to uncertainty about nature have the ambivalent force of taboo—attraction and repulsion. When they try to understand why they and their children enjoy watching disasters, Jack's colleague explains the attraction as normal, "natural. . . . Because we're suffering from brain fade. We need an occasional catastrophe to break up the incessant bombardment of information" (66). If this answer only increases their uncertainty, Murray Jay Siskind's paradox—"It's natural to deny our nature" (297)—is the ultimate statement of the circularity within which the Gladneys feel trapped. They are unable to know what they want, and unable to not know what they don't want.

The best systems treatment of the Gladneys' problems is Gregory Bateson's *Mind and Nature*, a book about what man can (and, particularly, cannot) know about living systems. Bateson succinctly diagnoses the kind of response the Gladneys have to their contemporaneity: "a breach in the apparent coherence of our mental logical process would seem to be a sort of death" (*Mind and Nature*, 140). The Gladneys' strategies for evading uncertainty overlap with their defenses against mortality—closed spatial, psychological, and social systems. The destructive consequences of their intellectual implosion are DeLillo's photo-negative methods for pointing to his systems-based conception of nature, mind, and mortality. Because nature, whether strictly defined as living systems or more widely defined as the world in its totality, is a complex of multiple, overlapping systems, many of which are open, reciprocal, and equifinal, the coherence of either/or logic, a major basis for delusions about certainty, should not, suggests DeLillo, be expected to apply to the simultaneous, both/and nature of phenomena. "My life," says Babette, "is either/or" (53). When the Gladneys attempt to impose expectations inherited from closed systems of entities on the open world of communications, what Bateson calls "the tight coherence of the logical brain" is "shown to be not so coherent" (*Mind and Nature*, 140). Unable to adapt to incoherence, the Gladneys verge toward the self-destructiveness and delusion that Bateson predicts for the "victims" of uncertainty: "In order to escape the million metaphoric deaths depicted in a universe of *circles* of causation, we are eager to deny the simple reality of ordinary dying and to build fantasies of an afterworld and even of reincarnation" (*Mind and Nature*, 140).

What the Gladneys refuse to accept and what forms the basis for DeLillo's understanding of systemic fact and value is the loop: the simultaneity of living and dying, the inherent reciprocity of circular causality that makes certainty impossible. Their refusal is rooted in mechanistic science, that extension of common-sense empiricism which defines the world as a collection of entities, a heap of things like the Gladneys' compacted trash, rather than as a system of energy and information. The way Jack expresses his question about fundamental reality—"the nature and being of real *things*" (my italics)—illustrates his epistemological error, which also leads to either/or categorizing, because "things" are separate and separable. Siskind tells the Gladneys that in Tibet death "is the end of attachment to things" (38). For DeLillo the detachment from "things" is not exotic transcendence but looping good sense, recognition of the systemic nature of nature.

Adaptation to uncertainty is a common theme in contemporary fiction. DeLillo gives it a "hopeful twist" in *White Noise* by demonstrating the benefits of systems-influenced uncertainty. If, as the Gladneys feel, the nature of the contemporary world is "strange," does not this fact, recognized and accepted, reduce the feared strangeness of death and even offer possibilities of hope? Put another way: If we are uncertain about life, wouldn't our uncertainty about death be natural and less feared? Discussing modern death in language that applies as well to modern science, Siskind sums up the Gladneys' dual fear: "The more we learn, the more it grows. Is this some law of physics? Every advance in knowledge and technique is matched by a new kind of death, a new strain. Death adapts, like a viral agent. Is it a law of nature?" (150). Later he leads Jack astray, drawing the conclusion that "fear is unnatural" (289). The alternative to Siskind's ultimately murderous conclusion is articulated by the elusive neuroscientist Winnie Richards. "I have a spacey theory about human fear," she tells Jack. "If death can be seen as less strange and unreferenced, your sense of self in relation to death will diminish, and so will your fear" (229). Jack asks, "What do I do to make death less strange?" He answers his own question with clichés about risking his life, thus missing the less dangerous and more intellectually promising alternative of admitting life's strangeness, its refusal to be consumed by human appetite or human needs for coherence, the human-invented "law of parsimony." Like the biologist Zapalac in *End Zone*, Richards advances a systemslike position that could, if accepted, make contemporary death "an experience that flows naturally from life" (100), as Jack says of death for Genghis Khan.

Also flowing from this pervasive strangeness or mystery might be a sense of hope, or at least the possibility that human existence could be open rather than closed. Jack and Babette have chosen, in a phrase used to describe their family, to "seal off" death and the dead. They choose to believe that death is the end of human identity. People around them believe in quite literal continuation, even in the apparently ridiculous tabloid versions of reincarnation and extraterrestrial salvation. While the senior citizens' appetite for "the cults of the famous and the dead" may well be a reversion to "superstition," a word repeated throughout *White Noise*, the elderly characters' belief could also be, as Jack implies in the shelter, the result of adjustment to the new natural world shot through with scientific implausibility. Their tabloids constitute a literalized bastardization of incomprehensible possibility, their "acceptance and trust . . . the end of skepticism" (27). Skepticism of the reductionist, mechanistic kind would be rid of all belief, but DeLillo suggests in *White Noise* that he shares Michael Polanyi's (as well as Gregory Bateson's) position that "in attributing truth to any methodology we make a nonrational commitment; in effect, we perform an act of faith . . . [that] arises from a network of unconscious bits of information taken in from the environment," what Polanyi calls "tacit knowing."[12] Mechanism believes the world is closed; systems theory assumes it's open and accepts uncertainty. The German nun tells Jack that she and her small band are keeping faith alive, but in fact contemporary science—not "fools, idiots, those who hear voices, those who speak in tongues" (319)—is the primary source and reminder of the necessity of faith. Many aspects of contemporary life that the Gladneys use to evade or master death and uncertainty could also be tacit means of man's adjusting to the inherent existence of faith and mystery in his experience. One working title of the novel was "The American Book of the Dead." Both the Tibetan and Egyptian Books of the Dead, as well as the Mexican Day of the Dead, are alluded to in *White Noise*. These sacred books, Siskind explains to Jack, prepare us for death. While the experiences of the supermarket, television, or scientific knowledge do not prepare contemporary man in specific and literal ways, as the Books of the Dead or the tabloids do, these everyday events can offer a communal experience of the invisible, a sense of mysteriousness that implies that neither life nor death has been settled, closed. Perhaps lack of conclusiveness means lack of conclusion.

Murray Jay Siskind is the tutor in mystery. DeLillo hedges Siskind's influence in several ways—by making him hyperbolic and occasionally wrong in his statements, by giving him an immoral influence—but I believe DeLillo means the reader to take seriously Siskind's analysis of essentially religious experience in secular forms. By immersing himself "in American magic and dread" (19), Siskind arrives at conclusions shared by Gregory Bateson. "The conventional view is that religion evolved out of magic," but, says Bateson, "I think it was the other way around—that magic is a sort of degenerate religion," a superficial but powerful way to answer the religious need "to affirm membership in what we may call the *ecological tautology*, the eternal verities of life and environment" (*Mind and Nature*, 232). It's in Siskind's realm, the supermarket, that the tabloids, which DeLillo states are "closest to the spirit of the book," are found.[13] These tabloids, DeLillo says, "ask profoundly important questions about death, the afterlife, God, worlds and space, yet they exist in an almost Pop Art atmosphere," an atmosphere that Siskind helps decode. In his family Jack experiences "magic," "secondary levels of life . . . extrasensory flashes and floating nuances of being" (34), the "debris of invisible matter" (64); however, he is slow to find a similar mysteriousness outside the home. To Siskind, the supermarket is packed not with the physical goods that the Gladneys consume, but with communications, messages: "This place recharges us spiritually, it prepares us, it's a gateway or pathway. Look how bright. It's full of psychic data. . . . Everything is concealed in symbolism, hidden by veils of mystery and layers of cultural material. But it is psychic data, absolutely. The doors slide open, they close unbidden. Energy waves, incident radiation. All the letters and numbers are here, all the colors of the spectrum, all the voices and sounds, all the code words and ceremonial phrases" (37–38). He finds the same plenitude in television: it "offers incredible amounts of psychic data. It opens ancient memories of world birth, it welcomes us into the grid, the network of little buzzing dots that make up the picture pattern. . . . The medium practically overflows with sacred formulas if we can remember how to respond innocently and get past our irritation, weariness and disgust" (51). Even technology has a similar, perhaps ironic mysteriousness: "New devices, new techniques every day. Lasers, masers, ultrasound. Give yourself up to it," Siskind tells Jack, "Believe in it. They'll insert you in a gleaming tube, irradiate your body with the basic stuff of the universe. Light, energy, dreams. God's own goodness" (285).

Two episodes, closing Parts I and III, suggest that Jack begins to learn to see as Siskind and, I believe, DeLillo do. When Jack views Babette on television, he wonders if she is "dead, missing, disembodied? Was this her spirit, her secret self, some two-dimensional facsimile released by the power of technology, set free to glide through wavebands, through energy levels, pausing to say good-bye to us from the fluorescent screen?" (104). He says, "I began to think Murray might be on to something. Waves and radiation" and confesses that "strangeness gripped me" (104). The last episode occurs at the supermarket and ends the novel. The confusion of the elderly in the aisles doesn't matter, Jack says, because the "holographic scanners" are in place, decoding "the language of waves and radiation, or how the dead speak to the living" (326). I have said that this ending was uncertain, and it remains so. However, considered as the culmination of the theme of nature and mystery, Jack's final words imply that he may be ready to accept the uncertain activity below the surface of our perceptions, activity that may—and only may—mean that the world of the living and the world of the dead are not wholly separate, closed off.

While satirizing how contemporary man uses and is used by his objects, his things, DeLillo also shows how a new perception of what is now natural—systems among systems, communications, inherent uncertainty, mysteriousness—can accommodate man to his condition as knower and even squeeze a modicum of hope from the junk into which a reductionist way of knowing has historically converted natural complexity. This is the looping accomplishment of *White Noise*. Morris Berman, in his study of science since the Rennaisance, asserts that the effect of systems thinking is a "reenchantment of the world," a sense of participation in systemic mysteriousness. Understated and uncertain, the ending of *White Noise* implies this possibility, this futurity—if not for Jack Gladney, then for the reader who knows more than he. Although *White Noise* seems most similar, among systems novels, to the collected noise of Gaddis's *JR*, I believe that DeLillo's is ultimately a larger-minded work, going beyond Gaddis's massive pessimism to ally itself with the more radically open system of Pynchon's *Gravity's Rainbow*, in which the voices of the dead—the long-extinct organisms that become petroleum, the recently dead humans who speak from the Other Side—are not wholly drowned out by the roar of the killing rockets.

The ambiguities of DeLillo's title and the pattern of reference composed around it summarize the doubleness of the novel. First, the phrase is itself a synesthetic paradox. In general scientific usage, "white noise" is aperiodic sound with frequencies of random amplitude and random interval—a term for chaos. In music, however, "white noise" is the sound produced by all audible sound-wave frequencies sounding together—a term for complex, simultaneous ordering that represents the "both/and" nature of systems (and irony). "Panasonic," a word that appears by itself as a paragraph on page 241, was another working title of the novel, one that indicates DeLillo's concern with recording the wide range of sound, ordered and uncertain, positive and negative.

The pattern DeLillo builds around noise parallels the thematic developments I've been discussing. The characters in *White Noise* consume sounds as they consume supermarket products. The sounds of home appliances, such as the "mangling din" (34) of the trash compactor, and the chatter of children give Jack comfort. In the supermarket he is "awash in noise. The toneless systems, the jangle and skid of carts, the loudspeaker and coffee-making machines, the cries of children. And over it all, or under it all, a dull and unlocatable roar, as of some form of swarming life just outside the range of human apprehension" (36). At the mall there is a similar "human buzz of some vivid and happy transaction" (84). The voices of radio and television, like the noise of stores, tell Jack he's not alone, allowing him to evade the feared silence of the cemetery he visits. For Jack, a sense of mastery comes from the private sounds of lovemaking, his voice lecturing, the chants of Nazi crowds, his voice as a weapon in Willie Mink's room, the explosion of the gun. The speculative dialogues he holds with Siskind initially distract his consciousness from mortality. But like the Gladneys' behavior in the novel, sounds have ironic effects and reversals. These are the alarms, commercial messages, confusing information, the "aural torment" (241) of cuckoldry, anxiety while pronouncing German, the news of secret plots, spoken ideas with deadly consequences, shrieks of madness from the asylum, and the noise of primal terror from airplane passengers who think they are about to crash: "terrible and inarticulate sounds, mainly cattle noises, an urgent and force-fed lowing" (92). With this negative evidence in mind, Babette wonders, "What if death is nothing but sound? . . . You hear it forever. Sound all around. How awful" (198). The opposite extreme is the tabloid hope that "some voice or noise would crack across the sky and we would be lifted out of death" (234) by UFOs.

While expressing polarities, the sound motif, like the novel as a whole, comes to signify a wide-ranging awareness of systemic mystery, a new knowing and non-knowing. In evolution, Anthony Wilden reminds us, noise is an intrusion "converted into an essential part of the system so as to maintain the relationship between system and environment"; the "efficient system" will "seek to maintain stability by ACCEPTING noise, by incorporating it as information, and moving to a new level of organization (evolving)."[14] In the human organism, as conceptualized by Michel Serres, noise is the constant internal background against which the organism transforms "disorder into potential organization" with language, thus creating what Serres describes as a loop: "negentropy goes back upstream," and the flow of time is bent.[15] In more everyday terms, Heinrich reminds his father of human perceptual limits: "Just because you don't hear a sound doesn't mean it's not out there . . . they [sounds] exist in the air, in waves. Maybe they never stop. High, high, high-pitched. Coming down from somewhere" (23).

What we experience as silence may be communication. What we hear as static may have meaning. Listening to Wilder cry for nearly seven straight hours, Jack thinks that "inside this wailing noise" might be "some reckless wonder of intelligibility" (78). An early sentence comparing traffic noise to the murmur "of dead souls babbling at the edge of a dream" (4) seems like a throwaway simile until, near the novel's end, Jack hears the sizzle of his freezer as "wintering souls" (258) and, listening to women talk, says, "All sound, all souls" (273).

In *White Noise* DeLillo collects the familiar sounds of American culture and universal fear; he then both turns them up, exaggerating their foolishness for ironic effect, and turns them down, finding in the lower frequencies a whisper of possibility, of uncertainty beyond our present range of knowledge. DeLillo's is the noise of disaster and the noise of mystery. Which shall we hear, which shall we make—in the loop? . . .

NOTES

1. Don DeLillo, *White Noise* (New York: Penguin Books, 1986; The Viking Critical Library, 1998), 60.
2. Don DeLillo, *The Names* (New York: Vintage, 1989), 313.
3. Don DeLillo, *Ratner's Star* (New York: Vintage, 1989), 4.
4. Don DeLillo, *Americana* (New York: Pocket, 1973), 198.
5. Robert R. Harris, "A Talk with Don DeLillo," *New York Times Book Review* (Oct. 10, 1982): 26.
6. In a letter to me, dated Nov. 8, 1985.
7. Ernest Becker, *The Denial of Death* (New York: Free Press, 1973), 7.
8. Gregory Bateson, *Mind and Nature* (New York: Bantam, 1980).
9. Don DeLillo, "American Blood," *Rolling Stone* (Dec. 8, 1983): 27.
10. Cleo Birdwell, *Amazons* (New York: Holt, Rinehart and Winston, 1980).
11. Michel Serres, *The Parasite*, trans. Lawrence R. Schehr (Baltimore: Johns Hopkins University Press, 1982).
12. Morris Berman, *The Reenchantment of the World* (New York: Bantam, 1984), 128–29.
13. Caryn James, " 'I Never Set Out to Write an Apocalyptic Novel.' " See page 333 of this volume.
14. Anthony Wilden, *System and Structure*, 2nd ed. (London: Tavistock, 1980), 400, 410.
15. Michel Serres, "The Origin of Language: Biology, Information Theory, and Thermodynamics," in *Hermes: Literature, Science, Philosophy*, ed. Josue V. Harari and David F. Bell (Baltimore: Johns Hopkins University Press, 1982), 81.

Frank Lentricchia

In addition to two volumes on DeLillo, Frank Lentricchia has published several critical books, including *After the New Criticism*, *Criticism and Social Change*, and, most recently, a memoir, *The Edge of Night*, and two novels, *Johnny Critelli* and *The Knifemen*, in one volume. He is the Katherine Everett Gilbert Professor of Literature at Duke University. This essay has been excerpted and adapted by the author from an essay that first appeared in *Raritan*, Spring 1989.

DON DELILLO'S PRIMAL SCENES

For obvious reasons Don DeLillo's publishers are pleased to advertise their man as a "highly acclaimed" novelist, but until the publication of *White Noise* in 1985 DeLillo was a pretty obscure object of acclaim, both in and out of the academy. He gives no readings,* attends no conferences, teaches no summer workshops in fiction writing, never shows up on late night television, and doesn't cultivate second-person narrative in the present tense. So he has done virtually nothing to promote himself in the approved ways. And the books are hard: all of them expressions of someone who has ideas (I don't mean opinions), who reads things other than novels and newspapers (though he clearly reads those too, and to advantage), and who experiments with literary convention.

What is characteristic about DeLillo's books, aside from their contemporary subjects, is their irredeemably heterogeneous esthetic texture; they are montages of tones, styles, and voices that have the effect of yoking together terror and wild humor as the essential tone of contemporary America. Terrific comedy is DeLillo's mode: even, at the most unexpected moments, in *Libra*, his imagination of the life of Lee Harvey Oswald. It is the sort of mode that marks writers who conceive

* As of October 1988.

their vocation as an act of cultural criticism (in the broadest sense of the terms); who invent in order to intervene; whose work is a kind of anatomy, an effort to represent their culture in its totality; and who desire to move readers to the view that the shape and fate of their culture dictates the shape and fate of the self.

Writers in DeLillo's tradition are never the sort who could buy the representative directive of the literary vocation of our time, the counsel to "write what you know," taken to heart by producers of the new regionalism who in the South, for example, claim parentage in Faulkner and Flannery O'Connor, two writers who would have been floored to hear that "what you know" means the chastely bound snapshot of your neighborhood and your biography. (An embarrassing sign of the esthetic times: one critic, writing for the *Partisan Review*, reported his happy astonishment that DeLillo could invent such believable kids in *White Noise* because, after all, DeLillo has no kids.) Writers in DeLillo's tradition have too much ambition to stay home. To leave home (and I do not mean "transcend" it), to leave your region, your ethnicity, the idiom you grew up with, is made to seem pretentious in the setting of the new regionalism, and the South is not unique. In the cultural setting in which Bobbie Ann Mason incarnates the idea of the writer and Frederick Barthelme succeeds his brother in the pages of *The New Yorker*, to write novels that might be titled *An American Tragedy* or *USA*—DeLillo's first book was called *Americana* (1971)—no doubt is pretentious. In this kind of setting, a writer who tries what DeLillo tries is simply immodest, shamelessly so. Apparently only the Latin Americans have earned the right to their immodesty. So American novelists and critics first look sentimentally to the other Americas, where (so it goes) the good luck of fearsome situations of social crisis encourages a major literature; then look ruefully to home, where (so it goes) the comforts of our stability require a minor, apolitical, domestic fiction of the triumphs and agonies of private individuals operating in "the private sector" of Raymond Carver and Anne Tyler, the modesty of small, good things: fiction all but labeled "No expense of intellect required. To be applied in eternal crises of the heart only." Unlike these new regionalists of and for the Reagan eighties, DeLillo offers us no myth of political virginity preserved, no "individuals" who are not expressions of—and responses to—specific historical processes.

Two scenes in DeLillo's fiction are primal for his imagination of America. The first occurs in his first book, *Americana*, in a brief dialogue the ostensible subject of which is television but whose real subject is the invention of America as the invention of television, which "came over on the Mayflower," as one of his characters says. And that is the first mark of his fiction: the presence of witty characters who talk obsessively about cultural issues in a funny and colloquial English and who do on a regular basis what Melville's characters couldn't keep themselves from doing: they think. And what they think about tends to be concerned not with what goes on domestically in the private kitchens of their private lives—small, good things, or even small, horrible things—but with what large and nearly invisible things press upon the private life, the various coercive contemporary environments within which the so-called private life is led. In the dialogue from *Americana* the genius of television emerges as nothing other than the desire for the universal third-person—it is *that* which "came over on the Mayflower," the he or she we dream about from our armchairs in front of the television, originally dreamt by the first immigrants, the pilgrims on their way over, the object of the dream being the he or she those pilgrims would become, could the dream be fulfilled: a new self because a new world.

So sitting in front of the TV in our armchairs is like a perpetual Atlantic crossing. For if, as DeLillo writes, "To consume in America is not to buy; it is to dream," then the pilgrims were the ur-American consumers in the market for selfhood. Which is to say that it is not the consummation of desire (for the pilgrims, the actual grinding experience of being here) but the foreplay of desire that is TV advertising's object. To buy is merely an effect, but to dream is a cause—the motor principle, in fact, of consumer capitalism. TV advertising taps into and manipulates the American dream; it is the mechanism which triggers our move "from first person consciousness to third," from the self we are, and would leave behind, to the self we would become. Unlike the movies, which blow up the image of the third person to larger-than-life proportions, the TV ad is realistic because it will never try to tell you that, like Richard Burton, you can go to bed with a movie star in Acapulco; instead, it will tell you "that the dream of entering the third person singular might possibly be fulfilled," that it is entirely possible for you to have "two solid weeks of sex and adventure with a vacationing typist from Iowa City." Advertising "discovered" and exploited the economic value of the person we all want to be, but the consumer dreaming on the original Mayflower, or on the new Mayflower in front of the television, "invented" that person.

If, in Fitzgerald's words at the end of *The Great Gatsby*, the "fresh, green breast of the new world" had "pandered in whispers to the last and greatest of all human dreams," if Gatsby's life is the meretricious but typical incarnation of that dream—the self he made out of the self he repressed: James Gatz become Jay Gatsby, the "first person" (in two senses) become "third"—then those pilgrims were his ancestors and we in TV land are his real-life progeny. The pilgrims, Gatsby, almost any character in Stephen Crane or Theodore Dreiser, ourselves in front of the television: the distinction between the real and fictional cannot be sustained; its undesirability is the key meaning, even, of being an American. . . . One thing our writers are saying is that to be real in America is to be in the position of the "I" who would be "he" or "she," the I who must negate I, leave I behind in a real or metaphoric Europe, some suffocating ghetto of selfhood figured forth repeatedly in DeLillo's books as some shabby and lonely room in America, a site of dream and obsession, a contemporary American origin just as generative as the Mayflower. The Mayflower may or may not have been the origin of origins—surely it was not—but, in any case, for America to be America the original moment of yearning for the third person must be ceaselessly renewed.

The second primal scene for DeLillo's imagination of America comes in *White Noise* in a passage which extends a major implication of the surprising history of television he had explored in *Americana.* "The most photographed barn in America" is the ostensible subject of this scene; the real subject is a new kind of representation as a new kind of excitement: not any given representation as some inert object upon which we might apply our powers of analysis (say, the particular barn in question), but the electronic medium of representation as the active context of contemporary existence in America. TV, a productive medium of the image, is only one (albeit dominant) technological expression of an entire environment of the image. But unlike TV, which is an element in the contemporary landscape, the environment of the image *is* the landscape—it is what "landscape" has become, and it can't be turned off with the flick of a wrist. For this environment-as-electronic-medium radically constitutes contemporary consciousness and therefore (such as it is) contemporary community—it guarantees that we are a people of, by, and for the image. Measured against TV advertising's manipulation of the image of the third person, the economic goals of which are pretty clear, and clearly susceptible to class analysis from the left—it is obvious who the big beneficiaries of such manipulations are—the environment of the image in question in *White Noise* appears far less concretely in focus (less apprehensible, less empirically encounterable) and therefore more insidious in its effects.

The first person narrator of *White Noise*, Jack Gladney, professor of Hitler Studies, drives to the tourist attraction known as the most photographed barn in America, and he takes with him his new colleague, Murray Jay Siskind, professor of popular culture, a smart émigré from New York City to Middle America who identifies himself as the incarnation of the problem of representation, as "The Jew. Who else would I be?" The tourist attraction is pastorally set, some twenty miles from the small city where the two reside and teach, and all along the way there are natural things to be taken in, presumably, though all the nature that is experienced (hardly the word, but it will have to do) is noted in a flat, undetailed, and apparently unemotional declarative: "There were meadows and apple orchards." And the traditional picturesque of rural life is similarly registered: "White fences trailed through the rolling fields." The strategically unenergized prose of these traditional moments is an index to the passing of both a literary convention and an older America. The narrator continues in his recessed way while his companion comments (lectures, really) upon the tourist site which is previewed for them (literally) by several signs, spaced every few miles along the way, announcing the attraction in big block letters. When they arrive the attraction is crowded with people with cameras. There is a booth where a man sells postcards and slides of the barn; there is an elevated spot from which the tourists snap their photos.

Gladney's phlegmatic narrative style is thrown into high relief by the ebullience of his friend's commentary. Murray does all the talking, like a guru of the postmodern drawing his neophyte into a new world, which the neophyte experiences in a shocked state of half-consciousness, situated somewhere between the older world where there were objects of perception like barns and apple orchards and the strange new world where the object of perception is perception itself: a packaged perception, a "sight" (in the genius of the vernacular), not a "thing." What they view is the view of a thing. What Murray reveals is that "no one sees the barn" because once "you've seen the signs about the barn, it becomes impossible to see the barn." This news about the loss of the referent, the dissolving of the object into its representations (the road signs, the photos) is delivered not with nostalgia for a lost world of the real but in joy: "We're not here to capture an image, we're here to maintain one. Every photograph reinforces the aura."

In between Murray's remarks, Jack Gladney reports on the long silences and the background noise—a new kind of choral commentary, "the incessant clicking of shutter release buttons, the rustling crank of levers that advanced the film"—and of the tourists ritually gathered in order to partake, as Murray says, of "a kind of spiritual surrender." So not only can't we get outside the aura, we don't want to. We prefer not to know what the barn was like before it was photographed because its aura, its technological transcendence, its soul, is our production, it is us. "We're part of the aura," says Murray, and knowing we're a part is tantamount to the achievement of a new identity—a collective selfhood brought to birth in the moment of contact with an "accumulation of nameless energies," in the medium or representation synonymous with the conferring of fame and charisma. "We're here, we're now," says Murray, as if he were affirming the psychic wholeness of the community. "The thousands who were here in the past, those who will come in the future. We've agreed to be part of a collective perception." We've come home to the world, beyond alienation. . . .

John Frow

John Frow is professor of English at the University of Queensland. He is the author of *Marxism and Literary History* (1986), *Cultural Studies and Cultural Value* (1995), and *Time and Commodity Culture* (1997). He is coeditor, with Meaghan Morris, of *Australian Cultural Studies: A Reader* (1993).

THE LAST THINGS BEFORE THE LAST: NOTES ON *WHITE NOISE*

> The edges of the earth trembled in a darkish haze. Upon it lay the sun, going down like a ship in a burning sea. Another postmodern sunset, rich in romantic imagery. Why try to describe it? It's enough to say that everything in our field of vision seemed to exist in order to gather the light of this event.
>
> —DON DELILLO, *White Noise*

Götterdämmerung. Why try to describe it? It's been written already, by Conrad, among others. Postmodern writing always comes after, the postmodern sunset is another sunset, an event within a series, never an originating moment but mass-produced as much by the cosmological system as by the system of writing. But the word postmodern here means more than this: this passage from *White Noise* refers back to an earlier one about the effects of an industrial (or postindustrial) disaster:

> Ever since the airborne toxic event, the sunsets had become almost unbearably beautiful. Not that there was a measurable

From *South Atlantic Quarterly* 89:2 (Summer 1990). Copyright 1990 by Duke University Press. Reprinted with permission.

> connection. If the special character of Nyodene Derivative (added to the everyday drift of effluents, pollutants, contaminants and deliriants) had caused this aesthetic leap from already brilliant sunsets to broad towering ruddled visionary skyscapes, tinged with dread, no one had been able to prove it.

The conditional clause structure and the repeated negation convey a pessimistic sense of undecidability, but it seems clear that industrial poison is a crucial component of the postmodern aesthetic, "rich in romantic imagery"—and vice versa. We could as well say "another *poisonous* sunset, or speak of an "airborne *aesthetic* event." It is not that the postmodern marks the return of aestheticism, a nonironic deployment of the full romantic cliché, but rather that it is the site of conjunction of the beautiful and the toxic, of Turner's *Fire at Sea* (1835), his "broad towering ruddled visionary skyscapes" and our postindustrial waste. This is thus, in Lyotard's sense, an aesthetic of the sublime: "With the sublime, the question of death enters the aesthetic question." It involves *terror* (the skyscapes are "tinged with dread") and ineffability, "the unpresentable in presentation itself." Why try to describe it? The twist here is that the sense of the inadequacy of representation comes not because of the transcendental or uncanny nature of the object but because of the multiplicity of prior representations. Priority of writing, priority of television, priority of the chain of metaphors in which the object is constructed. "We stood there watching a surge of florid light, like a heart pumping in a documentary on color TV."

Nor is there a lack of irony so much as a kind of self-effacement before the power of the stories which have gone before. The DeLillo passage I quoted at the beginning continues: "Not that this was one of the stronger sunsets. There had been more dynamic colors, a deeper sense of narrative sweep." Far from declining, the great nineteenth-century narratives continue to infuse the world with meaning, with a meaningfulness so total that the only possible response is ambivalence. The skies of this belated world are "under a spell, powerful and storied." They take on

> content, feeling, an exalted narrative life. The bands of color reach so high, seem at times to separate into their constituent parts. There are turreted skies, light storms, softly falling streamers. It is hard to know how we should feel about this. Some people are scared by the sunsets, some determined to be

elated, but most of us don't know how to feel, are ready to go either way.

Malign and beautiful, interpretable not so much to infinity as within an endless loop between two contradictory poles, this labile postmodern object causes "awe, it is all awe, it transcends previous categories of awe, but we don't know whether we are watching in wonder or dread." Singular but recurrent, an event (a change, a deviation, a production of newness) within the serial reproduction of sameness, it announces (but how typically *modernist* a gesture) nothing but its own gesture of annunciation: "there was nothing to do but wait for the next sunset, when the sky would ring like bronze."

In a town there are houses, plants in bay windows. People notice dying better. The dead have faces, automobiles. If you don't know a name, you know a street name, a dog's name. "He drove an orange Mazda." You know a couple of useless things about a person that become major facts of identification and cosmic placement when he dies suddenly, after a short illness, in his own bed, with a comforter and matching pillows, on a rainy Wednesday afternoon, feverish, a little congested in the sinuses and chest, thinking about his dry cleaning.

White Noise is obsessed with one of the classical aims of the realist novel: the construction of typicality. What this used to mean was a continuous process of extrapolation from the particular to the general, a process rooted in the existence of broad social taxonomies, general structures of human and historical destiny. Social typicality precedes the literary type—which is to say that the type is laid down in the social world; it is prior to and has a different kind of reality from secondary representations of it. First there is life, and then there is art. In *White Noise*, however, it's the other way round: social taxonomies are a function not of historical necessity but of style. Consider this description of the parents of Jack Gladney's students:

The conscientious suntans. The well-made faces and wry looks. They feel a sense of renewal, of communal recognition. The women crisp and alert, in diet trim, knowing people's names. Their husbands content to measure out the time, distant but ungrudging, accomplished in parenthood, something about them suggesting massive insurance coverage.

This type is not a naive given, an embodied universality, but a self-conscious enactment; the middle-class parents *know* the ideality they are supposed to represent, and are deliberately living up to it. But this means that the type loses its purity, since it can always be imitated, feigned; or rather that there is no longer a difference in kind between the social category and the life-style which brings it into everyday being: the type ceaselessly imitates itself—through the ritual assembly of station wagons, for example, which "tells the parents they are a collection of the like-minded and the spiritually akin, a people, a nation."

It is thus no longer possible to distinguish meaningfully between a generality embedded in life and a generality embedded in representations of life. The communal recognition that constitutes the social class is part of a more diffuse system of recognitions conveyed through an infinitely detailed network of mediations. When Jack tries to characterize the convicted murderer his son Heinrich plays chess with, he draws on a range of mass-cultural information, like those psychological "profiles" that construct, above all for television, a taxonomy of criminal types: "Did he care for his weapons obsessively? Did he have an arsenal stashed in his shabby little room off a six-story concrete car park?" A computer operator "had a skinny neck and jug-handle ears to go with his starved skull—the innocent prewar look of a rural murderer." Those who would be affected by the airborne toxic event would be "people who live in mobile homes out in the scrubby parts of the county, where the fish hatcheries are." The type of the bigot, embodied in Murray Siskind's landlord, is "very good with all those little tools and fixtures that people in cities never know the names of," and tends to drive a panel truck "with an extension ladder on the roof and some kind of plastic charm dangling from the rearview mirror." The whole of this world is covered by a fine grid of typifications, so detailed and precise that it preempts and contains contingency.

If the type is susceptible to minute description, then the traditional novelistic tension between detail and generality falls away, and Lukács's account of typicality becomes unworkable. For Lukács, typicality is best embodied in the category of particularity (*Besonderheit*), which stands midway between philosophical generality (*Allgemeinheit*) and descriptive detail, or singularity (*Einzelheit*); in a postmodern economy of mediations, however, where representations of generality suffuse every pore of the world, the opposition between the general and the singular collapses as they merge into a single, undialectical unity. The *petit fait vrai* of the realist novel, the meaningless detail whose sole function is to establish a realism effect, is no longer meaningless. Reconstructing the scene of his wife's adultery, Jack mentions objects like "the fire-retardant carpet" and "the rental car keys on the dresser"; the definite article here marks these—as it does in much of Auden's poetry—not as concrete particulars but as generic indicators; they are not pieces of detail broken off from the contingent real but fragments of a mundane typicality.

The complexity and intricacy of the type—whether it is a character, a scene, or a landscape—is made possible by the constant repetition of its features: it is reproduced as a sort of amalgam of television and experience, the two now theoretically inseparable. At its simplest, this inseparability gives us something like the image of the grandparents who "share the Trimline phone, beamish old folks in hand-knit sweaters on fixed incomes." This is of course a joke about typicality, or rather about its construction in Hollywood movies and television advertising. A somewhat more complex play with typification is this:

> A woman in a yellow slicker held up traffic to let some children cross. I pictured her in a soup commercial taking off her oilskin hat as she entered the cheerful kitchen where her husband stood over a pot of smoky lobster bisque, a smallish man with six weeks to live.

This description depends on the reader's recognition of the particular soup commercial, or at least the genre of commercials, that is being parodied by role reversal, and by the substitution of the traffic warden's yellow raincoat for the traditional and stereotyped fisherman's yellow raincoat—a substitution of the urban and feminine for the premodern world of masculine work. But part of the effect of this passage, as of that quoted at the beginning of this section, lies in its stylistic trick of pinning down the type (welcoming spouse at hearth) to an absurdly particular detail. What most of these typifications have in common, however, is their source in a chain of prior representations. Jack's dying, for example, is projected through a characterology taken from the movies, as in Murray's line to him that people "will depend on you to be brave. What people look for in a dying friend is a stubborn kind of gravel-voiced nobility, a refusal to give in, with moments of indomitable humor." The cliché is a simulacrum, an ideal form that shapes and constrains both life and death.

Let us say that this new mode of typicality has two features: it is constructed in representations which are then lived as real; and it is so detailed that it is not opposed to the particular. The name usually given to it in the genre of postmodernity is the simulacrum. Here are some notes:

(1) Early in *White Noise* Jack and Murray visit the most photographed barn in America. They pass five signs advertising it before reaching the site, and when they arrive there find forty cars and a tour bus in the car park, and a number of people taking pictures. Murray delivers a commentary: "No one sees the barn," he says. "Once you've seen the signs about the barn, it becomes impossible to see the barn. . . . We're not here to capture an image, we're here to maintain one. Every photograph reinforces the aura. . . . We've agreed to be part of a collective perception. This literally colors our vision. A religious experience in a way, like all tourism. . . . They are taking pictures of taking pictures. . . . What was the barn like before it was photographed? . . . What did it look like, how was it different from other barns, how was it similar to other barns? We can't answer these questions because we've read the signs, seen the people snapping the pictures. We can't get outside the aura. We're part of the aura. We're here, we're now." To this should be added another comment: "Murray says it's possible to be homesick for a place even when you are there."

(2) At the center of Walter Benjamin's argument about the mechanical reproduction of representations was the thesis that it would have the effect—the liberatory effect—of destroying the quasi religious aura surrounding the work of art. It is clear that the opposite has happened: that the commodification of culture has worked to preserve the myth of origins and of authenticity.

(3) In the main street of DeLillo's Iron City is "a tall old Moorish movie theater, now remarkably a mosque"; it is flanked by "blank structures called the Terminal Building, the Packer Building, the Commerce Building. How close this was to a classic photography of regret."

(4) The evacuation of Jack and his family is conducted by an organization called SIMUVAC, which is "short for simulated evacuation. A new state program they're still battling for funds for." When Jack points out to one of its employees that this is not a simulated but a real evacuation, he replies: "We thought we could use it as a model"; it gives them "a chance to use the real event in order to rehearse the simulation."

(5) For Plato, the simulacrum is the copy of a copy. Violating an ethics of imitation, its untruth is defined by its distance from the original and by its exposure of the scandal that an imitation can in its turn function as a reality to be copied (and so on endlessly).

The most influential contemporary account of the simulacrum and the chain of simulations is that of Baudrillard. His is a melancholy vision of the emptying out of meaning (that is, of originals, of stable referents) from a world which is henceforth made up of closed and self-referring systems of semiotic exchange. In a state of what he calls hyperreality the real becomes indefinitely reproducible, an effect, merely, of the codes which continue to generate it. From the very beginning Baudrillard has been hostile to the scandalous opacity of systems of mediation. His is a historical vision: there was a referent; it has been lost; and this loss, as in Plato, is the equivalent of a moral fall.

By contrast, the account that Deleuze gives of the simulacrum in *Différence et répétition*, while retaining the formal structure of the Platonic model, cuts it off from its ties to a lost original, and cuts it off, too, from all its Baudrillardian melancholy. The world we inhabit is one in which identity is simulated in the play of difference and repetition, but this simulation carries no sense of loss. Instead, freeing ourselves of the Platonic ontology means denying the priority of an original over the copy, of a model over the image. It means glorifying the reign of simulacra, and affirming that any original is itself already a copy, divided in its very origin. According to Deleuze, the simulacrum "is that system in which the different is related to the different through difference itself."

(6) The most horrifying fact about the evacuation is that it isn't even reported on network television. "Does this thing happen so often that nobody cares anymore?" asks one man. "Do they think this is just television?"

(7) The smoke from the chemical spill is initially called a "feathery plume," then a "black billowing cloud," and finally an "airborne toxic event." Steffie and Denise, Jack's daughters, keep experiencing the symptoms described in the bulletin preceding the current one. One of these symptoms is *déjà vu*, and Jack wonders, "Is it possible to have a false perception of an illusion? Is there a true *déjà vu* and a false *déjà vu*?" Later his wife Babette has a *déjà vu* experience of *déjà vu*.

(8) "The phone rang and I picked it up. A woman's voice delivered a high-performance hello. It said it was computer-generated, part of a marketing survey aimed at determining current levels of consumer desire. It said it would ask a series of questions, pausing after each to give me a chance to reply." Steffie, answering its questions, reads the label on her sweater: "virgin acrylic."

(9) Peter Wollen writes that in "an age marked by an ever-increasing and ever-accelerating proliferation of signs, of all types, the immediate environment becomes itself increasingly dominated by signs, rather than natural objects or events. The realm of signs becomes not simply a 'second nature' but a primary 'reality.' (The quotes around 'reality' mark the effacement of the traditional distinction between reality and representation in a world dominated by representations.)"

(10) Lighted by helicopters, the airborne toxic event moves like an operatic death ship across the landscape: "In its tremendous size, its

dark and bulky menace, its escorting aircraft, the cloud resembled a national promotion for death, a multimillion-dollar campaign backed by radio spots, heavy print and billboard, TV saturation."

The world of *White Noise* is a world of primary representations which neither precede nor follow the real but are themselves real—although it is true that they always have the *appearance* both of preceding another reality (as a model to be followed) and of following it (as copy). But this appearance must itself be taken seriously.

Consider these two passages about an adult looking at sleeping children: "I looked for a blanket to adjust, a toy to remove from a child's warm grasp, feeling I'd wandered into a TV moment." And "[t]hese sleeping children were like figures in an ad for the Rosicrucians, drawing a powerful beam of light from somewhere off the page." Both moments are mediated by another moment, a memory or a metaphor which shapes them, endows them with a certain structure; this structure is a part of their reality. It is quite possible to distinguish one reality (the sleeping children) from another (the TV moment, the ad for the Rosicrucians), just as we can in principle distinguish literal from metaphorical language; it is possible for the novel to be ironical about the gap between these two realities. But this distinguishing and this irony are insecure. Real moments and TV moments interpenetrate each other—and it is, in any case, another (novelistic) representation which offers us this reality and this distinction. The world is so saturated with representations that is becomes increasingly difficult to separate primary actions from imitations of actions.

Indeed, it seems that it is only within the realm of representation that it is possible to postulate a realm of primary actions which would be quite distinct from representation. During the evacuation Jack notices groups of refugees:

> Out in the open, keeping their children near, carrying what they could, they seemed to be part of some ancient destiny, connected in doom and pain to a whole history of people trekking across wasted landscapes. There was an epic quality about them that made me wonder for the first time at the scope of our predicament.

What he is seeing is of course a movie; and it is precisely because it is cinematic, because of its "epic quality," that the scene is real and serious to him. "Epic" here perhaps means something like "naive," lacking self-consciousness, and above all lacking any awareness of the cinematic nature of the experience. This paradox is even clearer in the case of Jack's fantasy about the death of Attila the Hun: "I want to believe he lay in his tent, wrapped in animal skins, as in some internationally financed movie epic, and said brave cruel things to his aides and retainers." The image is again of a heroic lack of self-consciousness, a naive immediacy to life and death:

> No weakening of the spirit. No sense of the irony of human existence. . . . He accepted death as an experience that flows naturally from life, a wild ride through the forest, as would befit someone known as the Scourge of God. This is how it ended for him, with his attendants cutting off their hair and disfiguring their own faces in barbarian tribute, as the camera pulls back out of the tent and pans across the night sky of the fifth century A.D., clear and uncontaminated, bright banded with shimmering worlds.

It is only in the movies, only through cultural mediation, that a vision of nonmediation is possible—and therefore absurd.

The central mediating agency in this world is television; indeed, for "most people there are only two places in the world. Where they live and their TV set. If a thing happens on television, we have every right to find it fascinating, whatever it is." The major statement is a speech made by Murray. He tells his students that

> they're already too old to figure importantly in the making of society. Minute by minute they're beginning to diverge from each other. "Even as we sit here," I tell them, "you are spinning out from the core, becoming less recognizable as a group, less targetable by advertisers and mass-producers of culture. Kids are a true universal. But you're well beyond that, already beginning to drift, to feel estranged from the products you consume. Who are they designed for? What is your place in the marketing scheme? Once you're out of school, it is only a matter of time before you experience the vast loneliness and dissatisfaction of consumers who have lost their group identity."

The assumptions are astounding: we know that human worth can't be measured in terms of our relation to consumption—to money and commodities—and that the order of things transcends "the marketing scheme." But all that Murray is doing is stating the central, the deadly serious principles of a capitalist society. This is really how it is, the marketing scheme really does work, for most purposes, in a capitalist society, as the scheme of things; the whole social organization is geared to this equation. The propositions are monstrous, but only because we find it so hard to believe in the true and central awfulness of capitalism.

Television comes into this because of its crucial role in marketing—and this is to say that its importance lies not in the sheer quantity of representations that it generates, nor even in their content as messages, but in the fact that they are always directly linked to commodity production and the generation of profits, and that in order to serve these ends they work as an integral part of a system for the shaping and reshaping of human identity. Murray's students are thus "beginning to feel they ought to turn against the medium, exactly as an earlier generation turned against their parents and their country." When he tells them that "they have to learn to look as children again. Root out content. Find codes and messages," they reply that television "is just another name for junk mail."

But cultural criticism—the moralistic critique of the mass media that has been the stock in trade of liberal journalism—is of course not an option, certainly not for this novel, which is much more interested, in its own ironic but unconditional way, in, for example, Murray's quasi-mystical experience of television. It is, he says, "a primal force in the American home. Sealed-off, self-contained, self-referring." Television

> offers incredible amounts of psychic data. It opens ancient memories of world birth, it welcomes us into the grid, the network of little buzzing dots that make up the picture pattern. There is light, there is sound. I ask my students, "What more do you want?" Look at the wealth of data concealed in the grid, in the bright packaging, the jingles, the slice-of-life commercials, the products hurtling out of darkness, the coded messages and endless repetitions, like chants, like mantras. "*Coke is it, Coke is it, Coke is it.*" The medium practically overflows with sacred formulas if we can remember how to respond innocently and get past our irritation, weariness and disgust.

A whole aesthetic is elaborated here, although unfortunately it's made up of the dregs of other aesthetic systems. Murray has the quixotic ability to disregard the banal surface of television and, with all the innocence of a formalist semiotician, to discover a cornucopia of aesthetic information in its organization. The key term here is "data," a meaningless word which suggests that the relevant level at which to decode the television message is that of the physical structure of light on the screen—but in fact the word has the effect of conflating this level with other levels of information. Gestalt and perceptual psychology mingle with genre theory and a mysticism of the proper name in Murray's postcritical celebration of the medium. For his students, however, television is "worse than junk mail. Television is the death throes of human consciousness, according to them. They're ashamed of their television past. They want to talk about movies." Murray is a postmodernist. His students, wishing to return to the high modernism of cinema, are postpostmodernist.

> The smoke alarm went off in the hallway upstairs, either to let us know the battery had just died or because the house was on fire. We finished our lunch in silence.

When the jug-eared computer operator taps into Jack's data profile (his history—but what history? "Where was it located exactly? Some state or federal agency, some insurance company or credit firm or medical clearinghouse?)" he finds that "[w]e have a situation": "It's what we call a massive data-base tally." This tally doesn't actually *mean* anything except that Jack is "the sum total of [his] data." Like so many signifying structures in *White Noise* it offers a profound interpretability but withdraws any precise meaning, or is at best deeply ambivalent. It's nothing but data, raw and unreadable. And what constitutes data is of course not something given, as the word suggests, but a set of constructs, figures whose significance lies not in their inherent structure but in the decision that has been taken to frame them in a certain way. The word embodies all the pathos of an impoverished and institutionalized empiricism. Its faultiness is caught in a joke about the search for contamination in the girls' school; the search is carried out by men in Mylex suits, but "because Mylex is itself a suspect material, the results tended to be ambiguous."

Whereas the sign causes unease, a sense that there is more to be known, the proper name is the site of a magical plenitude. Proper names tend to come in cadenced triads: "The Airport Marriott, the Downtown Travelodge, the Sheraton Inn and Conference Center." "Dacron, Orlon, Lycra Spandex." "Krylon, Rust-Oleum, Red Devil." They appear mysteriously in the midst of the mundane world of novelistic narrative, detached, functionless, unmotivated. At the end of a paragraph on Babette's fear of death, "the emptiness, the sense of cosmic darkness," occurs the single line: "MasterCard, Visa, American Express." The sonorous, Miltonic names lack all epic content, and they are intruded into the text without any marker of a speaking source. In a later episode the sleeping Steffie, speaking in "a language not quite of this world," utters two words

> that seemed to have a ritual meaning, part of a verbal spell or ecstatic chant.
>
> *Toyota Celica.*
>
> A long moment passed before I realized this was the name of an automobile. The truth only amazed me more. The utterance was beautiful and mysterious, gold-shot with looming wonder. It was like the name of an ancient power in the sky, tablet-carved in cuneiform.

Here there is a definite source for the utterance, but in another sense Steffie is not this source: the words are spoken through her, by her unconscious but also, as Jack recognizes, by the unconscious of her culture. Yet for all their commercial banality (the same that echoes gloriously through a phrase caught on the radio: "It's the rainbow hologram that gives this credit card a marketing intrigue"), the names remain charged with an opaque significance, so that Jack remarks: "Whatever its source, the utterance struck me with the impact of a moment of splendid transcendence."

The question of the source of enunciation of these proper names remains an interesting one, as there seems to be a definite progression in the novel from an apparently impersonal enunciation to more localized points of origin. In a description of the supermarket, "full of elderly people who look lost among the hedgerows," the words "Dristan Ultra, Dristan Ultra" occur on a separate line but are enclosed within inverted commas, which indicates a diegetic source—probably a public address system in the supermarket. The words have the same sort of status as the voices emanating from the television and the radio that punctuate the life of the house. At other times a psychological source seems to be indicated—when the words "leaded, unleaded, super unleaded" intrude into Jack and Babette's desperate lovemaking; or when the spelled out acronyms "Random Access Memory, Acquired Immune Deficiency Syndrome, Mutual Assured Destruction" cross the text as Jack is crossing the slum districts of Iron City. At other times there seem to be verbal associations flowing between the proper names and their textual context: "I watched light climb into the rounded summits of high-altitude clouds. Clorets, Velamints, Freedent." The movement is not just the phonetic one from clouds (perhaps "cloud turrets") to Clorets but is also a circuit between the novel's imagery of sunsets and the poetry of advertising. Another example: Jack experiences "aural torment" as he imagines Babette making love to the mysterious Mr. Gray:

> . . . Then gloom moved in around the gray-sheeted bed, a circle slowly closing.
>
> Panasonic.

Like the syllables of the Proustian name, the last word is multiply motivated. "Pana-" is the circle slowly closing, "sonic" is Jack's aural torment, and there are overdetermined traces of "panoramic" and, of course, television. But as with the name in Proust, the point is the excess of the poetic signifier over its component parts, its transcendental character, its plenitude. The poetic word comes from elsewhere, and if it seems to be spoken by a character (like the woman passing on the street who says "a decongestant, an antihistamine, a cough suppressant, a pain reliever"), this is nevertheless only a proximate source, a relay. The proper name is its own absolute origin.

At lunchtime Wilder sits surrounded by "open cartons, crumpled tinfoil, shiny bags of potato chips, bowls of pasty substances covered with plastic wrap, flip-top rings and twist ties, individually wrapped slices of orange cheese." Meals in this house lack the monumental solidity of the meals in *Buddenbrooks* or even in the James Bond novels; they are depthless, physically insubstantial. At times the staple junk food is opposed to the "real" (but never achieved) lunch of yogurt and wheat germ, but the truth of the matter is that eating has entirely to do with surfaces. Even chewing gum is described in terms of its wrappings.

The supermarket is the privileged place for a phenomenology of surfaces. Murray is a devotee of generic brands, and he takes their "flavorless packaging" to be the sign of a new austerity, a new "spiritual consensus." The packaging on supermarket goods, he says, "is the last avant-garde. Bold new forms. The power to shock." But even unprocessed and unpackaged foods take on the *form* of packaging: "There were six kinds of apples, there were exotic melons in several pastels. Everything seemed to be in season, sprayed, burnished, bright." And later: "The fruit was gleaming and wet, hard-edged. There was a self-conscious quality about it. It looked carefully observed, like four-color fruit in a guide to photography. We veered right at the plastic jugs of spring water." The kitchen, too, is a place of containers and packagings—the freezer, for example, where "a strange crackling sound came off the plastic food wrap, the snug covering for half eaten things, the Ziploc sacks of liver and ribs, all gleaming with sleety crystals."

But the force of this is not a sentimental regret for a lost world of depths, a nostalgic opposition of surface to substance. There *is* a depth to be found in this world (this house, this novel), but it is not a fullness of being; rather, it's the other end of the packaging process, a sort of final interiority of the wrapping. Jack comes across it when he searches through the trash bag of the compactor:

> An oozing cube of semi-mangled cans, clothes hangers, animal bones and other refuse. The bottles were broken, the cartons flat. Product colors were undiminished in brightness and intensity. Fats, juices and heavy sludges seeped through layers of pressed vegetable matter. I felt like an archaeologist about to sift through a finding of tool fragments and assorted cave trash.

This is the heart of domesticity:

> I found a banana skin with a tampon inside. Was this the dark underside of consumer consciousness? I came across a horrible clotted mass of hair, soap, ear swabs, crushed roaches, flip-top rings, sterile pads smeared with pus and bacon fat, strands of frayed dental floss, fragments of ballpoint refills, toothpicks still displaying bits of impaled food. There was a pair of shredded undershorts with lipstick markings, perhaps a memento of the Grayview Motel.

The list is of an accretion of wastes that have come full circle from the supermarket but which still retain the formal structure (and even the "undiminished colors") of the presentation of surfaces. At the heart of this inside is nothing more than a compacted mass of outsides.

White Noise is a domestic novel, continuously concerned with the secret life of the house—with the closet doors that open by themselves, with the chirping of the radiator, with the sounds of the sink and the washing machine and the compactor, with the jeans tumbling in the dryer. The narrator writes of the "numerous and deep" levels of data in the kitchen, and speaks of the kitchen and the bedroom as "the major chambers around here, the power haunts, the sources." But the center of the life of the house is the voice of the television. This is what it says:

> Let's sit half-lotus and think about our spines.
>
> . . . .
>
> If it breaks easily into pieces, it is called shale. When wet, it smells like clay.
>
> . . . .
>
> Until Florida surgeons attached an artificial flipper.

> . . . .
>
> (In a British voice): There are forms of vertigo that do not include spinning.
>
> . . . .
>
> And other trends that could dramatically impact your portfolio.
>
> . . . .
>
> This creature has developed a complicated stomach in keeping with its leafy diet.
>
> . . . .
>
> Now we will put the little feelers on the butterfly.
>
> . . . .
>
> Meanwhile here is a quick and attractive lemon garnish suitable for any sea food.
>
> . . . .
>
> Now watch this. Joanie is trying to snap Ralph's patella with a *bushido* stun kick. She makes contact, he crumples, she runs.
>
> . . . .
>
> They're not booing—they're saying, "Bruce, Bruce."

Television is about everything. It is about the ordinary, the banal, information for living our lives. It is rarely the voice of apocalypse.

John N. Duvall

John N. Duvall is professor of English at Purdue University. He is author of *Faulkner's Marginal Couple: Invisible, Outlaw, and Unspeakable Communities* (1990) as well as numerous essays on contemporary American fiction in such journals as *Novel*, *Modern Fiction Studies*, *Contemporary Literature*, *Studies in American Fiction*, and *Arizona Quarterly*.

THE (SUPER)MARKETPLACE OF IMAGES: TELEVISION AS UNMEDIATED MEDIATION IN DELILLO'S *WHITE NOISE*

Fascism sees its salvation in giving [the] masses not their right, but instead a chance to express themselves. The masses have a right to change property relations; Fascism seeks to give them an expression while preserving property. The logical result of Fascism is the introduction of aesthetics into political life.
—WALTER BENJAMIN, "The Work of Art in the Age of Mechanical Reproduction"

We know that now it is on the level of reproduction (fashion, media, publicity, information and communication networks), on the level of what Marx negligently called the nonessential sectors of capital . . . , that is to say in the sphere of simulacra and of the code, that the global process of capital is founded.
—JEAN BAUDRILLARD, *Simulations*

Reprinted from *Arizona Quarterly* 50:3 (Autumn 1994), by permission of the Regents of the University of Arizona.

Don DeLillo's *White Noise* comically treats both academic and domestic life. Yet both of these subjects serve primarily as vehicles for DeLillo's satiric examination of the ways in which contemporary America is implicated in proto-fascist urges.[1] In making this claim, I do not mean to erase the enormous differences between contemporary America and Europe of the 1920s and 1930s, particularly Germany and Hitler's National Socialists, which DeLillo's novel invokes. The United States, of course, neither maintains an official ideology of nationalism and anti-Semitism, nor overtly silences political opposition through storm-trooper violence and state control of the media. Nevertheless, our national mythology that tells us we are free, self-reliant, and autonomous citizens, when enacted as moments of consumer choice, produces a cultural-economic system that, in several Marxist and post-Marxist accounts of postmodernity, is more totalizing than Hitler's totalitarian regime. German fascism prior to World War II was a modernist phenomenon, linked to monopoly capitalism.[2] DeLillo's American proto-fascism, however, functions in what Fredric Jameson has identified as the cultural logic of multinational or late capitalism in which the social, the political, and the aesthetic flatten out into what Jean Baudrillard calls the simulacrum.

White Noise performs its critique not simply because its central character and narrator, Jack Gladney, is Chair of the Department of Hitler Studies at an expensive liberal arts college, but rather because each element of Jack's world mirrors back to him a postmodern, decentralized totalitarianism that this professional student of Hitler is unable to read. Jack's failure to recognize proto-fascist urges in an aestheticized American consumer culture is all the more striking since he emphasizes in his course Hitler's manipulation of mass cultural aesthetics (uniforms, parades, rallies). This failure underscores the key difference between Hitler's fascism and American proto-fascism: ideology ceases to be a conscious choice, as it was for the National Socialists, and instead becomes in contemporary America more like the Althusserian notion of ideology as unconscious system of representation. In *White Noise* two representational systems in particular produce this unconscious: the imagistic space of the supermarket and the shopping mall coincides with the conceptual space of television.[3] Both serve the participant (shopper/viewer) as a temporary way to step outside death by entering an aestheticized space of consumption that serves as the postmodern, mass-culture rearticulation of Eliot's timeless, high-culture tradition. Because of this linkage, the *market* within supermarket serves as a reminder that television also is predicated on market relations. The production and consumption of the electronic image of desire is a simulacrum of the images (aesthetically displayed consumer items) contained in the supermarket and the mall. This hinged relationship between the supermarket and the television is signaled by the twin interests of Murray Jay Siskind, the visiting professor in the Department of American Environments at the College-on-the-Hill. Siskind, a student of the "psychic data" of both television and the supermarket, acts as an ironized internal commentator on the family life of the Gladneys as both shoppers and television viewers. Siskind's celebration of the postmodern becomes highly ambiguous because, against his celebrations, *White Noise* repeatedly illustrates that, within the aestheticized space of television and the supermarket, all potentially political consciousness—whether a recognition of the ecological damage created by mass consumption or an acknowledgment of one's individual death—vanished in formalism, the contemplation of pleasing structural features.[4]

From the perspective of Walter Benjamin, this aestheticizing tendency in American culture suggests why it is appropriate that Jack should teach only classes—as the college catalogue describes it—on the "continuing mass appeal of fascist tyranny" (25).[5] For Benjamin, aestheticizing the political is a defining feature of fascism. Speaking particularly of German fascism, he notes in the epilogue to "The Work of Art in the Age of Mechanical Reproduction" that "the violation of the masses, whom Fascism, with its *Führer* cult, forces to their knees, has its counterpart in the violation of an apparatus [the media] which is pressed into production of ritual values" ("Work of Art," 243). Although the main thrust of the essay is Benjamin's celebration of the way in which reproductive technologies function to destroy aura in high-culture objects, he senses, in the passage just quoted, a countercurrent to his argument, which he elaborates in a note; that countercurrent is the link between mass reproduction and the reproduction of the masses. "In big parades and rallies, in sports events, and in war, all of which nowadays are captured by camera and sound recording, the masses are brought face to face with themselves" ("Work of Art," 253). Benjamin, in complicating his notion of mechanical reproduction, points the way toward DeLillo's America, where giving oneself over to a formal contemplation of the image matrix of either television or the supermarket denies one's insertion in the political economy and functions as but another version of Hitler Studies; it is learning how to be a fascist, albeit a kinder, gentler one. DeLillo's characters, as several instances of television viewing and shopping reveal, consistently fall into a suspect formal method when they interpret events in their world; such instances provide an important context for understanding both Murray's teaching of postmodernity and the specificity of American proto-fascism.

The conclusion of "The Airborne Toxic Event," the second section of the novel, typifies DeLillo's meditation on television as a medium constructive of postmodernity. Having fled their homes to avoid contamination from a railroad tanker spill, the Gladneys, along with the other residents of the small college town of Blacksmith, become quarantined evacuees in Iron City. At the end of the first day of their quarantine, "a man carrying a tiny TV set began to walk slowly through the room, making a speech as he went" (161). Like some tribal priest with a magic charm, the man "held the set well up in the air and out away from his body and during the course of his speech he turned completely around several times as he walked in order to display the blank screen" to his audience:

> "There's nothing on network," he said to us. "Not a word, not a picture. On the Glassboro channel we rate fifty-two words by actual count. No film footage, no live report. Does this kind of thing happen so often that nobody cares anymore? Don't those people know what we've been through? We were scared to death. We still are. We left our homes, we drove through blizzards, we saw the cloud. It was a deadly specter, right there above us. Is it possible nobody gives substantial coverage to such a thing? Half a minute, twenty seconds? Are they telling us it was insignificant, it was piddling? Are they so callous? Are they so bored by spills and contaminations and wastes? Do they think this is just television? 'There's too much television already—why show more?' Don't they know it's real?" (161–62)

John Frow notes that "the most horrifying fact about the evacuation is that it isn't even reported on network television" [see page 423 in this volume].[6] What is perhaps most horrifying about this absence of mediation is that, for those who experience the disaster, it is precisely this mediation (and this mediation alone) that could make their terror immediate. Because the evacuees are attuned to the forms, genres, and in fact the larger aesthetics of television, they experience a lack, a sense of emptiness. Strikingly, in the world of *White Noise*, immersed in multiple and multiplying representations, what empties experience of meaning for the evacuees is not the mediation but the absence of mediation. During the tv man's speech there comes a point at which his incredulity—and clearly he speaks for all his listeners—crosses a boundary line where understandable dismay at not being represented on network television becomes satire through the overdrawn particularity of his desired scenario; yet despite the satire, the speech accurately registers how fully mediated the evacuees desire the moment to be:

> "Shouldn't the streets be crawling with cameramen and soundmen and reporters? Shouldn't we be yelling out the window at them, 'Leave us alone, we've been through enough, get out of here with your vile instruments of intrusion.' Do they have to have two hundred dead, rare disaster footage, before they come flocking to a given site in their helicopters and network limos? What exactly has to happen before they stick microphones in our faces and hound us to the doorsteps of our homes, camping out on our lawns, creating the usual media circus? Haven't we earned the right to despise their idiot questions?" (162)

The problem the tv man articulates, deaf of course to the humor of his own speech, is how in the present one relates to one's fear. The evacuees intuit that their encounter with the poisonous chemical cloud far exceeds the bounds of the everyday. Their terror, however, cannot register in a Romantic sublime where origin is still attributable to the Godhead. The awe and terror of this man-made disaster can only be validated through the electronic media.[7]

What makes this speech humorous is that no one actually would articulate the situation as the tv man does. His language, however, gives voice to a portion of the postmodern unconscious. The masochistic desire to be exploited that passes as the collective desire of his audience seems almost as perverse as the Puritan desire to be scourged by God. And perhaps this analogy is not as strange as it seems. Just as the Puritans sought affirmation of their position through a sign from God (his chastisement) that would stabilize their sense of themselves (the chastisement, after all, meant that God found them worthy of his paternal attention and hence argued strongly that they were among the saved), so do DeLillo's postmoderns seek affirmation through television, the GRID who/that really cares and affirms the legitimacy of their terror. Those who encountered the airborne toxic event intuitively know that television is not a mediation; it is the immediate. Television, the intertextual grid of electronic images, creates the Real.

But if the tv man envisions television as some ideal unmediated mediation for the victims of the chemical spill, how would that same disaster, had it been televised, play at the receiver's end? A way to answer this question is suggested by one of the tv man's own questions: "Do they have to have two hundred dead . . . before [the media] comes flocking to a given site . . . ?" After concluding his speech, the tv man quite appropriately turns and looks into the face of Jack Gladney because Gladney's vacant gaze serves as a displaced reminder of the answer to the tv man's question; *White Noise* implies that the audience for the tv man's desired broadcast of the evacuees' story would be, figuratively, the Jack Gladney family, since they typify the American family's consumption of television images. The Gladneys' television habits illustrate the way the electronically reproduced image consistently empties its representations of content, turning content into pure form that invites aesthetic contemplation.[8] Each Friday night, Jack's wife, Babette, insists that the family gather to watch television. The attempt to create a family ritual is usually a failure—each would prefer to do something else—but one Friday their viewing begins with a repeated image of a plane crash, "once in stop-action replay" (64). The evening crescendos in a never-ceasing orgy of human suffering that mesmerizes the Gladneys:

> Babette tried to switch to a comedy series about a group of racially mixed kids who build their own communications satellite. She was startled by the force of our objection. We were otherwise silent, watching houses slide into the ocean, whole villages crackle and ignite in a mass of advancing lava. Every disaster made us wish for more, for something bigger, grander, more sweeping. (64)

The answer, therefore, to the tv man's question, then, is yes—at least two hundred dead, preferably more. Network and cable news programs, competing for a market, operate under capitalism's demand to make it newer, thus turning "news" into another genre of entertainment. As a form of entertainment, the distance between television news and the tabloids, a recurring presence in *White Noise*, collapses. Jack may find ridiculous those who believe in the tabloid stories, yet his own belief is predicated on distortions generated by his news medium of choice.

As disaster becomes aestheticized, another boundary blurs, that between television news' representation of violence and violence in film, creating a homogenous imagistic space available for consumption. Murray's seminar on the aesthetics of movie car crashes is a case in point. Jack is puzzled by Murray's celebration of car crashes "as part of a long tradition of American optimism" in which "each crash is meant to be better than the last" (218). Murray's advice on interpreting such filmic moments—"look past the violence" (291)—asserts that meaning resides in form, not content. And though Jack finds this advice strange, that is precisely what he and his children do instinctively when they watch television—they look past the violence and the human suffering of disaster and see only aestheticized forms, enhanced by repetition and technological innovation, such as slow-motion, stop action, and frame-by-frame imaging of plane crashes. Undoubtedly, the television coverage of Desert Storm confirms DeLillo's novelistic vision. Vietnam may have been the first televised war, but Desert Storm was the first war with good production values. Each network competed for its market share through high-tech logos and dramatic theme music as lead-in to their broadcasts. But not even the networks could compete with the technological splendor of American "smart" bombs, equipped with cameras that broadcast the imminent destruction of targets (and, incidentally, people). Never has death been simultaneously so clearly near and so cleanly distanced for the viewing public, turning the imagistic space of television into something more akin to a video game.

The repeated images of disaster that the Gladneys enjoy holds death at bay and participates in DeLillo's meditation on death in this novel. But what is more at issue is the sharply divergent role television plays for those who are televised and those who consume the image. The heart of the tv man's anger is that for those who experience disaster, the presence of the media makes the experience "real"; that is, as part of our cultural repertoire, people know, like the tv man, that the media is supposed to be interested in marketing disaster. Therefore, the airborne toxic event cannot be a real disaster if the media show no interest. Stripped of their imagistic knowing, the "victims" (but perhaps they aren't, since there is no media interest) are left without any way to understand their terror. The tv man hopes to enter the Real through imagistic representation but the Real can be received only as aesthetic experience and entertainment.

DeLillo's assessment of the postmodern media is reiterated in several other moments in *White Noise*. In discussing with his son Heinrich a mass murderer with whom his son carries on a game of chess via their correspondence, father and son reveal a clear sense of the genre of the mass murderer as depicted by the media. Jack's questions reveal the *langue* or the general system; Henrich's answers, the *parole* or particular articulation:

> ". . . Did he have an arsenal stashed in his shabby little room off a six-story concrete car park?"
>
> "Some handguns and a bolt-action rifle with a scope."
>
> "A telescopic sight. Did he fire from a highway overpass, a rented room? Did he walk into a bar, a washette, his former place of employment and start firing indiscriminately? . . ."
>
> "He went up to a roof."
>
> "A rooftop sniper. Did he write in his diary before he went up to the roof? Did he make tapes of his voice, go to the

> movies, read books about other mass murderers to refresh his memory?"
>
> "Made tapes." (44)

To all of Jack's many questions, Heinrich shows how Tommy Roy Foster signifies within the system "mass murderer." The questions and answers follow through a series of information that any story on a mass murderer must have—number of victims, killer's life history, type of weapon, site of killing, and posited motive. The genre then is predictable and formulaic. It is pleasurable because it is *form*ulaic. The final gesture in the mass murder story is, of course, the hypothesis, the reason for the killing, always woefully inadequate to the mystery and fascination of the killer's "real" motives. (Oddly, the assumption that a mass murderer must have real intention, however deviant, saves the concept of intention for everyone else; our meanings may be fluid and ambivalent but surely the mass murderer is motivated by a singular fixed purpose.) The answer to Jack's final question—"How did he deal with the media?"—is telling: "There is no media in Iron City. He didn't think of that till it was too late" (45). Here, as with the discontent of the tv man, the only thing that confirms the reality of experience is its construction as media event. Jack's and Heinrich's understanding of the aesthetics of mass murder underscore how deeply mediated that knowledge is.[9]

One of the effects of this intensely mediated knowing is a specious tv logic predicated on formalist interpretations of television. After returning to Blacksmith from the evacuation in Iron City, Babette can think about pollution in these terms:

> Every day on the news there's another toxic spill. Cancerous solvents from storage tanks, arsenic from smokestacks, radioactive water from power plants. How serious can it be if it happens all the time? Isn't the definition of a serious event based on the fact that it's not an everyday occurrence? (174)

But the illogic of Babette's argument is not that much greater than Jack's before the evacuation. He believes that disasters "happen to poor people who live in exposed areas," probably, one might add, the same people who rely on the tabloids rather than the television for their news. Jack remains calm, confident that his socio-economic status will protect him: "Did you ever see a college professor rowing a boat down his own street in one of those TV floods?" (114) Logic has been replaced by aesthetics, or perhaps more accurately it is a logic based on aesthetic perception.

Television, however, does not stop at structuring the conscious thinking of DeLillo's characters. More invasively, television and its advertising subliminally shape their unconscious. *White Noise* reminds us how closely related are the subliminal and the sublime. Listening closely to one of his daughter's sleeping verbalizations, Jack finally discerns the syllables that "seemed to have a ritual meaning": Toyota Celica. Jack is left with "the impact of a moment of splendid transcendence" (155). But if we recall Benjamin's concept of aura, then we can see Jack's false transcendence as a key moment in the production of consumers, those who then take their individual experiences of shopping as constitutive of the auratic self. Aura for Benjamin is a negative concept because it cloaks the work of art in its cultic and ritual function ("Work of Art," 225–26). For Jack and his family, reproducibility may have removed the aura of the work of art, but art's magic function has merely migrated to the marketing of consumer goods. The irony is clear: at the very time when reproduction destroys the false religious aura of high culture, those same techniques of reproduction establish tradition and aura in mass culture. If modernist art rushed in to fill the void created by the death of God, advertising has stepped in to fill the space vacated by modernism.

Jack certainly creates a ritualistic formula in his narration, repeatedly interjecting trios of brand names, always three products of the same kind. These interjections serve as clear bits of a modernist technique, stream-of-consciousness, used to portray the postmodern.[10] Such moments, inasmuch as they signify within the code "modernist fiction," invite one to tease at the signifying chain. One of these trios occurs, for example, when Jack describes a recurring conversation he and Babette have:

> She is afraid I will die unexpectedly, sneakily, slipping away in the night. It isn't that she doesn't cherish life; it's being left alone that frightens her. The emptiness, the sense of cosmic darkness.
>
> MasterCard, Visa, American Express. (100)

The apparently unmotivated series, however, has a logic of its own. Thinking of the "cosmic darkness," Jack's series unconsciously masters the moment. Mastery over death is what he strives for in his study of Hitler. He also wants to avoid death and loneliness and here is his exit visa for his vacation from such troubling thoughts. His transportation? A powerful locomotive, clearly, the American Express. Forms of credit, as we shall see, are crucial to Jack's function as a consumer, and it is through consumption that individuals in DeLillo's novel repress the fear of death. That each trio names specific brand names pushes us towards Jean Baudrillard's sense of consumption as a socially signifying practice that circulates coded values.

In *White Noise*, one might say, DeLillo fuses ideas from the earlier Baudrillard of *Consumer Society* with those of the post-Marxian Baudrillard of "The Orders of Simulacra." The earlier Baudrillard takes a number of categories of traditional Marxist analysis and shifts the focus from production to consumption, yet retains a Marxist perspective by seeing consumption as "*a function of production*" ("Consumer," 46). Thus, in analyzing consumption as a signifying practice, Baudrillard speaks of consumers as a form of alienated social labor and asks who owns the means of consumption ("Consumer," 53–54). DeLillo's novel proves an extended gloss on Jean Baudrillard's notion of consumer society. Baudrillard counterintuitively proposes that the broad range of consumer choices in today's shopping malls, which appear as the embodiment of individual freedom, is actually a form of social control used to produce the consumers that capital crucially needs.

Jack falls into his role as a consumer when his auratic self as Hitler scholar is threatened by a chance encounter with a colleague off campus. Without his academic robe and dark glasses, the colleague notes that Jack is just "a big, harmless, aging, indistinct sort of guy" (83). This deflation of self puts Jack "in the mood to shop" and the ensuing sense of power and control is immense:

> We moved from store to store, rejecting not only items in certain departments, not only entire departments but whole stores, mammoth corporations that did not strike our fancy for one reason or another. . . . I began to grow in value and self-regard. I filled myself out, found new aspects of myself, located a person I'd forgotten existed. Brightness settled around me. (83–84)

Jack replaces his inauthentic Hitler aura with the equally inauthentic aura of shopping, which he experiences, however, as authentic.[11] His sense of power in the mall, a physical space as self-contained and self-referential as the psychic space of television, is illusory for if Jack "rejects" one corporation, another is surely served by his purchases.[12] Jack says, "The more money I spent, the less important it seemed. I was bigger than these sums. These sums poured off my skin like so much rain. These sums in fact came back to me in the form of existential credit" (84). For Baudrillard, credit is a key element in the social control generated through consumption:

> Presented under the guise of gratification, of a facilitated access to affluence, of a hedonistic mentality, and of "freedom from the old taboos of thrift, etc.," credit is in fact the systematic socioeconomic indoctrination of forced economizing and an economic calculus for generations of consumers who, in a life of subsistence, would have otherwise escaped the manipulation of demands and would have been unexploitable as a force of consumption. Credit is a disciplinary process which extorts savings and regulates demand—just as wage labor was a rational process in the extortion of labor power and in the increase of productivity. ("Consumer," 49)

Credit allows Jack the exercise of auratic power, allowing a middle-class college professor to become briefly a conspicuous consumer like the wealthy parents whose children he teaches. Not surprisingly, Jack, the scholar of Germany's great dictator, imagines himself a little dictator in a benevolent mood: "I was the benefactor, the one who dispenses gifts, bonuses, bribes, *baksheesh*" (84). At the conclusion of the family shopping spree, the Gladneys, exemplary alienated consumers, are not satisfied; they "drove home in silence . . . wishing only to be alone." The final sentence of the chapter connects the mall as aestheticized site of consumption to television's imagistic space. In what appears to be an attempt to come down from the intensity of the shopping spree, one of Jack's daughters sits "in front of the TV set. She moved her lips, attempting to match the words as they were spoken" (84).[13]

If the Baudrillard of *Consumer Society* is pertinent to *White Noise*, the later Baudrillard of *Simulations* is even more so. Starting from Walter Benjamin and Marshall McLuhan, Baudrillard shifts the focus of technique away from a Marxist sense of productive force and toward an interpretation of technique "as medium" (*Simulations*, 99). Taken to its extreme, "the medium is the message" becomes Baudrillard's hyper-real, where the "contradiction between the real and the imaginary is effaced" (*Simulations*, 142). Jack Gladney lives in a world of simulations, modelings of the world tied to no origin or source. The clearest example is SIMUVAC; this state-supported organization, created to rehearse evacuations through controlled models of man-made and natural disasters, uses the chemical spill in Blacksmith as an opportunity "to rehearse the simulation" (139). But SIMUVAC is just the edge of the wedge. At the Catholic hospital in the Germantown section of Iron City, where Jack takes Mink after both are shot, Jack discovers what amounts to SIMUFAITH. The nuns who serve as nurses, Jack learns, pretend to believe in God for the non-believers who need to believe that someone still believes. One nun tells Jack, "Our lives are no less serious than if we professed real faith, real belief" (319), because the simulated belief serves the same structural function vis-à-vis the nonbeliever as actual belief. Jack himself is SIMUPROF. At "the center, the unquestioned source" (11) of Hitler Studies, Jack, who invents an initial to make his name signify in the system of scholarly names, successfully lives the erasure of the imaginary and the real; he is the world-famous scholar of Hitler who can neither read nor speak German.

II

While Jack is the ostensible teacher of fascism's appeal, he has much to learn about the subject from his Jewish "friend" Murray, who sees more clearly the possibilities of fascism for profit and pleasure. To focus on Murray's role might well seem unproductive. He is comic, a man who sniffs groceries, another of DeLillo's almost Dickensian eccentrics, as Murray's colleagues in the Department of American Environments most certainly are. Yet under the umbrella of DeLillo's meditation on the continuing mass appeal of fascist tyranny, Murray helps link the novel's various elements of matter—the media, shopping, the construction of aura—and points to the ways each of the preceding serve in the contemporary to allow individuals to imagine and to repress their sexuality and their death. These mirrored spaces of consumption, the television and the supermarket, are brought into sharper relief by Murray's explicit commentary; his interpretations are Baudrillardian, yet the very elements of simulation that make Baudrillard sad make Murray glad. Although Murray shows himself to be a shrewd semiotician of contemporary America, he is more than a character who comments on the action. Murray is an agent of action, the character whose goals and desires, more than any other's, become the occasion for plot. Much of *White Noise*, as Frank Lentricchia notes ("Tales," 97), is plotless, a fact not surprising given that the narrator, Jack, believes that "all plots tend to move deathward" (26). We have to turn to Murray Siskind to discover the desires that motivate plot, a sub(rosa)plot, if you will.

Siskind is the true villain of *White Noise*. Seductive and smart, he nevertheless encourages and fosters the worst in Jack. Murray is the man who would be Jack. Murray's very openness about his goals makes it hard to see the antagonistic role he occupies, yet Murray covets Jack's power within the college. In Chapter 3, Murray flatters Jack at length about his achievement:

> "You've established a wonderful thing here with Hitler. You created it, you nurtured it, you made it your own. Nobody on

> the faculty of any college or university in this part of the country can so much as utter the word Hitler without a nod in your direction, literally or metaphorically. This is the center, the unquestioned source. He is now your Hitler, Gladney's Hitler. . . . I marvel at the effort. It was masterful, shrewd and stunningly preemptive. It's what I want to do with Elvis." (11–12)

But Murray is already more Jack than Jack because Murray understands and sees the possibilities of professional aura in ways Jack does not. It is entirely appropriate that this scene is immediately followed by Jack's taking Murray to a local tourist attraction, "the most photographed barn in America" (12).[14] Murray's interpretation of the site reflects back on his reading of Jack's creation of the college as origin and source of Hitler Studies. Surrounded by people taking pictures of the barn, which is not billed as the oldest or the most picturesque but simply as the most photographed, Murray claims:

> "No one sees the barn. . . . Once you've seen the signs about the barn, it becomes impossible to see the barn. . . . We're not here to capture an image, we're here to maintain one. Every photograph reinforces the aura. Can you feel it, Jack? An accumulation of nameless energies. . . . Being here is a kind of spiritual surrender. We see only what the others see. The thousands who were here in the past, those who will come in the future. . . . What did the barn look like before it was photographed? . . . What was the barn like, how was it different from other barns, how was it similar to other barns? We can't answer these questions because we've read the signs, seen the people snapping the pictures. We can't get outside the aura. We're part of the aura. We're here, we're now." (12–13)

John Frow quite rightly points out that Benjamin's hope that mechanical reproduction would destroy the pseudo-religious aura of cultural artifacts has been subverted and that, instead, "the commodification of culture has worked to preserve the myth of origins and of authenticity" [see page 422 of this volume]. Here, as elsewhere in the novel, the myth of authenticity that is aura comes into being through mediation, the intertextual web of prior representations. Jack may object to his son corresponding with a mass murderer, but Jack's textual pleasure turns on his reading and writing about the world's most photographed mass murderer, Adolf Hitler. The difference underscores the role of mediation: Henrich's mass murderer failed to enter the media loop, while Jack's mass murderer is "always on" television (63) in the endless documentaries that our culture produces about the twentieth century.

The most dangerous element of the most photographed barn, finally, is the tourists' collective spiritual surrender precisely because it is a desired surrender. Here is the continuing mass appeal of fascism writ large. It is what Murray understands and Jack does not—the barn is to those who photograph it as Hitler Studies is to Jack; in both instances, an object of contemplation serves to legitimize the myth of origin, which creates a sense of purpose, which in turn serves to mitigate the sting of death. Murray, in a much more critically distanced way, sees the possibilities for institutional power and control by plugging into the aura of the world's most photographed rockabilly singer.

In addition to coveting Jack's position at the college, Murray also quite openly wants to seduce Babette. Even before he meets her, Murray's discussion about women prepares us for his relation to the Gladneys. He tells Jack: "I like simple men and complicated women" (11). Although Jack portrays Babette as a simple woman, the novel proves otherwise. Jack believes, for example, that "Babette and I tell each other everything" (29), yet he will learn later that her fear of death has driven her to answer an ad to become an underground human subject for an experimental drug, Dylar, that blocks the fear of death. Moreover, she gains access to the drug by having sex with the project coordinator, Willie Mink. The Gladneys, then, provide Murray ample range to take his pleasure: Jack is simple, failing entirely to understand the source of his own power, while Babette is more complex than Jack acknowledges. In his use of pornography—Babette reads pornographic texts to add spice to their lovemaking—Jack is straightforwardly heterosexual. Murray, however, despite his professed love of women, exhibits a more polymorphous sexuality, choosing as part of his reading matter *American Transvestite* (33). From the outset Murray announces his reason for being in Blacksmith: "I'm here to avoid situations. Cities are full of situations, sexually cunning people" (11). Yet clearly, Murray is one of those cunning people, a world-weary sexual sophisticate, who outside the evacuation camp bargains with a prostitute to allow him to perform the Heimlich maneuver on her (152)! Murray's seduction is a double one, in which he seduces Jack with his interpretive skills, all the while waiting for the chance to seduce Babette.

Murray's seduction of Jack yields tangible results because Jack soon proves willing to sanction Murray's bid to establish Elvis Studies by participating in an antiphonal lecture in which the two men speak of the similarities between Elvis Presley and Adolf Hitler.[15] Afterwards Jack recognizes what is at stake: "It was not a small matter. We all had an aura to maintain, and in sharing mine with a friend I was risking the very things that made me untouchable" (74). Even as Jack shows an awareness of his action, his language suggests the way Murray has infiltrated his thoughts, for Jack's choice of "aura" to describe his power is Murray's word and clearly depends on Murray's previous articulation of the concept while viewing the barn.

Murray's seductions are dangerous because he plots to supplant his rivals. At the college, this means Dimitrios Cotsakis, a colleague in the Department of American Environments, who has a prior claim on teaching Elvis Presley. On the sexual front, this means Jack. But after Cotsakis dies accidentally over the semester break, that leaves only Jack as an obstacle to Murray's desires. Significantly, Murray relates the news of Cotsakis' death to Jack at the supermarket, a key site of consumption. At this moment, Jack has a quasimystical experience:

> I was suddenly aware of the dense environmental texture. The automatic doors opened and closed, breathing abruptly. Colors and odors seemed sharper. The sound of gliding feet emerged from a dozen other noises, from the sublittoral drone of maintenance systems, from the rustle of newsprint as shoppers scanned their horoscopes in the tabloids up front, from the whispers of elderly women with talcumed faces, from the steady rattle of cars going over a loose manhole cover just outside the entrance. (168–69)

He responds to another's death because Jack is acutely aware that, as a result of his exposure to the airborne toxic event, death lives inside his own body, but the heightened perception Jack experiences again needs to be read in light of Murray's earlier interpretation of the supermarket. In Chapter 9, Murray runs into the Gladneys while grocery shopping and directs the majority of remarks directly to Babette:

> This place recharges us spiritually, it prepares us, it's a gateway or pathway. . . . Everything is concealed in symbolism, hidden by veils of mystery and layers of cultural material. But it is psychic data, absolutely. The large doors slide open, they close unbidden. Energy waves, incident radiation. All the letters and numbers are here, all the colors of the spectrum, all the voices and sounds, all the code words and ceremonial phrases. . . . Waves and radiation. Look how well-lighted everything is. The place is sealed off, self-contained. It is timeless. . . . Dying is an art in Tibet. A priest walks in, sits down, tells the weeping relatives to get out and has the room sealed. . . . Here we don't die, we shop. But the difference is less marked than you think. (37–38)

Although Murray is trying here to seduce Babette with his interpretive prowess, it is Jack's consciousness that becomes scripted by Murray. The pattern is clear in the novel: Murray's interpretations become Jack's convictions; Murray's speculations, Jack's experiences.

Given this pattern, it makes sense that the crucial moment of Murray's seduction of Jack should occur through an interpretation.[16] Confronted with the distinct possibility that his life will be shortened through his contact with the chemical cloud, Jack becomes increasingly depressed. Jack's three means of repressing death are television, shopping, and Hitler scholarship. During the academic year, Murray through his conversations has problematized Jack's relation to the first two, activities Jack shares with most Americans. During a long peripatetic conversation, Murray points out Jack's logically contradictory uses of Hitler to conceal himself in a transcendent horror in order to be outstanding in his professional life. Jack uses Hitler as a shield against death, and the correctness of Murray's interpretation is perhaps clearest when Jack, before going to face what he believes to be the Angel of Death (actually his father-in-law come on an unannounced early morning visit) grabs his copy of *Mein Kampf* (244). By exposing Jack's last best defense mechanism, Murray takes this simple man and shatters the very ground of his being. Having emptied Jack of his means of repressing death, Murray posits the best of all possible ways to respond to the fear of death: "think what it's like to be a killer. Think how exciting it is, in theory, to kill a person in direct confrontation. If he dies, you cannot. To kill him is to gain life-credit. The more people you kill, the more credit you store up. It explains any number of massacres, wars, executions" (290). Murray's theory of killing for life-credit substitutes for Jack's now untenable sense of shopping for existential credit. Although Murray emphasizes throughout their long conversation that his observations about the efficacy of killing are speculative, the point of his argument is to convince Jack of its correctness. To Jack's objection that if the world is composed exclusively of killers and diers, then he is clearly a dier, Murray asks: "Isn't there a deep field, a sort of crude oil deposit that one might tap if and when the occasion warrants? A great dark lake of male rage?" (292) Jack notes that Murray sounds like Babette and indeed she refuses to identify the man she had sex with on precisely those grounds (225). If Murray sounds so much like Babette, the possibility arises that Murray has succeeded in his intentions with Babette, pillow talk breeding the similar expression. Whether Murray has already bedded Babette, an intent of Murray's seduction would seem to be the following: if he can get Jack to commit a murder, Jack, if caught, would eliminate himself from both the college and from Babette's bed. Murray is a killer, even if his pleasure is psychological rather than visceral.

Beneath the happy exterior of Murray Siskind, the scope of his sinister intentions plays far beyond the specific seductions of Jack and Babette. In an analysis parallel to Baudrillard's sense of alienated consumption, Murray tells his students that "they're already too old to figure importantly in the making of society" because they are "spinning out from the core, becoming less targetable by advertisers and mass-producers of culture." The result is "to feel estranged from the products you consume" (49–50). Murray's lesson here, as elsewhere, is intended to seduce his students, just as he seduces Jack, into the postmodern flow. To follow Murray's celebration of the postmodern, however, grants him his desired mastery over others. Significantly, Murray only buys the generic items at the grocery, food packaged in black and white wrappers and, crucially, not advertised and hence not part of the signifying systems of culture Murray seeks to decode. They are outside the media and the very postmodern culture he ingenuously praises.[17] Everyone shall enter the postmodern flow—everyone except Murray, who will remain distanced precisely in order to plot, interpret, and control.

But truly to give oneself over to the imagistic flow of consumer information in the age of electronic reproduction is to become Fredric Jameson's schizophrenic, Willie Mink, who in exchange for sex gave Babette the experimental drug Dylar designed to eliminate the fear of death.[18] Jameson reminds us that if "personal identity is itself the effect of a certain temporal unification of past with one's present" and if "such active temporal unification is itself a function of language," then "with the breakdown of the signifying chain . . . the schizophrenic is reduced to an experience of pure material signifiers, or, in other words a series of pure unrelated presents in time" (*Postmodernism*, 27). Mink, whose subjectivity has been voided almost entirely and replaced by the signifying chain of television's language, watches television with the sound off when Jack comes to kill him. Mink's language, except for momentary lapses into thought, is a series of non sequiturs, word-for-word transcriptions of television moments:

> To begin your project sweater . . . first ask yourself what type sleeve will meet your needs. (307)
>
> The pet under stress may need a prescription diet. (307)
>
> Now I am picking up my metallic gold tube. . . . Using my palette knife and my odorless turp, I will thicken the paint of my palette. (309)

Even Mink's brief moments of quasi-lucidity are dialogized through the discourse of tv sports, weather, and late-night B movies. Before one of

"Mink's" utterances, Jack becomes aware of "a noise, faint, monotonous, white" (306). Throughout the novel, the voice of the television intrudes at odd moments, almost as if the television were a character. During a conversation between Jack and his daughter Bee on Christmas Day, for example, the television is on and at times seems to enter the conversation, though without purpose: "The TV said: 'Now we will put the little feelers on the butterfly' " (96). Such moments represent instances when the television, which is always on in the Gladney home, briefly catches Jack's attention. My point here is that when Jack enters Mink's motel room and hears the faint white noise—the hum of the tv—we are not surprised to hear the voice of television. The shock is that the "it said" of television become the "he said" of Mink; Mink *is* the voice of television. Metaphorically, then, Jack's sexual nemesis has always already been near to him and Jack is no closer now to the source of his pain and anger than he was before he confronted Mink.

Jack, who comes to the motel room in hopes of confronting origin—the origin of his male rage and the originator of a drug that will eliminate his fear of death—finds instead only an Oz-like shell of power and authority. Mink, a pill-popping wreck, offers no satisfying target of vengeance because there is no core or center to his personality. One of the side-effects of Dylar is a heightened sensitivity to suggestion, a fact that creates part of the scene's humor. Jack uses this symptom to terrorize Mink, saying such things as "falling plane," "plunging aircraft," and "hail of bullets," eliciting an exaggerated, mime-like response from Mink (309–11). Although Jack's suggestions and Mink's responses are humorous, their effect finally is disturbing, for here in displaced form is the tv man's dream of unmediated mediation revealed as postmodernity's schizophrenic nightmare. Mink experiences the mediation of Jack's language as pure material signifier—immediate and real. However exaggerated the exchange may be, we see in Mink's responses how media produce the consumer. Mink quite literally is the little man behind the screen of the great and powerful Oz. And the screen is tv.

DeLillo's name for the drug, Dylar, and the title of the third section of the novel, Dylarama, serve, it seems, as an indirect way of reminding us that Americans already have a more successful version of the drug Mink failed to produce. In *White Noise*, television itself, that means of forgetting death through aestheticization, is Dylar, an imagistic space of consumption that one accesses by playing dial-a-rama, turning the dial/dyl to the channel of one's choice. Such "choice" is illusory, however, since whatever channel one selects, the subliminal voice of advertising stands ready to produce the viewer as consumer in "substatic regions too deep to probe" (155).

Mink's role as a subject consumed by television recalls, oddly enough, Murray's relation to the electronic image. Other than the time he is on campus, Murray, like Mink, spends much of his time in a rented room sitting before the television. Nothing, however, could appear more different than the two characters' relation to the television image. Mink's viewing is more than passive. There is no distance for him; he is almost another piece of electronic hardware through which television's messages flow. Murray on the other hand attempts complete critical distance in his television viewing to produce his totalizing interpretations of postmodernity. Despite Mink's deterioration near the end of *White Noise,* he tells Jack, in the discourse of a Hollywood mad-scientist's confessional moment, "I wasn't always as you see me now" (307). Like Murray, Mink was a metaphorical killer, the designer of a plot. Mink sought control and totalizing power over death through his work on Dylar, just as Murray seeks power and control in his seductions of his students and friends. Even after the Dylar project had been discredited, Mink on his downward slide still managed another plot, the seduction of Babette, the same woman Murray wants to seduce. Mink's failure to produce a drug that would block the fear of death casts an odd light on Murray's plot to eliminate Jack, which in the end is also a failure. Instead of a relation of polar opposites (Murray actively distanced, Mink passively absorbed), it might be more useful to see Murray as a point in a continuum moving toward Mink.

Both Murray and Mink dislodge the signifier's context. When Jack tells Murray, "I want to live," Murray replies, "From the Robert Wise film of the same name, with Susan Hayward as Barbara Graham, a convicted murderess" (283). How different is Murray's shifting of context from Mink's claim: "Not that I have anything personal against death from our vantage point high atop Metropolitan County Stadium" (308)? The difference between Murray's motivated shifting of context and Mink's unmotivated leaps seems to figure the difference between structuralism and poststructuralism. Murray the structuralist semiotician seeks totality in his reflections on the forms of postmodern media; Mink the true postmodern can only register with a zero degree of interpretation the play of American culture's signifiers.

DeLillo's homologous reflections on the way the mediations of television map the realm of desire in the space of the supermarket and the shopping mall now seem prescient in ways that one could not have seen in 1985, the year *White Noise* was published. The Home Shopping Network combines exactly the intertwined spheres of desire that DeLillo's novel so suggestively connects. Today, personal aura is only a phone call away. As DeLillo contemplates the effects of mediations that pose as the immediate, *White Noise* posits the fear of death as the ground of fascism; such fear creates desire for God/the father/the subject, the logos/text, and the telos/intention. Hitler, Elvis, the most photographed barn, television, shopping all manifest a collective desire for "Führer Knows Best," a cultic aura to absorb the fear of dying. To acknowledge the continuing appeal of fascism, we need look neither to David Duke's strong showing in the 1991 Louisiana governor's race nor to Republican campaign strategists, who interpret the Los Angeles riots, precipitated by the court-sanctioned police mugging of Rodney King, as a sign that family values are weak. As *White Noise* argues, the urge toward fascism is diffused throughout American mass media and its representations.

NOTES

1. Paul Cantor also wishes to show how DeLillo in *White Noise* "is concerned with showing parallels between German fascism and contemporary American culture" ("Adolf," 51). He has a brief but interesting discussion of DeLillo's repeated use of Hitler in his fiction prior to *White Noise* ("Adolf," 40–41).
2. For Neumann, "monopolistic system profits cannot be made and retained without totalitarian power, and that is the distinctive feature of National Socialism" (*Behemoth*, 354). Neumann's belief that democracy would destabilize monopoly capitalism, however, does not anticipate the totalizing power of multinational capital.
3. Eugene Goodheart suggestively links these spheres of consumption when he notes that "the two main sites of experience and dialogue are the supermarket and the TV screen" and that the supermarket is "a trope for all sites of consumption" in the novel ("DeLillo," 121–22). Thomas J. Ferraro asserts that Don DeLillo's fiction "lies at the cutting edge of mass-culture theory because he struggles to imagine how television as a *medium* functions within the home as the foremost site for what sociologists call our 'primary' social relations" ("Whole Families," 24). Ferraro's sense of the ways in which television "reconstructs the nature of reality itself" ("Whole Families," 26) aligns his reading with the postmodernism of both Jean Baudrillard and Frederic Jameson.
4. Michael Valdez Moses, who reads *White Noise* against Heidegger, argues that "the technological media . . . alienate the individual from personal death" by "imposing an increasingly automatic and involuntary identification with the camera eye," which creates the illusion "that the witnessing consciousness of the individual television viewer, like the media themselves, is a permanent fixture possessing a transcendental perspective" ("Lust," 73).

5. Cantor, meditating on this course description, argues that DeLillo wants to suggest "that the spiritual void that made Hitler's rise possible is still with us, perhaps exacerbated by the forces at work in postmodern culture" ("Adolf," 49).
6. Frow's assertion is part of a larger claim about *White Noise* and DeLillo's relation to the postmodern. Frow sees DeLillo representing the postmodern sublime, a sublime in which our terror derives from "the sense of the inadequacy of representation . . . not because of the transcendental or uncanny nature of the object but because of the multiplicity of prior representations" (see page 418 of this volume). Frow convincingly argues that DeLillo is sensitive to the intensely mediated nature of contemporary experience.
7. Frederic Jameson, in opposing the postmodern sublime to that of Edmund Burke and Kant, suggests that "the *other* of our society is . . . no longer Nature at all, as it was in precapitalist societies, but something else which we must now identify" (*Postmodernism*, 34). And though Jameson resists simply substituting technology for Nature as the horizon of aesthetic representation, he does see such reproductive technologies as the computer and television as "a distorted figuration . . . of the whole world system of present-day multinational capitalism" (*Postmodernism*, 37).
8. Michael W. Messmer, using Baudrillard's and Eco's articulation of the hyper-real, argues that the blurring of boundaries between the real and the simulation creates "a distancing which is conducive to the fascination which DeLillo's characters experience as they witness disasters through the medium of television" ("Thinking It Through," 404).

   More pointedly, Goodheart notes: "We repeatedly witness the assassination of Kennedy, the mushroom cloud over Hiroshima, the disintegration of the Challenger space shuttle in the sky. Repetition wears away the pain. It also perfects the image of our experience of it. By isolating the event and repeating it, its content, its horror evaporates. . . . The event becomes aesthetic and the effect upon us anaesthetic" ("Don DeLillo," 122).
9. Jack later repeats exactly Heinrich's line when he picks up his daughter at the airport. Moments before, terrorized passengers deplane from a flight that had experienced a four-mile drop. Jack's daughter wonders where the television crews are, but Jack tells her, "There is no media in Iron City." Her response, though inflected as a question, is actually a statement, one that repeats the lesson of Heinrich's mass murderer and the tv man's outrage: "They went through all that for nothing?" (92). Once again *White Noise* reminds us that the medium of television has been so internalized in contemporary consciousness that experience can no longer be perceived as immediate without the electronic representation.

10. Of such moments Lentricchia wittily notes: "Jacques Lacan said the unconscious is structured like a language. He forgot to add the words 'of Madison Avenue' " ("Tales," 102).
11. Ferraro says of this scene that "Jack's urge to shop" is largely motivated by "a sense of disappointment in the supposed 'community' of the university" ("Whole Families," 22). Such a reading seems to psychologize Jack and shift the focus away from the productive forces that created Jack as a consumer.
12. DeLillo's Mid-Village Mall seems to come straight out of Baudrillard, who sees in such spaces "the *sublimation* of real life, of objective social life, where not only work and money are abolished, but all the seasons as well—the distant vestige of a cycle finally domesticated! Work, leisure, nature, culture, all previously dispersed, separate, and more or less irreducible activities that produced anxiety and complexity in our real life, and in our 'anarchic and archaic' cities, have finally become mixed, massaged, climate controlled, and domesticated into the simple activity of perpetual shopping" ("Consumer," 34).

    Because Jack shops in the corporate space of the mall, it does not matter what he buys, only that he buys: "Consumers are mutually implicated, despite themselves, in a general system of exchange and in the production of coded values" ("Consumer," 46).
13. This catalogue of consumption does not find its completion until Jack, raking through the grotesque and equally detailed catalogue of garbage compressed by the family trash compactor, confronts "the dark underside of consumer consciousness" (259). This confrontation occurs because the immediacy of the nebulous mass in Jack's body, the result of his exposure to the toxic cloud, overwhelms the aestheticizing power of shopping and television to repress death; he seeks in the trash the stronger anti-depressant Dylar. Jack the ironist is ironized for he sees in the garbage only an "ironic modernist sculpture," noting with formalist pleasure "a complex relationship between the sizes of the loops, the degree of the knots (single or double) and the intervals between knots with loops and freestanding knots" (259). By this aestheticizing, Jack misses the more relevant loop of production, consumption, and pollution that have created the very chemical spill that may cause the death he seeks to block from his thoughts. As is so often the case, Jack's sense of life's mystery is actually a mystification.
14. In his reading of the barn, Lentricchia argues that "the real subject is the electronic medium of the image as the active context of contemporary existence in America" ("Tales," 88); the scene opens up the question, "What strange new form of human collectivity is born in the postmodern moment of the aura, and at what price?" ("Tales," 92). For a parallel but differently articulated reading of the barn, see Lentricchia's discussion in "*Libra* as Postmodern Critique" (195–97).

15. See Cantor ("Adolf," 51–53) for a detailed comparison of the way Jack's Hitler and Murray's Elvis are paralleled.
16. My reading of Murray in part grows out of Tom LeClair's comments. LeClair registers the significance of Jack and Murray's final conversation, noting that "Siskind's advice promotes a profoundly immoral act" (see page 401 of this volume).
17. Since *White Noise* was published, the moment of the generic food product has passed, but not before it was thoroughly reified and commodified; the familiar white background with black letters used to sell everything from shirts to coffee mugs and even English basic courses (Robert Scholes, et al., *Textbook*).
18. For Lentricchia, "Willy [sic] Mink is a compacted image of the consumerism in the society of the electronic media, a figure of madness . . ." ("Tales" 113).

WORKS CITED

Baudrillard, Jean. "Consumer Society." *Jean Baudrillard: Selected Writings.* Edited by Mark Poster. Stanford: Stanford University Press, 1988: 29–56.

———. *Simulations.* Translated by Paul Foss, et al. New York: Semiotext(e), 1983.

Benjamin, Walter. "The Work of Art in the Age of Mechanical Reproduction." *Illuminations.* New York: Harcourt, 1955.

Cantor, Paul A. " 'Adolf, We Hardly Knew You.' " *New Essays on* White Noise. Edited by Frank Lentricchia. New York: Cambridge University Press, 1991: 39–62.

DeLillo, Don. *Libra.* New York: Penguin Books, 1991.

———. *White Noise.* New York: Penguin Books, 1986; The Viking Critical Library, 1998.

Ferraro, Thomas J. "Whole Families Shopping at Night!" *New Essays on* White Noise. Edited by Frank Lentricchia. New York: Cambridge University Press, 1991.

Frow, John. "The Last Things Before the Last: Notes on *White Noise.*" See page 417 of this volume.

Goodheart, Eugene. "Don DeLillo and the Cinematic Real." *Introducing Don DeLillo.* Edited by Frank Lentricchia. Durham, N.C.: Duke University Press, 1991.

Jameson, Fredric. *Postmodernism, or, The Cultural Logic of Late Capitalism.* Durham, N.C.: Duke University Press, 1991.

Hutcheon, Linda. *The Poetics of Postmodernism.* London: Routledge, 1988.

———. *The Politics of Postmodernism.* London: Routledge, 1989.

Huyssen, Andreas. *After the Great Divide: Modernism, Mass Culture, Postmodernism.* Bloomington: Indiana University Press, 1986.

LeClair, Tom. *In the Loop: Don DeLillo and the Systems Novel.* Urbana: University of Illinois Press, 1987. See also page 387 of this volume.

Lentricchia, Frank. "*Libra* as Postmodern Critique." *Introducing Don DeLillo.* Durham, N.C.: Duke University Press, 1991: 193–215.

———. "Tales of the Electronic Tribe." *New Essays on* White Noise. Edited by Frank Lentricchia. New York: Cambridge University Press, 1991: 87–113.

Messmer, Michael W. "'Thinking It Through Completely': The Interpretation of Nuclear Culture." *The Centennial Review* 32 (1988): 397–413.

Moses, Michael Valdez. "Lust Removed from Nature." *New Essays on* White Noise. Edited by Frank Lentricchia. New York: Cambridge University Press, 1991: 63–85.

Neumann, Franz. *Behemoth: The Structure and Practice of National Socialism.* 1944. Reprint, New York: Octagon, 1963.

Cornel Bonca

Cornel Bonca is associate professor of English at California State University, Fullerton. His essays and fiction have appeared in *Review of Contemporary Fiction*, *American Book Review*, *Saul Bellow Journal*, *College Literature*, and *Jacaranda*. He is books editor for *OC Weekly*.

DON DELILLO'S *WHITE NOISE*: THE NATURAL LANGUAGE OF THE SPECIES

White Noise is probably the only novel written by a white male American in the last fifteen years to have consistently broken through to reading lists at colleges and universities in the United States. Given the canon quakes of the last decade, this stands by itself as a cultural fact worthy of mention. And given the enormous range and high quality of writing by other white males—from old guardists like Mailer, Bellow, Roth, Updike, and Doctorow, to graying eminences of experimentation like Barth, Vonnegut, Pynchon, Coover, Hawkes, Gaddis, and Gass, to bold younger writers like Richard Powers, Ted Mooney, Steve Erickson, and William Vollmann—the book's emergence is all the more remarkable. It is my sense that *White Noise* has begun to replace *The Crying of Lot 49* as the one book professors use to introduce students to a postmodern sensibility. I have taught the book at two universities, to a wide variety of students from different backgrounds, to freshman, upperclassmen, and graduate students, and I can only describe their response to it as rousing. I can't say it is my teaching that makes this so; I've done my share of teaching good books to stone silence. Yet the novel seems to draw out a certain buried awareness in my students that the most familiar aspects of their lives—shopping malls, television,

From *College Literature* 23.2 (June 1996). By permission of *College Literature*.

families, and the languages of these things—harbor deep and resonant mysteries. It affects them, I think, as a sustained defamiliarization of their own lives. After reading it, it is (or should be) impossible to shop in a supermarket the same way, to watch a televised disaster the same way, even—and this is crucial—to listen to a baby's cry the same way. Preposterously funny, immediately accessible, yet deeply sophisticated on a formal and stylistic level, *White Noise* is one of the few novels capable of mastering—perhaps taming—our schizoid confusions about the mass media experience. It is a novel which, because of its wide-ranging explanatory power and uncanny compassion, somehow *helps.*

Critical appreciation for DeLillo and *White Noise* continues to mount. We have Tom LeClair's *In The Loop* and Arnold Weinstein's *Nobody's Home,* with their explicit or implicit intentions to put DeLillo in the company of the masters of contemporary fiction. Frank Lentricchia's two collections of essays, one "introducing" Don DeLillo's corpus as a whole and the other discussing *White Noise* alone, produce an array of superlatives. Finally, there is a growing number of so-far uncollected essays . . . [that] . . . celebrate the novel largely because it seems to illuminate reigning theories of cultural postmodernism, as if it were written as an example of what Fredric Jameson, Jean-Francois Lyotard, or Jean Baudrillard have been saying about our socio-cultural condition: *White Noise* as postmodern prototype. This tendency may have something to do with the fact that *White Noise* was published in 1985, seemingly in the wake of a number of exciting, much-Xeroxed and much-discussed theoretical essays, among them Baudrillard's "The Ecstasy of Communication," Jameson's "Postmodernism, or the Cultural Logic of Late Capitalism," and Lyotard's "Answering the Question: What Is Postmodernism?"[1] "*White Noise* and *Libra,*" writes Wilcox,

> with their interest in electronic mediation and representation, present a view of life in contemporary America that is uncannily similar to that depicted by Jean Baudrillard. They indicate that the transformations of contemporary secrets that Baudrillard described in his theoretical writings on information and media have also gripped the mind and shaped the novels of Don DeLillo. ("Baudrillard," 346)

In his "*Libra* as Postmodern Critique," Frank Lentricchia calls "the most photographed barn in America episode" from *White Noise* one of DeLillo's "primal scenes," insofar as it signifies that "the environment of the image is the landscape—it is what (for us) 'landscape' has become, and it can't be turned off with the flick of a wrist. For this environment-as-electronic-medium radically constitutes consciousness and therefore (such as it is) contemporary community—it guarantees that we are a people of, by, and for the image" [see "Primal Scenes," this volume, page 415]. This kind of analysis comes right out of Baudrillard, with his grandstanding hyperbole about the postmodern world as pure simulacral system, and also recalls Jameson, with his notation of "the fragmentation of the subject," "a new depthlessness," and "the logic of the simulacrum."[2] Finally, John Frow sees *White Noise*'s Airborne Toxic Event as an instance of what Lyotard calls postmodern writing (presenting the "unpresentable in presentation itself"), and sees a whole series of episodes in the novel through the lens of Baudrillard's and Deleuze's ideas of simulacra [see "Notes," pages 418, 421–24 in this volume].

Now all these analyses are certainly helpful, an apparent case of the visions of the novelist and the theorist happily dovetailing to mutually illuminating effect. I read *White Noise* along these lines for several years myself. Yet gradually the congruities between the novel and theories of postmodernism began to slip. It no longer seems to me accurate to call the world of *White Noise* a "mediascape" or a "mediocracy," for isntance, or to see a smoothly homologous relationship between the "white noise" of the novel and Baudrillard's concept of simulacra (Wilcox, 346; Crowther). Something else is operating in the novel that has been escaping our notice. That something is complicated and can't be reduced to a single statement, but let me begin by noting that DeLillo's ideas about language are quite different from those of the postmodern theorists I've mentioned. Beginning with *The Names*, and then in *White Noise*, *Libra*, *Mao II*, and the novella "Pafko At the Wall," DeLillo has been exploring the idea that language is something more than a ceaseless flow of signifiers with no resting place; furthermore, he's been suggesting that the "white noise" of consumer culture is saying something far more compelling than that our minds have been colonized by the static of late capitalism. I'd like to explore the proposition that the phenomenon of "white noise" is not merely the cultural dreck of consumerism, nor the demotic language DeLillo's characters use to shut themselves off from their terror that they will die—far from it, in fact. "White noise" is for DeLillo contemporary man's deepest *expression* of his death fear, a strange and genuinely awe-inspiring response to the fear of mortality in the postmodern world.

II

DeLillo doesn't articulate a systematic theory of language—few American novelists do—but he has focused increasingly on language not as a system of signifiers and signifieds (that is, as a system of denotation), but as something with a much grander scope: he now appears to see language as a massive human strategy to cope with mortality. In his first few novels, this isn't true: it was only with his second novel *End Zone*, DeLillo himself admits, that he even began to realize that "language was a subject as well as an instrument in my work" (Le Clair interview, 21). Subsequent novels like *End Zone* and *Great Jones Street* fit pretty comfortably into poststructuralist paradigms of language, in which linguistic systems and media culture rigidly constitute the self, reality, and meaning.[3] However, even from the beginning DeLillo has been fascinated by the kinds of language that elude systems, classification, or semiotic analysis: consider the hilarious pregame grunts of the football players in *End Zone*; Bucky Wunderlick's "pee-pee-maw-maw" lyrics in *Great Jones Street*; the babbling domestic intimacies of Lyle and Pammy in *Players* ("They jostled each other before the refrigerator. 'Goody, cheedar.' 'What's these?' 'Brandy snaps.' 'Triffic.' 'No you push me you.' " [53]); the glossolalia in *The Names*; *White Noise*'s media blips; the avalanche of unprocessable information burying Nicholas Branch in *Libra*; the ululating crowds in *The Names*, *Mao II* and "Pafko At The Wall." Gradually, I think, this fascination with non-denotative, perhaps "pre-linguistic" language has begun to occupy the center of DeLillo's curiosities as a novelist, as if these kinds of utterance speak to, and perhaps of, some mystery that is vital to understanding postmodern culture.[4] It is as if DeLillo now listens less to what his culture is saying than to the roar of its saying it. In *White Noise*'s supermarket, amidst "the toneless systems, the jangle and skid of carts, the loudspeaker and coffeemaking machines, the cries of children," Jack Gladney hears "over it all, or under it all, a dull and unlocatable roar, as of some form of swarming life just outside the range of human apprehension" (36). It is this mysterious "swarming life," whatever it is, swirling amidst us in the noises we make, that DeLillo seems to be after.[5]

At the conclusion of *Players*, Pammy Wynant only understands the meaning of the word "transient" (which defines her better than any other word) when the word itself takes on "an abstract tone" for her, and begins to "(subsist) in her mind as [a] language [unit] that had mysteriously evaded the responsibilities of content" (*Players*, 207). This swerve away from the denotative content of language evolves into something of a conscious strategy for both DeLillo and some of his characters starting with *The Names*. The novel is a breakthrough book insofar as it articulates for the first time a virtually religious sense of awe before the very fact that language exists, as if DeLillo had discovered an extraordinary mystery in the utterly familiar act of human utterance.[6] DeLillo has both James Axton and Owen Brademas learn to attend to language not as attempts to communicate specific meanings but as aural or palpably physical phenomena, whose meanings are less important than the "swarming life" or "being" that seems to emanate from them.[7] A fine example of this occurs early in the novel when James, in a typically uncontextualized eruption of wonder, listens to a crowd of Athenians "absorbed in conversation." It occurs to him that

> Conversation is life, language is the deepest being. We see the patterns drive the words, the gestures drive the words. It is the sound and picture of humans communicating. It is talk as a definition of itself. Talk. . . .
>
> This is a way of speaking that takes such pure joy in its own openness and candor that we begin to feel that people are discussing language itself. What pleasure in the simplest greeting. It is as though one friend says to another, "How good it is to say, 'How are you?' " The other replying, "When I answer, 'I am well and how are you,' what I really mean is that I'm delighted to have a chance to say such familiar things—they bridge the lonely distances." (*The Names* 52–53)

Here James lets language evade the responsibilities of content until it becomes something else—a broad signifier of something behind or immanent in all denotation ("over it all, or under it all" is another way to put it). In this case, language becomes that which "bridges the lonely distances" between people, that which literally consoles them in their mortal states.

This particular view of what language "really means," the message hidden though immanent in its very *sound*, becomes clearer as the novel proceeds. During their exhausting (and beautifully rendered) marital quarrel, James realizes that amidst the pettiness of their accusations, "the pain of separation, the fore-memory of death" hovers over and under their talk (*The Names*, 123). "Kathryn dead, odd meditations, pity the sad survivor," James thinks. "Everything we said denied this. We were intent on being petty. But it was there, a desperate love, the conscious hovering sum of things. It was part of the argument. It was the argument." Immanent in their language is the apprehension of death: "It was part of the argument. It was the argument."

Later, Owen and James (after his separation from Kathryn) become fascinated by the names cult, a terrorist group which randomly matches up the initials of towns with the initials of people passing through them, and then ritualistically murders the people because of the coincidence. The group is playing a nihilist end-game with the idea that language is arbitrary, that signifiers and signifieds lack any essential connection. Owen is at first transfixed with the cult's ideas, sensing a kinship between their mocking but inexorable terror-logic and his own haunting despair brought on by his sense that he himself can never link signifier to Signified, word to Word, as his tongue-speaking Pentecostal forebears were apparently able to do when he was a boy. He follows the cult to India, and in a capitulation to his own nihilism, does nothing while the cult murders one more victim. The game, he then realizes (too late), is up. He can no longer bear what the cult stands for, and makes his own stand against them. He tells James: "[The cult's] killings mock us. They mock our need to structure and classify, to build a system against the terror in our souls. They make the system equal to the terror. The means to contend with death has become death" (*The Names*, 308). This speech, one of the high moments in DeLillo's work, tells us that language, whatever it specifically denotes, and however it may be used to "subdue and codify" human beings, remains in the broadest sense a manifestation of "our need to build a system against the terror in our souls." Language is "our means to contend with death," and therefore the only responsible use of it comes from understanding that this terror dwells in all human utterance. Any other use mocks language. In the simplest terms, then, we need language because it bridges the lonely distances created by the fact that we are all going to die.

Owen's speech revivifies James Axton: "I came away from the old city feeling I'd been engaged in a contest of some singular and gratifying kind. Whatever [Owen had] lost in life-strength, this is what I'd won" (*The Names*, 309).[8] Upon his return to Greece, he is finally able to confront the Parthenon (as well as many other things), a monument he's avoided the entire novel because it has always felt to him too "exalted": "It is what we've rescued from the madness. Beauty, dignity, order, proportion" (*The Names*, 3). Yet this time, with the help of Owen's affirmation of what language's immanent message is, he can face it. The Parthenon no longer seems to him monumental, "rescued" from history and placed at an imposing remove from human discourse. Now he sees it as *part* of the human crowd that surrounds it, as part of the babbling white noise of human beings who congregate around beauty, dignity, order, and proportion as a way of handling their own death fears. The result? "I hadn't expected a human feeling to emerge from the stones but this is what I found, deeper than the art and mathematics embedded in the structure, the optical exactitudes. I found a cry for pity. This is what remains to the mauled stones in their blue surround, this open cry, this voice which is our own" (*The Names*,

330). It is a lovely passage, stripped clean of the studied neutrality or corrosive cynicism that has characterized the bulk of DeLillo's fiction till now. James is able to overcome the monument's authoritative aura, and to sense in the Parthenon a merely human cry for pity, a testament to our common mortal terror and longing. And he's able to do this not despite but because of the tourists who talk and snap pictures along the upright fragments of the ruin: "This is a place to enter in crowds, seek company and talk. Everyone is talking. I move past the scaffolding and walk down the steps, hearing one language after another, rich, harsh, mysterious, strong. This is indeed what we bring to the temple, not prayer or chant, or slaughtered ram. Our offering is language" (*The Names*, 331). This passage, which ends the novel proper (and precedes the excerpt from Tap's novel) is the culmination of the novel's exploration of what DeLillo feels lies immanent in language. Language is the organized utterance of mortals connecting themselves to other mortals. However humans may use language to exploit each other, it is also what binds them in life against the terror of death, and in that respect, it is "the deepest being." What is so powerful is DeLillo's serene sense of celebration. Nowhere in DeLillo's work have his narratives moved to such a sense of climax and epiphany. *The Names* is itself a kind of annunciation, a novel which takes delight in its self-conscious effort to *share* the cry of pity which is language, to speak language's death-echoes while announcing that to speak them is precisely to live most boldly.

The novel's coda, called "The Prairie" and written by James's son Tap, is a pure and generous "offering," a nine-year-old's effort to tell Owen Brademas's story of how as a boy he was unable to speak in tongues at his Pentecostal church meetings. The text, replete with misspellings, reveals not just language's slippery multiplicities (as a Joycean text does) but Tap's *own* cry for pity. Tap's own aliveness—his attempt to bridge the lonely distances—keeps poking through the curtains of standard English. Earlier, James says that he finds the "mangled words" of Tap's novel "exhilarating." "He's made them new again, made me see how they worked, what they really were. They were ancient things, secret, reshapable" (*The Names*, 313). "The Prairie" is about falling from grace, of course, about a boy's recognition that he's filled not with the Word, but simply words. While "worse than a retched nightmare," this very recognition brings him into the "fallen *wonder* of the world" (my italics)—which is finally the world of *The Names* itself, where language, fallen indeed, remains a matter of wonder because, with every utterance, it speaks the mystery of human beings grappling with time and nothingness. And with such a recognition can come the awareness that the human scene is everywhere and always a matter of pity and awe.

III

The ideas about language that surface in *The Names* and which pervade *White Noise* as well are not exactly commensurate with theories propounded by postmodernists. For DeLillo in his later work, language emerges from a definable though mysterious source—the human terror of death—and whatever it denotes, utters under its breath, "I speak to bridge the lonely distances created by our mortality." This may sound unnecessarily reductive, but there's good reason, aside from the textual evidence above, to suggest why DeLillo finds such ideas compelling. Tom LeClair notes that Ernest Becker's book *The Denial of Death* "is one of the few 'influences' [DeLillo] will confirm."[9] Becker's simple and powerful thesis is that "the idea of death, the fear of it, haunts the human animal like nothing else; it is a mainspring of human activity—activity designed largely to avoid the fatality of death, to overcome it by denying in some way that it is the final destiny for man" (ix). The death fear is with us from birth, and all human "projects"—especially the language we use to help us construct our belief systems—are designed to evade or deny or conquer the fear of death. Becker's ideas shadow *White Noise* at every turn, and help explain some key episodes in the novel.

However, before I explore these episodes, I want to flesh out what "white noise" means in this novel, since I think a limited idea of the term has kept many readers from appreciating the full range of DeLillo's exploration of postmodern culture. We can begin with the obvious. White noise is media noise, the techno-static of a consumer culture that penetrates our homes and our minds (and our serious novels) with ceaseless trinities of brand-name items ("Dacron, Orlon, Lycra Spandex") and fragments of TV and radio talk shows (" 'I hate my face,' a woman said. 'This is an ongoing problem with me for years' ") (*White Noise*, 52, 263). It includes "the human buzz" of transactions taking place at the shopping mall, the "incessant clicking of shutter release buttons" that surrounds the Most Photographed Barn in America, as well as the utterance of a phrase—"Toyota Celica"—by a girl who is coping in sleep with something as terrifying as the Airborne Toxic Event (84, 13, 155). Now, from the point of view of contemporary Marxism or the Frankfurt School, white noise is the manifestation of the final triumph of capitalist appropriation, specifically of late capitalism's "prodigious expansion . . . into hitherto uncommodified areas. . . . One is tempted to speak in this connection of a new and historically original penetration and colonization of Nature and the Unconscious." (Jameson, "Postmodernism," 78). From Baudrillard's perspective, white noise is the realm of the ecstasy of communication, of mass culture's signifying swirl which disperses the subject into links in the signifying chain, into a mere terminal in Communication's Mainframe. In such a scenario, life and death have no subjective reality unless they are confirmed by the System. Certainly DeLillo pays at least lip service to such powerful interpretations when he has Jack hear from a medical technician that "death has entered" his body. "You are the sum total of your data," the man says. "No man escapes that" (141). Jack thinks: "It is when death is rendered graphically, is televised so to speak, that you sense an eerie separation between your condition and yourself. A network of symbols has been introduced, an eerie awesome technology wrested from the gods. It makes you feel like a stranger in your own dying" (142).

Yet clearly Jack will not be a stranger in his own dying—the entire novel is about a man whose death sensations are all too familiar—and the phenomenon of white noise goes far beyond "neutral and reified mediaspeech" or capitalist appropriation (Wilcox, 347). White noise manifests itself in much subtler ways, in ways that have little to do with consumerism, mass media, or high technology. It isn't merely *imposed* from without by socioeconomic or communicational systems, but emerges from sources originating within the characters, from the same organismic death fear that we find operating in *The Names*. White noise, therefore, encompasses a wide variety of human utterance, both denotative and not. Examples are everywhere: the melancholy "homemade signs concerning lost dogs and cats, sometimes written in the handwriting of children"; the Gladneys' charmingly fact-bending family chats (the result of "overcloseness, the noise and heat of being"); the "low-level rumble that humans routinely make in a large enclosed space"; Vern Dickey's parting speech to Babette and Jack (" 'Don't worry about me,' he said. 'The little limp means nothing' "); the discussions of the New York émigrés ("Did you ever brush your teeth with your finger?"); the "love babble and buzzing flesh" that Jack imagines went on when Babette slept with Willie Mink (4, 81, 137, 255–6, 67, 241). What all these phenomena share is a passion for utterance to "bridge the lonely distances," to "establish a structure against the terror of our souls." It is language as the denial of death, as the evasion of what cannot be evaded. "Pain, death, reality," Murray Jay Siskind will say: "we can't bear these things as they are. We know too much. So we resort to repression, compromise, and disguise. This is how we survive in the universe. This is the natural language of the species" (289).

Let's take up one example of "the natural language of the species": Babette's father's speech to his daughter and son-in-law, which is a comic masterstroke of death-evasion. Now Vernon Dickey is on his last legs, a man with a horrible chronic cough, and the "look of a ladies' man in the crash-dive of his career" (245). Given the man's health and woefully erratic visiting habits, clearly the reason Babette cries so much when he's about to leave is that she's not sure she will ever see him again. But his speech, which rolls off his tongue with a hurling momentum that soon dwarfs the substance of what he's saying, is pure driven white noise. To capture this essential momentum, I quote at length:

> "Don't worry about me," he said. "The little limp means nothing. People my age limp. A limp is a natural thing at a certain age. Forget the cough. It is healthy to cough. You move the stuff around. The stuff can't harm you as long as it doesn't settle in one spot and stay there for years. So the cough's all right. So is the insomnia. The insomnia's all right. What do I gain by sleeping? You reach an age when every minute of sleep is one less minute to do useful things. To cough or limp. Never mind the women. The women are all right. We rent a cassette and have some sex. It pumps blood to the heart. Forget the cigarettes. I like to tell myself I'm getting away with something. Let the Mormons quit smoking. They'll die of something just as bad. The money's no problem. I'm all set incomewise. Zero pensions, zero savings, zero stocks and bonds. So you don't have to worry about that. That's all taken care of. Never mind the teeth. The teeth are all right. The looser they are, the more you can wobble them with your tongue. It gives the tongue something to do. Don't worry about the shakes. Everybody gets the shakes now and then. It is only the left hand anyway. The way to enjoy the shakes is pretend it is somebody else's hand. Never mind the sudden and unexplained weight loss. There's no point eating what you can't see. Don't worry about the eyes. The eyes can't get any worse than they are now. Forget the mind completely. The mind goes before the body. That's the way it is supposed to be. So don't worry about the mind. The mind is all right. Worry about the car. The steering's all awry. The brakes were recalled three times. The hood shoots up on pothole terrain." (255–56)

The remarkable effect of his deadpan speech is that Babette breaks up in helpless laughter; she "walk[s] in little circles of hilarity, weak-kneed, shambling, all her fears and defenses adrift in the sly history of his voice" (256). This is what white noise often does: it sets one's fears and defenses about death adrift *within* language (which captures and —somehow—neutralizes them), and for a time those fears are assuaged. They can even be turned to laughter, and redeem the moment from the death-fear's grip. Vernon Dickey knows what Murray knows about the responsibility of dying men: "What people look for in a dying friend is a stubborn kind of gravel-voiced nobility, a refusal to give in, with moments of indomitable humor" (284).

What the novel brings together, then, are two kinds of white noise: that which is a product of late capitalism and a simulacral society, and that which has always been "the natural language of the species"—death evasion—and which now gets expressed in the argot of consumer culture. The result is a vision of contemporary America that bypasses cultural critique in favor of recording awe at what our civilization has wrought. Because for DeLillo, while white noise certainly registers the ways in which Americans evade their death fear, it can also be heard —provided we learn to listen properly—as a moving and quite beautiful expression of that death fear. It becomes nothing less than a stirring revelation of the fear of death, a noise of great (and frankly, unpostmodern) pathos.

IV

At the height of their "major dialogue," Jack and Babette explicitly connect their fear of death to white noise. Says Jack to his wife:

> "How strange it is. We have these deep terrible lingering fears about ourselves and the people we love. Yet we walk around, talk to people, eat and drink. We manage to function. The feelings are deep and real. Shouldn't they paralyze us? How is it we can survive them, at least for a while? We drive a car, we teach a class. How is it no one sees how deeply afraid we were, last night, this morning? Is it something we all hide from each other, by mutual consent? Or do we share the same secret without knowing it? Wear the same disguise?
>
> "What if death is nothing but sound?"
>
> "Electrical noise."
>
> "You hear it forever. Sound all around. How awful."
>
> "Uniform, white." (198)

This is a breathtakingly loaded passage, and among its virtues is DeLillo's hint to the reader about how to listen to white noise—not simply as cultural detritus but as the manifestation of an attempt to communicate one's fear and hence to "bridge the lonely distances." Life, Jack says here, is lived in virtually unbroken terror that it will end. How do we survive? By repression, of course—by personal and culture-wide denial of the death-fear. But perhaps, Jack gropes, "we share the same secret *without knowing it*" (my italics): perhaps we speak our death terror all the time without realizing it. In the mysterious way some couples have of understanding the drift of one lover's words when even the lover himself doesn't quite understand what he's saying, Babette urges them both on to the notion that death itself might just be filled with white noise. And if that is so, what is all the noise—not just media/consumer noise but the noise they make while they "walk around, talk to people, eat and drink"—that surrounds them in life? It can only be their intimations of death; it is the death-fear expressed in the only terms that a postmodern media culture knows how to express it.

Three important passages in the novel reveal that there is wonder and a curious kind of revelation in the recognition that white noise communicates the death-fear. In each one, Jack hears a different kind of white noise, and by a mysterious *entrance* into its sound, he experiences what can only be called an epiphany. It is not the kind of epiphany which changes his character; Jack enters, each time, into a strange relation with the sound which is seemingly timeless, and has no after-effects in the temporal realm. The epiphanic revelations don't help him "deal" with his death-fear in any tangible way, especially because Jack doesn't know what it is he's experiencing. (This ignorance, incidentally, signifies the major difference betwen Jack and James Axton, who not only learns to read white noise as an expression of the death fear, but incorporates this knowledge into both his life and the text he writes.) Jack never gathers the revelations together into something he can use in the future.

The first moment comes during Wilder's seven-hour stint of crying. Ernest Becker spends some crucial early pages in *The Denial of Death* arguing that even for infants, the death-terror is "all-consuming."[10] When Babette wonders if it isn't a little silly to contact a doctor just to say "My baby is crying," Jack, in that marvelously panicked way of his, blurts out, "Is there a condition more basic?" (75). As Jack drives Babette to her sitting, standing, and walking class—Wilder wailing between them—Jack begins to feel that "there was something permanent and soul-struck in this crying. It was a sound of inbred desolation" (77). Becker would give a nod here. But the scene becomes most fascinating when, after Jack drops Babette off, he drives Wilder around. The boy's "huge lament continued, wave after wave."

> He was crying out, saying nameless things in a way that touched me with its depth and richness. This was an ancient dirge all the more impressive for its resolute monotony. Ululation. I held him upright with a hand under each arm. As the

> crying continued, a curious shift developed in my thinking. I found that I did not necessarily wish him to stop. (78)

Anyone who has ever borne the sustained bawl of a child will surely wonder about this "curious shift." What prompts it?

> The inconsolable crying went on. I let it wash over me, like rain in sheets. I entered it, in a sense. I let it fall and tumble across my face and chest. I began to think he had disappeared inside this wailing noise and if I could join him in his lost and suspended place we might together perform some reckless wonder of intelligibility. (78)

The boy's crying becomes a secret inhabitable space which is "strangely soothing." "It might not be so terrible, I thought, to have to sit here for four more hours, with the motor running and the heater on, listening to this uniform lament" (78). Why? Jack, I'd argue, has hit upon the secret we all share without knowing it. In his hysterical terror, Wilder is expressing (however unconsciously) his death fear, and in a primal way is trying to "bridge the lonely distances." He is doing what James Axton in *The Names* says all language does, only here it is in a "large and pure," prelinguistic form. The connection between Wilder's crying and language in *The Names* tightens in the chapter's last paragraph, when, the crying jag finally concluded, Jack notes that Wilder looks

> as though he'd just returned from a period of wandering in some remote and holy place, in sand barrens or snowy ranges —a place where things are said, sights are seen, distances reached which we in our ordinary toil commonly regard with the mingled reverence and wonder we hold in reserve for feats of the most sublime and difficult dimensions. (79)

I don't think there's a single note of hyperbole here. Wilder has come back from "a remote and holy place": the place where death is confronted without the benefit of the protections the ego establishes against it—just as Owen Brademas, who gradually strips himself of ego protections in *The Names*, confronts it while following the death-cult from Greece to India. And the religious language Jack employs evokes his exalted feeling that sharing his death-terror with his son is a primordial human moment.

A second epiphanic moment comes during the Airborne Toxic Event. Jack, having had a computer confirm just minutes earlier that "death has entered" his body, overhears his daughter Steffie whisper in her sleep the words "Toyota Celica." He responds by saying that "the utterance struck me with the impact of a moment of splendid transcendence" (141, 155). Critics so far have been baffled by what seems to them Jack's outsized response to his daughter's words, but if we see Steffie's outburst as an example of the death-fear speaking *through* consumer jargon, then Jack's wondrous awe will strike us, strange as it may seem, as absolutely appropriate.[11] It is tempting, particularly if one is used to ironizing any talk of transcendence in a postmodern novel, to say that Jack's desperation in hearing that Nyodene-D has entered his system has simply overcome him, and that he is already predisposed to expect the hieratic from sleeping children:

> Watching children sleep makes me feel devout, part of a spiritual system. It is the closest I can come to God. If there is a secular equivalent of standing in a great spired cathedral with marble pillars and streams of mystical light slanting through two-tier Gothic windows, it would be watching children in their little bedrooms fast asleep. Girls especially. (147)

However, the shock Jack feels when he hears what Steffie has spoken goes beyond even what he expected: "A long moment passed before I realized this was the name of an automobile. *The truth only amazed me more*" (155, my italics). Something splendid, if not transcendent, is indeed going on.

We have to remember, first of all, that Steffie is nine years old, and living without her real mother—which we know troubles her because, while perfectly capable of watching TV disaster footage with the rest of the family, she runs out of the room whenever a sitcom Dad argues with a sitcom Mom. The novel doesn't dramatize her vulnerability (DeLillo is never sentimental), but it hardly needs pointing out that the Airborne Toxic Event has terrified her. Steffie is less equipped to handle the cloud's terror than anyone in the novel, even Wilder, who is too young to register this external death-threat. Steffie incorporated the terror of the entire day's events, and in sleep communicates her fear in the only way she knows: by babbling "Toyota Celica." It is as if she has—with the wisdom that DeLillo attributes to Wilder in this novel and to children in general in an interview[12]—understood what the hopped-hysteria of mass advertising has really been saying all along (beneath, below or above it all), which is this: You are afraid of dying; let this phrase, this sound-bite, this whirling bit of language so pervasive worldwide that it can serve as common coin in Sri Lanka or

Schenectady, Rio de Janeiro or Reykjavik—let it soothe your fears; let your dread dissolve in the chanting of this media mantra.

The language DeLillo uses to lead up to Jack's moment is telling. Steffie's utterance "was beautiful and mysterious, gold-shot with looming wonder. It was like the name of an ancient power in the sky, tablet-carved in cuneiform" (155). This description recalls the hieratic language of *The Names*, of course, and Owen Brademas's desire to touch the stones that had been etched with hieroglyphics by ancient tribes. "It made me feel that something hovered," Jack says. "But how could this be? A simple brand name, an ordinary car. How could these near-nonsense syllables, murmured in a child's restless sleep, make me sense a meaning, a presence?" (155). Jack cannot answer, but a reader informed about DeLillo's sense of language surely can. Jack has touched the quick of his daughter's death-fear here just as he had with Wilder earlier. What is so splendid about the scene is that the most demotic language speaks the death fear in a way that is at once wondrous, comic, and pathetic (in both senses of the world). It is a moment of powerfully charged ambivalences: pathetic that Steffie has had to express her fears this way, but amazing that she does; awe-inspiring what strange psychic trails she had to follow to make her deepest fears heard, equally wondrous that on some level, they are heard.[13]

The third epiphanic moment I'd like to discuss takes place near the end of the novel, after Jack has shot Willie Mink and is being treated by Sister Hermann Marie for a flesh wound to his wrist. Jack has shot Willie in a psychological re-enactment of a Nazi's efforts to conquer his own death fears by killing others. Jack has wounded Willie in a state of psychopathic omnipotence—then is shot in return. However, this is not one of those shootings where a man discovers his own human connection to another person through the spilling of blood. Jack only comes to a sense of human connection later, in his chat with Sister Hermann Marie. What she tells Jack, in effect, is that priests and nuns of the Catholic church just speak another kind of white noise. They don't "believe" their teachings; they help people evade death with a torrent of doctrine, litanies, catechism—language. The church's job is to give comfort, and the white noise of religion provides that. At first, Jack rejects her argument, insisting that real belief is necessary, that it is the substance of the belief that counts, that the Church can't just be pretending. But Sister Hermann Marie scoffs at his naiveté. When Jack fails to understand her, she gives up any attempt to explain herself with denotative language. Instead she begins by "spraying [Jack] with German"—a language which Jack, despite his Sisyphean attempts to learn it, cannot understand. However, it is better that he can't, for from the nun bursts

> A storm of words. She grew more animated as the speech went on. A gleeful vehemence entered her voice. She spoke faster, more expressively. Blood vessels flared in her eyes and face. I began to detect a cadence, a measured beat. She was reciting something. I decided. Litanies, hymns, catechisms. The mysteries of the rosary perhaps. Taunting me with scornful prayer.
>
> The odd thing is I found it beautiful. (320)

Again, the question here is why Jack reacts the way he does. But by now we know the answer. He's heard the message immanent in the rhythms and patterns of this white noise, but he's had to hear it in a pure, babbling, glossolalic form before it can have an effect on him. He finds it beautiful because, once again, he's glimpsed the quick of the human death-fear, heard the naked cry for pity implicit in all human speech, heard "the offering" of "language" which is stripped of all meaning except the desire to "bridge the lonely distances."

V

The strategy of death-evasion—"the natural language of the species"—that characterizes white noise illuminates much of the novel. Jack's immersion in Hitler studies is clearly his attempt to bury himself in a discourse so horrible that his own death-fear is made puny. (Says Murray, "Hitler is larger than death. You thought he could protect you. . . .You wanted to be helped and sheltered. The overwhelming horror would leave no room for your own death. 'Submerge me,' you said. 'Absorb my fear' " [287]). Dylar is a kind of pharmaceutical reification of white noise: a pill to evade the death-fear. Heinrich's techno-nerd behavior—his pen-pal relationship with convicted murdered Tommy Roy Foster; his friendship with Orest Mercator and his attempts to immortalize himself in the Guinness Book of Records; his confident recital of scientific facts at the Red Cross center during the Airborne Toxic Event—all of these rehearse his attempt to diminish his death-fear. Finally, DeLillo explicitly associates Jack's attempt to kill Willie Mink (the ultimate strategy for evading death, as Murray makes clear, is to kill someone else) with white noise: after listening to one of Willie's rambling speeches, Jack "heard a noise, faint, monotonous, white"; getting ready to fire, Jack notes "[t]he precise nature of events. Things in their actual state . . . White noise everywhere"; finally, when Jack actually fires the gun, DeLillo describes it this way: "the sound snowballed, in the white room . . ." (306, 310, 312).

Yet there remains a problem with this reading, and its name is

Murray Jay Siskind. Murray is the one character in *White Noise* who isn't afraid of dying. Practically everyone else in the book walks through the novel in a state of suppressed terror, and it comes out in all manner of strange and lovely behavior. (In fact, the principle behind Jack's narrative voice—which in my view is the novel's greatest aesthetic achievement, and deserves separate treatment—is Jack's enormous awe at the most familiar events, an awe that comes from his knowledge that the backdrop for the familiar is the dark mystery of mortality.) Murray, however, manages to express only delight, or else mere semiotic interest, in the phenomena around him. When he takes Jack to The Most Photographed Barn in America, he tells Jack that in this prototypical simulacral scene, "We can't get outside the aura. We're part of the aura." While Jack doesn't need to fill us in on his own reaction to this—wondrous ambivalence, as always—he does add that Murray "seemed immensely pleased by this" (13). He, not Jack, is the true Baudrillardian man, the true ecstatic in the world of Communication. Immersed academically in "American magic and dread," he feels no dread himself (19). At the Gladney home, while the family watches in confusion, awe, and fear as Babette appears on the TV set, Murray is as removed and unmoved as a video camera. "[Wilder] remained at the TV set, within inches of the dark screen, crying softly, uncertainly, in low heaves and swells, as Murray took notes" (105). During the Airborne Toxic Event, while everyone else is wandering around terrified, Murray is soliciting prostitutes to perform the Heimlich maneuver on him (!). Finally, in his most fateful action, Murray carefully guides Jack through a thicket of rationalization into a psychological clearing where it appears that the only thing Jack can do about his death fear is to kill Willie Mink.

Throughout their "serious looping Socratic walk," Murray insists that "I'm only a visiting lecturer. I theorize" and that "We're a couple of academics taking a walk," which suggests he's oblivious to the "practical consequences" such a walk will have on a man whose death-fear is so powerful he's willing to try anything to overcome it (282, 293, 291, 282). Murray's logic has a brilliant inevitability to it: the death-fear seems unassailable. A "meaningful," "interesting" life won't help us deal with it, nor will love overcome it. Either one can place one's trust in technology ("Give yourself up to it, Jack. Believe in it. They'll insert you in a gleaming tube, irradiate your body with the basic stuff of the universe"), or "you can always get around death by concentrating on the life beyond," or one can put oneself under one "spell" or another to help one forget death (285, 287). When it becomes clear that none of these options will work for Jack, Murray goes on a tear of death-naming:

"The vast and terrible depth."
"Of course," [Jack] said.
"The inexhaustibility."
"I understand."
"The whole huge nameless thing."
"Yes, absolutely."
"The massive darkness."
"Certainly, certainly."
"The whole terrible endless hugeness."
"I know exactly what you mean." (288)

What *has* he communicated? Nothing, really. This kind of head-on denotation is impotent before the death terror. In *The Names*, this attempt to "bridge the lonely distance" might have been enough to temporarily ward off the death fear, but not here, not just because Jack's death fear is so much balder than James Axton's, but more importantly because Murray's own language is disembodied: it doesn't acknowledge a death-fear of its own, and thus Jack has nothing to "bridge" his own fear to. In Jack's mind, his only remaining option is to kill Willie Mink.

Murray, then, is both the novel's ecstatic seer and its evil presence. He mouths the most brilliant lines in the book, and clearly speaks many of DeLillo's observations about postmodern society. At the same time, he is the most compelling element in the plot's movement "deathward," and his clinical objectivity is unearthly. He may as well be from another planet. If every other character is actuated by his or her death fear, Murray's character is precisely defined by his lack of one. He is a man without a self, for in this novel to have no death fear is to have no self.[14] It is not Murray, but Jack, speaking with that disarmingly baffled voice, whose unintended humor gives off the novel's brilliant sheen of tender irony, who is capable of uttering the mysteries of white noise.

VI

I have tried throughout this essay to suggest that DeLillo's attitude toward the world of his novel is generous-spirited; it is not so much that he is uncritical toward a mass consumer society as that he has attempted to complicate the stiff categories of ideological or cultural critique. The novel does not "celebrate" the white noise of advertising and mass media—of course not. But it realizes that it is in that noise that our terrors and longings can be read. The effect of the narrative as a whole is similar to that achieved by Laurie Anderson in her performance piece, "Oh Superman." The entire song—a daring and very moving meditation on the need for us to let authorities (government, ideologies, "Mom and Dad") assume the responsibilities of our freedom in the postmodern world—has for its backing "rhythm track" a tape loop of Anderson imitating a vulnerable child's voice, chanting "Ah ah ah ah ah ah. . . ." Perhaps because the voice seems trapped in that tape loop, and because it serves as a backdrop for the adult terror enacted in the song, the effect is startling: a listener feels a terrible pathetic identification with the child, though the song itself is laced with cool synthesizers and a distancing irony. In *White Noise*, everyone is that tape-looped child, cooing its need and fear through a forest of technologized culture.

The novel also puts one in mind of Wim Wenders's extraordinary *Wings of Desire*. In that 1987 film, Bruno Ganz plays the angel Daniel, who listens with great tenderness to the internal and external conversations of human beings. Despite the enormous variety of the human utterances, it is impossible for the viewer to hear these utterances without attending to a gradual realization: all these people are going to die. Hearing human utterance from a caring angel's point of view, *we hear human language under the sign of eternity*. Under that sign, language cannot help but emanate its own mortal gleanings. Daniel decides in the end to give up his celestial status because he has fallen in love with a mortal, and he knows that without knowing what mortality is like, his love will mean nothing. For to know what it is to be human is to know what it is to die. Perhaps only an angel can truly understand such a thing—it is what makes an angel an angel. But for us humans, these are probably unbearable words: they are what make murder, suicide and all manner of violence conceivable. Yet they also send up gorgeous desperate flurries of white language, and make such amazing novels as DeLillo's possible.

ENDNOTES

1. Baudrillard's essay was first published in Hal Foster's *The Anti-Aesthetic* and later expanded into a monograph with the same name; Jameson's essay appeared first in *The New Left Review* and was later made the introductory chapter to his massive *Postmodernism, or the Cultural Logic of Late Capitalism*; Lyotard's essay was appended to his highly influential book, *The Postmodern Condition: A Report on Knowledge*. It was these texts, rather than the brilliant and innovative work of Ihab Hassan during the seventies and early eighties, that really broke down academic resistance to postmodernism.
2. Cf. Fredric Jameson's essay, "Postmodernism, or the Cultural Logic of

Late Capitalism," 63, 58, and 85. In the book of the same name, the page references are 14, 6, and 46, respectively, though Jameson alters the language slightly in the first case.

3. Surely the most persuasive and helpful chapter in LeClair's *In the Loop*—a book which runs DeLillo's novels through a host of theoretical paradigms which often wrench the life right out of them—is the one in which he looks at *End Zone* in terms of Derrida's critique of logocentrism. In that chapter, the fit between novel and paradigm is true.
4. Cf. Dennis A. Foster's "Alphabetic Pleasure: *The Names*" in Lentricchia's *Introducing Don DeLillo*, 157–173, particularly 159–160, for an evocative though all too brief exploration of DeLillo's interest in prelinguistic utterance, using Julia Kristeva's ideas of the semiotic, the symbolic, and the chora as markers in his theoretical grid.
5. Any explication of what DeLillo means by "mystery" and the "swarming life just outside the range of human apprehension" threatens to become portentous, swollen by metaphysical—and yes, German—rhetoric. I'm afraid this is unavoidable. DeLillo's tightest philosophical connections are not with Baudrillard or Lyotard, but with Heidegger. Consider the similarities in their outlooks: their shared conviction that it is the "familiar" or the "at-hand" that yields the deepest meaning: their shared fascination with etymology; Heidegger's explicit belief, and DeLillo's performative one, that the world must be viewed from a stance of "radical astonishment": the closeness of the statements "language is the deepest being" (DeLillo) and "Language is the House of Being" (Heidegger); their concepts of immanence—Being for Heidegger, intimations of "presence" or "something hovering" in DeLillo; their metaphors of "illumination" or "unconcealment" in epiphany; and finally, their preoccupation with death. This essay will not offer a Heideggerian reading; however, while Heidegger begins his philosophical system with a conviction about Being's presence, DeLillo is never less than racked with ontological doubt. The "presences" that hover occasionally in DeLillo's fiction appear as fleeting visitations which leave nothing behind but an awed sense of wonder in those who witness them. Still, Heidegger's ghost exerts a powerful presence in DeLillo's work; he hovers over it all, or under it all—a fitfully locatable roar.
6. In the *Paris Review* interview, DeLillo says "with this book I tried to find a deeper level of seriousness as well. *The Names* is the book that marks the beginning of a new dedication" (*Paris Review*, 284).
7. We must tread carefully here. *The Names* is a dense and complicated book that is almost entirely about language, and I will delineate in this essay mainly what I consider DeLillo's breakthrough affirmation of human utterance. Yet, as Michael J. Morris has pointed out, the novel

also engages the idea that language is profoundly dangerous, that in its zeal to name and denote, it "subdues and codifies" all that it touches (*The Names*, HO). Morris argues that in *The Names*, language, like international corporatism or the names cult itself, is repressive and murderous. Morris makes a fine case for this reading, but in the end he cannot explain the patently affirmative tone of the book's ending. As I'll try to show here, when DeLillo and his characters finally stop listening to language as denotation and listen to it as utterance instead—when at last language "evades the responsibilities of content"—what is immanent in language emerges, and the novel's powerful affirmation of language becomes possible.

8. James is really a changed man upon his return. He is able to quit his job immediately upon realizing he's been a CIA dupe, and he realizes that his own "blind involvement" in the CIA constitutes a "failure to concentrate, to occupy a serious center—it had the effect of justifying everything Kathryn had ever said about me. Every dissatisfaction, mild complaint, bitter grievance. They were all retroactively correct. It was that kind of error, unlimited in connection and extent, shining a second light on anything and everything. In the way I sometimes had of looking at things as she might look at them, I saw myself as the object of her compassion and remnant love" (*The Names*, 317). Finally, in quitting his risk analyst position, he's able to sit down and write the book we're reading: "These are among the people I've tried to know twice, the second time in memory and language. Through them, myself. They are what I've become, in ways I don't understand but which I believe will accrue to a rounded truth, a second life for me as well as them" (*The Names*, 329). James's reflections here are all life- and language-affirming, a far cry from his earlier cynicism and desperation. Owen is the immediate cause.
9. LeClair, see page 393 of this volume. DeLillo made this confirmation in personal correspondence to Le Clair.
10. Becker, 15. Becker makes the primary argument about children and the fear of death on pages 13–23, but I can summarize by saying that for Becker "the child . . . lives with an inner sense of chaos" whose root is the organismic "fear of annihilation." This fear, Becker goes on, quoting Gregory Zilboorg, "undergoes most complex elaborations and manifests itself in many indirect ways." The death fear becomes in fact "a complex symbol and not any particular, sharply defined thing to the child." Thus, children's "recurrent nightmares, their universal fear of insects and dogs"—these and other fears have at their base the terror of death. Becker takes pains not "to make the child's world seem more lurid than it is most of the time"—Becker is an enviably quiet and balanced thinker—but he does insist that phenomenologically, having

an infant's consciousness "is too much for any animal to take, but the child has to take it, and so he wakes up screaming with almost punctual regularity during the period when his weak ego is in the process of consolidating things" (Becker, 19–20).

11. LeClair calls Steffie's words simply "a product of consumer conditioning," but since that is all he makes of them, he cannot explain why Jack would sense something transcendent in them. He dismisses Jack's response by calling it "a delusion" and an attempt to escape consciousness [see page 399 of this volume]. Frow suggests that Steffie's words come from the "unconscious of her culture," but realizes that this recognition alone is insufficient to bring on Jack's "moment of splendid transcendence." Frow concludes his discussion of the issue with this: "The question of the source of enunciation of these proper names remains an interesting one" [see page 428 of this volume]. Arnold Weinstein quotes the episode only to say "One hardly knows what to make of such renderings, these epiphanic moments," except that they demonstrate the Frankfurt School chestnut that the "inner life" has been colonized by the "outer" life (Weinstein, *Nobody's Home*, 306). Finally, Wilcox, in passing, explains Jack's epiphany as an attempt to "glean meanings from the surrounding noise of culture. Jack is drawn toward occasions of existential self-fashioning, heroic moments of vision in a commodified world." However, Wilcox's entire article is about the end of the heroic narrative, and so his use of the adjective "heroic" to describe Jack is meant ironically (Wilcox, 349).
12. In his interview with Anthony DeCurtis, DeLillo says that "I think we feel, perhaps superstitiously, that children have a direct route to, have direct contact to the kind of natural truth that eludes us as adults. . . . There is something they know but cannot tell us. Or there is something they remember which we've forgotten (DeCurtis, 302).
13. In the 1993 *Paris Review* interview, when asked to comment on the Toyota Celica incident, DeLillo replied: "When you detach one of these words from the product it was designed to serve, the word acquires a chantlike quality. . . . If you concentrate on the sound, if you disassociate the words from the object they denote, and if you say the words over and over, they become a sort of higher Esperanto. This is how Toyota Celica began its life. It was pure chant at the beginning. Then they had to find an object to accommodate the words" [see page 332 of this volume]. The interviewer doesn't ask what that "object" is, but that doesn't take much effort. Given the scene's context, it can only be Steffie's fear of death.
14. The novel identifies selfhood explicitly in terms of the fear of death. Winnie Richards tells Jack that the sight of a grizzly bear is "so electrifyingly strange that it gives you a renewed sense of yourself—a fresh

awareness of the self—the self in terms of a unique and horrific situation." Jack responds, "Fear is self-awareness raised to a higher level." "That's right," Winnie answers. "And death?" Jack asks. "Self, self, self," she says. "If death can be seen as less strange and unreferenced, your sense of self in relation to death will diminish, and so will your fear." "What do I do to make death less strange?" Jack implores. "How do I go about it?" Winnie's frustrating answer: "I don't know." (229).

WORKS CITED

Anderson, Laurie. "Oh Superman." *Big Science*. Warner Brothers Records BSK 3674, 1982.

Baudrillard, Jean. "The Ecstasy of Communication." In Hal Foster: 126–34.

———. *The Ecstasy of Communication*. Translated by Bernard Schutze and Caroline Schutze. Edited by Slyvere Lotringer. New York: Semiotexte, 1987.

Becker, Ernest. *The Denial of Death*. New York: Free Press, 1973.

Crowther, Hal. "Clinging to the Rock: A Novelist's Choices in the New Mediacracy." *Introducing Don Delillo*. Edited by Frank Lentricchia.

DeLillo, Don. *The Names*. New York: Vintage, 1989.

———. *Players*. New York: Vintage, 1989.

———. *White Noise*. New York: Penguin Books, 1986; The Viking Critical Library, 1998.

———. *Libra*. New York: Penguin Books, 1991.

———. *Mao II*. New York: Penguin Books, 1992.

———. "Pafko at the Wall." *Harper's* (October 1992): 35–70.

———. "An Interview with Don DeLillo." Interview with Tom LeClair. *Contemporary Literature* 23 (1982): 19–31.

———. " 'An Outsider in This Society': An Interview with Don DeLillo." Interview with Anthony DeCurtis. In *Introducing Don DeLillo*. See also page 329 of this volume.

———. "Don DeLillo: The Art of Fiction." Interview with Adam Begley. *Paris Review* 35:128 (1993): 275–306. See also page 331 of this volume.

Foster, Dennis A. "Alphabetic Pleasures: *The Names*." In *Introducing Don DeLillo*, 157–73.

Foster, Hal, ed. *The Anti-Aesthetic: Essays on Postmodern Culture*. Port Townsend, Wash.: Bay Press, 1983.

Frow, John. "The Last Things Before the Last: Notes on White Noise." See page 417 of this volume.

Jameson, Fredric. "Postmodernism, or the Cultural Logic of Late Capitalism. *New Left Review* 146 (1984): 53–91.

———. *Postmodernism, or the Cultural Logic of Late Capitalism*. Durham, N.C.: Duke University Press, 1991.

LeClair, Tom. *In The Loop: Don DeLillo and the Systems Novel*. Urbana: University of Illinois Press, 1987. See also page 387 of this volume.

Lentricchia, Frank, ed. *Introducing Don DeLillo*. Durham, N.C.: Duke University Press, 1991.

———. *New Essays on* White Noise. New York: Cambridge University Press, 1991.

———. "Libra as Postmodern Critique." *Introducing Don DeLillo*, 191–213.

Lyotard, Jean-Francois. *The Postmodern Condition: A Report on Knowledge*. Minneapolis: University of Minnesota Press, 1984.

Morris, Matthew J. "Murdering Words: Language in Action in Don DeLillo's *The Names*." *Contemporary Literature* 30:1 (1989): 113–22.

Pynchon, Thomas. *The Crying of Lot 49*. New York: Harper, 1986.

Weinstein, Arnold. *Nobody's Home: Speech, Self, and Place in American Fiction From Hawthorne to DeLillo*. New York: Oxford University Press, 1993.

Wilcox, Leonard. "Baudrillard, Don DeLillo's *White Noise*, and the End of Heroic Narrative." *Contemporary Literature* 32 (1991): 346–65.

Wings of Desire. Directed by Wim Wenders. 1987.

Arthur M. Saltzman

Arthur M. Saltzman is professor of English at Missouri Southern State College. His most recent books are *The Novel in the Balance* and *This Mad "Instead": Governing Metaphors in Contemporary American Fiction*.

THE FIGURE IN THE STATIC: *WHITE NOISE*

In the course of naming contemporary novels he admires, Don DeLillo credits their importance to their common capacity to "absorb and incorporate the culture without catering to it" (Interview with Begley, 290). In DeLillo's own fiction, the challenge has always been to find a way of simultaneously engaging and resisting "the ambient noise," and that challenge has been answered by means of novels whose cunning does not compose its materials into some decorous conclusion. The DeLillo protagonist must locate some reliable avenue of free agency, some outpost of personal dimension, in face of ambiguous threats disclosed (although never completely elucidated) by the same sensitivities that recognize the need for aesthetic refuge.

For DeLillo himself, the paradox lies at the heart of the writer's profession: he must break the grip of idiom while continuing to exploit its pressures artistically. "Word on a page, that's all it takes to help him separate himself from the forces around him," he declares (Interview with Begley, 277). Nevertheless, even as the writer hammers privileged habitats and crafts vantages above the vague extratextual roil—"How liberating to work in the margins outside the central perception," claims archaeologist Owen Brademas in *The Names* (77)—his task is to assimilate, not to exclude.[1] Thus DeLillo goes on in this same

From *Modern Fiction Studies* 40:4 (Winter 1994).

interview to compromise the so-called ideal segregation of the novelist:

> You want to exercise your will, bend the language your way, bend the world your way. You want to control the flow of impulses, images, words, faces, ideas. But there's a higher place, a secret aspiration. You want to let go. You want to lose yourself in language, become a carrier or messenger. The best moments involve a loss of control. It's a kind of rapture, and it can happen with words and phrases fairly often–completely surprising combinations that make a higher kind of sense, that come to you out of nowhere. (Interview with Begley, 282)

Notice the trammeled quality of DeLillo's "rapture": he is describing a release saturated with words, which retain the effects of everyday use. Whatever transcendence he pretends to is derivative, obligated to the medium whose undertow he means to supervene.

As DeLillo redefines the terms of access and surrender to language, arbitrating his contradictory drives, he arrives at metaphor, which encapsulates the anxious status between planned exactitude and exhilaration, between decision and accident, out of which he prefers to constitute his projects. In *White Noise*, however, the task is further complicated by the way in which figures are disarmed by the flood of data, cultural debris, and otherwise indigestible stimuli that contribute to the condition that titles the novel. Whereas metaphor depends upon uniqueness and verbal defamiliarization to earn attention, white noise thwarts distinction, for the proliferation of language, typically through such vulgarized forms as advertisements, tabloid headlines, and bureaucratic euphemisms, submerges difference into the usual cultural murmur. There is always more, but always more of the same. The danger as it is defined in *Great Jones Street*, is "sensory overload" (252): technological fallout in all its multifarious forms, including such linguistic manifestations as secret codes, arcana, and all the kabbala of conspiracy. "I realized the place was awash in noise," Jack Gladney notes as he moves through the burnished interiors of the supermarket. Here everything has an exclamatory glow about it, a euphemistic sheen to needs manufactured and met. But dread penetrates: "The toneless systems, the jangle and skid of carts, the loudspeaker and coffee-making machines, the cries of children. And over it all, or under it all, a dull and unlocatable roar, as of some form of swarming life just outside the range of human apprehension" (*White Noise*, 36).[2]

Anxiety is awareness that remains on the far side of enlightenment. During an interaction with an automatic bank teller, Jack thinks, "The system was invisible, which made it all the more impressive, all the more disquieting to deal with." Hence, there is not much consolation in the sense that "we were in accord, at least for now. The networks, the circuits, the streams, the harmonies," if such congruities reduce their consumers (46).

Faced with that prospect, the DeLillo protagonist tends to respond with atavistic recoil, seeking out communes, caverns, and other enclaves of pristine, primitive behavior. Reacting to chemical disaster, Jack realizes that he and a fellow victim of the dispersal are speaking to one another from an "aboriginal crouch" (137), a posture of withdrawal that seems to suggest a kind of Ur-conspiracy on the most instinctive level of human exchange.[3] Ironically, then, efforts to escape depersonalization end up verifying its influence. For Gary Harkness in *End Zone*, the disease is "team spirit"; for rock star Bucky Wunderlick in *Great Jones Street*, it is the tide of adoration of his fans; for Bill Gray in *Mao II*, it is the phenomenon of the crowd, the reinforced huddle and animate pack in whose context, argues Elias Canetti in *Crowds and Power*, "liberation can be found from all stings" (Canetti, 327). Its mutuality and density are pitted against surrounding tensions, as seen in the phenomenon of the arena:

> There is no break in the crowd which sits like this, exhibiting itself to itself. It forms a closed ring from which nothing can escape. The tiered ring of fascinated faces has something strangely homogenous about it. It embraces and contains everything which happens below; no-one relaxes his grip on this; no-one tries to get away. Any gap in the ring might remind him of disintegration and subsequent dispersal. But there is no gap; this crowd is doubly closed, to the world outside and in itself. (Canetti, 28)

The crowd is an agreement whose main objective is to "form a shield against *their* own dying" at the cost of *one's* own dying (*White Noise*, 73; italics mine).

"There's something about a crowd which suggests a sort of implicit panic," DeLillo contends. "There's something menacing and violent about a mass of people which makes us think of the end of individuality, whether they are gathered around a military leader or around a holy man" (Interview with Nadotti, 87). It is a theme to which he often returns in his fiction, perhaps most memorably in *Mao II*, which is a novel obsessed by the terrifying *and* the numbing impact of human surfeit:

> The rush of things, of shuffled sights, the mixed swagger of the avenue, noisy storefronts, jewelry spread across the side-

> walk, the deep stream of reflections, heads floating in windows, towers liquefied on taxi doors, bodies shivery and elongate, all of it interesting to Bill in the way it blocked comment, the way it simply rushed at him, massively, like your first day in Jalalabad, rushed and was. Nothing tells you what you're supposed to think of this. (*Mao II*, 94)

Crowds may confer magnitude, or at least the illusion of magnitude, but its price is clarity—a hemorrhage in the field of vision. Images and ideals are exaggerated, leaving the human equivalent of white noise.

In his novella, *Pafko at the Wall*, DeLillo explains, "Longing on a large scale is what makes history" (35), and crowds (here, the crowd gathered at the Polo Grounds for the Giants' pennant-clinching victory) are the collaborative embodiment of that longing. Once again, the crowd operates as a self-conscious entity in search of historical dimension of its own, not just the satisfaction of standing witness to history. Indeed, the baseball crowd has historical reach: it is temporally extended through retellings of the game down through the generations and spatially extended through radio broadcasts into remote, anonymous precincts, later to be reborn as mythic coherences ("I remember where I was when Bobby Thomson's shot was heard 'round the world' . . .").[4] Once again, the media fortify this sensation of significant assembly, of "the kindred unit at the radio, old lines and ties and propinquities" on which the announcer bases his faith: "He pauses to let the crowd reaction build. Do not talk against the crowd. Let the drama come from them" (*Pafko*, 55, 58). And once again, the expense of team spirit is a waste of self, as our announcer realizes when, in the wake of celebration, he has to "get down to the field and find a way to pass intact through all that mangle" (*Pafko*, 62). In DeLillo's fiction, one tries to defect from the failure of differentiation, but his defection threatens disappearance.

A denuded language deprived of texture and abiding context is both another example and a means of disseminating the disease of attrition. Whereas the language of *Ratner's Star* constituted a naked assault on the sensibilities of the uninitiated—Billy Twillig is occasionally frightened by the "intimation of compressed menace" contained in scientific jargon—the language of *White Noise* is more threatening for being so commonplace. It lulls us into its death. Circumambient infection seems to have no origin, when in fact, no meditation escapes linguistic mediation; and because commercials, official press releases, academic pedantries, and the like foster verbal regimentation, that mediation must be viewed as co-optation of private motives. Even transcendence is leveraged at this level; satori is scripted according to the tawdriest common denominator, as Jack witnesses through his daughter

Steffie's talking in her sleep: "I was convinced she was saying something, fitting together units of stable meaning. I watched her face, waited. Ten minutes passed. She uttered two clearly audible words, familiar and elusive at the same time, words that seemed to have a ritual meaning, part of a verbal spell or ecstatic chant, *Toyota Celica* . . ." (155). The familiar is elusive on the one hand, inescapable on the other. Advertisers have pre-programmed the content and destination of our associations, so even when we imagine, we tend to imagine in the direction of media-induced debts, as evidenced by Jack's own relation of seeing his sleeping children to a "TV moment" or of cloud formations to brand-name mints and gums [see "Notes," this volume, pages 424, 428]. Although Steffie appears to be mumbling "a language not of this world," closer inspection reveals that it is utterly of this world, a carrier of the same grim stimulants, at once as synthetic and as deadly as Nyodene D.

Thus the novel is filled with disappointed verges—DeLillo builds to the point of revelation, only to resubmerge into the usual blather. Gladney's sentences exhibit "something like shock, a seeming inability to sort into contexts and hierarchies the information he receives and the thinking he does" [see "Closing," this volume, page 391], which is to say that they repeat what they mean to address critically. For instance, here is Jack completing a frantic bout of dispossession of his personal ballast:

> I stalked the rooms, flinging things into cardboard boxes. Plastic electric fans, burnt-out toasters, *Star Trek* needlepoints. It took well over an hour to get everything down to the sidewalk. No one helped me. I didn't want help or company or human understanding. I just wanted to get the stuff out of the house. I sat on the front steps alone, waiting for a sense of ease and peace to settle in the air around me.
>
> A woman passing on the street said, "A decongestant, an antihistamine, a cough suppressant, a pain reliever." (262)

The prophets are sick with the same disease; promises of solace, words of cure, are contaminated by the same plague of enervation. The same congestion in the house is in the air. White noise becomes the societal equivalent of cliché, the uniform influx in which particularity dissolves into static, and the metamorphic potential of words may not be heard above the universal monotone toward which all utterances tend.[5]

If routine tethers ecstasy, it also reins in raw panic. The death fears that assault Jack and Babette Gladney are more invidious for the illusion of inviolability in which they grow. Here in the quiet college town of Blacksmith, "We're not smack in the path of history and its contaminations" (85); television provides contact with trauma, of course, but it is a sublimely conditioned contact, filtered by the promise of distance. No wonder, then, that when the Airborne Toxic Event strikes, not only are the townspeople forced to rely on simulated behaviors, having had no other context to turn to, they are simultaneously threatened and mollified by the impenetrability of the experience. The cloud itself, an unpredictable, protean mass, is identified by inconsistent reports and linguistic evasions. Although it is designated by news reports as a "feathery plume," then recast as "a black billowing cloud," neither reliably approximates the threat whose malignancy is also a matter of its resistance to metaphorical compartmentalization: it is "Like a shapeless growing thing," Jack offers. "A dark black breathing thing of smoke. Why do they call it a plume?" (111). They do it to console the population with definition—to show that they have literally come to terms with the thing and to batten down our hunches with official rhetoric. So goes the romance of postulation. Uncircumscribable, nebulous in content, contour and consequence, the passage of the toxic event is assimilated with astonishing rapidity into the normative, where its ambiguities do not cease but rather function undetected among so many others. Consumers are returned to their polished matrices. Meaning restabilizes where the gravity of dailiness draws it out.

A similar irony infects the Gladneys' several strategies of psychic insulation against their death fears. With the urgency of addicts or patriots, they accumulate material possessions to defend their sense of presence, to lend them personal density and the illusion of spiritual "snugness" (20). Unfortunately, as Jack realizes, conspicuous consumption is self-defeating: "Things, boxes. Why do these possessions carry such sorrowful weight? There is a darkness attached to them, a foreboding" (6). Their daughter, a rapt collector of childhood memorabilia, seeks to protect her own history: "It is part of her strategy in a world of displacements to make every effort to restore and preserve, keep things together for their value as remembering objects, a way of fastening herself to a life" (103). But abundance numbs only so far, and stays against death seem deadly themselves.

From this perspective, Murray Siskind's rhapsodies on congestive kitsch contain warnings against the very swaddlings they celebrate and contribute to. Jack's colleague and confidant, Siskind has made a handsome career out of extracting "psychic data" from such concentrations of camp as cineplexes, malls, and ballparks.

> Supermarkets this large and clean and modern are a revelation to me. I spent my life in small steamy delicatessens with

> slanted display cabinets full of trays that hold soft wet lumpy matter in pale colors. High enough cabinets so you had to stand on tiptoes to give your order. Shouts, accents. In cities no one notices specific dying. Dying is a quality of the air. It's everywhere and nowhere. (38)

The burden of this informal lecture is that we can ride the exponential increase of the supermarket out of oblivion and shape identities that belie analogy to "soft lumpy matter in pale colors." Malls and supermarkets are our epiphanic parlors, bastions of spiritual purchase. Murray Siskind delights and prospers in "the trance of matter," to use a phrase of poet Sharon Olds ("The Swimmer"). However, as this analysis of the glamour of groceries progresses, plenitude proves just as lethal to uniqueness and individuality. Infinity is only the far pole of confinement—the anonymity of endless shelves of generic items. Fewer citizens may crowd the scope in smaller towns, but their distinctive markings—the Tide above the Maytag, the Mazda ticking in the garage—hardly distinguish them from their urban counterparts, nor are they spared. The appetite for favored brands robs us of contact even with our own dying. Shopping suffocates us in the fortifications it supposedly effects; the hollow men *are* the stuffed men.

If death is capitulation to rutted beliefs and behaviors, life is refutation of predictability. When Jack enters a state of frenzied dispossession, trying to slough the personal sediment that fills his house, he finds "an immensity of things, an overburdening weight, a connection, a mortality" (262). Blessed excess reveals its lethal propensities. We may recall Daniel Isaacson's creed in E. L. Doctorow's *The Book of Daniel:* "The failure to make connections is complicity" (*Book of Daniel*, 227). Here, the making of connections paradoxically complies with the Establishment because even meditation and desire are prechanneled. So it seems that when Jack determines to avenge the adultery of Babette at the hands of Willie Mink, alias Mr. Gray, to whom she has traded sexual favors for a supply of Dylar, he is inspired less by moral outrage than by the "advance of consciousness" occasioned by his decision (in deference to Siskind's logic) to become a killer rather than a dier—the most heinous manifestation of Jack's assimilation of Hitler Studies. Ideally, shooting Gray would be like smashing through the television: reclaiming immediacy by reviving the visceral.[6]

The precision of plotting exhilarates him: "With each separate step, I became aware of processes, components, things relating to other things. Water fell to earth in drops. I saw things new" (304). Here is discreteness wrested from the general slur. Single-mindedness enables Jack to approach the psychic plateau that his sleeping daughter could not:

> I continued to advance in consciousness. Things glowed, a secret life rising out of them. Water struck the earth in elongated orbs, splashing drams. I knew for the first time what rain really was. I understood the neurochemistry of my brain, the meaning of dreams (the waste material of premonitions). Great stuff everywhere, racing through the room, racing slowly. A richness, a density. I believed everything. (310)

That this advance results from a murderous commitment makes us hesitate to embrace it, and indeed, close reading reveals its insufficiency. For while the world lays out so invitingly, expansive and elemental at the same time, the effect—"I believe everything"—shows Jack to be overwhelmed by a wealth of stimulants.

There is really no difference between this open admission policy to every spectacle and a wholesale renunciation of the capacity for disbelief, as is indicated by Jack and Babette's willingness to accept as true the craziest headlines out of the supermarket tabloids. What more comfortable disease is there than adoration? How secure the transfixion by such glossy fictions, the dependable "grip of self-myth" (72)? The plausible quickly escalates into the portentous, until no speck, no deception, is large enough to cause the undifferentiating transparent eyeball to wince at all: "The extra dimensions, the super perceptions, were reduced to visual clutter, a whirling miscellany, meaningless" (313). In other words, Jack has not earned an unco-opted vantage point above the conditioned atmosphere of television antennae. His resolve is psychopathic, not poetical; he is as much a political zombie as he ever had been meekly encysted in his Hitler Studies chair.

Earlier in the novel, Jack experienced a myoclonic jerk that shattered his sleep, and perhaps that is what he is hoping to accomplish by shooting Willie Mink—a sudden, inarticulate decompression that breaks through the unremitting dial tone that is contemporary American consciousness (and which variously masquerades as theme parks, jingoism, or religious awe). The point is, however, that the myoclonic jerk is, like *déja vù*, untrustworthy, a synaptic glitch. It is likelier what preempts insight, not the insight itself. Similarly, the novel's typical refrains—the sound of clothes twisting in the dryer, a commercial announcement, the dance of taillights on the highway—seem heavy with prescience when they may actually represent nothing more than the sporadically detectable horizon of "brain fade."

As a random gathering of townspeople dispossessed by the toxic cloud sifts rumors, "We began to marvel at our own ability to manufacture awe" (153); when Jack later smuggles one of his wife's Dylar pills to a colleague in order to penetrate its chemistry, she explains, "We still lead the world in stimuli" (189). In each case, technology manifests breakdowns in distinguishability. White noise is a uniform distraction, so that, as with the malfunctioning smoke alarm that is *always* buzzing, no one knows how, or whether, to react. At one point Wilder starts crying with unnatural persistence. It goes on for hours unabated, as though the youngest Gladney were an early warning system of the atmospheric danger to come. Eventually, though, the urgency of his wailing gives way to something Jack interprets as keening, a practiced, inbred lament. Jack not only begins to get used to it, he finds it strangely soothing, and he thinks of joining his son inside this "lost and suspended place" where "we might together perform some reckless wonder of intelligibility" (78).[7] But the sound does not enlighten as it enfolds. When the crying ceases after seven hours, as inexplicably as it began—we might remember Emily Dickinson's "certain Slant of light / Winter Afternoons," whose massive impact is due in part to its indeterminancy—Jack ascribes mystical properties to the episode: "It was as though he'd just returned from a period of wandering in some remote and holy place, in sand barrens or snowy ranges—a place where things are said, sights are seen, distances reached which we in our ordinary toil can only regard with the mingled reverence and wonder we hold in reserve for feats of the most sublime and difficult dimensions" (79). Again, the assumption of metaphysical import is entirely a matter of faith, not unlike the faith that leads the citizens of Blacksmith to trust in anonymous officials to handle the airborne toxic event (or, for that matter, the faith that leads us to believe that salvation lies in the right combination of brand-name products). And Jack remains distant from the sublimity he imagines there.

Saturation by awe renders us immune to alert. "In the psychic sense a forest fire on TV is on a lower plane than a ten-second spot for Automatic Dishwasher All," Murray Siskind argues (67), nodding to the principal avatar of that awe. Television's *om* is carefully pitched to keep us tuned in to the All in whose ultimate impenetrability we trust. "Watching television was for Lyle a discipline like mathematics or Zen," we read in *Players* (16), but its electrostatic bath soon becomes an end in itself. So too does the surface brilliance of the local mall, wedding mass and pall, keep us sleepy with its friendly bombardment of light and promise. We become commoditized buyers, consumers consumed by pre-regulated passions, melded into the same matrix. Excess "is a sort of electrocution. . . . [t]he individual burns its circuits and loses its defenses," writes Jean Baudrillard (quoted in Keesey, *Don DeLillo,* 140). But the blissed-out buyer does not mind.[8]

The political implication of this is a sort of placidity of last resort, which during the airborne toxic event takes the form of the belief that the system responsible for engineering the crisis is also the best hope of assessing, digesting (with man-made poison-gobbling bacteria?), and rendering it harmless. The linguistic implication is the desolate voice of the novel, with its enormous clutter of gleaming cultural fragments and unborn insights that shimmer momentarily only to settle back into the collective hum. Metaphor implies a richer insistence, a greater command of hierarchy, resonance and relation, than we can marshal. Thus, white noise is literally an anaesthetic, paving the imagination for the transportation of sanctioned simulations. In this way, insulation is really infiltration, for the things we collect and consume in order to stave off mortality may be tainted by it:

> I walked up the driveway and got in the car. There were trash caddies fixed to the dashboard and seat-backs, dangling plastic bags full of gum wrappers, ticket stubs, lipstick-smeared tissues, crumpled soda cans, crumpled circulars and receipts, ashtray debris, popsicle sticks and french fries, crumpled coupons and paper napkins, pocket combs with missing teeth. Thus familiarized, I started up the engine, turned on the lights and drove off. (302)

Familiarity breeds content, a slew of duplication, our numbed slough. Everything is crumpled—DeLillo employs the same participle three times in the same sentence to emphasize the stultifying effect of modern fallout; there is nothing lyrical or empowering about familiarization in this mute, useless context. We recall Jack's being confronted by the electronic proof of his contamination by Nyodene D: graphically splayed on the computer screen, his fate seemed to him alien and beyond petitioning. "It makes you feel like a stranger in your own dying," he realizes. "I wanted my academic gown and dark glasses" (142).

Recoil is a conventional reaction to the brunt of understanding, which is to say that white noise is as likely to be treated by the characters in the novel as the cure as it is the curse. In addition to the ubiquitous bearings of personal property and media-shaped inducements, there are Jack's Hitler Studies and Babette's Dylar supply to personalize respective hiding places. By affiliating himself with Hitler, Jack pretends to guarantee himself a measure of mythical proportion; by taking Dylar, an experimental drug that presumably eliminates one's fear of death, Babette hopes to liberate her consciousness for life-affirming pursuits. However, neither tactic works. Because Hitler's posterity has to do with his perpetration of death, not with his transcendence of it—because in the end, killers and diers are tied to the same false criteria—Jack's absorption nearly destroys him. Only his human reflex—he takes the man he has accidentally wounded to the hospital—saves him. As for Dylar, not only does Babette's secret commitment to it undermine instead of enable her loving herself and her family, the drug does not work. Indeed, its side effects, grotesquely inflated in the ravenousness of Willie Mink, include extreme paranoia and the inability to separate words from things, which means that Dylar actually exacerbates what it was designed to quell.

The latter consequence in particular, a kind of Saussurean nightmare, represents the equally paralyzing converse of white noise—a murderous convergence of words and things. For if in the slather of white noise signs lose their signifying function, in the Dylar-induced psychosis (in which Jack need merely say the words "hail of bullets" to strafe his crazed adversary) signs afford no contemplative distance. Either way, we yield utterly.[9]

The consolation for both Jack and Babette is that the ambiguous sky left in the wake of the Airborne Toxic Event encourages "an exalted narrative life," which seems to render preconditioned responses obsolete—"it transcends previous categories of awe"—but has the advantage of inspiring new attitudes, new stories (324–325). In the end, neither homicidal nor pharmaceutical failures, respectively, relegate them exclusively to false electronic relations. There remain "the old human muddles" (313), which, for all the anxieties and misgivings they occasion, sustain personality with challenges to routinized beliefs and behaviors. To put it another way, not all of the "unexpected themes and intensities" buzzing in the deep structure of the commonplace are necessarily inimical to human growth even if they appear to evade human understanding (184).

To return again to linguistic consequences, DeLillo is peculiarly conscious among contemporary American writers of predicating his fictions in environments hostile to the individual's capacity to use words that have not been irrevocably sworn to prior manipulations, whose forms include official communiques and press releases (*Libra*), conventional bigotry (*End Zone*), commercialism (*Americana*), pedantry and jargon (*Ratner's Star*). To combat wholesale manipulation of language into "lullabies processed by intricate systems" (*End Zone*, 54), DeLillo proposes a creed of resistance. On the one hand, he intends to exploit the marginality of the serious writer as a posture of unassimilatability, as a means of avoiding becoming one more shelf item, which has to do not only with the thematic politicization of the novel but also with the tinge of dread that structural unresolvability instills. On the other hand, he hopes to create a sense of "radiance in dailiness" that restores the edge to everything we have accumulated. [See interview with DeCurtis, this volume, page 330.] In *White Noise* it is seen in the spell that seems to render the post-toxic event sky incandescent. "The sky takes on content, feeling, an exalted narrative life," but its effects oscillate between wonder and dread, between inspiration and angst (324–325). What *is* certain is that people linger, exchange, participate—instead of pressing heedlessly, habitually onward, they are moved to interpret and dwell upon the defamiliarized heavens.

"Symmetry is a powerful analgesic," postulated one of the crypticians housed in Field Experiment Number One in *Ratner's Star* (115). Dead metaphors deaden; clichés inspire clichéd reactions that keep ad executives, political spin doctors, and probability experts comfortable. Lyricism destabilizes the system of rutted assumptions, but because its radiance originates from dailiness, its departures actually restore the possibilities inherent in the ordinary by stoking its latencies—by extending, to use a favorite phrase of Stanley Elkin's, the range of the strange.[10] Tenor and vehicle—worldly origin and word-driven ambition—are interdependent components of successful metaphorical operations, which promise a livelier, more vivid transaction than what grocers or governments purvey. To be sure, if we accept the premise (borrowed from *The Princeton Encyclopedia of Poetry and Poetics*) that one of the defining roles of metaphor is to create "agreeable mystification" (Whalley, 490), the "powerful and storied" sky that concludes *White Noise* is a most accommodating setting for it.[11]

Although DeLillo does fashion startling metaphors in his novels, his vision of the abiding, empowering mystery of language does not solely rely on traditional metaphorical constructions. In fact, he consistently suggests that individual words have a kind of lambency at the core that goes beyond their referential employment. Owen Brademas, in *The Names*, is particularly attuned to the "beautiful shapes" of the physical constituents of words, finding letters themselves "so strange and reawakening. It goes deeper than conversations, riddles. . . . It's an unreasoning passion" (*The Names*, 36). Gary Harkness finds himself dismantling a slogan advocating rugged play to find a similar beauty beneath the meaning (*End Zone*, 18), just as Pammy Wynant intuits a discontented essence underlying a street sign (*Players*, 207), and Bucky Wunderlick turns to aleatory techniques that may discover novel, positive options outside "the mad weather of language" that society has contrived (*Great Jones Street*, 265).

I choose these examples because they are also precisely the ones alluded to by Bruce Bawer in his dismissal of such preoccupations in DeLillo's fiction as mere epistemological flap, which is to say, more of the very sort of rhetoric that DeLillo means to expose (Bawer, 41–42). Bawer is disappointed that DeLillo's characters seem to be incapable of real conversations, that they are primarily generators of theory who tend to preside like commissioned discussants or convention delegates.

Leaving aside for the moment the accuracy of this complaint—indeed, leaving aside the question of how many "real conversations" take place in, say, the drawing rooms of Henry James—let us consider just how exotic an office words are being asked to perform here. There is often an implicit dais beneath DeLillo's speakers; those who are not interpreters or social critics by trade are so by personal constitution. The fact is, we know how real people really talk, and I would maintain that DeLillo is actually exceptionally attuned to the rhythms and nuances of those conversations, not to mention the evidence of media fertilization they indicate.

As to the argument that these people do not so much talk as testify, perhaps their private verbal contrivances are efforts to extricate them from the contrivances they daily breathe and echo. Bawer's consternation that "when their mouths open, they produce clipped, ironic, self-consciously clever sentences full of offbeat metaphors and quaint descriptive details" comes from his failed expectations (Bawer, 37), but can DeLillo's assault on predictability rightly be faulted for not living up to standards of verisimilitude?[12] Perhaps no contemporary other than Thomas Pynchon is so assiduous as DeLillo when it comes to rooting out the menace that inheres beneath the smooth surfaces of contemporary America like buried drums of radioactive waste. Nowhere is that menace so insidiously compressed as in the language we absorb and employ—a menace made all the more effective by the comforts afforded by "uttering the lush banalities" (*End Zone*, 54). When speculation could be a carrier of the linguistic abuse that prompts speculation in the first place, a certain artificiality is likely to creep into one's diction. When people sense that the room is bugged, that their very vocabularies are tainted, that every utterance could itself become an airborne toxic event, a self-conscious weight accompanies even casual encounters. "What writing means to me is trying to make interesting, clear, beautiful language. . . . Over the years it's possible for a writer to shape himself as a human being through the language he uses," DeLillo argues (Interview with LeClair, 82), and a similar priority—deliberately shaping the self in the course and through the act of vocalizing the self—seems to have been bequeathed to his characters.

The question remains as to how we can counteract the haze when the haze is so inviting. "In societies reduced to bloat and glut, terror is the only meaningful act," confides a character in *Mao II*. Only the "lethal believer" has the force to resist absorption into the inertia of super-saturated cities, airwaves, consciousnesses (*Mao II*, 157). This is the source of DeLillo's reputation among detractors for reducing the spectrum of human options to either capitulation to enigma or murderous outrage (a la Lee Harvey Oswald in *Libra*). It is born out of the notion that, in the words of the chairman of the Department of American Environments at the College-on-the-Hill, "We need an occasional catastrophe to break up the incessant bombardment of information" (66), a sentiment that reiterates the suspicion voiced in *The Names* that "[t]he forces were different, the orders of response eluded us. Tenses and inflections. Truth was different, the spoken universe, and men with guns were everywhere" (*The Names*, 94). Fortunately, DeLillo also manages detonations more optimistic than bombings, yet more historically palpable than a myoclonic jerk. There are the products of the writer's imagination, which "increase the flow of meaning. This is how we reply to power and beat back our fear, by extending the pitch of consciousness and human possibility" (*Mao II*, 200). The way the athlete can suddenly invest his efforts with eloquence, "doing some gaudy thing that whistles up out of nowhere" (*Pafko*, 37), the writer can disarm the mundane, name-branded mentality and penetrate the collectivized comforts of customized buying, reading, and belief. By delivering the inexhaustible, incalculable facts of us, he has the knack of breaking through "the death that exists in routine things" (*White Noise*, 248) to restore us to wonder. Or to borrow again from *The Names*, the "hovering sum of things" remains tantalizingly aloft (123).[13] "So much remained. Every word and thing a beadwork of bright creation. . . . A cosmology against the void" (*White Noise*, 243).[14]

Not a wordless remove but a studied wonder is what may finally preserve by enlarging us. We may recall in this regard Robert Frost's idealization of the person who is educated by metaphor: while he is unafraid of enthusiasm, he specifically embraces enthusiasm that inspires the intellect and "the discreet use" of metaphor. Cruder enthusiasms—"It is oh's and ah's with you and no more"—are the stuff of "sunset raving" (Frost, 36), and are finally infertile, ineloquent (a pointed admonition, as it happens, to the rapt gazers upon the unprecedented sunsets that conclude *White Noise*). On the other hand, while Frost champions quality of expression, he recognizes that metaphor, as well as the "figurative values" it heralds, is not a permanent argument but a momentary stay: You need to know "how far you may expect to ride it and when it may break down with you" (Frost, 39). The poignancy, the beauty of metaphor is kept alive by the way that "we stop just short" of conclusiveness, as seen in the churning sky over Blacksmith and in the unsettled ending of the novel.

"Reality is not a matter of fact, it is an achievement," writes William Gass in "The Artist and Society" (282), and art is no less profound for its subtlety than other revolutionary activities. The irony is that while we admire works of art less for the theses they profess than for "the absolute way in which they exist" (Gass, 282), that absolute existence is not as simple as a political rally or an explosion. As DeLillo assesses them, the recurring themes in his novels are "Perhaps a sense of secret patterns in our lives. A sense of ambiguity." [See interview with DeCurtis, this volume, page 329.] Patterns attended by ambiguities—art posits the former while respecting the latter.

Throughout his canon, DeLillo discredits the "subdue and codify" mentality on two grounds: its sheer inadequacy and its imitation of absolutist behaviors (which also include the bright-packaging-to-blissful-purchase reflex). On the contrary, the artist "is concerned with consciousness, and he makes his changes there. His inaction is only a blind, for his books and buildings go off under everything—not once but a thousand times" (Gass, 288). Or as Richard Poirier puts it, skepticism is the lesson and the legacy of our greatest poets, artists, and intellectuals; it inhabits the words they use to interrogate the words we use, and it results in "a liberating and creative suspicion as to the dependability of words and syntax, especially as it relates to matters of belief in the drift of one's feelings and impressions" (Poirier, 5). When the revolution goes well, the sentences the writer hands down do not consign us to locked rooms but refute them. And so it is in *White Noise*, where DeLillo whistles in an undissipating but most precipitous dark.

NOTES

1. By contrast, the same novel relates through James Axton the risk analyst's lament: "We have our self-importance. We also have our inadequacy. The former is a desperate invention of the latter" (*The Names*, 5). The liberated artist may be the marooned artist.
2. In the following exchange, the possibility is advanced that this subterranean buzz is not just death's harbinger but the thing itself:

   "What if death is nothing but sound?"
   "Electrical noise."
   "You hear it forever. Sound all around. How awful."
   "Uniform, white." (*White Noise*, 198)

3. "At the edge of every disaster," we learn in *Great Jones Street*, "people collect in affable groups to whisper away the newsless moment and wait for a messenger from the front" (254). In this novel as well, people come to rely on tranquilizers to short-circuit input and to help "run the lucky hum through our blood" (138).
4. In an example of a simulacrum readily relatable to *White Noise* and meriting the attention of Jean Baudrillard, these were also the days of

"ghost game" broadcasts, in which nimble announcers had to re-create on radio the illusion of games wholly on the basis of inning-by-inning statistics received over the wire. "In this half-hell of desperate invention he did four years of Senators baseball without ever seeing them play" (*Pafko*, 45).

5. Consider in this regard the paradoxical tourist trap of the most photographed barn in America. The collective perception confers an aura of importance upon its object, but because its uniqueness is based on extraordinary familiarity, uniqueness is actually overwhelmed by the cumulative effect of a "maintained" image. We no longer see the barn so many see the same way (*White Noise*, 12–13).
6. Mr. Gray serves as a nominal and psychological precursor to Bill Gray, the shadow-dwelling author who is rudely thrust into the spotlight of world events in *Mao II*.
7. Compare the novel-in-progress being authored by Tap in *The Names*, whose dynamic, untotalizable progress of "White words . . . Pure as the drivelin' snow" (*The Names*, 336) offers an optimistic spin to DeLillo's consistent sense that language proliferates engimas it cannot dissolve. Art is not the antidote to the environment it derives from.
8. Arguably, he does not have the *ability* to mind. In "The Ecstasy of Communication," Baudrillard describes his pathology as "this state of terror proper to the schizophrenic: too great a proximity of everything, the unclean promiscuity of everything which touches, invests and penetrates without resistance, with no halo of private protection . . ." (Baudrillard, 132).
9. A related malady afflicts James, the mathematician's assistant in DeLillo's play *The Engineer of Moonlight*: instead of grunting, he says "grunt," or, panicked, says "Loud and prolonged cries for help" (44).
10. Similarly, DeLillo's refusal to tie up the numerous loose ends of his narrative (the result of Jack's diagnosis, whether Murray gets approval for his Elvis Studies center, and so on) actually helps to keep *White Noise* from the inevitable deathward progress to which, so it is rumored in the novel, all plots tend (Zinman, 77).
11. John Frow suggests that we might speak of an "airborne *aesthetic* event" in the wake of the toxic scare. He quickly notes, however, that this does not replace the poisonous cloud but joins with it [see page 418 of this volume]. In other words, the beautiful, protracted sunsets that conclude *White Noise* are, like good metaphors, mysterious incorporations, open-ended messages.
12. "I do sort of emit a certain feudal menace," concedes a character in *Players* (171), and this is the manner of expression Bawer indicts. In fact, this quality goes beyond the conversational arcane. At the end of that novel, for example, the sight of a naked woman asleep in bed

prompts the following considerations: how women "seem at such times to embody a mode of wholeness, an immanence and unit truth . . . "; how motels tend "to turn things inward" and serve as repositories of private fears; how bucolic street names constitute "a liturgical prayer, a set of moral consolations"; and how sunlight through the window reveals "the animal glue of physical properties and functions," thereby "absolving us of our secret knowledge" (*Players*, 209–212). Evidently, nothing is off-hand in DeLillo, every moment is richly textured and tilled, charged with scholarship and suspicion.

13. The trick, of course, is to distinguish this presumably enabling "hovering sum" from the tactical deceptions of the power elite, as David Ferrie puts it in *Libra*: "There's something they aren't telling us. Something we don't know about. There's more to it. There's always more to it. This is what history consists of. It's the sum total of all the things they aren't telling us" (321).
14. Capitulation to the void takes several forms in the novel, including Steffie's eager acceptance of the role of disaster victim during simulation exercises and competitions among Jack's colleagues as to who can drive longest on the highway with his eyes shut. This is the Zen of self-erasure without transcendent end.

WORKS CITED

Baudrillard, Jean. "The Ecstasy of Communication." Translated by John Johnston. *The Anti-Aesthetic: Essays on Postmodern Culture*. Edited by Hal Foster. Port Townsend, Wash.: Bay Press, 1983: 126–34.

Bawer, Bruce. "Don DeLillo's America." *New Criterion* 3 (April 1985): 34–42.

Canetti, Elias. *Crowds and Power*. Translated by Carol Stewart. New York: Viking, 1963.

DeLillo, Don. *Americana*. Boston: Houghton Mifflin, 1971.

———. "Don DeLillo: The Art of Fiction." Interview with Adam Begley. *Paris Review* 35:128 (Fall 1993): 275–306. See also page 331 of this volume.

———. *End Zone*. New York: Penguin Books, 1986.

———. *The Engineer of Moonlight*. *Cornell Review* 5 (Winter 1979): 21–47.

———. *Great Jones Street*. New York: Penguin Books, 1994.

———. "An Interview with Don DeLillo." With Tom LeClair. In *Anything Can Happen: Interviews with Contemporary American Novelists*. Edited by Tom LeClair and Larry McCaffery. Urbana: University of Illinois Press, 1983: 79–80.

———. "An Interview with Don DeLillo." With Maria Nadotti. Translated by Peggy Boyers. *Salmagundi* 100 (Fall 1993): 86–97.

———. *Libra*. New York: Penguin Books, 1991.
———. *Mao II*. New York: Penguin Books, 1992.
———. *The Names*. New York: Vintage, 1989.
———. " 'An Outsider in This Society': An Interview with Don DeLillo." With Anthony DeCurtis. Lentricchia: 43–66. See also page 329 of this volume.
———. *Pafko at the Wall*. *Harper's* (October 1992): 35–70.
———. *Players*. New York: Vintage, 1989.
———. *Ratner's Star*. New York: Vintage, 1989.
———. *White Noise*. New York: Penguin Books, 1996; The Viking Critical Library, 1998.
Dickinson, Emily. "There's a certain Slant of light." *The Poems of Emily Dickinson*. Vol. I. Edited by Thomas H. Johnson. Cambridge: Harvard University Press, 1963. 185.
Doctorow, E. L. *The Book of Daniel*. New York: Random House, 1971.
Frost, Robert. "Education by Poetry." *Selected Prose of Robert Frost*. Edited by Hyde Cox and Edward Connery Lathem. New York: Holt, Rinehart and Winston, 1966: 33–46.
Frow, John. "The Last Things Before the Last: Notes on *White Noise*." See page 417 of this volume.
Gass, William. "The Artist and Society." *Fiction and the Figures of Life*. Boston: Godine, 1971: 276–88.
Keesey, Douglas. *Don DeLillo*. Twayne's United States Authors Series 629. New York: Macmillan/Twayne, 1993.
LeClair, Tom. *In the Loop: Don DeLillo and the Systems Novel*. Urbana: University of Illinois Press, 1987. See also page 387 of this volume.
Lentriçchia, Frank, ed. *Introducing Don DeLillo*. Durham and London: Duke University Press, 1991.
Olds, Sharon. "The Swimmer." *The Father*. New York: Alfred A. Knopf, 1992: 56.
Poirier, Richard. *Poetry and Pragmatism*. Cambridge: Harvard University Press, 1992.
Whalley, George. "Metaphor." *Princeton Encyclopedia of Poetry and Poetics*. Enlarged edition. Edited by Alex Preminger. Princeton: Princeton University Press, 1974: 490–95.
Zinman, Toby Silverman. "Gone Fission: The Holocaustic Wit of Don DeLillo." *Modern Drama* 34 (March 1991): 74–87.

Paul Maltby

Paul Maltby is associate professor of English at West Chester University, Pennsylvania. He is the author of *Dissident Postmodernists: Barthelme, Coover, Pynchon* (1991) and has had articles published in *College Literature, Contemporary Literature,* and *Centennial Review*. He is currently at work on a book for the State University of New York Press that examines the narrative convention of the visionary moment from the standpoint of postmodern theory.

THE ROMANTIC METAPHYSICS OF DON DELILLO

What is the postmodern response to the truth claims traditionally made on behalf of visionary moments? By "visionary moment," I mean that flash of insight or sudden revelation which critically raises the level of spiritual or self-awareness of a fictional character. It is a mode of cognition typically represented as bypassing rational thought processes and attaining a "higher" or redemptive order of knowledge (gnosis). There are, conceivably, three types of postmodern response which merit attention here.

First, in recognition of the special role literature itself has played in establishing the credibility of visionary moments, postmodern writers might draw on the resources of metafiction to parodically "lay bare" the essentially literary nature of such moments. Baldly stated, the visionary moment could be exposed as a literary convention, that is, a concept that owes more to the practice of organizing narratives around a sudden illumination (as in, say, the narratives of Wordsworth's *Prelude* or Joyce's *Dubliners*) than to real-life experience. Thomas Pynchon's *The Crying of Lot 49* is premised on this assumption. Pynchon's

From *Contemporary Literature* 37, no. 2 (Summer 1996): 258–277. Reprinted by permission of the University of Wisconsin Press.

sleuthlike protagonist, Oedipa Maas, finds herself in a situation in which clues—contrary to the resolution of the standard detective story—proliferate uncontrollably, thereby impeding the emergence of a final enlightenment or "stelliferous Meaning" (Pynchon, 82). It is a situation that not only frustrates Oedipa, who is continually tantalized by the sense that "a revelation . . . trembled just past the threshold of her understanding" (Pynchon, 24), but which also mocks the reader's expectation of a revelation that will close the narrative.

A second postmodern response might be to assess the credibility of the visionary moment in the light of poststructuralist theory. Hence the representation of a visionary moment as if it embodied a final, fast-frozen truth, one forever beyond the perpetually unstable relationship of signifier to signified, would be open to the charge of "logocentrism" (where the transient "meaning effects" generated by the endless disseminations of language are mistaken for immutable meanings). Moreover, implied here is the subject's transcendent vantage point in relation to the visionary moment. For the knowledge that the "moment" conveys is always apprehended in its totality; there is no current of its meaning that escapes or exceeds this implicitly omnipotent consciousness. As if beyond the instabilities and surplus significations of language, the subject is assumed to be the sole legislator of meaning. (All of which is to say nothing of any *unconscious* investment in the meaning of the visionary moment.)

A third postmodern response might deny the very conditions of possibility for a visionary moment in contemporary culture. The communication revolution, seen by sociologists like Baudrillard to be the key constitutive feature of our age, has aggrandized the media to the point where signs have displaced their referents, where images of the Real have usurped the authority of the Real, whence the subject is engulfed by simulacra. In the space of simulation, the difference between "true" and "false," "actual" and "imaginary," has imploded. Hence Romantic and modernist conceptions of visionary moments—typically premised on metaphysical assumptions of supernal truth—are rendered obsolete in a culture suffused with simulacra; for under these "hyperreal" conditions, the visionary moment can only reproduce the packaged messages of the mass media.

What these three responses to the truth claims of the visionary moment share is a radically antimetaphysical stance. We see the visionary moment, with all its pretensions to truth and transcendence, exposed as (1) a literary convention, (2) a logocentric illusion, and (3) a hyperreal construct. In short, the metaphysical foundations of traditional conceptions of the visionary moment cannot survive the deconstructive thrust of postmodern thinking.

This essay will examine the status of the visionary moment in particular, and of visionary experience in general, in three of Don DeLillo's novels, namely, *White Noise* (1985), *The Names* (1982), and *Libra* (1988). DeLillo has been widely hailed as an exemplar of postmodernist writing. Typically, this assessment rests on readings that focus on his accounts of the postmodern experience of living in a hyperreality.[1] But to postmodernize DeLillo is to risk losing sight of the (conspicuously unpostmodern) metaphysical impulse that animates his work. Indeed, the terms in which he identifies visionary experience in his fiction will be seen to align him so closely with a Romantic sensibility that they must radically qualify any reading of him as a postmodern writer.

In part 2 of *White Noise*, the Gladney family shelters at a local barracks from the toxic cloud of a chemical spill. As Jack Gladney observes his children sleeping, he recounts a visionary moment. It begins as follows:

> Steffie . . . muttered something in her sleep. It seemed important that I know what it was. In my current state, bearing the death impression of the Nyodene cloud, I was ready to search anywhere for signs and hints, intimations of odd comfort. . . . Moments later she spoke again. . . . but a language not quite of this world. I struggled to understand. I was convinced she was saying something, fitting together units of stable meaning. I watched her face, waited. . . . She uttered two clearly audible words, familiar and elusive at the same time, words that seemed to have a ritual meaning, part of a verbal spell or ecstatic chant.
>
> *Toyota Celica*. (154–55)

Before I continue the quotation, consider the following issues. Up to this point, DeLillo has manipulated his readers' expectations; what we expect from Gladney's daughter, Steffie, is a profound, revelatory utterance. Instead, we are surprised by (what appears to be) a banality: "Toyota Celica." Here it looks as if DeLillo is mocking the traditional faith in visionary moments or, more precisely, ironically questioning the very possibility of such moments in a postmodern culture. After all, a prominent feature of that culture is the prodigious, media-powered expansion of marketing and public relations campaigns to the point where their catchwords and sound bites colonize not just the public sphere but also, it seems, the individual unconscious. Henceforth, even the most personal visionary experience appears to be constituted by the promotional discourses of a consumer society. However, the irony of this apparently postmodern account of a visionary moment proves to be short-lived as Gladney immediately recounts his response to Steffie's words:

> A long moment passed before I realized this was the name of an automobile. The truth only amazed me more. The utterance was beautiful and mysterious, gold-shot with looming wonder. It was like the name of an ancient power in the sky, tablet-carved in cuneiform. It made me feel that something hovered. But how could this be? A simple brand name, an ordinary car. How could these near-nonsense words, murmured in a child's restless sleep, make me sense a meaning, a presence? She was only repeating some TV voice. . . . Whatever its source, the utterance struck me with the impact of a moment of splendid transcendence. (155)

The tenor of this passage is not parodic; the reader is prompted by the analytical cast and searching tone of Gladney's narration to listen in earnest. Gladney's words are not to be dismissed as delusional, nor are they to be depreciated as those of "a modernist displaced in a postmodern world" (Wilcox, 348). The passage is typical of DeLillo's tendency to seek out transcendent moments in our postmodern lives that hint at possibilities for cultural regeneration. Clearly, the principal point of the passage is not that "Toyota Celica" is the signifier of a commodity (and as such has only illusory significance as a visionary utterance), but that *as a name* it has a mystical resonance and potency: "It was like the name of an ancient power in the sky," a name that is felt to be "part of a verbal spell or ecstatic chant." For what is revealed to Gladney in this visionary moment is that names embody a formidable power. And this idea is itself the expansive theme, explored in its metaphysical implications, of *The Names*, the novel that immediately preceded *White Noise*. Indeed, when read in conjunction with *The Names*, the metaphysical issues of *White Noise* can be brought into sharper relief.

The Names addresses the question of the mystical power of names: secret names (210, 294), place names (102–3, 239–40), divine names (92, 272).[2] For DeLillo wants to remind us that names are often invested with a significance that exceeds their immediate, practical function. Names are enchanted; they enable insight and revelation. As one character explains: "We approach nameforms warily. Such secret power. When the name is itself secret, the power and influence are magnified. A secret name is a way of escaping the world. It is an opening into the self" (*The Names*, 210).

Consider the remarkable ending of *The Names*—an extract from the manuscript of a novel by Tap, the narrator's (James Axton's) nine-year-old son, replete with misspellings. In Tap's novel, a boy, unable to participate in the speaking in tongues at a Pentecostal service, panics and flees the church: "Tongue tied! His fait was signed. He ran into the rainy distance, smaller and smaller. This was worse than a retched nightmare. It was the nightmare of real things, the fallen wonder of the world" (*The Names*, 339). These lines conclude both Tap's novel and *The Names* itself. "The *fallen* wonder of the world" connotes the failure of language, in its (assumed) postlapsarian state, to invest the world with some order of deep and abiding meaning, to *illuminate* existence. More specifically, the language that has "fallen" is the language of name, the kind of pure nomenclature implied in Genesis where words stand in a necessary, rather than arbitrary, relationship to their referents.[3] The novel follows the lives of characters who seek to recover this utopian condition of language. For example, people calling themselves "abecedarians" (*The Names*, 210) form a murder cult whose strategy is to match the initials of their victims' names to those of the place names where the murders occur—all in a (misguided) effort to restore a sense of the intrinsic or self-revealing significance of names. And note Axton's response to the misspellings in his son's manuscript:

> I found these mangled words exhilarating. He'd made them new again, made me see how they worked, what they really were. They were ancient things, secret, reshapable.
>
> . . . The spoken poetry in those words. . . . His . . . misrenderings . . . seemed to contain curious perceptions about the words themselves, second and deeper meanings, original meanings. (*The Names*, 313)

The novel suggests that the visionary power of language will only be restored when we "tap" into its primal or pristine forms, the forms that can regenerate perception, that can *reveal* human existence in significant ways. Hence the novel's inquiry into "original meanings," the concern with remembering "the prototype" (*The Names*, 112–13), when "[i]t was necessary to remember, to dream the pristine earth" (307). The "gift of tongues" is also understood as a primal, and hence visionary, language—"talk as from the womb, as from the sweet soul before birth" (306)—and, as such, it is revered as "the whole language of the spirit" (338), the language by which "[n]ormal understanding is surpassed" (307). (And far from DeLillo keeping an ironic distance from such mystical views of glossolalia, he has endorsed them in interviews.)[4] Moreover, one can hardly miss the novel's overall insistence on the spoken word—especially on talk at the familiar, everyday, pre-abstract level of communication—as the purest expression of primal, visionary language:

> We talked awhile about her nephews and nieces, other family matters, commonplaces, a cousin taking trumpet lessons, a death in Winnipeg. . . . The subject of family makes conversation almost tactile. I think of hands, food, hoisted children. There's a close-up contact warmth in the names and images. Everydayness. . . .
>
> This talk we were having about familiar things was itself ordinary and familiar. It seemed to yield up the mystery that is part of such things, the nameless way in which we sometimes feel our connections to the physical world. *Being here*. . . . Our senses are collecting at the primal edge. . . . I felt I was in an early stage of teenage drunkenness, lightheaded, brilliantly happy and stupid, knowing the real meaning of every word.[5] (*The Names*, 31–32)

The affirmation of a primal, visionary level of language which, moreover, finds its purest expression in "talk" (glossolalia, conversation) is vulnerable to postmodern critique on the grounds that it is premised on a belief in original and pure meanings. Suffice it to say here, such meanings are assumed to exist (as in some transcendent realm) outside the space of intertextuality, or beyond the "logic of supplementarity" whereby, according to Derrida, "the origin . . . was never constituted except reciprocally by a nonorigin" (*Of Grammatology*, 61).

The idea that language has "fallen" or grown remote from some pure and semantically rich primal state is characteristically (though not exclusively) Romantic, and most reminiscent of views held by, among others, Rousseau and Wordsworth. In his "Essay on the Origins of Languages" and *Confessions*, Rousseau identified speech, as opposed to writing, as the natural condition of language because it "owes its form to natural causes alone" (Rousseau, "Essay," 5). In the face of a culture that conferred greater authority on writing than on speech, he affirmed the priority of the latter on the grounds that "Languages are made to be spoken, writing serves only as a supplement to speech" (quoted in Derrida, 144). While writing "substitut[es] exactitude for expressiveness" (Rousseau, 21), the bias of speech is toward passionate and figurative expression which can "penetrate to the very depths of the heart" (Rousseau, 9). Indeed, "As man's first motives for speaking were of the passions, his first expressions were tropes. . . . [Hence] [a]t first only poetry was spoken; there was no hint of reasoning until much later" (Rousseau, 12). Moreover, it was "primitive," face-to-face speech—as opposed to the sophistications of writing, and especially the tyranny made possible by the codification of laws—that, according to Rousseau's anthropology, once bound humans together naturally in an organic, egalitarian community. And recall that in his "Preface" to the *Lyrical Ballads*, Wordsworth deplored the "arbitrary and capricious habits of expression" of poets who, following urbane conventions of writing, had lost touch with the elemental language of rustics. The latter, by virtue of their "rural occupations" (that is, their regular intercourse with nature) are "such men [who] hourly communicate with the best objects from which the best part of language is *originally* derived" (emphasis added). Furthermore, this is "a far more philosophical language" than that used by poets (*Poetical Works*, 735). Of course, all this is not to suggest that DeLillo would necessarily endorse Rousseau's or Wordworth's specific claims. But what all three share in is that familiar Romantic myth of some primal, pre-abstract level of language which is naturally endowed with greater insight, a pristine order of meaning that enables unmediated understanding, community, and spiritual communion with the world around.

If we return to Jack Gladney's visionary moment, we should note that while "Toyota Celica" may be a brand name, Gladney perceives it as having an elemental, incantatory power that conveys, at a deeper level, another order of meaning. He invokes a range of terms in an effort to communicate this alternative meaning: "ritual," "spell," "ecstatic," "mysterious," "wonder," "ancient" (155). Similarly, for Murray Siskind, Gladney's friend and media theorist, the recurring jingle "*Coke is it, Coke is it*" evokes comparisons with "mantras." Siskind elaborates: "The medium [that is, television] practically overflows with sacred formulas if we can remember how to respond innocently" (51). DeLillo highlights the paradox that while so much language, in the media society, has degenerated into mere prattle and clichés, brand names not only flourish but convey a magic and mystical significance. Hence they are often chanted like incantations: "Toyota Corolla, Toyota Celica, Toyota Cressida" (155); "Tegrin, Denorex, Selsun Blue" (289); "Dacron, Orlon, Lyrca Spandex" (52).

Earlier passages in *White Noise* derive their meaning from the same Romantic metaphysics of language as Gladney's "moment of splendid transcendence." First, consider Gladney's response to the crying of his baby, Wilder (and note, by the way, the typically Romantic impression of the mystique of desolate spaces, and the appeal to "the mingled reverence and wonder" of the Romantic sublime):

> He was crying out, saying nameless things in a way that touched me with its depth and richness. This was an ancient dirge. . . . I began to think he had disappeared inside this wailing noise and if I could join him in his lost and suspended place we might together perform some reckless wonder of intelligibility. . . .
>
> . . . Nearly seven straight hours of serious crying. It was as though he'd just returned from a period of wandering in some remote and holy place, in sand barrens or snowy ranges—a place where things are said, sights are seen, distances reached which we in our ordinary toil can only regard with the mingled reverence and wonder we hold in reserve for feats of the most sublime and difficult dimensions. (78–79)

And, for Siskind, "Supermarkets this large and clean and modern are a revelation to me"; after all, "Everything is concealed in symbolism, hidden by veils of mystery and layers of cultural material. But it is psychic data, absolutely. . . . All the letters and numbers are here, . . . all the code words and ceremonial phrases" (38, 37–38). Evidently, for DeLillo, language operates on two levels: a practical, denotative level, that is, a mode of language oriented toward business, information, and technology, and a "deeper," primal level which is the ground of visionary experience—the "second, deeper meanings, original meanings" that Axton finds in Tap's childishly misspelled words; the "ancient dirge" that Gladney hears in Wilder's wailing; the "language not quite of this world" that he hears in Steffie's sleep-talk; the "psychic data" that Siskind finds beneath white noise.

In communications theory, "white noise" describes a random mix of frequencies over a wide spectrum that render signals unintelligible. DeLillo applies the metaphor of a circumambient white noise to suggest, on the one hand, the entropic state of postmodern culture where in general communications are degraded by triviality and irrelevance—the culture of "infotainment," factoids, and junk mail, where the commodity logic of late capitalism has extended to the point that cognition is mediated by its profane and quotidian forms. Yet, on the other hand, DeLillo suggests that within that incoherent mix of frequencies there is, as it were, a low wavelength that carries a flow of spiritually charged meaning. This flow of meaning is barely discernible, but, in the novel, it is figured in the recurring phrase "waves and radiation" (1, 38, 51, 104, 326)—an undercurrent of invisible forces or "nameless energies" (12) that have regenerative powers. And how do we "tune in" to this wavelength? Siskind says of his students, who feel alienated from the dreck of popular television, "they have to learn to look as children again" (50), that is to say, to perceive like Gladney's daughter, Steffie, or Axton's son, Tap, are said to perceive. In an interview, DeLillo has observed, "I think we feel, perhaps superstitiously, that children have a direct route to, have direct contact to the kind of natural truth that eludes us as adults" ("Outsider," 302). The boy protagonist of *Ratner's Star* (1976) is considered, by virtue of his minority, more likely than adults to access the "primal dream" experience of "racial history," or "pure fable, myth, archetype"; as one character tells him, "you haven't had time to drift away from your psychic origins" (*Ratner's Star*, 264–65). And here it must be remarked that this faith in the insightfulness of childhood perception is a defining feature of (but, of course, not exclusive to) that current of Romantic writing which runs from Rousseau's *Emile* (1762), through the writings of Blake and Wordsworth, to De Quincey's *Suspiria de Profundis* (1845). For Coleridge, "To carry on the feelings of childhood into the powers of manhood; to combine the child's sense of wonder and novelty with the appearances which every day for perhaps forty years had rendered familiar . . . this is the character and privilege of genius" (*Biographia*, 49). And recall, especially, the familiar lines from Wordsworth's "Intimations of Immortality" which lament the (adult's) loss of the child's "visionary gleam," that "master-light of all our seeing"; which celebrate the child as a "Seer blest! / On whom those truths do rest, / Which we [adults] are toiling all our lives to find, / In darkness lost" (*Poetical Works*, 460–61). In *The Prelude*, Wordsworth also argued that adult visionary experience is derived from childhood consciousness, the "seed-time [of] my soul," a consciousness that persists into adulthood as a source of "creative sensibility," illuminating the world with its "auxiliar light" (*Poetical Works*, 498, 507).

The Romantic notion of infant insight, of the child as gifted with an intuitive perception of truth, sets DeLillo's writing apart from postmodern trends. For, of all modes of fiction, it is postmodernism that is least hospitable to concepts like insight and intuition. Its metafictional and antimetaphysical polemic has collapsed the "depth model" of the subject (implied by the concept of *inner* seeing) and, audaciously, substituted a model of subjectivity as the construct of chains of signifiers. In such fiction as Robert Coover's *Pricksongs and Descants*, Walter Abish's *In the Future Perfect*, and Donald Barthelme's *Snow White*, for example, we find subjectivity reconceived as the conflux of fragments of texts—mythical narratives, dictionaries and catalogues, media clichés and stereotypes.

In an interview, DeLillo has said of *White Noise* that "Perhaps the supermarket tabloids are . . . closest to the spirit of the book" [see "I Never Set Out," this volume, page 333]. What one might expect from any critique of postmodern culture is a satirical assault on the tabloids as a debased and commodified form of communication. Yet the frequency with which DeLillo cites tabloid news stories—their accounts of UFOs, reincarnation, and supernatural occurrences (see, for example, *White Noise*, 142–46)—suggests that there is more at issue than simply mocking their absurd, fabricated claims. For he recognizes our need for a "weekly dose of cult mysteries" (*White Noise*, 5), and that, by means of tabloid discourse, "Out of some persistent sense of large-scale ruin, we kept inventing hope" (*White Noise*, 146–47). In *White Noise*, the tabloids are seen to function as a concealed form of religious expression, where extraterrestrials are substituted for messiahs and freakish happenings for miracles. In short, on a wavelength of which we are virtually unconscious, the tabloids gratify our impulses toward the transcendental; "They ask profoundly important questions about death, the afterlife, God, worlds and space, yet they exist in an almost Pop Art atmosphere" [see "I Never Set Out," this volume, page 333].

White Noise abounds with extensive discussions about death and the afterlife (38, 99, 196–200, 282–92, and elsewhere), a concern of the book that is surely symptomatic of a nostalgia for a mode of experience that lies *beyond* the stereotyping and banalizing powers of the media, a mode of experience not subject to simulation. In a culture marked by an implosive de-differentiation of the image and its referent, where "Once you've seen the signs about the barn, it becomes impossible to see the barn" (12), the nonfigurability of death seems like a guarantee of a domain of human experience that can transcend hyperreality.

In another visionary experience, Gladney has mystical insight into the force—a huge, floating cloud of toxic chemicals—that threatens his life:

> It was a terrible thing to see, so close, so low. . . . But it was also spectacular, part of the grandness of a sweeping event. . . . Our fear was accompanied by a sense of awe that bordered on the religious. It is surely possible to be awed by the thing that threatens your life, to see it as a cosmic force, so much larger than yourself, more powerful, created by elemental and willful rhythms. (127)

This "awed," "religious" perception of a powerful force, which seems in its immensity capable of overwhelming the onlooker, is characteristic of that order of experience explored by the Romantics under the name of "the Sublime." The concept of the sublime has had a long and complex evolution since Longinus's famous treatise on the subject, and here it must suffice to note just one key statement that has served as a foundation for the notion of the Romantic sublime. In his *Philosophical Enquiry into the Origin of Our Ideas of the Sublime and the Beautiful* (1757), Edmund Burke advanced the following definition: "Whatever is fitted in any sort to excite the ideas of pain, and danger, that is to say, whatever is in any sort terrible, or is conversant about terrible objects, or operates in a manner analogous to terror, is a source of the *sublime*; that is, it is productive of the strongest emotion which the mind is capable of feeling" (39). Burke identified the *sources* of "terrifying" sublimity in such attributes as "power," "vastness," "infinity," and "magnificence," and among the effects of the *experience* of the sublime, he identified "terror," "awe," "reverence," and "admiration." It is remarkable that Gladney's experience of the sublime yields almost identical terms: "terrible," "grandness," "awed," "religious," "cosmic," "powerful." Moreover, such terms are familiar to us from descriptions of sublime experience in Romantic literature. For example, in *The Prelude*, in such accounts as his epiphany at the Simplon Pass and the ascent of Mount Snowdon (*Poetical Works*, 535–36, 583–85), Wordsworth frequently invokes impressions of the "awful," the "majestic," "infinity," and "transcendent power" to convey his sense of the terrifying grandeur of nature. In the violent, turbulent landscape of the Alps, he perceived "Characters of the great Apocalypse, / The types and symbols of Eternity, / Of first, and last, and midst, and without end" (536). Wordsworth's invocation of "Apocalypse," like the sense, in *White Noise*, of a life-threatening "cosmic force," reveals a defining property of the experience of the sublime: the subject's anxious intimation of a dissolution of the self, of extinction, in the face of such overwhelming power. "[T]he emotion you feel," says Burke of such "prodigious" power, is that it might "be employed to the purposes of . . . destruction. That power derives all its sublimity from the terror with which it is generally accompanied" (Burke, 65). And here it should be added that the experience is all the more disturbing because such immense power defies representation or rational comprehension (hence the recourse of Wordsworth, DeLillo, and others to hyperbole—"cosmic," "infinite," "eternal," and so on).[6]

The Romantic-metaphysical character of DeLillo's rendering of sublime experience is evident in the pivotal place he gives to the feeling of "awe." Not only is the term repeated in Gladney's description of his feelings toward the toxic cloud, but it is used three times, along with the kindred terms "dread" and "wonder," in a later account of that characteristically Romantic experience of the sublime, namely, gazing at a sunset.[7]

> The sky takes on content, feeling, an exalted narrative life. . . . There are turreted skies, light storms. . . . Certainly there

> is awe, it is all awe, it transcends previous categories of awe, but we don't know whether we are watching in wonder or dread. . . . (324)

Given the Romantics' valorization of "I-centered" experience (in respect of which, *The Prelude* stands as a preeminent example), the feeling of awe has received special attention in their literature. After all, that overwhelming feeling of spellbound reverence would seem like cogent testimony to the innermost life of the psyche, an expression of what Wordsworth, in "Tintern Abbey" and *The Prelude*, called the "purer mind" (164, 506). However, that deep-rooted, plenitudinous I-centered subject of awe is a far cry from postmodern conceptions of the self as, typically, the tenuous construct of intersecting culture codes. As noted earlier, this is the model of the self we find in the quintessentially postmodern fiction of Abish, Barthelme, and Coover, among others. It is a model which accords with Roland Barthes's view of the "I" that "is already itself a plurality of other texts, of codes which are infinite. . . . [Whence] subjectivity has ultimately the generality of stereotypes" (Barthes, 10). Evidently, DeLillo's awestruck subjects contradict the postmodern norm.[8] Finally, why create such subjects at all? Perhaps they may be regarded as an instance of DeLillo's endeavor to affirm the integrity and spiritual energy of the psyche in the face of (what the novel suggests is) late capitalism's disposition to disperse or thin out the self into so many consumer subject positions (48, 50, 83–84). In short, we might say that sublimity is invoked to recuperate psychic wholeness.

Studies of *Libra*, which identify it as a postmodernist text, typically stress its rendering of Lee Harvey Oswald as the construct of media discourses and its focus on the loss of the (historical) referent and the constraints of textuality.[9] And yet for all its evident postmodern concerns, there is a current of thinking in the novel that is highly resistant to any postmodernizing account of it. Consider, for example, this observation by David Ferrie, one of the book's anti-Castro militants:

> Think of two parallel lines. . . . One is the life of Lee H. Oswald. One is the conspiracy to kill the President. What bridges the space between them? What makes a connection inevitable? There is a third line. It comes out of dreams, visions, intuitions, prayers, out of the deepest levels of the self. It's not generated by cause and effect like the other two lines. It's a line that cuts across causality, cuts across time. It has no history that we can recognize or understand. But it forces a connection. It puts a man on the path of his destiny. (*Libra*, 339)

Observations of this type abound in *Libra*: elsewhere we read of "patterns [that] emerge outside the bounds of cause and effect" (44); "secret symmetries" (78); "a world inside the world" (13, 47, 277); "A pattern outside experience. Something that *jerks* you out of the spin of history" (384). Clearly, repeated invocations of invisible, transhistorical forces which shape human affairs do not amount to a *postmodern* rejection of empiricist historiography. Rather, this is the stuff of metaphysics, not to say the occult. Indeed, in a discussion of *Libra*, published in *South Atlantic Quarterly*, DeLillo seriously speculates on supernatural interventions in human history:

> But Oswald's attempt on Kennedy was more complicated. I think it was based on elements outside politics and, *as someone in the novel says, outside history*—things like dreams and coincidences and even the movement or the configuration of the stars, which is one reason the book is called *Libra*. . . .
>
> . . . When I hit upon this notion of coincidence and dream and intuition and the possible impact of astrology on the way men act, I thought that Libra, being Oswald's sign, would be the one title that summarized what's inside the book. ("Outsider," 289, 293–94; emphasis added)

I also cite this interview as evidence that DeLillo is more likely to endorse his characters' beliefs in transcendent realities than to dismiss them as, in the words of one commentator, a "fantasy of secret knowledge, of a world beyond marginalization that would provide a center that would be immune to the play of signification" (Carmichael, 209).

Libra appeals to the truth and sovereignty of "the deepest levels of the self," that is, the levels of "dreams, visions, intuitions" (339). Indeed, alongside those readings of the novel that point to its postmodern rendering of the subject without psychic density—"an effect of the codes out of which he is articulated" (Carmichael, 206); "a contemporary *production*" (Lentricchia, "*Libra*," 441)—we must reckon with the books' insistent focus on "another level, . . . a deeper kind of truth" (*Libra*, 260), on that which "[w]e know . . . on some deeper plane" (330), on that which "speaks to something deep inside [one]. . . . the life-insight" (28). Such appeals to insight or intuition are common in Romantic literature and conform with Romanticism's depth model of subjectivity. That model is premised on the belief that truth lies "furthest in," that is, in the domain of the "heart" or "purer mind"; the belief that truth can only be accessed by the "inner faculties" (Wordsworth), by "inward sight" (Shelley), or, recalling the American Romantics, by "intuition." "[W]here," Emerson rhetorically inquired, "but in the intuitions which are vouchsafed us from within, shall we learn the Truth?" ("Nature," 182).[10] The comparisons may be schematic but, still, are close enough to indicate that the mindset of *Libra* is neither consistently nor unequivocally postmodern. No less emphatic than the book's evidence for a model of mind as an unstable "effect" of media codes is the evidence for a model of it as self-sufficient and self-authenticating, as an interior source of insight or vision.

What are the ideological implications of DeLillo's Romantic metaphysics? A common reading of Romanticism understands its introspective orientation in terms of a "politics of vision."[11] This is to say that, first, Romantic introspection may be seen as an attempt to claim the "inner faculties" as an inviolable, sacrosanct space beyond the domain of industrialization and the expanding marketplace. Second, the persistent appeal to the visionary "faculty" of "insight" or "intuition" or "Imagination" supplied Wordsworth, Blake, and others with a vantage point from which to critique the utilitarian and positivist ethos of capitalist development. But the crucial component of the "politics of vision" is the concept of what M. H. Abrams has called "the redemptive imagination" (117–22). Abrams notes how Blake repeatedly asserts that "Imagination . . . is the Divine Body of the Lord Jesus" (Abrams, 121) and quotes from *The Prelude* to emphasize that Wordsworth also substituted Imagination for the Redeemer:

> *Here must thou be, O Man!*
> *Strength to thyself; no Helper hast thou here;*
> ....
> *The prime and vital principle is thine*
> *In the recesses of thy nature, far*
> *From any reach of outward fellowship[.]*
> (quoted in *Abrams*, 120)

What needs to be added here is that this faith in the "redemptive imagination" is premised on an idealist assumption that personal salvation can be achieved primarily, if not exclusively, at the level of the individual psyche. Indeed, this focus on salvation as chiefly a private, spiritual affair tends to obscure or diminish the role of change at the institutional level of economic and political practice as a *precondition* for the regeneration of the subject.[12] And it is a similar "politics of vision" that informs DeLillo's writing and that invites the same conclusion. DeLillo's appeals to the visionary serve to affirm an autonomous realm of experience and to provide a standard by which to judge the spiritually atrophied culture of late capitalism. Thus against the impoverishments and distortions of communication in a culture colonized by factoids, sound bites, PR hype, and propaganda, DeLillo endeavors to preserve the credibility of visionary experience and, in particular, to validate the visionary moment as the sign of a redemptive order of meaning. He has remarked, "The novelist can try to leap across the barrier of fact, and the reader is willing to take that leap with him as long as there's a kind of redemptive truth waiting on the other side" ("Outsider," 294). Yet, as we have already seen, that "leap" is into the realm of the transhistorical, where "redemptive truth" is chiefly a spiritual, visionary matter. And it is in this respect that his fiction betrays a conservative tendency; his response to the adverse cultural effects of late capitalism reproduces a Romantic politics of vision, that is, it is a response that obscures, if not undervalues, the need for radical change at the level of the material infrastructure.

The fact that DeLillo writes so incisively of the textures of postmodern experience, of daily life in the midst of images, commodities, and conspiracies, does not make him a postmodern writer. His Romantic appeals to a primal language of vision, to the child's psyche as a medium of precious insight, to the sublime contravene the antimetaphysical norms of postmodern theory. Moreover, while there is, to be sure, a significant strain of irony that runs through his fiction, it does not finally undercut his metaphysics. As Tom LeClair has noted in a discussion of *White Noise*, "DeLillo presses beyond the ironic, extracting from his initially satiric materials a sense of wonderment or mystery" [see "Closing," this volume, pages 393–94]. "Wonder" and "mystery," to say nothing of "extrasensory flashes" (*White Noise*, 34), are frequently invoked in DeLillo's writing as signifiers of a mystical order of cognition, an affirmation that the near-global culture of late capitalism cannot exhaust the possibilities of human experience. But it is precisely this metaphysical cast of thinking that separates DeLillo's fiction from the thoroughgoing postmodernism of, say, Walter Abish or Robert Coover, and that should prompt us to qualify radically our tendency to read him as an exemplary postmodern writer.

NOTES

1. See, for example, Lentricchia, "Tales" and "*Libra*"; Frow [page 417 of this volume]; Messmer; and Wilcox.
2. Perhaps the choice of title for the novel is, among other things, calculated to evoke that long tradition of Neo-Platonist and medieval mysticism which meditated on divine names. One might cite the writings of pseudo-Dionysius, author of *The Divine Names*, or the Merkabah mystics, early Kabbalists who speculated on the secret names of

God and the angels. For such mystics, the way to revelation is through the knowledge of secret names.

3. This is precisely the theme of an early essay by Walter Benjamin, who, reflecting on the degeneration of language into "mere signs," observed: "In the Fall, since the eternal purity of names was violated, . . . man abandoned immediacy in the communication of the concrete, name, and fell into the abyss of the mediateness of all communication, of the word as means, of the empty word, into the abyss of prattle" (Benjamin, 120).
4. "I do wonder if there is something we haven't come across. Is there another, clearer language? Will we speak it and hear it when we die? Did we know it before we were born? . . . Maybe this is why there's so much babbling in my books. Babbling can be . . . a purer form, an alternate speech. I wrote a short story that ends with two babies babbling at each other in a car. This was something I'd seen and heard, and it was a dazzling and unforgettable scene. I felt these babies *knew* something. They were talking, they were listening, they were *commenting*. . . . Glossolalia is interesting because it suggests there's another way to speak, there's a very different language lurking somewhere in the brain" (LeClair, "Interview with Don DeLillo," 83–84). And "Glossolalia or speaking in tongues . . . could be viewed as a higher form of infantile babbling. It's babbling which seems to mean something" (DeCurtis, "Outsider," 302). (Such comments help explain the significance of the crying of Baby Wilder in *White Noise* [78–79], an episode I shall discuss later.)
5. A little later we read: "People everywhere are absorbed in conversation. . . . Conversation is life, language is the deepest being" (*The Names*, 52).
6. Kant formulated the following succinct definition: "We can describe the sublime in this way: it is an object (of nature) the representation of which determines the mind to think the unattainability of nature as a presentation of [reason's] ideas" (Weiskel, 22).
7. Recall these lines from Wordsworth's "Tintern Abbey": "a sense sublime / Of something far more deeply interfused, / Whose dwelling is the light of setting suns" (*Poetical Works*, 164). I am indebted to Lou Caton, of the University of Oregon, for drawing my attention to a possible Romantic context for the sunsets in *White Noise*.
8. Here, I anticipate two likely objections. First, the "airborne toxic event" may seem like an ironic postmodern version of the sublime object insofar as DeLillo substitutes a man-made source of power for a natural one. Yet Gladney's words emphasize that that power is experienced as a *natural* phenomenon: "This was a death made in the laboratory, defined and measurable, but we thought of it at the time

in a simple and primitive way, as some seasonal perversity of the earth like a flood or tornado" (127). Second, I disagree with Arthur Saltzman (*Designs of Darkness*, 118–19) and others who see postmodern irony in the account of the sunset insofar as (to be sure) (1) the sunset has been artificially enhanced by pollution and (2) most observers of the spectacle "don't know . . . what it means." After all, the passage in question clearly insists on the sense of awe irrespective of these factors.

9. See, for example, Lentricchia, "*Libra*"; Carmichael; and Cain.
10. In his lecture "The Transcendentialist," Emerson asserted, "Although . . . there is no pure transcendentalist, yet the tendency to respect the intuitions, and to give them, at least in our creed, all authority over our experience, has deeply colored the conversation and poetry of the present day" ("Nature," 207).
11. Jon Klancher notes that it was M. H. Abrams who tagged Romanticism as a "politiics of vision." However, he argues that insofar as Romanticism is an uncircumscribable, historically variable category, one whose construction alters in response to "institutional crises and consolidations," its "politics of vision" can be, and has been, read as not only radical but also conservative (Klancher, 77–88).
12. It is often argued that social history gets repressed in Wordsworth's "extravagant lyricizing of the recovered self" and in his " 'sense sublime' " (Klancher, 80).

WORKS CITED

Abish, Walter. *In the Future Perfect*. New York: New Directions, 1975.

Abrams, M. H. *Natural Supernaturalism: Tradition and Revolution in Romantic Literature*. New York: Norton, 1971.

Barthelme, Donald. *Snow White*. New York: Atheneum, 1967.

Barthes, Roland. *S/Z*. Translated by Richard Miller. New York: Hill and Wang, 1974.

Benjamin, Walter. "On Language as Such and on the Language of Man." 1916. *One-Way Street and Other Writings*. Translated by E. Jephcott and Kingsley Shorter. London: Verso, 1985.

Burke, Edmund. *A Philosophical Enquiry into the Origin of Our Ideas of the Sublime and the Beautiful*. 1757. Edited by J. T. Boulton. University of Notre Dame Press, 1958.

Cain, William E. "Making Meaningful Worlds: Self and History in *Libra*." *Michigan Quarterly Review* 29 (1990): 275–87.

Carmichael, Thomas. "Lee Harvey Oswald and the Postmodern Subject: History and Intertextuality in Don DeLillo's *Libra, The Names*, and *Mao II*." *Contemporary Literature* 34 (1993): 204–18.

Caton, Lou. "Setting Suns and Imaginative Failure in Don DeLillo's *White*

Noise." Twentieth-Century Literature Conference. University of Louisville, Louisville, Ky. 1995.

Coleridge, Samuel Taylor. *Biographia Literaria*. 1817. Edited by George Watson. London: Dent, 1975.

Coover, Robert. *Pricksongs and Descants*. New York: Plume, 1969.

DeLillo, Don. " 'I Never Set Out to Write an Apocalyptic Novel.' " Interview with Caryn James. See page 333 of this volume.

———. "An Interview with Don DeLillo." With Tom LeClair. *Anything Can Happen: Interviews with Contemporary American Novelists*. Edited by Tom LeClair and Larry McCaffery. Urbana: University of Illinois Press, 1983: 79–90.

———. *Libra*. New York: Penguin Books, 1991.

———. *The Names*. New York: Vintage, 1989.

———. "An Outsider in This Society: An Interview with Don DeLillo." With Anthony DeCurtis. *Introducing Don DeLillo*. Edited by Frank Lentricchia. Special issue of *South Atlantic Quarterly* 89 (1990): 281–304. See also page 329 of this volume.

———. *Ratner's Star*. New York: Vintage, 1989.

———. *White Noise*. New York: Penguin Books, 1996; The Viking Critical Library, 1998.

Derrida, Jacques. *Of Grammatology*. Translated by Gayatri Chakravorty Spivak. Baltimore: Johns Hopkins University Press, 1976.

Emerson, Ralph Waldo. *Nature, Addresses and, Lectures*. Cambridge, Mass.: Belknap-Harvard University Press, 1971. Vol. 1 of *The Collected Works of Ralph Waldo Emerson*. 4 vols., 1971–87.

Frow, John. "The Last Things Before the Last: Notes on *White Noise*." See page 417 of this volume.

Klancher, Jon. "English Romanticism and Cultural Production." *The New Historicism*. Edited by H. Aram Veeser. New York: Routledge, 1989.

LeClair, Tom. *In the Loop: Don DeLillo and the Systems Novel*. Urbana: University of Illinois Press, 1987. See also page 387 of this volume.

Lentricchia, Frank. "*Libra* as Postmodern Critique." *The Fiction of Don DeLillo*. Edited by Frank Lentricchia. Special issue of *South Atlantic Quarterly* 89 (1990): 431–53.

———. "Tales of the Electronic Tribe." *New Essays on* White Noise. Edited by Frank Lentricchia. New York: Cambridge University Press, 1991: 81–113.

Messmer, Michael W. " 'Thinking It Through Completely': The Interpretation of Nuclear Culture." *Centennial Review* 32 (1988): 397–413.

Pynchon, Thomas. *The Crying of Lot 49*. 1966. New York: Perennial-Harper, 1990.

Rousseau, Jean-Jacques. "Essay on the Origin of Languages." Translated by John H. Moran. *On the Origin of Language*. Edited by John H. Moran and Alexander Gode. Milestones of Thought. New York: Ungar, 1966: 5–74.

Saltzman, Arthur M. *Designs of Darkness in Contemporary American Fiction*. Penn Studies in Contemporary American Fiction. Philadelphia: University of Pennsylvania Press, 1990.

Weiskel, Thomas. *The Romantic Sublime: Studies in the Structure and Psychology of Transcendence*. Baltimore: Johns Hopkins University Press, 1976.

Wilcox, Leonard. "Baudrillard, DeLillo's *White Noise*, and the End of Heroic Narrative." *Contemporary Literature* 32 (1991): 346–65.

Wordsworth, William. *Poetical Works*. Edited by Thomas Hutchinson and Rev. Ernest de Selincourt. Oxford: Oxford University Press, 1978.

Topics for Discussion and Papers

GENERAL QUESTIONS

1. What are the chief characteristics of Jack Gladney's style? What kinds of sentences does he most often employ? Does this style change over the course of the novel?
2. DeLillo's dialogue has been much praised. To what degree is it "realistic"? In what ways does it depart from documentary realism?
3. Some critics and reviewers have perceived Jack and Babette's family as a typical American family. To what degree is the family typical in its structure and interactions? To what degree is it eccentric or unusual? What other families—for example, those in television sitcoms—does it resemble? How is it different from such families?
4. Does the *White Noise* family watch a lot of TV? What kind of TV do they seem to watch? Consider the Friday night ritual of TV viewing. Does this help to bring the family together? Why or why not?
5. Compare the children's attitudes toward television with those of the faculty in the American Environments Department at Jack's college. Do any of these attitudes reflect your own views? Which of them seem most genuine or true?
6. Analyze the three-part lists that punctuate the narrative. Where do they come from? Are they Jack's commentary, or do they emerge from the "noise" around him? Could any of these lists be moved around, or does each seem to belong where it appears? Do any of them comment on the events that surround them? What does the presence of these lists of brand names and places imply about the role of advertising and television in the postmodern world?
7. What is the role of public spaces such as motels, supermarkets, and college classrooms in the novel? How are these places alike? Different?

8. Is Murray Jay Siskind right that the supermarket is full of "psychic data"? What kind of data does it present? Explore his notion that supermarkets are like temples.
9. One of DeLillo's working titles for *White Noise* was "Panasonic." Another was "The American Book of the Dead." Consider the appropriateness of all three titles. Which aspects of the novel does each emphasize? How does each open new avenues for possible exploration? Which title seems most suitable?

THINKING ABOUT THE CHARACTERS

1. Murray Siskind has been called the "villain" of the novel. What, if anything, seems "villainous" about him? What is attractive about him? How persuasive are his ideas or his ways of arguing?
2. Does Jack change in the course of the novel? Find evidence for or against this possibility.
3. To what degree does Jack see Babette clearly? What does he want from his relationship with her? How does she change in the novel, if at all?
4. Analyze each of the children's habits and behaviors. Why does each one act as he or she does? Do they change after the airborne toxic event? If so, how?
5. Is Wilder a realistically depicted child? In what ways does he seem realistic? What is his symbolic role? What does his presence provide for his mother and stepfather? Is it important that he can't speak?
6. What is Vernon Dickey's role in the novel's plot? Compare and contrast his and Jack's attitudes about mortality.

QUESTIONS ON EACH PART

"WAVES AND RADIATION"

1. Describe the various types of waves and radiation that the characters experience. Which ones are damaging? Are there any that seem beneficial? What kinds are we subjected to in our daily lives?
2. Why are the children so attracted to disaster footage? Why is it upsetting to them that the disaster that they actually experience is not televised?

"THE AIRBORNE TOXIC EVENT"

1. How do the various names given for the toxic spill change? What do these names do besides, or instead of, describing the toxic leak?

2. What does Jack mean when he says that he is a "stranger" in his own dying (142)?
3. How does Jack's attitude toward technology differ from Heinrich's? Are these just generational differences?
4. Why is Jack so impressed with Steffie's "ecstatic chant" of "Toyota Celica"? What could be perceived as "beautiful and mysterious" in her words (155)?
5. Why does the "TV man" at the end of part 2 become so upset? How might his attitude relate to Murray's comments on the "most photographed barn in America"?

"DYLARAMA"

1. Compare and contrast Murray's and Winnie Richards's comments about death. Do you agree with either one?
2. Is Willie Mink a symbol? What does he symbolize? How does his behavior resemble or differ from that of the other characters? Is Jack's confrontation with Willie Mink satisfying as a plot device?
3. Consider the nun's words about belief. Is she right that we need something to believe in? Why? Is she right that religious beliefs have all but vanished from today's world?
4. Consider the three main events in the final chapter: Wilder's tricycle ride across the interstate, the collective viewing of the sunsets, and the final visit to the supermarket. What does Wilder's ride signify? What are people looking for in the sunsets? To what degree are the novel's final words ironic? Do they show a change in Jack's attitudes about death or tabloids or supermarkets?

WORKING WITH "CONTEXTS"

1. In the interview with Anthony DeCurtis excerpted in this volume, DeLillo states that in writing *White Noise* he tried to discover and portray "a kind of radiance in dailiness." What do you think he means by this phrase? Find moments of such "radiance" in the novel. How is this "extraordinary wonder" related to "extraordinary dread"?
2. DeLillo states in " 'I Never Set Out to Write an Apocalyptic Novel' " that the tabloids are "closest to the spirit of the book." Test this statement by analyzing the role that tabloids play in the airborne toxic event chapter. Do the stories in the tabloids share any common features? Why do people read such stories? What is their "spirit"?
3. In the *Paris Review* interview DeLillo expands upon Jack Gladney's declaration that "all plots tend to move deathward" (26). Is Jack right? Think of examples that support or contradict this notion. If the state-

ment is true, what may it suggest about our reasons for reading novels? What is the relationship between Jack's comments on plot and the plot of the novel in which he exists?

4. Consider the comment from the *Americana* excerpt on page 335 of this volume that television is "an electronic form of packaging." What does this mean? To what degree does this description ring true in *White Noise* or in your own experience?
5. What does the character in the *Americana* excerpt mean by "the universal third person" (see page 335 of this volume)? Do any scenes in *White Noise* depict this person?
6. Are there any characters in *White Noise* who share the views about disasters and technology expressed in the excerpt from *End Zone* on pages 339–41 of this volume? Who? How are the attitudes in the two novels different?
7. Compare how the characters in *White Noise* watch television to Lyle Wynant's way of viewing in the excerpt from *Players* on pages 342–43. Does he resemble Jack Gladney? Jack's children?
8. Does Jack Gladney's way of turning Hitler into a pop cultural icon do justice to Hitler's actions and effects? Does he take Hitler and the Holocaust too lightly? Does DeLillo? Read "Silhouette City" (pages 344–352 of this volume): what does this essay tell us about DeLillo's attitudes toward Hitler and Nazism?
9. Compare the millennialists in "Silhouette City" to those whom Jack encounters during the airborne toxic event. Why do such people seem to welcome disasters? Are such beliefs and movements becoming more common? If so, why?
10. Read the news stories on the Bhopal toxic leak (pages 353–362).
    a. How is DeLillo's treatment of the airborne toxic event different from a journalistic report? How is it similar? How is the behavior of his characters similar or different from the reality portrayed in *Newsweek*? How do you think you would react to such an event?
    b. Compare the contents and effects of Nyodene D to those of methyl isocyanate. Would the novel be more or less effective if DeLillo had created a more obviously lethal toxin?
    c. Many early reviewers were struck by DeLillo's seeming prescience. How likely do you think a toxic spill such as the one in Bhopal, or the one in *White Noise*, is today?

USING THE CRITICAL ESSAYS

1. Frank Lentricchia isolates two "primal scenes" in DeLillo's work: the discussion of television in the *Americana* excerpt (pages 335–37), and "the most photographed barn in America" scene in *White Noise*. How,

according to Lentricchia, are these two scenes related? What makes them "primal" for Americans?

2. In his essay on pages 387–411, Tom LeClair describes the Gladney family's trash compactor as a "metaphor in the novel for the novel." To what degree does *White Noise* fit LeClair's description as a "novelistic heap of waste"? Does DeLillo, as LeClair later suggests, find in the "seeming rubbish . . . a kind of knowledge that would provide a more livable set of systemic expectations about life and death"? What knowledge is he referring to? What expectations, if any, about life and death would this knowledge seem to provide?
3. LeClair argues that the Gladney family is oppressed by uncertainty about nature, about their bodies, and about knowledge itself. In applying mechanistic or fragmented forms of thought to phenomena, he claims, they fail to see the "systemic nature of nature." What does LeClair mean by "systemic"? How can such an understanding transform uncertainty into a positive condition? What is the relationship between uncertainty and what LeClair calls "mystery," or what DeLillo, in the excerpt from the *Rolling Stone* interview (see pages 329–330 in this volume), calls a "sense of transcendence"?
4. John Frow analyzes what he calls a "new mode of typicality" in *White Noise*, and lists several scenes that dramatize this condition (see pages 421–424). What is this new typicality? Choose three scenes (drawn either from Frow's examples or from elsewhere in the novel) and analyze how each one exemplifies that typicality. Is this typicality truly new?
5. John Duvall ties together Jack Gladney's obsession with Hitler and the novel's treatment of consumerism by claiming that *White Noise* depicts an America implicated in "proto-fascist urges." (See page 433.) What does he mean by this term? How persuasive is his argument? Are there any other ways of looking at the conditions he describes?
6. According to Duvall, *White Noise* repeatedly demonstrates how televised or filmed images empty events of content and turn them into pure form. That is, television encourages us to perceive actual events in terms of prepackaged formulas. Discuss Duvall's argument. Can you think of examples from our own world that support his thesis? What sort of formulas do these examples follow? Why do we desire such formulas?
7. Frank Lentricchia and Duvall remark on Murray Jay Siskind's use of the word "aura." The current sense of the word in literary and cultural criticism derives from Walter Benjamin's famous essay. "The Work of Art in the Age of Mechanical Reproduction," which is cited by Duvall and even by DeLillo in interviews. Obtain a copy and read Benjamin's essay. How does his use of "aura" resemble or differ from DeLillo's? Is his argument applicable to *White Noise*? How?

8. Frow's and Duvall's essays in this volume discuss the influence of Jean Baudrillard on *White Noise*. Like Lentricchia, they find the "most photographed barn" incident to be highly significant. Obtain and read Jean Baudrillard's writings on "simulations" and discuss why this scene is pertinent. Which critic provides the most helpful links between DeLillo and Baudrillard? How accurate is Baudrillard's notion that reality has been supplanted by simulacra?
9. According to Cornel Bonca, *White Noise* presents language as a "massive human strategy to cope with mortality." To what degree does language operate this way in the novel? How does Bonca's assessment contrast with the Baudrillardian ideas about language and representation advanced by the other critics?
10. Find the various definitions of "white noise" in the review by Yurick and in the articles by Frow, Bonca, and Saltzman. Compare their interpretations of the title. What thematic aspects does each one emphasize? Is there some significance to the title that all of these critics miss?
11. Saltzman cites DeLillo's admiration for art works that "absorb and incorporate the culture without catering to it." (See page 480.) How, according to Saltzman, does *White Noise* perform this difficult feat? Do you agree that the novel manages to avoid merely "catering to" our culture? Why or why not?
12. Saltzman believes that DeLillo's use of language counters the deadening effects of the clichés and "rutted assumptions" that the novel depicts. Find some examples of such formulaic language in the novel. Does DeLillo's style function as Saltzman suggests?
13. Maltby portrays DeLillo as adhering to a "Romantic" understanding of visionary moments. Is DeLillo a Romantic, as Maltby argues? Find instances in *White Noise* or in his other works—particularly *End Zone*, *Great Jones Street*, *Ratner's Star*, *The Names*, or *Underworld*—and show how they support or contradict Maltby's thesis.
14. How, according to Maltby, does DeLillo's depiction of children conform to Romantic ideas about childhood? You might begin by comparing his children to those of Wordsworth. Or, using Maltby's article as a guide, compare the role of Tap in *The Names* to those of the children in *White Noise*. Does anybody serve a similarly redemptive role in *White Noise*?

RESEARCH TOPICS

1. Read DeLillo's earlier novel *Running Dog* and compare the treatment of Hitler in it to the treatment in *White Noise*. You will also want to read "Silhouette City," the essay included in this volume on pages 344–52.

2. Compare the first-person narrative of Jack Gladney to those of DeLillo's earlier novels *Americana, End Zone*, and *The Names*. What do the narrators have in common? How is Gladney's style and sensibility different from those of these earlier characters? What problems do they share? Do any of them discover a solution?
3. Read DeLillo's play *The Day Room*. Consider the fact that the "television" is played by an actor in a straitjacket. Does this character resemble anyone in *White Noise*? Why might it be significant that the television is "insane"? How does DeLillo's treatment of television here help us understand *White Noise*?
4. DeLillo has acknowledged the influence of Ernest Becker's book *The Denial of Death* on *White Noise*. Peruse Becker's book and find passages that DeLillo seems to have used. How does he shape Becker's ideas for his own work? The essays by LeClair and Bonca will be helpful here.
5. Read DeLillo's story, "Videotape" (also chapter 1 of Part 2 of *Underworld*). How does the depiction of the relationship between violence and television resemble that in *White Noise*?
6. Compare and contrast the treatment of waste and garbage in *Underworld* and *White Noise*.
7. Compare the relationship between advertising and religion in DeLillo's story "The Angel Esmeralda" (now adapted into *Underworld*) to that in *White Noise*. Would *Underworld*'s Sister Edgar agree with the nun in *White Noise*?
8. Read other news stories on environmental disasters, such as Three-Mile Island or Chernobyl. How does DeLillo's portrayal resemble them? What has he emphasized? What has he underplayed?
9. Go on a shopping trip to the mall with a friend or family member. Take notes on the atmosphere, signs and kinds of purchases you make. List your purchases, distinguishing between those made for what Jack calls "immediate needs" and those made for their own sake (84). Which of the two kinds of purchases does the mall most encourage? How do the mall's signs, features, or special events attempt to promote a sense of community? What aspects of it seem to defeat that sense? Can you discover, as Jack says he does, "new aspects" of yourself by shopping in malls (84)? What, if anything, are they? Take notes on how you feel when you return. Do you too "wish to be alone" (84)? Write a brief account of your trip and what you discover.
10. Go on a half-hour shopping trip to the local supermarket with a friend or family member. List the different sounds that each of you hears. List the other forms of "psychic data." Compare notes. Write a brief account of your findings.
11. Collect three or four tabloid newspapers. What kind of stories predominate? Does *White Noise* offer an accurate picture of their stories or of the needs they seem to serve?

12. Read the works of other twentieth-century satirists such as Evelyn Waugh, Thomas Pynchon, or Joseph Heller. What are the satiric targets in each? How does DeLillo's humor differ from theirs? What underlying ethical, political, or moral values does each author seem to espouse?

Selected Bibliography

WORKS BY DON DELILLO

NOVELS

Americana. Boston: Houghton Mifflin, 1971; (Paper) New York: Penguin Books, 1989.

End Zone. Boston: Houghton Mifflin, 1972; (Paper) New York: Penguin Books, 1986.

Great Jones Street. Boston: Houghton Mifflin, 1973; (Paper) New York: Penguin Books, 1994.

Ratner's Star. New York. Knopf, 1976; (Paper) New York: Vintage, 1989.

Players. New York: Knopf, 1977; (Paper) New York: Vintage, 1989.

Running Dog. New York: Knopf, 1978; (Paper) New York: Vintage, 1989.

The Names. New York: Knopf, 1982; (Paper) New York: Vintage, 1989.

White Noise. New York: Viking, 1985; (Paper) New York: Penguin Books, 1996; The Viking Critical Library, 1998.

Libra. New York: Viking, 1988; (Paper) New York: Penguin Books, 1991.

Mao II. New York: Viking, 1991; (Paper) New York: Penguin Books, 1992.

Underworld. New York: Scribner, 1997; (Paper) New York: Scribner Paperback Fiction, 1998.

PLAYS

The Engineer of Moonlight. Cornell Review 5 (Winter 1979): 21–47.

The Day Room. New York: Knopf, 1987; New York: Viking/Penguin, 1989.

The Rapture of the Athlete Assumed into Heaven. The Quarterly 15 (1990); *South Atlantic Quarterly* 91 (1992): 241–42.

UNCOLLECTED SHORT FICTION

"The River Jordan." *Epoch* 10:2 (Winter 1960): 105–20.
"Take the 'A' Train." *Epoch* 12:1 (Spring 1962): 9–25.
"Spaghetti and Meatballs." *Epoch* 14:3 (Spring 1965): 244–50.
"Coming Sun. Mon. Tues." *Kenyon Review* 28 (1966): 391–94.
"Baghdad Towers West." *Epoch* 17 (1968): 195–217.
"The Uniforms." *Carolina Quarterly* 22:1 (Winter 1970): 4–11.
"In the Men's Room of the Sixteenth Century." *Esquire* (Dec. 1971): 174–77, 243, 246.
"Creation." *Antaeus* 33 (1979): 32–46.
"Human Moments in World War III." *Esquire* (July 1983): 118–26.
"The Runner." *Harper's* (Sept. 1988): 61–63.
"The Ivory Acrobat." *Granta* 25 (Autumn 1988): 199–212.

ESSAYS

"Notes Toward a Definitive Meditation (By Someone Else) on the Novel *Americana*." *Epoch* 21.3 (Spring 1972): 327–29.
"Total Loss Weekend." *Sports Illustrated* (27 Nov. 1972): 98–120.
"Notes on 'The Uniforms.'" *Cutting Edges: Young American Fiction for the '70s*. Edited by Jack Hicks. New York: Holt, Rinehart, and Winston, 1973 [532–33].
"American Blood: A Journey through the Labyrinth of Dallas and JFK." *Rolling Stone* (8 Dec. 1983): 21–22, 24, 27–28, 74.
"Silhouette City: Hitler, Manson and the Millennium." *Dimensions* 4:3 (1989): 29–34.
Salman Rushdie Defense Pamphlet. New York: Rushdie Defense Committee USA, 14 February 1994.
"The Artist Naked in a Cage." *New Yorker* (26 May 1997): 6–7.
"The Power of History." *New York Times Magazine* (7 Sept. 1997): 60–63.

FILM

Don DeLillo: The Word, the Image and the Gun. Broadcast 27 Sept. 1991. Directed by Kim Evans. British Broadcasting Corporation.

SELECTED INTERVIEWS AND PROFILES

Arensberg, Ann. "Seven Seconds: An Interview." *Vogue* (Aug. 1988): 337–39, 390.
Begley, Adam. "Don DeLillo: The Art of Fiction." *Paris Review* 35:128 (Fall 1993): 274–306.

Burn, Gordon. "Wired Up and Whacked Out." (London) *Sunday Times Magazine* (25 Aug. 1991): 36–39.

Champlin, Charles. "The Heart Is a Lonely Craftsman." *Los Angeles Times*, Calendar section. (29 July 1984): 7.

Connolly, Kevin. "An Interview with Don DeLillo." *The Brick Reader*. Edited by Linda Spalding and Michael Ondaatje. Toronto: Coach House Press, 1991: 260–69.

DeCurtis, Anthony. "Matters of Fact and Fiction." *Rolling Stone* (17 Nov. 1988): 113–22, 164. Longer version published as "An Outsider in This Society." *South Atlantic Quarterly* 89 (1990): 280–319, and in Lentricchia, *Introducing Don DeLillo*. Durham, N.C.: Duke University Press, 1991: 43–66.

Harris, Robert R. "A Talk with Don DeLillo." *New York Times Book Review* (10 Oct. 1982): 26.

Heron, Kim. "Haunted by His Book." *New York Times Book Review* (24 July 1988): 23.

Howard, Gerald. "The American Strangeness: An Interview with Don DeLillo." *Hungry Mind Review* 43 (Fall 1997): 13–16. (Online address: http://www.bookwire.com/hmr/hmrinterviews.article$2563)

James, Caryn. " 'I Never Set Out to Write an Apocalyptic Novel.' " *New York Times Book Review* (13 Jan. 1985): 31.

Kamp, David. "DeLillo's Home Run." *Vanity Fair* (Sept. 1997): 202–4.

LeClair, Tom. "An Interview With Don DeLillo." *Contemporary Literature* 23 (1982): 19–31. Reprinted in Tom LeClair and Larry McCaffery, eds. *Anything Can Happen*. Urbana: University of Illinois Press, 1983: 79–90.

Nadotti, Maria. "An Interview with Don DeLillo." *Salmagundi* 100 (Fall 1993): 86–97.

Passaro, Vince. "Dangerous Don DeLillo." *New York Times Magazine* (19 May 1991): 36–38, 76–77.

Remnick, David. "Exile on Main Street." *New Yorker* (15 Sept. 1997): 42–48.

WEBSITE

Don DeLillo's America. Address: http://www.haas.berkeley.edu/~gardner/delillo.html. Contains much useful information on DeLillo's novels and on critical studies of his works. For a more complete listing of interviews and profiles, readers are encouraged to consult the bibliography compiled by Curt Gardner and Philip Nel at this Website.

LITERARY CRITICISM

BOOKS

Hantke, Steffen. *Conspiracy and Paranoia in Contemporary American Fiction: The Works of Don DeLillo and Joseph McElroy*. Frankfurt: Peter Lang, 1994. *White Noise* discussed: 46–59.

Keesey, Douglas. *Don DeLillo*. Twayne's United States Authors Series. New York: Twayne, 1993.

Solid, informative overview of DeLillo's career. *White Noise* discussed on pages 133–150.

LeClair, Tom. *In the Loop: Don DeLillo and the Systems Novel*. Urbana and Chicago: University of Illinois Press, 1987.

Insightful, at times brilliant analysis of DeLillo's novels through *White Noise*, with emphasis on depicting DeLillo as a "systems novelist." *White Noise* discussed, pages 207–36.

Lentricchia, Frank, ed. *Introducing Don DeLillo*. Durham, N.C.: Duke University Press, 1991.

Reprint of a special issue of *South Atlantic Quarterly* (89.2 [Spring 1990]) on DeLillo. First-rate collection of essays on DeLillo from a variety of critical viewpoints, covering most of the novels through *Libra*. Its usefulness for students and scholars is slightly mitigated by the absence of footnotes.

Contents:

Lentricchia, Frank. "The American Writer as Bad Citizen—Introducing Don DeLillo," 1–6.

DeLillo, Don. "Opposites." Chapter 10 of *Ratner's Star*, 7–42.

DeCurtis, Anthony. " 'An Outsider in This Society': An Interview with Don DeLillo," [Longer version of *Rolling Stone* interview, cited on page 527.] 43–66.

Aaron, Daniel. "How to Read Don DeLillo," 67–81.

Crowther, Hal. "Clinging to the Rock: A Novelist's Choices in the New Mediacracy," 83–98.

McClure, John A. "Postmodern Romance: Don DeLillo and the Age of Conspiracy," 99–115.

Goodheart, Eugene. "Speculations on Don DeLillo and the Cinematic Real," 117–30.

DeCurtis. "The Product: Bucky Wunderlick, Rock 'n Roll, and Don DeLillo's *Great Jones Street*," 131–41.

Molesworth, Charles. "Don DeLillo's Perfect Starry Night" [on *Ratner's Star*], 143–56.

Foster, Dennis A. "Alphabetic Pleasures: *The Names*," 157–73.

Frow, John. "The Last Things Before the Last: Notes on *White Noise*," 175–91. Revised in Frow book cited on page 529.

Lentricchia, Frank. "*Libra* as Postmodern Critique," 193–215.

———, ed. *New Essays on* White Noise. Cambridge and New York: Cambridge University Press, 1991.
Contents:
Lentricchia, Frank. "Introduction," 1–14.
Ferraro, Thomas J. "Whole Families Shopping at Night!" 15–38.
Discusses the depiction of Gladney family and shows how in shopping and supermarkets "consumer capitalism brilliantly exploits the need for strengthening family bonds that it has itself, in part, destroyed."
Cantor, Paul A. " 'Adolf, We Hardly Knew You,' " 39–62.
Wittily analyzes DeLillo's treatment of Hitler in both *White Noise* and his earlier fiction.
Moses, Michael Valdez. "Lust Removed from Nature," 63–86.
Reading *White Noise* in tandem with Heidegger, Moses discusses the relationship between technology and nature in the novel.
Lentricchia, Frank. "Tales of the Electronic Tribe," 87–113.
Focuses on Jack Gladney as first-person narrator and protagonist as a "human collage of styles," both literary and pop-cultural.

BOOK SECTIONS

Applen, J. D. "Examining the Discourse of the University: *White Noise* in the Composition Classroom." *Miss Grundy Doesn't Teach Here Anymore.* Edited by Diane Penrod. Portsmouth, N.H.: Boynton/Cook, Heinemann, 1997. 136–46. Pedagogical essay, giving examples of how *White Noise* can be used in composition courses to enable students to think and write about the discourse communities that define contemporary culture.

Chénetier, Marc. *Beyond Suspicion: New American Fiction Since 1960.* Translated by Elizabeth A. Houlding. Philadelphia: University of Pennsylvania Press, 1996.
Contains several brief passages discussing *White Noise*; see 130–32, 183–86.

Dewey, Joseph. "The Eye Begins to See: The Apocalyptic Temper in the 1980s—William Gaddis and Don DeLillo." *In a Dark Time: The Apocalyptic Temper in the American Novel of the Nuclear Age.* W. Lafayette, Ind.: Purdue University Press, 1990: 180–229. Praises *White Noise* for offering hope and reassurance in replacing the white noise of "language" by silence. Emphasizes the hopeful aspects of the ending. *White Noise* discussed, 205–229.

Frow, John. *Time and Commodity Culture.* Oxford: Clarendon Press, 1997. 13–15, 23–36, 38–39, 45, 49, 59–61, 67–69, 79, 88–90. Revision of Frow article in Lentricchia, *Introducing Don DeLillo*, cited on page 528, and reprinted in this volume, pages 417–31.

Heffernan, Teresa. "Can Apocalypse Be Post?" *Postmodern Apocalypse: Theory and Cultural Practice at the End*. Edited by Richard Dellamora. Philadelphia: University of Pennsylvania Press, 1995 [171–81]. Reads Jack Gladney's confrontation with death in the light of "nuclear criticism" as an attempt to move beyond apocalyptic narratives and meanings.

Mottram, Eric. "The Real Needs of Man: Don DeLillo's Novels." *The New American Writing: Essays on American Literature Since 1970*. Edited by Graham Clarke. New York: St. Martin's Press, 1990: 51–98.
Survey of DeLillo's novels through *Libra*. *White Noise* discussed, 86–90.

Reid, Ian. *Narrative Exchanges*. New York and London: Routledge, 1992 [59–63].
Sharp narratological reading of pages 191–92.

Simmons, Philip E. "Don DeLillo's Invisible Histories." *Deep Surfaces: Mass Culture and History in Contemporary American Fiction*. Athens, Ga.: University of Georgia Press, 1997: 41–81.
Traces the influence of filmed images and simulacra on DeLillo's artistic vision. *White Noise* discussed, 55–65.

Weinstein, Arnold M. "Don DeLillo: Rendering the Words of the Tribe." *Nobody's Home: Speech, Self and Place in American Fiction from Hawthorne to DeLillo*. New York: Oxford University Press, 1993: 288–315.
Well-written analysis of DeLillo's use of language; finds DeLillo's depiction of family life to be heroic. *White Noise* discussed, 298–311.

White, Patti. "Toxic Textual Events." *Gatsby's Party: The System and the List in Contemporary Narrative*. W. Lafayette, Ind.: Purdue University Press, 1992: 7–27.
Reads the novel in terms of information theory, with illuminating remarks on the "trilog" lists peppering the text.

JOURNAL ARTICLES: ON *WHITE NOISE*

Bawer, Bruce. "Don DeLillo's America." *New Criterion* 3.8 (April 1985): 34–42.
Negative survey of DeLillo's fiction, focusing on *White Noise*.

Bonca, Cornel. "Don DeLillo's *White Noise*: The Natural Language of the Species." *College Literature* 23.2 (June 1996): 25–44.
Illuminating essay linking the novel to DeLillo's recurrent demonstration of the redemptive powers of language. See pages 456–79 of this volume.

Bryant, Paula. "Extending the Fabulative Continuum: DeLillo, Mooney, Federman." *Extrapolation* 30 (1989): 156–65.
Brief discussion of how *White Noise* coincides with certain aspects of "fabulative"—science-fictional—themes and strategies.

Caton, Lou F. "Romanticism and the Postmodern Novel: Three Scenes

from Don DeLillo's *White Noise*." *English Language Notes* 35 (Sept. 1997): 38–48.
Gladney recognizes but mourns the emergence of a constructed political postmodern culture, and DeLillo "maintains a romantic uncertainty throughout *White Noise*."

Conroy, Mark. "From Tombstone to Tabloid: Authority Figured in *White Noise*." *Critique* 35.2 (Winter 1994): 97–110.
Interprets Gladney's malaise as a "crisis in authority" deriving from the demise of traditional forms of cultural transmission.

Duvall, John N. "The (Super)Marketplace of Images: Television as Unmediated Mediation in DeLillo's *White Noise*." *Arizona Quarterly* 50.3 (Autumn 1994): 127–153.
Forcefully argued analysis of the "proto-fascist" role of TV. Particularly good on the use of Baudrillard and Murray Siskind's role. See pages 432–55 of this volume.

Frow, John. "The Last Things Before the Last: Notes on *White Noise*." In Lentricchia, *Introducing Don DeLillo*, reprinted from *South Atlantic Quarterly* 89 (Spring 1990): 414–29. Helpfully addresses issue of typicality, simulacra, and brand names. See pages 417–31 of this volume.

Hayles, N. Katherine. "Postmodern Parataxis: Embodied Texts, Weightless Information." *American Literary History* 2 (1990): 394–421.
Offers *White Noise* as an example of "parataxis," in which the relationship between terms is emphemeral and decontextualized.

King, Noel. "Reading *White Noise*: Floating Remarks." *Critical Quarterly* 33.3 (Autumn 1991): 66–83.
Shows the close relationship between the novel's discourses and current theories about postmodernism. Argues that *White Noise* denies us a "preferred reading position" from which to evaluate its presentation of "unverified information."

Leps, Marie-Christine. "Empowerment through Information: A Discursive Critique." *Cultural Critique* 31 (1995): 179–96.
White Noise "registers some of the difficulties of agency associated with the Information Age while inscribing the possibility of resistance and alteration."

Maltby, Paul. "The Romantic Metaphysics of Don DeLillo." *Contemporary Literature* 37 (1996): 258–77.
Persuasively examines DeLillo's depictions of visionary experiences and suggests that he espouses a metaphysics much indebted to Romanticism. Treats *White Noise* as well as *The Names*. See pages 498–516 of this volume.

Messmer, Michael W. " 'Thinking It Through Completely': The Interpretation of Nuclear Culture." *Centennial Review* 23.4 (Fall 1988): 397–413. Uses *White Noise* to exemplify DeLillo's understanding of nuclear culture via his treatment of the sublime.

Moraru, Christian. "Consuming Narratives: Don DeLillo and the 'Lethal' Reading." *Journal of Narrative Technique* 27 (1997): 190–206. Focuses on instances of misreading in *Mao II*, *Great Jones Street*, and *Libra*, as well as in *White Noise*, to show how such "lethal" readings menace inherited notions of textuality and authorship.

Parks, John G. "The Noise of Magic Kingdoms: Reflections on Theodicy in Two Recent American Novels." *Cithara* (May 1990): 56–61.
Compares the treatment of belief in *White Noise* and Stanley Elkin's *The Magic Kingdom*.

Pastore, Judith Laurence. "Marriage American Style: Don DeLillo's Domestic Satire." *Voices in Italian Americana* 1.2 (Fall 1990): 1–19.
Suggests that beneath DeLillo's satire lies a more traditional view of marriage and divorce stemming from his Italian-Catholic heritage. Also discusses the early stories "Spaghetti and Meatballs" and "Creation."

———. "Palomar and Gladney: Calvino and DeLillo Play with the Dialectics of Subject/Object Relationships." *Italian Culture* 9 (1991): 331–42.
Argues that both Calvino's and DeLillo's protagonists seek "to escape from the subjectivity of modern relativism" but end up shifting to "some quasi-religious approach."

Peyser, Thomas. "Globalization in America: The Case of Don DeLillo's *White Noise*." *Clio* 25 (1996): 255–71.
Argues that *White Noise* exemplifies how global forces impinge on old cultural boundaries and disable the concepts of boundaries and community.

Reeve, N.H., and Richard Kerridge. "Toxic Events: Postmodernism and DeLillo's *White Noise*." *Cambridge Quarterly* 23 (1994): 303–23.
Perceptive analysis suggesting how most events are incorporated into formulas or packages in the novel; "toxic events" are those that spill out and violate categories.

Saltzman, Arthur M. "The Figure in the Static: *White Noise*." *Modern Fiction Studies* 40 (1994): 807–26.
Elegantly written and incisively argued essay addressing DeLillo's use of language and the role of art and the artist. Locates *White Noise* amidst DeLillo's other work. See pages 480–497 of this volume.

Wilcox, Leonard. "Baudrillard, DeLillo's *White Noise*, and the End of the Heroic Narrative." *Contemporary Literature* 32 (1991): 346–65.
Persuasively links DeLillo's work with the analyses of Jean Baudrillard and other postmodern theorists; argues that the world of simulacra depicted in *White Noise* disrupts subjectivity and precludes the possibility of heroic narratives.

JOURNAL ARTICLES: GENERAL CRITICISM ON DELILLO

Bell, Pearl K. "DeLillo's World." *Partisan Review* 59.1 (Winter 1992): 138–46.

Bosworth, David. "The Fiction of Don DeLillo." *Boston Review* 8.2 (1983): 29–30.

Bryson, Norman. "City of Dis: the Fiction of Don DeLillo." *Granta* 2 (1980): 145–57.

Carmichael, Thomas. "Buffalo/Baltimore, Athens/Dallas: John Barth, Don DeLillo and the Cities of Postmodernism." *Canadian Review of American Studies* 22.2 (Fall 1991): 241–49. Compares *The Names* and *Libra* to John Barth's *LETTERS*.

———. "Lee Harvey Oswald and the Postmodern Subject: History and Intertextuality in Don DeLillo's *Libra*, *The Names*, and *Mao II*." *Contemporary Literature* 34 (1993): 204–18.

Edmundson, Mark. "Not Flat, Not Round, Not There: Don DeLillo's Novel Characters." *Yale Review* 83.2 (April 1995): 107–24.

Hantke, Steffen. " 'God save us from bourgeois adventure': The Figure of the Terrorist in Contemporary American Conspiracy Fiction." *Studies in the Novel* 38 (Summer 1996): 219–43. [Discusses *Players* and *Mao II*.]

Ireton, Mark. "The American Pursuit of Loneliness: Don DeLillo's *Great Jones Street* and *Mao II*." *Don DeLillo's America*: Online: http://haas.berkeley.edu/~gardner/ireton_essay.html

Isaacs, Neil D. "Out of the End Zone: Sports in the Rest of DeLillo." *Arete* 3 (Fall 1985): 85–95.

Johnston, John. "Generic Difficulties in the Novels of Don DeLillo." *Critique* 30 (1989): 261–75.

———. "Post-Cinematic Fiction: Film in the Novels of Pynchon, McElroy and DeLillo." *New Orleans Review* 17:2 (Summer 1990): 90–97.

Kucich, John. "Postmodern Politics: Don DeLillo and the Plight of the White Male Writer." *Michigan Quarterly Review* 27.2 (Spring 1988): 328–41.

Lentricchia, Frank. "Don DeLillo." *Raritan* 8.4 (Spring 1989): 1–29. [Discusses mostly *Libra*.] Excerpted in this volume, pages 412–16.

McClure, John A. "Postmodern/Post-Secular: Contemporary Fiction and Spirituality." *Modern Fiction Studies* 41 (1995): 141–63.

O'Donnell, Patrick. "Engendering Paranoia in Contemporary Narrative." *Boundary 2: An International Journal on Literature and Culture* 19 (1992): 181–204. Dicusses mainly *Running Dog*.

Oriard, Michael. "Don DeLillo's Search for Walden Pond." *Critique* 20 (1978): 5–24. Discusses the early novels.

JOURNAL ARTICLES ON SPECIFIC TEXTS

AMERICANA

Cowart, David. "For Whom Bell Tolls: Don DeLillo's *Americana*." *Contemporary Literature* 37 (Winter 1997): 602–19.

Osteen, Mark. "Children of Godard and Coca-Cola: Cinema and Consumerism in Don DeLillo's Early Fiction." *Contemporary Literature* 37 (Fall 1996): 439–70. Also discusses early short stories.

END ZONE

Benton, Jill. "Don DeLillo's *End Zone*: A Postmodern Satire." *Aethlon* 12.1 (Fall 1994): 7–18.

Burke, William. "Football, Literature and Culture." *Southwest Review* 60 (1975): 391–98.

Osteen, Mark. "Against the End: Asceticism and Apocalypse in Don DeLillo's *End Zone*." *Papers on Language and Literature* 26 (1990): 143–63.

Taylor, Anya. "Words, War, and Meditation in Don DeLillo's *End Zone*." *International Fiction Review* 4 (1977): 68–70.

Thornton, Z. Bart. "Linguistic Disenchantment and Architectural Solace in DeLillo and Artaud." *Mosaic* 30.1 (March 1997): 97–112.

GREAT JONES STREET

Osteen, Mark. " 'A Moral Form to Master Commerce': The Economies of DeLillo's *Great Jones Street*." *Critique* 35 (1994): 157–72.

RATNER'S STAR

Allen, Glenn Scott. "Raids on the Conscious: Pynchon's Legacy of Paranoia and the Terrorism of Uncertainty in Don DeLillo's *Ratner's Star*." *Postmodern Culture* 4:2 (January 1994): n.p.

RUNNING DOG

Johnson, Stuart. "Extraphilosophical Instigations in Don DeLillo's *Running Dog*." *Contemporary Literature* 26 (1985): 74–90.

O'Donnell, Patrick. "Obvious Paranoia: The Politics of Don DeLillo's *Running Dog*." *Centennial Review* 34:1 (Winter 1990): 56–72.

THE NAMES

Bryant, Paula. "Discussing the Untellable: Don DeLillo's *The Names*." *Critique* 29 (1987): 16–29.

Harris, Paul A. "Epistémocritique: A Synthetic Matrix." *SubStance* 71/72 (1993): 185–203.

Morris, Matthew J. "Murdering Words: Language in Action in Don DeLillo's *The Names*." *Contemporary Literature* 30 (1989): 113–27.

THE DAY ROOM

Pastore, Judith Laurence. "Pirandello's Influence on American Writers: Don DeLillo's *The Day Room*." *Italian Culture* 8 (1990): 431–47.

Zinman, Toby Silverman. "Gone Fission. The Holocaustic Wit of Don DeLillo." *Modern Drama* 34 (1991): 75–87. Also briefly discusses *The Engineer of Moonlight*.

LIBRA

Bernstein, Stephen. "*Libra* and the Historical Sublime." *Postmodern Culture* 4:2 (January 1994): n.p.

Brent, Jonathan. "The Unimaginable Space of Danilo Kiš and Don DeLillo." *Review of Contemporary Fiction* 14.1 (Spring 1994): 180–89.

Caesar, Terry. "Motherhood and Postmodernism." *American Literary History* 7.1 (Spring 1995): 120–40. Treats *Libra* alongside Doctorow's *Billy Bathgate* and Pynchon's *Vineland*.

Cain, William E. "Making Meaningful Worlds: Self and History in *Libra*." *Michigan Quarterly Review* 29 (1990): 275–87.

Civello, Paul. "Undoing the Naturalistic Novel: Don DeLillo's *Libra*. *Arizona Quarterly* 48 (Summer 1992): 33–56. Reprinted in Civello book; see page 536 in this volume.

Johnston, John. "Superlinear Fiction or Historical Diagram?: Don DeLillo's *Libra*." *Modern Fiction Studies* 40 (1994): 319–42.

Kronick, Joseph. "*Libra* and the Assassination of JFK: A Textbook Operation." *Arizona Quarterly* 50.1 (Spring 1994): 109–32.

Michael, Magali Cornier. "The Political Paradox within Don DeLillo's *Libra*." *Critique* 35 (1994): 146–56.

Millard, Bill. "The Fable of the Ants: Myopic Interactions in DeLillo's *Libra*." *Postmodern Culture* 4.2 (January 1994): n.p.

Mott, Christopher M. "*Libra* and the Subject of History." *Critique* 35 (1994): 131–45.

Thomas, Glen. "History, Biography, and Narrative in Don DeLillo's *Libra*." *Twentieth Century Literature* 43.1 (Spring 1997): 107–24.

Wacker, Norman. "Mass Culture/Mass Novel: The Representational Politics of Don DeLillo's *Libra*." *Works and Days* 8 (Spring 1990): 67–87.

MAO II

Baker, Peter. "The Terrorist as Interpreter: *Mao II* in Postmodern Context." *Postmodern Culture* 4.2 (January 1994): n.p.

Bizzini, Silvia Caporale. "Can the intellectual still speak? The example of Don DeLillo's *Mao II*." *Critical Quarterly* 37.2 (Summer 1995): 104–17.

Hughes, Simon. "Don DeLillo: *Mao II* and the Writer as Actor." *Scripsi* 7.2 (1991): 105–12.

Scanlan, Margaret. "Writers Among the Terrorists: Don DeLillo's *Mao II* and the Rushdie Affair." *Modern Fiction Studies* 40 (1994): 229–52.

PAFKO AT THE WALL

Duvall, John N. "Baseball as Aesthetic Ideology: Cold War History, Race, and DeLillo's 'Pafko at the Wall.' " *Modern Fiction Studies* 41 (1995): 285–313.

OTHER CRITICISM

BOOK SECTIONS

Aldridge, John. *The American Novel and the Way We Live Now*. New York: Oxford University Press, 1983: 53–59. Discusses *Players*.

Atwill, William D. *Fire and Power: The American Space Program as Postmodern Narrative*. Athens, Ga., and London: University of Georgia Press, 1994: 139–56. Discusses *Ratner's Star*.

Berman, Neil David. *Playful Fictions and Fictional Players: Game, Sport, and Survival in Contemporary American Fiction*. Port Washington, N.Y.: Kennikat Press, 1981 [47–71]. Discusses *End Zone*.

Brooker, Peter. *New York Fictions: Modernity, Postmodernism, and the New Modern*. London and New York: Longman, 1996 [229–36]. Discusses *Mao II*.

Chénetier, Marc. *Beyond Suspicion: New American Fiction Since 1960*. Translated by Elizabeth A. Houlding. Philadelphia: University of Pennsylvania Press, 1996. *Passim*.

Civello, Paul. *American Literary Naturalism and Its Twentieth-Century Transformations: Frank Norris, Ernest Hemingway, Don DeLillo*. Athens, Ga., and London: University of Georgia Press, 1994 [112–61]. Discusses *End Zone* and *Libra*.

Day, Frank. "Don DeLillo." *Dictionary of Literary Biography: American Novelists Since WWII*. Vol. 6. 2nd series. Edited by James E. Kibler, Jr. Detroit: Gale Research, 1980 [74–78].

Frow, John. *Marxism and Literary History*. Cambridge: Harvard University Press, 1986 [139–47]. Discusses *Running Dog*.

Gardaphé, Fred L. "Don DeLillo's American Masquerade: *Italianità* in a Minor Key." *Italian Signs, American Streets*. Durham, N.C.: Duke University Press, 1996. 172–92. Only substantial discussion of early story "Take the 'A' Train"; also treats "Spaghetti and Meatballs," *Americana*.

Ickstadt, Heinz. "Loose Ends and Patterns of Coincidence in Don DeLillo's *Libra*." *Historiographic Metafiction in Modern American and Canadian Literature*. Edited by Bernd Engler and Kurt Müller. Paderborn, Germany: Ferdinand Schöningh, 1994 [299–312].

Johnson, Diane. "Terrorists as Moralists: Don DeLillo." *Terrorists and Novelists*. New York: Knopf, 1982 [105–110]. Discusses *Players*.

McClure, John A. "Systems and Secrets: Don DeLillo's Postmodern Thrillers." *Late Imperial Romance*. London: Verso, 1994 [118–51]. Discusses *Players, Running Dog, The Names, Libra, Mao II*.

Mullen, Bill. "No There There: Cultural Criticism as Lost Object in Don DeLillo's *Players* and *Running Dog*." *Powerless Fictions? Ethics, Cultural Critique and American Fiction in the Age of Postmodernism*. Edited by Ricard Miguel Alfonso. Amsterdam and Atlanta: Rodopi, 1996 [113–39].

Nadeau, Robert. *Readings from the New Book on Nature: Physics and Metaphysics in the Modern Novel*. Amherst: University of Massachusetts Press, 1981 [161–81]. Discusses DeLillo's novels through *Running Dog*.

Oriard, Michael. "Don DeLillo." *Postmodern Fiction: A Bio-Bibliographical Guide*. Edited by Larry McCaffrey. New York: Greenwood Press, 1986 [323–36]. Discusses the novels through *White Noise*.

———. *Dreaming of Heroes: American Sports Fiction, 1868–1980*. Chicago: Nelson-Hall, 1982 [241–50]. Discusses *End Zone*. Incorporates Oriard, cited on page 533.

Saltzman, Arthur M. *Designs of Darkness in Contemporary American Fiction*. Philadelphia: University of Pennsylvania Press, 1990 [45–51]. Discusses *The Names*.

———. *The Novel in the Balance*. Columbia: University of South Carolina Press, 1993 [83–96]. Discusses *Ratner's Star*.

Storoff, Gary. "The Failure of Games in Don DeLillo's *End Zone*." *American Sport Culture: The Humanistic Dimensions*. Edited by Wiley Lee Umphlett. Lewisburg, Pa.: Bucknell University Press, 1985 [235–45].

Tabbi, Joseph. *Postmodern Sublime: Technology and American Writing from*

Mailer to Cyberpunk. Ithaca, N.Y.: Cornell University Press, 1995 [169–207]. Discusses mainly *Libra* and *Mao II*.

Weinstein, Arnold. *Nobody's Home: Speech, Self and Place in American Fiction from Hawthorne to DeLillo.* New York: Oxford University Press, 1993 [288–315].